I0598132

Trickin' Wit' the Virus

A NOVEL

THE WRITE MESSAGE

Karla Denise Baker

First Edition

This is a work of fiction. The characters and events in this book are fictitious. Any similarity to real persons, living or dead, is coincidental and not intended by the author.

ISBN-13: 978-0-692-25432-5
ISBN-10: 0692254323

E-mail: karlabakerd@yahoo.com

Formatting/Editing/ Creative concept/Model: Karla Denise Baker
Photographer: Don Sherrill
Cover graphics: Toni (tirvolino@aol.com)

Printed in the United States of America
10 9 8 7 6 5 4 3 2 1

All poetry written by Karla Denise Baker

Also by Karla Denise Baker

Anonymous

Sleepin' Wit' the Virus

Kreepin' Wit' the Virus

Trickin' Wit' the Virus

Spittin' 'Em Out Like Babies

Does God Have Toys in Heaven?

I Cried B'tween My Legs- Lust, Love, and Life Lessons

Toys in the Attic

Buried Within My Ribcage

Author's Note

Pain is all I know.

I was never told I couldn't do it
Yet I was ridiculed because I did
Because I took of the mask of HIV/AIDS
And attached a fictitious name to an incurable disease
Because I exploited myself in photograph
To bring reality into focal view
For that I have been stigmatized
For caring and sharing through the written word
I have been ostracized by rumors
By cynicism and slander as if I backslapped yo' mammy
And sucked yo' pappy's big toe
I've done no wrong
Wrongs done me
Yet, I am being belittled by closed-mindedness
Have you forgotten?
I am a dream
A figment of free-spoken

In loving memory of:

Poppa

Ma'am

Epidemic

Johnnie

Tyde a.k.a Storyteller

Therron

Jewell

Antwone

Teka

Daisy

DADDEE'S LULLABY

Hush, li'l bitch, don't you cry

Daddee's gonna buy you'a crack pipe tonight

Daddee's gonna make you smoke dis rock

Daddee's gonna make you work da block

Daddee's gonna make you smile 'n' laugh

Daddee's gonna make you sell dhat ass.

"*Ev'ry Ho Gotta Daddy*
It's hard out here for a hoe. A must, must read!"
-Pink Khocolate, author of *Spittin' 'Em Out Like BABIES*

Trickin' Wit' the Virus

Two women, two separate lives, one epidemic...

The Manuscript

Ev'ry Ho Gotta Daddy

Foreword by

Pink Khocolate

It was Christmas Eve, if I'm not mistaken. AnthonyHamilton's "Magnolia's Room" was blaring through the car speakers as I was riding through Paterson, New Jersey.

There on the corner of Carroll and Van Houten Street stood this young dark-skinned girl. Her thin body was hunched over with her bony arms strapped around her stomach like she was hurt or hurting or hungry. She looked to be about 5'5". I don't know why but something told me to stop. That gut instinct, I guess. Normally I wouldn't, especially since it was in the wee hours, and plus, I was in unfamiliar territory, but I did anyway.

I rolled down the passenger's side window to ask her if she was okay. She was barely able to nod her head, yet she spoke in a sultry tone. "The angels are singing in my head. Can't you hear the music?" Is she high, I asked myself? Most definitely, she was. Even though she appeared to be high she fascinated me. I put my car in reverse and parked my hunter-green Honda Accord and got out to talk to her. I know I was taking a huge risk by doing so, but there was something about her. Something unique. I was being inquisitive because I felt something inspiring from her. And the curiosity made me want to know more—more about her.

First, I asked her her name. "Everybody calls me Lil' While," she replied in a raspy, soft-spoken voice.

"My name is Pink," I told her. She twisted her lips and kind of nixed me off.

Here it was midwinter, bitterly cold. I'm out shivering in my Northface jacket and Lil' While was ho-strollin'. She didn't even show an inkling of fear. Wasn't she aware of the violence that lured between 12 a.m. to 4 a.m.? Heck, even broad daylight. There was nothing but madness and maliciousness out at that time of morning. It was apparent to me that she was in dire need. *Was it sex, drugs, or money? Or was it something so unfamiliar to her?* Emphatically, I couldn't say. Was I her guardian angel or was she mine? Or were we both crazy to be out so late? I contemplated, and then came to the obvious conclusion that we both were *nuts*, especially me because she was a total stranger.

As I had that thought, her eyelids folded as her glossy eyeballs rolled underneath. She looked smashed. She sniffled in the snotty drool that was running out from her nose. I inhaled the stench of waste permeating through her pores. Moisture trickled down the sides of her temples, down and over the rise of her high cheekbones, lowering to the pitters of dry ashen skin on her scrawny face. Her lips were ashy white. She walked doubled over, achy cramps twisting her insides. Smelly perspiration soaked to the skin as her stomach rumbled of hunger. I offered to get her something to eat if she'd allow me to interview her. Out of the blue, she began to sing. *"Ey, Miz-tah, you gotta dimeeeee..."* as a hint that she wanted cash instead of food. Her laden feet treaded through the thick, slushy snow as her half-nude body paced back and forth dressed in a fake white faux, turquoise halter-top, hot pink mini-skirt, and white four-inch hooker boots. Her hair weave was matted and unkempt. I inhaled. And as I did, *woo-woo-woo* I could literally smell her body that reeked of musky skunk as her frostbitten fingers curled shielding something in her hand. I tried to see what it was but she was holding it so tightly like she was guarding it with her life. Lil' While diligently awaited any passersby to come and indulge in her. I was repulsed, angry, pissed!

I tried to reason with her because I knew in my gut that she had a message to share with her being so young and all. She looked to be at least fifteen, no more than sixteen. I was humble about it. Didn't want to come off as parental, you know. "Listen. Instead of me giving you cash why don't you let me go and get you something to eat, and then we can talk about *us* writing your story." I figured if I said 'us' she'd see that I was genuinely sincere. "You'd get royalties for the lifetime of the *book*," I told her. She smacked her chapped lips together, and said. "What if I die? Who gonna get the royalties then, huh?" She rotated her neck and placed

11

her hand on her small waist. *Well, at least she ain't stupid,* I thought. "Do you have family?" I asked her. She shook her head no. "What about any children? No boyfriend?" She shook her head no. She scrolled her droopy eyes up and down me slowly like she was trying to size me up. "What you'a journalist or something? You want to write a story and put it in the newspapers?" I shook my head no. Didn't I just tell this chick that I wanted to write a *book*? I sighed, softly. "I'm a writer. I want *us* to write your story and make it into a *book*." I told her. She cut her eyes to the side like she was thinking. What the hell was there to think about? I wondered. Then I weighed out the pros and cons of it all: *trickin' or book? Degrade yourself or respect yourself?*

I couldn't understand the logic in her thinking. But then it dawned on me that I didn't live *her* life. I had no reason to judge. There was no way for me to comprehend her struggles. If I had literally walked in her shoes, okay, I had a legitimate reason that could substantiate how I felt about the situation but I didn't. There was no possible way for me to relate to her issue. Yes, I had done my dirt (*Spittin' 'Em Out Like Babies*), but I had no idea, no clue, as to what she had endured up 'til this day. So again, I had to take a few steps back and chill.

Lil' While distracted my train of thought. "You don't know nothing about me, lady. You think I'm stupid or something. All you wanna do is git rich offa my shit. For real, though, what you gittin' outta it? You ain't doin' this fo' nothin'," she said, while rolling her sleepy eyes at me. "You're right. I'm not doing it for nothing." I replied, "I know you gotta story to tell. There is something...I can feel it in my bones. But I don't wanna waste your time and I sure as hell don't want you to waste mine." I paused. "Answer this, how many people stopped to ask you if you were okay, needed something to eat, huh?" I had to go there to prove a point. She remained quiet. "Uh-huh. Just as I'd thought," I said. "So what do you have to lose?" She took a second or two to respond. "So when do you want to do this *lady*?" I didn't need time to think about it, so I said, "Why not start now?" She looked up the desolate street, bit down on her cracked bottom lip and said, "A'ight." Then right before my eyes she transformed into this sweet, innocent child. She lowered her voice kinda baby-like and said, "Can you git me a bagel wit'a cream cheese and grape jelly and a large hot chocolate?" I nodded my head yes. "I'll be right back." I told her, as I hopped back in my car, and drove off hoping she'd be there when I got back.

Oddly enough, she was.

I knew that there was something unique about her. For one, just because she worked the streets, didn't make her street. She appeared to have a good head on her shoulders. And I knew once she was cleaned up she'd look and smell better too. I didn't think twice about my decision because I knew that I was on to something good. My only reservation was that she'd dip on me and 'we' wouldn't be able to complete the book. This was when I really had to put faith in my task and trust in her. It may sound a little iffy that's because it was. I mean I didn't know her and she didn't know me. Either one of us could've bailed. The ultimate goal was to make sure we both were comfortable with one another in order for this to work. I put everything I had in me to show and prove that I was a woman of my word, and so did she.

What really struck me with Lil' While was her philosophy on *Hoes*. I never looked at it the way she did.

"Do you know that Hos come in all shapes, sizes, occupations, and ethnic groups? Hos are universal. A married woman can be a hoe. Even a godly woman can become a hoe. Even the President's First Lady can become a *hoe*. No one is exempt from becoming a hoe, male or female," she said.

I had no idea of how many types of hos there really were out in the world. And I think she knew that by the dumbfound lock on my face. This chick was really schooling me on...*hos*!

"Most of the chicks out here ain't got nobody to love 'em, no daddy to protect 'em, and they ain't strong 'nough to love 'emselves, so they settle for the little they can git, which ain't nuthin' but an overused dick. And you wanna know the funny part of all of this...?" she looked me dead in my eyes. I nodded my head yes. "As my gurl, Rocka-Bye Bitch usedta say, 'Ev'ry Ho gotta Daddy. Ev'ry Pussy gotta Past.' Whether it is husband, pimp, john, boyfriend, or significant other, hell, even yo' own mammy could be a Daddy. It really don't matter."

My brow rose.

"That's deep." I said.

The girls who are deprived of a "daddy" find one in the boys or men that come into their lives. I comprehended exactly where Lil' While was coming from. It made perfect sense to me. See, the gut never lies. I knew that she had something special to give. I just knew it.

During our first meeting, I was out till the wee hours, Dunkin' Donuts large hot chocolate in one hand and recorder in the other freezing my butt off.

"If you don't mind me asking, how *old* are you?"

"Fifteen," she replied, with a mouthful of bagel.

I wasn't too surprised because some girls I saw were much younger than her. I didn't want to make her feel funny so I kept my comments to myself. But if I did share I'd probably asked her: "Don't you want more than this?" Like I said I didn't want to make her feel bad. If anything, I wanted to help her, not belittle her. Everybody had skeletons. Everybody.

The timeframe of interviewing Lil' While took me less than two weeks. After interviewing *her*, I took the liberty of tracking down others that she had mentioned in our interview: Scoop, Detroit, D.C., Blue-Bird, Lottery, and her estranged dad, Lime Brooks to authenticate her story. They all agreed to interview with me and gave me some information on themselves as well as how they met, felt, and looked at Lil' While.

Lastly, I reached out to Durdy-Dog (owner of the gentleman's club: THE NAPPY DUGOUT), but he declined to be interviewed.

During the process of getting my story together, tragedy struck. Lil' While along with four other young girls were brutally murdered. All five of their lifeless bodies were found in an abandoned building on Fair Street in Paterson. All killed execution style.

P. K.

Fuck whatchu heard!

In all honesty I'm probably that last bitch you should be listenin' to. But I ain't got shit to lose. And I sure as hell ain't got no reason to lie. I got a lil' schooling. Don't git it twisted, I ain't no uppity bitch. No. I come from dirt poor. Lived in dirt. I gotta dirty mouth too. And I act like a hood rat at times. Well, I used to. Ain't never been called pretty or beautiful or nuthin' good from my mama. That triflin' ho. Ain't never had a mama, if you ax me. Shit. All she teaches me was how to use my ass, titties and pussy to make a hustle. And in all of my years I used the hella outta it. That ain't no mama to be proud of.

Dunno my daddy. Can't tell you nuthin' about him. Not even his name. Mighta fucked him, dunno. I got some shame in me and that's why I choosin' to tell my story. Hope to help a stupid bitch. Some wounded, fucked up girl roaming around these goddamn muthafuckin' streets high as a muthafucka sellin' her pussy like it's studded with diamonds 'n' shit. I wanna help her see how grimy peoples can be. Help her see that life got mo' to offer than just dick and money and sweet bullshit. Help her see herself if it ain't no mirror in her view. I'm yo' muthafuckin' mirror. You heard what I said lil' bitch?! I'm yo' mirror!

Listen, fo' the young girls who read this here book I hope you git something outta it—something that will save you from this type of bullshit.

Cos, if not, I feel that I have failed y'all. And fo' that, babies, I am truly, truly fuckin' sorry.

—Magnolia "Daisy" Wily aka Rocka-Bye Bitch

Durdy-Dog
The Emperor of 'NAPPY' Hoes

"Yo', what's good, Durdy-Dog?"

"Nothin', Hook-Head."

"You straight?"

"Nah, Son, I ain't pullin' nothin' but lint out of my pockets, yo'," I said with the straightness of face. I was twenty with a game plan. I didn't have time to be hanging out in the streets. And plus, shit was live in P-town.

"Me, too."

"You stayin' in, right?" Hook-Head asked.

"Yeah, might as well 'cause ain't nothin' out here but bullets, my nigga," I told him. Plus, I was expecting company. My woman always came to me. Shitttttt ain't nothin' betta' to a nigga than a bitch with some trite pussy.

"I ain't tryna get caught up in that shit."

"Yo, hit me up later." I said.

"A'ight."

That was the last conversation I had with my boy Hook-Head. We'd known each other since we were kids rockin' Chuck Taylor's 'n' shit. Now, we don't even chill. Not since that *bitch* ditched me.

Hook-Head and I had been through a lot. Back then we used to have mad fun with the crew. It was Hook-Head, me, Gutter, Rasta, Cocky, Whiteout, Filly and Klutz. We'd all been through our share of life's downfalls, but we made a pact to always stay tight—to never let a bitch come between us. But we were boys. We had no clue as to how influential pussy, head; lust-slash-love could stroke a nigga's ego. No clue. But that was in the past—the young me. I'd matured since then. Nigga got his priorities in check.

As a young *boy* growing up in the ghetto I realized some bad shit you just gotta let go of. Yeah. Some shit. And as a *man* some shit you can't find the strength to let go of. It's different when it's your *boy* compared to your *bitch*. A bitch knows how to fuck a man's head up without him even seeing it happening. I guessed, no, I know that was what happened to me. All the fellahs saw it. And everyone told me, including my mom, but

I was too far-gone to smell *her* bullshit. No doubt, I was sprung. I was knee deep in her hole. And now, neck high in debt. Let's just say...*10 G's short.*

Fallen in love ain't shit. Especially when the one you loved don't love you. See I had to learn this the hard way. I had to fall deep in order to feel the pain. And trust a nigga that shit hurt like a muthafucker. It hurt even more when I got a letter in the mail from the Internal Revenue Service stating that I was being audited for ten G's. A brother had to come up from the kick back. Nigga had to do what a nigga had to do to get his paper in check. I was going to come back strong—stronger than ever. I was going to get myself out of debt. Regain my dignity and stick-'n-move. Yeah. That *was* the plan. But I felt naked. Broke as hell! I felt like I had nothin' but a shriveled dick and a muthafuckin' toothache that was kicking my ass.

In other words, I didn't feel like the man I used to be. I let my heart get in the way, and my pockets got dry from all the giving I had done. That bitch took advantage of my soft spot. I was breaking that bitch off nice. And in the end, I fell off quickly. I was barely able to afford drawers to cover the crack of my ass.

I wasn't one of those dumb jokers. I was a hard working black man who earned his keep. Never stole from anyone, yet I got caught up in what I thought was a good thing. Women. Or shall I say one bitch. Mom always told me to beware of the "pretty bitches." She always used to say that they had mo' shit wit' 'em than the ugly ones. And she ain't lie either. Man, they sure knew how to cover up their shit and make you *think* that they were who they said they were. But their game had mad flaws. Because when a *man* hits a speed bump in life and he ain't got no money to come up on his feet, that's when you know what type of bitch you got. Either she's a "ride-to-die" who got your back or she's a "trick-a-dick" and some other nigga is doing your backbreaking for you. Either way you see it, it's fucked up.

They say, "Nice guys finished last," I almost believed that shit until it happened to me. That's when I decided to turn that shit around. But what really made me see the muthafuckin' light was when she mailed me pictures. Pictures flaunting her shit in my face. New tattoos, her trip to Las Vegas with some metro-sexual nigga, new shoes and designer clothes, while I was sitting home on a Friday night pinching pennies to make ends meet. It was then that I told myself: "nah, it ain't going down like this!"

17

Here I was being the gentleman of the situation making $40.00 monthly payments. All I asked was that she breaks me off $20.00 a month. She was getting a welfare check every month. I was trying to help her out by making sure she had. That was the only reason why I put her down as my dependent when I filed my taxes. The only reason! She said that she loved me. That I was the best boyfriend she had ever had. She said a lot of things that she never meant.

For a year I did what I had to do to keep my nose clean. But the situation was getting stressful, not to mention tight on a nigga's wallet. And it was only going to get tighter because come January, the stakes had been raised. Try adding $160.00 to the $40.00. Yeah. A $200.00 monthly payment until the debt was paid in full. There was no way I was going to be able to maintain this alone. And she didn't seem to have a care in the world for my predicament, or me. Fuck Durdy-Dog, was basically what she'd said. So I scratched my balls, instead of my head. I really needed to think, you know. Was she worth it? Hell, no!

The first time I filed my taxes she spent $5800.00 of that money like it was water. I only saw $1200.00. The second time I filed I added her daughter as well as her. I gave her the full amount of $3000.00. No. I saw none of that money, but I didn't care because I had *her*. Yeah. I was played a fool.

This was no longer a laughing matter to me. Something had to be done because I did it for *her*. This woman I was planning on asking to marry me. This woman I had already picked out an engagement ring for. Yeah. Daddee. Yep. That simple-minded ghetto-bitch that *tricked* me. I truly blame it on matters of the heart 'cause had I not felt anything for her, this would never had happened to me.

See I'd be damned if I'd suffer the consequences of the IRS garnishing my wages because of her refusal to help a brotha' out—out of debt she *helped* put me in. Nah. *Fuck that!* Retribution was *now* the name of the game. Daddee had to pay!

One way or the other the IRS was going to get their money, and so was I, by any means necessary.

***

Malik FREEMAN

"It's quite simple," I said, while checking me out in the full-length mirror of my bedroom, "in order for me to indulge in a woman she has to possess 'swagger.'" I told my fifteen-year-old brother Akee, as I tied my silver striped tie and attached my sterling silver cufflinks onto the light blue button down dress shirt. Then I reached for the soft gray suit jacket I recently bought and put it on. Spitz a little cologne on my neck, and then reached for the soft bristle brush and brushed my jet-black hair. Then I marveled at myself and said back to my reflection: "damn, that's a fine dark chocolate muthafucka."

Akee laughed while sitting on the black leather loveseat. "Malik, you are so messed up." Akee said with a perplexed look upon his caramel-complexioned face. He cocked his head to the side and asked, "What do you mean by...swagger?" he blinked his light-brown eyes waiting for a response.

"Swagger." I stopped getting dressed and took a moment to explain my philosophy to lil' bro. I bent back each individual finger: (1): looks (2): how she carries herself (3): how she dresses (4): intellect...all of these above equates to...swagger, my brother." Akee nodded his head as he listened.

Lil' bro always admired me. He looked up to me because I never allowed the streets to get the better of me. I always knew growing up that I was going to be successful. I applied myself and the end result came into fruition. At the age of thirty-five I owned several food franchises, beauty salons as well as barbershops in New York, Atlanta, Chicago, Washington and Detroit. My bank accounts were overflowing and as a result my ego was only getting bigger and bigger. It would take a confident woman to be able to stomach a man like me and bring my 6'3" of massiveness back down to size.

"Lil' bro, a woman has to know when her man wants to fuck and how he wants it. Men don't want to hear nothing about: 'I got a headache,' 'Maybe later,' 'I gotta stomachache,' none of that. Women must understand that what she won't do, another willing, able, ho will. See, women are ears and mouthpieces. Men don't give a shit about the bullshit women is talking about. We basically tune her ass out. All we see is what we want, and wonder what she is holding underneath that dress. The body. The face. The pussy. That's all a man is first interested in. Talking? We leave that up to the ladies. See, a man needs QT (quality time). Some women fail to adhere to this. There is nothing more irritating than a woman who doesn't allow her man to breathe freely. Insecure women, they're the worse, especially those barracuda bitches.

19

They hear that biological clock and are itching to get hitched. Not going to happen with me. I'll wine and dine, but I'd be damned if I'm going to father a child with a bitch that is twice my age. Nah. They cause a lot of drama and cost too much money to get rid of. Lil' bro, your best bet is to be an 'in-the-meantime' type of nigga. Don't let yourself get caught up in the hype of the pussy. 'Cause if you do, nigga, you're done, remember this shit 'cause Dad isn't going to school you the way I will. He's still living in that chivalry era. Shit has changed since chivalry." I paused. "Listen, lil' man, most of the time our 'QT' is spent with the fellahs doing men shit. See, if a woman knows her man's sex cycle she will go above and beyond to please him, to keep him." I told him. I shook my head. "When it comes to sex, huh, these chicks out here got shit twisted. A man gets tired of missionary. Arch your back. Stretch your legs. Give me more than just the hole. Okay, it's wet! *So!* Do something with it. Don't expect me to hump you for an hour or two. Don't think you're just going to ride my dick and grind my balls, and think that that's supposed to satisfy me. I can't stand a lazy fuck. Talkin' 'bout, 'Come get it.' Lying on your back for 30 minutes like that is supposed to excite me. Bitch wants to suck dick all the time! I need more than a dick sucker! Fuck me! And I don't mean in one fuckin' position either. See, this is why women need to stay in shape so that they can maneuver their bodies during sex. These bitches out here got guts just hanging over and pussy just dry and gray-haired. The crack of their asses so tight you gotta spray it with Febreze to cut through all that stank. And they have the audacity to wonder why they can't keep a muthafucker like me. I need to be stimulated." I brush a piece of lint off of my right shoulder of my suit jacket and admire myself in the mirror.

"How'd you get so wise, man?" Akee asked, "I mean Dad never schooled us on this woman stuff."

"Man, I listen and study...women. See women love to gossip and share their heartaches and pain. If you take a moment to listen, you'll learn a lot about what women go through from other women, or, the woman herself. Even more so about what they have or have not done for or to their man. Men want love too, but we don't want to have to ask for it. We want our women to know. Get to know me as your man and you won't go wrong with me." I concluded.

"I see your work." Akee said. "But didn't you say something about this new woman in your life. What was her name, again?" he snapped his fingers three times, in deep thought.

I blurted out, "Rocka-Bye Bitch. But I call her...Rocka 'cause the bitch can suck da hell outta my dick!"

Akee cocked his head back and laughed. "Yeah, that's it! Yo', man you ain't fuckin' a dude, are you? I mean I ain't ever heard of a chick named Rocka before."

I sucked my teeth and shook my head. "Nah, man. She's all woman the last I saw her. All woman." I smirked.

"How did you meet this one? Whatever happened to Giselle?" Akee asked.

"Giselle is history. That bitch had too much lip. Spanish chicks gotta lot of shit wit' 'em. For some strange reason they seem to think just 'cause they can cook, fuck, and look good that that's all you gotta do to keep a nigga happy. Nah. Bitch you gotta have a job and good fuckin' credit to get this here dick. Giselle was the exception to the rule 'cause in spite of her delusions she had a good head on her shoulders. I saw potential, you feel me.

I continued, "When I met Giselle she was unemployed. She had a five-year-old son, who mind you, she didn't have custody of. Her grandmother was raising him. It's funny how she used to always claim that she was an *independent* woman. Nigga, tell me how you 'independent' when you depend on the system to make ends meet, huh? Fuck that! Women got it twisted, Akee. They think looks going to make a nigga spend, spend, spend, not this muthafucker. 'Cause at the end of the day you got to show-'n-prove that you are worthy of two things: (1): *my money.* (2): *my heart.* Havin' good looks ain't gonna cut it with me. I prefer a woman who I know got my back. When I'm sick, down and out, broke, or on my deathbed I need to know that she gotta nigga. Listen, from my past experiences all these chicks seem to know is 'gimmee'. What happened to...Get-Your-Own? Instead of constantly trying to ride my dick! You gotta be alert, lil' bro. 'Cause if you don't you'll be a got nigga. All 'cause you let a bitch hoodwink your heart and suck your pockets dry." I exhaled, inhaled. "And that's another thing." I did a full circle in the mirror making sure my shit was tight. Listen, Akee, if a woman who is 'sposed to be your woman, *and* won't give you no *head...* cut her ass loose! A man needs to get his dick sucked on the regular. I don't want to hear nothing about, 'I don't do that,' 'Ooh, that's nasty,' none of that bullshit. And I definitely don't want an 'Ow-Ow-Ow' bitch. Those are the worst! All a bitch can do for me is fuck me and shut the fuck up. Now that might make a nigga break a bitch off with a little something...something. Word up! But on the real, lil' bro, I like a woman

21

with a strong mental. That is sexy to me! Oh, and as far as Rocka is concerned, I met her at THE NAPPY DUGOUT. She's a stripper. After her performance we got to talkin' and I asked her for her number. She was cool. I could tell that she was a mellow type of chick. She's not hard up for a nigga. I like that."

"What time is your flight?" Akee asked.

"1:30 p.m."

Akee shook his head, "Man, you have the life. You get to go wherever you want. It must feel good to have money to burn."

I nodded my head. "Spend wisely, my brother, and you'll be well off too. Women love a successful black man."

We both laughed.

"Are you taking, Rock, along with you to Vegas?" Akee asked.

I sucked my teeth. "Akee, its Rocka. And hell no, man! Did you not hear me say that she is a *stripper*? I can't be seen with her out in public. I could see if she was a 'Closet Freak' but her shit is out in the open. I will say this though, she can suck my dick any day of the muthafuckin' week. That bitch likes to *swallow*."

***

Greig STEVENS

"I'm leaving work now, Mom. I'll see you in about thirty minutes. I have to stop and buy a suit before I come home, okay." I told her.

"Okay son," My mother, Virginia replied, in a feeble tone. Mom had been sickly and with the recent passing of my dad, McBride Stevens, her health was vastly depleting. With high blood pressure, diabetes and obesity, I had a lot of responsibility. Sure, I always yearned to move out of Jersey, and get my own place but I could never seem to take a stand and do so, because for one, there was almost always something blocking my blessings. So I simply accepted my fate feeling as though one day I'd get the opportunity to free myself from captivity, but that moment had yet to arrive.

"I'll stop at the pharmacy to get your medication too." I said to her as I was putting some cleaning supplies back in the closet.

"All right. Be careful out there."

"I will, Mom."

We hung up.

I exited out of the redbrick building and hopped into my old, rusty beat-up gray Chevrolet.

Being the youngest of *nine* children, I was the only responsible sibling and carried the weight on my shoulders like a trouper. I was never the type of man to turn his back on family, especially my mom and dad. With my father's passing I was indeed the man of the house. The thought of leaving my mom in her destitute state was inconceivable. How could I turn my back on the woman who had given me precious life, food, clothes and a roof over my head? Working as a custodian for the school system was not my dream job, but it helped pay the taxes on the old house on Fair Street. It kept the lights on as well as food in the fridge. My dreams, aspirations all had to be put on the backburner. Family came first. It was how I was raised and often spoken upon by my departed dad.

Growing up a lot of the girls around my neighborhood often liked me, but most considered me to be a "momma's boy." I was okay with it because it was nothing far from the truth. I loved my mother to death and no one, not for the life of me, was ever going to stop the love I had for her. I could never see myself becoming "that" guy to turn my back on the woman I treasured more than my own life.

Forty-seven years old, six foot one inches tall, I always had a desire to get married and move south but long-term relationships that I'd had never lasted no more than four to six months. I'd meet women from all walks of life: teachers, investment bankers, principals, lawyers, doctors, nurses, even an evangelist, but I had standards that I was just not willing to bend. Not even for love. I wanted my special lady to have certain qualities, morals and values, and self-respect. Looks were never top of my list. I learned years ago, way back in my teen years to look beyond the superficial. My mom always lectured me on the inner beauty of a woman. Well, I guessed it sunk in.

Women with loud mouths always turned me off. I despised women with no sense of direction. A "yes" woman used to trigger a migraine for me. I wanted someone with some discipline—someone with ambition. I wanted someone who was independent but not to the point where they felt like they didn't need a man. Oh, those types of women...the "I-can-do-it-without-a-man" usually irked my last nerve. The overconfident butterflies who felt they could wear the pants and skirts. The ones with the bossy attitudes, possessiveness, and cocky dispositions, I'd frown upon. I was a simple man with simple taste. I was a single father of two

23

six-year-old little girls, by two different women. I was seeking a woman of wife material—someone who wouldn't mind being a stepmother to my girls, Jada and May. I wasn't eager to have any more children but would consider with the right woman for the future. The most important thing with me was that my woman had to be honest. And it was imperative that she had good hygiene and took pride in the way she looked. Clothes certainly didn't make the woman but I wanted her to dress in a becoming fashion. I was never one to want a woman who had multiple sex partners. Women like that were whores to me. I never wanted to take a whore home to meet my mother.

Not having a social life, I often felt displaced. With me being a care provider for my mom, a father to my daughters, and having other responsibilities, besides, work, and chores around the house took up most of my time. My life had become everyone else's life. Due to the untimely passing of my dad, my life was placed on hold.

I parked my car in the lot of SUIT YO'SELF reached over in the passenger seat for my bag of pork skins and opened them. Snatched out about a handful and stuffed them in my mouth before exiting out of my car. I was walking swiftly to get inside before they closed the store at 7:00 p.m.

Without paying close attention to where I was going I nearly knocked this gorgeous woman down dressed in a fitted red strapless dress off of her sexy feet. But with my quick reflexes I managed to grab her by her small waist before her pretty face met the hard concrete.

"Ma'am, are you okay?" I asked alarmingly. "I'm so sorry. I didn't even see you right in front of me."

She took a minute to calm herself down. "I'm fine," she said; exasperatingly while swallowing the rock-size lump of spittle back down her throat. "Yes, I'm fine. It's okay."

"Are you sure?" I asked again.

She nodded her head, yes, and walked down the street. As she walked away I noticed she dropped a business card on the ground. I picked it up and read the bold print.

DAISY
Private Dancer
(973) BED-ROCK

A brow raised as I slipped the card in my front pants pocket, then entered the store.

***

Bo MONTGOMERY

I can't remember the last time my dick got hard having a woman lying beside me in bed. It damn sure ain't get hard with Shirley or Lola or Leslie or Patrice or Nancy or Sherita or Beth or Desiree or Kayla or Janice or Peaches or Frieda or Jennifer or Gwen or Faith or Lauren or Beatrice or Ruby or Marlene or Veronica or Helen or Rose or Rosalyn or Peggy or Joice or Evelyn or Justine or Joelle or Donna. And none, except Sierra ever got fucked in this bed. But that was so long ago. Sierra and I hadn't screwed in God knows when. I can't even remember what the hell her pussy looks like. Nope. I couldn't even tell you if you asked me to describe it, go to show that I wasn't feeling her in a sexual way. We had a good relationship for the time that it lasted, but a man with a high sex drive as me needs a woman who can multitask. Sierra just couldn't hang.

Now, back in the day, Sierra had her shit down.

That woman was holding a man up. Now I always had a job but when a nigga was low on cash Sierra made sure my pockets stayed swoll. She fed me even though she couldn't cook worth a damn. She washed my dirty boxers, bought me suits and ties and shoes to keep me looking good. And I looked out for her too. Nah. This was not a one sided thing. We were partners. That's how I saw it. And I think she did too because she started to get that itch. Yep. Marriage. Now Sierra had great potential, but there was a gap in our ages. Not that that mattered much.

Let me stop lying. It did matter. To a certain degree it did. Especially when things that used to stand on their own began to flop. Yeah. Her tits. She used to be able to showcase those babies without the need of a support bra, but then something changed and not only did she need a bra she also needed control top panty hose and girdles to hold all of that flabbiness in.

Now, I am not one to knock a sistah but damn, damn, damn, what the fuck happened to the woman I met eleven years ago? What...all of a sudden she got comfortable and just said fuck it! I got my man, so, what the fuck! Nah. That's not how you're supposed to do it. You're supposed to keep that shape in check. Not let yourself go.

Honestly, it was a complete turnoff for me. But since I did care for her, I pushed all of that superficial bullshit to the wayside. Sierra cared for me too. That woman loved me to death. Me, well, I never wanted to see anything happen to her, but I was not in love with her as she had thought. And no, I never divulged that to her, but I'm more than sure she felt it. How could she not? I mean when the flames burned out in the bedroom and a brotha' comes and goes as he damned well pleases and barely spends time with the woman he has at home, what does that tell you? Exactly.

I never asked her to stay with me. Never pleaded and begged. Sierra was a very intelligent woman. She could've left at any given time. I'd never hold her back. But as she had stated numerous times, why go fishing when she'd invested time in molding me into the man that I am today. She gave me too much freedom and I ran with it while she chose to stay home and eat Big Mac's and Sing-Sing chicken wings. And she wondered why she was blowing up like the Good Year Blimp. That was not attractive to my eyes. And I guess she kind of knew it, but she was too far in to stop her indulgences. Since I wasn't there to stroke her back, she preoccupied herself with other things, things that only changed her outer appearance and pushed me farther and farther away.

I was happy with a lot of things except one...my eleven-year relationship with wife, Sierra Preston.

Our relationship was a little shaky but I was doing my best to try to repair the brokenness. But the cracks were too deep to salvage with communication alone. We were in need of passion—hot nasty sex to rekindle our flames. And neither was stimulated enough to take it there. So, we lived as a sexless couple. More like roommates, if you asked me. But I was okay with it. I had accepted the fact that what we had was now contentment—a relationship of convenience, nothing more, nothing less. But that didn't sit well with Sierra.

She wanted to buck this horse like she used to back in the day. But with all of her oochin' and ouchin' her body was not equipped to handle all that I had to offer. I'd rather choke my own chicken to relieve myself, than have her attempt to try. And that was mostly what I did. I invested heavily in bootleg porn DVDs, as well as a family sized container of Vaseline. It was better than cheating. And plus, Sierra knew where I was at night, downstairs beating my dick so she simply accepted what we had become.

Was she happy? No. But she had invested so much time, money and energy into building a meaningful relationship with me. And she wasn't about to throw that all away just because of what we lacked in the bedroom. She truly loved me. And to her, love conquered all. But that was her theory because I saw things differently. I adored Sierra. I would bend over backwards to please her, but the more I laid beside her in bed, the more repulsed I began to get at the sight of her, especially when she was naked. You can't fault a man for liking what he likes. Back in the day, Sierra had it going on.

What used to be a small waist were now rolls of fat. What used to be toned hips and apple-shaped ass were now wide hips and dimpled ass. And what used to be a flat-board stomach was now an oversized stomach that required a girdle to tuck in the rolls of fat.

I was completely turned off, but I never had the heart to tell her with words so I showed her with actions. There was no action happening in our king-sized bed.

"Ev'ry Ho
Gotta
Daddy,
Ev'ry Pussy
Gotta
Past"

—DADDEE

DADDEE'S LULLABY

Hush, li'l bitch, don't you cry

Daddee's gonna buy you'a crack pipe tonight

Daddee's gonna make you smoke dis rock

Daddee's gonna make you work da block

Daddee's gonna make you smile 'n' laugh

Daddee's gonna make you sell dhat ass.

Daisy aka Rocka-Bye Bitch

MUTHAFUCKIN' BASTARDS!

Those po' innocent li'l muthafuckin' bastards never stand a chance in hell of hasin' a good life. Muthafuckin' bastards, who suffered, dunno nuthin' 'bout good, all we know is that the bogeymama is comin' to eat us up, and we scared outta our fuckin' minds. We left out in this cold ass world all by ourselves to fight that ugly monster off before she destroys what li'l good might be left in us. Good, bad, don't matter much. To me, seemt like the bad outweighed the good any fuckin' way.

I was a li'l bastard barely able to say my name, let 'lone my ABC's and 1 2 3's, but I member some bad thangs that don't seemt to go away. Yeah. It jus' don't seemt to go the fuck away.

I member yellin' between my mama and some old white lookin' dude named Shoe. He had a scruffy-looking face. Beady eyes were yellowish and bloody red. And he smelt like whiskey and piss or piss and whiskey. He walked wit'a limp and supported his balance wit'a makeshift cane. He stood tall likea streetlight pole and he towered over her like one of 'em ghostly trees you seent on the *Adams Family*. He gave her this-this mean look that made her body tighten up. I was standing in the far corner of his dirty ass kitchen. My back and heels of my sneakers pressed against the wall, teeth chattering, scared shitless.

The man smacked his pink lips and started talkin' real loud and tough like, "You gonna come up in my house and ax to come back! Ain't nobody tells you to take your fast ass out there and get knocked up by some sorry muthafucker. Look, lil' mama, I done paid my dues by keepin' a roof over your trifling ass. Then you go and gits knocked up. And if you think I'm gonna play 'daddy' to your bastard, huh, I got news for you, li'l mama. It ain't gonna happen! You opened your legs fo' that nigga! Now you keep opening 'em! Hell, you're actually pretty good at it." He grinned slyly. "Now if you don't mind carry you and your whiny ass bastard and git the hell outta my house! Git on. Scoot. Go! That's right. Git on and git the fuck out!"

Daddee grabbed my hand and pulled me out of that old dude's house. She was mad as hell. It was written all over her face. And it triggered

30

some anger towards me. I could see it in her eyes. She hated me. But as a little girl I loved her. I loved how she looked, how she dressed, how she smelled like baby powder. Sweet and lovin' but that-that was far from her. Daddee had love for only one. Daddee.

I'm sure it wasn't easy for Daddee practically being a baby herself and having a baby of her own. And I'm sure her options had run out of what to do, where to go? She hadn't no money. No family. No baby daddy as far as I could tells. All she had was her pride and soon even that was up for bargain. Yeah. So easily the streets became her home—her haven.

As far as family went, well, that developed rather quickly. This big time pimp named Roscoe took us under his wing. The prostitutes, drug dealers, hustlers, number runners all pooled together to take care of her. They looked out for her and me I guessed you could say she fit right in as if the last piece to an unfinished puzzle. The only problem was I didn't seemt to fit in her new world. I was like a bad lucky charm. And every day of my natural born life she made that known to me.

DADDEE WAS BEAUTIFUL. She was every man's pussy. She was thickframed wit' big, firm breasted, and flawless vanilla cream skin, seductive hazel eyes, wit' sorta wavy shoulder-length scarlet-colored hair. She was what one would thank a Madonna bombshell would look like. But she was no Madonna. *Fuck no!* She was wicked. Behind closed doors her beauty quickly vanished. I thank I was the only one who seent the evil in her eyes. And even though I was lighter than her is, she always used to call me mean and hurtful names. I never understand why. It always made me wonder, thank that my dad mighta been *black*? He had to be black if she called me *nigger baby*. All the lies she'd tell. Who my daddy is? Where my daddy is? What his name is? What he look like? Daddee never uttered one word. And it it liked to kill me every fuckin' day.

Daddee was spiteful as a ferocious Rottweiler on the inside. Those who really didn't known her thank her to be street smart. Okay, I had'ta give it to her, she knew how to fuck men's heads up and bleed 'em outta they's money. Of course, she used her beauty and curves of shapely hips to lure men's in. But once they gotta taste of her and what she was a lot of 'em dropped her like a bad habit. She was a user and abuser—an insensitive womens who was as cold-blooded as a serial killer. Knowing this, they's left her. But there was always somebody who didn't seent her

31

for who she was. That one somebody happened to be this foolish man named Coop Jonesy. He looked beyond her exterior and was tempted to get to knows her. If you ax me, that was one stupid muthafucka.

Coop was a hardworking countryman who'd come up north from Rocky Mountain, North Carolina, to start a new life. He was a widower. Said his lovely wife died from some type of woman's disease. He never said exactly what kind though.

Coop had to be in his mid-fifties. He was a solid framed man, stand about 6'2", blue-black complexion. His mahogany eyes looked like small marbles. And he had this winning smile like on game shows that shined bright in darkness like a flashlight or a star. Real bright. He was a nice type of fellah—real down-to-earth and laid back—a free-spirit type of guy.

Coop owned a thrift store over on Curtis Place called Thrifty that he had for several years. He was doing pretty good for hisself. That was till Daddee switched her whorish ass in his store axin' 'bout a used TV he had on sale dressed in a body fitting fiery red spaghetti strapped dress with four-inch red stilettos on and red lipstick lips. One look at her, Coop lost his damn mind. He was hooked in.

Daddee and Coop went on a couple of dates. By the following year we moved into another slum. Coop wanted to move into a betta' neighborhood, outside of Paterson, but Daddee fought against it. Said she didn't want to forget where she comes from. If it didn't have piss, rats, roaches, mold and mildew, garbage, beer cans, cigarettes buds, crack vials, dirty syringes, junkies, prostitutes, gang-bangers, used condoms on the sidewalks, it was too suburb for her blood. Daddee was always comfortable 'round filth. Since she was filthy she felt right at home.

I found it kinda strange that Coop wanted to marry her, but Daddee preferred to live together. He respected her wishes and settled for shacking up. I don't know if they were truly in love. But what I did knows was that Daddee loved Coop's money mo' than she liked him. She tolerated him 'cause he'd spoil her rotten with fine trinkets; fur coats. He catered to her every want.

From what I member, Daddee was a naïve girl in search of a something. Coop happened to fall into her trap—her beauty simply memorized him. But what come with beauty also come a loud mouth. Daddee never knew when to shut the fuck up! She was always up in someone else's business. She had a fucked up stank-ass attitude. She was always sleepin' wit' somebody else's boyfriend or husband or bitch. She

32

had no loyalty or respect when it came to her relationship with Coop.

I used to feel sad for him. I never understand why he stayed wit' her. Musta been love. Musta been 'cause he was the only man, I 'sposed, who could stomach her and her devious ways. Oh, she was a menace. She'd stomp all over his manhood. Treated him like he ain't has a dick between his legs. And yet, he never left us high and dry. I figured he musta been a very, lonely, lonely man to halfta willingly endure so much pain and destruction. He musta had low self-esteem too, 'cause if he truly loved her, he shoulda taught her how to treat him like a man. But he didn't do that. He allowed her to wear the pants. And she took full control of the situation.

Coop was a cool dude—a father figure to me. I member how he used to watch cartoons wit' me and read me stories 'bout street livin'. He played fun games wit' me too. He used to take me for ice cream. Sunday afternoon walks wit' me in the park. He played in the park wit' me too. Yeah. He could be a big kid. That's what I loved 'bout him. Sometimes we'd go to the bookstore at the mall or to the library. He always gives me fatherly advice. He'd ax me questions like: "Magnolia, if it were your last day on earth, what would you do?" And I'd always give him the same response: "Find my real dad." Oh, he'd smile so wide showing off all of his twenty-six teeth and wrap his big arms 'round my half-pint frame, and land a wet one on the side of my face wit' his soft, thick, cocoa butter lips.

Yeah. In all honesty, I always looked at Coop as a father. He always made me feelt acceptable. Like no matter how much I disappointed him, fucked up, he'd still loved me. That always gives me hope, you know. And I feelt that I could never let him down. That he would look past all of my mistakes, my fuck-ups, and never turn his back on me. That he would always seent me as his "daughter." That he'd always loved me. I treasured that shit.

Often I wondered why he loved Daddee so much 'cause she didn't seemt to feelt the same 'bout him or me. She'd talked down to him, slap him 'round like a nigga-bitch. Throw his clothes outta the window or kick him out at any given chance she could git. She'd always find something wrong just as an excuse to git rid of him. That didn't last too long. 'Cause as soon as she was low on cash she'd lure him back in. Use her feminine ways. Her *pussy*. Those sweet devious sides of her always seemted to git her her way.

Coop was weak minded in so many ways when it come to her. He took his relationship seriously. He wanted to please her. I guessed in the back of his mind he figured she'd come 'round. Come to her senses and realize that she had a good dude at home. But it never happened. Daddee couldn't see beyond herself. I always seent the li'l girl in the mirror staring back at me. Every time I looked into hers eyes, I seent me. That *fucked-up* me.

Coop was a good provider for the family. I mean he made sure we always had. I feel he coulda done so much betta' in his choice of women's. But Daddee, huh, she had that "thang" that men latched onto. Well, actually she had coupla thangs in her favor: looks, body, and boldness to do whatever her mind tells her to. All I could tell was that she had to have had some good ass pussy to keep that man 'round. I say that 'cause she had nuthin' else going for her. Nuthin'.

She was a welfare mama and a high school dropout. She had no ambition of being anythang other than a whore and a trophy on any dudes arm. She never talked 'bout her dreams or nuthin'. All she seemted to talk 'bout was... money. How much mo' money she needed for this or that. She'd bash Coop for not having enough money to keep her looking stylish. From what I could tells Coop did the best that he could do. But his best in Daddee's eyes was never good enough. She wanted mo', mo' than what he could give. She always had that thirst for something. If it wasn't jewelry, clothes, shoes, it was something someone else had. Something she feelts she should have. She liked to bite off of peoples. And she also liked the bad-boy type: thugs and hustlers and pimps. Coop was none of those types of men's. He was a decent man wit' a great big heart filled wit' love. How he got fooled into thanking that Daddee was the 'love of his life'? I had yet to figure that shit out.

Our household was neglected from the git-go, so I wasn't too surprised. It upset Coop though. I mean c'mon, she was a girlfriend, a mama. She was 'sposed to be settin' an example for me. But she didn't. Not in the eyes of Coop.

According to Daddee, huh, I was a hindrance. A burden. A mistake. An un-want. Garbage.

Let everyone else who knowed her tells it, she was the most popular piece of ass in the streets of Paterson, New Jersey. I ain't gonna say that it didn't bother me to have peoples' whisperin' snickerin' gossipin' laughin' 'bout her 'cause it did. It hurt. After all, she was my mama.

I tried to help out 'round the house to take the load off of Coop. He'd come home dead tired after tryna keep his business afloat. I'm mo' than sure it discouraged him knowing that his womans was out chasin' her youth. He heard rumors in the streets 'bout mama hanging in bars gittin' loose wit' young and old cats, it was an embarrassment, but Coop carried on wit' life.

I always wondered how he does it. Let shit like that roll off of his shoulders. Not wear his pain on his sleeve or face. I didn't knowed if I could do it. I didn't feelt that I was that strong. But Coop was. That was one strong black man. He had to be to deal wit' the shit Daddee would pull. He jus' had to be.

I guessed he thought by given her a weekly allowance that that would be enough. Shit. He was given me an allowance too. Five dollars was a lot to me. I was happy as could be. 'Cause nobody give me nuthin' but a hard ass time, so I was happy that he thought so much of me. I used to git five dollars every Friday too! I don't knows how much Coop was givin' Daddee but whatever it was surely was not enough. She was tightlipped 'bout thangs concerning her money, it was mo' in her actions that give her away. She was ungrateful. She never said thank you. She never showed him any type of affection. She never did anything nice for him. She simply dismissed him as if he didn't exist. Yeah. My mama was nuthin' but a tricked out Ho!

After a while, Coop didn't have to wonder anymo' 'bout what Daddee was doin' 'cause the dark come to muthafuckin' light. Daddee's face seemeted to age wit'in weeks. Her hazel eyes weren't as pretty as they's used to be. Her complexion lost its glow. She looked dusty pink. Her hair was neglected, thin wit' split ends. She stopped doing the thangs she done in the beginning that wooed Coop in. Yet, to him she was still a very beautiful woman. Yeah. He seent her from the inside out, not outside in. But if you'd axed me, Daddee looked like shriveled up raggedy shit.

I guessed me seent too much for a kid, huh? Yeah. I took inventory on a lot that went on in that house on Choice Street and in my neighborhood.

To put it mildly, my mama was a *crackhead-two-penny-bitch*. And the worse of the worse was that eventually I was too. Yeah. I became her twin. Her double. No different than the other girls in my neighborhood. I don't knows 'bout 'em, but it wasn't *my* choice. I was a chile. Daddee. She-she stole my purpose. And there is nuthin' that I could do. Nuthin' that I could say. Nuthin' to do but pray to a God that Coop talked of. A godly man, I never really knowed of or ever heard of in my house. Not until Coop.

Coop taught me how to believe in something even though I couldn't physically see it. And I tried. Slowly but surely I began to believe, but

35

wit' everything happening in that house it was hard to believe. I grew bitter. I had no one to call—no one to protect me from the bogeymama. Yeah. Exactly. I was doomed.

"Girlllllllllll, if you don't sit yo' silly ass down 'for I give you sump tin' to jump 'round 'bout." Yeah. That was her response. She could care less 'bout how I was feelin'; 'bout how much pain I was in. It didn't bother her at all.

I was coughing up a storm. You thank she cared. Hell, no! I nearly choked to death.

"Li'l giiiirrrrrllllll, I done told you. Carry yo' ass in yo' room! Git the fuck outta my face wit' all that noise—coughin' 'n' shit! Messin' up my high!" She'd say while cutting her eyes over at me realll sharp. I'd zoom into my room. I looked in the cracked mirror and seent that my bottom lip had black spots on it. It looked so ugly that I started crying. I stayed in my room for the rest of the day.

By the time Coop comes home, he axed 'bout my whereabouts. I overheard Daddee tellin' him that I didn't felt good. Instead of him checking in on me, she did. She didn't want me to snitch on her. She knowned that if he comes in to see me that she was going to have to explain what happened to my lips. He never come in to say, "Good night, suga dumplin'," like he normally done. I was so sad, so mad, so hurt that he ignored my feelings likes that. Why he do that? Why didn't he come in and check in on me? I wondered. I needed to tell him what had happened. I needed him to seent what she had done to me. *Why did he have to put so much trust in her?* I axed myself. But then I knowed that answer 'cause she was his woman...and 'cause she sucked his *dick*... that's how come.

Wit' Daddee everything came wit'a price. Even for Coop. 'Specially for me. I came last.

The next day, Daddee made me stay home from school. It took coupla days for the color of my lips to come back to normal.

By that time, the truant officer, Mrs. Rowena started makin' visits to our house. Daddee would never let her in.

Mrs. Rowena, a petite black woman wit' big lips and big bifocal glasses would ring our doorbell, nonstop. That old lady played by the book. Yeah. She took her job very seriously. And that really got under Daddee's skin. "Why can't this old bat beat it," she'd say annoyed. "Oh, my God, don't she git the fuckin' hint that we ain't home, shit!"

Buzz! Buzz! Buzz!

Mrs. Rowena was very pesty and it fucked wit' Daddee's head. Her body would quiver full of hotness. Her face would git red as hell. "Oh, she is gittin' on my last damn nerve!" She'd snap, while pacing back and forth in the living room. Her nerves would git so frustrated that she'd start chain smoking. The house would be full of smoke it could gag you.

Mrs. Rowena knowed how to tick Daddee off. But I'd take the heat for it every time. Daddee used to turn and look at me wit' cunning eyes and say; "Yo' ass is gon' back to school tomorrow. Fuck dis shit!"

In times of ailments Daddee normally made an appointment for me to be seent by Dr. Herringbone, another one of her many johns.

By the next day, I had my fake doctor's note ready for the nurse. Like I said, my mama made sure she covered all of her tracks, including the one's that grew on her arms. The tattoo marks left from the syringe needles. The one's she called her "birth marks."

How excited I was the second time I saw Daddee smoking her crack pipe. Yeah. It sounds stupid now that I thank back. But I was soooo young, so naïve, so unworldly. My li'l palms clapped and I pursed my little lips like a gold fish so happy. I said, "Ooh, Mama, the angel is dancing in the bubble!" I was memorized, giggling in my small frame. Seent the cloud of smoke dance inside that clear bubblehead was like a-m-a-z-i-n-g to me. Damn-fuck. I couldn't wait to grow up and become somebody cool.

When I reached 'bout age *six* or *seven* years old, Daddee bought me a gift home. It wasn't my birthday or nuthin' like that, so I was just surprised that she thought of me. Seent how she hated me so. I was jumping up and down on my tip-toes wit' my li'l arms stretched up in the air, anxious, "Yeh! Yeh!" Daddee handed me the gold rectangular box and I tore that red wrapping paper open so eager to seent what Daddee had gotten me.

As soon as I laid eyes on it my eyes widened so big. "Yehhhhhhhhhhhh!" I sang so happy. I had butterflies swarming 'round in my tummy; so very excited that Daddee gives me a gift. Up and down I jumped. "Yeh, Mama, I got one too! I got one too!" I said so happy.

Inside of that rectangular box was a glass bubblehead wit' what looked like a hard chunk of rock-sized chalk? You knowed the chalk teachers used on the blackboard. "What are you going to name *her*," she axed me. I was straining my brain tryna thank of a name.

Daddee was fidgety in her seat. "Why don't you name *her*...Ol' Durty," she said.

I stand still, thanking. She lifted her forefinger up and tapped it against her top lip, three times like she was in deep thought too. Then she spoke in a faint tone, "Shhh...she's our little secret, okay. You know Ol' Durty loves you, don't you?" I nodded my head up and down, and smiled so big. From her given me that gift I believed her every word.

That day, me and Daddee sat in that dirty ass kitchen wit' roaches crawling on the kitchen table, dirty dishes in the sank, molded pots sitting on the stove, a mouse stuck to a mouse trap and mice running throughout the house. Daddee cooked the hard chunk of chalk and we'd smoked the night away.

After a few good pulls from the bubblehead my head spun. I was feelt dizzy, nauseous. I was so sick to my stomach. I started throwing up. It quickly became the worse feelin' in the world to me. But within a couple of days' time, after Coop had finally had enough and packed his bags and left us, Daddee and I was smoking chalk almost every day.

And in times when we were broke as hell, I means those desperation times, Daddee, she'd make me do thangs that ugly little girls do to gits money to feed *her* drug habit. Instantly her eyes would sag and her lips would poke out lookin' like she'd lost her very best friend. She'd looked downright pitiful. I feelt pity for her.

Once she knew she had me where she wanted me she undressed me till I was butt naked, put cute barrettes in my hair, put makeup on my small innocent face, and then she'd get dressed up in her big red teddy, made her hair looked pretty wit' big loose curls and put makeup on to make her looked sexy, and then she'd call up one of her old male companions and invited him over to have a nightcap.

After a few shots of tequila we'd all end up in her bedroom, both taking turns wit' this grown ass hairy scary lookin' man. I always wanted to ax her if it was okay for that man to be putting his hands on me—to be touching my *privacy* wit' his wet tongue and then sticking his large finger in my opened hole. But Daddee looked content as she climbed on top of his hard dick and rode him so whorishly wit' intent to please. I didn't want to spoil her fun, her fuck. I wanted her to be happy 'specially since Coop was gone.

You see, in spite of how she feelt 'bout me, I still looked to her as my mama. A fucked up mama, but mama.

"Li'l girrrrrrrllll, you betta' git yo' ass out in 'em streets and work 'em corners, while you still got function in you. I keeps tellin' yo' ass to come out with me, you coulda made some cash fo' coupla hours of blowjobs. What you thank you too good to give blowjobs? What you too good to git fucked in the backseat of a john's car? It's called makin' a livin' so don't knock the hustle. You gotta eat, don't you? Shit. Piss. Li'l girl, I ain't

38

got no damn money to be wastin' on yo' tired ass. Buyin' shit to wipe yo' ass wit. Spending my backbreakin' money on buyin' yo' ugly ass pads 'n tampons fo' yo' bloody pussy—wastin' my damn money on gittin' you fuckin' bras, drawers, like I'm rollin' in muthafuckin' dough. Lemme tells you sump tin'. These bitches out in the world, out here in these here streets don't believe in wearin' drawers. It's against they's religion. That's why they's let their pussies breathe cuz when they's come into this world they's ain't have no drawers on. They's was butt ass naked. Stupid! I dunno why you can't seemt to git this through that rock head of yours. They's hos' like you and me. You gots that, li'l girl. Hos! Why you gotta be so goddamn stupid? Every time I turn 'round you gots to need sump tin'? That's all I hears. 'Daddee, I need. I need. I need.' Act like you sump tin' special. I dunno who lied to you cuz, bitch, you ain't shit! You ain't no betta' than me. Huh. Give me a fuckin' break. Shit. I needs too!

She go on and on, "You listen. And you listen reallllllll goood cuz I'ma 'bout to school yo' ass. You ain't gonna learnt this shit in no classroom. Look at me when I talkin' to you, li'l girl, so I knows you hears me straight. Now, you can take dis any way you want, but it's the honest truth. You listenin' cuz I'ma only tells you dis once. *Ev'ry Ho gotta daddy, ev'ry Pussy gotta past.* And when yo' Dad ain't 'round you gotta be nasty to git what the hell you want in this fucked up world. You hears me? Fuck what you learnt in that sorry ass school. 'Em fake ass teachers dunno nuthin' 'bout survivin' in the mean streets of the ghetto. Out there is a muthafuckin' jungle, you hears me? 'Em bitches dunno nuthin' 'bout livin' in no damn jungle. Tells 'em to call me. Daddee, at your service! I'll taught 'em sump tin'. I know what the fuck I'm talkin' 'bout cuz I'm livin' the shit. What the fuck they's knows? They's got all the schoolin' and dunno... shit! Dumb bitches!

"Listen to me li'l girl; using yo' pussy wills git you far in life. Use it and find the fuck out. Don't let 'em bitches fuck yo' head up wit' that talk 'bout gittin' a good education, fuck grammer school, college, too. If they's know like I knows, huh, pussy and dick go hand in hand. Listen. Pussy is yo' bread 'n butta, chile. Pussy is the bread. Cum is the butta. Don't you know dis shit? That makes a sweet fuckin' sandwich! So, if you knows what the fuck you doin' you can git paid jus' fo' lying on yo' back. That's right. I said it! Let a nigga climb in that pussy and tap tap tap on that young ass. Educate yo'self wit' that! And see what 'em bitches say then. Ain't nuthin' wrong wit' fuckin' fo' a livin', ev'rybody's fuckin'. How you thank all these badass muthafuckers windup in this world? Fuckin', that's how! Use that head of yo's, 'n realize. Oh, you too goddamn stupid to realize anythang. Dumb ass! I dunno why the fuck I had you in the first damn place. I shoulda aborted yo' ugly ass when I first found out I was knocked up. If it weren't fo' that sorry muthafucker yo' ass wouldn't be here right now. Yeah. He left. And I didn't shed one measly tear. I did what the fuck I had to do! Me.

"Look-a-here, li'l girl, you just holdin' a crackhead trick down, you hears me! You holdin' my muthafuckin' ass down! DO YOU *hears me*?!!!! You'a burden to my soul, girl! A burden to my muthafuckin' soul!"

***

"KNEEL ON YO' knees, *bitch*. Magnolia, don't play with me!" Shot out of Daddee's mouth. I stood stiff. She pierced a frigid look at me with her dull hazel eyes. She wore her favorite red teddy wit' no panties. Resting between her index and middle finger was a lit Pall Mall cigarette. She'd tilt her head back, long bleached blonde hair touching her supple skin. She'd stare at me with disgust in her eyes. Then take a pull off of her cigarette and blow out; still sternly piercing those cat eyes at me.

"Li'l girl, kneel yo ass down and put yo head between Unc's legs." Daddee demanded. She sat up and looked at me, hard. "Do it, girlllll!" Her facial expression of stoic eyes unemotionally locked in on me. All I can tell you is that she'd pimp me out in a heartbeat.

"Li'l girl, don't make me fuck you up." She'd narrow-eyed me. I plopped down like a stiff body to my bony knees. Scooted myself closer to Unc as he stood before me. His feet were spread apart in his worn construction boots, as my face was eye level to his shriveled dick. I sniffed. And as I did, I could smell the stench of sour sweat from in-between his hairy legs. The pubic hairs around his balls looked nappier than the kitchen of my next-store neighbor Abita's head.

I figured after Unc: #10, #15, #23, she'd learnt her lesson of bringing stragglers home. Knowing her, she could never pick a decent fellah. No. Only the nasty ones wit' deep pockets seemted to attract her eyes.

Unc reached his large grungy hand down in his tattered gray boxers and scratched underneath his plum-size balls. I could hear his jagged nails scraping against his ashy dry skin. It sounded like sandpaper scratching against a spackled wall.

"Unc!" Daddee snapped. "You want yo' *dick* sucked or what?" Unc nodded. He then pulled his boxers down to his ankles. His dick swung low, as it was slightly erect.

I frowned. Closed my eyes wishing I could disappear. Just drop dead and be done wit' it all.

My mouth filled wit' spit. I was nauseous and shivering. Tears engulfed in my innocent kid eyes and streamed hard and fast down my scrawny face. All I could thank about was, why couldn't I have been a stillborn?

Since I was in the livin' I chose to change my mindset of myself. *You're mo' than a Ho. You're mo' than a Ho. You're mo' than a Ho. You'sa girl. You'sa bright girl. You'sa bright, pretty girl. You'sa girl wit' imagination. You'sa girl wit' hopes and dreams.*

I paid mo' attention in class when I did go to school. Even though Daddee stayed in my ear I tried to tune her out 'cause she was steady knockin' me for wanting to betta' myself. I wanted to learnt how to talk betta', act betta', look betta', conduct myself in a betta' way. I wanted to have friends who wasn't ashamed to hang out wit' me. Or who parents didn't talk ugly of me 'cause of Daddee.

I guessed I wanted to set myself apart from Daddee. You know, separate how people's looked at me. It was hard. Reallll hard. I wanted to be my own me. Daisy. So I started working on Daisy.

***

"I seent you lookin' at Driven. He don't want yo tight pussy." Daddee said sitting at the kitchen table with her freshly painted crimson toes propped atop a rusted kitchen chair, smoking a vanilla-scented blunt. I tried to ignore her as I headed straight for the fridge to get me a glass of milk.

"I knows you hear me, bitch! I seent you lookin' at Driven. He don't want yo tight pussy," she repeated in a retort tone as if I didn't hear her the first time. Her chapped and blistery lips pursed together as she sucked in another drag.

I opened the fridge and reached for the quart of milk.

"Why da fuck would he want yo young ass when he got me?! I'm all he needs." She grabbed her tits and squeezed 'em so nastily. "I give that man wet pussy, so if you know what's best fo' your bitch-ass you betta' keep yo eyes to yo'self 'fore I fuck you up. Yo li'l pussy can't handle a big dick like Driven's anyhow. He too much nigga fo' yah. Got too much dark meat. That nigga'a split yo li'l stank ass pussy open, bitch!"

All I could think at the moment was if I had a shotgun I would've pulled the muthafuckin' trigger and blew her trifling ass away. But instead I grabbed a dirty Welch's grape jelly jar out of the sink. I washed it with watery no-refills laundry detergent 'cause we ain't have any mo' lemon Ajax. And I tried with everything in me to block her out of my head, her sultry voice, her milky white face, her presence, but she kept on running off at the muthafuckin' mouth, as usual.

"Lemme school yo ass on sump tin' up in this here crib...the dick that comes walking through that muthafuckin' door is mine! You ugly bitch!" she snapped and squinted her eyes at me to get her point across. I heard her loud and clear. I kept quiet.

I turned on the kitchen faucet and rinsed the Welch's grape jelly jar to use as a glass and reached for the milk and poured in a half of glass. I guessed the silence was killin' her 'cause her brows knitted and she sneered at me stirring up mo' drama.

"Oh, you gonna act like you'a fuckin' mute. You jus' 'member what I fucks I tells yah. Fuck 'round and look at Driven again and see what happens to you." She held the blunt between her lips and just stared at me.

I didn't flinch, at least not that time. I guessed I was beginning to get used to it. Somewhat.

I gulped down the milk, washed the Welch's grape jelly jar and headed back to my bedroom. I shut the door, sat down on the edge of my disheveled bed, and cried like nobody's business. I was *eight*.

The door slammed, hard.

In walked Daddee dressed in her white mini skirt, psychedelic halter-top wit' thigh-high hot pink hooker boots on. Her shoulder-length blonde hair was tucked under a strawberry-colored wig that really brought out her features, especially her eyes. Her face was all twisted up, which meant someone had pissed her off. Which meant I was gonna catch a case.

Daddee cut her eyes sharp at me. "Lemme school you on sump tin' li'l girl. You betta' use the hell outta that body, that pussy, that ass, and those tits and stack you up some bank cuz I can't help yo stupid ass. I ain't got the time or the patience to potty train you. I've done my job given birth to yo ugly ass. Now I gotta look out fo' me, bitch! Me!" she snapped, then sashayed her nasty-looking self back out the door. I held back the tears, as often as I could.

Thirteen.

"Git yo ass out here!" Daddee snapped. I tried to hold my breath hoping to die before she came bum rushing through my bedroom door. Knowing that I probably couldn't kill myself in time I rose from my bed with this bad feeling in my gut. I was sick again. It seems I was always sick, but she never cared.

"Hurry up! Time is money!" Daddee barked.

I rushed into the living room in my holey pajamas where she was with a man I had never seen before.

The man was sloppily dressed in a pair of dingy jeans and a dirty T-shirt. He was fat, short, and dark-skinned with rotten teeth. He looked like he was the nasty type. I could always sniff out the nasty types. They always had this daunting look in their eyes and this stench to 'em.

"Drop yo bottoms for Unc." Daddee's voice was nonchalant as if she was axin' me to change the TV channel. Or bring her her *fuckin'* beer.

I didn't budge.

"I said drop 'em, bitch!" She yelled at the top of her lungs, which made me flinch in my skin. She sneered at me.

"Li'l girl, don't play wit' me."

I shut my eyes. Body shook.

"Daisy!"

She rarely called me *Daisy*. It musta been a full moon.

Unc stood, eyes chewing at me. Slowly, my thumbs sunk in the sides of my raggedy pajama bottoms and I eased 'em down to my knees, then ankles.

"Drop the drawers, girl; this man ain't got all day. He wants some pussy! I can't fuck him cuz I gots my period."

Unc scrunched up his nose when she said that. I guessed he didn't want no bloody pussy. I couldn't very well blame him.

I swallowed, and then stepped out of my pajama bottoms and holey drawers. I was shaking like crazy by just the thought of him touching me. *Oh, the man in the sky...God.* I thought in my head. I wanted to just pass out on the floor and hoped that when I woke up he'd be long gone or stone-cold dead.

The unknown man unzipped his pants, and reached inside of 'em and pulled out his long, skinny, black, old lookin' monster.

I exhaled.

Daddee rolled her eyes with hatred embedded in 'em. She then shifted those eyes over to the dusty lopsided clock on the wall. She slithered her bony fingers in the pocket of her coffee stained housecoat and pulled out a cigarette. Then she reached over on the three-legged coffee table and grabbed the lighter and lit it. She leaned back on the couch as if she was watching a television show. There was no empathy in her eyes. She was heartless.

"Okay, now git yo ass over by the couch! Bend over. This man wants some pussy. Bitch, I gotta git some money so you betta' not fuck this up cuz if you do, if you do, it's yo ass! Do you hear me, li'l girl? Don't have me embarrass you. I'll make yo bitch-ass git on the floor and purr like a stray kitten. Keep playin' wit' me. You want that *plunger stick*," she'd threatened.

Vigorously, I shook my head no. I didn't want no plunger stick stuck up my ass. *No mo'! No mo'!* I screamed in my head.

My eyes flooded with tears. I leaned over the raggedy couch. I raised my knees up on the couch, my face and eyes facing the wall. I felt this brush of heat against my butt. I knew Unc was behind me. I didn't even have to open my eyes. I smelled his body odor that smelled like sweaty feet. His callous hand rubbed my butt wit' roughness. And his large middle finger rubbed against the lips of my dry pussy. His motion was rough and vigorous that eventually my pussy creamed, yet my body stiffened.

Daddee sucked her teeth. I hated when she did that shit. "Look, li'l girl," she spoke in a stern tone. "I teached you how to do this...now spread 'em so that this man can give me my money and git the fuck outta my house. I ain't got all fuckin' day," she squinted, then rolled those eyes of hers, slow. "I know you know how to work that tight ass body of yours. What a waste of fuckin' pussy," she huffed, while shaking her head as if I was a pity case. She folded her skinny arms about her chest and laughed as her floppy titties jiggled. "All that fuckin' and you still don't know how to work the pussy. Girlll, you should be ashamed of yourself. You ain't my muthafuckin' daughter, not fuckin' like that! Move your ass, bitch! Pump the pussy, bitch! Gyrate! Rotate those hips! Dig your middle finger in your pussy! Finger-fuck yo'self! Shit! Make-believe it feels good to you! Squeeze your ass cheeks! Play wit' your nipples! Pull those muthafuckers! Lick your lips! Rub on your clit! Tug on your small tits! Squeeze 'em! Moan! Scream! Yell out his name! (But I didn't know his name, other than to call him...Unc like all the rest). Shout! Git into it! Do sump tin' to arouse him! Make him want the pussy, bitch! Make him want it enough to come, shit! I want my damn money! This is some fuckin' bullshit!" Daddee snapped, totally upset with my sexual performance. I was 'sposed to be her legacy—to please her and her john. Keep the "fuckin' tradition" going in our family. I was 'sposed to make her proud since she was the one who had mentored me since birth. I was 'sposed to boost her name up as well as her ego and make her standout so that others would be envious of her. But who would be envious of a mama pimping out her kid, huh? Who?

I tried so many times to block her outta my mind, my heart, but I just couldn't. Somehow Daddee knew how to invade every part of my existence. I despised *her* even mo' for that. How could it be so easy to just throw away your biological chile like that? I wondered.

To me, my life was no longer mine to live. It became everyone else's. And it made me *think* way beyond my imagination: *Was I already dead inside but just didn't know it?* I had to pay for every deal that went bad. Consciously...I had to pay. And trust you me, I did.

Still *thirteen*, I remember Daddee only came out when it was dark. Other than that, I rarely saw her. And when I did she looked scary to me. Her once gorgeous face was sunken in and her curvaceous figure was now skin and bone. Her hazel eyes were yellowish-gray and big, round saucers in her head. She no longer had that pretty brunette hair either. It was now strings of thinness. She sure as hell didn't look like the mama I knows, or didn't know. Slowly, she was dryin' up.

Two days had past when I discovered my thirty-something year old trick-ass-crackhead-heroin-addict mama...*dead*. And no, I didn't shed one measly tear. Nope. If anything, I smiled. Yep. I smiled so freely. Man in the sky...God. I was happy that that bitch had died. And for me, ME, to have had the pleasure of finding her bony ass slumped over sitting on the toilet was the best gift I'd ever been given. I felt uplifted, light. That was until...

Until I viewed a page from a journal in her hand. Yes, at that moment I felt a whole lotta things. I thought how naïve was I to be a dreamer. Nothin' I ever wished for come true. Or so I thought. But Daddee was dead. *Dead!*

Somehow that brought a little piece of joy to my fucked up life. But then something happened.

I read the sheet of paper. And that fucked my head up. And for the first time in my young life I had mixed feelings for Daddee. Yeah, I hated her, but then a small part of me still wanted to love her. But my heart was near brick. It seemed too late.

"Dear Daddee,

In the years that we have been courting I've given you 95% of me and you couldn't even find it within yourself to give me 5% of a "hello," "how was your day?" or "love yah, baby." Ever since I lost my business I could never hangout with the fellahs drinking beer and playing pool because you needed to have your lo-jack on my every move. I chose you because I felt you were my soul mate. You completed me. But it seems I'm nothing more than a puppet on a string to you. You just don't know how good you had it. I understand now that you never appreciated me. I swallowed my pride to keep you happy, but through all of the pain and suffering and the verbal abuse, I have lost myself.

I have tried numerous times to crawl out of the hell that you put me in, to prove to you how good I could be for you and your daughter, but yet you kept me locked down. What is wrong with you, Daddee? Personally, I think your father has scarred you. You can't realize a good man when you see him standing right in front of your face, lying beside you every night in your bed. Woman, I prayed and asked God to release me from this hell. I cried because I felt worthless and ashamed. I allowed you to dictate my life. I am a man whose heart has been placed in your manipulative hands. I have lived in denial for so many years, hoping that one day you would truly see what you have in me. I am a good man. Faithfully, I have loved you unconditionally. But you have never reciprocated, you only asked for me to do more for you. I've been waiting for you to show me that you loved me, to let me know that you even cared.

I finally asked myself, 'Coop, when was the last time your woman actually told you she loved you?' Answer: 'Never.'

My mind, body, and spirit were all speaking to me in one voice this morning. That inner voice said you are resilient and powerful. Don't shortchange her one bit. So Daddee, I made you dinner, washed, pressed, and neatly folded your clothes, cleaned your house for the last time.

After that, I walked over to the calendar on the wall and marked an X on today's date. I cried when I walked into your bedroom, packed my suitcase, and left your key on the kitchen table. This good man is moving on.

Farewell,

Coop"

I come to. Wiped my tear-streaked face. And thought, *that bitch!*

AFTER THAT TRIFLIN' HO died, and before Child Services could get a hold of me, a man everyone called Ghetto-Man got involved. He was kind enough to take me into his home.

Ghetto-Man was well known, very friendly and polite. He was like a father figure to most of the underprivileged kids in the neighborhood—a very givin' man.

Ghetto-Man stood about 5'10", fair-skinned with big, round gray eyes and fine silver hair that looked liked wool covering his head. One thing about him was that he was very soft-spoken. He never raised his voice even if he was upset. I always liked to be in his presence. It was just something about him that I really took to. It was something in his eyes that said: *I'll never hurt you.*

Ghetto-Man knew mama. He knew that Daddee was a *junky*. He knew that she was the neighborhood whore, too. He knew Coop. And that he had left us.

Word usually traveled quickly in the streets of Paterson. So knowing that, he knew that I didn't have any close relatives to help me out. So he took it upon himself to do so.

I tell you no lie. I never felt so *accepted.*

Ghetto-Man treated me like the dad I once had. I'm talkin' 'bout Coop. Ghetto-Man fed me home cooked meals every day. He enrolled me back in school. He helped me with my homework. And he spent quality time with me. He talked to me. He axed me questions to see where my head was. I'm sure he knew that I was deeply troubled, and he tried with everything in him to make me feel at ease. I really felt like he cared 'bout me. I hadn't felt that way since Coop left.

Ghetto-Man owned a big house out in Montvale, New Jersey, out in the boonies away from the hustle and bustle of Paterson. He had a big old-fashioned house. A big yard, too. He lived in comfort. Quiet. So quiet where you could hear the birds chirp. Hear myself think. Could hear the leaves flutter against the tree branches. Hear the wind sing. And in the spring hear the bees buzz. You smelled the scent of nature, sandalwood and honey. Man, it smelled so sweet to my senses. He also had a cat named Lena Horne (named after the singer) that kept him company. She was a housecat with a fluffy white coat and cornflower blue eyes. Goodness, I loved his cat. She was so pretty and playful.

"Daisy," Ghetto-Man spoke in a mellow tone.

"Yes, sir."

"Tell me what you're thinking at this moment."

47

I remained silent.

"I won't judge you." He said softly.

I felt he wouldn't. He had such genuineness to him.

I raised my self-esteem. Made eye contact with him and said, "*Men* craved her. Knowing that she was a whore only intensified their lust. It was like an addiction. Something I could never understand. I wanted to have a relationship with her, but sadly to say, she never seemed to want one with me."

I sighed, and then continued, "Often I felt as if she hated me for being her *daughter*. She had me. I didn't make her fuck. She wanted the dick. And whoever she fucked gladly gave her some dick. Honestly, I really don't think she was happy about being pregnant with me. I think I put a damper on her lifestyle. To have to endure stretch marks, weight gain, swollen feet. No. She wasn't happy at all."

I lowered my head, then immediately lifted it back up.

I continued, "In spite of how she made me feel I still managed to get through each grueling day under her roof. How? I couldn't tells you. I guessed I had this inner strength that kicked in when it wanted to. But I seemed to never be able to kick my habit of smoking *crack*.

"Damn, it got so bad I was eating out of Dunkin' Donuts dumpsters 'cause I was soooo hungry. I had no shame. Fuck. I didn't care.

"After the fact of selling my soul I'd feel like shit. I wasn't thinking. I was too busy craving to even care about the aftereffects of my actions. I was *a junky*! And junkies do what junkies do to feed their pain. I felt like I had no choice in the matter. It wasn't like I was going to one-day walk into a Detox program or Narcotic Anonymous-NA program in the near future or anything like that. I was already too fucked up.

"Truth be told.

"All I wanted was Ol' Durty and all Ol' Durty wanted was for me to continue to want and need her. And I did. I desperately needed her to continue to fuck my life up."

I sucked in the tears before they managed to leak from my eyes, while Ghetto-Man listened.

I continued, "The things Daddee used to do to me would make one think I was her worst enemy. I never liked her. I know she couldn't stand the sight of me, but I tried with everything in me to love her. But I could never bite down hard enough to find that opening in my heart to do so."

His eyes widened in surprise. "You don't really think that, do you?"

I nodded my head.

Ghetto-Man gently wrapped his thick arm around me, and hugged me so very tight. I never wanted him to let me go. For once I felt safe. I felt loved.

"God. He'll see you through, my child. He'll see you through. Trust and believe."

I wanted to trust and believe in the man in the sky. But—

THINKING BACK, I recall when Daddee used to barmaid at Ghetto-Man's hole-in-the-wall called MO'-WHISKEY. It resided on a side street of Whiskey Street, a few blocks from us. It was in a secluded spot primarily for: members only.

Before you even stepped foot in the place Ghetto-Man had a license plate made up that he hung on the front door the read:

MO'-WHISKEY
If you please...
Proprietor: Ghetto-Man

Boy, I used to get a kick outta that sign.

MO'-WHISKEY USED TO be packed Monday through Sunday like clockwork. From eleven in the morning till whenever that place would be jumping. Ghetto-Man ain't had no set time to shut down. He was about making money and making people happy. He'd leave when his customers were good and drunk. Damned near falling off the barstools. Once they got tired of hearin' the jukebox playing, they'd take their drunken asses home. Come back the next day and do it all over again.

Daddee used to complain almost every day when she worked at MO'-WHISKEY. The manager, Old Lady had given her a run for her money. Oh, she couldn't stand that lady. When she'd get home she'd rant like nobodies business.

"The shit a bitch gotta go through jus' to make a fuckin' dollar is fuckin' unreal! It don't make no fuckin' sense! I'd rather sell my pussy than go through this bullshit! Lemme tell you sump tin' li'l piss-bitch, peace of mind pays more than a barmaid paycheck any day fo' me. And the tips, yeah, they come in handy, but the thangs you gotta go through, the 'she say she say' bullshit, the lies, smart ass comments, looks, sucking of the teeth, rolling of the eyes, and the drunk ass nosey bitches wit' their fuckin' loud mouths is not sump tin' that I'm gonna tolerate much longer. I'll rather fuck a *broke down nigga* more so a *broken soul nigga* any day of the fuckin' week. I can't do this shit! But I refuse to let Old Lady break me. I refuse!"

I honestly think Daddee was trying to change her ways, but since her and Old Lady never got along it only pulled her back to what she knew best: ho'in.

Every time she'd come home she'd vent. "Man in the sky," I said under my breath, "boy, I'd wished she'd quit that barmaid job." But like Daddee said that would've given Old Lady too much satisfaction, too much power. Daddee wasn't 'bout to do that. So she played the game, but she changed the players.

The mo' Old Lady toyed with *her*, the mo' Daddee toyed with Old Lady's old man Rooster. Oh, she flirted with him like crazy just to get under Old Lady's skin. And she did.

Daddee bought Rooster drinks. She knew how to lure him in. She'd sweet-talk him. She made him feel like a king. Rooster easily took the bait. That only inflamed mo' drama at the bar. Ghetto-Man didn't play that shit. He didn't care what you did in your own backyard, but he didn't want that shit brought to his front door. He'd nip that shit in the bud right then and there.

Eventually Rooster left Old Lady and started seeing Daddee on the side. That only enraged Old Lady but there was nothin' she could do. Daddee had body, looks, and pussy that her man had been missing since Old Lady had gotten all big and fat. Yeah. They were very open about their relationship. Rooster used to come to the bar and sit while Daddee worked. Talk 'bout wicked. That was Daddee fo' yah.

Needless to say, the relationship between Daddee and Rooster didn't last for long. Daddee got bored with playing with his little dick and dismissed him with the quickness. Rooster ended up crawling back to Old Lady. And she took him back too. But best believe on everything certain she made that old man suffer.

Besides, Daddee and Old Lady, Ghetto-Man had four other barmaids on his roster: Stank-Booty (but her real name was Lullaby), Juicy, Fierce and Strawberry.

At MO'-WHISKEY, Old Lady called the shots. That was one *ugly* woman. Her whole flow was jacked up. She was dark-skinned wit'a blonde 'do. No, it did not do her justice. She was wide-hipped and flabby, big ass gut hanging over her spandex. But she could make a mean ass blue margarita and could sang her ass off. Sounded like another

Aretha in the makings. I kid you not! Taught herself how to barmaid during the time she was a runaway. Said she read in some book of how to make mixed drinks. She also said her Pops used to beat her with a steel bat. He slapped her Mom around a couple of times with a brick, too. He had broken her jawbone. She'd come a long way from sleeping in the streets and selling drugs on the corners to support herself. Going through some hard times really toughened her up. It's funny 'cause she only stood about 4'11". But she wasn't anyone to be messin' with. Old Lady had a handful of babies. Most of their daddies' gon' left her to fend for herself. But from what I could see she'd done just fine on her own.

Sometimes some of the barmaids would share personal stories about their past with me. That only happened when Daddee was off doing whatever she did.

Often I wondered why? What did *they* see in me to tell me such personal things? Things they wouldn't even tell their own mothers. I'd never forget how much of an impact it made on me. Never. Why couldn't I have been as strong as them women's? I guessed 'cause I was still a child in mind.

Most of the patrons took to *Stank-Booty* 'cause she was a high yellow gal. She was so-so in the looks department, but she had a body build like a brick house. All 5'5" of her, with long reddish-brown hair that she kept slicked back in a ponytail. And girlfriend loved to wear those tight breeches. She fit 'em good. She had a pleasant attitude and pretty much got along with everybody that got along with her.

Juicy wasn't really blonde, just to let you know. Her tall, thin frame put you in mind of a skinny ass crackhead model. She was caramel complexioned with chinky-looking, black walnut eyes and honeyed-toned-colored hair. She had mad issues. I think she'd been beaten too many times as a child and it done affected her mentally. Heard DFYS took her children away from her 'cause she wasn't fit to be nobody's mama. Heard she was into females that looked like dudes. She didn't look like no bull-dagger, but what I know. She didn't fuck wit' me. And if she'd tried I'd cut her without a second thought. I didn't play that shit. If I were interested I'd let it be known. No. I didn't play that creepin' up on a bitch shit.

Fierce and Strawberry happened to be related. Uh-huh. Somehow they met by accident. Both were working the streets for two different pimps.

One night *Fierce* was gettin' her ass whooped by her pimp Tinsel. Strawberry, wit' her crazy ass self, intervened after working her john.

51

Said she had to do something 'fore (Tinsel) beat Fierce, five foot of bony ass to a pulp.

Come to find out after *Strawberry*, a thick chick, who stood about 5'6" in mocha skin convinced him to let her complete the job that Fierce had fucked up. The two of 'em became like blood sisters. After talkin' they found out that they were related: *aunt and niece.*

Don't get me wrong, MO'-WHISKEY mighta looked like a hole-in-the-wall on the outside, but on the inside it looked like the Brownstone. Well, not exactly, but you get my drift.

Ghetto-Man had that place sparkling. From the mahogany bar wit' granite marble counter, to the chandeliers that dangled like tear-drop diamonds, to the cherry wood leather bar stools, polished hardwood floors, laminated bar menus, not to mention how neat and clean he had his barmaids looking in their uniforms. He stopped 'em from wearing their plain clothes 'cause he thought they looked tacky. So he had 'em wear black tank tops with "MO'-WHISKEY" in pink lettering with pink mini-skirts and pink high-heeled shoes. No one give him a problem, not even Daddee. That was surprising to us all.

Everything was upscale in that place. It was liked Ghetto-Man always used to say: "You can't judge a book by its cover." And it was so true. He put his heart and soul into that place to make it what it was. It was his. And he treated it as if it was his *old lady*.

Mostly every day MO'-WHISKEY was flooded with peoples. Ghetto-Man was a very well off man, but he wasn't rich as in millions. He was wealthy within. He wasn't a superficial man. He was a very practical one. Now his son, on the other hand, Durdy-Dog was just the opposite. He was a ruthless son-of-a-gun.

Every time Durdy-Dog stepped foot in, MO'-WHISKEY he always gave me this eerie feeling. I used to sit in the corner of the bar with a Harlequin romance novel in my hands. Call myself gettin' my romance on. And every time that fool would see me he'd come and snatch the book out of my hands. Ghetto-Man would kindly tell him to stop actin' so foolish. Durdy-Dog just ignored him. That man used to make my toes tingle in his presence. I always took that as a sign that he was no good.

Durdy-Dog had his own vision for MO'-WHISKEY. He felt his vision could build an empire, if only his father would allow him to take over, but Ghetto-Man was adamant about how he wanted to run his own business. MO'-WHISKEY was established back in the late '50s, way before I was even thought of. Ghetto-Man wanted it to remain as he saw fit. His patrons were used to a certain kind of treatment. They felt good in the hands of Ghetto-Man because he was not only a businessman, but also a friend. He treated people like people. He was very hospitable. He cared deeply for his community 'specially the less fortunate. He gave back to feed the hungry. He did all sorts of things for his Black people. He was a man of great integrity. And people gravitated toward him 'cause he was a good person. He made his establishment make you feel welcomed, especially with the jukebox blaring the likes of: Little Milton "Annie Mae's Café," Johnnie Taylor "Last Two Dollars," Howling Wolf "The Red Rooster," Little Richard "Lucille," Marvin Sease "The Candy Licker," Jimmy Reed "Big Boss Man," and Bobby "Blue" Bland "You've Got to Hurt Before You Heal." The joint would be packed with people listening to music that made 'em feel good. They'd bob their heads, snap their fingers, sing along, or tap their feet or dance, step or swing. It was music to soothe a weary soul. Yeah. And that's what MO'-WHISKEY represented: *a place of comfort wit' some down home blues.*

It was like a family at MO'-WHISKEY. And that's what Ghetto-Man wanted his place to feel like, a place his patrons could and would consider a home away from home.

By now, we were livin' in a new day and era. Durdy-Dog couldn't wait to get his grimy hands on MO'-WHISKEY, so that he could change everything that it meant to his dad. Durdy-Dog was about making connections and he didn't care whom toes he'd stepped on, not even Ghetto-Man. I can only assume in his mind, MO'-WHISKEY could generate some real loot, if only his seventy-five year old father would just step aside and handover his life's work. But what, Durdy-Dog failed to realize was that MO'-WHISKEY was what was keeping his dad alive. MO'-WHISKEY became his everything, especially after his wife, Bluesy of forty-something years had passed away.

MO'-WHISKEY was what had gotten him through those bad days and lonely nights. The people he'd come in contact with were also a value to him 'cause without them, the legacy would have died a long, long time ago. Ghetto-Man would've died a long time ago, too.

MO'-WHISKEY really gave him hope—strength to carry on with life as a widower. People respected and trusted Ghetto-Man to the utmost. So it seemed rather bizarre of his untimely death. He was never a sickly man. He kept a clean bill of health. I never saw him with a cold or as much as a runny nose. He was very cautious about what he ate. He stopped drinking after Bluesy had taken ill with ovarian cancer. He never smoked. So it seemed rather bizarre for this healthy man (in spirit and in mind) to suddenly drop dead. I found him lying face down on his living room floor. I was startled and so heartbroken. It was my second time witnessing death. Don't know why but death seemed to have a strong affect on me. It was like death was all around me. Everywhere I turned death was always watching.

Everyone assumed that Ghetto-Man was poisoned but no one was sure. An autopsy was performed, which came back as: death from natural causes. People suspected that Durdy-Dog had something to do with his father's death, but they had no concrete evidence to back it up. So the case went cold.

I really had taken a strong liken to Ghetto-Man. He was a good guy, unlike some that I had come in contact with, 'specially his son, Durdy-Dog.

When Durdy-Dog took over a lot of things changed. First, being location. I can't 'member the square footage of the place, but I know it was real big and spacious. It was a redbrick bi-level building on Straight and Ellison Street that he transformed it into a lucrative investment.

The space was off the hook! From the wrapped around bar in the center of the room, to the marble granite counters, mahogany bar stools, solid oak wood floors, two pool tables, Jacuzzi, chandeliers, strip poles, claw foot bathtubs, spiral staircase, mirrors on every wall. He had an upstairs where the VIP Purple "NUTT CRACKER" Room, Rainbow "CANDY LICKER" Room, Pink "BACK DHAT THANG UP" Room and Red "PIPE DREAM" Room were. Each room was used for something different depending upon the clients' sexual appetite. All I can tell you is that whatever Durdy-Dog's heart desired, that nigga made it happen. The place was top-notched. Laid the fuck out! He had surveillance cameras throughout the place. Any place Durdy-Dog thought a nigga could get slick and try to hoodwink him, he'd put a camera up to watch everybody. Yeah, I would say that he was a little paranoid too. I mean it made perfectly good sense to me 'cause Durdy-Dog was making a killin'. Jokers knew he had crazy loot. And if he wasn't willing to part ways with it, best believe they'd find a way to get some of that paper, even if it meant catchin' a body.

Personally, I thought Durdy-Dog went too far when he changed the business name from: MO'-WHISKEY to THE NAPPY DUGOUT. The part that really disgraced his dad's honor was that he made it into a gentleman's club (similar to a burlesque, but not quite so). I know Ghetto-Man was sitting upright in his grave. Of course, the old loyal patrons left and a new elite crowd flowed in. Durdy-Dog was gettin' paid! And that only inflated his head. He thought he was the muthafuckin' "Swagga King" fo' real.

Durdy-Dog used to pay us girls to sit at the bar and work the customers over. Rub a little here, squeeze a little there; you know what I'm tryna say. Pretend that we just got in town (from God knows where) and stopped to have a nightcap before heading upstairs to the VIP Purple Room (NUTT CRACKER). Most of the men loved out-of-town pussy, so they'd fall for it every time. And each and every time they'd get got. Durdy-Dog had us doing some dirty, dirty shit.

Some of the girls tried to get new thinking that they were going to outsmart Durdy-Dog. You know, do him dirty by working independently. But it almost always backfired in their faces. Durdy-Dog had clout, reputation, was held in high-esteem in the 'hood. His peoples would rat a bitch out just to get on his good side. Everybody wanted a piece of that pie. Everybody. Play with Durdy-Dog or his money and you were definitely axin' to get smoked.

Durdy-Dog was one man I never liked. Actually, I hated him. He was tall, honeyed-toned, with an athletic build. He was a sharp dresser—mostly in business suits. You'd never catch him dead in jeans or sneakers, T-shirts or du-rags neither. Oh, and he loved his stingy brim hats too.

Durdy-Dog was a clean-cut looking brother—clean-shaven too. He kept a low, detailed haircut, trimmed mustache and goatee. One thing about Durdy-Dog was that he didn't mind spreading his money around but only when he wanted to. He couldn't stand beggars. He attracted people from all walks of life even with limited education. He dropped out of school in the seventh grade and worked with his dad fulltime. The other thing about him was that he never entertained jokers who talked the talk and didn't walk the walk. He'd watch jokers like a hawk. He'd ear hustle too. Time was always money to him. He was determined to live a lavish lifestyle.

Durdy-Dog spoke with a lisp, but he had mad confidence about himself. In other words, Durdy-Dog was very vain and he could come off as arrogant too. He had this sort of dry humor—the kind that would leave a bad taste in one's mouth. A lot of people didn't take to him 'cause they felt he thought he was betta' than everyone else. Some of the fellahs he grew up with felt he had forgotten where the fuck he'd come from. Durdy-Dog carried himself like a businessman. He dressed and talked the part. So yeah, it did set him apart from his past niggas.

One thing about Durdy-Dog that didn't change was that he was still a crazy muthafucka. He was a daredevil type of joker—fearless and vengeful. He didn't have a soft spot in his lanky body. Durdy-Dog was a monster, unlike his dad, who was a sweet and kindhearted man.

For Durdy-Dog to be in his early thirties, he had a mind of a loan shark. People clung to him 'cause they envied him. Knowing this, only inflated Durdy-Dog's ego even mo'.

After Ghetto-Man died, Durdy-Dog took the role of becoming my guardian. It was 'cause of *him* that my life was of great sacrifice.

The day of the funeral, Durdy-Dog came home drunk. I cried myself to sleep that mournful day. I was in my bed. Durdy-Dog walked into my bedroom and nudged me to wake up, and once I did, he unzipped his pants, pulled 'em down to his ankles and forced himself on top of me. I tried to fight him off. I screamed. I swung. I kicked. No, no, no... I never wanted to have sex with him, but he made me do it. I can't tell you how that made me feels. I can't even describe how that one moment affected my life forever. I thought Daddee had done me wrong. No. She had merely broken me in. Durdy-Dog, he abused me into what he wanted me to be.

And every day that I think back, *Man in the sky, I wished that my mama had made betta' choices. Why, why in Johnnie Walker Red's name did she have to be a prostitute? But since she was, I had taken the punishment 'cause of whom she was. Judge me not based on me; Judge me on the basis of what my DNA consisted of. I had ho blood running through my veins. It was like I parted ways with the "jealous angles" in heaven and pounded fists wit' the devil hisself.* Durdy-Dog.

"Rocka-Bye, listen, when you get onstage you gotta work that ass!" Durdy-Dog spoke assertively dressed from head to toe in Gucci.

Durdy-Dog had given me the stage name "Rocka-Bye Bitch." I was fifteen, at the time. I looked older for my age, so no one suspected that I was a minor. I never wanted to dance. I was always self-conscious of my body. I hated the way I looked, from my face to my feet. My *body* inflicted mo' and mo' and mo' pain in my life.

Around this time in my life, Durdy-Dog had made me drop out of school. I was in the *eighth* grade. He felt it was a waste of time for me to be trying to get an education, he said that I could do betta' working for him making *him* money.

After being told of what I'd be doing, I'd slip in the ladies room and took a hit off of Ol' Durty. It was either that or, stays sick for the rest of the day. And I couldn't afford to do that. Sick or not, Durdy-Dog expected me to make those niggas drool by enticing 'em with my cupcake. It was the only way to get 'em to throw their crumpled money up onstage. It was 'bout the money—the mighty dollar-dollar bill.

I was the finale of the show. Men paid top-dollar to see me perform. I'd come out all glistened down in beaded baby oil. My head shining to perfection, exotic eyes, sensual lips, and high cheekbones set me apart from the rest in THE NAPPY DUGOUT. I was Durdy-Dog's "lucky bitch"—a moneymaker—his one and only baldhead snowflake that worked the hell out of the strip pole.

Durdy-Dog showed me how to work my pussy. He also taught me how to give excellent head. He taught me how to make love to the pole—to pretend that it was Ol' Durty. I'd pump; pop, gyrate, and grind the pole—ass and pussy drippin' hot sex juice down my legs. The men's used to love to sniff my sweaty cupcake. My ass used to be on fire while onstage. I had to feel myself up with bullshit to make it through the night. I had to set myself apart from the rest of the girls. I had to be hotter, sexier, and fiercer!

The hot pink, amber, and violet fluorescent lights made me feel the heat. My body was sweltering. Even my insides were sweltering hot. In between my thighs my lips were clinging together. I was sticky wet! I'd masturbate onstage by rubbing my clit and teasing my tits to arouse those sorry ass muthafuckers I had to become somebody else to stop myself from breaking down. Ol' Durty, she held a bitch down. Yeah, she was my bottom bitch!

"'Ey, Rocka-Bye, bring yo sweet ass over here so I can lick that cunt." This joker named Five (Ellis Hertzberg) said. His white ass was fine, so I didn't mind fulfilling his fetish. If it was sweet cunt he wanted, then it was sweet cunt he was going to get. I loved the tall and distinguished. Five was easy on the eyes too. He was a regular and he loved hisself some me.

I sashayed my curvaceous body over to him. He leaned forward and stuck out his long, sodden tongue; I placed my fingers between my legs and pulled my pussy lips apart, and let him lick, lick, suck, slurp, lick. He was lickin' my shit like a thirsty ass dog. My body trembled. I squirted juicy cum in his mouth. He went fuckin' crazy! That investment banker threw two hundred and fifty dollars onstage. I kissed him on the forehead and worked the other niggas pockets for the rest of the night.

The place was normally full from the time the doors opened at 8:00 p.m., until they closed at 3:00 a.m. A lot of the men's who came to THE NAPPY DUGOUT had sick cash. That was one thing about Durdy-Dog, he didn't fuck around with broke ass niggas. He mostly entertained businessmen; jokers with money who considered a grand or two play money to squander at NAPPY's.

Durdy-Dog knew that good pussy was hard to come by, so he made it his business to break each and every girl he hired in. He knew exactly what to do to keep his patrons happy.

For one, he knew what his girls were capable of doing in between the sheets. He knew their strengths and their weaknesses. I mean whom betta' to know than the man who was fucking 'em all.

Quite often things would get rough in THE NAPPY DUGOUT. Niggas wanted to fuck raw. That was one thing about Durdy-Dog, he was conniving like that. Having unprotected sex with his hoes was something he'd turn a blind eye to.

I'd get dizzy onstage, but there was nothin' that I could do but dance until I dropped. I had to do what I had to do to survive. Yeah, Durdy-Dog had threatened me plenty of times, but see the only thing that saved my ass was that I was the *only* white meat on the menu. I bought in mad cash. Durdy-Dog knew it to be true too.

The music was thumping with Sweet Pussy Pauline's "Work this Pussy" which was my theme song to get dirty. Durdy-Dog loved to drop bombs like that. You know to catch bitches off guard 'n' shit. It was the hype of the night. Everybody roared with excitement. Howled and hollered and hooted at the top of their lungs. Everybody was lit— smoking weed, snorting coke and drinking.

The lyrics to the music spoke to my body as it moved to its beat. I had to look convincingly out to the crowd of horny men. I was glistening under the light, my fingers gripping around the smooth silver pole and slowly squatted down, prying my legs open for all to see my trigger-happy-bitch. I eased backup in slow motion, spun my tongue around my lips a couple of times, then flipped my body upward as my legs stood mid-air, wrapped my ankles around the pole, and slowly eased my body back down like a spider. Yeah, I was doin' da shit!

While the crowd of men was throwing money up onstage, I cut my eyes over to Durdy-Dog in the far corner of the room. I could see the shining whites of his teeth grinning from ear to ear. He was rubbing his palms together making money count. He nodded alerting the deejay to flip the tunes. The deejay, a young cat from Newark, New Jersey, named Ziggy-Iggy turned the turntable out. The crowd went wild. "Stank Pussy in This House" was blaring through the speakers. The walls were vibrating from the surround sound. I grabbed my ass and spread my cheeks apart.

One joker named Six (Luke Garrison) a Certified Public Accountant slipped a hundred in the crack of my ass. He rubbed my booty for good luck and squeezed on my firm tits, then maneuvered his massive ivory-colored hand down to my hard clit and stroked it back and forth. My pussy was throbbing. I felt like I wanted to fuck right then and there. I got on my knees and crawled across the floor like a baby. Durdy-Dog was already making his way over to the stage. He handed me a Coke bottle. The deejay switched the music. "Fuckin' Twat, Twat" was my shit!

I got loose—buck fuckin' wild!

I seductively stuck the Coke bottle all the way inside my pussy until it completely disappeared. Eight, this Italian dude named (Joey Sorrento) the CEO of a Fortune 500 Company skillfully pulled the bottle out with his drunken ass. My pussy squirted with juice spraying out into the crowd. Those horny bastards went nuts!

My body was jerking to the music. I was feeling the groove. My body drenched down in hot sweat, watching those men lusting over me. It was crazy!

The remainder of the night grew crazier and crazier. Denominations of fifties and hundreds were thrown onto the stage. With all the excitement, somehow I survived another night of utter disgrace.

Three o'clock had come and I couldn't have been happier. The crowd had faded out into the night and we girls were getting freshened up to head out. We usually got paid on Tuesday. It was an odd day to get paid, but Durdy-Dog was odd. Throughout the week I had to live off of my tips to make ends meet, but come payday it was well worth the wait. I was clocking at least a grand and sometimes more a week. Yeah, the money was good, but the lifestyle was a stigma on me.

I always had ambitions of going to college, but before that I had to get my GED first. With Durdy-Dog on my ass those ambitions were buried with everything else I had wanted to do. It was tough.

The metallic silver stretched limo pulled up alongsid the redbrick building. Normally the bouncer Juice would escort us girls out to the car. Each girl would get dropped off and escorted to her apartment. Durdy-Dog was a stickler for this because *his* girls were an investment to him. And he took extreme care of his investments.

The driver, Royce, a short, older gentleman with deep dark skin and silver hair got out and opened the back door for me. He was a true gentleman. He always treated me like a lady in spite of what he knew I did for a living. He never made me feel lower than I already felt for myself. I don't know if anyone understood what I was going through. I don't know if anyone could see the hurt outlined on my face, buried beneath the pupils in my eyes, but I was miserable.

As soon as I had gotten to Chosen Street, apartment 3H, Royce waited for me to get inside safely, and then he headed toward the stairs and showed himself out.

As soon as I got inside my apartment, my body, habit began to crave. I walked into the bathroom, reached underneath the sink and pulled out my faded red duffel bag. I unzipped it and cradled Ol' Durty. I locked myself in, and then sat on the edge of the bathtub in the dark. It was just Ol' Durty and I dissolving in our bliss, trying to forget all the bullshit I had endured. All the nightmares, night sweats, all the creepy crawlers gnawing at me.

My drug addiction stemmed from my upbringing, so I felt no need to be ashamed. I think I was mo' ashamed about being a stripper turned trick than a crackhead. Yeah, that sounded pretty fucked up. But that was me...I never saw myself as nuthin' else, but a *junky*.

By the time I got to THE NAPPY DUGOUT I was high as a fuckin' kite. Durdy-Dog grabbed me by my forearm and dragged me across the floor like a dust mop, up the stairs, and into the Red Room (PIPE DREAM). He slammed the door behind us. He didn't have much to say. I could see the anger burning in his eyes. My feet moved backwards toward the wall, away from the king-sized bed. He walked up to me and started jabbing me with closed fists punching me in my stomach, ribs and face.

Wham!
Wham!
Wham!

I felt the stinging sensation rise between my eyes. Eyes watered. I vomited all over myself.

"Didn't I tell you to lay off of that pipe, bitch?" he snapped, eyes still burning with bitterness.

I couldn't speak or look him in his eyes or face. My body was doubled over trying to stop the room from spinning—the vomit from spewing out of my mouth.

"How the fuck are you going to dance looking like shit, huh, Rocka? Do I pay YOU to come in here looking like...SHIT! ANSWER ME!"

Whack!

Wham!

Whap!

I dropped down to my knees.

"ANSWER ME! Stand up!"

I was trying to, but I couldn't.

His patience had run short.

Durdy-Dog snarled at me. "What you gettin' new on a nigga?"

Smack!

Wham!

Whap!

Slap!

With one hand Durdy-Dog lifted me up off the floor and body slammed me like I was some joker on the block. I couldn't move. I literally couldn't move. I thought he had broken every bone in my body.

Durdy-Dog stepped over me. "Now clean yourself up, so that you can make my muthafuckin' money, bitch!"

I never felt so scared. I lay on the floor for what seem like twenty minutes tryin' my hardest to stop crying. Every part of my body hurt. I struggled to get up on my feet but I kept falling back down to the floor. Everything before me was blurry. I was pretty fucked up.

"Get it together, girl. Hurry up before..." I told myself. I was so sore inside and out. I placed my hand on the mirrored wall and tried to lift myself up. I felt so woozy. That *crack* had me sailing. I was floating.

Within a second or two one of the girls came into the Red Room (PIPE DREAM) to prep it for a client. Her stage name was Dexxter (Halima Holman). She was one of the main dancers too. Yeah, she had been working for Durdy-Dog since I had. I think she was the oldest out of all of us girls. Twenty. She was smart, too. I could tell even though I never spoke to her. We weren't allowed to interact with one another

Not even as much as a hello. All of us girls looked at one another as competition, so therefore, none of us even tried to bond. There was no *"girrrrlllll, did you hear 'bout..."* going on at THE NAPPY DUGOUT.

Durdy-Dog didn't want us to get close and start gossiping about shit that was poppin' out in the streets. Nor did he want us to start cat fighting over niggas or tips either. The less attention we attracted the betta' for him. He preferred that we kept our distance. Just 'cause we all had something in common (dancing) didn't mean that we 'had to share our dreams, aspirations, or life goals with one another. Hell, we couldn't even think on that level in his place. Whatever Durdy-Dog wanted Durdy-Dog got. Us being anti-social kept a lot of that "she says she says" shit out of everyone's path. Shit, we didn't even eat together. It wasn't a family affair like it was at MO'-WHISKEY. All we did do was dance and kept Durdy-Dog's money flowing in to keep him happy.

"Rocka-Bye, are you all right?" said Dexxter. She stood over me covered in flawless caramel skin, dressed in a leopard and black baby-doll and G-string with cherry apple red stilettos on. I noticed she changed her hair from strawberry red to platinum. It looked good on her. Her eyes were fixated on me. I sniffled in before snot ran down my nose. "I-I-I...." I stuttered. She extended out her hand to help me stand to my feet. I stood up feeling woozy. I felt like I was about to plop back down to the floor. Dexxter grabbed me and helped me over to the bed.

It was something about her that was different, like me. She had sweetness to her. Something I never noticed before. It enhanced her sexiness. Yeah, Dexxter was hot. Fine...*hot!* She had big bazooka titties (I wondered if she had a tit job done) that stood perky without a bra. Small waist. Nice cute ass. And her legs...shit; she had long, silky legs like me. She was definitely competition, but in that moment we both put our egos aside.

"Listen, Rocka-Bye, I'm not trying to get all up in your business, but you have to deal with that pipe situation." She looked me directly in my eyes. She didn't bite back her words. She stood strong. And I really admired her for that. I never really noticed that she had light-brown eyes with a hint of amber before. I knew she was right, but I still saw no way out. Even with her bringing it directly to my face. It registered but I guess not enough. People always had something negative to say but no one ever took me by the hand and guided me straight to rehab. And I most definitely didn't have the strength to do it myself. I was a junky looking to get high, not stop getting high.

I looked Dexx in her face; the girl was super model gorgeous. I bowed my head ashamed. She kind of made me feel a bit uncomfortable, her knowing my business and all.

Dexxter patted me on the outer skin of my hands and said something that really took me by surprise. "My mom was a junky. You don't want to die a junky, Rocka. If you're going to leave this earth, leave it with something for someone to learn from. Leave a message of purpose behind, girl." Then she stood up.

Before she walked out the door I lifted up my head and asked her a question. "What's your purpose, Dexxter?" She stopped, and turned and looked at me and said, "I'm gonna be a doctor so that I can open up a free health and wellness clinic." She nodded her head, turned back around and slowly walked out of the door as if she was waiting for me to say: "Come rescue me. Help me, Dexxter, help save me!" I didn't utter a word.

I rose from the bed and stood in front of the wall, which was plastered with tile-size mirrors. I looked like broken pieces, which was a depiction of my inner self. My face was swollen and purple. Durdy-Dog had whooped my ass again.

At that moment in my life, I guessed you could say that I was at a crossroad—between faith and disbelief. I sighed, tryin' figure out what to do with my life. But then it dawned on me, as it often did, my life was still not my own. I think, rather I know, that that was the reason why I was wasting myself away.

If Durdy-Dog had control then he could also control my death. When was he going to put me out of my misery? He was 'sposed to be God. Or so he thought. No. I didn't want to live anymore. And if I should've died it would've been blood on his fuckin' hands, not mine. I had surrendered a long time ago. *Fuck it!* I thought. *Fuck it all!*

I know. I know, it sounded stupid, but I wasn't wrapped too tight. I was scared, confused and frustrated about a lot of things. The one person I needed mo' than anybody else was my dad. But of course, he was nowhere to be found. I couldn't for the life of me understand, okay, he left Daddee, but why did he leave me? Suddenly, my eyes began to well up. I let the tears fall. I couldn't hold the pain in any longer. The li'l girl in me needed to cry. And as I did, memories of Daddee appeared and I could hear her sangin' that fucked up lullaby while dangling me by my ankles out of her bedroom window.

Hush, li'l bitch, don't you cry

Daddee's gonna buy you a crack pipe tonight

Daddee's gonna make you smoke dis rock

Daddee's gonna make you work da block

Daddee's gonna make you smile 'n' laugh

Daddee's gonna make you sell dhat ass...

"Rocka-Bye Bitch, get your muthafuckin' ass out here!" Durdy-Dog commanded.

I snapped back, wiped the tears from around my swollen eyes and off of my bloodied and bruised face, straightened myself up. Before I exited out of the door I cracked a smile even though it hurt like hell. Then I walked out with my head held high. I couldn't let him see me weak even though deep down he knew I was. I had to act the part. Believe that I was that vixen bitch and work the fuck out of my pussy. And I did. I showed a side of me they had never seen before.

THE NAPPY DUGOUT had a full house. All I saw was polished suits in the joint. This dancer named Coda (Karen Betsy) went onstage first. She was a thick chick, dark chocolate, with a fierce body. She was 5'7", angle wing hips, perfectly round ass, and bone straight honey-blonde hair that dangled down to the small of her back. She loved to wear glittered pasties on her nipples. The niggas went crazy for her sixteen-year-old ass. Coda was sleazy onstage and the niggas loved her. She could make her body do things I had never seen before. She could make her ass jump. I don't mean no booty clap either. She had those muscles working. She had her own style. She'd let you do whatever you wanted to her. Girls, guys it didn't matter to her. She was nasty like that: professionally and I assumed personally.

One white guy was doing her in the ass, while the other, a black guy was licking the clit. And another was sucking on her plum-size titties, while everyone's eyes were engrossed in them getting their fuck on. Coda had those niggas going insane! Men were throwing hundreds up onstage. Hundreds! Coda had those men eyes locked in on her freaky ass. That chick knew how to put on a good show!

Just the sound of her moaning everybody in the room started rubbing on their dicks while rubbing on the girls' clit and titties. Some were in the corner doing it doggy-style or getting head or eating pussy. The room smelled like sex. Coda had started some shit. And I loved every minute of it!

Coda gave me what I needed to keep the momentum flowing. I was ready. Ready to do da shit! I needed Durdy-Dog to see that I was still his #1 bitch! The only white baldhead exotic dancer who had those men's eyes fixated on the pussy that did tricks. I was going to get downright freaky wit' it! Fucking, sucking, and squirting until my pussy dried the fuck up!

"Fuck Me Up, Over, Under, and Inside Out" by Leash was playing and the crowd was getting their buzz on. Before I got onstage I asked Dexx to do a number with me. I knew Durdy-Dog wouldn't mind 'cause we had never done a show with two girls before. Considering we had recently opened this was the perfect time to liven things up a bit. Dexxter agreed.

I was instantly attracted to her. And honestly, I wanted to taste her. I wanted to smell her, feel her soft supple skin against mine, and her luscious lips. I wanted to kiss 'em and stick my tongue down her throat. I didn't want to just fantasize. I wanted to do her. Right there onstage. I wanted those niggas to respect my position. I wanted 'em to be envious of me...yeah, me..."Rocka-Bye Bitch."

As the music played, Dexxter and I walked onstage naked, glistened down in honey oil. She kneeled down on her knees, stuck her tongue out, looked up at me, and I parted my lips so that she could gently lick my clit. Her tongue was hot and so was her saliva. I tilted my head back, my hands met my nipples and I started tugging on 'em. Everyone in the room was quiet. It was like they were hypnotized or something. I moaned loudly 'cause she was hitting spots I never knew existed in me. I was wet, and it was oozing out of me and down my legs. She had me going fuckin' crazy! I wet the tips of my fingers with my tongue and tugged on her nipples. We switched positions. Dexx lay back on the pillows that were already on the floor as our prop. She spread her sexy long legs open. I kneeled on my knees and kissed from her feet to her ankles to her inner thighs, getting the men's revved up.

Dexxter closed her eyes; her tongue wet her lips as she was anticipating the feel of my tongue against her flesh. I wanted to take my time with her, to savor her. I spit a glob of spit on the outer lips of her pussy. Men started hollering and carryin' on. I cut my eyes to the side and saw Durdy-Dog stroking his seven inches. The men who stood near the stage were jerking off too. Some of the girls were heading upstairs with their clients. Some were against the walls getting it in. Everyone was damn near naked, with no shame. I saw short dicks, long dicks, skinny dicks, fat dicks, thick dicks, and some with hardly any dick. It was a fuckin' affair!

Dexxter's pussy tasted like sweet and delicious raw sugar. I played with the clit with the edge of my tongue—tickled it as she moaned softly. Yeah, she was feeling it. And so was I. I did it once, twice, three times, she reached her hand out and squeezed on my left tit and tugged on my nipple. Just her touching me I felt this volt of electricity shoot through, around, and down to my pussy. I wanted her. She gave me a rush like Ol' Durty did. I was slippery wet.

I inched my face down in the garden of her hairy pussy and I sucked her, hard and strong. She lifted her feet up and on my back, inviting me in mo' and mo'. I stuck my tongue inside of her hole, rotated it around and around so sensually. She moaned louder and louder. Everyone in the crowd dicks was hard brick. I stopped licking her pussy and inched my body up meeting her face-to-face, eye to eye and tongue kissed her wildly. I heard someone in the crowd say, "Dammmmmmmnnnnn, that shit is sexy as hell!"

While we were fucking one another I reached to the side and pulled out Pasture Deacon (dildo) from the box that I had hidden on the floor. I greased it down with Vaseline.

I said, "Baby, turn over." Dexxter did so willingly. All the men eyes got wide and they started grinning like schoolboys. We talked dirty talk to get the shit flowing.

"How you want it, baby?" I asked her in a seductive tone.

"Ooh, baby, give it to me...*hard*," Dexxter replied in a child-like voice. She sounded so innocent.

"Can you handle it?" I asked.

"Baby, fucks me, and sees if I can handle it...fffffucks me, baby, fucks me!" Dexxter replied so sensually.

I cut my eyes to the side to watch the men's eyes, watch us. They were literally slobbering at the mouth.

Dexxter got on all fours and raised her pretty ass mid-air. She stroked her middle finger down the seam of her crack, up and down it went and then she stuck her middle finger in her hot mouth, rotated her tongue around her sexy lips like it tasted so fuckin' good. That move was sexy to me!

Dexxter spread her ass cheeks apart and I reached for my 13-inch silicone black cock (Pasture Deacon), grabbed some mo' baby oil and rubbed Pasture Deacon down as well as lubricated her asshole. Then I caught everyone off guard when I reached for Flexi Felix (anal toy) and slowly inserted it in for anal pleasure before I teased her with Pasture Deacon.

Dexxter head leaned forward, then back. I grabbed her by the meaty part of her ass cheeks and did inward and outward motions. Those men were jealous 'cause I was getting the ass. I made them suffer. I licked her ass, stopped, and stuck that black cock all up in her. She winced and squinted her eyes. I was the muthafuckin' bitch and I was taking my position seriously. I wanted her to know what it was like being with a crackhead trick. Then I reinserted Flexi Felix. Slowly I released Flexi Felix from her ass and she turned over on her back. The crowd was still engrossed in us, with their mouths dangled open. Dexxter raised her legs up and put 'em on my shoulders. I grabbed one of her ankles and sucked on her toes, while this was going on; Durdy-Dog was making rounds with a bucket collecting his dough with his long dick swinging from side to side.

Dexxter smiled as her body quivered. I licked in between each toe with my wet warm tongue. She quivered. I swallowed the big toe. She quivered. I inched my body down on top of hers and grinded Pasture Deacon against her skin. I sucked on her titties, licked, and pulled on the nipples with my teeth. She bellowed out a loud moan. I inched myself back down to her pussy, licked it, and then I grabbed Pasture Deacon by the head and slowly, and very gently inserted Pasture Deacon in her juicy pussy. Her eyes rolled back, and her legs trembled. Inward and outward Pasture Deacon motioned. "Harder! Harder!" she screamed. I pumped her harder, faster; I tried to hit the pit of her pussy with Pasture Deacon. She reached for my baldhead and massaged it and that move turned a bitch on. My hips were rotating, the muscles in my ass were tightening, and my pussy was throbbing mo' and mo'. Dexxter bit down on her bottom lip as she gritted and grinded down on her teeth. "Shhhhhhhiiiiiiiitttttttt," she sang. She couldn't function like the Dexxter I had just met. I had her going fuckin' crazy with Pasture Deacon. It was so sexy! So fuckin' sexy! She busted several nutts. And the niggas went wild!

AS I WAS 'BOUT to get ready for my next performance, Dexxter approached me with tears in her eyes. "Are you okay?" I asked her. She took me by the hand and pulled me into the ladies' room. "What's wrong?" I asked her again.

"What's right," she replied. "It's been a long week, very, very stressful for me."

"Did something happen?"

She shook her head from side to side, and then nodded her head up and down.

"Talk to me."

"I almost didn't make it here today. Just what Durdy-Dog did to you, could've happened to me. Or worse," she said.

I had a perplexed look upon my face. "What do you mean?"

"I stay with my aunt. She's kinda off in the head. Her husband left her and she ain't been the same since. Every time, just before we leave here I have to call her to let her know that I'm on my way home, otherwise, I can't get in. Well, the other day I couldn't get in. I had gone home to get my clothes ready for work, but she never answered the phone. I kept calling her back, but she never picked up."

"Well, maybe she wasn't home." I said.

"No, she was there. I ended up walking there anyway. I put my key in but the door was locked. I think she might've had a chair blocking it. I banged on the door several times, rung the bell several times, even called from the hallway. This is an ongoing thing with her. I'd rather her tell me she doesn't want me to live with her than to treat me like this. You don't know the half of it. Whatever food I bring into the house, she eats it from me. Her mind is so screwed up. She won't let me get any sleep. Sometimes I come into a house of lights. She'll have all the lights on and sit in the living room where I sleep on the couch and watch TV. I never get any rest. In order for me to study I have to either go to the library, bookstore, or a café, and most of the time my mind has drifted. I can't seem to concentrate because I keep thinking about how bad things are for me. I don't have any peace in my life. No privacy. If you really think about it, girl, I'm homeless. I'm miserable, too. I get nothing done. I can't afford to fail another test. My tuition is so expensive and I'm paying out-of-pocket too. Sometimes I just feel like giving up, but then I think about my mom, and I can't allow myself to do that. I just can't, because every time I think about it, I realize she gave up. I don't want a life like this."

I nodded my head.

Dexxter continued, "A friend of mine had asked me what I was doing to change my circumstances. I told him that I had put in for housing. I had gotten approved, but now I have to wait for a vacancy, but in the meantime, I have no other alternatives but to wait, and keep on pushing forward. God, it is so hard." Dexxter eyes got teary. She wiped her eyes smearing tears all over her cheeks. "So, anyway, a friend of mine named Deejay had called me earlier in the day. I called him back to let him know that I couldn't get in the house, and to see if he'd let me sleep over there. He said okay." She sniffled.

"That was nice of him." I said.

Dexxter cut her eyes sharp at me. "I asked him to meet me downtown, so that I wouldn't have to walk alone. He said okay. I said call me and let me know when you are close to the college. He said okay."

"Did he meet you?"

"Yeah. He did. But stupid wasn't on College Boulevard like I had asked him to be. Rocka, I'm cutting my eyes over my shoulders while on my cell phone with another friend of mine. This asshole calls me from Van Houten Street. I hung up with my friend. I saw Deejay approaching me. He stood about 5'8", butter cream complexion, and jet-black hair, with hypnotizing green eyes. He was all smiles, dressed in black jeans and a T-shirt and loafer shoes. But by then I was agitated. I really didn't want to talk. I was tired."

I nodded my head.

"Deejay walks ahead of me, which kinda ticked me off too. Where had the gentleman in men gone, huh?"

I shrugged my shoulders.

"Well," Dexxter said, "we finally got to his apartment. We took the stairs to the third floor. We entered his apartment. 'Excuse the small mess,' Deejay said. I didn't care about that as long as it wasn't dirty, you know. Deejay goes upstairs. I sat down on the rust leather couch. I fiddled with my cell phone because I felt a little uneasy. I mean I hadn't gone over to his apartment in years. Deejay usually called me but I never felt the urge to go over. Anyway, he comes downstairs bringing me a mint-green washcloth and a black tee and faded red towel. He goes into the bathroom. He comes back out and goes into the kitchenette to wash the little bit of dishes that were in the sink. I grabbed some things out of my satchel bag and entered the bathroom inhaling the incense that he had burning. I screamed because I saw a bug. I think it was one of those centipedes crawling across the back of the toilet. It crawled out to the hardwood floor and Deejay walked over and stepped on it and shut the bathroom door for me. I turned the nozzle to the shower on and stepped inside the bathtub and under the showerhead and let the warm water flow down my tired body.

"After I took my shower, I got dressed in the T-shirt, and headed out of the door, back into the living room. By now the room was dark, yet the

TV from upstairs gave me a little light. I lay on the couch and covered my feet with my jean jacket, and snuggled against the rust pillow, and closed my eyes. Deejay yelled out in his boyish voice, 'You okay?' I replied, 'Yeah.' I closed my eyes again to settle in to a good sleep, but he distracted me with, 'Why don't you come upstairs?' I shook my head no and said, 'I don't want to come upstairs.' Within a few minutes Deejay came running down the steps barefoot in a T-shirt and boxers or they could've been shorts. 'Why don't you come upstairs,' he said again. I replied, 'I'm fine on the couch.' Then he said, 'Well, I don't let people sleep on my couch. Lemme get the air mattress.' So he goes to his closet and reaches for what looked like a bag, but before he pulled it out he took one hard look at me. I stared him dead in his face from where I was laying. Immediately I felt a shift in the air. Something wasn't right. Something was about to go down. Something bad. I don't know exactly what happened but he changed faces on me. 'Fuck that! It's either we fucking, or nowhere!' Deejay snapped. All I could think was wow! This can't be happening. But it was. And it did. I said, 'Well, I guess it's nowhere.' I grabbed my clothes out of my satchel bag. He turned the lights on. I walked passed him and entered the bathroom and got dressed. As I exited out of the bathroom, he was sitting on one of the bar stools. I zipped up my bag, walked passed him and said, 'Thank you.' He said, 'Did you put the towel on the shower rail?' I said, 'No, I put it next to your other towel on the towel rack.' I walked out the door. He locked the door behind me without a care in the world. I took the elevator downstairs and exited out of the building at 12:10 a.m. What was the purpose of him saying yes that I could come over, huh? I mean I told him my situation. I thought Deejay was cool, you know, but everyone has their own motives. The fact that I'm a stripper gives them the wrong perceptions of me. They don't know me. And most of the times they won't attempt to get to know me because they have already labeled me as a hoe. But I'm not a hoe. We are actresses. We play roles to give these assholes a fantasy." Dexx paused. "Girl, I got big dreams, big dreams. I won't be shaking my ass for the rest of my life. You watch and see."

"Damn." That was all I could say. "That's pretty fucked up, girl." I told her.

She shook her head with a crumpled forehead. "Tell me about it. I've known Deejay for years. Never thought he'd do me dirty like that, but I guessed that's what I get for trusting, you know. I just thank God I made it out safe. It could've really gotten out of hand. I'm blessed, girl, truly blessed to be here talkin' to you right now."

I nodded my head in agreement. "So where did you end up going? Weren't you scared out there all by yourself?"

Dexxter lowered her head. "Yeah, Rocka, I was, but he didn't even care enough about me being out there in the streets late at night. It was dark as hell and so quiet. There were a few guys out hanging near the old folks' complex, sitting on the front porch chillin'. He couldn't get what he wanted from me; so therefore, I didn't matter much to him. It's funny because most of the time when he'd call me I'd never go over to visit him. I guess I knew subconsciously that he was full of shit, but I was in a situation I had nowhere's to go. I assumed that he would come through for a sistah, you know. I didn't want to have sex with him. That was not my intention. All I wanted was a safe haven to lay and rest my head."

"Yeah, I know exactly what you're talkin' 'bout." I told her.

She raised her head and looked me dead-on in the eyes. "Do you? 'Cause I ended up sleeping up near the train tracks. The only good thing about it was that it was muggy out. Imagine if it were winter. Yeah, I was scared out of my mind. There are a lot of homeless people and druggies who sleep up there. All I could do was ask God to help me out of this situation. I swore on my mother that once I got out of this situation I'd never live this way again. So I went where my mom had died."

"What do you mean...*where she died?*"

Dexxter lips quivered. She sighed. "It was about 4:30 a.m. My mom's name was Faith. She had been hooked on coke since I can remember. She used to dibble and dabble with heroin but it got to be too expensive for her pocketbook. The funny part of this is that she used to be a registered nurse." She lowered her eyes. "She met the wrong guy and got caught up. She lost her job. Got caught stealing morphine from the hospital. There was no income coming in, so we ended up getting evicted. She went her way and I had to go mine. She stayed with her junky boyfriend and her drug addiction only worsened. I don't know for the life of me why she'd be sleeping on the train tracks. It still doesn't make sense to me. Anyway, the train was coming full speed, the conductor saw them on the tracks and honked his horn, but it was too late. The rest is a grisly scene that I try to block out of my mind. Some people seem to think that someone put them on the tracks—that someone killed my mom, but only God knows the truth. I don't want to go down that same path. I want better. I deserve better." Dexxter couldn't hold back her tears, she sobbed so uncontrollably and all I could do was hold her in my arms. "Shhhhh, it's gonna be alright." I said, with tears flooded in my eyes. "I-I-

71

I am so sorry for your loss, Dexx."

Dexxter shook her head. "It's not go-nn-a be al-right," she stuttered in between each word.

"Why?"

Dexxter explained. "I'm in school trying to do something with my life. Do you know how hard pre-med is? It's hard, girl, real hard. Between here, school, and me finding another job so that I can get out of my aunt's house, I'm a walking zombie. I'm always tired; I can't seem to get a break! You think I want to be here dancing? No, I don't. It's just a means to an end. I have dreams, you know, but no one wants to see me make it. Wait, wait and see when I do, girl. Wait!" she rubbed her crimson eyes and laid her head on my shoulder.

I felt her pain. Literally. So I let her cry until she couldn't cry anymore. Dexxter was hurt and I could understand why. Why did it have to be about looks, body, or tryna get over on someone 'cause they were vulnerable? Why couldn't people just be there for you without wanting something from you? I know I was contradicting myself, but I kept my shit on the up and up. The only thing I hadn't done was, tell Devin Rogers the truth about my nightlife, but soon it would all be revealed. That's what I kept telling myself. *"Soon, Daisy, soon, you betta' tell that man if you expect to keep him in your life. Don't let him find out from someone else."* But then I had this funky attitude as if I didn't care about him: *"If he doesn't want any more to do with me, well, then, I guess it wasn't meant to be."* I was straight trippin'.

Truth be told, I was tired. Tired of shaking my ass for those horny ass niggas, but I was in a situation worse than Dexxter. Durdy-Dog owned me. And as much as I wanted to tell her that, I couldn't. I didn't have anyone for me where I could empty myself out on. I couldn't be completely myself. People didn't know that it hurt to be so confined. Living like that would make anyone go fuckin' crazy. Even commit suicide.

I patted her on the shoulder. "Look, Dexx, you gonna be alright. I gotta go get ready for my next show, okay." She nodded her head up and down.

I did a solo off of "Scarlet Pussy" by Prince for my second performance. I was open, completely nude and vulnerable before a room full of doggish dicks. I allowed them to see a softer side of me, more subtle side of me. I captivated my audience with slow body movements as if I was making love to each and every one of those niggas behind closed doors. It touched me. I got misty-eyed. Yeah. I got emotional. I didn't care. I didn't care one bit 'cause I felt myself cracking open and spilling outside of myself. And it was so liberating, so fuckin' liberating. It was the most incredible thing that had ever happened to me. I had exposed myself raw, up close and personal. I was translucent, not invisible. And they were able to feel my anguish. I was playing the role of a scarred girl who needed to be in control of her destiny. I was playing the role of a girl who was sexually assaulted, yearning for her daddy's touch, to feel him loving her in a fatherly way. It was all I could think about. Yeah. My heart craved for my dad.

Dexxter was right. Most of the niggas who came to THE NAPPY DUGOUT came to live out their sexual fantasies that they, otherwise, weren't getting at home. But either way you sliced it men's would always look at us as hoes. We'd never really be wife material in their eyes, unless they were open to getting to know us, and not condemn us for what we did to make our loot.

I WOKE UP AT 6:30 a.m., lying on my bathroom floor, still fully dressed in a fetal position with slobber along the crease of my mouth. As soon as I tried to sit-up my body felt weird. I felt dizzier than I'd ever felt before. I saw blind spots before my eyes. It was pretty scary. I swore, I thought (well, it doesn't matter. It never happened).

With feeling the way that I did, it didn't stop me from taking another hit off of Ol' Durty. I'd smoked more than I'd eat and gradually it started affecting my weight. Durdy-Dog noticed a drastic change and he was not feeling it one bit. He stepped to me with the quickness.

"Listen, bitch, I told you once before to lay off that pipe." Durdy-Dog snapped dressed in his Armani suit. I couldn't. No matter how much I tried (which I never did) I just couldn't leave Ol' Durty alone. She was my...*everything. She understood me: how I felt, what I needed, when I needed it...she was all I had to get through the shit I was going through.* What could I do to maintain my size four figure? Shit, if it were up to me I'd starve and smoke my life away.

I had to keep my shape because niggas were already accustomed to seeing me that size. Now I could go up in my weight but I damn sure couldn't go down. The first thing they'd think was that "Rocka-Bye Bitch" had gotten sick with some dreadful disease of some sort. If I started to fall off the money would've stopped rolling in. And my tips would've dwindled down too little of nuthin'. Not to mention, Durdy-

73

Dog would've been on my ass. To keep everyone at bay I did what was expected of me. I ate, smoked, ate, and smoked myself to a state of unbearable nausea and constant diarrhea.

I entered the ladies room and hid in one of the stalls. I fell to the floor. God, I felt so sick to my stomach. I struggled to get up off the floor. Managed to pull myself up, then sat on the toilet seat, and let the flush of loose bowels flow out of me. God, I felt lousy. All I could think about while sitting there was how my life had become. *This can't be it*, I thought. And if it is, then I was destined for a fatal downfall. How could I break free? I saw no way out. With Durdy-Dog still breathing in good air, my life would be indebted to him. Why? What had I done to make him punish me so? I wondered.

***

TALL, DEEP DARK complexioned Finesse Witherspoon stood in the far end of OPEN YO' EYES bookstore putting trinkets and candleholders atop the glass counter.

I arrived promptly at two o'clock. Mr. Witherspoon was there alone.

"Where's Mr. Eugene?" I asked as I walked in.

Mr. Witherspoon turned around and looked up from the counter. "Oh, Ms. Wily, he doesn't work on Sundays. He usually goes to church." He said while tidying up.

I nodded in acknowledgement.

"Ms. Wily, don't be shy. C'mon in. Have a seat. Take a load off of your feet. It's good to see you. Really, really good to see you on this glorious day," he said overly excited.

I cut my eyes at him wondering if he was feeling ok. I sat down on the amber-colored couch dressed in my olive-green corduroys, oatmeal turtleneck sweater, furry fudge-colored suede boots, and waist-length olive-green suede jacket with a camel-colored knit hat on my head. And of course, my big hoop earrings to accentuate my vanilla cream skin.

"Mr. Witherspoon..." I began to say.

"Please, please, call me Finesse," he said slyly. I didn't want to be informal. That always caused me problems with men, but I gave in anyway.

"Finesse," as I began to speak again he interrupted me with this funny look in his big, doe-eyes. I glanced at the bangle on my right wrist that read: "Trick-of-all-Trades" in bold black letters, feeling a bit impatient, wanting to talk about what I had come over here for, which was, but—

"Are you in a rush," he asked me.

"Kinda."

"Take the load off. It's Sunday. The Lord's Day! Relax for a bit."

Is he always so hyper, I wondered?

Finesse walked up to the entranceway of the well-lit store and locked the door. I sat still. I take it as if he wanted to give me his undivided attention—to listen to me talk about what I had come for. How wrong was I to think that?

Finesse walked to the back of the store where I was sitting. Then he walked through this other door that was behind the counter and suddenly the music switched to something a little more intimate, like love ballads of Freddie Jackson. Again, I didn't think anything of it until the bright lights went dim—this "Sexual Healing" Marvin Gaye kind of dim.

What is he doin'? I thought to myself.

As I was having this thought, Finesse stood before me in his dark sweat pants with a thick sweater on and a pair of black Timberland boots on his size ten and a half feet. His body gyrated in a sexual motion. My eyes widened then narrowed, baffled as to what was going on. His right hand gripped the bulge that had swelled in his sweats. He massaged it forth and backs as to arouse me as well as himself. I sat up, planted both feet on the floor, eyes sharply cut toward the front door.

All of a sudden, his sweats fell down to his ankles. There before me, stood this dark-skinned man in his white Hanes underwear.

I blinked, twice, completely caught off guard. Is this how he runs his business, I wondered? Oh, I was heated!

Finesse continued to massage his sex tool. The bulge increased into a hard erection. A grimace quickly outlined my face. My left brow rose. "Damn, look at that," I said to myself.

I stood. "Let me out of here." I snapped, feeling this rush of adrenaline zoom throughout my sexy body and straight down to my clit. "Let me the fuck outta here! Open that door!" *The door to my pussy*, I thought. I was trying to convince myself—trying to avoid the images of us getting our fuck on. Honestly, I thought Finesse saw right through me. Yes, I believe he saw right through me. It was easy to detect a hoe. Yet, I felt I had no choice but to put up a good front. So I demanded to be released from his man cave. "Open the door...!" I snapped again. *To my pussy*, I kept rethinking in my head. "Let me outta here. Open that damn door!" My voice rose above the soft music playing. The heat between my thighs rose too. My body was afire.

"Ms. Wily, calm down," Finesse said, still massaging his dick as if everything was fine.

Everything was not fine! *I don't get down like this!* I thought to myself. Obviously he had other things in mind that I was unaware of.

I was quite agitated and turned on all at the same time.

Is this premeditated? Did he orchestrate this to test my business ethics? How many others? I wondered.

"I want you to watch me..." Finesse said, his eyes closed, full thick dark lips pressed together. His hand motion on his dick was slow and sensual like he was making love to himself.

God, I was drooling in my thong.

This man is sick! I thought.

I scowled at him. "Watch you...what...?" I asked with attitude in my tone.

"Won't you let me masturbate with you watching me," he said with a grin on his face. "C'mon now, look at all of this...big...thick...juicy...black...dick." He gripped it firmly, wrapped his fingers around it and palmed it like it was a priceless heirloom past down from generation to generation.

Finesse stood before me with a hard ass dick. And I-I was pissed the fuck off! Yes, I was pissed but I was also yearning for the feel of that dark chocolate ass man—to have him stick his hard dick all up in my sloppy hole. I wanted it to go in my pussy and come through my mouth. Yet, I had to compose myself. I silently screamed in my head: Daisy, concentrate on something else! But in all honesty, I couldn't. That dick was a *huge* distraction.

Inside, I throbbed to feel his thick meat swallowing up my hole. Flip me. Motion my body in all sorts of directions. Taunt. Tease. Squeeze. Suck. Taste me like I was a vanilla éclair oozing out of myself.

I was hot, thirsty hot between my thighs. Finesse made my clit rumble. My nipples were harder than his dick. I was hurting. It was unbearable.

Beads of sweat formed and slowly slithered down past the small of my back, down to the crack of my ass, then dissolved in the fabric of my lace hot pink thong. I was feverishly hot.

Eyes rolled. And as they did, Finesse was all in me—drooling from the mouth and smiling from ear to ear as if he was reading my mind and body language.

I swallowed. And every time I did I felt a puddle of wetness squirt out of me. With Finesse eyeing me down I had to keep it together, not show that I was possibly interested in fucking him. I had to be strong in my time of weakness. But I felt like he was winning me over with that succulent dick of his dangling between his legs and them doe-eyes of his steady gaping at me. Man, he was a deep dark-skinned Mandingo standing before me. Gripping his dick like it was a trophy. I was so, so, turned on by him. Shit!

Suddenly, I felt sick. Not sick as in the common cold. Sick as in if I didn't get me some dick I was going to spit up in my thong. Just the thought of vomiting made my stomach growl. I was hungry—in dire need of something thick and juicy to eat. I wanted his dick to spit. Just splatter come all over my baldhead, then put it back inside me, and come all over my walls. Pullout and splatter me in the face. Then let it dribble down my chin and onto my turtleneck sweater. I blinked again—tried to distract myself from gawking at the big, wide dick dangling so confidently. But I just couldn't do it. My eyes were glued as if I were hypnotized. That dick had fucked my head up.

My legs pried open and zipper crept down. Finesse thick eyebrows rose. My hand inched in my pants. My head leaned back against the couch and my waist and hips did a rotating motion as my fingers tried to scratch that annoying itch. My body gyrated. I called myself calling his bluff by pretending to pleasure myself. But I was not doing such a good job of it. I got caught up in my own shit. My lips pursed together and as they did, Finesse continued to slowly eye me down from my boots to my face detailing every motion of my body to see if I was weakening to his advances. It was clear that I was.

I moaned, and then bellowed out sexy groans that aroused him to move in a little closer. His eyes still gaped at me, watching me get off.

"Ugh, ugh, ugh," my lips parted and an echo of erotic sound bellowed out. My index and middle finger were taking turns eager to satisfy my clit. They rubbed it vigorously and as they did I felt the tip of it harden. Oh...my...! They had no mercy on the clit. I gritted my teeth. I wanted it to explode between my legs. I bit down on my bottom lip because I felt the urge to roar out my sexual frustrations. The feeling was so, so, so, tempting! I couldn't contain myself. My fingers were working overtime trying to get me to that point of orgasm. Shit. I was so fuckin' close. So close to feel wet juice spit out of me, but as I opened my eyes I saw Finesse enjoying it. He wet those thick African lips and kept on stroking himself.

"Fuck dis shit," I said to myself.

Karla Denise Baker

I inched my corduroys down my sheer legs, down to my ankles, then pull down my thong. I stood before him with wet pussy. Finesse eyes widened and his bottom lip drooped. He wanted to fuck just as much as I did. I was butt naked standing before him. I wanted to put my moist lips on that firm erection of his, swallow it whole, pullback, twirl my sodden tongue around it and have my hot spittle drench it to a shine of glistening ebony silk. Shit! It was there for the taking. And I wanted to take full advantage of that opportunity that was being presented to me.

That ebony silk was calling my name. It was talking to me. Asking me to c'mere and choke it—begged me to *come* on its head. Everything in me wanted to. I was horny like that too. Ooh, that dick had me fucked!

By this time I was slippery wet. My lips were sliding against each other, too. Shit it was on. That was, until I told Finesse how much I charged for the pussy. He looked at me like I had shit on my upper lip.

"What you think you getting this coochie for free?"

"Well, yeah," he said all nonchalant.

"What you think I'm going to give you my pussy just on a whim without getting paid, nigga?"

"I figured we'd both get some enjoyment out of it. It ain't like it won't be worth it. Look at this muthafucker." He gripped his thick meat. Damn, that dick did look good, but could he work it? That was what was on my mind. Every nigga talk a good game about how they work their dick but does that muthafucker comply. Does he obey your muthafuckin' command by staying...*hard*? Besides, sticking me in the doo-doo hole and pussy what else does it do? Other than slipping it in and out of my mouth and having me deep-throat it, can it accommodate all of my sexual needs? Those were the questions I needed to know before I was all willy-nilly with my pussy.

"Listen, pussy like mine doesn't come every day, I gots to get paid," I told him.

Finesse looked a bit frazzled. I guess he was so used to getting what he wanted that he finally met his match.

"Can we talk about this rationally?" He said trying to humble himself.

I laughed. "Rationally? Are you serious? Lemme school you on something so that we don't waste each other's time. No money. No pussy. How 'bout that?"

Finesse started pacing and as he did his meaty dick was swaying from side to side like a church bell.

I couldn't seem to take my eyes off of it. If only he knew how much I wanted that dick. I would've fucked him for free, but I thought against

78

it. This cat and mouse game was beginning to turn me on. I needed to see what he was willing to do or at least give up for some of my juicy pussy.

"How much do you think it's worth nigga? What's your bid?" I asked him.

He laughed.

"Throw out a number. I gotta go soon so you betta' think quickly."

He called my bluff.

"Let me sniff it first. 'Cause I don't want no stank pussy," he said.

I smirked.

"No problem. Go ahead." I stood still while he moved in close and knelt down and sniffed. My shit was clean and it smelled like clean money. I had no worries at all.

He smiled real big.

"So, what you sayin'?" I asked.

"Wait a minute. Let me stick my finger in it. I need to know that it smells good inside too."

"Do you." I said.

I stood still and Finesse stuck his middle finger in my sloppy hole When he pulled it out it was glistening with my wet juices.

"Now what?" I asked.

"All right. But I need to know how it tastes."

"So what you sayin? You sayin' you want to eat me out?"

"Nah. I just want to lick it a coupla times. See how it tastes on my tongue. That's all."

"Do you."

I didn't budge.

Finesse pulled my sticky lips apart and stuck the tip of his slippery wet tongue in and out of my fleshy folds. Shit, his hot tongue felt soooooooo good.

"Damn! Your pussy tastes good as hell." He said.

"So what you sayin'? Listen, time is money and my time is running out. What you gonna do?"

"How much you talkin'?"

"It depends on how long you want it."

"Alright. You take food stamps?"

"What you trying to insult me? Sayin' I got welfare pussy. Hell, no What you think I got time to waste with your broke ass! Nigga... I got shit to do."

"Okay, lighten up. I was just kidding. Shit. You're feisty for a white chick."

I laughed.

"Were you ever a cheerleader in school?" he asked.

"What?"

"A cheerleader. You know with the pom-poms and little skirt."

"No."

"Oh. Scratch that idea."

I heaved, loudly.

"Okay. Okay," he said.

"What does that mean?"

"You win."

"You know you really take the fun out of this game, Mr. Witherspoon. This theme is getting old. It's time to think of something else, okay."

He nodded his head, then leaned over and grabbed his sweats and pulled out his wallet.

"Here you go," he said.

I counted out two hundred dollars. I let him squeeze my ass a couple of times. I got dressed. And headed for the door and let myself out.

"See you next week." I said.

"Same time, okay." he said.

"Okay."

***

IT WAS SATURDAY. Devin Rogers had come by to get some morning cream in his coffee. To be perfectly honest I was not in the mood to be entertaining but seeing that he was my cash flow, I had to get in the mood.

I winded a ball of tissue around my hand and wiped from front to back, flushed the toilet, pulled up my thong, and washed my hands, and sprayed the bathroom with Glade Summer Breeze, and hurried to answer the door.

Devin was self-employed. He owned a men's wear store SUIT YO'SELF downtown Paterson. We had been dealing with one another for about six weeks. He was looking for an exclusive relationship. I, on the other hand, was looking for finances—his finances. With rent, and all of my other expenses, I needed a steady cash flow coming in. Devin was that steady cash flow.

Devin stood about 6'5", medium build, flat-board stomach, and drop dead, strong manly features. He was dark complexioned with muscular frame and memorizing coffee-colored eyes. He had a mellow tone that was very inviting to me. It was smooth, soft, and yet still masculine. The one thing I loved about Devin was that he knew how to please a girl's body.

I opened the door and invited Devin in. God, he looked so good dressed in black trousers with a white button down dress shirt on, and a pair of black leather shoes on his feet. I noticed he had this sadness in his eyes, though.

"Is everything alright?" I asked him.

"It pains me," he said, staring into my bloodshot red eyes as he stepped inside of my one-bedroom apartment.

I reached for his massive dark hand and led him into my bedroom.

"Do you want to talk about it?" I asked, groggy.

"I had this conversation with this friend of mine. Um, he's dating this girl, well, woman, and he is beginning to have these feelings for her. Feelings he never thought he would have for someone like her." He said.

"Is he in love with her? Or is he just fucking with her head?" I asked as I sat down on the edge of the bed. Devin sat down next to me.

"Yes, no, yes..." Devin dropped his head, and then he lifted it back up. "Yes, he's deeply in love with her." He said.

"I see." I said.

"He's hurting right now." He told me.

"Where exactly does it hurt?" I asked him.

He didn't hesitate to respond. "Man, it hurts him everywhere. Even when he breathes, it hurts."

"How'd he get so sprung, so quickly?" I said.

"I dunno. She lured him in with her truth." He told me. "He felt free. She let him breathe. She let him be him." He smirked, and then sniffed in the scent of Summer Breeze that lingered in the air. "Damn," he continued, "he can still smell her scent of Daisy (by Marc Jacobs) on her supple skin. Smell the Alberto VO5 shampoo in her hair." He exhaled. "I can't really explain it, but she had this 'thing' about her. Something so unique that it just drew you in, and once you got a taste of it...BAM! You're done. Hooked, lined, and sinking your tongue in her pussy."

"Shit!"

"Yeah, shit is right. She had him doin' shit he'd never done to a woman before."

"Uh-huh. Question," I asked him, "How does he plan on getting this woman out of his system?"

"I dunno." Devin replied.

81

"Soooo in other words he's *fucked*."

After that, there was silence between us; off came his clothes and then mine. I kneeled on my knees and wrapped my lips around his bulging head and sucked him damned near dry.

THE SPAGHETTI STRAP to my red teddy dangled on the cherry wood bedpost as I lie on top of Devin's hard body. Daybreak broke through the tangled mini-blinds and awakened me out of a peaceful sleep. I opened my eyes gaping at him, while inhaling the fragrant scent of Dove's pomegranate and lemon verbena lingering on my skin. Instantly I felt a sense of contentment. I gently brushed my smooth backhand against his supple dark skin and delicately massaged the nape of his head. Devin loved when I'd massage his smooth head. I wet my lips and tenderly pecked him on the earlobe. The feel of my lips upon his skin roused him to open his eyes. And when he looked at me I saw lust engulfed in flames. He was drooling for me and I was drooling for him.

My mind drifted.

I had my silent moments when I would talk to God. And I would express to Him that all I ever wanted and felt I needed was a man with mind, heart, and potential. And to me, Devin fit the bill to a tee. It was evident to me that he was the one. He was everything I didn't expect. He was odd. And that intrigued me. He was an introvert. You know, a man who kept to himself. He kept his business just that...his business. He had minimal friends. And the ones he did have were mostly women. Men. Well, he kept them at a distance for various reasons.

Having a man who supported any aspirations was like trying to find a needle in a haystack. Devin was the answer to my prayers. He was a man of patience. He had a good eye for quality. When it came to women, he could pick out the freaks, gold-diggers, and snooty bitches from miles away. Women were like vultures when it came to him mainly because he owned his own business. The mid-forty year old entrepreneur was struggling to make ends meet, but I was attracted to his drive, tenacity to keep growing. With good looks, brains, and a little bank, women desired him mainly because they assumed that he was rolling in the dough. I didn't care about the other women. They were no threat to me. I was in it for the money and mere pleasure of being caressed by a good looking man.

I wasn't looking for love, babies, marriage, or the white picket fence fairytale. I had made that perfectly clear upon our first date, which was a tranquil ride to the outskirts of Philly. He took me to an exquisite restaurant called BEEHIVE. Oh, the food there was delicious! I had a wonderful time just eating and talking.

Devin was not easily convinced. He figured all women talked that talk, and later ended up eating their words because they'd wound up barefoot and pregnant and professing their love (something they claimed they'd never let happen) so he assumed that I was the same. If he'd given me a couple of more months more than likely I'd change my mind. So he thought. But Devin was in for a rude-awakening because I was adamant about how I felt. It was my life, and nothing and no one was going to change that unless I was ready for change. I loved me enough to not be swayed by a man or his dick. FYI. I had Du-da-Trick (vibrator), to take the edge off, if needed be.

I was not trying to get caught up in the hype of happily-ever-after. Yet I devoted "quality time" to Devin, which was every Saturday. As much as Devin was slightly discouraged by that, he adapted rather quickly to keep the peace as well as me in his life. Had it been anyone else, he'd stick to his motto: "Men don't share their meat!" He was not the desperate type. He was headstrong. His morals and values were important to him, but his devotion to me made him bend a bit. Me, being straightforward was quite a turn on for him. He was zealous to indulge in me. I was a no-nonsense type of girl. Something he was not accustomed to, but was willing to explore. I didn't hide my other encounters I'd indulged in from him. I was open about my life. And I reassured Devin that I wasn't ready to get into a committed relationship by my actions. I didn't give him an ultimatum to be with me. If anything, I gave him an option. Stay or go. I wasn't the type of girl to shed tears, whine, or plead to keep a man. I was hard. It would take a bulldozer to get through to me. But that came from past experiences. I'd endured a lot of pain in my lifetime. Of course, I knew that I was spreading myself thin by having a man for every day of the week. But the way I saw it there was nothing wrong with playing the field as long as everyone on the team was well informed. To me. a girl getting her feet wet along with her pussy was not uncommon. If anything, it seemed practical to me. My way of thinking was to be honest about my intentions—to not mislead or spoof my johns. I'd never play the damsel in distress. It was not my style to use one only to abuse 'em later. I was on the up and up—a simplistic-type of girl merely interested in having a good time as long as I got compensated for it.

I rolled my curvaceous body off of Devin and wrapped my arms around the goose down pillow and snuggled up. Devin rose out of bed and sat on the edge; his sleepy eyes gaped at the 4 x 6 picture that sat on the nightstand of us all hugged up in Bryant Park, with big smiley faces.

I rolled back over and gazed at Devin's strong, flawless back, "Baby, are you okay?" I asked sensing that he might be troubled. Devin cracked a smile, "I couldn't be better, baby. It couldn't be better." I reached out my arm and touched the small of his back and twirled my forefinger in a circular motion. Devin loved when I touched him. He'd never deny me of that. "Well, I have to go to the writing workshop today." I said in a raspy voice.

I never divulged my nightlife with Devin because I didn't think he'd understand. It was obvious that he was catching deep feelings for me. I cared for him, but I had to keep some things private. Devin nodded his head letting me know that he was listening. "Sounds great!" He replied. I smiled, because he always made me feel heard. I loved how easy going Devin was. He wasn't the clingy type. He gave me as much space as I needed. Seldom had I felt bad about my double life. But a slither of guilt crept in, and then quickly disappeared from my consciousness. I couldn't allow my conscience to get the better of me. Devin was a confident man—very secure about himself. Another man was never a threat to him, so he said. I found that to be so damn sexy. We had great chemistry and as long as that continued I had no reservations about seeing him.

I loved Devin's style. He carried himself like a professional. He wasn't overdone. He was well rounded. I was drawn to his aura and his power. To me, Devin was the whole package, but I often had to remind myself that our relationship was purely physical. He was there for the mere need of fulfilling my sexual appetite. The less I saw of him, the better. I wasn't trying to get caught up and on that emotional love coaster like some older women did. And I was determined not to.

I stretched out my long arms and released a loud yawn. Then rose out of bed and headed toward the bathroom to take a hot shower. As I crossed paths with Devin, he extended out his right hand and gently reached out for my small wrist pulling me closer toward him. I lost my balance and fell my bare-skinned body onto his lap brushing my ass against his soft penis. He wrapped his arms around my twenty-nine inch waist and placed his salivating tongue upon my navel, rotating the edge of his tongue in the crevasse. I felt my juices flowing but tried to restrain myself from arousal. I squirmed trying to get my body a loose, but Devin held onto me.

I closed my eyes and submissively surrendered to the passion burning between us. I eased my legs open as Devin lowered his head down and gently kissed the outer skin of my lower lips, sniffling in my essence. He teased the clit so sensually stimulating every vessel in my body. He caressed my clit with tender love as I opened my legs wider inviting him to eat. He caressed my ass; gently dug his fingers into the meat as I rotated my hips to the sweet sensations that whooshed throughout my famished and feverish body.

Devin released his hands from my ass as he maneuvered my body to fall back onto the bed and gingerly placed me on my back, while he gazed into my eyes. He rose to his feet, marveling my natural beauty. His deep, dark eyes soaked in every inch of my girlhood. He then climbed upon the king-sized bed and knelt on his knees, memorized as he leaned over shadowing my body with his and suckled on my right coral-pink nipple, taunting and teasing it with his sodden tongue as moisture formed tiny bubbles between my fleshy folds. I reached my right hand out and wrapped my searing fingers around his hard, thick, black dick and gently massaged it.

Devin closed his eyes, as did I. I clenched my teeth to the feel of Devin's finger fondling my clit. I moaned. Devin's body glowed with sweat streaming from his clean-shaven head, face, down to his chest, and lowering to his scrotum, testicles, and then dissolving into the woven white linen sheets. The feel of his forefinger stroking "Honey Walls" drove me mad. I stretched my head back in the goose down pillow. elongated my neck as I weakened. My legs trembled as my toes spread and then curled under. I toiled his manhood with vigorous strokes of back and forth motion until it intensified and beads of sweat formed on his forehead. Not able to contain myself, I wet my lips with spittle and grinded down on my teeth as my eyelids fluttered to the deliverance that Devin was giving me. It was a feeling I had never felt before.

Devin cocked his head back and then leaned forward as he vigorously motioned his finger against "Honey Walls." Both of us were near our peak. Our bodies quivered. My eyes squinted. I pursed my lips, while my fingernails scratched the headboard. "Ooh, I'm gonna cum! You gonna make me cum!" I shrilled, while Devin kept caressing "Honey Walls" as he pressed his lips tightly watching me squirm like a snail against the moist, disheveled sheets.

"Let it go!" Devin spoke in a mellow, yet firm tone. I squeezed my legs together as his finger continued to delight "Honey Walls." I clenched my teeth and clawed at the sheets with my fingernails. I arched my back as my head rose from the goose down pillow. The muscles in my stomach and legs tightened up as I heartily clasped his manhood. Both of us glowed with hot, sticky sweat as we passionately contented one another. We gawped at one another, and then simultaneously burst outside of ourselves.

I fixed my eyes on Devin engrossed in him ejaculating a pearly cream onto my forearm, him, and the sheets. "Oh, shitttttttt!" Devin sung through his teeth. I panted, with pure delight. "That was so, so, se-xy! Se-xy as hell!" I exclaimed with excitement and then fell back against the goose down pillows completely immobilized. Devin depleted all of my energy. He gazed at me with fulfillment in his eyes and enormous love and respect for me in his heart. Knowing how much he cared for me, how could I ever divulge my double life to him, let alone my age?

Before Devin left, he placed three hundred dollars on my dresser. Gave me a forehead kiss, and then said, "See you next Saturday."

I nodded. Rolled over onto my stomach and went to sleep.

***

"Can I speak to, ah...Rocka?" the female disgruntle voice asked.

"Who's calling?"

"This is Mrs. Montgomery. Bo Montgomery's wife of twenty-five years that's who the *fuck* is calling."

"*And...*"

"And I'm calling to let you know that Bo is my husband."

"As if I didn't know..."

"Well, know enough to leave my man alone...before..."

"Hold up, bitch, did you just threaten me?"

"Call it what you like, Ho; you just remember what I said!"

Click!

This was usually how it ended. Another desperate wife calling me, trying to hold on to the only man she's ever really loved. Those wives used to kill me with that bullshit—trying to stake their claim. All of a sudden as soon as they smell another woman's perfume or pussy they want to act as if they really care. Now he's their "everything." Pleasssseeeeeeeeee...if you asked me it was always 'bout finances, perhaps stability too. But love, huh, I begged to differ.

Of course I was not in the least bit intimidated by the wives or girlfriends. Little did they know, while wifey was calling me, her so-called husband was in the shower washing away the residue from our steamy sexcapade nearly fifteen minutes ago? Wifey's like her, gave me all the power to do what I did...*fuck... her... man.* Yeah, I kept it gritty.

See, I was not interested in knowing 'bout *her.* Nor did I care 'bout the fact that he was married. Because contrary to what those wives knew, that's what I preyed on...MEN. Single men. Married men. Happy men. Unhappy men. Separated but living in a household of convenience men, too.

You see Rocka liked men period! I liked men who talked to me, not at me, about their home life with the missus. These ears listened attentively to them bicker 'bout what she was not doing in the bedroom. Child support. Her weight. Her sexual performance. Her cooking. Her not cooking. I gave those men every bit of: pussy, pussy, and more sweet/sweaty pussy. I gave them some of my time and energy too. I reeled them in, oh...so...nicely, and catered to their every wish. I gave them everything that she wouldn't or couldn't.

So with that being said, I was not the one wives needed to be calling...ho. You gotta understand how this shit worked. Every time wifey fell short, I tripped on his dick and giddied up horsy. Every time wifey bitched, I screamed out his name. Every time wifey did anything that would piss him off...where did he come? He came running to me. I knew how to calm him down with the feel of these "Honey Walls." I knew how to appease and please him. It was no deep dark secret that I was a "repeat offender." Rehab couldn't do a thing for me. I was an addict for a dick with or without a ring on his finger.

"Who were you talking to, Rocka?" Bo asked as he stepped out of the granite bathroom of Hittin'-the-Skins Motel, dripping wet. The hunter-green towel wrapped loosely around his forty-four inch waist.

"You really want to know?"

He nodded his head as he removed the towel and towel dried his broad back.

"Well, it was your wife."

Underneath my bare feet felt like the earth had just shook just by the 'oh, shit' look on his face.

Bo cut his chestnut-brown eyes over at me. "Listen, I-I-I never gave her your number," he said in an unnerved baritone voice.

"Baby, why would I think that? Obviously she's been snooping and found my number in your cell phone."

"Obviously," he repeated his voice still a bit shaky as he gaped at his nude dark-skinned body in the mirror.

"Don't let that stress you," I told him as I rose from the edge of the king-sized bed and I walked over to him. I pressed my hot body against his sexy, damp skin.

"Don't start something you can't finish," he said with a smile on his handsome face.

"Oh, baby, you of all people know that I can finish anything I start." I said, rubbing my blond-haired hairy pussy against his hairy buttocks.

"Rocka, I'm *warning* you."

"I'm listening to every word your body is saying, baby." I said seductively.

My fingers made their way up to his massive chest and I massaged the damp hairs and gently tugged on his nipples. I stood on my tiptoes and softly teased his earlobe with my teeth, and slowly maneuvered my fingers down to his thick six-inch sex organ.

"Rocka, I'm *warning* you," he said in a faint whisper, as his tongue glided across his thick bottom lip.

I grazed my baldhead against his back, moaned seductively, and maneuvered my warm fingers down to pleasure his manhood. Instantly, the blood rushed from his feet and up to his meat. I made my way to the front of him, licking his face with my warm, slimy tongue, gliding my spittle from his nose to his top lip, and slowly made my way down, down, down, as I knelt on my knees, feet imprinted in the plush carpet, toes spread, and tongue teasing the tip of his bulged erection.

Bo tilted his head back and yelped. "Damn, baby, you give great head. Shit!"

The sound effects of sucking his meat were like background music.

"Oh, mmmm, shit." Bo groaned.

I loved it when he'd let me know how good I made him feel. The more he'd let me know, the more I aimed to please him.

"Ah, shit, baby, baby, I'm about to throw up on you!" He moaned.

"I know," I said to myself. "Throw up, baby, throw up!"

"Ahhhh, shiiiittttttttttttttttt, don't let me throw up in your mouth, baby. Relinquish, relinquish!"

This only made me keep going. *Throw up, baby, throw up,* I thought.

"Rocka, st-op," he sung. He squinted his eyes tightly, a wrinkle formed on his forehead and his hands maneuvered my head to keep going. So I did.

"Aw...sh...it! Aw, sh...it, Roc—"

Within seconds, his coconut cream exploded in my mouth. I swallowed, and then tongued him down, recklessly.

By the end of the night, Bo placed two hundred twenty dollars on the nightstand, gave me an endearing forehead kiss, and headed out the door with a big ass grin on his face, while I leaned my bare back against the headboard, misty-eyed.

***

MY CELL PHONE rang, while Devin was taking a shower.

I answered it on the first ring. "Hello?"

"What's up, Rocka?"

As soon as I heard *his* voice I knew it was Malik.

I whispered into the phone. "Just resting before I have to go in for work."

"Well, I'm out-of-town so I won't be able to see your fine ass tonight."

I wasn't surprised. Malik was always calling me when he was out-of-town.

"Where are you *this* time?" I asked him.

"Vegas."

I knew doggone well that he wasn't in Vegas alone, not that it really mattered. We rarely spent time together and the one time we did, Malik seem too eager to get in my drawers. But when he reached in his pants pocket and pulled out his gold money-clip and placed three hundred dollars in my hands for fifteen minutes of *head*, shittttttttttt, it was on. I got mine. That was how I got down!

Don't get it twisted...yeah, I was a stripper, but that didn't always mean that I didn't respect my body. That's the first thing people say and thank. You gotta be a whore to be a stripper. That's not necessarily true. There are some educated women's who have stripped to get to where they wanted to be. I ain't mad at 'em for that. They had to do what they had to do. Look, I knew who the hell I was. I was Magnolia "Daisy" Wily, not Rocka-Bye Bitch. I wasn't livin' in denial, *they* were.

I think people got things misconstrued about strippers. Working the pole was damn hard work. The strippers had to stay in tiptop shape to work at THE NAPPY DUGOUT because Durdy-Dog didn't play that shit. You think he was gonna let his hos work for him with bullet holes in their ass, cottage cheese caked up on their pussies, and cellulite. Hell no! He expected his strippers to look like fuckin' money.

Listen, some of the girls who worked at THE NAPPY DUGOUT were in college, single mothers, or were tryna get money up to pay their bills. I wasn't there for none of those reasons, 'cause I never chose that lifestyle. It was chosen for me. If it were up to me I'd probably be working with crack babies like myself. But that wasn't the case. I had no say.

"Hmm...how's the weather there?" I asked.

"Nice," Malik said.

"Baby, you ready....?"

I heard this female's voice say.

I rolled my eyes. "It sounds like you're preoccupied; don't let me hold you up." I told him.

He laughed. "Nah. It ain't like that."

I shook my head from side to side and twisted my lips. "Whatever. Do you."

"Always, lady, always...."

"Talk to you...whenever." I said and hung up the phone.

As I put my cell phone down, Devin was walking out of the bathroom with a towel tightly wrapped around his waist. My eyes were glued to his muscles popping out of his chest, upper arms, and legs. Man, did he have a nice ass body. I always used to tease him about how fine his body was just to see him blush. It was cute to see him feel a bit uncomfortable. It said a lot about his character. He wasn't full of hisself, like Malik. I really found that to be very attractive.

Devin checked his voicemail. Then he looked over at me and said. "I have to head to SUIT YO'SELF to check on the store. Harlem is working by himself today because my sales associate Sean called out again. Jackson can't come in because he is sick. Jasmine can't find a babysitter. And Sarah, well, she got drunk as hell last night and has a hangover. I can't win. I mean I try to give these young kids a chance but they are so unreliable, you know." He pulled up his boxers.

I nodded my head. "You'll figure it out, baby. Don't stress yourself. Kids will be kids. Listen, I have to get ready to get out of here too."

Devin tilted his head to the side like he was thinking as he was putting on his socks. "Ey, Daisy, did you write your essay, yet?" he asked me.

"Huh?" I said with a dumbfounded look upon my face.

"The essay. The essay *you* said you had to have done by...*today*."

I had completely forgotten about the "lie" I had told him. "Oh, yeah, that."

"Well, did you finish it? Can I see it? Maybe I can see if you have any grammatical errors or typos before you submit it in," he said while pulling up his trousers. "In high school I was pretty good in my English class."

I was at a loss for words. "Now, how I am going to get out of this one," I asked myself. "Well, um, ah...."

"You don't have to be embarrassed." He said, "Listen, I don't care if I see misspellings, it's okay, at least you are trying to do something you love. I admire you for that."

"Really?"

"Really."

I felt like a complete idiot for lying to him. "Would it be okay if I look at it again before I show it to you?" I said hoping he would say okay.

"That's fine. See that's what I'm talkin' about. You really care about everything you do. It says a lot about you. I hope you know that."

I was naïve. Everything that Devin said to me didn't register right away. But I always knew how to make it seem like it did. I looked at him with this distance in my eyes. "What does it say?"

He stood still to explain. "It says that you take pride in your work. That you are the type of woman who wants to put your best foot forward."

I smiled.

Devin really knew how to make me feel special. No man has ever made me feel that way before.

While Devin was putting on his V-neck T-shirt and dress shirt, I grabbed a pair of thongs and bra out of the top dresser drawer and headed to the bathroom. I left my cell phone on the bed, not really thinking anything of it. Well, while I was in the shower my cell phone rang and Devin took it upon himself to answer it for me. That really rubbed me the wrong way. I can't tell you how pissed I was by that. What would make him think that he could just invade my privacy like that, huh? He was my john/lover, at least one of 'em, so to him I was his woman at least on Saturdays, so he felt there was nuthin' wrong with answering my phone. We shared no secrets. I totally disagreed! I had a secret that was burning my insides to tell him, but I just didn't know how to get the words out of my mouth.

"Hello?"

"Ah," The male voice on the other end said, "Ah, may I speak to Daisy?"

"Who's calling?" Devin asked

"Oh, this is Mr. Stevens."

"Hold on, let me get her for you."

The one thing I absolutely admired about Devin was that he was honestly not a jealous man. And if he was I never saw it, with the exception of when I told him about my other encounters. He knew that he was not my one and only. And he appeared to be fine with it; at least that was what he had said. Did I believe him? No, but I respected the fact that he was willing to accept it—to have me.

Devin walked into the oatmeal-colored bathroom, pulled back the maroon, gold, and olive-green silk-like shower curtain and said, "Baby, ah, Mr. Stevens is on the phone. Do you want to talk to him now or should I have him call you back later?"

I quickly rinsed off, toweled dried my body down, and answered the call. Devin walked out of the bathroom giving me some privacy.

"Hello?"

"Daisy?"

"May I ask whose calling?"

"My name is Greig...Mr. Stevens, um, we met, well, I had bumped into you the other day. You remember?"

I took a minute to think back. I smirked. "Oh, yeah, but..."

"I got your number off of your business card. The one you dropped that day. I slipped it in my pocket. Anyway, it says that you do 'private dancing' well, I was wondering if you could meet me at a hotel (of your choice), one night."

"Exactly what do you have in mind?" I asked him.

"Nothing that you wouldn't normally do for your clients," he said.

I pursed my lips, "I see. Well, can I get back to you...I'm kinda in the middle of something at the moment, but if you'd like you can come to THE NAPPY DUGOUT and we can talk more about it."

"I prefer not. I'll wait for you to contact me. You have my number on your phone?"

"Yes."

"Well, you have a blessed day."

"You too."

I hung up the phone feeling a little leery about meeting Mr. Stevens, but then the other part of me was a little curious about him too.

As I was about to walk out of the bathroom I heard Devin say, "Babe, I'm heading out. I'll call you later, okay."

"See you, honey." I yelled back.

I heard the door close, and just as it did I felt this urge to take a hit. So I did. I swear I felt like Ol' Durty was calling my name. That nigga had a serious hold on me—one that I couldn't seem to shake, alone.

I wanted something to get into. I mean after my performance at THE

NAPPY DUGOUT I was in the mood for someone that would fulfill my sexual appetite. I was tired of chicken, fish, steak...I wanted me some pork. So, before everyone was to leave out I went into the bathroom and hid in one of the stalls and called Mr. Stevens. For someone reason. I remember sniffing in pork skins when he bumped into me.

The phone rang, twice.

Someone picked up.

"Hello?"

"Yes, um, may I speak with Mr. Stevens, please?"

"This is he."

"This is Daisy." I heard heavy breathing over the phone. "Hello? Hello? Are you there?"

"Yes, ah, I didn't think you'd call."

"Why?"

"I don't quite know, but I'm glad you did."

"You mentioned something about...motel or hotel. Oh, I forget which one you said."

"Hotel." He said.

"Well, is this a bad time?"

"No, it's actually a very good time."

"Well, I'll be getting off at 3 00 a.m. Is that too late for you?"

"No, no."

"Well, what you can do is reserve a room and calls me back to let me know where you'll be. And I can come to you."

"Sounds like a plan."

Before I got a chance to tell him my fee, he asked the question.

"How much do you...um, charge?"

"I start at one thousand and work my way up. It all depends on what you want, and how long you want it."

"I see."

"Is there a problem?" I asked him.

"No. Everything is fine, just fine. I'll call you with the place and time."

"Okay." I said, and then hung up.

My cell phone rang as Royce was opening the door to the limo. It was Mr. Stevens. Good thing I was in front of my building. I answered the call and said, "Can I call you back?" He responded, "Yes."

Royce did his normal routine of escorting me upstairs and making sure I got in safely.

As soon as I shut the door to my apartment, and heard Royce's footsteps going downstairs, I called Mr. Stevens back.

"Sorry about that. I know you said that you wanted things to be discreet. I just got home." I told him.

"Well, thanks for returning my call. I'm at the Private Stock Inn in Wayne."

"Okay. Which one?"

"The one on.... It's the only room I could get on such short notice. I hope that is okay with you."

"It's fine. I'm gonna have to catch a cab. It may take an hour or so for me to get there."

"Ah, if you want I can come and pick you up." He said.

I paused, not certain if I wanted him to know where I lived. I guessed he picked up on it because he said, "It's no problem. We have all night. I'll see you when you get here. It's room 312."

I can't tell you how good that made me feels to hear him not badger me on coming to pick me up.

"Let me call the cab now, okay."

"Okay. Call me when you are here."

"Okay."

We hung up and I called a cab. Then I entered my bedroom and grabbed my satchel bag from out of the closet and packed my black 3-piece halter and mini-skirt set in it, sexy 5-inch thigh high boots with one and a half inch platform. I walked into the bathroom and reached under the sink for my toiletry bag, exited out and back into my bedroom and packed a pair of raggedy faded blue jeans, white V-neck T-shirt, and a pair of black heeled boots. I then changed into something a little sexier...a black halter dress that wrapped around the neck. By the time I finished doing that I heard the cab honking its horn.

I exited out of my apartment, took the stairs and exited out of the building and into the yellow cab.

When I arrived at the Private Stock Inn, it was quiet as a mouse. I called Mr. Stevens letting him know that I had arrived. I took the elevator up to the third floor and he was standing in the doorway waiting for me.

"Hello." I said.

"Hello." He said, and then smiled.

God that man had gorgeous white teeth, dark chocolate brown eyes, and tall, with deep dark skin. There was something mysterious about him too. Something about him caught my eye. Mr. Stevens stepped to the side dressed in a pair of jeans and a button down navy-blue dress shirt tucked in his pants with a black leather belt, and allowed me to entry into the room. I looked around the spacious room and everything was neat and clean. There was a bouquet of assorted flowers sitting on the coffee table in a crystal vase. Tall rose, yellow, and peach colored candles were lit and the lights were dimmed, but I was still able to see that near the wide window was a table filled with cheese, crackers, strawberries, and two bottles of wine: white and red.

I cut my eyes toward the bathroom and saw on the counter chocolate kisses and a bottle of White Rain bubble bath. I smirked 'cause I was flattered that he had done all of that for us. The room had a slight chill to it from the air being on, but I didn't mind. It looked so lovely.

I placed my satchel on the rose-colored loveseat, and as I did, I noticed sitting on the nightstand was a bottle of Male Sexual Enhancement and a penis ring. Interesting, I thought. Mr. Stevens was telling me a lot about his sex life. He had none. I found that to be quite strange. It was different from the norm of men's I'd normally fucked.

"Relax yourself, I'm sure you're tired from a long day's work," Mr. Stevens said giving me direct eye contact.

I smiled.

"Yes, Mr. Stevens, it has been a tough day, but I made it here."

"Please call me...Greig."

"Sure."

"Would you like a glass of wine?"

"Yes, please." I said, as I took off my shoes and got comfortable.

"Which would you prefer...white or red?"

"White is fine."

As he poured the wine, he pushed play on the CD player that was sitting alongside the silver ice bucket. "Let Me Make Love To You" by the O'Jays came streaming out of the small speakers.

I could see that Mr. Stevens. well, Greg wasn't in a rush to get down to business. I was glad 'cause I was pooped. I worked the hell out my body and I felt everything hit me all at once.

After Greig poured us a glass of wine, he took a few steps back over to me and we made a toast. "To the moment..." We clanked our glasses, and then sipped. I reached for a piece of cheese and a dark red strawberry. I bit into the cheese, which was slightly bitter and then took a bite into the strawberry, which was sweet, and then, another sip of wine to wet my palate. Greig placed his glass down on the nightstand. I sat on the loveseat nearest the window viewing the scenery. It looked so pretty.

Greig knelt down on one knee and reached for my swollen feet, but I pulled them away. I was a little hesitant to let him touch my feet, but the look in his eyes comforted me that he would do me no harm. I extended my feet back out to him and let him have his way. And boy, am I glad I did. Greig had some magical fingers. It felt so good to have his hands on my feet. Everything that hurt slowly escaped from my mind. He massaged under the soles with long, hard strokes like they do in the nail salons. He popped my toes and massaged each one individually. I tell you when that man got done with my feet, *ooh; girl* was all I could think.

His hands rose up to my calves, legs, and inched his strong fingers underneath my dress, up to my hot thighs. Then he began to sing. Such a soulful voice he had. It brought chills to my spine. I was so charmed by him. He reached for my hand and asked me to stand up and turn around. And I did. He lowered his hands down the small of my back and massaged his fingers into the deep tissue. I was so tense I know I felt like rocks were inside of me. I could feel his warm breath against the nape of my neck. I exhaled, as his soft lips pecked upon my neck so mildly. He inched down to my bare-skinned back, and kissed it. Then slowly he unloosened the strap wrapped around my neck. Instinctively my hands rose to grab the front of my dress before my breasts were exposed. The pecks were still inviting as he spun me around and gazed piercingly into my eyes and kissed me so passionately I saw stars. Butterflies fluttered in my stomach as the CD changed to "I Can't Say No" by Natalie Cole, and I felt I couldn't. This man was so charming that I felt willing to oblige his wishes. Impulses raced throughout my body and that tingle I normally got triggered something in me. I knew with everything in me that I wanted him. Just as I had that thought Patti LaBelle's "If You Ask Me To" vocals sprung from the speakers and so welcomingly into my ears. I was open to the invitation.

Greig took me by the hand and escorted me to the entrance of the bathroom. "May I undress you?" he asked. I nodded my head yes. I released my hands from my tits and fully exposed myself. He knelt down and pulled the dress from over my head and tossed it to the floor. He peeled my thong off of me like a banana and I stepped out of them. And then there was quiet as he intently gazed at every inch of my naked body. The look wasn't lustful. It was mesmerizing. God, I found that to be so damn sexy.

That moment of silence between us was the best thing I had ever experienced from a man. Something I'd never forget.

"I want you to be relaxed. Release all that tension so that when we make love we have each other's mind and body."

"Make love?" I whispered, with my eyes lost in him.

"Yes." He said in his deep husky voice. "That's what I want us to do...make love. I haven't been with a woman in years and I want this experience to be well worth it No disrespect, but I'm sure most men want to manhandle your body instead of caressing it. I don't want our experience to remind you of what you do or where you work. I want it to be something that will uplift you, not degrade you. You are a vibrant and beautiful woman, Daisy."

I bowed my head when he spoke of me being beautiful. I never really saw myself as that, yet men's often used the term in addition to: sexy gorgeous, fine...words that were somewhat foreign to me. My ears heard it often but the inner me had yet to believe it to be true. I knew I had a lot more growing to do within. No, I was not living in denial. I was slowly and steadfastly coming into my own girlhood. It was different from when I was performing onstage 'cause it was all an act to me, but in real life I had a lot to uncover about myself. It's funny how you see yourself and how others see you. It's hard for someone who never had that type of guidance, you know. I was not raised with praiseful words so I had to learnt from my surroundings, from others who were in my inner-circle, from men's, from women's, basically from life experiences: whether kind or not so kind that's how I learnt. So here I was in the presence of this man named Mr. Greig Stevens, who desired me in a way I had never been desired. Did I feel fireworks for him? I felt something that I could not really put into words, but it wasn't for him. It was for Devin.

I can't say that Greig didn't have me melting, 'cause he did. His words, God, they spoke of everything I ever wanted to hear a man's say to me. I didn't know if he was playin' me or not, but I tell you what...I didn't care. That moment was for us. And I wasn't about to mess it up by analyzing his every word. No, I was going to enjoy him and have him enjoy me; at least that's what I told myself.

Greig scooped me up off of my feet and carried me over the threshold of the bathroom entrance. He then lowered me into the bath of warm coconut milk and let me soak my yesterday away. I leaned my head back on the fluffy white bath pillow, closed my eyes, and hoped and prayed that this night was not a dream. For good measures I opened my eyes just to make sure. Greig had shut the door behind him and left me alone for a little "me" time.

After about a half hour I rose from the milky waters, towel dried, and wrapped a white towel around me, and drained the bathtub, then exited out of the bathroom. Greig was sitting on the loveseat with his head leaned back and his eyes closed listening to music. The heat from my eyes gaping at him awakened him out of his daze. He lifted his head up and our eyes met. He rose to his feet and I walked toward him feeling so renewed.

"How do you feel?" he asked.

I smiled. "I feel brand new."

He entered the bathroom and shut the door behind him. I reached for the cheese and crackers, sat down on the loveseat and nibbled while soaking up the ambiance.

About twenty minutes past, then the bathroom door opened. Hot steam cascaded in the air. Greig stepped out of the bathroom with a towel wrapped around his waist. I noticed he had a slight potbelly. And he was rather hairy. There's something sexy about a man's with hair on his chest. I happened to love it!

Our eyes met just as I was about to take a bite out of the juicy strawberry. With him eyeing me down I felt just a tad bit uncomfortable, so I placed the strawberry on one of the napkins that was setting next to the crackers and cheese.

Greig smiled. I smiled. And then I don't know what came over us, but the towels dropped to the floor and we ended up on the bed humping the shit out of one another. All I could tell you was that I was on all fours with my ass mid-air on the edge of the bed. Greig was standing behind me. With his massive hands he squeezed my ass cheeks apart, sniffed my asshole, and stuck his dick in my soaking wet pussy. While he was fucking my brains out, he was also stroking my back and the soles of my feet. Like I said I don't know what happened. Maybe the anticipation built up and got the betta' of us both. And if you're wondering, yes, we both forgot about the condom. So that meant I had to make a trip to the clinic to make sure I didn't have another STD. After you got gonorrhea in the throat once, who wanted to get that shit again?

Now at the time I wasn't concerned about an STD. Greig had me lay on my back with my knees pressed against his hairy chest as he was pumpin' the hell out of my hot pussy. My titties were jiggling as the bed was squeaking. I was purring like a cat. Purring and sweating like a feline in heat. Damned that nigga snuck up on a bitch! I couldn't say that I didn't love it. But I must admit I was a little worried after we took a breather. Why? Well, for one I loved a man with a wide, thick dick, 'specially one who knew how to work his shit. Greig said that he hadn't been with a woman's in years. And I couldn't say that I didn't believe him, but I must admit I was a little skeptical. The man's was a wild beast in bed. I felt his cock all the way up in my stomach. God, his dick...ah man, his dick had me jonesing fo' real.

Round two.

Greig played with my clit. My shit got hard real quick. I was oozing come juice out of me. Then he knelt on his knees and stuck out his long pink tongue and scooped my shit up. Damn! His tongue felt soooo good against my clit. I started yanking on his dick until it got hard. Then I said, "I wanna suck you." He lay on his back. I spread his legs wider than they were and I sucked from his balls to his dick, up and down and all around. Yum, yum, yum!

Next thing I knew he was calling out my name. Talk about an ego booster. Shit. You couldn't tell me nuthin'! His body shuddered, legs tightened up, toes sprung under and curled, and the fireworks shot in my mouth...he was cumming like a water fountain! I nearly gagged 'cause there was so much cum. I had drained him completely dry. Or so I thought.

Greig wasn't done yet.

Round three.

He took some of that sex enhancer shit and put that penis ring on his dick and it was on. My eyes kept rolling in the back of my head every time he'd make me come. God. I'd come so fuckin' hard I got a cramp in my leg and big toe. I had to leap up and pace the floor to get the cramps out and while I was doing that, Greig was on my ass, literally, fingering my pussy. I felt like I was about to pass out. I had no more come in me. But he wouldn't stop. He wanted to get his monies worth of pussy, so I had to get my second wind and ride his dick like I had just robbed it from a federal bank.

I pushed him back on the bed, climbed on top of him, my "honey walls" were clinging to his dick, and I rode him cutting my eyes over my shoulder as if someone was chasing me until the juices poured from my heavens. I raised my ass off of him and squirted all over his hairy chest. Then I moved up to his mouth and let the juice flow in. Yeah, he had drunk my *come* as if it tasted like holy water.

After I had exhausted myself, I grabbed my makeup case and headed for the bathroom to get my hit on. Shit, Ol' Durty had been calling me from the time I left home, walked into the hotel, took the elevator up to the third floor, got off the elevator, saw Greig waiting for me, entered the room and shut the door. I had to get my hit on. I just had to.

I locked myself in the bathroom, sat on the toilet seat, and did me. I was crack piping—getting my buzz on. Nuthin' could compare to the nutt I got from Ol' Durty. When I took that hit it was total b-l-i-s-s! That bitch knew how to make my pussy talk. My middle finger was rubbing my clit, almost rubbing the skin raw. My middle finger was waggling inside my pussy. I could hear the swooshing sound of my juices. It turned me on so much that I released my finger and stuck it in my mouth and tasted my own sweet stuff. And it felt and tasted good to me. It felt reallll good to me. It felt too good to me 'cause the next thing I knew I had fallen off of the toilet seat and dropped to the floor. Greig heard the loud thump and rushed to knock on the door, but I couldn't answer him. I was flying; head was twirling, eyes were fluttering, mind was drifting. I was gone. He tried to open the door but it was locked, so he ended up taking the hinges off the door. That's when he found me on the floor fucked up with Ol' Durty clenched in my hands.

I was at a loss for words. I didn't know what to say. The next thing I knew, Greig peeled back my fingers from Ol' Durty, helped me get up, and then asked me the strangest question: "Do you have anymore?" I was limp but somehow I managed to nod my head. And from there we got fffffffffffffffffffffffffucked up.

As we were getting our high on, something came over me, and this soft, sultry bluesy sound streamed out of my mouth.

"Hush, li'l bitch, don't you cry

Daddee's gonna buy you'a crack pipe tonight

Daddee's gonna make you smoke dis rock

Daddee's gonna make you work da block

Daddee's gonna make you smile 'n' laugh

Daddee's gonna make you sell dhat ass..."

Next thing you knew, Greig started humming and I started scatting like that of Jill Scott. We snapped our fingers, cranked our necks, and tapped our bare feet.

"*Hush, h-h-huuuuuuuu-ssssssssh*

Li'l, li'l, bit-ch, don, don, don, don't

yooooooouuuuu crrrrrryyyyyyy

Daddee's, I's say a Daddee's gon'na buyyyyy

yoouuu'a crack pipe tonight

Daddee's, I's say a Daddee's gon'na makkkeeee, makkkeeee,

youuuuu smoke disss, disss rock

(Shakin' my head, scrunching my nose, tightening my lips)

(Pursing my lips) OOOOOOHHHHHH, Daddee's gon'na maakkkkkeee

youu work da block

Daddee's gon'na maaakkkkeee you

smile 'n' laugh

Woo, Daddee's gon'na makkkkeeee yyyyyouuuu sell dhat, dhat assssss... yea, yea

yea-yea, yea..."

We laughed our asses off, high as hell. Then our high slowly wore off and we both got quiet. I guessed we were both dazed in our own shit, you know, staring in space, drooling from the mouth, fucked up. One thing I do know we had us a hit record called "H-H-H-ush Li'l Bitch."

I didn't have any more cookies so all we did for the rest of the morning was fuck, fuck, f-f-fuck!!!!

We rose from our dead sleep around 11 a.m., just before checkout time. I was hungry as hell and so was Greig. We took a shower together and did it doggy-style. I got on my knees and gave him some head; we got dressed. Afterward, before I was getting ready to head out of the door, Greig placed one thousand dollars in my hands. Then we parted ways and returned back to our regular lives.

By the time I arrived home, I hit the "PLAY" button on my recorder and listened to several messages from Devin. He sounded like it was an emergency as much as he had called. I brushed it off to be nuthin'. Nope. I never called him back. And plus, it was the middle of the week. We only met on Saturdays. I took another shower, put on my favorite raggedy nightshirt, and made myself some scrambled eggs with cheese and beef sausages and poured me a tall glass of orange juice, but before I could get a chance to eat, my cell phone rang.

I searched through my satchel bag to retrieve my phone. I found it on the third ring.

"Hello?" I said hastily.

"Is everything okay?" the male voice asked.

"Oh, yes, I was just fumbling with the phone." I told him.

"Well, I just called to tell you that I had a wonderful time with you," the male voice said.

I didn't pick up on the voice right away, but then I realized that it was Greig. "Well, sweetie, it was an adventure. We must do it again." I told him.

"Yes. How 'bout *this* weekend?"

"Ah, it will have to be on a Sunday."

"Sunday? I don't know about...Sunday. I have my daughters and I normally take them to church on Sunday."

"I understand, but that is the only day I have available." I told him. "Oh, you have daughters? You never mentioned 'em."

"Well, it didn't seem like the topic of discussion, you know."

"Yeah, you're right. We had other things on our minds."

"I'll see what I can do. I really need to see you again." He told me.

"Work it out and then give me a call. If I don't pick up just leave me a message."

"Why wouldn't you pick up?" He asked with a hint of aggressiveness in his tone.

I picked up on it right away. So I had to mellow him out. You know, make him feel special. "Babe, I could be at work when you call, that's all. We can't have personal calls at work." I told him.

"Oh."

All he could say was, oh. Normally I wouldn't even go as far as explaining myself, but Greig was new to all of this. I should've known betta' than to think that he wouldn't get caught up on our first meeting. Yeah. I should've known betta', but I let that slip away from my mind. He's a grown ass man's, not a boy, I told myself. Grown ass man's or not, the nigga still got sprung. I knew that he might become a nuisance. And I really didn't need that in my life. I had to somehow convince him that everything was cool with us. Did I mislead him? Of course, I mean c'mon, the man's ain't have good pussy in years. Enough said.

"Please, don't think that I don't want to see you again, 'cause I do. I'm just giving you the heads up, okay."

Immediately I could sense that he was smiling on the other end of the phone.

"I understand. It's cool." He said.

That's what he said, but did he really mean it was something that I would have to see. I tried to give people the benefit of the doubt, but you could never be too sure, you know. I enjoyed his company, as well as the money, but it really wasn't all about that when it came to me. I felt like I was searching for something, you know, something that I never had before, but felt like I had, possibly in a pipe dream of some sort. All I knew was that I had to keep both eyes and ears open when it came to Greig. My gut was telling me that he might be a problem—a little more than I could handle. I hoped that I was wrong. But that girl's intuition kicked it. And I took that as a sign. I might've let some things slide but not that.

"Well, I have to be going now. I need to get some sleep so that I won't look so tired for this evening."

"Okay. Stay beautiful."

I remained quiet, and then I said, "Talk to you later."

"You have a blessed day."

"You too."

After getting off the phone with that nutcase, I wiped the sweat off of my forehead. Shit, that was hard work. I laid my cell phone on the kitchen counter and ended up putting my food in the microwave to nook it for a few seconds. I couldn't stand cold eggs!

Beeeeeep! Beeeeeep! The microwave sounded off. I opened it and pulled out the steamy hot ceramic plate, sat down, and ate, thinking about my evening with Greig. I was kind of shocked that he wanted to get high with me. I mean, on our first meeting and all. I knew that he was a man's of mystery, but damn. I was curious as to how far he was willing to go to be in my company. And I found out too. Since he knew more about me than met the eye, how would he look at me now, was what I wondered.

My cell phone rang.

"Hello."

"Rocka-Bye, I need you to come down to NAPPY's." L.D. said in an agitated tone. What is this about? I wondered.

"Okay. What time?"

"Now!" He demanded.

"Al-right. Lemme get dress. I'll be right down." I told him while shoving in the food in my mouth.

I quickly put my empty plate in the sink and hurried to get dressed. I grabbed a pair of black leggings and an oversized sky-blue men's shirt and slipped my bare feet in a pair of old low-heeled pastel pink cowgirl boots. Then I called a cab.

By the time the cab arrived I was on pins and needles. So many thoughts raced through my head. Did I do something wrong? Did I say something wrong? Did someone rat on me about something?

By the time I arrived at THE NAPPY DUGOUT I had a friggin' headache.

I paid the Hispanic cab driver and exited out of the cab a little hesitant to walk into NAPPY's. I took about three breaths and then walked in like everything was cool.

As soon as I got inside, Durdy-Dog was sitting at the bar drinking a Heineken. He had a grimace on his face. I really didn't know how to approach him, so I waited for him to notice that I was standing behind him. He looked up and said, "Rocka, have a seat." I can't tell you how scared I was to even sit next to him. But I played it cool and sat down, but inside, my bones were rattling like crazy.

"What's up?" I asked him.

Durdy-Dog wasn't smiling at all.

"Some things have changed around here." He said with his head dangled low like he was praying or something.

"What do you mean?"

Durdy-Dog talked with his hands. "Well, there's been a change of events that recently took place."

Why is he rambling? This is not like Durdy-Dog to be beating around the bush. I'm so used to him getting straight to the point.

I interrupted him. "Um, I'm sorry, but I'm not following you, Durdy-Dog."

He took a swig of the beer and turned his face looking directly into my eyes. The look he had on his face, I'll never forget till the day I die. His eyes were bloody red and swollen. He looked flushed in the face too. And he was sweaty on his nose, forehead and upper lip.

"We loss one of our girls today, so I expect you to step it up one."

I blinked, three times. I didn't know what to say. All I was wondering was who? Who did he get rid of? So I swallowed one big glob of spit down my throat and asked.

"Who?"

Durdy-Dog remained quiet. He just sipped on his beer.

I asked again, "Who, Durdy-Dog?"

He took one hard look at me. I mean, hard. I noticed he had five o'clock shadow, which was not like him at all. He seemed jittery too.

"Dexxter."

I liked to die right then and there, but I had to play it cool. I couldn't let him know that Dexxter and I had become friends. I was stunned.

"How...when...where...why?" I said stuttering.

"It doesn't matter, how, when, where, why...she's dead, bitch! I figured I'd do a good deed by telling your fuckin' ass face-to-face instead of you hearing about it through the streets."

I lowered my head. Dead! I had to play it off. I swear I thought he was going to say that he fired her or something along those lines. Not dead. I had to keep it together. And I did.

"Well, thanks for calling me, Durdy-Dog." I murmured.

Durdy-Dog cut his eyes over at me, as my head was still dangling staring at my reflection. "Make sure you're back here by 8:00 p.m., and be on time, Rocka. I'm not in the mood to be fucking nobody up today. You got me? Oh, and don't even bother to go to the service. I can't have ya'll comin' in here cryin' 'n shit over no low-down bitch. You got me?"

I nodded my head, but deep down I was so hurt. Dexx was my friend and this monster couldn't even find a smidgen of compassion to let me go to her funeral. I can't tell you how distraught I felt over that. I was the one who was low-down 'cause she was my friend—my one and only friend.

I stood with a blank look upon my face. As I was walking toward the door I heard Durdy-Dog say, "Now I gotta get another bitch before the week is up, shit!" His fist pounced the bar counter. I flinched from the sound and quickly kept walking out the door.

Instead of me calling another cab I decided to walk home. I needed to breathe. And I also needed to find out exactly what happened to Dexxter. I knew a couple people around the way who kept their ears to the streets. Yeah, they were ear hustlers and they knew the upcoming news about every an anything that went down from last night to last week.

My feet were moving fast to get to Curtis Place. This kid named, Self, usedta hang out over there. Most of the time Self would be in the park chillin' with the pigeons. He had this fascination with birds.

Anyway, by the time I got to Lou Costello Memorial Park, to my surprise, Self was there sitting on the park bench sipping on a bottle of spring water. I walked up to him, "Yo', Self, what's going on?"

"'Sup, Rocka?"

Self sat leaned back in his twenty-two year old frame. He was dressed in a pair of shaggy jeans and oversized white tee and a pair of white Air Force Ones. I noticed, as I got closer he had a blunt in his hand. His blond hair was pulled back in a ponytail. Self had features of a girl but he was a boy, at least I think he was. His flawless light-skin, light-brown eyes and heart-shaped lips probably made one think that he might've been gay, but I wasn't too sure. Either way it didn't matter to me.

"Listen, Self, I need to know if you know anything 'bout what happened to this chick they called Dexxter. She used to strip at THE NAPPY DUGOUT? Her real name is Halima Holman. You know anything 'bout it?"

Self didn't hesitate to respond. "Yoooooo, chick was setup. I know who you talkin' 'bout. We were chill. She was like my road dawg."

My eyes spread wide. "What do you mean...setup?" "She lived over on...." He snapped his fingers, "Damn, I forgot the name of the street. Anyway, she lived wit' her aunt, right?"

"Yeah."

"Well, word on the streets is that she was planning on moving. Something came through for her. I think she got a letter stating that she could move in her apartment. I remember because she was so fuckin' happy when she told me. I was like, yo', that's wassup. She said something 'bout telling her aunt that she wouldn't be able to pass off any more loot. I mean she had to do what she had to do. I remember she used to be stressing. She used to sleep up near the train tracks some nights too. Chick was going through it. So when the time came for her to let her aunt knows about the dough. Aunty snapped. She went ballistic on Dexx. I don't know how much she was supposed to pass off to her aunt, but aunty wanted her dough. Your girl stormed out of the house, she didn't even bother to take her belongings. She just had the clothes on her back and that bag she always carried around with her. She had gone to the building to sign her paperwork and pickup her keys, but she never made it there. Word is that aunty had someone follow her. They did

Dexx dirty, Rocka, real, real dirty. She was a nice girl, you know. She had big dreams, big dreams. I think if she would've gotten in that apartment her whole life would've changed. All she needed was a break."

I nodded my head up and down. "Yeah, I know. What exactly did they do to her?"

"Man, based on what I heard, two jokers snatched her up and threw her in the back of this white van. One of the dudes stayed in the back and did her in. He had been watchin' her onstage at THE NAPPY DUGOUT for a minute. He been said that he was gonna wax dhat ass. Well, the opportunity presented itself. After he got his shit off, he cut her throat with a butcher knife, and they wrapped her body in a tarp. Then drove around until they found a desolate spot and dumped her body in a dumpster over near the REDBIRD."

"REDBIRD?" I said with a perplex look upon my face.

"Yeah. You know where Burger King is across from the Paterson Museum?"

I nodded my head.

"Well, that small brick building next to Burger King is the REDBIRD."

"Oh. I never paid it any mind." I told him.

"When did this happen? She was at work yesterday." I said baffled.

"Well, I saw her earlier today. She stopped and told me the good news. All I know is some homeless guy found her and he had someone waiting in line at the Burger King's Drive-Thru call the police."

I pressed my lips together. My forehead crumpled. "Around what time, do you know?"

Self took a moment to think. He cocked his head to the side. "I can't really say for sure."

"Did they arrest her aunt?"

"Nah. Ole boys never rat her out. They took the bid. The bitch is still free as a fuckin' birdie."

"Damn." I said, "Thanks for the heads up, yo."

"One."

I left Self, then cut across the Main Street Bridge and walked across Presidential Boulevard, through the Main, and onto Chosen Street. All the way home I kept thinking about Dexxter and the last conversation we'd shared. My eyes welled up on me 'cause I really felt bad for her. Why'd she have to die like that? Why did people have to be so damn greedy about money to go as far as killing someone? How could her own blood do something so heinous and not even care? So many thoughts

107

raced through my head. All 'cause of money! I was completely beside myself by the time I reached my front door. My body was limp. I had the shakes and my armpits were sweaty.

In order for me to calm my nerves I pulled out my bitch, Ol' Durty. I got lit. I couldn't help it. I had to do something to be able to stomach performing tonight. To be in the same place that Dexxter was. To dance on the same stage and use the same props that we used. To look out at the slew of horny niggas wondering what they thought of me. Did they feel the same as the jokers who killed Dexxter—mouthwatering for some of my pussy too?

The other thing I thought about was how I would react when looking Durdy-Dog in the face. I mean he didn't seem to be too concerned about Dexxter, but more so about whom he was going to get to replace her. That's fucked up 'cause the girl wasn't even in the ground yet and already he had money on the fuckin' brain. Didn't he realize that Dexxter was a human being, not a dollar sign? Obviously not! Just when I was about to have a girlfriend someone had to come and take her away from me. It seemed so surreal, but it was real. Dexxter was dead! That shit really hurt me to my heart.

I tried to take it down a notch and get some sleep, but my mind was thinking too much. I was most definitely on edge. I was a little leery about stepping foot back in THE NAPPY DUGOUT too. *You just don't know who's watching you*, I thought to myself. *You don't know a person's motive, intentions, or where their heads are at either. Some people you could know for years and then, out of the blue they flip the script on you. Look what happened with Dexxter and that guy named Deejay.* My mindset had flipped. I was on this: no one could be trusted. I was fidgety all day, peeking out of my bedroom window, kitchen window, bathroom window, and double-checking the locks to the front door. Making sure the windows were locked too. Paranoid was more like it. "Relax," I told myself, but that was like talking to the dingy white walls in my apartment. I simply couldn't relax. This was too close to home for me. Nervous? Shaking my head, no, I was beyond nervous. Dexxter's death really fucked me up. I guessed 'cause we were doing the same thing...exotic dancing. The only difference between us was that she was doing it to pay for her education, pay rent to her aunt, eat, and buy the necessities to keep herself up. I, on the other hand, was being forced into the industry. And I wanted out, but my back was against the wall. I didn't see a way out, at least not at that moment.

I didn't know how all of this would play out. Eight o'clock I had to be at NAPPY's. There was no doubt about that. Durdy-Dog was not in the mood for no drama today. He made that perfectly clear. My hands met my distraught face and I massaged it in a circular motion as I tried to hold back the tears that were welling up in my eyes. "How'd things get so bad? Why is this happening," I asked myself, as a pear-shaped tear rolled down my face? I just let them fall. I needed to release some of the stuff that was deeply troublesome to me. Being in the situation that I was, it was lonely. I was alone. I had no one to talk to—no one to run to. Ghetto-Man was dead. Dad was missing in action. Dexxter was dead. It was too much to take in.

My cell phone rang. I damned near jumped out of my skin. Hands shook as I reached for it off of the kitchen counter.

"Hello?" My voiced cracked, eyes cut from side to side, spooked.

"'Ey, finally you answer your phone."

I sighed, relieved.

"Devin, I'm so sorry. I've been busy with..."

"I know your essay. By the way, how did that go? I guess you were too busy to answer your phone and let me know that you were okay, huh?"

"Why'd he have to say it like that," I asked myself. I felt bad enough for keeping the secret from him. I wanted to beg him to come over, but then I didn't want to be too forward, especially since I never did it before. Here it was Thursday. It would seem odd for me to ask him over on a Thursday, I said to myself.

"Are you there," he asked. "You seem preoccupied. Is everything alright?"

I exhaled.

"Yeah. Yeah. Everything is fine, baby. What brings this call other than you being concerned about me?"

"I miss you."

"Really?" My eyes watered. I was a complete train wreck.

"Yes. I need to talk to you, face-to-face."

"O-kay."

"Is it okay if I stop by? Are you already home?"

"Yes!" I said in a desperate tone, but then I caught myself and pulled myself back by tryna act all cool and calm. Deep down I was a basket case. "Yes, yes, I'm home."

"Okay, I'm on my way." He said.

We hung up.

Within two seconds my cell phone rang again.

"Yessss, Devin..."

"Devin?" the male voice said. "Who's Devin, Daisy?"

The only two men's who called me Daisy, besides, Devin, was Greig. Damn. How was I going to get out of this with him? I could tell that he had already caught feelings for me, but I didn't feel the same for him. I had to play along. And the best way for me to do that was to take ownership, which was exactly what I did.

"Yes, that's what I said, Greig."

"Oh. I was just asking. You seem a little tense. Maybe we need to see each other before Sunday. What do you think? Do you want to see me?" he said.

Silence.

"You make my dick tremble with the anticipation of rubbing the head against the folds of your pussy. Then slowly, pressing myself deep between those long, sexy legs till I feel the hot liquids flow from that glossy pussy onto my glistening dick."

I blinked, twice, not really in disbelief of him wanting to have phone sex, but it was too early to be having it. At least I thought it was, but I still played along to keep my john satisfied.

"Shiiitttttttttttttttttttttttttttttttttttttttttttttt!!!" I sang. "Gotta take the edge off...pussy sloppy wet...I'm gonna finger-fuck myself."

"I wanna lick ya finger," he said.

"Here, baby, lick, lick, lick. My eyes are rolling in the back of my head. Screaming 'cause it feels soooooooooooo fuckin' good. Ah, ah, baby...gimme more!!!!..."

"Ummmmm...taste sooo good! Ride the dick, you sexy gorgeous warrior dick ridin' muthafucka!"

"I'm ri-din'...giddy up giddy up. Oh, oh, oh, damn, fuck, shit, shut the fuck up and gimme that pleasure...feed this thirsty pussy. Oh... my... God!"

"Slap some of that pussy juice on my balls, lickin' those lovely tits."

"Take that! And that! And that...gushing my juice all over your balls...now lickin' 'em...taste like fuckin'. My tits want to be sucked...stickin' my two fingers in my wet hole...dripping...head dizzy, lightheaded...just came...fuck this shit...I need the real shit! Pussy popping bubbles."

"Put this dick in your hot, wet mouth...please!"

"Make it talk to me, baby, make it ooze...speaks that poetry I love to hear...make it feel the motion...make it tremble...!"

110

"Oh, shit, D-a-i-s-y! I like that. I wanna suck your whole entire ass."

"You stroking. I'm throbbing...nipples like bricks...pussy slobbering...I'm h..u..n..g..r..y for the chocolate."

"Oh, Daisy...you make me feel alive and young, shittttttttttttttttt...Oh, shit!"

I could hear his heavy breathing. I had given him a snack to hold him over till later.

I wanted to see anyone who wanted to see me. I knew that I didn't want to stay in that apartment alone. But I also knew that I didn't want to invite Greig over to my place either. He was already acting weird. It was too late to change things between us. His first taste of my pussy drove him over the edge. And it didn't take long either. Yeah. I blamed myself for having good pussy. How could he not get hooked? Hopefully Devin would be willing to stay but there was one problem with that idea. I had to work. How was I going to explain my whereabouts from 8:00 p.m. to 3:00 a.m.? There was only one option for me, well, two. Have Greig meet me at our spot. Or, go get a room by myself. I knew that I didn't want to be alone so that second option was out of the question. I felt that I could stomach Greig another night. So I told him to meet me at the Private Stock Inn around the same time as before.

"Sounds like a plan," he said.

"Okay, well, we can talk later. I'll see you tonight."

"Are you rushing me off the phone to be with Devin?" he asked me.

"No, no, Greig, I was just in the middle of something." I told him.

"Oh."

"I'll see you later on tonight ...okay."

"Fine!" he said hostilely, then hung up on me before I could say... "Bye."

What is his problem? I thought as I heard what sounded like Devin gently knocking at my front door. I dropped the phone and rushed to answer it. It was Devin. I can't tell you how relieved I felt when I opened the door and saw his pleasant face. I completely lost my grip and fell into his arms like a wounded damsel. Yeah, I surprised myself. And I know I baffled him.

Devin's eyes pierced mine. "I take it that you missed me, too." His smooth palm stroked my baldhead so delicately, as if I was a newborn baby. I closed my eyes and took all of him in. I planted my head in his shoulder blade and remained there for what seem like a second. I inhaled his scent of Gillette deodorant. He smelled so fresh and clean. As I inhaled his body scent I thought about Dexxter in that split second I thought about the first conversation we'd shared. It was as if I could hear her saying: *"My mom was a junky. You don't want to die a junky, Rocka. If you're going to leave this earth, leave it with something for someone to learn from. Leave a message of purpose behind, girl."* Her sweet voice rang in my ears. It was as if she was standing right next to me, staring me dead in my face. I literally shivered in my skin as Devin continued to massage my back.

"Are you cold, baby, because you're shivering."

I remained silent. I just wanted to be held.

In that moment all I wanted to do was get high. I heard Ol' Durty calling me, askin' me to c'mere, to c'mon, to do *her* right. And I wanted to do her, any, which way I could. I wanted her to fuck me good 'cause I was already fucked up sober. I didn't want to remember a damn thing. I wanted to disremember every bad thing that had ever happened to me in the course of me living this fucked up life. I yearned to be in bliss: mind, body, and fucked up soul.

I held onto Devin like I've never held him before. I pecked him on his neck, earlobe, cheek, and his luscious lips. He pecked me back on the lips and neck. His silky hands rubbed my back. My right hand lowered and rubbed his crotch. I was squeezing his manhood. I was pulling it, gently, wrapping my long fingers around it arousing it to hardness. I wasn't really in the mood for sex, but I needed something to take my mind off of my troubles, so I lured Devin in like the feline that I was.

I placed his hand down to my crotch area and had him fondle me through my spandex. He could feel the wetness building through the thin material. I moaned for sound effects. I pecked him some more, then unbuttoned his shirt and pecked his bare chest. Then I unzipped his trousers. Lowered myself down and pecked his bulging dark-skinned cock. He didn't reject me. If anything, Devin embraced me with open arms and allowed me to drive his stick shift this go-around. And I drove that dick recklessly. I needed to be in control of something especially since my life was in disarray. Devin gave me that control. And it only increased what and how I felt for him. I never divulged those feelings to him, but I know deep down he knew that I was feeling something stronger than I could ever imagine. My body language spoke very loudly. My body movements spoke even louder. And when I fucked him, my heart was thumping so fast in my chest and my voice was screaming so loudly in my head...I'm feelin' you...Devin Rogers! Goddamn am I feelin' you! But I just don't know how you'll feel about me...when—

I tried to distract my thoughts with his *johnson*. And I did. I think, no, rather I know I fucked him too good. I could see it in his eyes. Devin had fallen deeply in love with me. And so, so did I. It wasn't intentional. I wasn't tryna play him out. I truly liked him. But never did I think I'd fall in love with the man's. I didn't think I had it in me to fall so hard for someone. I really didn't. But I did. And somehow that experience did something to me on the inside. It's kind of difficult to explain, but I felt strange in my own body, like I was a different girl. Maybe I just wanted to be "that" girl—a girl who could erase her past and start new and fresh with a man's who truly cared for me. Yeah. I wanted that, but I knew that it would never happen. Not with Durdy-Dog in my life. He'd never relinquish his grip. I was his. He was never going to let me go. I kept telling myself. Never. Unless—

My mind was plotting. I dreaded to leave home but I knew soon I would have to. Durdy-Dog was expecting me to be on time. Perky. Sexy. Smoking hot! Everything that was going to make his money, he expected me to be.

I rose from the bed, headed toward the bathroom to vomit. God, I felt so sick. I looked in the mirror and I looked flushed in the face. I didn't know how I was going to pull this off. How could I? My girl, Dexxter was dead. Dead! Dead! Dead! This was not a time to be celebrating. Shaking what bitch-ass Daddee had given me. No, no, no! This was a time to be crying, screaming, mourning, shouting...WHY, WHY, WHY, WHY DEXTTTEEER?!

But I couldn't. I fuckin' couldn't 'cause Devin was there. I couldn't share my pain, past or present life with him. God, it hurt so badly. I loved that man's with all of my heart. I couldn't tell him the truth to save my own life. I just fuckin' couldn't do it!

Within a few minutes, Devin entered the bathroom finding me slumped over with my face in the toilet bowl puking my guts out.

"Honey, are you okay?"

I remained silent. I didn't know what to say or how to say it.

He grabbed a washcloth, wet it with cold water, and gently reached for my bare waist. I was barely able to stand on my own.

"Come, sit down, baby, let me help you," he said.

Oh, I wanted him to help me in any way he could. *Take me away from all of this, Devin! Take all the pain away. Help me, Devin! Help me get away from the bad man. Love me, Devin. Love me up and down and all around and never let me go. Please, Devin. Please.* I thought.

Devin touched my forehead with the back of his left hand. "You feel hot. Do you have a thermometer?"

I shook my head no. I didn't think I had a fever. I was deeply depressed, lost, and I felt completely alone even with Devin in front of me. I felt like I had no one. No one who would or could understand what I was going through and what I had to go through for the rest of the evening. "How am I going to pull this off tonight?" I asked myself again. I felt myself breaking. I couldn't hold back the tears any longer. No matter how strong I thought I was or could be I simply couldn't remain a rock. So I let everything that I was feeling flow out of me. I sobbed. Devin held me so close to his heart. I didn't want to talk. I didn't want to think. I didn't want to feel. I didn't want to live. In all honesty, I wanted to die. Bury me and be done with me. I was depleted.

Devin had a concerned look in his eyes. They were watery. I knew without a shadow of a doubt that that man loved me. I felt like a fraud duping him like that. Where was my courage? Hidden. Everything about me was hidden. I wanted to be freed. But how? "How bad do you want out?" I asked myself. "Bad." I told myself. "Yeah, but how badly?" I took a moment to contemplate. Well, enough to do something drastic—something that could potentially harm someone—something that would set me free from agony. My mind was all twisted with foul thoughts. Things that I would have never imagined I'd think. Me? Yeah. Me. I was in a desperate situation and I wanted out.

Devin helped me get into bed, but I knew I couldn't fall asleep. Time was moving fast and the more it did the more paranoid I got. I never felt so sick before. The last time I felt that bad was when Coop left. Oh, I cried and cried for him to come back and save me. But he never did. He completely vanished from my life. And I began to feel ill feelings toward him. Why, Coop, why?! I already knew why. Daddee.

I used to talk in the mirror askin' him questions like that. Stupid, it was stupid of me to even care. He didn't, so why should I. I said that to myself plenty of times. I guessed I was hoping to convince myself to hate him. To wish a stroke, heart attack, or just for him to drop dead. But every time I thought of something bad happening to him it made my insides hurt even more. There was no way I ever wanted anything bad to happen to him. Coop was a good man—a good father figure for the time that he was in my life. And like I said before, I'll always treasure him for that. I missed him so much. And often, I wondered if somewhere in the back of his mind, he missed me too. All I could do was hope he did. Hope and pray that one day he'd reenter my life...before—

I tossed and turned in the bed.

"Relax, baby." Devin said sitting beside me. He stroked my hot forehead so gently with his smooth hand. It brought tears to my eyes.

"Do you want to talk about it?" He asked.

I remained silent and just stared in outer space.

"Are you hungry? Do you want me to cook you something? Or go out and get you something to eat? Baby, talk to me, tell me what you need. what you want," he asked so compassionately.

Tears rolled and zigzagged across the middle of my nose and down my face and dissolved in the goose down pillow. I had nuthin' to say. What could I possibly say to this man's who was clueless of this girl he was involved with? Nuthin'. All I could do to save myself was to tell him the truth. But the girl in me just could not find the right words. It was on the tip of my tongue, almost ready to escape from my mouth, but I just didn't have the courage to take that chance. I wanted Devin in my life. He brought joy and peace and calmness to my life. I needed him more than he wanted and needed me. Why couldn't he see? Why couldn't he see through the eyes of a young, naïve, and fragile girl that I needed guidance? I needed protection, knowledge, and peace of mind. He couldn't see 'cause I had camouflaged myself. He couldn't see, 'cause he couldn't see me. I mean my true self. I was hidden too deep within that curvaceous body of mine. I was drying up. Slowly and painfully, I was dying. And Devin was none the wiser.

I just stared into his eyes, allowing the tears to break free. I cut my eyes over to the clock that was mounted on the wall. It was 5:00 p.m. Three more hours before show time, I told myself. I shut my eyes trying to block it all out of my mind, my sight. But it was there, waiting with diligence.

Devin rose to his feet, stood over me and gaped at me like I was some small child. In essence, I was. "I'm going to see what you have in the cupboards. Maybe some soup will make you feel better, okay." I remained quiet. I lay there seemingly lifeless.

My mind and body drifted to a place I had never been. I jolted out of my sleep, sat up with my mouth opened wide and sound loud and shrieking came bellowing out as if someone was stabbing deep incisions in my flesh. I breathed erratically. Daddee had arisen from the dead. She just couldn't leave me be! My temples throbbed like a heartbeat. She just had to come and disrupt my life! Even from the grave she refused to grant me peace. Why?

Why won't that evil bitch—? I paused, and then clasped my lips together. My eyes narrowed as I sneered at the floor. I wished her to rot and never revisit me again. Just leave me be!

Devin came charging into the bedroom nearly tripping over my black stilettos. "Baby, baby, what is it!" I opened my mouth, muteness, as my eyes bulged, frightened and paralyzed. "Daisy, honey, is you okay?" I couldn't speak. My eyes seem locked, but I could see him standing before me. He waved his hand in front of my eyes. I didn't even blink. "Babe, say something." What could I say? I couldn't very well tell him that my mama arisen from the dead just to haunt me. Nor could I tell him things about my past. I wanted to. I really did.

My body was stiffened for what seem like an hour, but was more like minutes. I felt a tingle in my fingers and toes. My breathing had reduced from utter panic to slow beats of normalcy.

"Baby, are you okay?" Devin asked again with a look of fret on his face.

I wiggled my big toe. "Yes." I said haltingly.

He sat on the edge of the bed. His backhand touched my forehead. "You're burning up."

I didn't feel like I was burning up. I felt hot because of the unwelcoming visit from a bad spirit. Daddee had gotten me mad.

"You need to lie down and let me take care of you." He told me.

I can't. I have to start getting ready for work. I have to figure out what I am going to wear. Take a shower. Do my hair. Put my makeup on. Look fierce. Durdy-Dog is expecting me at 8:00 p.m. I can't be late. I have to still pack my overnight bag and meet with Greig. I can't afford to stay home, I thought.

"You don't have any soup in the cupboards. Let me see what I can find." He said, as he stood and walked out of the bedroom.

I heaved.

This overwhelming pressure seems to clasp my chest. My whole body felt heavy. I was woozy with thought of how I was going to get rid of Devin. If I ask him to go, he probably wouldn't. If I pretended to be asleep, maybe he'd leave on his own.

6:40 P.M. I closed my heavy eyes and dozed off.

I awoke. My eyesight was a bit fuzzy. I turned my stiff neck and gaped at a container of chicken fried rice, which I had every intention of taking to work for my dinner.

There was a piece of my acid-free writing paper lent against the container that read:

I didn't want to wake you up. I'll call you later.
Eat.

Devin

Slowly, I sat up. And as I did my eyesight became clear. I glanced at the clock and jumped out of my skin, wide-eyed. 10:30 P.M.! I leaped up and fast paced the floor, toes cracked, arms swung, head pounded trying to figure out what to do. I needed an excuse as to why I was late. My eyes shifted from side to side Where's my cell phone? I lifted up the pillows, palpated the sheets with the palms of both hands, and lifted and flung the comforter onto the floor only to find it at the foot of the bed, blinking red.

My heart was beating rapidly. God, I was afraid to look. But I had to. I had *five* missed calls and *seven* text messages all from Durdy-Dog.

"Where da fuck you at, bitch!"

"Didn't I say 8:00 p.m.!"

"Didn't I tell you not to be late?!"

"Get your ass down here!"

"You better have your ass down here in fifteen minutes, or else!"

"Bitch callllllllll me!"

"Don't call and see what da fuck happens! Try me if you want to."

How come I didn't hear my phone ring? I mumbled. I checked my phone it was on silence. Shit! I smacked my forehead. Devin! Devin, what did you do! I grunted.

As I was trying to calm down and think of something, anything remotely believable for an excuse to give Durdy-Dog, I heard a hard knock at my door. Suddenly, the knock became heavier pounds. Then I heard, "ROCKA-BYE! I KNOW YOUR BITCH ASS IS IN THERE. OPEN THIS MUTHAFUCKIN' DOOR!"

I cowered in the corner near the bedroom closet with my butt close to the wall, knees bent up to my chin, and my head sunk between my legs, quivering uncontrollably. My cellular seemingly glued to my clammy palms praying that Durdy-Dog wouldn't break down my door. Oh, God, please, please, don't let him get in here, please. The edge of my teeth bit into my bottom lip as hot tears engulfed in my eyes and rolled down my somnolent face. I was so scared.

My cellular lit up and buzzed like a bee. I cut my eyes to see who it was. It was Devin calling me. I didn't dare answer the phone.

"ROCKA-BYE, I SAID OPEN THIS MUTHAFUCKIN' DOOR! I KNOW YOUR BITCH ASS IS IN THERE! " Durdy-Dog said with salty venom in his tone.

I could picture the look on his face: mean grimace, narrow-eyed, sweaty crumpled forehead, curled upper lip and flared nostrils.

BANG! BANG! BANG!

His fists pounded the door so hard I felt it vibrate. I trembled even more. I contemplated on calling the police, but then I thought against it. What would I tell 'em? Someone's trying to break into my apartment! Someone's harassing me! Someone's threatening me! He's coming to kill me!

BANG! BANG! BANG!

The pounds grew violent.

I flinched. Pressed my back against the dingy wall wishing I could disappear.

"YOUR ASS IS MINE, BITCH! ROCKA, YOU HEAR ME! YOUR ASS IS MINE! YOU GONNA DEFY ME, HUH? BITCH, YOU MUST'VE FORGOTTEN WHO THE FUCK I AM...I'M Durdy-Dog aka LORD. I'M YOUR MUTHAFUCKIN' GOD!"

My body shuddered as my teeth chattered. Tears poured from my crimson eyes. I clamped my legs together. I was afraid to even blink or breathe.

I rocked back and forth and hummed, "Holding Back The Years" by Simply Red as if time was still. And in that quiet moment my mind drifted. I thought about this woman named Miss Praline. She was a sweet old lady, tall, rotund frame, with the smoothest dark skin I'd ever seen. She had Aretha Franklin eyes and Maya Angelou lips. Her voice reminded me of Loretta Devine. She was my eyes, my ears, and my security blanket for that one day. She really cared. Took me under her wing and tried to school me on some things. Life shit. Women shit.

I remember when she said: "You have to *know* which company to keep. Not everyone is out for your best interest, you remember now." She stroked my chin. Placed the side of her face atop of my head, shut her eyes, and took a moment of silence. Then she opened her eyes and nodded and spoke so gently in my ears, "You's gonna be a miracle. You's gonna make a difference. You's just believe it and it shall come to pass. God says so. And only He..."

I kid you not, that was the first time I ever felt validated by anyone. It's a shame our meeting was so short-lived. Miss Praline was a sickly woman, but she didn't die from sickness. A stray bullet, bullet that was meant for me, killed her.

The heavy banging ceased but I wasn't sure if Durdy-Dog had left. I was frozen stiff with fear. I knew if he had gotten a hold of me, my life would've been over. What was I gonna do? I didn't know, but then my cell phone buzzed again. It was the answer to my silent prayers.

I flinched, and then sighed, relieved that it was... Greig.

I swallowed the rock that was lodged in my throat, and then answered in a whisper. "Hello?" My voice cracked.

"Are you okay?" Greig asked me.

"No, no, um, someone's banging on my door. He's yelling and threatening me." I told him.

"Who?!"

"My boss...Durdy-Dog. He says he's gonna kill me!!!"

I could hear heavy breathing on the other end of the phone.

"Is he still there? Did you call the police?"

I remained silent.

"Daisy, are you there?"

"Yes, yes, I gotta get out of here. I'm afraid for my life. He's crazy like that...CRRRRAAZY!"

"I'll come get you. Don't leave by yourself. What's your address?"

"He might be out there. Don't come. It's too dangerous." I told him.

"Daisy, baby, I'm a grown ass man. Please, let me protect you. Let me help you, honey."

I didn't want to get him involved but I felt like I had no other alternative. Greig was insanely jealous and I knew that he'd flip once he found out that someone was threatening me. I couldn't let Devin get involved. I loved him too much. Greig was just something to do, a pastime to make a dollar. Devin *was* the man for me.

I surrendered. Relinquished all my will and handed it to Greig. It was a weight lifted off of my shoulders. Or so I thought.

"Okay. I'm at ... on 666 Chosen Street." I told him.

"I'm on my way!"

"WAIT!"

"Yes," he said hastily.

"I live on the third floor, apartment H."

All I heard was the phone slam down and a loud ...CLICK!

I bit my nails. Slowly, I rose to my feet and entered my bathroom to wash my hands. I tiptoed back into my bedroom, eased my dresser drawers open to get me some clothes, grabbed my satchel bag and shoved some clothes in it. I flinched at any sound I heard.

Durdy-Dog had me freaked.

Within fifteen minutes Greig arrived, exasperated. "Daisy! Daisy!" I heard a *voice* calling out for me.

I rushed to open the door, glided my fingers to slide the deadbolt unloose, untwisted the double locks, and quickly opened the door. And as I did, I nearly fell back off of my feet!

It was no stretch of the imagination. I literally saw me standing before me. And in my hands was this book. A book I had recognized. A book I had held in my bare hands. Read with my own eyes.

She opened the book, and then opened her mouth, and words, words that I had heard before came softly streaming out as if scriptures from the Bible. She said:

"The *first* step is for the addict to admit that they have a problem and that they are powerless over it.

"The *second* step is to believe in a higher power which can bring back sanity.

"The *third* step is to turn their problem over to that higher power.

"The *fourth* step is that the addict must take a moral inventory of themselves-recognizing bad behavior, faults and patterns that encourage substance abuse. This step is usually guided by sponsors.

"The *fifth* step expands on moral inventory; the addict has to admit their faults, confess them to their higher power and to another person (usually the sponsor).

"The *sixth* step is to tell the higher power that the addict is ready.

"The *seventh* step has the addict asking the higher power to take away their faults.

"The *eighth* and *ninth* steps have the addict asking for forgiveness from those they've wronged, and to offer restitution.

"The *tenth* and *eleventh* step continues the moral inventory and the connection to a higher power.

"The *twelfth* step (final) is where the recovering addict tries to help other addicts.

She slowly closed the book. She then looked at me with this despondency embedded in her eyes.

She then reached inside her back pants pocket and pulled out a yellow Post-it with printed red letters written on it and extended her *sixteen* year old arm out to me.

I then reached out to *accept* it.

At first I felt this feeling of anxiety come over me. I really didn't want to read what it said, but she insisted with this look of earnestness in her bluish-green eyes.

I swallowed a big gulp of spit down my throat.

I looked at her.

I took a couple deep breaths.

I looked at her.

Tears flooded in my eyes.

I looked at her.

I swallowed again.

I looked at her.

I blinked, closed my eyes, opened them, swallowed, deep breath. Tears overflowed and streamed hard down my face.

Silently *we* recited The Serenity Prayer (Reinhold Niebuhr):

"God grant me the serenity to accept the things I cannot change; courage to change the things I can; and wisdom to know the difference.
Living one day at a time;
Enjoying one moment at a time;
Accepting hardships as the pathway to peace;
Taking, as He did, this sinful world
as it is, not as I would have it;
Trusting that He will make all things right
if I surrender to His Will;
That I may be reasonably happy in this life
And supremely happy with Him
Forever in the next.
Amen."

The look of earnestness she once had in her eyes changed to *hopefulness.* Just from the look in her eyes I was able to build up my courage and faith. And from that I *received* whatever was written on the yellow Post-it. It read:

(x)- Positive for HIV

I received, and then believed that the man in the sky...God, that He still had love for me. That He did not disregard my efforts. That He understood my life's purpose. That He understood that I would fall short of myself from time to time and relapse, but that I knew that He would continue to guide me back to the starting point allowing me to try again 'cause I believed in Him. That He would give me the opportunity to make a difference through the written word to help those still standing on those cross streets of Choice and Chosen. That He would embrace me with open arms once He called upon me. I had to believe in the Higher Power to get me through the next phases of my life. And I did just that. *I believed, and then I surrendered.*

The End.

1

The Beginning

"HELLO, TIA, this is Avery. May I speak with Mr. Clausen?"

"Avery, hold one moment please."

"Sho'."

"Byren, speaking."

"Hi, Mr. Clausen, it's Avery. I-I was wondering if you could spare me some of your time to discuss a-a personal matter. Right now I really don't know who to trust. Things are so challenging lately. Um. Jeez. Where do I begin? Well, within the last couple of days I've been receiving some usual text messages from an unfamiliar number. I called it back several times but no one picked up. I only got the automated voice mail that just repeated the number. Each time I receive a text it's from a different number. I wrote all the numbers down. I'm frazzled at this point because I don't know who it is or why they are harassing me. I keep to myself. Don't get too personal with folks. Um, its nerve wracking to think that someone is possibly watching me." I cut my eye over my left shoulder. Am I paranoid? I guess. This whole ordeal almost paralyzed me, but I have come too far to just give in and give up. Daisy would be furious with me if she knew I'd coward out. *Furious!*

"Hmm. Yes, I can understand that. Avery, what does the text messages say?" he asks in his strong baritone voice.

I bow my head, eyes gaze at the floor. Biting on my bottom lip I say, "Disturbing things—things that I'm a little embarrassed to share with you over the phone. But majority of the texts are about my creditability. How they want to expose me with the truth, whatever the means. It also said something about divulging my sex life and disclosing my 'secret' in explicit detail. Again, whatever that means. It also said something about damaging my name and reputation. Oh. And they also threatened something about writing an (unauthorized) kiss-and-tell book about me and my dirty little secrets and selling their story to a publishing house. I really don't know what secrets they're talking about. As you know, it's no deep secret about me being HIV-positive, anymore. The word is out."

"Defamation of Character," Byren says, adjusting his wire-framed glasses while running his free hand through his thinning salt-and-pepper hair.

"Yes. It's crazy to think that someone wants to destroy my character. Crazy."

"Uh-huh. I see."

"Mr. Clausen, I know that you don't handle these types of cases. As a former paralegal I know that I would need a Personal Injury lawyer, but quite frankly, I also know that not all lawyers are honest folk like you. I cannot afford to be taken and not see any results in the end. That's the reason why I called you. I trust you to guide me in the right direction and um, you know, give me the name of a reputable attorney should I need to hire one for this-this slander. I have really worked hard to get where I am and I don't need this getting in my way. I'm just getting back on my feet. It's been a hard grind but I managed by the grace of God to pull through. This comes at an impromptu time. With me starting my independent publishing house (*PINK PINSTRIPES PUBLISHING*) ah, things could get ugly." I sigh.

"Do you think it could be someone from your past?"

"I really don't know. Could be, could not. It's hard to say."

He sighs.

My voice cracks. "I really didn't want to get you involved but I-I've endured enough. I'm tired of going through unnecessary stuff. Sure I could say, 'say what you want to say,' but folks don't always tell the truth. Folks embellish things that never happened—things that were never said or done just to ruin someone's life. That's my only concern. You know putting my reputation and me out there like it means nothing—like it's not hurting anyone. But it's hurting me. One thing I pride is my name. So I can't just let this slide. Not anymore. I just can't."

"Understood. You are one tough cookie," he says, humorously.

I nod. "Yes. I guess I am. It's been a journey."

"Yes, Avery, I know it has. Let's meet on Thursday at noon."

"I'll be there. And, Mr. Clausen thanks."

"Anytime."

We hang up.

I sit back on the saffron sofa deep in thought. Who? Who would go to great lengths to get my attention like this?

2

I SLEPT HARD. The hardest I've ever slept in weeks.

When I open my eyes I wipe the sleep from their corners and the sticky drool from the corners of my mouth. And as I do this surge of energy comes over me. I've never felt this-this way before. This warmth that I am presently feeling, it's so soothing that it literally pulls me out of bed.

I climb out of bed and walk toward my window. A light breeze caresses my bare skin and a sense of calm sweeps across my bare breasts and gently fades away.

As I am standing still I hear this faint, yet sweet angelic voice whisper in my ear. "Go. You haven't gone, but it is time for you to go. Go and say your *final* words. Go and tell 'im how you feel. Go. Go now."

Tears well up in my eyes as soreness swells in my throat, the thought terrifies me. Why now? I shake my head, flustered. Why now? Questioning doesn't help.

The voice whispers. "Go. Go now. Don't question what needs to be done. Go. Go, and relieve the pain."

I sniff in the snot before it runs down and out of my nostrils. Breathe, Avery, breathe.

"It's time," I whisper underneath my breath. "Don't make it any more difficult than it already is. Just go and relinquish it all. Trust and believe in yourself. You'll be fine. Just fine."

With that being said, I don't bother to shower or wash my face or brush my teeth or comb my hair, I quickly open my dresser drawers and pullout a pair raggedy jeans and pull overhead a worn T-shirt, then pull from underneath the side of the bed my black flip-flops and slip them on my bare feet. I then rush to the living room to call a Yellow cab, and wait.

I sit fidgety on the saffron sofa. As I wait, I bite down on my unpolished thumb nail as anxiety zooms throughout my body.

Ten minutes later, I hear the cabdriver impatiently honking his/her horn.

I leap up off the sofa and rush downstairs before he/she pulls off and leaves.

Exiting the lobby door, taking six steps forward, I open the door to the Yellow cab and climb inside. "Can you take me to 911 Mourn Ave in Kearney, New Jersey?" I say to the frizzy dark-haired woman.

"That's gon'a cost you, lady." She says in a Hispanic accent.

I lower my eyes. "Ma'am, it already has."

3

PANTING.

Quickly I sit upright. My clammy bareback presses against the warm headboard, eyes spread wide. With the nail on my forefinger I gently scrape out sleep from the corners of my crimson eyes. I then spread open both hands and with the smooth inner skin of my palms I glide them down my pained face smudging the glistering sweat that beads it. Deliriously disoriented I shake my head; blink my eyes. "I must've had another one of those awful nightmares," I say to myself. Lately I've been having 'em more frequently. It's like he's everywhere, everywhere I am—just watching my every move—waiting to lurk out of darkness to disrupt my life all over again.

The devil stays on my heels. Every time...every single solitary time something good is coming he always tries to block my blessings. Lips quiver uncontrollably. Pain engulfs me. Why, why I won't just simply surrender? And let him *win*? No. He had his chance! He blew it by running off. He coward out! Not me.

I had to walk through raging flames of fire, get third-degree burned, and come out a different woman. And I did. I had to really look deep within myself and see with clear eyes my fate. And I did.

I don't hate myself anymore. I don't blame myself either. I had no notion, no inkling, no forewarning...he just appeared from nowhere.

Back then, why, why didn't he just say *fuck it* and finish me off? I often wonder. Constantly wonder: *when, where, what*? It seems he doesn't play fair. He never plays fair. He just invades and runs off into the night. It's not amusing to have to live in fear. But I guess it pleases him. It makes him feel untouchable, empowered and strong. Where I feel irrevocable at times, but each day brings a little bit more of me to me. I see me. I feel me. And I pray that each day I become *whole* again.

I raise my hand to feel the rattling in my chest. My heart is beating so fast, too fast. I breathe in and out slowly trying to calm myself down. He gets me all discombobulated where I can't seem to function. Think. Live with normalcy. I don't feel like myself and it really agitates me. Yet I keep allowing him to invade my space, cloud my judgment, and manipulate my thoughts that make me vulnerable, feeble. Why? Why do

127

I purposely give in to his bullshit!

All I want to do is sleep. Sleep and forget all the rest. Just let me breathe and take it from there. But it is not that simple. He purposely makes things so complex, so unreasonable. He is not that generous. He refuses to let me go. He refuses to break the ties. What more can I give him? What kind of animal is he? I bow my head, and then shake it bewildered. He hurt me so badly, so brutally.

His forcefulness made my delicate skin sting and burn around my vagina like he had poured acid on me. God, I screamed at the top of my lungs, helppppppppppppp! I tossed and turned my body trying to get away. Shut up bitch! He snapped, followed by a backhand slap that nearly knocked my two front teeth out of my mouth. He hit me so hard I thought I was going blind. I felt helpless as he tortured me while breathing heavily in my ear. It left me feeling stagnant, and so full of fear. I shut my eyes because I did not want to see his face. I did not want it etched in my mind.

I come to.

My forearm swipes across my moist lips as if his spittle lies upon them. I frown to the thought of his hands wandering about my breasts, tugging and pulling on my nipples—his sweaty, sticky nakedness against my nakedness. Brows knit. God. He infuriates me!

The act seemed long and agonizing. His thrusts were more aggressive, whispering in my ear that he was coming. I grew bitter. I screamed for help! He tried to muffle my screams by forcing his smelly hand over my mouth, as he released his demonic semen in me, but I continued to scream, muffled and all. He panicked and ran off, leaving me. He left me traumatized, and shaking like a junky. I couldn't move my legs or my body for that matter, for what seemed like hours. I was in shock. I wiped the snot that was running from my nose with the tail of my torn blouse. My face was throbbing and blood stained from the blunt punches.

I blink, and then swallow spittle down my throat.

Inhale.

Exhale.

Why do I continue to give him power? He took so much from me. Tears well up in my eyes when I rethink of all he took. They slowly roll down my sweaty cheeks. Exhale. Close my eyes and try to disremember what he took me through. Why me? What had I done to deserve it all? What had I done?

He ruined my life. And since then to now nothing has remained fulfilling. Every time I get close to having pleasure, joy, something terrible happens and steals it all away from me. I remember when I was once on top and now I'm damned near crawling trying to stand back on my own two feet.

I push the magenta duvet away from my clammy skin and climb my juddering body out of bed. Wobbly, I stand still for a minute or two to regain myself as well as drift him as far away from me as possible. Once I feel unshaken I then make my way downstairs, bypass the kitchenette, bathroom, and amble barefoot toward the front door. Thumb and forefinger twists the top lock, then bottom as I clench my hand around the doorknob, twists to the right, then pull it open.

My eyes shift downward. Dang no HeraldNews in sight—only a colorful promotional card is laying face up on the burlap doormat. I kneel down and pick up the 4 x 6 card and briefly glance over it.

THE FIRST ANNUAL
RED BUTTERFLY
HIV/AIDS FUNDRAISER

DECEMBER 1
(RED ATTIRE ONLY)
ADVANCED V.I.P TICKETS $50
INCLUDES** 3 COURSE MEAL & TABLE SEATING
ADVANCED TICKETS $25 | MORE AT THE DOOR
LIMITED AMOUNT OF TICKETS WILL BE SOLD
DOORS OPEN @ 6 PM | SHOWTIME 7-10 PM
FEATURING PATERSON'S POETS:
LATE NIGHT SEDUCTION,
WOMEN AS THE FACES OF BROKEN SILENCE:
MINERVA WEAVER, MAXINE STILES, BURN BENTLEY,
WYNDOW PAIN,
WITHER-ME-NOT,
MY SENTIMENTS EXACTLY:
PURNELL WEAVER, KENYATTA J. BENTLEY,
MR. FUCK-YOU-NOW-DISS-YOU-LATER,
SOFT JUSTICE & BEYOND-THE-EXTERIOR,
JAZZ BAND: KUT THE PHAT
JAZZ VOCALIST: SOOTHE-THE-WEARY-SOUL

THE HUSTLER 'n' the POET NIGHTCLUB

85-85 Page Turner | Paterson, NJ

Maybe someone dropped it at my front door by accident, I think. I peek down the hall from left to right to see if anyone else has one lying at their front door, but no one does. Suddenly it dawns on me that it is after five o'clock in the evening and I have pretty much slept through the day.

I shut the door and lock it.

As I am making my way toward the kitchenette my first initial thought is to throw the card in the garbage because I am not in the mood to be going anywhere. And I especially am not in the mood to be getting dressed up in some red getup to go parading around at some fundraiser with a bunch of snooty folks. I'd rather sit home and watch *Lackawanna Blues* DVD for the umpteenth time.

I set the promotional card on the kitchenette countertop. Go to the bathroom to pee before making myself a hot cup of peppermint herbal tea.

As I exit out of the bathroom I cut my eyes at the promotional card. *Nope. Not going*, I tell myself. *I am not going anywhere. I am going to sit my tired ass home and watch DVDs until my eyes droop and boredom knocks me out cold.*

I enter the kitchenette and lift up the silver teakettle and fill it with cold water. Set it on the first burner to heat up. I begin babbling in my head. *It's too cold outside*, I think. *And plus, I don't have a thing to wear. Okay. That's a boldfaced lie. With my fashion sense I can put something together.*

I turn the teakettle off before it starts whistling. And make my way back upstairs to my bedroom to see what I have to wear that would be appropriate for this evening's event. Sliding my closet door to the right I tug on a few outfits but nothing speaks to me until I come across a unique vintage halter back to the '50s red cotton swing dress I bought from the Red White and Blue Thrift Store a couple of years ago. I've only worn it once and hopefully I can still squeeze these hips into it.

I reach down and pullout a shoebox of vintage red four-inch stilettos and place the box on the bed alongside the dress. I open my dresser drawer and pullout a red lace thong and matching lace brassier. In the second drawer I pullout a pair of sheer french coffee pantyhose and place them alongside the dress. I make my way back downstairs to take a warm shower.

It is already 5:30 p.m., and I know it is going to take me at least a half hour to forty-five minutes to get dazzling.

I enter the bathroom, pull overhead my nightshirt and place it in the wicker hamper. I stare at my African breasts in the mirror. Marvel myself for what feels like a nanosecond then proceed to the turn the nozzle to the shower on. Hearing the lukewarm water sprout out, I continue to stare at my body. The steam cascades and fills the bathroom, and as it does I kneel down to open the cabinet to retrieve a fresh white washcloth and oversized burgundy towel. I stand. Reach my hand in the shower to test the water. I turn the nozzle to adjust the temperature to make it a little hotter, and then step in feeling the beads of moisture against my dry thirsty skin.

Raising the bottle of coconut milk body wash I squeeze as the creamy liquid flows out and onto the washcloth, I begin to lather myself down. Inhaling the insatiable fragrance of freshness I am beginning to wake up from sleeping part of the day away.

Moping, that's what I've been doing for the past couple of days, weeks. I sleep to pass the time, the loneliness. There hasn't been any excitement in my life. No drama. It's been kind of dull. But a good dull because usually things constantly happen and I find myself overwhelmed with grief. For once I can honestly say that I wish I had something going on—nothing dramatic. Just something to keep me preoccupied during this quiet time.

Xavier and I haven't really been spending much time together. I don't know what is going on between us, but I know it's something. We talk over the phone more than we see each other. I don't want to crowd him so I wait for him to contact me, come to me, but that hasn't been happening much lately either. I know I shouldn't think like this but with everything that has happened I often wonder if JaVonna Banks wasn't incarcerated would he still crave her presence, her coochie. I wonder how he'd be with her still in the picture. I know it sounds like I am insecure and I guess to a certain extent I am. I mean right now JaVonna has the upper hand with being pregnant. And as much as I try to block it out the fact of the matter is she is carrying his baby—Xavier's baby. I have no ties, no attachment other than what I feel in my heart for him. And often I wonder, I truly wonder if that is going to be enough. I try to fake myself out and think positively but the baby situation really gets the best of me. Rebuilding trust is hard. Especially when you are betrayed as I was. I am not putting all the blame on him, but to go to great lengths as to have *sex* with her, that's a challenge for me. I can't seem to get past it. It's not easy but every day I try a little harder. Love a little lighter.

I stand underneath the showerhead and rinse myself thoroughly then step out of the shower and towel dry. Lubricate my damp skin down with hydrocerin cream. I wash my face. Glide my Dove deodorant under each armpit. Brush my teeth. Stick a Q-tip in my ears to clean them.

Then reach for my frayed makeup case that sits on the bamboo rack and lightly apply my makeup making sho' I still look natural. I then head back upstairs to my bedroom to get dressed.

By 6:10 p.m., I am finally ready to paint the town red. I stand before the full-length mirror lent against the wall making sho' I look sensational. I hope I am not wasting my time going to this thing. "Think positive," I say to myself as I reach for the three dollar bottle of oil atop my dresser. I dab a smidgen of African musk on my neck and behind both ears.

In my imitation snake-skinned jewelry box I reach for my flowerily crimson earrings that complement my ensemble. I glance at myself in the mirror one last time for final approval and then head back downstairs. Grab my keys, wool coat, knit hat, red sequin clutch, and strut my fine self out the door.

I exit out of the taxi, and enter the luxury lounge.

The place is packed with a mixture of faces, none of which I am familiar with seeing. I make my way to the line that has already formed. I unzip my clutch and pull out my last thirty dollars debating if I should hold onto it just in case I need it for something more important.

Standing next in line, I am still debating: should I or shouldn't I? As I am thinking I look at the flow of folks come walking in blowing warm air on the hands and shivering in their skin. A group of four ladies stand behind me dressed to kill in their red getups with no coats on. Two are light-skinned with long honey-blonde weaves. The other two are darker skinned with natural hair. All of them are strikingly attractive, but dumb as hell. It is too cold to be trying to be cute.

Behind them stands an elder couple engaged in small talk. They turn to see folks dining at the restaurant. Some are at the bar sipping on drinks, laughing, and enjoying the ambiance.

The fair-skinned man takes his missus coat and dangles it from his arm. The mocha-complexioned woman makes her way to the ladies room sporting a basic red dress with a red ribbon broach pinned to it and three-inch red pumps. I watch them both. Noticing how the man's eyes are still captivated by his woman's dainty walk.

The man who looks to be well in his late fifties still has on his black overcoat and lipstick red stingy brim so I can't tell what he is wearing but I know that he has on red trousers that enhance his red Cole Haan shoes. I realize that if they can come out in this bone-chilling cold I may as well stay. I must admit it does feel good to get out of the house. And plus, it is for a good cause. Something I can definitely relate to. I may as

132

well show some support.

At the winding stairway entrance sits a dark-skinned young lady with bushy afro dressed in a red spandex dress that looks like it was painted on her curvaceous body. She greets me with a smile as I hand her my last thirty dollars. She stamps the outer skin on my left hand that leaves a highlighted RB in red letters. I frown inside because she doesn't give me any change back. I then make my way upstairs to the event.

As soon as I open the door all heads turn in my direction. A handful of women roll their eyes at my presence while the men gawk at me like I'm a piece of rib-eyed steak. I act as if it doesn't bother me, but underneath all of this dazzling I am nervous as hell. "Shake it off, girl," I say to myself. Look confident. I slowly and sensually make my way to the bar hoping I can find at least four dollars at the bottom of my clutch to buy my first drink.

Instead of standing in everyone's eye view I about face and enter the ladies room to check my clutch. I smile with my eyes because not only do I find a twenty dollar bill I also find my pair of rhinestone earrings I had been looking for since last month. Suddenly I feel myself cheering up. *This might turn out to be a great evening after all.*

I exit out of the bathroom with a little switch in my hips and make my way back to the bar. I order a glass of red Sangria. Pay the Dominican bartender. Then I make my way over to a table and bar stool meant for party of one.

I remove my coat and place it on the back of the chair and tuck my hat in its side pocket. I sit down with my legs crossed and posture straight.

The show is supposed to start at 7:00, but you know how black folks do, we are never on time. I shake my head, then take a sip of Sangria, and try to relax.

My mind drifts as I look at the many couples here this evening. I wonder what Xavier is doing right this very minute but I don't pullout my cell to call him. If he wants to talk he'll eventually call me. Sometimes I wonder if I should just stop while I am ahead. Possibly join one of those dating sites like *PositiveSingles.com.* But then I think against it. I'm not that desperate, at least not yet. And plus, I'm trying to see where this goes with Xavier. See if we are indeed marriage material. Sometimes I wonder. I mean, I'm pretty sho' me being positive had a lot to do with Xavier's infidelity. It hurts just thinking about it, but I cannot deny the truth no matter how much I wish I could.

I am distracted out of my daze as this young caramel complexioned guy with a red fitted on his head and red Gucci jeans with matching sneakers and red hoodie walks up onstage. He has a baby face, which puts me in mind of the R&B singer Miguel. He has big Orlando Jones brown eyes and Maxwell lips. He's tall and lanky and looks to be in his early-to-mid-twenties. He reaches for the mike and says in a guttural voice.

"How's everyone doing this evening?"

Everyone yells back, "Fine! Great!"

"A'ight. A'ight," he replies with a winning smile on his oblong face. "For those of you who don't know who I am. I'm better known as Emcee Cradler. Paterson is my hometown. I was born and raised here. I left here back in '86. Did the college thing, graduated, and then was fortunate enough to get into the music industry. Networking really helped me meet some good people who have pulled me up with them in a positive way. People like Drake, ah, Queen Latifah, Alicia Keys, will-i-am and Erykah Badu. I feel privileged to come out and support the cause of HIV/AIDS. I, myself, have had some family members, friends who have departed from this life due to the disease so I wanted to give back to the community in any way I could. Um, we have some former Patersonians like me who have come all the way from: Hampton, VA, Charlotte and Durham, NC, Atlanta, GA, Kissimmee, FL, New York, NY, Washington, D.C., to show some love to their stomping grounds. It is going to be a wonderful show so I hope you really enjoy it. We have some talented poets who are raw so I hope you can handle their self-expression. Um, we are not here to offend anyone, but as you know in the world of what I call Lyricist it is known for straight talk. So I'm just giving you a heads up beforehand so no one will be surprised by whatever comes out of these poets mouth. This cause is to raise money for those who have been inflicted with the disease and to provide assistance with: medical bills, medication, treatments, food, clothes, and housing, anything that will help lighten the load off of someone who is sick or facing hardships. We are not here to judge. We are here to make a difference. This is our first annual fundraiser and our goal is to continue to support the cause. Just to let you know RED BUTTERFLY is a nonprofit organization so you know we have to do the footwork to make this happen. We had to pull together as a community and build to get to this point and we are continuing to build because there are millions of people who are living with this disease." He pauses, covers the mike with his hand, and then nods his head to someone in the far corner. "Okay. So without further ado let's get this party started. Eat up. Drink up. And enjoy the show."

He adjusts the mike, then says, "Ladies and gents, let's give it up for my manz...'Late Night Seduction!'"

Hands clap, as the ladies in the front row whistle loudly. I am beginning to warm up to my surroundings. I lift my glass and take another sip of Sangria. I liked to choke on my drink as this handsome specimen of a man steps out of the dark and into the light. "Oh...my...God, what do we have here? Ooh, chocolate wine." I say to myself. *Annoyingly, Avona purses her lips, and shakes her head from side to side. "Girl, close your mouth! I said close... chile, your...mouth... Avery! You ain't ready for a man like him. Trussssssst."*

LATE NIGHT SEDUCTION

Brotha' don't hold anything back, I think to myself as I walk up onstage. My left palm grazes against my Caesar haircut. I straighten out the collar to my red dress shirt. Brush a piece of lint off of the shoulder of my red suede sports jacket, jiggle the pants leg of my red leather pants and gaze down at my red suede shoes as I place the headset on. Bring the miniature mike to my moist thick burnt umber lips. I crack a dazzling white smile to the honies. Wink my eye at this *fine* brown sugar sitting in the front row. Then I spit my shit.

I GOTTA FEEL U, BEFORE I ENTER U

I blow into the mike, gaze at the ladies, and then say, "*I am woman. I am man. No, don't get it twisted. I am a depiction of spiritual life. I make love on a spiritual level. I am better known as: 'LATE NIGHT SEDUCTION.'*

"I am soft and supple body that quench on a whim. I am a sensual curve that fluctuates between pain and joy. I am an eye that tears happily-ever-after. I am mouth that water for something delicious as chocolate covered strawberries. I am an ear that hears everything but what needs to be heard: 'I don't want you anymore. Nah. I said I love you. Weren't you listening?' I am feet that walk into the arms of masculinity and manipulation and pretend to be in love—in love, with someone unknown to me.

"Do you know my name? C'mon, girlllllll, have you forgotten it that quickly? Well, allow me to refresh your memory.

"I am MR. FUCK-YOU-NOW-DISS-YOU-LATER, nice to meet you too.

"I can be as suave as the next joker. Pull out your chair. Help you with your coat. Open the door for you. Walk you to your doorstep. I can electrify your mind with fake

promises, sweet kisses on your frontal lobe, I can ride you till the sunsets, sing you a sweet-ass melody, having you think I'm going on tour with Keith Sweat. And I-I wanna take you with me, baby. Fly you to the moon and back again. 'Cause you know you is a Nefertiti queen. I know how to make you smile with your eyes, then your lips. I've studied you enough to know how to get you in the mood. Serenade you some Barry White nightcap. As I watch you guzzle down that love shit. Feels good, don't it. Real good. Good enough to have you eating out of the palms of my hands. Yes, now you're beginning to understand MR. FUCK-YOU-NOW-DISS-YOU-LATER's men-tal-ity.

"So, so, you are feelin' my vibe, huh? Yeah. Brotha' knows how to layer that sugary shit on thick. Gotcha wet between those maple brown thighs. Yeah, I like it moist, wet.

"And see; see you'll give me all I need as many times as I want it because I've made your muthafuckin' day. I've kept my word to keep you smiling. And when you're down on your luck, here I come a runnin' to help my baby out. I'd never see you fall 'cause I need you just as much as you need me. Just don't need my need too much. Never be that 'need' for any nigga, not even your sugar daddy. Notice I didn't say...MAN. 'Cause when a nigga 'bout to jet, trust and believe you're that last person on his mind. Nah. He doesn't have time to drop a dime 'cause his funds done ran low. He gotta go. Brotha' is gone, while you're home stressin' 'n' bitchin' 'n' twitchin' 'n' itchin'—crying over some nickel and dime muthafucka that you never knew. Just losing your goddamn mind because you thought you had a man who was going to give you the world out of his cruddy little hands. But all it seems he has done is shown you how naive you've become. How desperation got you all fucked up in the head. He took you on a sexual ride that you thought was everlasting and you submissively lost your inner-woman and gladly gave him your body, then soul. Now you're left on broken heels tryna fill those shoes with heartache baggage. Giiiiirrrrllllll, he done cut you so deep you can't even find the wound. And every time you think of him, mention his name...you begin to consume with gloom. You begin to ache. You allowed him to eat and drink on every floor of that department store he took you to. He sold you a fantasy. And you bought it right away, didn't even bother to check the price tag. So easily you became a trick to his trade...."

I pause. "Ladies, I see I have to feed you in moderation. I don't want you to get too full, too fast. Let's take a fifteen-minute intermission my mouth is parched."

Palms applaud loudly as I exit offstage.

A blonde-haired woman yells, "I can wet it if you'd like, baby! Let me do that for yah," she puckers her heart-shaped glossy lips and makes a poppin' sound with her mouth.

I ignore her and walk to the right side of the room as the crowd scatters about mingling, eating from the colorful buffet, and getting their drinks at the bar. All I see is lips flapping a mile a minute with wide smiles on their faces. All I hear is laughter filling the room. It's good energy, exactly what I need to help me regain my inner strength. If only they knew. Tonight is taking a lot out of me, more than I care to admit, but the truth of the matter is I had to learn the hard way of how to respect a woman. I had to lose to gain a better perspective. It took a great deal for me to grow into who I am today. No. This newfound "*me*" did not happen overnight. I had to feel the weight of agony on my shoulders and back for many, many years. Guilt can do a number on a joker, especially a hardheaded joker. I used to be that that dog, that refused to bow down and listen and console my mother's cry. I would never cave, never come down off of my high horse to meet her halfway. I had something to prove to somebody. Today, I really couldn't tell you who. No one asked me to be the *coldest muthafucker ever* (son of a *bitch*) that I was. I chose to be because of whom was missing in my life.

I needed a man to teach me, preach to me, get in my face and let it be known of who was the boss of the house. I needed a man to whoop my ass when I got too big for my own dirty drawers. I needed a man to knock me down with one mighty hard punch and demand for me to get on my knees and thank God he didn't kill me for talking back. I needed a man to pull me up by my shirt collar and instill in me the rules of: "Fly the Fuck Right" OR "Get Knocked the Fuck Out." I needed repetition of a father's physical existence. To know that he was just a door away, or down in the basement, or in the garage or backyard, I had neither. So I became this irate young boy who defied his moms every word. I disrespected her—looked down on her too. Bitter. I was very bitter. Had I known then what I know now maybe, just maybe she'd be here listening to a man speak his shame.

After wetting my palate and filling my belly with a little pasta salad and one chicken wing I make my way through the congestion run to the bathroom to empty out my bladder. I think I drank more than I ate this evening. I don't really have that much of an appetite. Once things resume back to normal and my worries become few and far between I'll be able to enjoy food again, life again.

I return to the stage.

"Okay, Ladies, I gave you the appetizer, but here is the full course meal." With my forefinger and thumb I wipe the creases of my mouth. I then crack a smile and begin to have my last say.

"So easily you became a trick to his trade...

"Pimpin' that suit like the Mack-Daddy that he is. He used every tactic in his PLAYER manual. He wooed you. He schooled you. He fooled you. And by the time he was through with you, sistah, you were dick whipped. You relinquished all your good shit for some muthafuckin' bullshit! You willingly handed over your dignity and integrity just to fuck him again and again and again. But again, you weren't listening. No. You let him fuck you from your head to your curled toes. He made you scream out his name to boost his ego. And then, then he wore your ass out till the point of insanity. He had you dangling from his puppet string. Then he dissed you. Dismissed you, yet he warned you with the look of lust filled eyes. He laid out every clue. But you turned and looked the other way. He told you. But you ignored every word he would say, other than: 'I love you,' that was all you heard. He swept you off of your feet and into his bed that reeked of new pussy. Then y'all walked hand in hand back to that department store where you thought he was claiming to be your man. Y'all took the escalator six floors up. Then took the elevator thinking he was going to elevate your mind but instead he shopped for another bedmate. You witnessed it all. Yet you refused to bail out and restore your sanity. He gave you plenty of opportunities to say: ENOUGH ALREADY! But the words would not leap off of your tongue. And your feet would not EXIT OUT. You were hypnotized. Memorized. Delusional too. I LOVE YOU stuck like glue to your heart even though he was ripping it apart.

"See, you honestly thought that he was deeply in love with you. You could no longer see the truth staring you right in the face. He practically fed you the: T.R.U.T.H. But you, you rebelled and refused to swallow it down. You refused to stand your muthafuckin' ground.

"So sluggishly you dragged that pain around like a hand-me-down coat. You cried and cracked simultaneously all because you allowed him entry into that sacred place. And he, he ate it up and left you with a cavity not even a dentist could fill. He played you fo' real.

"See if only you allowed time to lapse. Not be so eager to please, fall to your knees to SUCK UP all of his BULLSHIT.

"If only you'd had that mindset of: I Gotta FEEL U, Before I ENTER U...you would've been straight—you probably would've had a brotha' eating off of your pussy plate.

"And you have the audacity to ask: where you went wrong? You and you and you and you and you...you didn't FEEL ME, Before I ENTERED YOU. You pretended to. You gave me ENTRY into your paradise, before thinking, twice. I must admit that shit was like that. You had a brotha' licking his lips. Kissing his fingertips. Poppin' his collar. *Gripping his mighty mighty dollar. I was in there like Powwow! And then I dissed you—dismissed you from my peripheral vision. In other words: I gave you the BOOT! Goodddbyeee!*

"*Excuse me, but do you remember my name? Of course you do. I'm that brotha' patting himself on the back. How could you forget someone as debonair as me? I'm MR. FUCK-YOU-NOW-DISS-YOU-LATER.*

"*Ladies, Ladies, Ladies, is it sinking in yet?*

"*Do I need to spit this shit?*

"*Are you inebriated or constipated that you can't grasp my flow? Let a brotha' know.*

"*Girl, say it ain't sooooo...'cause I'm not done as of yet...*

"*Who am I? I see you still weren't listening.*

"*But if you must know...*

"*I'm that man every woman should long for. But see, you have to come with more than just an open-door-pussy. I need to read the fine print that is in scripted on your lips. And if it happens to read: TRICK. Then my reply would be: DECLINE. Sorry, I need to be mind-fucked. I know that shit went right over your head. Enough said. See, I want a woman—a realllllll woman who knows how to please her man virgin style. No, baby, I'm not an easy catch—I'm the type of brotha' that has to be approached from a different mindset. And SEX, my lady, is not what makes my nature rise. Uh-huh. What catches my eye is a confident woman who can stimulate my mind and take me on a spiritual journey and get me spiritually high off of her inner beauty. Ssssshhhiiiittttt, she can have my undivided attention. Not to mention every other attribute that I possess. For her and only her I will give my heart, my soul. And we would become an intertwining climax of freedom. Mmmmmmmm. Stop frontin'. 'Cause you don't know nothin' 'bout that. Your shit is whack fucking around with every low-life. You can't even spell...MAN. Don't even know the definition. All you know is: 'open sesame,' 'baby, do me,' 'baby, please, baby, please'...then drop to your knees giving the wrong muthafucker praise.*

"*Aren't you tired of lying on your back? Getting fucked in the crack? Aren't you tired of getting dick slapped? Aren't you tired of being used? When are you ever going to see the light that shines around you, that halo that hovers above you? I guess it's too high above your head. When are you going to stop and think? Think about the consequences of your actions? When are you going to love yourself enough to stop the muthafuckin' madness?*

"*Why do I care? Because when I look at you, I see a beautiful black sistah that lacks woman. Do you know who you are?*

"'Cause I know who the fuck I am. I'm your male eyes, which you refuse to utilize. What more can I do for you that you won't even do for yourself? Tell me?

"Silence... likes a typical bitch.

"I'll leave you with this ...now you can either take heed or keep feeding that empty need.

"I'm your LATE NIGHT SEDUCTION, but I have to tell you all something I am tired of fucking you bitches mind 999 times! I am tired of you allowing niggas to stick their dick in you abusing your pussy black and blue! Reducing you down to a sex slave with dirty feet, have you no shame? Is this the price for fame? Allowing yourself to be diminished by the control of a nigga with no soul. Got you swinging from pole to pole, twisting and switching your shit. While he pockets all the rewards and leaving you bone-dry and stone-cold high. I am tired of listening to jokers run the same ole lines; dropping shit like it's theirs when they know they got it off of a record that some smooth talkin' R. Kelly wannabe wrote. I am tired of seeing niggas cut your throat every time you swallow their piss. I am tired of watching you shrivel up and become their broke down bitch.

"But see, see I realize why, why you act the way you do. Pain is all you know. And he, Mr. FUCK-YOU-NOW-DISS-YOU-LATER drew you in to believe it so. I mean, you done heard: trick, slut, and jump-off so many times you're immune to it. Done been called a thousand bitches and hundred hos to the point where you don't even know your name. Every nigga who claimed to have loved you has degraded you. All, all he did was fuck you, fuck you, fuck you in ways you can't comprehend. He had you convinced that you were 'the one' that made him feel like a king. And you dropped down on your knees and you aimed to please...sucking him so endearingly, passionately like his dick was dipped in gold. So I've been told...

"Tell me. Did he make you cum? Did you ever get your shit off? Or are you still starving, waiting to wake yourself up, and finally come to the realization that you no longer give a fuck about a dick 'n a smile!"

"There is more to you. But first, U Gotta Feel U, Before U Feel Me.

"See, a real gentleman will work for his. Let me earn my keep. Let me crawl, then walk to your paradise. Let me knock on the door or ring the doorbell before you allow me entry into your sanctuary. Let me woo you with wisdom. Let me school you with truth. Let me love you in a way that only a soul mate can make love to you: slowly, sensually, and unconditionally. Let me do my manly duty and elevate you into a strong black woman, not some trick sniffin' fo' some dirty dick.

"Woman, I Gotta FEEL U, Before I ENTER U. And U, U Gotta FEEL ME TOO.

"Who am I? My name is LATE NIGHT SEDUCTION stroking you ladies twelve *inches of fuckin' commonsense!"*

I debonairly walk offstage with this aura of confidence. The ladies near the stage swoon as I walk pass them and head to the guest room.

Emcee Cradler hops back onstage, "You ladies a'ight in the front row? I see you, yeah, *you* in that sexy red number. You are drooling at the mouth. Look at you. LNS got you all hot. Lemme stop messin' wit' you, girl. Yo', LNS, it is kind of hot up here. I see why she drooling at the mouth. Damn! Okay. Before I sweat to death let's give a round of applause for my girlllllllllllllllllll, Wither-Me-Not."

The applause is overwhelmingly loud as a woman in a formfitting red dress that complements her curvy figure walks up onstage. She has long wavy chestnut brown hair that dangles down to the small of her back. Oh, my! I wet my lips. There is a white gentleman sitting near the stage that grasps my attention. Red does him well, I say to myself. It complements his dirty blonde hair. He turns in my direction and I gaze at his beautiful gray eyes. Immediately he puts me in mind of *Fifty Shades of Grey*...Christian Grey and a charge of exhilaration creeps up my thighs.

Broken out of my trance I focus my attention back to her flawless fair-skin tone and Kerry Washington scandalous lips and high cheekbones that makes me a tad bit envious. She stands about 5'8" but with heels on she looks to be about 6'2".

"Hello, everyone," she says in a soft-spoken Brooklyn accent. "I'm so glad you came to support the cause. It really, really means a lot to all of us. I'm very open about my life so with that being said I can share that I am HIV-positive. I have been for more than six years now.

"As a way to deal with my illness I began writing in my journal. It was difficult to share with others what had happened to me. I started coming out of my shell after meeting some wonderful people who embraced me with open arms. And it chan me for the better. After a few years of dealing with my illness I began to reach out to others who are inflicted. And over the years we created a support group called WITHER ME NOT. Currently we have about one hundred and fifty supporters and every day we are constantly growing. After birthing the support group I began to reflect back on when I was first told that I was HIV-positive. And in retrospect I, um, I started to release the pain through the written word never really thinking that I'd be sharing my most intimate thoughts with anyone. But here I am. So, here it goes. The title of these two poems is: Woman on the Couch (Part 1) and Step Out/Step In (Part 2).

"The first poem explains how a woman will extend herself for her friend with benefits, but at the end of day she realizes that she's only been stagnating herself to keep the peace between them."

Wither-Me-Not closes her eyes and strokes her arms in an up and down motion. She then stares out into the crowd and instantly you see her transform into this other person. When she speaks into the mike her voice even sounds slightly different. It is the craziest thing I'd ever seen. One thing I will say she knows how to capture an audience's attention.

"I sleep on the couch so that I don't have to hear myself talk
"There R times when I feel the urge to walk as far away as my mind will take me
"2 keep the peace
"We were all I ever needed, but lately that need has diminished
"No, I'm not one 2 start something N not finish
"U got me confused w/someone else
"I'm an unwed, black woman
"Single as a sensual 'S'
"Sometimes my thoughts drift N I wish I had wings 2 fly into Ur arms
"Knowing that Ur arms won't catch me
"B cuz of the grudge U housed inside
"We were never in love, just friends w/benefits
"A man N a woman mending broken ends
"Obviously our broken ends have a shelf-life that neither knew
"Would expire
"I didn't take the higher road
"I chose to sleep on the couch
"2 bite my tongue
"Chew on the blame framed around Ur face
"U blames me for Ur dysfunction
"For the fact that Ur car won't start
"U knew that rusty, old El Camino needed a new transmission,
"New engine
"As it got older, slower, U got colder
"Sometimes the frigid leaves a frost-bite
"I grow numb

"N I blame me for expecting romance
"Something more than anger and pain
"I bite my tongue
"Keep my true feelings hidden in the glove compartment of my heart
"N the soreness in my throat
"I try to cope
"Cope with the inevitable
"We've grown apart
"Decades ago
"N no, no, I am not acting out of anger
"I try to douse out the flames that burn from Ur tongue
"The look of disappoint that pierces my eyes
"The truth that lies between our sheets
"The connection was long gone but not the friendship
"But lately, lately that seems to B dissipating too
"Yes, there used to B a love
"Love for me, Love for u
"Who r we kidding?
"Y r we pretending?
"We were untouchable, inseparable
"Magnetic
"Alive N free-spirited
"But somewhere it all disappeared into thin air
"N no, no, no, I am not
"Putting blame on old age
"I'm just saying that what used 2 b is no more
"N I can't make it spring shower
"If it desires to downpour
"I can't relive in Ur past
"N makes what we currently have last
"I cannot accommodate Ur needs
"Make U feel like a king in Ur castle
"Those wheels have rolled on
"Simply got in the car N drove off
"So, I lie on the couch to prevent myself from walking out on a man
"Who cannot follow simple instructions?
"But see, it's not only about that

"What U r lacking is a personality?

"It's about how U talks at me, not 2 me

"All that does is push me back

"N I grab my pillow

"Snuggle up tight with the imagery of a good loving man

"Wishing I had arms to hold me at night

"But I don't

"You won't

"Unless U gets what U need

"Having my naked ass in Ur bed

"Waiting diligently for U to sock-it-2-me

"Prove 2 Urself that U're still the 'man'

"But see, this is where the problem lies

"Between the centers of Ur attention

"Not my thighs

"I try to empathize

"But U chose not to listen

"Thinking that herbs N the 'blue pill' R gonna straighten out Ur

"Condition

"But I know

"N you know

"That that is not so

"I can't make a sore bleed if there is no flesh wound

"Make nature rise if there is no arousal

"Yet, we can still do other things

"But even that is not good enough

"So, what r U saying in so many unspoken words

"Wait!

"Put that shit on pause

"B 4 U can't take it back

"I'll crawl under my comforter N act as if this conversation never happened

"B cuz if I don't

"Won't B no: us, we, our

"Will only B: me, myself, N I

"I won't tell a lie N says that I am happy B cuz

"Truthfully, I am not

"Here I stand scratching my ass instead of my head

"Trying to remember the last time you touched it

"N made it clap

"See; see I am searching in my mind for a man who is willing 2

"Understand what I need

"Fill my skies w/yellow, bright light N take all of this

"Attitude, blues, mood swings far away from here

"Allow me the pleasure of greeting romance

"Let me have one dance under the moonlight

'Let me smile

"Give me the things I've been missing

"I want to dress myself in Vera Wang

"Put my face on

"Slip my feet in a pair of high heels

"N marvel myself

"Then say to me, 'I know that neighbor next-store

"Yep. She moved in w/ a man decades ago

"N since then to 5 years ago she has been curled up on the couch

"Wishing 2 walk barefoot out the door; get in her car, N drive

"Into the arms of another man

"A man, a real man that will appreciate her

"N understand her frustrations

"Instead of settling 4 someone who no longer sees her as a woman

"But now as a trick in nightwear

"'Where is my money?'" Since U feel the need 2 degrade me. 'Come 2 bed?!' U'd say
as if a command. "N I'd reply, 'I'd rather hug my pillow, squeeze my thighs together, N
make myself come. I get more pleasure this way.'

"I dunno. I... don't... know... Y I stay in this unfulfilled room.

"Consumed w/gloom N temperament.

"It has 2 B more out there.

"I believe it has 2 B.

"So, I've come to the conclusion...that I am no longer willing 2 "pretend that this
couch is my man,

"While U hold a grudge w/Ur man in Ur hand

"Still trying 2 wake him up."

Wither-Me-Not pauses, and stares out at the crowd. "The Part 2 to
this poem explains how the same woman will leave one relationship,
find her soul mate, and try to live happily-ever-after with this new man.

145

A man she'd later married only to realize in the end that she is still unfulfilled and trapped in something she never saw coming her way." She shakes her head, then bears her soul so profoundly, so candidly.

STEP OUT STEP IN

"Jus' for a day I wish you could feel my inner rage
"'Cause, baby, I don't think we are on the same page
"Deep in my heart I know you are trying to drive me insane
"With all the self blame
"Playing with my emotions
"True devotion
"Just to see if I'll leave or stay
"What more is there to say travels through my mind
"Every single day
"He doesn't care about me or the vows that we made
"Or the fact that I am carrying a token of his deepest affection
"As he punctured her with his firm erection
"That makes me bleed a toxic red

"STEP OUT/STEP IN
"Into my world of woman, wife, lover and friend
"Wear these shoes worn, torn at the soles
"Walk 'n hear them talk up a storm
"And see if you can stomach all that is going on
"Feel the trickery that invades me, changes me
"I am not the woman I used to be
"Relinquish, set me free
"Allow me to be the woman I yearn to be

"STEP OUT/STEP IN
"Turn the pages to this book
"Read all of the revised chapters of misery
"Engross yourself in the epilogue
"Realize what deprivation has done to me

"STEP OUT/STEP IN
"These high-heels and feel the strain
"Yes, our love has weakened
"Infidelity has deepened
"Then comes home reaping all of my rewards
"Stringing me along
"Breaking me more and more
"While you're out screwing whores

"STEP OUT/STEP IN
"Share how it feels to carry all of this dead weight
"To feel unappreciated every fuckin' day
"To go to bed cold, longing for her man to come home
"To wither in pain
"Counting, recounting each second that melts a part of her away
"And tell me to my face that you'd stay
"Knowing, unknowing your mate
"Is out trickin' and treatin' himself to every pussy that catches his "eye
"While I sit home contemplating if and when I am going to die

"STEP OUT/STEP IN
"Into my world of woman, wife, lover and friend
"Wear these shoes worn, torn at the soles
"Walk 'n hear them talk up a storm
"And see if you can stomach all that is going on
"Feel the trickery that invades me, changes me
"I am not the woman I used to be
"Relinquish, set me free
"Allow me to be the woman I yearn to be...Happy."

Emcee Cradler steps back onstage. "C'mon y'all, let's give it up for my girrrrlllllll. She doesn't pull any punches." Wither-Me-Not walks offstage and blends in with the crowd. "Yo' my peoples we have a newcomer in our home. Let's give it up for the intriguing...Wyndow Pain."

Everyone claps to show some support. And as we do, this young woman heads onstage dressed in a pair of red skinny jeans and a red pullover sweater that hugs her skin. She is slender framed with big doe hazel eyes. Her jet-black hair is pulled back in a ponytail which accentuates her strong facial features on honey-toned skin. Besides, her beauty I notice she is rockin' some funky red boots.

When I look at her I notice she has a strange look upon her face like she is a thousand miles away or wishes she were. I know that look all too well.

She breathes warm air into the mike, and then speaks in what sounds like a child's voice. "Hi. Um, y'all bear with me 'cause I'm a little nervous standing up here. I feel like I'm about to faint."

A male voice in the crowd yells out, "Don't be, if you fall I'll be the first one to catch you. We gotchu baby, do your thang."

She cracks a smile. She then looks over the crowd with that same strange look upon her face and stillness in her eyes as if she has drift off somewhere she really doesn't want to be. She parts her full thick lips, presses them together, shakes her head and then sets herself free into the mike.

"I'm gonna detoxify my PAIN
"I'm gonna Check myself in rehab and reclaim what was
"Rightfully mine in the first doggone place
"I'm gonna Go through withdrawals that repeatedly stab me with
"Sharp cuts of reality
"I'm gonna shake, quiver and cry
"I'm gonna feel like I just wanna drop dead and die
"But once, once I do my 30, 60, 90 days clean
"I'm gonna sing, even off key
"I'm gonna hug myself
"Kiss the outer skin of my hand, and I'm gonna look up at the
"Ceiling and thank Him again and again and again
"And yes, tears they, they may run from my eyes down my cheeks
"My lips may quiver just a bit
"My heart may ache
"My body may even feel like it's going through withdrawals
"'cause I'm shaking like a leaf
"I got the shakes!!!!!

148

"I'm shakin' all of this GRIEF up outta me
"I got PAIN that that feels like an unwanted tenant who just won't
"Vacate the premises
"Even with an eviction notice stamped to my heart, it refuses to
"Leave
"So I continue to grieve
"I continue to cry
"I continue to feel like I just wanna drop dead and die
"I sigh as tears drip from my chin
"And I wonder...
"I wonder, is this the end?
"The END to all hurt, desert that intrudes
"Leaves track marks on my skin
"Is this worth reclaiming?
"This life of stress, of strain, of strife
"'Cause if it is I'd rather be a junky
"For the rest of my life."

Inaudible silence fills the room, as this young woman remains standing onstage with her head held high, tears bursting to flood from her eyes. But she holds them back. You would think someone just died in here.

I glance to my left and a woman has her head bowed. To my right another woman stares at the ceiling with tear-filled eyes. Something happened within these walls. I feel it. And I see plain as day that even Emcee Cradler feels it telling by the teary look in his eyes. Noticing me noticing him he wipes his eyes with his hoodie sleeve and drops his face in the palms of his hands.

Sometimes, sometimes other people will give you a window to look through just for future reference of how bad things could potentially be. I feel the connection. And all it does for me is gives me the courage I need to keep looking ahead.

Wyndow Pain walks offstage and heads straight toward the ladies room leaving a lasting impression behind.

With no introduction needed a couple walks up onstage. Emcee Cradler walks up behind them and adjusts the mike for the female since she stands about four feet ten inches tall. She is dressed in a simple red dress with light skin and honey-colored hair styled in a Doobie. The male accompanying her looks to be about six feet. He is built like a football player with deep dark skin tone and a Brooklyn haircut dressed in a red two-button suit with red leather shoes on his size fourteen looking feet. Jeez.

"Hello," the female says in a sweet angelic voice. "I'm Beyond-The-Exterior. And this is my man Soft Justice. He's kind of shy so bear with him. Ah, we, ah, normally do a duet to express our inner selves. Sometimes I find it difficult to express myself vocally. So, ah, just as, ah, Wither-Me-Not was saying, I, too, began to write in a journal. One day I, ah, showed my man some of my deep feelings especially when we were having problems in our relationship. It was easier to write than to talk because talking didn't help us at the time. We didn't know how to communicate without raising our voices at one another. We lived in a hostile environment which was our home. It was very unhealthy. But, but sharing with him how I truly felt kind of opened us both up. He, too, began to jot some of his feelings down and it opened some dialogue for us to communicate in a tone that was relaxed as well as cathartic enough for us to maintain and salvage our relationship because we were on verge of an ugly, nasty breakup. It was just that bad. But God is good. And here we are...still together, still communicating, still very much in love, still learning, and still willing to learn how to love. I think this piece we are about to perform was the first thing my man had written to me. It was unique because he spoke for me and me for him. It was the way he had written it to let me know that he saw, he heard, he understood."

Soft Justice removes the mike from its stand. He penetratingly looks his lovely lady in the eyes, as he recites the poem. I feel myself slipping, wondering, and yearning for a love such as theirs.

Soft Justice and Beyond-The-Exterior bond in a loving hug and walk offstage. Everyone stands to their feet, whistling with hard claps. It is an emotional moment especially for me. I miss my man. As the poetic couple exit's the stage, three men, two white, one black hop up onstage dressed in red tuxedos. One untamed blonde-haired man with pale skin sits in front of a set of drums. The other mousy-brown-haired man with tanned skin and crystal blue eyes lifts up the saxophone. The tall, blue-black skinned man with shiny baldhead and captivating smile sits in front of the piano.

Emcee Cradler stands onstage, "Before we leave this evening I would like for you to leave with an open mind. And who better to express openness than Founder/CEO of RED BUTTERFLY. Let's give a warm round of applause for the one, the only, Ms. Java Sparks."

I think I have just died three times over when this six foot of smooth ebony skin, seductively attractive—one-hundred and sixty-seven pounds of sophistication walks up onstage with such, such grace and poise. And that dress, dang, she is wearing this full-length crimson body-hugging dress, and she is wearing it well. But the main attraction is her crystal baldhead. The woman is simply ravishing—a goddess to marvel.

With everyone in this room, from a distance I feel a connection that I haven't felt with any other woman. This woman I do not even know, yet something unexplainable is happening between us right at this very moment. And no, I am not dreaming. I am wide-the-hell-awake!

Ms. Sparks gazes out at the audience with her large dreamy copper-colored eyes. The voices die down giving her her due respect. She stands straight postured and begins to speak into the mike, a sexy English accent. "Hello. It's such a colorful array of shades in this room, such beautiful people. I say to my sistahs in this here room, find yourselves, complete your journey, and don't, don't allow your past to hinder your future. Trust in God. He'll guide you to the right man, at the right time. And when He does just be mindful of who you are and what you feel your worth is. If love is what you desire then be open when it comes into your life. Don't shut the door on it. Simply breathe, and ask it to c'mon in."

Java raises her hand to wipe the small tear away from her right eye. I don't know why but I feel her words as if she was speaking directly to me. *Whoa!*

Java continues, "My sistahs and brothers we are fortunate this evening to have this trio of men come from West Africa to join our Nubian sistah in a soulful rendition of 'Red Butterfly.'" She pauses, and then smiles showcasing pearly white teeth, she then lowers her eyes as her long black lashes flutter. Raising her head high she looks out to the audience, smiling with her eyes. "Let's give it up for the vivacious Soothe-The-Weary-Soul and the trio, Kut the Phat!" She then walks offstage and blends in with the crowd.

The applause roars thunderously loud.

I sip my last drop of Sangria, and exit out to head home.

As I am making my way down the steps, upcoming is a man with a pretty young *thang* clenched to his arm. Instantly my heart thumps and my eyes become misty as I view in plain sight Zaelyn Homes with an enigmatic look in his eyes.

Disoriented, I lose my footing and nearly tumble my way down the stairs, but a burly man walking behind me manages to catch me before I fall flat on my face.

I whisk out the door, hyperventilating, hearing nothing but the click-clack of my heels as I stagger down the street. Of all people to run into, it just had to be *him*.

Past thoughts spiral around in my head like dust flurries as I am thinking about all the things I yearned to say to Zaelyn after our night of ecstasy. After my findings, goodness, I couldn't and still can't seem to get him out of my head. I was doing so well up till now. Seeing him triggered some old feelings that have yet to die. It's really not that serious. That's what I keep repeating in my head. Lies. Maybe I'm experiencing a little chocolate rush. Yeah. Maybe. I shudder in my skin. Nearly on the verge of breaking down as I stagger from block to block. If only I was that woman that rock that didn't let situations like this get the better of her. If only I was *her*, that used-to-be-me woman that man would not still has power over my heart, and I wouldn't be feeling as I am.

God, I know you are here walking with me. Please, Lord. Please. I'm not... I can't revert back to that feeble woman. Yes, what Zaelyn and I shared was magical, but that was *then*...

"Zaelyn, I really enjoy your company and I would like to have the opportunity of getting to know you even more." I fake a cough. "I have thoughts about us being intimate."

Zaelyn's hand caresses me gently.

"But unfortunately there is something that needs to be said first. Zaelyn. Zaelyn...I'm...I'm...HIV-positive." I shut my eyes not wanting to see the grimace on his face. I pull back my hand, but he gently pulls it back and massages it ever so gently. Then I open my eyes. I feel relief from within. He doesn't react in the slightest way and that frightens me.

"Avery, I've also been thinking about us connecting. Lord knows it's been difficult smelling your lovely scent and admiring your beauty. It has been traveling through my mind since our last date. I am feelin' you like no other woman."

I close my eyes feeling his words. He swallows me with his affection.

"Avery, the chemistry is here and by you being honest with me it only assures me that this is fate. I want to be inside you, floating my juices around with yours, as we make love 'til dusk turns to dawn. I don't have an issue about using precautions. I just want to indulge in you like a bowl of chocolate pudding." He moistens his lips.

I smile. Zaelyn has wooed me right off of my feet.

The truth has been told and Zaelyn still stands before me with open arms. He starts undressing me with his eyes as he unbuttons his burgundy suede dress shirt and holds his arms down as it slips off his skin showing off his biceps of steel. They look plump and juicy. And then he unzips his black trousers and they rush to his feet. He has some meaty thighs. He steps out of his burgundy suede shoes, and pulls off his socks, showing me clear toenails. I just hope the soles of his feet are not scaly, rough, and I hope there is no fungus. He lifts up one leg at a time, standing before me in his silk boxers that show off a huge bulge. He wraps his arms around me breathing his Altoids breath on my already burning hot skin and unzips my dress as it caresses my body and falls to my feet. We are face-to-face as my breasts protrude and my sexy black thong makes him drool. I am ready to be fed! Zaelyn takes my hand and I lead him to the bathroom. He turns on the shower, drops his boxers and pulls off his wife beater. I step out of my thong. He stands close, cuddling me as he touches my breasts, squeezing, and pushing both of them together as he kisses them. The water is steaming up the bathroom making our bodies aroused. Zaelyn places one foot in the shower as he helps me in; the water beads against our bodies. He runs his fingers through my hair. He whispers in my ear, "You are so beautiful." I touch his back and spiral down to his third arm massaging as its size increases enormously. His blood flows quickly. He strokes my clitoris building secretion making me sloppy moist. I moan. He moans. The intensity grows and his third arm is as hard as a rock. He becomes aggressive in his burning desire to be within me. We make animal music. We lather each other allowing our hands to explore. I kiss his neck and lick his nipples, as the tension in me creates a friction that ignites. I am on fire. He teases me by gently biting my nipples and palming my ass. Foreplay makes us two horny dogs. Zaelyn turns off the water picks me up and carries me to the bedroom. And all I hear at this moment is Etta James singing, "At Last." Our bodies are dripping wet. He lays me on the bed, spreading my legs apart, and sitting in between. Cuffing my wrists like a crab with claws, he teases me with the touch of his penis up and down my thigh. The feeling makes my mouth open, his tongue meets my lips and I moisten them. Its finally gonna happen. I point to my nightstand indicating for him to get a Magnum condom. He reaches over in and pulls one out, tears it open with his teeth, and rolls the lubricated latex condom on. I want him badly. Zaelyn lies on top of me and slowly tries to enter my walls, while kissing my neck, breasts, and navel, but the entrance feels cemented. I squint because the pressure is not pleasurable. I feel as if I am a virgin. I inhale with anxiety as he tries to enter for the second time and my eyes close as the walls partially open. I exhale. He is larger than I thought. Then he tries a third time and he strokes once, twice, until the rhythm moves my body along. He palms my shoulders giving him more of grip and spreads my legs with his legs allowing him to have his way. Suddenly, I am in the driver's seat positioning on top riding him forward, backwards, sideways, and in a circular motion.

His arms extend on both sides of the bed and he pulls on the comforter for support. Sweat is dripping from my face, down my breasts and onto his stomach. He sits up and I continue to giddy-up horsy on his long, hard, stiff penis. Zaelyn flips me on my stomach and I am taking it doggy style. My head bobs as he thrusts with forcefulness. I moan loudly. That triggers him to go faster, harder, faster, and harder.

"Who's my baby?! Who's my baby?!" he stares at me with sweat dripping from his chin onto my back.

"Ooh baby, I am! I am," I mumble loud enough for him to hear while grinding my teeth into the goose down pillow. Zaelyn flips me on my back and places my legs on his shoulders getting a full workout; inward, outward, inward, outward until hip-hop beats formulate, pop, pop, pop! The wetness makes my vagina make beautiful music. My eyes roll back. He stands up and puts me on his hip as he pumps, and grabs my ass imprinting it with his fingerprints, as I palm his back and place one arm around his neck. His stamina is incredible! A loud howl cries out of him as he shuts his eyes tightly almost biting his lip. He is trembling out of control. I'm out of breath. But he is full of energy as if he has taken Viagra beforehand. I grit and grind my teeth some more, eyes fluttering and I wet my lips because my mouth's dry.

"I'm – c-c-c-, cu-, ccccuuummmiiinnn'!" I clamp both arms around his neck, tears scream down my face, at that second he releases while our bodies are sticky with our tropical juices. We both lean back wanting a smoke, but settle for a glass of water. Frantically we both realize that the condom has come off. I reach inside of myself and pull it out. Some of his thick semen resides in the tip, but the remainder is left inside of me. I rush to the bathroom to douche, hoping it will leak out. Zaelyn remains still until I return from the bathroom. I'm cautious not to say the wrong thing. I discreetly look towards him but he remains silent. He sits up and palms his face with his left hand, and shakes his head. I massage my face and began to pray silently. A moment of absolute pleasure may have turned into a life of regret or weeks of agony because the last thing I want is to become a single mother. Zaelyn stands up and walks into the living room for his clothes. I follow him. He gets dressed and stares at the rug as he buttons his shirt, never looking me directly in the eyes. I swear he makes me feel like he just paid for sex. Like, I'm some trick. Delicate walls start building up inside of me, but I don't let it show on the surface. Zaelyn states that he's getting ready to go, and this is when he looks me in my face and gives me a counterfeit smile. I see right through it. I nod in acknowledgment and lead him to the door. I give him a kiss on his cheek, say goodnight and slowly close the door. Zaelyn seems too calm, which throws up red flags. I may never see him again.

I come to.

And this is *now*.

I can't allow myself to be submissive and swept into his world again. I can't lose control and fall like a hopeless damsel in his arms. I can't let his charm persuade me. Or his handsomeness distracts me. Please, please, please Lord; give me the strength I need to fight the temptation? Give me something, anything to preoccupy my mind from thinking of him and his big black dick.

4

Dear Sis,

"I am too much of a mess right now," I say to myself. There is power in these words because I feel the strain in my voice. The crackling sound as I spit the words out of my mouth. I feel the lump form in my throat, the ache that shoots up to my eyes. They well up because the truth hurts that much.

Just yesterday I heard this gospel song coming from Mrs. Silva's apartment, echoing through her thin walls. A song by Jessica Reedy, "Blue God" and it really made me think about how I treat Him. That thought only seemed to last a split second and then I drifted in thought of me. Reminisced about me, and how close I was to having it all. I simply pushed Him aside. It was about me, me, me, and me...not realizing how I made Him feel, how blue He must've felt by my treatment toward Him. And I'd feel a smidgen of sadness, but then I'd revert back to me, me, me, me, me, and I'd get angry with Him feeling as though He didn't protect me as his daughter—feeling as though He rejected me as his daughter. Oh Father, I'd mumble so low as if I didn't want Him to hear me speak His name. Knowing deep down I needed Him, but how I couldn't expect Him to console me in my time of need when I called Him and then slammed the phone in His ear.

I felt as if I had stepped out of my womanhood shoes and stepped into my girlhood shoes and I'd realized that as a child, a young little black girl I believed that He could work miracles. My faith in Him was so strong, unbreakable. But somewhere in the midst of my troubles, my blues, I gave up on Him. I let go of that bond we'd shared because I was so hurt by Him not protecting me from harm. I needed His protection and He closed his eyes and allowed this to happen to me. I pushed Him aside. Shut my door—closed my windows. And I locked them both. And said the hell with Him!

But then I felt so bad, so low that I tried to reel myself back and put Him first, but all I seemed to continue to do was put me first. Cry, complain, bitch, moan and groan because I was not happy with myself. I mean, He showed me the light, of how promising it all would be and within a flash of a second everything disintegrated around me. And I darkened with animosity toward Him. I weakened. And my faith diminished down to the size of a mustard seed. I was black, no longer blue. No longer seen, no longer heard.

156

And then my mind drifted again and I thought about how He continued to work on me in spite of my behavior toward Him. How He helped lift me out of my darkness to see the light of opportunity. The things that seemed so far out of my reach He encouraged me to see the bigger picture and try to reach them anyway. He assured me that I could achieve any and everything I put my mind to. All I had to do was come back home. He'd welcome me with open arms. All I had to do was believe. Believe in Him, believe in me—believe in the power of unconditional love.

As a little girl He used to be the love of my life. As a woman He seemed to be an acquaintance of mine.

Honestly, Sis, I feel like I'm failing Him. And it makes me question: what will come of me? I know that I need to build up my faith but sometimes I just lose that part of me that used to be so faithful. With everything that has previously happened in my life I often wondered, how much more do I have to endure, Lord, before I begin to feel worthy again?

My mind started rambling and I found myself listening to those little voices in my head. It's hard to shut them off. Tune them out.

Slowly I tuned them out and began to listen to Jessica's song, "What About Me?" and in between the lyrics I heard Him asking me that one question. And then I asked myself, what about Him that makes me not lean toward Him? That makes me so afraid?

And then I revisited that me, me, me...again. And He left me where I was. And I left Him wherever He was. And since that time to now I have been struggling to talk to Him. Why? I don't really know.

Sis, will I die leaving no legacy behind? Will anyone remember me if I die? Care? Cry? Pray for me? Wish me to hell? Glory me to heaven?

Here I am in this big world all by my lonesome trying to find my purpose and fulfill it with pride. Lately I seem so flustered. Many questions find no resolution. I feel as if I exist only in my mind, my heart, my spirit, my soul. Others don't see me. You know what they see? HIV.

(Breathing out) Where do I go from here? Up? Down?

Throughout my life I never really asked myself those questions, seem strange to be thinking about it now. I guess back then I always knew that my life would be full and that I would be successful. There was never any doubt because that was what I was working toward. Yeah. I was on the right track, and then everything that I worked so hard to achieve seemed so much harder to hold, to grip, to keep. My will had weakened, girl. I crumbled. Yep. Crumbled.

After being tormented and beaten and violated, after being shunned, ridiculed, abandoned, ostracized, and stigmatized because of having HIV I began to question my abilities, capabilities. I began to self-doubt my potential. I began to realize that I no longer had options to pick and choose men anymore. Used to be where that was so easy—a given. He liked me. I liked him. Okay, let's see where this leads, I thought. I felt more in control to pick and choose who I wanted to spend my time with. Nowadays I'm the one who has to sit back and diligently wait for the phone to ring. Wonder if it will ever ring. I'm the one who now wishes to be chosen as someone's lover or friend or wife. Not someone's bitch, trick, slut, skank. Me. Avery—the woman who once had men eating out of her hands—flocking at my feet—snuggling up with me in my bed, twisting and tangling with me between my sheets, and drooling on my pillowcases. It's mind-boggling to me now as to how one is treated because of a life alteration. It's not like it was self-inflicted but folks don't care about that. They draw their own cliffhangers of this life that I live leaving me in suspense.

Don't get me wrong, I get it. I do. 'Cause if the shoe were on the other foot, I'd have some reservations too, I'd question. I'd ask. I'd probe. I'd research. I guessed it is different when you're the one wearing both shoes. I know. I know that I cannot expect someone to just whisk me in their arms and not be afraid of what I carry around in my body. Heck, I'm afraid. Truth be told, I'm afraid every day of my life. I'm afraid that one day I might wake up and instantaneously go blind. Or, can't speak or move. I'm afraid that this disease may debilitate me. I'm afraid of getting deathly ill and can't take care of myself. I'm afraid of many things, but mostly I'm afraid to be afraid.

Oh, I feel plenty of burdens, and I try with all of my might to be optimistic but sometimes my troubles get the best of me. And when they do, I find myself cowering within the little black girl hidden inside padlocked in my heart.

I nod my head up and down. Hmm. I think I made a grave mistake. Yes, I do. And it pains me so. Just tears me in two because I meant well. I had all this stuff bogged inside me that I needed to rid of because it was wearing me out. I felt I had no choice in the matter. I needed to find an escape. And I did. I sho' did.

You see, I don't know if me coming out and sharing my ordeal, I don't know if it was the best decision I'd made. It was impulsive of me. An imposition that I chose. Often I-I feel like I created more of a burden for myself. More of headache. More stress than I need. But what is a woman to do with so much stuff buried inside? Who does she confide in when her life has been turned upside down? Who will understand her anguish and agony? Women. That was my first initial thought. Other women. Women who have endured what I have. Women, who wish to share but can't find the strength within to do so. I carried the torch because I felt compelled to. Where is she supposed to release it all? How can she move onward with all of this stuff bottled up crippling her? Someone had to open up and release. So I did. I took that first step and let it out and I felt so light because I was so heavy. Initially I thought I was doing right by exposing myself, but it leaves me to wonder. Did I just make matters worse? Should I have kept my mouth shut and let pain stress me out to my grave? Just carry on with everyday life and act as if nothing ever happened?! I don't know. I'm not sho'.

I didn't think about myself when I released Anonymous, Sleepin' Wit' the Virus, and Kreepin' Wit' the Virus. I didn't think about the ramifications of my actions by using me as the cover model. I honestly didn't think anyone would want to read them. I didn't think it would make an impact on someone else's life. I didn't think about the negative aspects that would later empower me as the writer/author. I didn't think beyond that point. I merely wrote the books because they gave me as sense of purpose and peace of mind. I wanted to relinquish. Just let go, be done with it all, and move forward. But all I seem to be doing is going in circles. I see no open door for me to walk out of. I feel so trapped within, so confined, so vacant. Where is the light that so many folks speak of? Where is the sun? Where is the moon? Everything around me is so gray, so hazy, so dreary I feel like I'm already dead, or, perhaps, walking a thin line on death's trail.

I feel alienated after hearing of the rumors. The looks, whispering, snickers, stares made me feel segregated from my own black people. Women look down on me without even knowing me. All they seem to do is gossip and stare in my passing. Talk about me with folks who don't even know me on a personal level. I'm sho' they have questions but instead of approaching me they rather draw their own conclusion which is usually wrong. For some strange reason they feel as though they have to put their finger on something that doesn't even pertain to them. Or does it? Does it pertain to them and they are in denial or are they simply trying to put their finger on themselves without being found out? Hmmm. Men grow even more curious. Some ask questions. Not directly to me but to their buddies who may have seen me from time to time. Others remain quiet and try to study me. Try to figure it all out. But there is nothing to figure out because I have already exposed myself. And even then I have some folks still questioning, still digging, still probing to find something to satisfy their curiosity. Not curiosity about what I have shared but curiosity about is it her. Her? Meaning is it: Avery? Karla? Karla? Avery? At this point does it really matter? Can anything be changed? I can't be changed back to the woman I once was. Disease-free.

All I wanted was to free myself from the pain. And all I seem to have gained is more pain, more hurt, more havoc, more heartache.

Why can't I just be accepted as I am? Why can't I just be loved and nurtured and protected for the woman I am? Tell me, what more do I have to do? Should I stop while

I'm ahead? Should I just pretend that I'm fine and live my life with normalcy and never divulge my status to anyone new, I meet? Should I lie to myself? Should I lie to them? What should I do that I haven't already done? I wrote the books. I thought I was opening some dialogue for folks to talk about. I thought God was using me as a voice, a face, and just maybe I was making a difference. Suddenly I don't know if I made a difference. Women are still getting infected. Women are still dying from AIDS.

I tried my best. I gave in and kept trying, but I'm running out of purpose to fight. I'm running out of patience and understanding and motivation. I'm running out of words to express myself. What I'm trying to say is... I'm spiritually dying.

But then I reflect back to Daisy's life and I remind myself of how blessed I really, really am.

Who am I? Avery? Karla? Avery? Which?

You know what, Sis; some questions are better left unanswered.

Talk to you later, Sis

Avery

5

THIS WEIRD SENSATION SWEEPS across my chest. Within seconds I feel nauseous. Simultaneously I develop a throbbing headache. The pounding feels like someone is repeatedly hitting me over the head with a sledgehammer, nonstop. It is so excruciating that I have to sit still on the sofa until the pounding wanes.

There is an eeriness that smolders the living room like black smoke. I sit upright. Raise my feet and plant them on the soft cushion as my arms wrap around bare-skinned legs, chin rests upon knock-knees, mind dangling on past thoughts.

Face hangs haggard as an unwanted image appears in my head. Brows knit. *That stupid bitch! If she weren't already dead I'd kill her myself,* I think.

Deep-set brown eyes motion downward toward the grooves in the hardwood floor. Suddenly a series of wicked thoughts and hardhearted emotions envelop inside me.

My body stiffens. Lips tighten. Eyes squint. "Teka Teka Teka...you just couldn't leave well enough alone, now could you?" I express with bitter contempt in my tone. Eyes shift from side to side. "No. You just had to spring this on me as if I don't have enough on my plate. I guess this was your way of getting back at me for not wanting to be your friend. And you wonder why. This is your dirty little secret, huh? All this time *you* knew. And you never said a word to me. You wait until after you're dead to make amends! What kind of shit is this, Teka?! You grimy bony bitch! I should've known. Come to think of it, huh, I did know that you were always envious of me." Dead stare like to burn a hole in the floor. "Tell me, Teka, what got under your skin? Was it his spontaneous approach or, ah, his aggressive, erratic behavior for the likes of me that got your panties in a wad? Was it the thought of his *dick* ripping my insides out? Penetrating me? Was it the fact that he enjoyed squeezing my buttocks, my breasts, sucking and teething on my dark nipples? Which part, Teka? Was it his jealousy? Was he thinking about me, while he was *fuckin'* you? Tell me, did he say something to you that made you think of me? Is that what this is all about...your little insecurities, huh? Chile, I was *raped*!!! RAPED! It wasn't a moment of *consensual* sex. He *violated* me! Why couldn't you get that through your pretty little head? HE took something from me! And then, then HE gave me HIV! *Sicko!* You gotta be kidding me if you were jealous of that! You sick bitch!" I snarl and pace the floor burning hot. Breathing hard and heavy, I persist to give Teka a piece of mind.

Tight lines along my jaw line even out as my dark eyes light up with suspicion. Shakily, I say, "I wondered why you were constantly dangling your ring in my face. You wanted to make sure I didn't trespass your territory. That should've been the least of your worries, Teka. Every dang day you showed off that big ass rock! 'Ooh, Avery, look at this...' No. You didn't say it directly. You implied it. And every dang day I bit my tongue. I should've told you how I really felt, but I didn't want to hurt *your* feelings. But you, *you* couldn't stand the freedom I had—determination to not let *him* break me. Obviously, he broke you down. He had you running rampant with different men—out here selling yourself short. He pimped you out, controlled you and manipulated you to do things his way. What I can't figure out is what he said to convince you that he was in love with you. How stupid could you have been, Teka? Why, why, would you give all of your power away, especially to him of all people? Why didn't you fight? Tell me, why didn't you leave? Why did you stay? Now you're dead. Dead! I can't believe you did this to me! And then, then you had the *audacity* to send me a necklace with the initials: A.L." I huff, then narrow-eye the ceiling with tears welling up in my eyes.

"Johnnie, I can't seem to trust anyone. Why should I trust Teka? Give me one reason why I should? She got me stressing all out. Not knowing if this crazy man is lurking about, just waiting to strike again." I roll my eyes and wipe the tears that flow down my cheeks with the back of my right hand. "Why didn't she give me more to go on? Why did she leave me hanging like this? A part of me feels like she's lying about the whole thing like she conjured up all of this just to drive me crazy." A perplex look outlines my face. My tone reduces down to a whisper as I say to myself. "But how would she have known?" I purse my lips, and ponder in my head. *Oh, I get it.* Head bobs up and down. Slowly it begins to make more sense to me. *I'm 'sposed to know. Just fan my magic wand and his face will magically appear. How the hell am I 'sposed to know who the hell raped me!* My face and eyes burn with fury. My right foot stomps down hard on the floor. *Stomp! Stomp! Stomp!* "Tell me, Teka, how the fuck am I 'sposed to know that?"

Wide-eyed, face is dang near purple. I get tongue-tied in my head. It was dark in the back of that Electronics store." I ball up both fists and swing at the air. *Swish! Swish! Swish! Swish!* Exasperated. I keep swinging. *Swish! Swish! Swish!* Tears rush harder down my enraged face. "I just want to forget. Forget you! Forget him! Just forget it! Why, why, why can't I forget? God, please, just let me forget?" I drop to my knees and bawl even harder.

After about a thirty minute meltdown I pull myself up on my feet and walk toward the butter cream leather chaise longue and sit down. Head sways from side to side, puzzled. Tears continue to stream from my eyes as I ponder over every detail, every minute, every second, every hour of January 9th.

Click. Click. Click.

I hear the keen sound of my high heels. Simultaneously, my lips tremble, chin quivers, tension builds in my pensive face.

Click. Click. Click.

My hands rise to cover my ears to block out the sound. Then cover my eyes to block out the scenes I drop my hands to my sides and scream at the top of my lungs. "Stop! Stop! Stop!" Breathing erratically, I have to calm myself. God, I am losing my way again. Help me? I plead. Help me?

Feeling overwhelmed and hopeless I surrender all faith and fortitude. I dangle my head and whisper in a faint tone, "Teka, I can't do this anymore. I won't allow him to dictate my life. Destroy my progression. You were weak, vulnerable, and desperate." I lift up my head with an evil glare in my eyes. "I'm not. If anything, I'm mad as aw hell!"

I lean back against the chaise longue. Bloodshot red eyes stare at the high ceiling, restless and pained. I think to myself: *how many times are you going to relive this pain, Avery? How many times are you going to submit to the same ole bullshit? For what, closure? Revenge? Which is it? Are you ready to let go or get even?* Apprehension clouds my better judgment. Do I or Don't I? Do I really want to know? Don't I have a right to know? It's been so long ago. Maybe I should leave it alone and continue where I am. Leave the past in the past. Let the pain stagnantly lie where it rests.

Right leg hangs off the chaise longue. Right arm is tuck under my side as I sleep, lightly. I am hung-over with grief. As much as I try I can't seem to forget JaVonna confessing her pregnancy: *"That's right muthafucker. I m carrying your baby! What you got to say now?"* Over and over I keep hearing her ghetto ass slapping me in the face with this. And each and every time I feel myself breaking more and more, crying more and more, aching more and more. How could *Xavier* do this to us?

"*Look at the pot calling the kettle—*"

"*I'm not in the mood, Karma!*" I say aloud. "*Need you always have to throw up in my face what I've done? I know. Stacy Blazman. But I had no strong feelings for that man. He drugged me—coerced me into believing that he had fallen in love with me. Yeah. I was duped.*"

"*How do you know that for sure?*"

"*What are you trying to say, K? WHAT! You think I asked for this! No, no, that's not what, happened. From what I can tell Stacy has some mental issues.*"

"*As handsome as he...*"

"*Let me stop you right there, Karma! Looks have nothing to do with it. Stacy is a womanizer.*"

"*So you're telling me that you weren't attracted to him physically first?*"

"*No. Yes. Okay, yes, but it wasn't everything. I was actually trying to get to know him as a person. Look, the only reason I was willing to open the door was because I thought Xavier stopped loving me. It was time, Karma. It was time for me to move forward in my life. I have no regrets about moving forward. But I do ache over the fact that Stacy and I are still married. Mr. Clausen referred me to an attorney, ah, Mr. Norman Fest, who is currently working on getting this 'marriage' annulled. Okay. I get your point; K. Xavier wasn't just at fault.*"

Karma interjects, "*Why do you say that he was at fault at all? Think about it. All those men you screwed back in the day: Therron Bolton, Heath J. Efferson, Brian Adler, Zaelyn Homes, Grand and Fletcher. Oh, and let's not forget...Christopher Morehouse, which Xavier knows nothing about. Let's not be naïve here. You know just as well as I do that Xavier snooped and read Anonymous and Sleepin' Wit' the Virus, and that, my dear, is what turned him off. Men want to feel like they're the only one even though realistically they know that they're not. He could've been #101, but in his mind he's already accepted others, but he doesn't want to be reminded of them. The fact that your story is written in a book gives everyone access to knowing your business publicly. Imagine how that made him feels. I'm more than certain he had some doubts about how you really contracted HIV. Think about it, Avery. Think hard on that.*"

"*But, but, he could have easily asked me or called me to find out.*" I snap.

"*Stupid! How he gonna call you in a coma! Now, if you had come to, okay, then he could've if he had the strength within to do so. Xavier loved you for real. This wasn't any puppy love. That man was broken, girl, especially after he read about your life. The life you wrote, not some pseudonym you call yourself (Karla Denise Baker), you girl, you! He was hurt.*" Karma snaps back.

"*But, but...*"

"But, but, hell, Avery! You should've been the one to give him copies of those books."

"Wait a minute! Those books were written for me. I never told anyone that I wrote those books. It was merely for my own personal needs. They were written as a way for me to remember, and then forget. How else could I move forward? I didn't see any other way for me to move forward without family, friends, everyone I knew had died. How'd he get the copies anyhow?"

"Girl, you can be so slow sometimes. Detective Crenshaw found them in your house in one of the drawers and made Xavier aware of them. He interrogated Xavier to death. Practically threw the books in his face. Detective Crenshaw hammered him about your past."

I shake my head.

"My intention was never to hurt Xavier. I love him."

"That you may, but now you should understand how easily it was for JaVonna Banks to manipulate a vulnerable man. So, you can't fault him because he didn't know when or if you were going to come back to him. Whether you came out of the coma or not, you could've chosen to leave him. He was scared just as much as you were."

"Love is love. He should've waited for me, but instead he left me in the cold to rot away alone—to die alone. That hurt me. And then you see what happened. YOU see, don't you! She's PREGNANT by my man!"

"So you're jealous?"

"Did you not hear me?! Xavier abandoned me when I needed him the most. He walked away and forgot I ever existed. I guess I am a little jealous. You have to understand I've loved this man with everything in me, and this skank comes and ruins everything!"

"Didn't you do the same thing to her? Wasn't it you who ruined her relationship with Danell?"

"I had nothing to do with her relationship with Danell. I never came on to Danell. She came on to me!"

I shake my head again. "No. That was not my doing." I say with a scowl outlining my face.

"Okay. Okay, calm down. I believe you. So, do you wish any harm to JaVonna or her unborn baby, maybe just a little?"

I take a second to think about this question. 'Do I wish JaVonna or her unborn baby any harm?'

"I plead the fifth."

"You plead the fifth. What kind of answer is that?"

"Listen, don't you have something to do besides get on my nerves?"

"Actually, no, no, I don't. Answer the question, Avery."

"NO! I don't have to answer such an ugly question. Won't you just leave me alone?"

"I'd rather stay and continue to pick your brain."

"I am 'bout to tune you out."

"Oh, really?"

"Yes, really. You can't never just be on my side for a change, Karma. You always gotta psychoanalyze me with all these doggone questions. If it ain't you, it's Avona. Why don't you two just leave me alone?"

"All you had to say was: 'Karma lay off a bit because I'm going through something.' But, no, you don't know how to do that without hurting my feelings."

"Your feelings!"

"Yes, bitch, my feelings! How quickly does one forget? I'm all you got. You better learn how to appreciate me."

"I got better things to do than to sit here and take this abuse from you, Karma."

"Really?"

"Yes, really."

Hands land on my forehead as I smack smack smack and yell, "Get outta my head! Disappear. Leave me the hell alone!"

"How you plan on living with him still in the picture?" Karma asks.

"Who?"

"Him."

"Him who?"

"Him! Avery, stop acting like you don't know whom I'm talkin' about. Do I need to spell it out for you? R. A. P. I. S. T."

"Now why'd you have to go there, Karma?"

"Look, girl, you need to deal with what is coming next. You can't run. You can't hide. You need to handle this because you don't know when or where he may strike again."

6

W-W-WHAT THE HELL! I tilt my head slightly to the right trying to get a good angle of the image. Who could've been so bold as to send *it* to my cell phone? I wonder. Can't be anyone I know. Hmm, can it?

The image is crystal clear—might be about eight or nine inches long, thick width and deep dark-skinned with bulging veins. Goodness. It's standing firmly erect. Uninhibited. Shit!

I cannot believe someone would be so daring as to text me an image of their *penis*. Here I am at my peak of my womanhood and some stranger sends me a picture of his pecker as if to say: "I know what you've been missin'. Look at it. Be honest with yourself. Don't you miss it? Miss the way it feels deep inside you."

All I can do is nod.

Yeah. I miss it. I miss the hell out of it, but—

Looking at it, dang, it's like, like it's talking to me through that little pee-hole sayin': "Avery, come and get this big black dick. You know you want it. Girllll, c'mon, it got your name written all over it." Dang! Even his voice sounds confident.

Yeah, right! It is not that simple. Maybe back in the day I had it like that, but now...please! I'm lucky if I can still get a wet tongue kiss. That's the highlight of my foreplay.

Folks these days are no longer discreet. Shame is a thing of the past. Who would do such a thing? Only someone who is not embarrassed—someone vain. I gotta give it to 'im. Whoever he is, he sho' is blessed. I clamp my legs together. Sho' is blessed! Dang.

I am tempted to send a reply back, but I think against it. With all these perverts out here I don't want to send off the wrong message and find myself in a situation. So I take a few more glances, and then finally hit, Delete.

"What's it gonna be, Avery?!" Avona snaps. "Are you really gonna sit here and stuff your face with Edy's ice cream, Entenmanns (butter, chocolate, marble loaf) pound cakes, Famous Amos cookies, tortilla chips and spinach dip, a foot-long hoagie and a six-pack of Coronas while sitting your frumpy behind in front of the flat screen

doing nothing but having a pity party, breaking wind, gaining weight, and sulking about shit you can't change? I can't believe you, girl! I really can't. What you need to do is take your greedy ass in that kitchen, open your freezer and pullout either that salmon or tilapia and make yourself a healthy meal. Hell, make a green salad for all I care! Eat some fruit. Steam some fresh vegetables. Yogurt. Eat something other than that shit you're eating now. If my memory serves me right wasn't it you who said something about watching your dietary intake. You said something about wanting to watch your cholesterol. You were the one saying that you were going to stop eating red meat and cut back on the potatoes, white rice, and pasta because you were getting a little pudgy around the midriff section. It was you who said that you were going to commit to only eating fish and chicken, but that you really wanted to stop eating chicken and just eat fish. Then you have the nerve to pullout the baking pans. In here getting your Betty Crocker skills on with those doggone cheese and carrot and German chocolate cakes you make from scratch. And you know how you like to make them cakes rich as hell. How you expect to watch your weight if you keep eating like you is? And then you wonder why you can't fit your clothes. What do you expect if you keep getting up at midnight making honey turkey and Swiss cheese sandwiches and drinking soda pop? Then you have the nerve to take your ass to bed like you haven't eaten anything. When the last time you actually drank some water? Cleanse yourself out, huh? And what's up with the head? Don't you own a comb? Because those naps on that head of yours need to be popped! When the last time you've seen some clippers, huh? All these damn barbershops around the way and you mean to tell me you can't find one. Is that what you're tryna tell me? How you expect to keep that handsome man of yours, huh? I'ma tell you right now, I don't wanna hear shit if Xavier leave your fat, nappy-headed funky ass! Not one damn thang! Av, I thought you had shit under control but I can clearly see you don't. Don't make me do it! Don't make me press the speed dial button and call Dr. Cristal. 'Cause you know I will! I'll have her here so fast it'll make your head spin. Girlfriend, you are in desperate need of an intervention! You really need to get back in the driver's seat and take charge of your life. I don't know what's going on with you, but by the looks of things it surely ain't good."

"Mind your business!" I bark back while crunching on a mouthful of tortillas.

Avona huffs. "Hold up! Wait a damn minute! I know you ain't getting new on me! Look. I'm only looking out for you. I don't see anyone else knocking on your door or ringing your buzzer to see how you're doing. They could care less, bitch!"

Huff. Huff.

I look to my right and gaze at the flickering flames coming from the blue sage and vanilla candles setting on the saffron coffee table that invites a delicate fragrance throughout my place. At least before I fell into my slump I managed to cleanup my apartment. That's one thing I can say I like about myself no matter what I am going through I make certain there are no leftover dirty dishes in my kitchen sink overnight. The Hotpoint stove doesn't have any grease popping residue on it 'cause I wipe it down every day and night after I use it. The Cuisinart pots and lids are neatly placed in the cupboards. All of my condiments, sauces, soups and assortment of herbal teas are aligned on the top, middle, and bottom shelves. The RCA microwave is cleaned every day. And the carousel seasoning rack is fully restocked.

The bathroom sink is clean 'cause I softly scrub it with Comet and sometimes wipe it good with Clorox bleach. My toilet bowl is fresh and clean 'cause I scrub it and then pour some bleach in it to kill any germs that might've lingered. I lift up the toilet seat to make sho' ain't no splotches of urine or feces visible. And if it is I make sho' I put some extra elbow grease in it and clean that grime away. My bathtub doesn't have any dirt rings around it. I make sho' it shines a pearly white. That bathtub is my sanctuary. I decorate the corners of the tub with an eclectic assortment of candles and I keep an extra bottle of bubble bath handy 'cause I never know when I may run out, especially on those tiresome, burdensome days. I am a stickler for a hot bubble bath. Just the feel of the soothing water against my body, hurtin' head leaned back on the fluffy bath pillow makes me think I'm in another place and time. Slowly the lids of my eyes close and my mind drifts. I drift far away. Sometimes I reminisce about Johnnie and me slow dancing off of India Arie's "Ready for Love." That memory gives me so much peace, so much comfort when I feel overwhelmed with blues. It nourishes my spirits 'cause it truly depicts Johnnie as a human being. Truly does. That song speaks so highly of him and every time I listen to it it brings me to tears 'cause I had such a selfless, beautiful friend who loved me so much. I don't know how, and I often wondered if it were possible for his spirit to have journeyed to India's mind, heart, and soul 'cause she knew him well. Better than I *ever* did or could.

The bathroom gets swept and mopped every other day. Kitchen floor too. And the hardwood floors never neglected 'cause I mop them with Murphy oil soap at least once a week. I dust mop it every other day, too to keep it clean 'cause I have a tendency to walk barefoot. I like to feel the wood under the soles of my feet. The GE (General Electric) refrigerator gets cleaned out every Saturday. And I make a habit of putting a fresh box of baking soda in the corner to keep it smelling fresh.

I don't bother to do anything to the freezer 'cause it defrosts itself. Everything from the: bedroom, living room, kitchenette, bathroom, closets and pantry stays tidy. I pride myself on keeping an immaculate place. Mostly 'cause it is a reflection of how I view myself. Yes, I *now* view myself as a woman HIV-positive. Down to the artifacts, knickknacks, vibrant colors, mixed-matched furniture, lamps, utensils, plates, glasses, mugs, towels, books, any and everything that is set in this living space is a reflection of me.

I stare in outer space, thinking, Avona just doesn't get it. She can't possibly understand what I am currently going through. No one can unless they have experienced all the loss that I have.

I'm hurting right now. I'm horny and hurting and hungry, shit! And it ain't a damn thing I can do 'bout it but soothe my pain with comfort food.

Okay. I'll agree I'm not quite myself. But what does she expect me to do. It's like loss after loss after fuckin' loss. There is only so much I can take. I mean, I feel like I've had my share over the years. Poppa. Ma'am. Johnnie. Jewell. Antwone. Every birthday! Every anniversary! Every Thanksgiving, Christmas! Every memory! It's a lot to take in, a lot to swallow. I'm just tired of losing out—never gaining anything but another loss. I'm stressed and downright depressed. Sue me.

I tune Avona out and revert back to watching television.

"She knows she wrong." I belt out. What gets my panties in a wad is that she has the nerve to—

I know. I gotta bad habit of talking back to the television, but this hussy is wrong. Dead wrong!

For some strange reason the Maury Povich Show has a tendency to tick me off. It pushes buttons in me I never knew could be pushed. My face gets all hot along with my body and I start acting like it's me sitting in the hot seat listening to this, this...nonsense! *Then why do you keep watching it if it disturbs you so?* I hear a voice say in my head.

I don't know why I keep watching these shows. I guess 'cause I don't have anything else better to do. Its entertainment, and right now I need to be entertained.

My bare feet move backwards toward the saffron sofa, my eyes still engrossed in the show. I sit down as Maury begins to explain the situation between the ex-couple.

Maury is neatly dressed in a grayish-blue cashmere V-neck sweater and brown slacks as he faces his guest, Shaniqua Loutish who is seated with her thick legs crossed at the ankles.

"Shaniqua Loutish," I say back to myself. "Isn't she *white*?" I purse my lips. These white girls kill me wanting to be black. You ain't gonna sit here and tell me that her white momma named her Shaniqua. I can't see it. 'Cause for one she don't look like no dang Shaniqua. Maybe Peggy-Sue, Heather, Tiffany, Kati, Marybeth...maybe, but not Shaniqua. Chile, please. She done got a piece of some black dick and don't know how to act. That black dick done blew her mind that the girl can't remember her birth name. Dang!

According to Shaniqua somebody's been creeping and sleeping with her man and she intends to get to the bottom of it. I can tell she's a bit insecure—more than a handful. Yep. Her body language is definitely giving her away. And plus, she hasn't stopped flapping her gums since she came out onstage. She looks like she is ready to duke it out. Her hands are balled and resting on her lap. Her eyes look dark and her face is a crimson color which means she is burning up inside. I got a feeling this ain't gonna be good once the man comes strolling out. It is just a gut feeling.

In one hand Maury has a cue card gripped between his thumb and forefinger and in the other hand he holds the mike. "Well, let's hear the other half of this story, shall we." Maury says looking out toward the audience. "Okay, Shaniqua, your baby daddy is here. Swag, come on out."

The audience claps as they see Swag with his chocolate self strolling out all smooth and casually dressed in saggy jeans with matching jean jacket, white T-shirt and camel-colored Timberland boots making his way to the stage. All of a sudden the audience is divided as some boo Swag to get offstage and take his good-for-nothing-ass home. Others seem to want to hear what he has to say.

Maury extends out his hand to shake Swag's and invites him to have a seat. But before Swag has a chance to sit down Shaniqua jumps out of her seat and gets all up in Swag's face talking smack. All you see is a million unkempt cherry-red dreadlocks swaying from side to side and her mouthpiece moving a mile a minute. Swag is standing still trying to block her pointed finger out of his face.

"Give the brother a break," I snap back at the screen. Finally, Maury intervenes and Swag sits down. Shaniqua sits down too but she ain't satisfied. Her face is all twisted up. And her outfit is atrocious. I believe she came on this show to make an ass out of herself. And thus far, she is doing a fantastic job!

I rise off the sofa to go to the fridge to get another beer. As I am walking toward the kitchenette I turn my body around and snap again.

"What! C'mon now. Honey. And you have the nerve to bitch about him. Girlllll, have you looked in the mirror 'cause um you could stand to hit *Weight Watchers-Jenny Craig-Lucille Roberts* yo damn self. He's a nice-looking fellah." I grimace, and then shake my head. These young girls really crack me up.

While looking for the bottle opener I vent aloud.

"See, see, Shaniqua, you starting off on the wrong foot," I snap back at the screen. "What's with all the yelling, huh? The man is sitting right next to you, just as calm as he can be so there is no need for you to be trying to shine in front of your girls by yelling like you ain't got no goddamn sense. Chill." I roll my eyes and tighten up my lips but it's hard because this girl is soooo dense!

I have to remind myself that she's young. And even though she looks like a woman, mentally she hasn't grown into her womanhood. The 'hood part, yeah, she has that down pat, but the woman, no, she still has more growing to do. And that mouth of hers needs to be washed out with turpentine!

I frown. She just disappoints me every time she opens her big mouth. Where is the logic? Commonsense? Something?

"Shaniqua! Shaniqua Loutish. Oh, you just gonna act like you can't hear me, huh?" With my big toe I turn the sterling silver toe ring on my second toe in a circular motion, then snuggle my long toes in the thick paisley throw rug. Point my index finger toward the television screen and snap back at it again. "I SEE why he stays quiet. He CAN'T seem to get a word in edgewise. You just GOTTA have the last word, DON'T you? You KNOW WHAT, Shaniqua, you got too much mouth with very little to say because all I am hearing is you rambling on and on about nothing! Get the story straight. Get the dang story straight 'cause, Shaniqua, you lyin' up a storm on national television."

I narrow eye her. "Girl, please. You just are making a complete fool out of yourself. It don't make no doggone sense!" My head sways from side to side with spit flying out of my mouth. "You're a mother! That's why he wants your ghetto ass home with the baby. Leila is only two! Two, hussy! But no, you'd rather be up in some club getting your freak on with some fool you don't even know! Dropping it like it's hot. And you wonder why Swag's upset. C'mon now. You sound realll childish. Real childish!" I pause to try to compose myself, but—

I sit back down on the sofa. My eyes stretch, head moves all around like a bobble head doll and my forehead crumples up real tight. "Well, then, you should've kept your legs closed if you weren't ready to have a baby! Stop fucking and you won't have to worry about this shit happening again! What you think motherhood is a joke? A friggin' game! Motherhood is a fulltime job, tramp!" I cut my eye sharp at her. "What *you* say?" I could've sworn I heard her say something slick back to me.

I twist up my face and get up off the sofa and walk closer toward the television set as if I am all up in her redbone face. I scrunch up my nose and slowly my eyes scroll her up from her wide feet to the flabbiness around her stomach to her no bra wearing droopy breasts to her no neck self until I finally reach her rotund face painted with all sorts of colors of cheap makeup and back down to her wide feet that are too wide for her cheap Rainbow Shop shoes. I look at her like the white trash that she is. I continue to stare her down. "What?" Again, I thought I heard her say something slick back to me. I roll my eyes in disdain. "Look at you! Let's talk 'bout that, why don't we." I smack my lips ready to give her another piece of my mind. "YOU'RE on NATIONAL television, broad, dressed as a 'hood rat! That getup you're wearin' ain't even cute! You have no home training. How you gonna be a mother to your daughter Leila when you can't even conduct yourself as a lady on television or out in public, huh? How old are you *eighteen, nineteen, sixteen, seventeen?*" This chile is working my last dang nerve.

Shaniqua sucks her teeth and flings her dreadlocks as if she is the fuckin' bomb.

Oh... no... she... didn't!

With narrowing eyes I scan the floor until I eye one of my fluffy lavender slippers sticking out from under the sofa. I pick one up with the intent to pop her in her big mouth.

With all the arm strength I can muster up I throw the slipper at the television screen popping her *hard* in the left eye. My whole body shakes in laughter. "Now, shut the hell up! Don't listen to her, Swag. Swag. Swag. J-just leave the stage. Get up and walk off, dude. You don't need this type of abuse from this melodramatic chick. She buggin'. Move on. Forget that hussy!"

Quite perturbed by the fact that Swag is still sitting next to Shaniqua I grab the remote and flick the television OFF!

These trifling bitches that go on these talk shows make me sick especially on the Maury Povich Show. Why must young girls and women go on national television to air out their dirty laundry? It's so simple to have these dragged out arguments and catfights behind closed doors at home. Why act a fool in front of the whole wide world? It is an embarrassment toward family as well as themselves.

I just don't get it. I mean, if Swag doesn't want to be with Shaniqua anymore, what is the big friggin' deal? Okay. They have a beautiful daughter together. Swag's paying child support, so why can't *they* seem to move on and let that shit go? Drama. That's why. They like the drama. 'Cause drama keeps them *fucking*. Drama is like an aphrodisiac for them. You aint gonna sit here and tell me that Swag ain't still tappin' that fat sloppy ass.

For one, Shaniqua is too upset. Dead giveaway. Why you think that is? I'ma tell you why. 'Cause she ain't getting the dick on the regular. Yeah. She used to be his queen. But now, honey, that dick is being shared and Shaniqua don't like it one bit. But 'ey, wait a minute. She brought that on herself.

I'ma tells you how.

Shaniqua had this hardworking strong black man supporting her and their baby. All she had to do was: keep the house clean, cook dinner, wash his dirty drawers, give him some pussy whenever he wanted it, and put the check in their bank account. But no, she's too busy listening to her trifling girlfriends—talkin' about Swag doin' this, and Swag doin' that. How they know what the hell he doing? She should've asked herself that pertinent question. But see, Shaniqua was too slow in that department. It didn't even occur to her that she broadcasted her business and opened the door for one of her girlfriends to step in and *fuck* her man. How did that happen, you ask? Well, Shaniqua was too busy running her fuckin' mouth about all the *good* things Swag was doing for her. Now this piqued her so-called girlfriend, Nikki's curiosity, especially after her man, Khool had walked out on her for her good friend, RaRa. It ain't nothing but...drama.

This is the kind of shit that pisses me off with women. It does not take Ugly Betty to figure this here shit out. All you have to do is a few things to keep your man satisfied: cook, clean, look good, smell good, talk with some commonsense, act like a lady, be a freak behind closed doors, and when a dispute... shut the fuck up and allow him to have the last damn word. (Okay. Lemme stop lyin' on that one 'cause if a joker talkin' crazy I gotta set him straight) But you don't do as I do, okay.

Now, if you do all these things, best believe you'll keep that man and he'll keep you laced up and down in fake furs, fake diamonds and fake pearls. You know what you got, girl, so you can't expect the real shit if your man is only making DPW (Department of Public Works) money, honey. His money is looking quite funny these days but he does what he gotta do to please your fake bougie ass!

You still don't get it, huh? Lord has mercy. You young hussies kill me! Okay. Sighing.

Let me try a different approach to get through to you dumb asses. I'm going to keep it real for a moment. And please, please don't take this the wrong way. Are y'all listening?

Now, if you have *good* pussy you automatically have a steady paycheck, full access to both savings/checking bank accounts (plus his little play money bank account), ATM card, credit card, pension and 401k, and any insurance policies. Now you may be insulted by that, and its okay, but for some women that's how they survive. That's how they make their hustle—make ends meet. You know support their habits, children, man or men, or women, and repeat the cycle day in and day out. I ain't too surprised because this has been going on since the beginning of time.

Women use what they got to get what they need. I even hustled a few men in my day, but never to the point where I was getting compensated for sex. Let me backtrack 'cause some men may beg to differ.

Okay, I've gone on dates where men have paid for the meal and drinks, jazz club, and have taken me home and all I'd do was give him a good night kiss on the lips, no tongue, call him the next day, and that was it. There was no sleepover's, no quickies, no fucking in the backseat of his Mercedes, none of that. If I felt highly respected, that only led to me possibly having a second or third date with him. And if he didn't pressure me like some men do today, huh, I *might* have obliged his curiosity, especially if he was a gentleman and if I was physically attracted to him in a sexual way.

If he had that "something extra" that tasted like filet mignon...you know how it melts in your mouth and made me tingle between the legs and he treated me like a lady I'd perhaps *fuck* him. But best believe that's all it would be simply because I wasn't looking for a "permanent" man. Back in the day "temporary" was mo' my speed.

7

WITH MY RIGHT HAND I slide the oatmeal-colored cloth shower curtain to the side. Index finger pushes the lever down as I turn the nozzle and steamy hot water sprouts out and fills the bathtub. Setting on top of a wooden elephant coaster alongside the tub is a flute glass filled with chilled *Papi* Cabernet. To the rear of the tub is two lit candles on each corner, burning a delicious fragrance of sandalwood jasmine. A bar of *Dove Summer Care* with lotus petal and seagrass scent soap is set in a soap dish on the edge of the right-side of the tub. A white and hot pink polka dot spaghetti strapped Victoria's Secret satin negligee hangs freely from the hook attached to the door. A pair of worn black checkerboard boy shorts and wife beater tee is sprawled across the shaggy oatmeal-colored bath rug that accentuates the tiled earth-tone floor.

An olive-green Cynthia Rowley wash cloth and hand and bath towel hangs from the towel rack.

Facing front the medicine cabinet to the right of me there is an Art.com print of a deep dark-skinned African woman with a natural cut and big hoop earrings walking barefoot along the beach in a leopard-print string-bikini with a black panther walking alongside her as she admires the crystal blue-green waters.

To the back of me are two more prints of African women dressed in dashikis and matching head wraps against the egg-shell colored walls.

The sink is cluttered with a fresh tube of Colgate Baking soda and Peroxide toothpaste, neon pink toothbrush stands erect in the holder, a container of Dermasil hand wash is set near the faucet handles, an opened container of Dove cleartone deodorant, a tube of Retinol Correxion Deep Wrinkle Daily Moisturizer, Nivea almond and Hydro IQ body lotion, a bar of honey and almond goat milk soap sets in the soap dish, and a black Conair wide-toothed comb lays on its side along the sink counter along with a bottle of Palmer's moisturizing hair milk.

The basin of the sink is speckled with dry hair dandruff from me scratching my scalp with the wide-toothed comb. I am in a need of a shampoo and deep conditioning, but I am not in the mood to do it this evening, maybe tomorrowor the day after, probably next week. Last I heard a little dirt never killed anybody.

I test the temperature of the water with my index finger to make sure it is not too hot. I then slip my nude body into the body of water and lean all the way back feeling as though I am floating on air.

With all the stresses of the week, fatigue seeps through my achy body and crackling bones.

My right hand extends reaching for the flute glass of wine. I take a sparse sip and let the wine ease down my throat. I open my mouth and let out a soothing aaaahhhhhhhhh sound. It's been some long days, some heavy burdensome days too. Lately I've been feelin' completely worn-out from doing simply nothing. Nothing but fantasize of "Mista Maybe" "Mista Someday" "Mista Do-Okay" comin' to sweep me up off these here tired feet and gets me away from all of this, this nothingness.

Well, not nothingness I should say. Between keeping house and running errands and doctor visits, picking up my refills of medication from Mr. Clyde's Pharmacy and my bi-weekly sessions with Dr. Cristal I'd say my plate is overflowing with things to do. I guess I wished I was tired from working a nine to five.

No one has called as of yet. And quite frankly I'm on the verge of giving up on hoping that someone does call in regards to a position. Right about now I'd take just about anything paying an honest wage, because this GA (General Assistance) check ain't putting a dent in shit. Lord knows if my rent wasn't subsidized I'd be one homeless chile.

Erasing all the stresses from my mind I indulge in thinking about nothing at the moment. I guess this is what some call meditation. Clearing your head of all that clutters and starting from a clean slate.

Hmm.

It sho' feels good to have nothing to think about. No worriation. Sho' feels mighty good.

After my bath I reach for the bottle of Lysol cleaner alongside the toilet and spray the bathtub and wipe it down with a thick blue sponge to a sparkling shine.

Still in the nude I kneel down and pull from underneath the sink a container of Cantu shea butter hair dressing pomade. With the wide-toothed comb I part sections of my tightly coiled salt-and-pepper natural hair and grease my itchy, dry, and thirsty scalp.

177

8

MEGABUS.COM IS MY FIRST initial route to visit Sisal and Tyree in North Carolina, but the closest I can get to North Carolina is either Durham or Charlotte and I don't know how much of a distance that is from Clarkton. Already I am gaining a headache.

Traveling can be a pain in the butt sometimes. But what would I really know 'bout traveling. I haven't been as far as my living room for the past several years. Imagination traveling, I do very well. Heck...let me tell it I've been some of everywhere: London, Italy, Texas, Africa, Atlanta...I mean I'm a *traveling fool*!

I tilt my head back and chuckle 'cause that is hilarious. Chile, don't get me started 'bout traveling out of this place. I'm 'bout tired of staring at these four walls and talking to myself in the bathroom mirror.

I rise to my feet and take three steps into my living room. I lean over and pullout my Jill Scott's "Beautifully Human" CD from the CD holder. I know she has a new release out but I haven't been out lately. And when I did go to Record City to purchase some new CDs I was rudely surprised that it was *now* a hair braiding place. That's how long I've been chillin' at home. Uh-huh.

I slip the CD in the Samsung CD player.

As soon as I hear her voice I feel myself opening and her positive reinforcement inspiring, lifting me out of my gloom. Goodness. She really knows how to feed my spirit.

With my arms swaying in the air and my hips swirling in circles I feel the rhythm hit me in all the right spots: my mind, my heart, and my soul. Yeah, I should be living my life like its golden. What's stopping me? I don't quite know the answer to that question as of yet. I'd have to get back 'atcha with a response. And please, don't trip. I ain't gonna leave you hangin'. I just need a little time to figure it out. I don't wanna mislead *you* into thinking one thing, and then I realize it's another. I just need a little patience and time. Once I figure it out I'll be sho' to let you know. Yes, I promise.

"Sing it, girl!" *La, la, laaaa...yes, it does take mo' than diamonds to woo me. La, la, laaaa...it takes mo' than money to groove me. Sho' you're right, Jill!*

Material things don't get my panties wet either. Shit. I can't remember that last time I had a puddle in the seat of my thong.

"I Keep" oh, that's my jam!

Girl, I know 'bout smiling when I come through and crying when I need to, too. Jill you ain't said nothing but the truth.

The invite to get away comes, unexpectedly. If Tyree never tried to find me on Facebook I would have never known how they were doing or that they wanted me to come and visit. It slipped my mind that Sisal might've lost my cell phone number. Really, it did. I'm not that bad that I wouldn't want him to have it. And yes, I could've kept in touch, but I just was moving on, you know. Trying to patch up those open wounds from when they were here. It's still hard, but I'm doing okay.

I will admit, lately, I've been in this funk. Not so much feeling bad as in sickly, but feeling bad in general. I really don't know what is wrong with me. Lately, everything seems wrong. I feel weird in my own skin. Food tastes weird. I look weird. Blah, blah, blah. Lord knows I need new scenery just to clear my head—de-clutter all of this disheveled mess scattered 'bout in my brain.

I *never* thought that I'd be here again, but here I *is* as these country folks say. I sniff. Mmmmmm. Just the smell of cleanliness in the air lets me know I'm far away from home. It feels pretty dang good.

I stand to my feet, smooth out the crinkles in my heather-gray cardigan merino sweater that overlaps my light-gray jersey tee. The twenty dollar pair of dark denim jeans I am wearing is snug to my hips and buttocks. Just the way I like 'em to fit. My body feels rested. Thus far this trip seems to be doing me swell.

I step one rust Italian leather boot off the train and then the other. Amtrak Train Station in Fayetteville, North Carolina, is quite congested for 2:00 p.m. It kind of reminds me of Paterson, during the first of the month.

The enclosed waiting area is flooded with folks and luggage and backpacks and duffel bags and business suits and leisure wear and high-heels and sneakers and long, short and shoulder-length assorted hair colors on women of varies ages, shapes and sizes and a slew of whiny children, both infants and toddlers. There are few adolescents sitting on the floor talking on their cells and texting their fingers off. There are ticket booths, vending machines, ATM's and restrooms. I must say the women here look like they eat well. Some are so plump and thick I wonder how they can stand the summer, especially when temperatures rise to 105 degrees. I'd have to relocate because there is no way in hell I'd be able to stand the sweltering heat waves and all that cushion of blubber upon rolls of blubber. I shake my head. Ain't no way! I'd like to die. Just suffocate in my skin.

I spoke to Sisal while on the train. I could hardly hear his country self with the poor reception but I was able to make out him saying that he'd be here to pick me up. There was no way I was driving here again. That was too long of drive when I came the first time for Jewell's Home-Going. I took the easier route this go-around and hopped on a train. It was bus, train, or plane. And Avery doesn't do planes. Not with all these talks of plane catastrophes. Uh-huh.

Sisal say to look out for a white Lincoln Continental. And that he should be pulling up in less than forty-minutes 'cause he gotta stop and get Tyree from his little under the table job. Job? Say he work in some convenience store called Willow-Bee not too far from here. I can't believe that boy working now. I smile, and then think to myself, *I know you'd be so proud of him, Jewell.*

The way Sisal talk about that boy he sho' sound like a proud father. Tyree has been doing real good in school. I think he's in high school, but I'm not sho'. Lord, time sho' flew by. It was just Sunday, December 16, 2008, when I found out I had a sister. Unfortunately she was taken before I had the opportunity of getting to know her. But God, he looked out for me because I was able to connect with her sons, my nephews. How sweet is that?

Sisal say Tyree help out around the house. Mow the lawn, shovel the little snow they do get, help in Sisal's garden, and wash the cars, and take out the trash. Pretty soon he'll be talking, if he ain't already, about getting his driver's license, then a piece of a car.

Suddenly my smile turns upside down as I wonder how Antwone would've turned out had he still been here. Quite often that travels through my mind. But I gotta bad habit of shutting it out 'cause it's still raw. Still sore—tender to the touch, but I have to look on the brighter side of things. He's in a better place. No mo' sufferin'. No mo' silent pain.

Waiting for Sisal I find myself pacing. I made reservations to stay at the Comfort Inn Fort Bragg-Fayetteville Hotel. There ain't no way I can stay in his house. I just ain't got the stomach to do it, especially with Jo-Ruthie there. Don't get me wrong, she seems like she could be a nice lady, but if I had to keep it real. That woman is bitterer than apple cider vinegar. I just ain't willing to compromise by putting up with her shit. So

I prefer to stay in a hotel to keep the peace. And plus, I heard that there is a Books-A-Million in the vicinity, which is good because I am in the mood for a good read while on this mini vacation.

I am a little jittery. North Carolina, can't believe I came back for the second time. Clarkton was like a quiet walk—kinda peaceful. I guess one would look at it as a good place to write. I guess I would too had I been a novelist. Kind of makes me wonder if this is how that author Nicholas Sparks gets inspired. Sho' is beautiful.

I glance at my Timex wristwatch and saunter inside to the waiting area until Sisal arrives. As I sit down and stretch out my legs Sisal pulls up in this shiny white Lincoln Continental. Only reason I know its Sisal is because Tyree jumps out of the car and pulls open the door yelling my name like a damn lunatic. Under other circumstances I'd act like I don't know him, but since I am in a new setting I don't mind one bit. If anything, I'm happy he still remembers what I look like.

I stand to my feet and greet him as he opens his arms wide and gives me a bear hug. "Look at you," I say to him, "You growing like tree, young man." Tyree smiles from ear to ear. Goodness! He looks so grown up and well-groomed. I swear he looks like that rapper DMX. And he gotta little facial hair going on too. And a few pimples on his forehead but nothing a little ProActiv can't get rid of. His hair is light-brown and cut low on his scalp. He looks like he just got a fresh cut. He's dressed casual in a pair of tan Dickies and a white polo shirt that has Willow-Bee embroidered on the shirt pocket and a pair of icy-white Air Force Ones. "Single-aunty," Tyree says in a crackling puberty voice, "Aunty Av, I'm so glad you came. I wasn't sho' if I'd be able to find you. Grampa couldn't remember your number. He knew he wrote it down but he couldn't remember where he'd put it. So I figured I'd try Facebook. I wasn't sho' if you had a profile or not. Grampa Sisal say try it anyhow since you have your business and all. *Had my business.* I think to myself. He said maybe you had some advertisement on there like Mr. Witty with his garden vegetables. I prayed on it. And look, here you is." I smile and drape my arm around his broad shoulders as we walk toward Sisal's car.

Tyree opens the passenger's-side door and I climb in. He shuts the door like a true gentleman and hops in the back seat.

Sisal looks the same with the exception of dark rings around his eyes like that of a raccoon. "Avery, gal, it's really good to see yah." He says in a southern drawl.

I lean my head back on the head rest and close my eyes as I say, "It's good to be seen, Sisal."

Sisal puts the car in reverse and we head to the hotel so that I can freshen up and take a nap before I go over to his house to have dinner with his family.

After checking in at the Comfort Inn, I tell Sisal that I will phone when I am ready for him to come back to pick me up.

Sisal and Tyree head out.

9

AS I PERUSE THROUGH Books-A-Million, I immediately come across a wooden table with the latest new releases: *She Too Ghetto for Amaretto*, *Pulling Back the Covers over Sin*, *Ain't No Sugar in My Milk*, and the cutting-edge erotica *The Darker Side of Pussy*. That book has been setting off quite a buzz. Heard the big dogs like: *Boy Shorts* and *Hot Babes*, *Lick-Stick*, *Wet Burn* and *Ooze Mate* are anxious to sign the author to a multi-million dollar three book deal. But the self-published author is not enthused to sign over copyrights as of yet, according to several articles in the *New York Times*. Pink Khocolate wants to bask in her success a little while longer. Shoot. I ain't mad at her. Girlllll, do you!

Talks of a movie deal are in place, but according to Editor Rainey Fox of WIDE magazine that will be put to the wayside for now. In addition, rumors spread like wildfire that PK is in search of a screenwriter/film director/producer to put her nasty girl sex-filled imagery to film has everyone biting their bottom lip with anticipation. Film Director Quentin Tarantino was named one of her top potentials. Nothing has been confirmed as to if Tarantino wants to take a bite into this scintillating teaser.

Now in popular demand everyone from the: Queen Latifah Show, Ellen DeGeneres Show, Wendy Williams Show, Arsenio Hall Show, Late Show With David Letterman, and a segment on OWN Network and ABC's Nightline have been raving about *The Darker Side of Pussy*, the provocative novel. The tabloids have been eating the story up. Inquiring minds seems to believe that the tale is a self-portrait of the author. But no one is for certain—mere speculation.

I locate the book displayed on a small easel on the front of the wooden table. Set behind it are ten books neatly stacked with candy apple red letters captioned across the front cover and spine and a jet-black background which makes it ooze with sex appeal and scandal. It most definitely grasps your attention as soon as you walk into the store. Especially with the suggestive illustration of a pierced tongue dripping golden honey and the tip licking the center seed of a peach. Wow.

I lift up the paperback, turn it over to the back cover, and read what all the hoopla is all about.

Distracted by my cell phone buzzing and my own yearning I place the book back on the table, exit the store, and head back to Sisal's car with a puddle in the seat of my panties.

10

SO QUICKLY MY MINI vacation is cut short. Seems Jo-Ruthie and I get into a heated discussion. One that I feel was long overdue. 'Ey I've been suppressing some ill-feelings myself but you don't hear me blurting any of 'em out. I figured why bother to bring up old baggage, but apparently it needed to be uprooted by *her*.

Jo-Ruthie holds animosity towards me for whatever her reasons are. I'd done nothing to this woman, but I guess the fact that I resemble a woman her man once loved is enough to make an insecure country gal bitter. I'm not too surprised because when I first met her I sensed something. I just couldn't put my finger on it. Oh, she tried on several occasions to make it seem like she was understanding of the situation between Ma'am and Sisal but underneath that shit was eating at her. And now she is truly showing her true colors by reverting back in time as if anything can be reversed. Whatever happened happened. It is time for her to get over it. What I don't understand is how can you let a dead woman still till this day put a wedge between what she claim as hers and what used to be? And if for some reason she thinks a marriage certificate sets nuptials in stone, she better think again. If that were the case the divorce rate wouldn't be so high. And infidelity wouldn't even be an option. Everyone who is married would be living in friggin' marital bliss.

Anyway, Sisal tries to intervene but Jo-Ruthie is too longwinded. Some things need to be said and I assume she can't hide her inner feelings about me, Ma'am, Poppa in any longer. I resent the fact that she chooses now to display her frustrations. Why'd she wait so long? This could've been resolved years ago had I'd known about my sister Jewell and them, but I guess she was still in the process of reeling Sisal in.

I try with everything in me to respect this trifling heffa, but when she hits below the belt by talking trash about my momma it is time to strike back. Whether my mom *was* battier than a fruit cake is not her place to say, especially not her place to tell me. Hell! I lived in that household up till the age of *seventeen*. What did she think she was going to tell me that I didn't already know?

With her lips just'a flapping: "You mammy was a simple-minded gal."

"Your mammy was a crazy nut," "Your mammy was unfit to be somebody's mammy," "Your mammy was a quack," "And you wonder why they put her in that straitjacket," "Sisal did the right thang by leaving her and you too," with hot blood boiling and quick reflexes pumping me to knock this old biddy out I restrain myself by balling up my fists and asking God to hold on to me before I let loose and put this old lady in a body cast. I bite down on my teeth, grab my purse, and with my head held high in the sky and my hips swaying east to west I simply walk out of Sisal's home and slam the back door. I saunter around to the front of the house and bump into Tyree sitting on the porch.

"Aunt Av, what's wrong?" He asks.

"Nothing!" I snap.

"C'mon, Aunty, talk to me."

"I should've stayed home." I motion my hands up to my face and try to massage the tension away. Take a deep, deep breath to try to calm my nerves because I am about to pop.

"I know the feelin'," he says, then sighs.

I look at him perplexed. "What feeling?"

"That feelin' when you feel like poppin' somebody. It's written all over your face. I usta feel like that after momma died. I was angry, hurt. and sad. I felt all mixed up and confused. Momma's gone, brother died, and then my dad jetted. I lost them all around the same time. At least that's how it felt. Now I feel like I have no choice but to stay strong, but sometimes I dunno how I keep standing, Aunty. I jus' dunno. But I gotta believe that God gotta purpose for me. I mean this country life ain't all it's cracked up to be. It's not for me anymore, but I'll stay to help Grampa until it is his time to go to heaven. It's only right. He's helping me. Doin' mo' for me than my own dad had." Tyree pauses, just stares in outer space.

"Why are you about to pop? Is something wrong? You wanna talk about it?"

"Nah, Aunty. You got 'nough to worry 'bout I don't wanna add mo' on you."

"No, really, Tyree, if something is troubling you, I'm here. Really."

He exhales deep. "Well," he pulls this marble covered notebook out from his side. "I have this essay I've been working on. It's due on Monday. I get frazzled. I was going to ask Grampa to help me, but you know."

"Yeah, I know. Him...being illiterate is not much help to you." I say to myself.

Tyree continues, "I'm not sure if it is any good. I'm trying to keep my grades up. I don't want to get a low grade because of it. You think you can read it and tell me what you think? Give it to me straight, Aunty."

I nod my head. "I don't know any other way, Tyree."

Tyree stretches out his arm from his chair and hands me the notebook. I wipe the first step with a swipe of my hand to brush off the orange dirt and sit down, open the notebook and begin to read:

His Name Is Slip
Written by Tyree Love

I skim through the essay, but when I reach the last paragraph I slow down. My heart nearly drops to my feet.

It reads:

Nah. I didn't dodge that bullet as I had thought. Crazy part is I never felt the bullet. I never heard the gunshot. That's how silent it was. It caught me by surprise. That silent killer caught me off my guard. I'm only 17 living with HIV.

Do yo'self a favor. Don't slip. Grow up to be somebody other than an AIDS patient.

The End

After I finish reading the essay somehow my anger turns melancholy. All I can think to say is Wow. So badly, so very, very badly I want to share. Tell Tyree the truth. Tell him that aunty knows more than she cares to know about HIV. Tell him that he is looking directly at HIV. That he has held HIV in his arms. That he breathed in HIV's air, but the words, those sour words won't form into a sentence. I sigh, feeling this abundance of guilt boiling inside me. I turn and look Tyree in his beautiful eyes and force a smile as I ask, "Ty, why did you choose to write about the *virus*?"

Tyree sits upright in his seat. "I dunno, exactly. Um, Mom usta tell Antwone and me stories 'bout all the homies she knew who had died from it. I thought it would be a tribute to her. You know, to let her somehow know that I was listening. That she was heard. I couldn't really think of anything else to write 'bout here. There's disease everywhere but I never experienced knowing of someone who had it. So I figured I'd use this brain of mine and imagine this young fellah who contracted it. An imaginary friend, a fellah I personally never met, yet felt a strong connection to. Sounds crazy, right?"

I shake my head and smile. "No, Tyree. It sounds like you're a *writer*. You are truly an inspiration. Don't *ever* change. Don't ever lose sight of that."

Tyree nods his head and smiles.

I hand him back his notebook and head up the road realizing more about me than I care to tell.

11

I LIE BACK on the hotel full-sized bed. With a feverish body I pin my legs together with hopes to calm the want that is throbbing mercilessly for a certain male attention. But the throbbing only exacerbates the longing for his well-endowed member to abate the uncontrollable yearn that has escalated into an insufferable pine.

Resting my head back in the micro fiber organic pillow, squinting my eyes, and shoving pillow into pillow between my thighs and squeezing, doesn't help much either. The intensity has increased. It is now unbearable. And the desire to touch myself and caress my clit with delicate erotic strokes is totally out of the equation at this point. It is a pointless effort to use a: vibrator, porn flick, dildo to resolve my predicament. And plus, I don't own one of those things anyway. Moreover, Hella is too much in heat for some play thang. Blistering inside my love tunnel is a raging inferno screaming infuriatingly to be doused down.

Beads of moisture dot across my forehead. Mouth is bone-dry. Natural coiled hair is drenched from the roots. Sweat trickles down from the nape of my neck, down to my bare-skinned back, down to the crack of my derriere and into the cobalt blue sheets.

Pure misery, yearning for his touch, he left me in the cold of night. Just rose from the bed and slipped on his boxers, socks, T-shirt, jeans, dress shirt, ankle boots, and hat and simply walked out the door. No goodbye. No see you later. No talk in few. Nothing. It seemed so rehearsed. As if he'd done it many times before. I guessed this was his exit out of my life.

Oh, he tried. He tried to turn the tables on me by saying that it was my fault with my ranting. I'm not the only woman who rants especially when I'm upset. It's *not* like I do it for kicks or because I'm starved for attention. No. I do it to vent and scream when I feel that I am not being heard. And if I have to repetitively speak it over and over and over again until it is heard, then so be it! Ranting? What planet is he living on to not have a woman rants? I narrowed that down to him not having a reasonable explanation for his little debut. It was so uncalled for,

189

unnecessary. All he needed to do was communicate with me. But I guessed that would've been asking for too much.

Dang! What the hell am I talkin' 'bout? I must've dreamt up this imaginary man again. What I can't seem to understand is why he pisses me off sooooo much?!

12

Paterson, New Jersey

"*Do you really think that I would put you at risk? Really? After the conversations we've had on the subject? Really?*" *he said.*

"*I felt very uncomfortable when talking about, but I trusted you. Look. Don't worry about it. I know what I have to do.*" *she replied.*

I can only imagine the dialogue sounding something like this between a man and a woman. How many times do we slip? A lot. We are so attracted to the physical that we tend to forget that there are diseases out here. We get caught up in conversation that we often forget to slide in that one question: "*Have you been tested?*" Yeah. It's a difficult one to ask. Often we do things backwards. Sleep with first, and then ask questions later. Or don't ask at all.

I thought I was doing the right thing when divulging myself to: Blu, Travar, Zaleyn, and the others but deep down, chile, I felt like dirt. Like it didn't really matter to 'em how I was *really* coping. I say that because none of them came knocking on my door. It was bittersweet. Mostly bitter because I had to deal with the pain on my own. I don't think they realized how hard it was to come forth—to be forthright. Don't get me wrong, I'm glad I did. I know I did the right thing. It's just, just so much to take in when you are face-to-face with someone you are attracted to, possibly interested in. How does the conversation even begin? Do you just blurt it out? Mumble it? Whisper it? Or do you simply wait for him to bring it up? Most men don't or won't. None of the ones I've encountered asked. So that leaves it in the hands of the *woman*.

You don't have to tell me. I already know that I haven't always followed protocol. Hell, I'm the one who told you. And yes, yes, yes, I let loneliness get in my way—emptiness and insecurity too. Successful *white* men were my weakness. I'm not ashamed to admit that. But it wasn't the men it was the power that they possessed that I was addicted to. The power was the drug for me. So from experiencing all of that is the reason why I can say what I say. I am living proof of what I speak, what I feel, how I see certain things that *we* as women do. More importantly women of color because women of *color* have an issue with uniting with other women, especially *black* women.

Black women will fight tooth and nail so not to get along. And it's sad. Actually pathetic but every 'sistah' has a mind of her own. And if she so chooses to be influenced at least be influenced by a powerful 'sistah' like myself.

I think I've earned that role. I mean for as long as I've been "Avery Love" which has been all of my life I've never watered down my words to save face. I've always kept it on the up and up. Why? Because this is some serious shit and if you don't take heed things can get ugly very quickly.

Something is troubling me. All this hatred, killings, self-destruction is really a downer on my creative spirit. It affects me in ways I never knew it would or could. And it hurts too. I literally hurt. I don't know these people, personally, but just the thought of life being senselessly taken pierces my heart. It's so unfortunate that these youths can't or won't comprehend the significance of life. Where have we gone wrong? Parents. Community. People. How can we unite and bring love back into the Black families? Where do we start? How can we convince our youth to see beyond the bloodshed? How? How can we get them to at least listen? How used to be so hopeful, but now I beginning to wonder if even How knows how come.

I reach over on the nightstand for my journal, Sis. I skim through the pages until I come across the passage I wrote last night. Street. He would've known...*how.*

Dear Sis,

My mind won't let me sleep.

I got some bad news today that made my heart nearly drop to my feet. Can't believe he's gone. God seems to always take the good ones first. And leave all these demons behind. Just don't make any sense to me. Just don't seem right.

A good friend of mine, well, let me rephrase that: a good "platonic" friend of mine has passed away. I couldn't believe it when I saw his picture in the local newspaper. But it was him. Street. That was his name. He was a good man. Amicable. Real. He was a man of community service. I say that because he was the neighborhood's barber. Oh, we have several barbershops. But none had someone like him. He just possessed a lot of goodness you don't really see today.

Street was one of kind. Especially when the single mothers used to come in with their nappy headed sons who were in desperate need of a haircut. Street would give 'em that and mo'. He took time to talk to those children like they were little soldiers. He instilled some kind of goodness in 'em. I used to just sit back and listen to him talk to 'em as if he wished they were his sons. He had sons but they all grown with families of their own, moved out of the ghetto. Some moved out-of-state. But they kept in touch by phone.

Anyway, the children looked up to him because he made 'em feel important, special Something their own daddies didn't do for'em, especially the boys that rarely saw their daddies. Street became a father figure to 'em. It used to make me smile 'cause he truly cared about the black children in the community. Truly cared. Something I hadn't seen in a good while. The children respected him—looked up to him as a man to honor. And that he was.

He took pride in being a barber. Demonstrated diligence, worthiness, most of all he respected the single mothers. Especially this single mother named Justine Mosley.

Justine was a slender, dark complected woman. She was probably around mid-twenties or early thirties. She worked at a convalescent center as a nurse's aide. And she held a second job as a sales associate for JC Penny (jewelry section) in the mall. She never married. But word was that she'd hoped to. Her and her baby daddy had fallen out of love when her son was just a newborn. But he was still living with her. I say about close to her son turning one year s old, that's when all hell broke loose. Justine caught him in her bed with the landlord. Brotha' claimed since Justine was a month behind on the rent he'd slept with the landlord to buy her some time instead of getting his broke ass out and finding a legitimate job.

Sometime after finding out that her baby daddy had a lot of sugar in his tank, she brought her son Wes in for his first one year old haircut. I'd seen Justine before because she used to come in to get a shape up. She always looked drawn in the face. Just the look on her face told all. Trying to be both parents had taken its toll on her, especially with her baby daddy not fulfilling his fatherly duties. That chile used come in every Saturday that I was there dragging her feet. Oh, she was dead tired. But she faithfully made sho' her son had a haircut for church come Sunday.

Street took one look at her and kinda shook his head. He knew Justine was going through it. Working double shifts trying to find someone reliable to watch Wes so that she could make ends meet. But she needed time to rest. And that time was not there. The baby daddy wasn't trying to help her. He could care less of how she was burning herself out. But Street with his quiet demeanor asked her if she'd mind if he took her son to the park that day. And after the park he'd feed him. They'd watch some cartoons and he'd bring him home straight after. Way before dark. Street said, "Don't worry about cooking dinner." He handed her a fifty dollar bill. "Treat yourself today. I'll make sure he eats. Go home and relax your tired bones. Take a hot bubble bath and maybe have a glass of wine to unwind your nerves. Just relax. Lil' Wes is in good hands with me." Justine. She didn't know what to think. First time any man had ever said anything like that to her. First time any man had ever given her money to treat herself. She was flattered and slightly embarrassed. But just the look in Street smoky black eyes said that she had nothing to worry about. There was no motive behind his kindness. So she took him up on his offer. Kissed Wes on the forehead and said, "I'll see you later, Son." Just makes me think of how God seems to take the good ones first.

Well, Street took Wes home as he'd promised.

He rang the doorbell and then knocked on the door a couple times. Justine's hoopty (Hyundai) was parked in the front of the house. Maybe she's sleep, he thought. He peeked in the front window only to find Justine lying face down on the living room floor. He immediately called 9-1-1.

When the paramedics and police arrived Justine was already dead. Just the thought of her taking Wes home, made Street realize his purpose in life, especially when one of the police officers showed him the fifty dollar bill. Justine had written on it: "Last Will and Testament. Should anything ever happen to me I would like Mr. Street (the barber) to be the parental guardian for my child, Wes Mosley. Here are my fifty reasons why... " Then she signed it: Justine Mosley.

Something unfamiliar came over Street just by those words. He felt the emotions brewing in him. Tears rolled down his face. Wes touched his hand and held it for dear life. He knew he was a barber for a reason. Since his children were grown. And since Justine's baby daddy wanted nothing to do with Wes. And since Street was a single dad back in the day, he knew how important a father was needed to a growing boy. With that being known, he decided with God's guidance to take that child and place him into his home. Within a couple months' time, Street adopted Lil' Wes.

It's funny how history repeats itself.

Street maybe gone, but his legacy still lives in the eyes of the child. It still lives through the gifted hands of his son, Wes. Him watching his father figure day in and day out run his business really inspired him to follow in his father's footsteps. Wes realized that barbering was much more than just cutting hair.

As a barber you cut into lives. You had to have a steady hand and a keen sense of what was going on around you. You had to have an open ear. Open mind. And a sense *of responsibility to the community for which you served. It was all instilled in Wes since being a little boy going to the barbershop. So when he began to grow into his manhood Street gave him his first pair of clippers. Oh, Wes was beside himself with delight. You'd think he'd be disappointed 'cause he didn't get a pair of Air Force Ones or X-Box or Playstation or an expensive pair of jeans. None of that mattered to Wes.*

He'd practice every Friday night after he'd come home from school. After he graduated from high school, he enrolled in Cosmetology school to get his license. And by the time he'd graduated Street had a surprise for him. He placed his keys is Wes's hand, and retired. May he rest in peace?

Talk to you later, Sis

Avery

13

STANDING BESIDE MY BED, I kneel down on my knees, clasp my hands together, and bow my head and I have a good ole ugly cry. After I'm done crying my eyes out I say in a shallow tone of voice:

"Anguish, it seems we meet again. You know we must stop meeting like this. Next time pick up the phone and call before you invite yourself over. At least give me the courtesy so that I can prepare brunch. You always seem to catch me at the most impromptu times. I guess that's your way of staying on top of things. My life is not that interesting for you to have to constantly badger me. I'm sure you have more entertaining things to do—more women, perhaps to see? Anyway, you know the drill. There is no need for me to go over it once again. Wow. I thought I had it. I thought I was so close to having it again. Closure. And yet again, I was misguided by what appeared to be right, but was oh, so very wrong. Patience. Perseverance. God, I know those words very well. Practice them like crazy throughout my life. I guess I got sidetracked by the feel of companionship. Missing what I used to have with a best friend. It was pure, genuine. But I should've known. I should've known that a love like that doesn't come that easy. It takes work to achieve a love like that. It takes initiative. It takes wanting and needing and reaching out to achieve a friendship like that. Call me spoiled, I don't care. But I yearned for someone who would uplift my life and sweep away all the debris of past and bring golden into my view. Maybe my standards were a little too high. No, my standards were where they were supposed to be. It was the person who standards were too low for me. His intensions were never to see me grow, bloom, become this beautiful flower. He preferred that I kept my distance, not to take the spotlight off of him. All he had to do was talk to me. Instead of treating me like a tramp. I finally see that he saw me as 'Black Death.' Wow. That's hitting wayyyy below the belt.

"I have to recant when I stated that I hated you because had I hated you none of the things that have transpired in my life, none of them would have ever happened. And some of the things that have happened really changed my life.

"Since all of this madness has festered in my life, there are only two men in my lifetime that I loathed: (1): Poppa. (2): Rapist.

"What I dislike about you most, Anguish, is the mistreatment. I don't feel deserving of it. And when you do it, it does set me back to a time that I try to forget. Writing it out doesn't always help especially when the one that hurt you is asking to now be a part of your life, indefinitely. It's even more difficult when they have no explanation as to why. This is how you make me feel. What have I done to be treated as if I'm not deserving of goodness? How can you sit at the kitchen table, eat off my plate, drink from my glass, share my living space, my body, and knowingly leave me dangling from a string of madness and mayhem? How can you turn your head as if you disown me? It hurt. It hurts even more when you take the things I love so dearly and bring this gloom into my home. I've starved before. Have been told and shown how to starve. And it didn't break me. It just made me aware of what your intentions are. You, Anguish, are destined to destroy me, and eventually send me to an early grave.

"I'm not asking for anything from you. Not friendship. Not anything. I thought if I didn't ask then maybe you'd like me more. See that I'm not like *most* women that are strung out on blues. You'd see that I know how to survive. And I'm proud of that, that I don't have to open my legs to pay my rent or put food in my fridge or clothes on my back. I'm proud that I struggled, believe it or not. And I'm proud that I am able to express myself even if it is on deaf ears.

"Through all of the suffering I do realize that life is not fair. And no matter how good of a person you try to be or want to be something or someone will shake you up and bring you back to remember something or someone you've tried your hardest to forget.

"Sometimes you just have to keep walking through the pain to get to your destiny. I do declare. I guess I'm still walking in these worn-down shoes.

"Amen."

14

RAISING MY LETHARGIC body upright, legs stretch over the side of the bed, bare feet plant firmly on the throw rug, legs spread apart, toes stretch and wiggle, head dangles low as I sit on the edge of my full-sized bed contemplating. Clarity. All of my life that's all I ever wanted from folks. But I never got it. Even Poppa left me in a fog as to why or what caused his rage to put me out of his house. Clarity. He gave no reasonable explanation. Only thing I remember him saying was that I had to venture out into the world. What I didn't and still don't understand is why not let me stick to my plan, and then venture with some money saved and a foundation set. It wouldn't have felt so cold and callus as it did if he'd tried to reason with me. But I guess in his eyes he saw fit to do as he damned well pleased. And he did. Oh yes, he did. But never did it seem that he wondered to himself as to why he was so cold to his little girl. What had I done to deserve such mistreatment? To this day I still wonder. And the only thing that seems to come to mind for me is that I sense he saw "great potential" and he didn't want anyone to tarnish it, especially not the *white* man. But his approach did just that. I had to find and redefine who I was/am. Still till this day I am in search of...me.

Clarity is such a beautiful thing.

After my ordeal with the rape I felt so victimized, so out of touch with reality. I didn't even want to touch my own skin—my own skin. Then when I was told that I had contracted the virus...I felt like now who's going to want to touch my skin. It changed me—changed my perceptions of myself. Of course I wasn't the same woman as I'd been. I even looked different—same to the world, but different to me.

One night I guess around 11:59 p.m., I was brushing my teeth. For some reason I paused and just gazed at myself in the mirror. Would I have thought that my own *black* daddy would have thrown me out in the naked cold? Never.

Warm tears flood in my eyes as I feel an overabundance of grief building inside me. God. So much regret climbs and crawls in my heart.

'What if'...zooms through my thoughts like a car drag racing at high speed up Route 80 West. The thoughts clutter my mind as if a hoarder stuck amongst all the rubbish. How can I be found if I can't be seen? I wonder. Yes, he's seen me in so many awkward positions, but has he really taken a good, hard look at me? Can he see beyond the surface? *Forget about him for a moment*, I think to myself. *What if someone else saw me? What if someone finds out what I have done? What if it leaks out? With all the enemies I have it could happen.* Folks don't particularly care for me, and my difference. I nod. I know. They'd be happy to make my life more of a living hell. I will never recover from the low that I am presently feeling. *What was I thinking?! How could I? When did I lose complete faith? Avery, what's going on, girl, what's really going on with you?* I sigh deeply. *And then, then I come home and have the audacity to look myself in the mirror, as if I'd done nothing wrong. As if...*Oh, I've done it this time. I've really done it! This I'd have to take to my grave.

What more can I possibly go through? Put myself through. I guess I shouldn't ask that question but it is heavy on my mind. What made you do it? Different reasons. Everything. Some things. Many things. It all played a major part in my decision-making. I mean, what was I trying to prove? To whom was I trying to prove it? I don't know. I was on this high for a while. Then I quickly came crashing down and found myself at a low nearly kissing some scumbag off the streets. Since that time it has been a struggle trying to climb back up to where I used to be. Um, I stammer, and then think. *I've fallen as far as one could go. Any further I might as well be lying in a six-foot hole.*

For the last couple of days I've been experiencing premonitions of things that haven't yet occurred. It's scary to see images of folks you know who might not be here tomorrow or next week or next month or next year. It's especially scary when you see yourself as one of those people. Scared the hell outta me.

My head is throbbing. The back of my eyes hurt too. Anxiety. I get up off the bed and head downstairs to go into the bathroom for some Bayer aspirin. I open the medicine cabinet and reach for the bottle and twist it open. I shake two aspirin in the palm of my hand then twist the cap back on. I put the bottle back in the cabinet and close it shut. Then make my way back to the kitchenette as I pop the dry pills in my mouth and swallow.

In the kitchenette, I pull open the top cupboard and reach for the box of Celestial Seasonings Herbal Tea Sampler. Which do I want? Chamomile? Lemon Zinger? Peppermint? Honey Vanilla Chamomile?

Sleepytime? I open the box and take out a packet of chamomile.

With my two front teeth I tear open the packet and with my thumb and forefinger I pullout one teabag and set the box on the granite countertop.

The silver teakettle is set on the back burner of the electric Hotpoint stove so I lift it up and fill it with cold water. Then place it back on the same burner and turn the knob on to simmer.

As I stand there I feel a bone-curdling chill run up my spine. I shiver as if a brisk of cold air sweeps past me. Standing in place for a few more minutes I try to decide what I want to eat for breakfast. I pull open the fridge. I see nothing but a plastic container of crumbled Feta cheese. Other than that it is totally bare. Dang! I gotta go grocery shopping. "How'd I would forget to do that?" I say to myself.

My eyes scroll upward to the top of the fridge. Croissant. I settle for a five day old plain croissant. No butter. No marmalade. Just plain croissant.

I sit on the barstool and contemplate what I truly want in this life as my fingers pull small pieces off the croissant and feed the hunger. Is it fame? Fortune? Both? Or simply peace of mind? Marriage? Single and free? Kids? What? Everything is so cluttered that I can't focus; think straight to save my life. Lately I've been down and I can't seem to find the endurance to will myself back to me. It's so frustrating.

I stand to my feet and walk over to the stove to turn the knob to: Off. I squeeze an adequate amount of Golden Blossom honey into the hand painted mug and drop in the teabag. I lift the teakettle and pour the searing hot water over the honey and teabag and let it steep.

I wrap my fingers around the handle of the mug and return back to my seat on the barstool.

Deep in thought I stare in outer space. I lift the mug and take a sparse sip nearly burning my tongue. I sigh, deep. Shake my head as if I am in disbelief. I swear it feels as if I am reliving it all over again. It never, never seems to go away—the feeling the panic the red, blue, purple, black the act itself. It all plays back, then freezes in time. Yeah. (Nodding my head.) I'm speaking of the rape. And when it does...when...it...do I find myself crawling in this small compartment of the little girl inside me— that innocent little black girl. Sweet Jesus. Hiding. Hibernating. Doing whatever it takes to survive the anguish. Tears well up in my eyes, chin quivers. It is all I know how to do. I've trained, or, shall I say, programmed myself as if a robot pushing: stop, go, stop, and go...until I feel complete exhaustion. I don't care what anyone else seems to think, but it is mighty difficult being a woman. Look. It really makes no difference at the end of the day. But what does, what really makes an impact on someone's life is the skills to conquer whatever comes into one's life, unexpectedly. Never. Never in a million years would I have thought that I would've been a woman who was raped. Never. I just never thought of it happening to me. Never suspected it would, but it did. It sho' 'nough did. So here I am trying to rebalance a traumatized woman. And it's hard as fuck!

Sometimes I wished...

I wipe the tears that stream down my face with the back of my right hand. Sometimes I wished I would've stayed trapped in the bubble that I had formed around me. But I didn't. I allowed myself to interact with others, some good folks, some bad. And during that time I met someone as women often do when we're in that mode of transition. He was there...waiting, diligently awaiting my arrival. He was someone as you know I had met at one of my photo shoots during the time I was working as a model for IMG. He was someone who found me intriguing, different, and special, however you choose to word it. He was someone who later became a friend, then more than a friend. Yes, Stacy Blazman, you got it.

In the beginning I thought I was seeing the truest essence of him. But I was so very wrong.

Where did I go wrong? Chilllllleeeeeee. I have to catch my breath on that question. Well, I went wrong when I treated him like a man should be treated. I introduced him to things that no other woman had. I wined him. I dined him. I spent my hard-earned money on him. Even put gas in his car. No. I wasn't trying to buy his affection nor him. I just wanted him to know that all *black* women were not the same. Not all of us were gold-diggers or welfare recipients or junkies or whores or vagrants or uneducated black bitches.

Who was I talking about? Aden Thomas? I think.

I get sidetracked sometimes. Stacy Blazman? He came after all the rest. He was the last man I'd dealt with. Or was it Christopher Morehouse? So many men it becomes scrambled in my head. Who came first, second, third...? It really didn't matter because they all came. Ok I tried to make light of things by making a funny, but funny it was not. Aden Thomas? He was someone from my past, past. Someone I just knew I'd live happily-ever-after with but—

Let me break it down by saying this. I had no time for indigent men. No time. You had to come with something lucrative for me to even give

201

you the time of day. It had to be something for you, not me, because I had my own, and I was content with working harder to reach my level of comfort. I wanted someone who was ambitious and hardworking too. I do believe around that time, which was late-'98, I was open-minded, eager to embark on something new, exciting, challenging. I met Aden. We complemented each other. But we had a major setback. Let me tell you something, when a man who is not fully developed in mind—that man can often be persuaded to go against what his heart speaks. Aden was one of those men. Some men, they get beside themselves and begin to show a different side that is not so pleasant. Aden was one. And when I began to see those behavioral changes that were not there before I began to probe. And when I began to probe I realized it was not all his doing. Someone was behind it. Someone close. Someone influential. Someone he trusted. Someone he loved dearly. That's when I began to say to myself that maybe he was *not* the man for me. And when I began to realize *that* I didn't hesitate to remove myself from the relationship because I felt like I *was* no longer dating Aden. No, no, no...I was dating someone else who had slipped in Aden's pants. Who might *that* have been? His *mother*! Need I say anymore?

How did *he* get my number? Business card. He got it off of my business card that I had left at several local businesses downtown Paterson. Well, Aden called me. How did *he* know it was me? He didn't, at first. He took a chance to see, which really surprised me because he was *never* (with me that is) the risky type. I see that has changed.

As soon as he heard my voice, he knew it was me. Just as I knew he was still living in the past. But of course *now* he wants to explain. *What is there to explain?* I say to myself. Nothing. It was. It's not anymore. Folks move on. Some folks, I should say, because others seemed stuck in time, hoping to recapture a moment that no longer exists. I am not that woman I used to be. Things have changed dramatically in my life. None of which he knows. Plus, I *vowed* to never go back to him. I no longer cared about his dashing good looks, his impressive family background, him being well-off, suburbia, country clubs, the finer things in life, traveling around the world, fringe benefits, knowing the who's who, crab cakes, lobster and caviar, Tiffany's on Sunday, and fine wines and gourmet foods, butlers and maids and nannies. Nor did I care for the flock of well-educated *handpicked* women who merely made a mockery of him. They used him, abused him, and discarded of him like he, his name, meant nothing. Money. Money meant nothing to them simply because they had their own money. Me, the woman with no money, no luxurious lifestyle, yet, I was pure in every word that I spoke, in every feeling that I felt, struggling to make something out of myself, giving, yet, not receiving the truest part of him. His heart. I was no longer experiencing those same feelings I once felt for this man. If anything, he was unseen in my memory—out of mind, out of heart, out of soul, out of spirit. There was nothing left but memories that I have not thought of since today. But for some reason he felt compelled to call me on this day, to express himself, to be heard, validated, and understood. Whatever.

"Let it go, Aden. Move on." I say with a pinch of agitation in my tone.

"You are special to me. I was feeling things that I didn't want to feel for you, Avery. My feelings were strong and I knew it would be a distraction. I was so close to graduating from college. I needed to stay focused." He declares. "And I told you, I told you that once I graduated we could pick up where we left off."

I interject. "That's not how I recall it."

"Don't interrupt me." He says in aggressive tone of voice. "Let me finish saying what I was saying. Avery, you didn't want to hear it. You weren't willing to listen to me—just like you're not listening to me right now."

I stand my ground and say. "That's not how it went down, Aden. As I recall..."

"Baby, don't do this to us." He pleads with hurt in his voice.

"I'm not your baby. And furthermore I am not doing anything. There is no us..." I retort with a crumpling forehead and throbbing temples. "Obviously you've forgotten a lot that was said. Remember the letter I wrote to you? I expressed my truest feelings to you. I purged. Do you remember?"

"Baby, don't ...."

I chuckle. "Mmmmmm, baby, don't. That's one of your favorite lines. But, Aden, I remember. I remember exactly what I wrote. It goes like this: 'Day 5 was yesterday. I usually give myself 5 days to mourn over something that is troublesome to me. I vent, cry, write, bubble bath...do whatever it takes to get that person out of my system. I purged, baked yet another carrot cake, drank a few glasses of the Remy Martin cognac you left in my fridge, which by the way had a pungent taste going down my throat (it felt like it was burning), slept later than usual because I was up most of the night. I wrote long chapters in my journal letting the person know how I'm doing and how foul they might've been to me. On the 6th day, this is today. I peel those soiled layers off and start anew. I'm good now! Refreshed! Ready for whatever He has in-store for me. I hope you have a great day! Because I sho' am!' Remember that?"

All I hear is Aden's soft breathing.

"May I continue?"

"Sure."

"As I recollect, Aden, your response to me was: 'It's good to know that you have coping skills. Conflict that stems from such an intimate moment speaks volume about a personality. No matter how 'real' you are...there is a time, a place, and method of addressing any problem or feeling.' I laugh. "So then I said: 'Time was in the moment. Place was in my sanctuary. Method was heated because of how you made me feel. I don't think you realize certain things that you do. Possibly people don't tell you the truth about yourself. That situation was no different than you coming over to my place on scheduled visits. Remember that day? The *day* my phone wasn't working properly. You called from the payphone outside. I never heard my phone rang. Eventually I called you at home. It so happened that I could make calls but I couldn't receive incoming calls. We had just had a terrible storm that week. You answered the phone with an attitude then *pretended* that you were about to go to sleep. We hung up. It annoyed me so I called you back. And you basically asked me if I were interested in someone else would I tell you. As if to imply that I had another man in my home. As if to imply that I was so sexed starved that I could not wait on you. You accused me of something that never even crossed my mind. All this came about because I didn't answer my phone. Because 'Aden Thomas' could not have his way I told you the truth. You said all of this stuff to me without any regard to my feelings. Ok. Let's fast-forwarding shall we. We make up. Or so I thought. While lying on top of me, butt-ass naked I asked you a question. So what, if it was during sex! So what! You got your nutt and you were off running to the next bitch. You thought I didn't know. I mean it was sooooo obvious. I fulfilled your sexual desires and you left me hanging. You didn't even attempt to try to please me. So selfish. And you had the audacity to make it seem like it was me doing the dirt. Aden, you were so big on yourself that you really didn't need me in your life. There was no room for the both of us.'"

"Look. I didn't know then what I know now." Aden says.

"Doesn't matter," I snap. "You opened a can of worms. You called me. I didn't call you. Ooh, Lord, give me strength. It was about you all the time. But Aden, it was about me and you. If you were looking for fellatio I'm sure you could've gotten that with no problem. If you were looking for unwinding, food, drink, conversation, music...you had all of that with me, and more. I didn't pressure you. Maybe I was going through something. Do you know that my body ached just like blue balls? No. You couldn't have known that. You know why? You never took the time to know. I used to hurt when I didn't have sex on the regular. I mean from going to three, four times a week, to zero. I mean c'mon. Let's be real here. I suffered. Me. Aden. I reached out to you and you told me you couldn't and wouldn't be there for me. So I stayed in a fetal position, legs clamped together, and pussy throbbing unbearably...aching for you to come and soothe me, comfort me in my time of need. And *you* didn't because it was all about you."

"Sorry."

"Sorry. That's all you can say? You know what, Aden, Thank you. Yes...," I let out a deep, hard breath. "Yes, Aden, you were in school. As I recall you had two years left. Man, I used to think that you were the smartest man on campus. I used to think that, but now I'm beginning to wonder. Now, had you said what you're saying right now, back then, I wouldn't have had a problem with any of the things that we were going through? But you didn't say that. As I recall I was focused too, but you always found a way to weasel yourself in to distract me when you were having baby mama drama, separated from your wife drama, kids drama. momma drama, and you took your anger out on me. I tried to be supportive—to give you a shoulder to lean on. An open ear, but it didn't matter to you. And after a while it *didn't* matter to me. I said that hell with it all. And you! I left. I packed my shit and left. And I changed with no desire to look back, to come back to you. I was done. You were history to me. It was the mistreatment that pushed me away. The selfishness that pushed me away, *and*... I was *good* to you. And you let *her*...You gave me a urinary tract infection messing around with those wealthy dirty whores. Suppose you'd given me something else, huh? Did you *ever* think about that? Did you?! Did it *ever* cross your mind while you were out gallivanting with your whores? But then you...Ooh..." I pause, "You know what...I'm not doing this. That's in the past. I've since moved on. And you should too."

"We had something good. C'mon admit it." He says trying desperately to reel me back. "Something I know we can have again if you would just give us a chance."

I yawn, loudly. "Are you listening to yourself? No! We can't. I don't feel anything for you. Why aren't you listening?"

He murmurs, "You don't care. It meant nothing to you?" he lowers his voice down to whisper. "I get it. I get it. Then answer this for me, why'd you *fuck* me so well? Huh? Huh, Avery? Why'd you give me all of that chocolate pussy? Answer that for me, why don't you. Huh?"

I raise my left brow. "Why'd I *fuck* you so well? Listen to me clearly. Everything Avery does she gives a 110%. I don't do half-assed! And furthermore, Aden, that was damn near *sixteen years ago!* You'd think you'd be over it by now." I roll my eyes in disdain.

Aden chuckles, "Get over it? Huh. Men never forget good pussy. It is what keeps us coming back. And even though I've been gone for quite some time now, I know that that chocolate pussy ain't changed. Do you realize what you have, baby. You have a turn-a-motherfucker-out pussy. You'll have that soldier doing shit he ain't ever done before just to get another taste of you."

I scowl. "Do you hear yourself, Aden? Do you get it?" I get indignant. "I gave you the *best* of me. Good pussy and all. I gave you that softer, sensual, subtle woman and you basically shitted on her as if she was supposed to bow down to your bullshit. Because of all that you were going through. N-not once, once, Aden, did you consider what I was going through. You never asked. You didn't care. You never talked to me. You talked at me. You showed your anger by treating me like dirt. Like some bitch dangling from a string. And I took it for a little while as women often do when they care but then I rediscovered something about myself. And I quickly let it go. I dug deeper within myself and I found something good and nurturing and wholesome for my heart, for my spirit, for my mind, for my soul. You wanna know what that was, Aden? I found *contentment.* And I was looking forward to greeting *happiness.* It was hard after I let a man see me for who I really am. But since *you* I've kept her under lock and key. And no, no, it's not fair to the new man who is willing to give of himself to have to be subjected to that kind of treatment, but I refuse to allow another man to take me there. I refuse." I sigh.

Aden lets out a deep, hard breath. "Don't be angry, Avery. Don't become whom I used to be. It eats you up, spits you out. It leaves you all alone, bitter. Listen. I didn't call to upset you. I just wanted you to understand where I was coming from. I felt the need to tell you. And express how much I feel for you. You're a good person, a wonderful woman. I thought we had a connection. I felt we did. But I guess it didn't matter to you. We can salvage what we shared. Start anew. I know that I can make you happy. I have everything in place now. I got my head on straight. My heart still desires you, Avery. After all these years I still think of you. I still feel those strong feelings for you. The shit won't go away. You, Ms. Avery Love, you were 'the one' that got away."

I purse my lips. *I ain't falling for this shit.* I think to myself. "Well, listen, I have to go." I tell him.

"It was good talking to you I still care deeply for you. I told you once I finished school...we...."

I roll my eyes. "I have to go, Aden."

Click!

I grab my thigh-length taupe-colored Parka jacket, keys, purse, and head out the door.

15

The Hustler 'n' the Poet Nightclub

Paterson, New Jersey

SNARLING IN MY Bobbi Brown compact mirror, I slam it shut nearly cracking the glass. I then turn to my left, scroll this hefty specimen of man up and down. My lips twist, highly disappointed. "Same ol' shit," I say to myself. Can't a woman come out looking half-way decent, walk into an establishment, sit down at the bar by herself and order herself a drink without a person assuming she is looking for a quick fix or some quick dick. How many times do I have to reiterate that I am not a *gold-digger*? I carry my own weight as heavy as it might be. I do for me! If he really opens his eyes he should be able to see that I'm a woman of class. I *don't* have time to be trying to *pimp* myself out for these broke clowns. I got too much going for me to degrade myself for pennies. Too much!

I can't blame him. No. I cannot. It's the women's fault. The half-naked women who strut in these bars looking for some quick action, yesssss, I blame *them* because these men just assume that all women who come into bars are the same. And that's simply not true.

I don't come looking for shit! I come to unwind with a drink, think, listen to some music, laugh, and take myself home.

Understand this; if a woman *does not* know how she wants to be treated by a man, I'm going to tell you what you do. Are y'all listening? This is exactly what you do...*take yourself out on a date*! Wow...is right. And you'll soon discover what you want and how you want to be treated by a man. I discovered a lot by doing this simple task.

So every now and again I take myself out to dinner, to the movies (when I do go), out to have a drink (as I am doing now), or if I feel like hearing some good music I'll go to a nice jazz spot. There is no man here with me. Shit. I haven't had a date where two people sit across from a table in an exclusive restaurant, converse, go dancing, and he walks me to my front door since, since...Zaelyn!

So, now I get dazzling (although I'm not today) but when I do I get dazzling for me. Date me. Then safely bring me home.

Women have a difficult time adjusting to being seen alone. Those types of women have major issues that only they can address.

A man does not define me; stop me from enjoying "me" time. I cannot allow myself to be drawn backwards. I cannot.

I used to put men on high pedestals because that was how I viewed them externally, but internally some of them were just as lost as a stray dog. There was nothing there, nothing but uncertainty. It was not attractive. So I began to see men for who they truly are. My expectations of men haven't grown. If anything, it's diminished over the last few years.

I purse my lips together, annoyed. Let one of those bigheaded men step to me right now! I'll show 'em how this shit is really done. I'll have 'em eating out of my hands. Scratching my back, rubbing my feet and clipping my toenails and polishing them too, kissing my toes, cooking my dinner, scratching, shampooing and conditioning, and greasing my scalp, washing, folding, and ironing my clothes. And I dare 'em to try to use anything that I do against me. I double dare 'em. 'Cause for one he approached me, so therefore, he should've known better.

But see most of these fools out here don't do their homework. They just assume that if it worked once, it will work twice. That's only if you are dealing with the same type of chick. But if you are dealing with someone as supreme as me, then you better come with your A-B-C-game or don't come at all.

It seems after a man gets what he wants from a woman she is disregarded. Her time is devalued. That irks my last dang nerve.

The simplest things in life seem so complex for a man to do. I mean, I have a lot of pet peeves but I personally feel that they are valid peeves when it comes to man and his dealings with me.

You see, I've learned over the years that you have to show folks, especially men what you want. Telling 'em gets you nowhere because they only hear what they want to hear. I have a major issue with non-responses, and men taking me and my time for granted. I'm not the type of woman who likes to be disregarded because I feel that I am important. Important enough to reply to a text or show-up if asked out on a date or phone if you are going to be late or choose to cancel. Give me my due respect.

In order for a man to know what I like I have to show him by example. I cannot expect him to just know, because some women don't lead by example. Some women just settle and accept whatever a man brings. I have done that in the past, settled and accepted, but I'm not that woman any more. And any man in my inner space has to respect what I like and/or dislike. Of course, not all men will take heed to do as I ask or care how I feel, but at least they can't say that I didn't show 'em how I want to be treated. At least I know what I will and will not settle or stand for.

See, I'm *not* expecting perfection. I'm *not* expecting him to profess his love for me. Hell, I'm *not* even expecting good sex. All I'm expecting is for him to *live up to his word.* And if he can't live up to that, then he becomes a waste of my time. And anyone who happens to know me knows that my time is not to be wasted on any tired ass man. Either you come with something more than a $250 prepaid credit card and Enterprise rental car. Or joker, don't come at all 'cause I'm 'bout tired of the slick talk and bullshit.

A woman has to have standards. If not, she'll settle for just about any man walking. My expectation of men, in general, is very, very low. Never thought I'd feel this way, but I do. I expect 'em to do as they will without any regard for me or my feelings. And from that I've learned to leave a man where he is and simply walk away.

I cut my eyes to the side with a grimace on my face. Men! I cannot keep my thoughts to myself. 'Ey he asked for it by gawking at me like I'm some cheap sleaze. He should've kept his eyes to himself. But he didn't, so therefore, I feel I have a right to vent. And he gon' listen.

I lift up my glass and take a sip of red sangria, then turn full circle in his direction. I want to give him an eyeful. Look while you can, mister, 'cause you ain't getting any of this luscious chocolate. "You wanna know something, *mister*," he turns in my direction with a sort of grin on his chubby face. He gives me his undivided attention. Damn, he ain't even fine! He's an average looking, receding hairline, mustache and beard, no neck, potbelly looking fellah. *Where is his waistline?* Oh, he is entirely a little too overweight for my taste buds. But hell, the man has ears (that I hope are not filled with buildup wax) and that's all I need. My brows knit. "It is mind-boggling to me when a man that *I* have encountered insinuates that I am *not* being one hundred percent truthful about whom the fuck I *fucked* in my past and present life. C'mon. I don't appreciate it! *Avery* is the first name. *Love* is the last. That's who *I* am! Look, mister, you don't know me like that, so you may wanna step off before you catch a case that ain't even meant for you. There is definitely no love-connection here. *Love* ain't looking for me and I ain't looking for *love*." I snap with a rotating neck. Evidently he wasn't paying close enough attention to see that I was not in the mood to be stared down. I just wanted to sit here, have a drink or two, calm the hell down, then take my crazy self back home to do...whatever.

The man hurries and gulps down his drink of screwdriver (vodka and orange juice), rises from his seat, and quickly heads for the exit.

Within seconds the kitchen door swings open and out comes the Head Chef Hector walking towards me with an amicable smile on his plump mango-colored face.

He greets me, "Hello, baby. How are you? Good to see you Everything okay?"

I nod. I am not in the mood to talk to anyone. I just want to drink in peace. Not wanting to be rude I say, "Yes. Everything is good. How have *you* been?"

"Oh, so-so. Work work work... I need a vacation."

"You and me both," I say.

"Go back to my country."

"Which is...?"

"DR...Dominican Republic."

"Oh. Okay."

"Hector, my friend!" A gray-haired man dressed in a suit and tie yells out at the end of the bar.

"Excuse me, Love."

I nod as Hector greets the elder man.

"Wow. That was brutal." This brown-skinned, detailed low-cut wearing mid-thirty year old lithe woman dressed in a pair of denim Skinny jeans and silk fuchsia-colored blouse with thick bright yellow custom-made necklace with matching tear-drop earrings that is seated to the right of me says in a raspy tone of voice. "Boy, aren't we hostile. What had that man who stormed out of here done to you? Please. Do tell," she says hungry for some gossip.

I turn in her direction and narrow eye her. "Me? *Hostile!* Look. Why you all up in my business?" I catch myself before I fly off the handle and snatch this chick up by the collar and wring her chicken neck. "Do we know each other? Have we met before 'cause I don't *ever* recall seeing you around *here*? I frequent this place, sooooo I would know. And I do know that I haven't seen *you*." I emphasize.

"I've been here. A coupla times. Normally I come with my girlfriends but lately with our busy schedules we can't seem to hookup."

My heart is beating pretty fast.

The woman takes a sip from her glass and begins to babble. "Rachel, she's a personal assistant and her boss, Natty keeps her chained to her desk. Monica, well, she's a lawyer. She is always in court or working on new cases, so she pencils us in whenever she can. Blanche, well, she owns a health food store and can never catch a break. But that's a good thing because her business is doing very well. And plus, she's a single mother of four. We never saw that coming. The divorce, I mean. Her and her husband seemed so happy. But looks can be deceiving. Sophie, well, she's married. Her husband, Crazy, I call him that because of how he acts. His real name is Lamm. Lamm won't let her out of his sight. He is so insecure. Once a man gets a gut and realizes he doesn't look as he did ten years ago it starts to toy with his ego. I guess he thinks if Sophie hangs out with the girls too much she may meet someone else and leave his controlling ass. And as for me, well, I'm Vanity. I'm the spontaneous one. No leashes. No chains. Single and free. I've been here more than you know. You just didn't notice me," she says, "but I know I've seen you here, and in passing. I never forget a face. Girlfriend...you get around." She says as if insinuating something negative.

Girlfriend? Girlfriend? This hussy doesn't know me well enough to be calling me...*girlfriend*. I roll my eyes. And keep my cool on a simmer. "Well, who hasn't seen me?" I stretch my neck feeling a heat wave zoom throughout my body. The delayed reaction has kicked in. I am 'bout to slap this skinny heffa!

I turn slightly to my right and say with a hint of sass in my tone. "Hold up! Wait a minute! What you tryna insinuate heffa?"

She stretches her eyes and quickly opens her mouth. "No, no, I didn't mean it like that. I'm just saying I've seen you at a lot of places. That's all."

I purse my lips. "Uh-huh. No disrespect, sweetie, but I'm going through some shit right now, so you might wanna back off. Why don't you go over there and talk to one of those gentlemen. I'm sure they'll entertain you."

She turns her body around in the barstool and glances at the three men in business suits. She turns back around facing the bar with a blank look on her attractive face. "Not my cup of tea," she says. "What's on your mind? You want to talk about it?"

212

I don't bother to look in her direction. I lower my head and stare at my reflection in the granite countertop. I lift my head back up and say, "Talk to you? Why would I want to do that? I don't know you. By the way, who the hell are you, Vanity?"

Vanity remains silent.

I shake my head from side to side, finding myself getting annoyed with this chick. "Uh-huh. Like I said I got some shit on my mind and I'm just tryna get my drink on, if *you* don't mind!"

"Snappy. Snappy. Must be men troubles," Vanity says matter-of-factly.

The simmer has heated up and I give this chick a piece of my mind. "You don't know *me* well enough to be telling me that I have *men* troubles! What are you a...*shrink*? Stirring up conversation just to pick my brain? For your information, *Miss Thang*, I don't have any *men* troubles. That's in the past. I'm just tryna get the bastards out of my system. Well, one bastard in particular. You know you really need to mind your business!"

"What happened?" Vanity asks without as much as a concern as to what I have just said to her.

I clasp my eyes shut before I reach out and snatch this chick up and throw her slim-trim ass across the room. "Girl...!" Suck my teeth. "Giirrrrlll. Giiiirrrrlllllll, you do not have enough time to listen to me babble on and on about my troubles. Trust me."

"Yes, I do."

"Oh, you do? Don't you have somewhere to be? Someone to meet, perhaps...?"

"No one."

"Really?"

"Talk. Tell me why such a beautiful black sistah is in this bar trying to drink her pain away?"

"Mind your business. Has anyone ever told you that you are a nosey bitch?"

"All the time," Vanity replies coolly. "I have this gift of reading people and my gut tells me that you really don't want to be alone. You've been alone too long. And it sucks! It really, really sucks. You actually want someone to care enough to come and sit next to you and talk to you. And no, it doesn't have to be about you, per say, but at least acknowledge the fact that you are sitting here looking stunning as ever. It kind of reminds me of that scene in *Waiting to Exhale* when Bernadine Harris (Angela

Bassett) is sitting at the bar and James Wheeler (Wesley Snipes) comes in and asks is anyone sitting here, remember that scene?" She asks, cuts her eyes over her right shoulder then blows out a deep breath. She turns back in my direction. "Tell me you've seen the movie."

"Uh-huh. More than once," I reply. "But if you read the sequel *GETTING TO HAPPY* you'd know that Mr. Wheeler was full of shit. Not to mention a compulsive liar, thief, and bigamous. *And* if you read the book then you'd know that if it weren't for his *first* wife, huh, chile Bernadine wouldn't have found out about his secret double life."

All of a sudden Vanity seems deep in thought. But when the bartender accidentally drops a glass she seems to snap out of her daze, "What about ahhhh...*Temptation*?" she asks.

I shake my head no. "I haven't been to the movie theaters lately. Actually I haven't been in years. I heard about the movie though. That's the one with Brandy Norwood in, right?"

Vanity nods.

I get this funny feeling in my gut. Anytime that happens it makes me wonder about a person. I'm curious about this chick named Vanity. "C'mon. Tell the truth, Vanity. One thing I've learned about black women is that we can't seem to get along. We can't stand each other. And we love to feed off of drama. It's about competition. What the next chick got and who she's doing and how she got that position and who she fucked to get it. Your pain and heartache is my pleasure. I get pleasure out of seeing you fail. Ridiculous! It's all ridiculous. Black women don't know how to be there for other black women. I mean sincerely be there for a sistah without trying to either throw her under a bus or stab her in the friggin' back. You get where I'm coming from? It's sad. But true. Hispanic women can get along. White women can get along. Asian women can get along. Jamaican women can get along. But we black women; some of us can't hold water. And it's sad because you can very well be one of those 'sincere' sistahs but in this time there aren't many like you, like me. So you can kinda understand why I am so skeptical, you know?"

I can see the frustration building in Vanity's eyes, face and body language.

"But-but-but..." she stammers. "I'm serious." Vanity emphasizes. "Whether you care to believe it or not. What motive would I have? Honestly. I don't know you, like you've said. I'm just being me. You know sometimes God brings people together for a reason. This may just be a brief encounter but I do believe there is a reason for everything in life. Sometimes you just have to take heed. Believe that God is caring for you by bringing someone, a total stranger, into your life, momentarily. Believe that He has a message specifically for you. Do you believe in God? Do you own a Bible? 'Philippians 4:3: And I urge you also, true companion, help these women who labored with me in the gospel, with Clement also, and the rest of my fellow workers, whose names *are* in the Book of Life. 4:4: Rejoice in the Lord always. Again I will say, rejoice! 4:5: Let your gentleness be known to all men. The Lord *is* at hand. 4:6: Be anxious for nothing, but in everything by prayer and supplication, with thanksgiving, let your requests be made known to God. 4:7: and the peace of God, which surpasses all understanding, will guard your hearts and minds through Christ Jesus. 4:8: Finally, brethren, whatever things *are* true, whatever things *are* noble, whatever things *are* just, whatever things *are* pure, whatever things *are* lovely, whatever things *are* of good report, if *there is* any virtue and if *there is* anything praiseworthy— meditate on these things. 4:9: The things which you learned and received and heard and saw in me, these do, and the God of peace will be with you.'" She smiles with such an illuminating glow. Lifts up her paper napkin and dabs at the beads of moisture on her upper lip and nose.

My eyes scroll her from her suede Jessica Simpson pumps to her narrow face wondering what the hell is wrong with this chick. Has she gone mad? Has she suddenly been possessed by a demon? Or is she possibly a messenger from God? I can't say for sho' but I'm guessing this chick needs a valium. I allow each scripture Vanity has just recited to penetrate. It's a struggle within to believe that someone would go through such lengths to get through to someone else, but then again, it doesn't because I remember someone so near and dear to me who went above and beyond to express how much I meant to him. Yep. Johnnie. Maybe I'm overreacting, just a tad bit. Maybe she is who she says she is? Maybe I need to ease up and find out. No, no, no... There is something fishy about her coming out reciting scriptures in a lounge. Why isn't she at Bible study, or, or some Revival? Hmm, makes me wonder.

I straighten up my posture; purse my lips as I often do when I feel someone thinks they're pulling wool over my eyes. I say in a voice of skepticism, "You're actually concerned for a total stranger. Please. Sorry, but I ain't fallen for the bullshit, lady. Nice try though."

As quick as those words are released from my mouth and into her small ears a grimace outlines Vanity's face. She quickly turns herself around and pierces my face with those eyes of hers until I finally turn myself fully around giving her eye to eye contact. Her thin lips go a flapping. "Well, it's true. You know, you really have to learn how to follow your instincts when it comes to people. I'm a people person! I work with people all damn day! I know what the hell I'm talkin' about."

You may know people but I know bullshit when I hear it. And this is some bullshit!

Woosa! Woosa! This heffa don't know. She don't know that I am about to leap off of this barstool and leap on her. Lord. Lord. "Whoa! Sister, who the hell you think you're talkin' to?"

Vanity closes her eyes. Takes a deep breath, and then lifts her glass to take another sip off of her drink. With her glass still in hand and her face erect she says in a mellow tone, "All I'm sayin' is that you should go with your gut. If it doesn't feel right, it's probably not. But if it does, it probably is."

She has a point, I think. "Hmm. Question, why? What you want to analyze me? Process everything that I share, just to throw it all back in my face and tell me where I went wrong. Contrary to what you may think, sugar, I know where I went wrong. I don't need you to tell me that."

Vanity stares in outer space as if she is ignoring my every word. She grips the wine glass and swallows down the last drop of her drink.

To play it off as no big deal I wave my hand in the air and then continue, "See, I went wrong by *loving* a man. I went wrong by *seducing* a man. I went wrong by *trusting* a man. And in the end *love* burned me raw. Yes. So, here I am sitting at this bar drinking my problems away. Of course, of course, I know that the problems will still be there once I sober up. I'm not stupid. But for now I have to do something to soothe me." I can feel myself getting choked up. It's been a long haul pulling all of this misery on my back.

Vanity crosses her legs and leans in close and says, "I'm at your disposal." I get a good whiff of the perfume she is wearing. God, it smells so inviting. Not too strong, not too mild, just meets in the middle—a soft and subtle fragrance.

I repeat her words in my head: *"I'm at your disposal."* It's more than the words, but in the way that she says it that convinces me that she really is willing to listen. Finally, I cave.

I scratch my throat. "Well, if you insist on hearing my drama tale. At least let me buy you another drink?" Snap, snap of my fingers. "Excuse me, Carlton. Excuse me. When you get a chance can you give this sistah here a glass of...?"

Vanity finishes my request. "Hennessy, please, thank you, Avery."

"You're welcome. It's nice to meet you, Vanity...?"

"Singleton. That's my last name."

"Well, Vanity Singleton, I appreciate you. Not too many sistahs are willing to listen to another sistah's drama. Well. Dang. I don't even know where to begin. I guess I'll start with Johnnie Rivera." I lift up my wine glass and take another sip.

"Who is he?" says Vanity.

I place the wine glass down on the bar counter.

Suddenly, I feel that choked up feeling come on again. "He used to be my *very* best friend." I sigh.

"What happened?" she asks.

I stare in outer space. "He died. But if he were still alive that crazy *bitch* would have me cracking the hell up right 'bout now!"

"Oh, I'm so..." Vanity pauses, lowers her head as if embarrassed.

"Yeah. It's crazy, you know. Life is crazy." I sigh, deep. "He's no longer suffering. That's all that matters. Then there was Zaelyn Homes. Sometimes I wonder how we lasted as long as we did. Uh-huh. Yeah. When a joker starts pouring his heart and soul out to you and you two have only gone out on two dates that is a red flag that something might be up. Things go sour reallllll quick, especially if the Negro is a player. Zaelyn was the ultimate player. And might I add...*very married*. But he was sloppy with his. Things were shaky between us. One reason was because Zaelyn was a liar. Hell, Blu McDowell wasn't any better. That was one gorgeous ass man. Those muscles on him! Chile, please! Travar Atkin was *finne* as hell too. Something about a man who loves to rub a woman's feet. Not to mention cook her home cooked meal. That right there is sexy to me. But the truest love for me was Xavier Combs III. Jesus. Losing him nearly ripped my heart out of my chest. Lord has mercy. That man loved me. Me. Girl, I never thought it would happen to me, but it did. But then other stuff began to happen too. Things changed between us. I felt like I was losing him. You feel a lot of things when you truly love someone. It's like you're connected in some way. Our love was strong while it lasted. Then someone came and put a wedge between us. That someone was none other than...JaVonna Banks trying get back at me for her breakup with Danell Owens. That was not my doing. Not my fault. I didn't pursue Danell. She was just going through something and needed someone to be there for her. I tried. But things got a little out of hand when Danell leaned in and kissed me. Yeah. *Kissed* me. Uh-huh.

Sometime after Xavier and I got back together JaVonna shot me. Shot, girl, shot!" I nod my head up and down.

Vanity's eyes widen.

I continue, "I did a little modeling in my day. Yeah. For a modeling agency in New York called IMG. You ever heard of them?'

"No." Vanity replies.

I continue, "Well, chile, the experience was something to remember, at least some of it. See, I met this guy named Stacy Blazman. He told me he could take me places in my modeling career. Don't ever believe that shit, okay. Anyway, we started dating. Things were good for a while. But then I felt like I was being pushed in front of an oncoming train. He wasn't who he said he was. He treated me like crap. He beat me down like I stole something. And, let me not forget got me hooked on cocaine. Then jetted. Oh! B-but not before stealing my money. Then he came back into my life and kidnapped me. Yeah, girl, I said *kidnapped*. He held me hostage *after* marrying me without my consent. He drugged me. It was pretty bad. So now I am in the process of getting our marriage annulled."

"Really?" says Vanity.

I nod my head. "Really. Come to find out Stacy had some issues. Issues that I don't want to talk about right now. Currently I am in therapy, but I've missed a couple of sessions with Dr. Cristal. She's persistent. She keeps calling me, but I haven't returned any of her calls. I just need a break; you know what I'm saying? It's difficult trying to deal with all of this. And on top of this, there is so much more that I have to come to terms with." I nod my head up and down. "Would you like another drink? Excuse me, Carlton, another drink for the lady, please?"

Vanity and I sit and chit-chat for thirty more minutes. I feel myself getting tired so I am about to tell her that I'd be leaving.

Ring. Ring. Ring.

"Avery, hold that thought." Vanity says as she answers her cell phone. "NOW!" She sucks her teeth, and then presses her lips together in a hard line. "Ok. I said OKAY!" she barks in a belligerent tone, then "ends" the call. She takes a deep breath, and then sighs unevenly. "Sorry about that, Avery. Listen, I gotta get up outta here and take care of some business." she pauses. "You've been so open with me about your life so I feel the need to do the same. That was my boss, Philip. He's such a pain in my ass. I moonlight as a chanteuse over at this nightclub, Bag Lady Blues in Montclair. Maybe if you're in to that type of thing you can come and check me out." She raises an arched brow. "We should exchange numbers. Keep in touch. Have a few laughs and a few drinks. Talk. Get to know one another."

I smile. "I'd like that."

Vanity reaches her right hand deep in her handbag and pulls out a business card and hands it to me. I reach in my purse and scramble my fingers around at the bottom for a business card. Finally, I find one and pull it out. The edges are dog-eared but it serves its purpose. I hand it to her. She reaches in for it and slips it in her handbag.

"Well, I have to be off. I'll call you within the week," she says, "Take heed to what I've said. You just don't know what may come." She laughs, and then sprints out the door.

I smile, and then take a sip off of my drink.

16

MY MOUTH OPENS WIDE and a loud yawn sings. I peel back the organic sage-colored quilt and autumn floral flannel sheets from my nude cinnamon skin. I lie still, dazed. Head turns slightly to my left. Sleepy eyes stare, nearly burning a hole into the wall as the lyrics from Mrs. Silva's apartment permeate the barricade that separates us and flows into my ears, then slithers down to my heart and cradles it with such loving gentleness.

Turning fully from my back to my left side, eyes is now gaping at a picture hanging on the egg-shell colored wall of a dark-purple complexioned African woman with a jet-black complected nappy-headed little girl strapped to her strong back. Eyes fixated on the picture; suddenly I am distracted out of my trance. I hear the words, feel the words soaking through to the tenderness of me as if a sponge soppy wet. Instinctively I find myself zoned in as if hypnotized. This achy in my heart alerts me that something tangible has penetrated the delicateness of me.

The vibration of the walls is symbolic to a heartbeat pumping at a rapid pace. Simultaneously my heart is racing in my chest thinking of him. *Calm.* I tell myself. Calm before I start to hyperventilate from all the excitement that is circulating throughout my body. I breathe in and out, out and in, slow and steady breaths.

My left hand lifts and gingerly grazes my coiled hair as a reminder of how his smooth, silky, strong manly skin felt to my fingertips. *Calm. Breathe slowly.* I coach myself. Remember it *was* only a fantasy. It's not real. He, he doesn't exist. He was just a figment of your imagination. A lustful thought of a man you materialized in your head as your soul mate, bedmate, ideal lover, even dream man.

I beg to differ. He exists in my mind, in my mouth, in my love tunnel. He exists in my bed, on my pillows, on my sheets, on my lips, neck, breasts, earlobe...he exists in my heart.

The silhouette of him etches in my mind, then recaps as if a movie being rewind. The images are so abridged, yet as exact as it occurred in my thoughts. *"If I could...could forget him/I would...please believe me."* And I would in a heartbeat, but I can't. I can't let go of what Xavier and I have achieved thus far. Xavier. He is a godsend. The most wonderful man I know, and have grown to love, but something is missing. Pieces no longer fit. Feelings have slightly altered due to the turn of events. I want him. I want him in the worst way, but deep in my gut I don't feel as though Xavier wants me. Wants me as in make love to me. He never says. He hardly shows. What am I supposed to do? Continue to wait for him to realize what he has? I've held myself down for too long. It's time to take off these handcuffs and shackles and just...be...free.

17

FOR EVERY WOMAN who has visited my Message Board: Avery♥hiv.2000 I'd like to say thank you for your continuous support in my endeavors. My hope is to keep the message of awareness ringing in your ears. I cannot stress enough how important it is to get tested!

Ladies, ladies, ladies, please, love you enough to protect yourselves from: HIV/AIDS, STDs/STIs and Hepatitis A, B, and C. Just think beforehand. Put yourself before others.

While it is on my mind I would like to request a favor from you all. Now the favor that I'm going to ask of you all is to write a letter that is not addressed to *your man*, but to your girl, *Vajajay*. Yes, your *vagina*. It may sound silly but it is important to be aware of what your body needs along with your mind and spirit. You'll be surprised of how you truly feel about yourself.

By me writing to my vagina I was informed of things I hadn't really thought about. Ain't gon' lie, I wasn't *exactly* thrilled in what she had to say.

See, the other night I had an "aah haa" moment. It was then that I realized that Hella (that's what I call my vajajay) and I were having some intimate issues that needed to be addressed. Now both of us are some stubborn heffas. Neither of us wanted to make the first move and initiate any conversation. Hellacious was pissed at me. But I didn't know why. She never divulged that need-to-know information to me, so I carried on as I always do. But then I started back tracking. Counting the months that had gone by. Six months or longer was pretty much what it summed up to. It was ridiculous as far as I was concerned. I mean what could I have done that was sooooo bad to have her stop speaking to me? We were supposed to be girls. Well, I guess Hella realized it too. We really needed to sit down and girl talk. But again, who was going to initiate the conversation without it turning into a screaming match. Well, one morning to my utter surprise was a florescent pink Post-it stuck to my (vagina) lips from Hella. She addressed her many concerns. I, on the other hand, walked into my bathroom, pulled down my boy shorts, sat down on the toilet seat, and took a dump. It was evident to me that Hella was full of shit!

Um, as you know I've been through my share of disappointments, heartache, you name it. You frequent Message Board Members pretty much know my story and you have expressed empathy, anger, and encouragement. Some of you even told your own stories to enlighten other women. I found it very powerful, empowering.

So here we are, Ladies, faced with another challenge to better understand ourselves and what our bodies really want and need.

I stayed up most of the night trying to figure out exactly what to say to my girl, Hella (short for Hellacious). Ah, it wasn't easy to admit a lot that I had, but after the fact of divulging my truth I had a better understanding of how we both felt. And I am willing to share what I had written for your benefit. After reading it I hope to either inspire you or at least open a window for some healthy dialogue that will encourage safer sex.

Dear Hella (aka Hellacious),

Listen, ah, I read your lips, as you stated on the Post-it. You said a lot. Ah, I was well aware of my circumstance—of my actions. Reading front and back of the Post-it allowed me to really hear you, want to listen to what you had to say, how you truly felt, and how you are adapting to celibacy life. But I sensed some self-loathing too. That's how I see it. Um, you say you're content. But I-I beg to differ.

First, let me just reiterate that I would never do anything to jeopardize us. I feel that we are well connected enough where we should be able to communicate without all the yelling and screaming. I know it's something we haven't taken the time to do lately. I think in the beginning the conversation was too invasive and I really didn't know how to explain my point-of-view to you at the time. You pretty much set the tone, as you often do. And I followed. But now I feel confident enough to voice some things that you may not like or want to hear. Girl, we grew up together. And we've been tight ever since. We shared periods. Remember how you used to hate wearing those Kotex Maxi pads because they were so bulky and so obvious on your bony behind. We shared yeast infections, too. And remember how nervous we were when we had to go to the GYN for our first Pap smear? Girl, we were petrified! Hell, we shared our first sexual experience, even though that was nothing to brag about. Remember the miscarriage? We were a nervous wreck. Sad. Withdrawn. Yeah. That was difficult but we hung in there for one another. I had mixed feelings on that too. Still till this day, I do. Of course we should've waited on having sex, but, 'ey, you live and learn.

223

Look, Hella, we are not always going to get along. Women, you know. That's just how it is on any given day. But I want you to know that I respect you, and I love you, and I want us to explore and enjoy life while we still have life in us. And I get that we can always make better choices in the men we choose. I realize that sometimes it takes time to really find the right companion. But sometimes time seems to be flying by and it makes me wonder if I'll ever truly be happy. Lord knows I've had a taste of some good men with good intentions, but somewhere along the way I'll admit I've fallen off. Settling was never an option of mine. I don't know what happened. Well, I do, but rather not say. A lot changed in me. In us. I see it. I feel it.

I heard you, Hella. I heard a lot in your voice, things you said and didn't say. Every word you expressed had depth. However, I challenge if it all had truth. For some reason I think you're afraid—afraid to lose yourself in someone. Afraid to be vulnerable and seen and explored without feeling threatened. You used to be so lively and easygoing. Sex. It used to be so spontaneous and thrilling. But now it's mundane and kind of predictable. Romance. That's what's missing. The romance between you and me. We don't share moments like some women do. I mean we don't go there—to that place of solitude and self-gratification—enjoyment of that moment of intimacy that a man and a woman share. Nowadays folks just have sex just to have sex. There's no meaning behind it. Just sex. And I guess a woman such as me should want more than just sex. I should want to explore you, but... What if the only connection you can have with a man is to open your legs to know if he truly wants you in his life. In my case, in all women's cases we want to believe that, but in all honesty it's just another lie behind closed doors. Because the truth of the matter is, if he can't be seen with you after the fact of fucking you, then there was never a deeper connection. There was never even the thought of a relationship. Women make is so easy for men. Men don't have to work for it like they used to back in the day. Now it's too commonplace. No sparks. No stars. No moonlight. Love as I remember from my parents was like poetry. Not easily read but known.

Some folks considered me "wild" but I never saw myself as "wild". I considered myself "free-spirited". Someone who enjoyed spending time with men without all of the hoopla attached to it. I was never drama material. Everything was pretty simple when dealing with me. At least I thought it was compared to other women that I've heard about or seen out in public get raved up because they were rejected. It wasn't a pretty sight. If anything, it gave me a reason not to flip. Why give him the satisfaction of knowing that I care that much? No. I'd rather disappear. As I've done many, many times.

Even knowing all of this, the longing to be wanted seems to override everything. My situation puts me at a standstill. I'm at a crossroad between Ask and Don't Ask. It's not easy being me. Wasn't easy being me before, but then I didn't have this stigma attached either.

Hella, even with depth I don't think you comprehend what I am currently going through. Okay. I get that you don't want to be conditioned. Controlled. You don't want to feel like someone is being territorial with your stuff. And I also get that there is more to you than just pussy. Trust me, I get it. That's why you're so aloof. To be honest I think you're frustrated with rejection. 'Ey, no one likes to be rejected, but it comes with the territory. Not every man is going to want you for your mind. That is the very reason we make sure we have our own supply of condoms. And we know that we shouldn't depend on a man to have what we should already have for ourselves. Hella, all we can do as women is be upfront and let the cards fall where they may. Do you know how challenging it is for a man to adapt to strong-minded woman, responsible woman, intelligent woman? I am a woman who cannot and will not be controlled. Girl, women, like that go through obstacles to find and keep a man—a man who will respect her and still love her at the same time—dating is not easy. And lately, casual sex is not easy either. Women are seeking relationships. They are tired of giving it up on a whim—going home to an empty house to sleep in an oversized bed, alone. Women are beginning to wake up and see that they have options. Single and sex-free. Yep. It is an option. But just as me, women get that lonely itch. Dating, you remember how it was for us. Yeah. Exactly. Hypnotic, LoJac ...we had our share, didn't we. But dating can be fulfilling with the right two people who have a strong mental. Look, I know how sensitive you are. That's one of the reasons why I'll choose my words carefully. I don't want to burn any bridges between us.

Hella, I understand that you feel extremely undesirable. Your mood-swings can be a slight turn off. One minute you are hot, the next cold. But listen, I feel that I have been most understanding when it comes to you, girl. I mean you are my very best friend— the only friend that truly knows me. But I need you to reflect back on how you used to feel with that thick piece of meat inside you. Girl, you can't tell me you didn't feel good and wanted with that dick. I never said a word when you were getting your groove on. But over the years I noticed a difference in your sexual appetite. You can't be on a dick-free diet. Baby, you looked too fabulous to be on somebody's diet. I gotta give it to yah, girl, you used to keep yourself well-groomed—skin as soft as a baby's bottom. Immaculate. And the scent smelled like sweet golden honey. But lately you've been hidden. Please don't take this wrong, but girl, I can't find you anymore. The bush has gotten thick! I think, no, rather I know it's time for a BIC, baby. You used to let yourself breathe. You had no inhibitions. Hella was free-spirited. Now you keep *yourself covered up with pajamas and sweats. What's going on? You used to talk. Even in your quiet moments I knew exactly what was on your mind. Body language, girl, and the way you used to pulsate. The way you used to ooze those juices. The way you used to get so hot and bothered. The way your flesh used to get moist and soppy wet. All of that seems to have dissipated. Almost as if you've given up or shut down or are on the verge of giving up or shutting down. What I don't understand is why? Honey, you are in your fun-in-the-sun years! These years are priceless! So why do you continue to wear those granny drawers? What happened to feeling free and sexy and young and vibrant? It's like you choose to wither and cluster yourself in gray hairs. We are too young to be acting old and losing vitality and elasticity.*

Hella, don't do this to me, to us. For once in your life look at it from my perspective I'm not a vegan. Never practiced being one either. It is so easy to fill that request of celibacy, which you know I have done before. I'm not rushing anything at this point. I have my reasons. Two reasons as to why I choose to stick with what I know. Although, sometimes I wish you would really understand where I'm coming from. Hell, I'm not coming at all. And quite often I feel like you either don't care to or there are other reasons that I won't get into. Like I said I try very hard with you but I continuously get the door shut in my face. After a while of getting the door shut in your face you begin to remove yourself and preoccupy your time and mind with other things. But I'm stressed out. And I need and want to be felt and loved and cuddled and kissed. Why won't you just let go and let your sweet berry juice flow?

I'm tired of all of this. You can't control every aspect of my life! You won't allow entry for your own selfish reasons. It's that list again, isn't it? Hella, (girl, you gonna make me call you out your name), when are you going to get it through your clitoris that that penis does not exist! Sho' you want that one and only. What woman doesn't? But sometimes I wish you would stop dreaming, living in a fantasy world! And realize that majority of the penises out here are shared, honey. Or gay. No disrespect. And even the gay ones are shared. Sometimes, girl, sometimes you have to take what God is giving. Your dream penis may not come in a full package of single with attractive extras specifically for your taste buds. He may not come with all of those perks. What are you going to do, then, huh? Continue to shrivel up because you can't have what or whom you want? Is that fair to me?! Why should I have to continue to suffer, huh? All I'm asking for is for you to be reasonable and realize. Realize that I am in dire need of a well-endowed penis!

Sometimes, Hella, you can be pompous ass. You expect so much from me. Too much. Yeah. I should devote more time and focus on what is important to me. I should take this quiet time and embrace it. I should smell the single and free roses, if you will.

Meditate. Appreciate the freedom. And I do, except the meditate part. I haven't taken the time to learn that yet. And I know that you think that whatever comes with a penis should also come with more to offer than just penis. You'a trip. That strikes me as odd coming from you. I mean all of a sudden Ms Hella gotta conscience. Before this new transformation you used to get down. You never worried about quality time because you, my dear, required space. You called the shots. I know. I know that you were never the clingy type. And yes, you were always selective, but let's keep it real by saying you never missed an opportunity. You indulged plenty. Okay. You had an acquired taste White meat. That's true. But you can't tell me that those penises didn't fulfill your needs. At least some of 'em did. That was up and until—

I agree. I do understand. A lot has changed.

But do you see yourself? Do you see how you treat me? You shut the door in my face. Padlock it. Hibernate. I sensed way before now that you were depressed. And I know you have good reason to be. If anybody knows, I know. But it's not a healthy way to live, sweetie. All of that pent-up frustration eventually needs to come gushing out.

Haven't you noticed in the shower…the way I caress you? That, that something is missing in-between my legs. Haven't you noticed how I ache?! I know you can feel it?! You just choose not to. You've always been good at blocking things out. But then you expect me to understand. How can I, Hella? Your response is always the same. You abruptly shut the door in my face. And I, me, Hella, I wallow in anguish hating me because of what happened to us—hating me because we were raped—hating me because we have HIV.

But you know what, girl, FUCK you! I'd be damned if I'm gonna shrivel up and die. I'd be damned!

Sincerely,

Avery

227

18

"C'MON NOW, WOMAN! Av, get your stank-ass up and go wash that funk! Your armpits smell like musk. I know your ass smells like butt-butt. It's probably glued to that chair. I can't believe you, girl, that computer ain't going nowhere, so please go into that bathroom and take care of that." Akil says, while scrunching up his nose.

I don't even bother to raise my eyes. I simply erase him from my mind and continue on with what I am doing.

Akil paces back and forth trying to think of a way to break my train of thought, "Listen, Avery, no offense but I can smell your coochie from all the way over here." I continue to ignore him because now he's being mean to me. He didn't have to say that. With my head focused on the computer screen and my fingers fast clicking to finish the last sentence that I'm currently working on, Akil plants himself alongside me with his arms folded about his chest. He seems pretty annoyed with my unkempt display. I am in a zone and I don't want to lose this charge of energy. Shower can wait.

Akil won't let up. He keeps on nagging, which is really beginning to tick me off. I don't show it on my face but I am about to pop inside if this man doesn't leave me alone. *Last straw, Akil! Please. Please don't say anything else. Not another word. Have mercy.* But he can't help it. Inspector Gadget just keeps running his trap. Yap, yap, yap! I simply tune him out before I leap up and sneak him with a left hook cracking his jaw. Never underestimate me. I move pretty swiftly since Hellman. I'd promised myself to never allow another man to diminish me like he'd done to me. Punch, slap, humiliate me in such a way. I had to learn how to defend myself. Kickboxing really disciplined me. But for some reason my skills did not kick in that evening with Hellman. I froze. Merely froze and allowed that man to beat me without cause. I loved him. And he beat me down because he loved someone else.

The feel of my eyelids are extremely heavy. Barely able to keep my eyes open I try to fight the sleepiness. I can't remember last when I actually slept four or five hours. Was it yesterday? Or, or the day before that? Don't know. I've been a busy bee.

I tilt back my head open my mouth wide and I let out a loud yawn. Oh, God what I do that for because Akil goes in for the kill. He fans his hands in front of his nose and scrunches it up like I just passed gas. "Damn, girl, when was the last time you brushed your teeth?! Smells like somebody died up in here." I frown. "And I know," Akil puts emphasis on "and" with a stretch of his eyes, "you're not still sipping from that same mug of cold lemon ginger tea from three days ago. Girl, what is happening to you? It's like you've become obsessed with this, this manuscript. All you do is, sit there clicking away. You don't cook. Your hamper is overflowing with dirty clothes. Smells like death walked in here and farted and bounced! This apartment is a mess! Your fridge is bare. All you have is a bottle of spring water, seltzer water, two eggs, a package of Borden's $2.79 shredded cheddar and Monterey Jack cheese. You haven't even gone food shopping! You have dishes piled high in the sink. The bathtub has a black dirt ring around it. The kitchen floor is sticky like you spilled juice on it and didn't bother to mop it up. Look at this place, girl!" His arms rise and stretch out wide as he shakes his head from side to side. "Just look at it!" He takes a deep, deep breath. "This is not you, Avery. I don't know what that manuscript is all about, but damn, if it has you like this maybe you need to put that shit down and come back to earth 'cause, girlfriend, you got it bad," he snaps with a crumpled forehead.

I completely shut down. Why does he always have to be the center of attention? Why can't he leave a little room for me? I don't think I'm asking for too much. Am I?

Here I thought that Akil would be supportive. But I see I was wrong. If he doesn't like what's happening to me, why doesn't he just leave! I didn't ask him to come over here. Actually he invited himself. I mean, dang, can't he see that I'm trying to accomplish something here? At this point in my life I really don't have anything else worth doing. And when I did everything pretty much slipped through my fingers. And I so willingly gave up. I'm not used to living a destitute lifestyle. To come from living in a home to living any and everywhere I can fit in. To fall so far and to have no one to help lift my spirits or me up is devastating. To see my potential just bury itself for fear of failing again and again. So much has happened in my life—things that Akil knows nothing about— things that I do not wish to share. I need a new start—a new beginning to prove to myself that I can bounce back to a lifestyle that I am accustomed to living. I'll admit I have spoiled me. And to taste it once, only teases me to taste it again, but this time on His terms. I just have to follow His lead. I know that I can have all the things my heart desires as long as *I* work hard. Akil has no idea of who "Avery Love" really is. I am more than just a black woman. I am a testament of faith. I am a book to inspire. This time I have to fulfill my destiny. If I give up, where will it leave me? Back where I was before I ever started—on a dead-end street to nowhere.

Akil's a platonic friend. But for how long...honestly, I really can't say. I guess it all depends on what other insensitive thoughts come spewing out of his big mouth. Why do folks do that? Speak of every thought with no regard for the person they're speaking about? I could have fragile skin and bones. I could be so sensitive that I threaten to slit my wrists. Akil doesn't know much of anything about me. So therefore, he should watch what he says to me. I could snap and slap the shit outta him. But then, I'd be wrong. I wouldn't do it for the simple fact Akil does have a point. And as much as I hate to admit it, I am obsessed with this manuscript.

Akil doesn't understand the bond, the connection, or the purpose. He doesn't understand how this manuscript is giving me the strength I so desperately need. I can actually breathe again. Think. Smell life again. See a better tomorrow. See myself moving forward. This is a big deal—a huge imposition—a godsend.

I have a lot riding on this manuscript. Akil just doesn't know how much. He doesn't understand me. I have to keep reminding myself: he is not Johnnie. Johnnie knew me like the back of his hand. Akil is a novice at knowing me. I'm different, as folks tend to tell me every day.

Akil and I are like complete opposites. We have nothing in common, other than teaching. I would like to think that I teach by being open about my life—the obstacles that I've faced. I consider myself a window, a mirror; glass...a metaphor for anything that is translucent and easily broken. Akil is outgoing, wild, and dare-devilish. Me, well, I am pretty predictable.

I remember the first day I invited Akil over to my apartment.

It was the weekend, a Saturday, if I'm not mistaken. Akil came over around seven o'clock. He was casually dressed in a black Adidas sweat suit with white shell-toe Adidas on. We sat on the sofa in my living room chitchatting about back in the day, while sipping on flute glasses of Riesling and nibbling on hor d'ourves of hot spinach dip with warm cube-sized pieces of baguette wheat bread.

Malcolm Cobb & Six Shoes Band CD "Maya" was playing in the background. The lights were dim. It was cozy and quaint ambiance—strictly two friends getting reacquainted.

Akil placed his wine glass down on the saffron coffee table. "So, Av, what do you do besides: read, write, watch DVDs, oh, and listen to your CDs?"

I shrugged my shoulders. "I guess that's pretty much it. Oh, besides, cooking, baking, and an occasional poetry reading in Montclair."

I was content with that. But Akil seemed a bit baffled. I swear he reminded me of Travar Atkin with his many questions.

"No. I mean...what you do for *fun*?" he asked.

He put a lot of emphasis on the word...*fun*. All I could do was suck my teeth.

Akil just kept pressing, digging for an adequate answer. I guess one that would suit him, not me.

Didn't I just tell him? I thought.

"That is fun, Akil." I expressed.

"For you," he mumbled.

I took a sip of wine and disregarded his insensitive comment.

My thoughts bounce from one thing to another: house chores, food shopping, laundry, but I have a deadline that I can't afford to miss. I have to stay focused. I mean so much is dependent upon me. So much pressure left in my hands. I have to make a good first impression or I might as well call it quits at being a novelist. No. Writing was not my first career choice. This unexpected gift was kind of placed in my hands. Now I feel obligated to complete what I've started. Yes, that's how I truly feel. Don't get me wrong; it's not a bad thing. It's just, just something I never expected to be doing.

Poetry is one thing. But writing a book is a totally different dress size, shoe size for me. I don't know if I have what it takes. I mean without the proper tools how can I possibly make this manuscript into a masterpiece, let alone expect folks to want to buy it. I sigh. I guess all I can do is put my best foot forward and believe that anything is possible. And you know what, that is exactly what I am going to do. No more second-guessing. No more doubt. No more negativity. I am going to remain positive and hope for the best. Actually, I'm praying for a miracle.

Why am I so on edge? I guess 'cause it is something new. I don't know what the heck I'm doing. I mean the longest poem I've ever written was like two pages long. And that was pretty easy because the words just flowed. A book is completely different. You have to put a lot of thought into it. It has to make sense in order to follow each scene, sort of like a movie. It is pretty doggone scary for a novice like me. Who am I kidding? Everything I seem to touch turns sour. Okay. Okay. Maybe I'm being a little too hard on myself. It's the pressure. It's beginning to get to me. Folks expectations are high, and, and, I don't know if I have what it takes to pull this off. There goes that doubt again. Well, I can't help it! This is huge for me. I can't even fathom it. I'm a poet, not a writer.

I lift up the thick manuscript while sitting at my desk. Sorting through the pages I check to make sure the title page is first, copyright page follows, odd header has the title of the book, and the even header has the names of the authors. Scroll my eyes down to the footer to make sure all the pages are numbered. I sigh, relieved, smile; lean my body backs against the soft black leather swivel chair feeling a sense of feat for nearly completing my task.

I sit silent for what seems like a nanosecond, then turn to look at Akil standing by the high-rise window, staring out.

My voice raises one octave to distract Akil from his trance. "Ey, tell me how this sounds? This is what I wrote for the front cover of the book."

"It sounds good," he says in a husky voice.

"I haven't read anything yet, knucklehead. Listen to this, Akil: 'Her mind was filled with imagination but her life was anything but...If you have daughters, clench em to your bosom and never let em go!' whatchu think?"

Silence.

I disregard him and say, "Oh, I forgot to mention to you that I was lucky enough to get that author Pink Khocolate to write a: Foreword for the book. Isn't that great! I never thought she'd respond to my email but she did. She really did!" I smile from ear to ear.

Akil smirks, still gazing out of the window.

I cut my eyes up to the high white ceiling.

"Johnnie, I hope I didn't wake you. I know how you like to get your beauty sleep. You can be cranky in the morning when you don't get enough rest. Oh, by the way Happy Birthday! Yep. It's that time again. December 18th. Such a Sagittarius, you are. J, how old is you now? I know what you're going to say: 'Avery, that's my business, gurrrrrrrrlllll.' Then you'd snap your fingers and laugh. I was just reading your horoscope off of Horoscope.com. And it had you pegged. One thing it said, well, a couple of things were that you're an extrovert, optimistic, and enthusiastic. Can't keep a Sagittarius down and that is so true. Your life motivated you, Johnnie. You were always up for change no matter how painful it might've been you lit up with energy. And you were always searching, wandering to find the meaning of life. Now that I think about it you were always a traveler in spirit. God, I miss your laugh, Johnnie. I

miss your silliness. I miss your free spirit too. Well, on a more serious note. Ah, remember the package I told you about? I finished typing the manuscript today. But now I have the tedious job of proofreading and editing it. As you know I am not an editor. And currently I can't afford to hire one. I can only do what I can do. I'm, as you would say: 'holding it down' on this project. I've been going to the library to research other books. I've been checking out book covers too. I figured it would give me some ideas for my book cover, you know. So much pressure, Johnnie, so much pressure I feel. You're the only one I can really talk to about things like this. I love you, Johnnie Rivera. Tell God I said hi. Oh, and tell Him I didn't mean to do it. He'll know what I'm talking about."

Writing a book is not easy. I don't care what anyone else says. It is not a piece of cake. You need all of the ingredients or the cake will fall. I don't want to fail at this. I want it to be a success. I'm a complete worrywart. I know. I know.

"Akil, I need your honest opinion on if I should leave it as it *is* or *finagle* with the wording a bit. I don't want to take too much from it, you know. I want it to still be in Daisy's voice, not mine." I say, and then rise from my seat with what feels like a stack of bricks in my hands.

I pace about the hardwood living room floor, engaged in thought.

"What's the title of this book again?" Akil asks with his back facing me.

"Pay attention. The *title* is *Ev'ry Ho Gotta Daddy*." I roll my eyes a tad bit annoyed. I mean I've told him the title like three times already. You'd think he'd remember. If he'd get his mind off of that car he'll be able to retain something in that thick head of his.

Akil nods his head.

I stand still and just gaze at him. My tongue glides across my bottom lip. Mmmmmm. Look at him, all sexy 'n shit. He's dressed in a pair of Lucky Brand jeans, V-neck white tee with pinstriped blazer and square toed chocolate brown leather shoes. His dreadlocks are pulled back in a neat ponytail. His skin looks so dewy. I wonder what he uses to make it look like that.

Why didn't he just put a ball and chain on that car if he's so worried about it getting stolen? Ain't nobody tell him to go out and buy that expensive ass cherry apple red Mercedes-BenzS500 anyway. My left brow rises. *How can he afford it off of a teacher's salary? Is what I'd like to know?*

Finally, Akil turns away from the window and gives me his undivided attention.

It's about time! I think.

Akil has been my friend for 'bout, oh, five months now. It's a different kind of friendship than what I shared with Johnnie. Johnnie and I were best, best, best friends. Akil and I were classmates in grammar school.

We reunited by coincidence. No, I won't say it was fate.

As I recall it was a Friday evening. I was at the Garden State Plaza mall in Paramus, New Jersey, and I happened to notice this guy who I *thought* looked like Akil. Still, I wasn't too sho'.

I was in Macy's buying my favorite bare mineral foundation (Dark Deep) by MAC. This guy was over at the next counter, buying Weekend by Burberry. He was lanky, dark chocolate skin tone with deep burnt sienna eyes and shoulder-length salt-and-pepper dreadlocks. I kept saying to myself that it was Akil, but I still wasn't too sure until I walked over in his direction.

As soon as I got up close the man cut his eyes to the side, and then turned fully around staring me dead in my face.

His eyes widened as if surprised. "A-Avery?"

I nonchalantly looked in his direction to acknowledge him.

"Akil?"

"Hey! Long time no sees!" he said.

"How long has it been? Ah, since...grammar school, right?" I said with excitement in my tone.

"Yeah." he nodded. "Look at you." His eyes scrolled every inch of my tall frame. "You look amazing!"

"You too," I told him with a big ass, stupid grin on my face.

Akil sure looked eatable that day. He was sporting a pair of dark blue Skinny jeans and a button down white-collar shirt, which made him look like a model in one of those men fashion magazines.

We chatted for a little over forty-five minutes, exchanged numbers, which took another five minutes, then parted ways.

Who'd ever think Akil Jojoba would become a fifth grade schoolteacher, I think to myself. *I* certainly didn't. I guess 'cause back then he was a bully in school. He always started trouble with my classmates to gain some type of respect. I figured by now he'd be either dead or behind bars for the rest of his life. It had come to my attention years later that Akil had joined a gang. That's why he was acting so out of control. I did know that he lived in a fatherless household. Missing his dad could've brought on many ill feelings that he acted out on the outside. Whatever changed him for the better, I am so glad it did.

I sit back down in the black leather swivel chair and engross myself in the manuscript. I read a passage, aloud. Each word, I swear, I can hear

Daisy's voice coming through—clear and stormy. I can hear the emotions building as she relinquishes her anguish. I feel it as I am reading. I hear it so loudly as if she is screaming in my ears. It is horrendous.

Akil breaks my train of thought. "It's sounds very straightforward. It's kind of in your face. If that's what you're going for, then it works. I guess." He pauses. "By the way who's Daisy, Avery?"

I pause. And as I do, a feeling of apprehension comes over me when asked about Daisy. I don't know why. Or maybe I do, and just am a little embarrassed to say. Why bother to keep it all to myself?

It could have something to do with her lifestyle as a prostitute and a junky. I don't want to give Akil the wrong impression of me. You know how it is. Folks often judge you based on the folks you associate with— the company you keep. I know that sounds pretty shallow, but I have had enough of folks judging me based on my own personal life. I don't need any more added to my already toxic profile.

The last time I heard Daisy's voice was when she'd called in to Red Alert to talk about her kids. You remember Daisy, right? You know whom I'm talking about—the white chick with the legs to die for like Tina Turner—yeah her. And let me *not* forget about her boyfriend, Jessie. The one she kept yelling at about her fuckin' beer.

Well, anyway, a package was addressed to: C/O RED ALERT, Mr. Xavier Combs III/Avery Love. Xavier must've put it away in the storage boxes around the time I was in the hospital and completely forgot about it. Apparently someone wanted me to read *her* story—a story that would hopefully awaken the youth. *Heck, I'll give it a shot*, I thought since I was unsuccessful at being a motivational speaker. Those students took me for a doggone joke.

There was a letter enclosed in it stating that she wanted *me* to get her story out to the world. Why me? I wondered. That was, if I survived through my own ordeal. Obviously, time seemed to be drifting away for Daisy. Funny, Xavier never opened the package. I'm a little surprised. I happened to stumble upon the package a few weeks ago, while I was looking for something in some boxes in the bedroom closet. I can't remember what though.

I did some digging and I found out from someone that works at Hopkins Hospital and Medical Center that Daisy was hooked up to a respirator. Her three children (two daughters and a son) found her and they could not find the strength within to pull the plug. I'm not quite sure how they found her, but at least they did. I wonder if Daisy knew that they were in the room with her. I surely hoped she felt their presence. Like Poppa used to say: "I guess a little time is better than lost time." It really saddened me when I saw her obituary in the Sunday, HeraldNews. It brought tears to my eyes when I saw the lovely picture of her. And read about all the activities she was involved in. The churches she attended. The places she used to work. How she took time out of her daily schedule to volunteer. Reading about her and seeing her picture, huh, Daisy used to be a very attractive woman in her day. Yeah, it's a shame how one minute you can be riding high on life, and then the next find yourself in a crack house getting high. Yep. Magnolia "Daisy" Wily is finally at rest. She will truly be missed.

The funeral is scheduled for next Wednesday. I think I may go. Go and pay my respects properly.

Akil waves his hands in front of my face. "Ah, earth to, Avery."

I flinch. "Huh?"

"Are you ok?"

I nod.

"'Cause you seem a bit on edge," he says. "As I was saying, who's Daisy?"

"Oh, she's the name of the woman in the book."

"I know that, but who *is* she? Do you know her or know of her through someone else?"

"I know of her." I stress to him. I don't want to get too personal with Akil. Some things I like to keep to myself. I guess Daisy is one of those things, at least for now.

Akil has a strange look on his face like he's deep in thought.

"Is something wrong?" I ask, with a look of concern on my face.

"Maybe you should consider writing it in third-person opposed to first-person," he says.

I nod with my left thumb tucked underneath my chin. "I'll probably write it in first-person. It will make it seem more personal, you know, similar to the books *Anonymous, Sleepin' Wit' the Virus* that that author Karla Denise Baker wrote. You know she lives here in Paterson, right? Well, last I heard she was."

Akil dismisses what I've just said. He sits down and stretches out his long legs, as he gets comfy in the saffron leather chair.

I feel the heat from his eyes burning through my skin. Why is he staring at me? I wonder.

Akil places his hands on his lap. "Soooo, is this a self-portrait?"

"What?" I say a little guarded. Why is he digging? If this were about me I would say so. I mean I have nothing to hide. I've pretty much exposed myself in *Kreepin' Wit' the Virus*. Obviously he hasn't read any of Karla's books.

"Is this another Chick-lit book? I think I heard about her. She's the chick everyone was saying wrote the book as fiction to hide the truth—something about the story being about her true life. Now that you mention it, I do remember some talk about her and that book. It was the first book she wrote." He nods his head up and down. "Yeah, Av, people are a trip, you know what I'm sayin'." He cuts his eyes to the side. "What you think?" He asks.

"About what?"

"Do you think it's really about her or not?"

"Can't say. I mean if she wrote it where she made you feel like it was a personal story, I say great for her. Does it really matter? I mean her whole objective was to tell a dang story. I don't know why folks are making more out of nothing. It's a story—a great, uplifting, powerful and compelling story."

"But doesn't it make you wonder how far a person will go to seek fame?"

"Yes and no. When I read the book I didn't think of that question. If anything, I felt a connection to the writer as she told of her horrific ordeal. It really made me open my eyes to men, relationships, trust, family, self. I commend her. I'm sho' telling the story wasn't easy. And whether it is true or not is irrelevant to me."

"You sound like you're taking offense to my question."

"Because you sound like 'them', listen to yourself."

"My bad."

I nod, once, while keeping my head low as I focus on what I am doing. "Yeah. She caught some heat for it. But I admire her because she took a risk. She didn't let what folks thought discourage her from pursuing her dream. She really inspires me, you know. Women are readers. Who better to write about than 'em, huh? Did you read any of her books, Ak.? If you want I have all three over there on the bookshelf."

"Nah. Like I said it's Chick-lit. Fiction is not really my thing. I like nonfiction. Like Richard Wright's *Black Boy* or James Baldwin's *No Name In The Street*. No offense."

"None taken," I say. "I was reading a novel by Ernest J. Gaines, *A Lesson Before Dying*. I haven't finished it yet, though. I figured once I finish this project I can go back to it. I think I left off on page 124."

Akil continues, "I gotta give it to yah, Av. Women are readers. It's sad that some men won't even pick up a book, let alone read one. I try to instill that reading is important to my students, especially the boys." Akil scrunches up his nose. "Can I ask, what's up with the title, *Ev'ry Ho Gotta Daddy?*"

My eyebrows rise as I raise my head. "You don't think it's catchy?"

"Catchy, yes, but is it going to grasp your audience attention? I don't see you as an urban writer, Av. You're normally subtle. You know, more so a contemporary women's fiction writer, not as straightforward as this. You see how that author, oh, what's her name," he pauses for what seems like a second or two, and then snaps his fingers, "Ntozake Shange."

"Who? Ntozake? The playwright and poet, what about her?"

"She writes movie material. That's how you want to write and think. Think big," he says enthusiastically.

Why is it that folks who don't have talent always wanna add their two cents in? I always wondered but I never asked that question because I felt it would be rude to put someone on the spot, but if Akil don't stop running his choppers it's about to get ugly up in here.

"All due respect, Akil, it took like thirty-something years for her book to become a movie. And as I recall Oprah and Tyler Perry had a lot to do with that. Need I remind you her poetry was made into a play first? It made it all the way to Broadway. And plus, I'm not Ntozake. I've read her poetry book, *For Colored Girls Who Have Considered Suicide/When the Rainbow is Enuf.* It was deep. But everyone is different. Their writing styles are different. I'm not trying to mimic anyone, because for one, I will never be able to write like anyone else. My experiences are different from others. My speech. My tone. My struggles. My desires. My anger. My fears. My anguish. Akil, you fail to understand that a traditional publisher is not picking me up. Do you realize how many hands the raw cut version of a manuscript goes through? Listen, I sent sample chapters of this manuscript out to 10 different literary agents and not one offered to read the entire manuscript. That's 10 rejection letters! Oh, sure *one* thought I had a compelling story but she wondered how she would market it. I'm self-publishing this book under me: *PINK PINSTRIPES PUBLISHING.* I don't have time to wait for them. *Opportunity* and *life* waits for no one." I smirk, and then narrow-eye him.

Akil remains quiet. He just nods his head. I guess he knows what's best.

I am on a roll. "Don't get me wrong, Ntozake was fortunate. I do not hate one bit. When it is time for me to make it there, then it shall come to pass, but for now I'll do it my way. Ntozake has her way and I have mine. With this being my *first* book (which is actually my fourth) I have to go with my gut. I understand where you're coming from Akil, don't think I don't. But I want this book to reach young girls who live in urban cities—even the ones who don't—girls who don't come from close-knit families—girls who feel lonely and alone—girls who are suffering in their skin—girls who live in deplorable conditions—girls who grew up on welfare—girls who have no concept of what being "independent" means—girls who have dreams and aspirations—hopes of going to college and getting out of their environment. Girls who yearn to be another: Oprah, Whoopi Goldberg, Toni Morrison, Angela Bassett, Aretha Franklin, shoot, Queen Latifah or even the recently departed Ms. Whitney Houston. I want this book to reach girls who were not prepared for the obstacles of what it means to have a *vagina* between their legs."

Akil eyes widen. "Whoa. Who said anything about *vagina*?"

"I did. Listen. Some girls don't know their worth. Some women don't either. Some girls and women don't understand the sacredness of their bodies because their mothers never explained it to 'em. Probably never lived by example. Who were their mentors? Grandmothers? Aunts? Sisters? Boyfriends? Some girls don't even understand the value of their vagina. Some don't even know how to clean it properly. These young girls are under the impression that if you wash it once then that makes it clean. But they don't realize throughout all the activity in a day, a girl needs to wash her body thoroughly."

"Yeah," Akil says, "Listen, the way I see it a girl doesn't know how to wash her ass and pussy until she reaches womanhood at least in her mid-thirties into early forties. And *even* some of them don't. I tell you no lie. I met this fine honey. Oh, she was divine to the naked eye. She had body, a job, and her own crib. Sad to say, she was faking the funk. I didn't find this out right away. She tried to keep me at a distance. But one day I said to her, 'Glitter, how come you've never invited me to your house?' That's when I found out. She told me that she was going through something and she didn't want me to look at her in a certain way. I was like, what you mean? She said, 'well, last week I felt weird. Um, I had to run to the bathroom, like I had this urgency to pee. Then when I did it burned. I had this pain that wouldn't go away. I didn't know what was wrong with me because I had never experienced something like that before. So I went to the emergency room. Come to find out I had a urinary tract infection. I was like, 'a what? Where did this come from?' She said she knew she wasn't a dirty person. She said the doctor explained that UTI (urinary tract infection) is usually caused by a germ. And that it is cured with antibiotics. But you have to make sure you take all the medicine until it is gone because if you don't the infection may not get well. It can become more difficult to treat. She said the doctor told her to prevent further infections she should pee often. That after a bowel movement, women should wipe from front to back. Use each tissue only once. And that she should pee before and after sexual intercourse. She said she was drinking a lot of cranberry juice and water to keep fluid in her body. I was like, 'Glitter, you could've told me that. I wouldn't have looked at you as being dirty or out here fuckin' like a rabbit with some dirty muthafucker. I don't see you as that type of chick. Look. I get it that most men jump to conclusions, but not every man is that ignorant to the fact that y'all women got shit going on. And no, I can't sit here and vouch for every man when I say that some men are just plain ignorant. Some men don't think before they speak. Some men are just uneducated when it comes to women issues. They don't understand and they don't want to understand. Women go through shit all the time. Look, Glitter, I've experienced this before so we good as far as I'm concerned.' She was like, 'yeah, women do. A whole lotta shit.' I told her to let me see her for her. Yeah, you're beautiful but let me see how you *really* livin' behind closed doors. No, I didn't want her to go home and cleanup shit. I wanted to go straight to the house, right then and there, and see what *she* was workin' with. Before we even walked into her crib I could smell this foul odor seeping through the door. I wanted to vomit. I took my chances and walked in trying to give her the benefit of the doubt 'cause she was soooo *fine*. Her upkeep appeared to be in immaculate condition based on her form of dress. You know the bumptious type of chick. Avery, the place was filthy. I took the liberty of opening up her fridge, while she went into the bathroom to call herself freshening up. Baby, I kid you not; I slammed the door and bounced. She didn't have to *ever* worry about seeing my black ass ever again. You know, some women may look clean and keep a dirty house. And some women may look dirty and keep a clean house. And some women may look clean and keep a clean house, like you Avery. I'm baffled by this shit. I know one thing every time I come to your crib it's clean. Bathroom clean. Kitchen clean. Therefore I know you keep the pussy, clean. I mean I'd eat off your floor that's how much I trust you. You don't see me buggin' when you cook for me. Hell, no! I eat that shit 'cause you can throw down in the kitchen. Fuck what you heard! Any brotha' who don't appreciate a woman who can maintain her house, her body, and her duties in the bedroom is a dumb muthafucker. I'm just sayin'. See, Av, I didn't bounce because of the urinary tract infection. Nah. I bounced because of her dirty ass crib."

I double over in the chair cracking up, slobbering and all. "What was in the fridge?"

Akil rolls his eyes, while I'm still laughing. "You really want to know?"

I nod, while I am still doubled over.

"*Maggots!*"

I cringe from the thought.

Akil continues, "Now, you know that didn't make no goddamn sense and you out here walking around like *Foxy Brown*. I feel you on that. If you can't smell your own ass and armpits when it is funky and pussy when it is fishy or smells like death, then that is evident to me, that you don't know yourself. Know yourself enough to know that you stink. These young girls don't have a clue about personal hygiene. Using Norforms Vaginal Suppositories is not the answer to all. Wash your ass!!!! Douche! Got white discharge caking up in the seat of your panties and you walking around strutting like your ass don't stink. Get one of them DNC or DMC's whatever you call that shit. That's why I don't mess with these fast-ass young girls—they too fast for their own damn good. I prefer a woman in her mid-to-late forties—a seasoned kind of woman whose pussy smells sterile. But honestly, I prefer a woman who allows a man to be the man. You know the type of woman who doesn't chase a man. I can't stand a pushy or needy woman. That is a turn-off for me."

This grasps my attention. So I stop what I am doing for a sec. "What do you mean by chase or needy? Explain?" I say.

"You know the kind of women who chase but probably are not aware that they are chasing after him. They have a tendency to beat a man to the finishline and then they wonder why he doesn't express himself. When did he have the opportunity to do so with her constantly running the show? If she'd lean back a bit and slow her roll possibly he'd feel more incline to meet her halfway, you know, um, but if she continues to call before I call her or initiate contact like texting me to death or emailing me too much or Facebooking me like crazy or the worst dropping by uninvited, man listen, I'm no longer interested. She'll get the hint if she doesn't hear from me."

"That's foul. Why can't you just be man enough to tell her what you really think of her?"

"'Cause I don't want to, that's why. Call it what you want." He shrugs his shoulders.

I suck my teeth. "Wow."

"Hear me out, Av. If she makes suggestions or plans before I do, where do I fit in? Or constantly asks me how I feel or how I feel about her. When did all of this take place? How did feelings come into play? I never got that far to feel a thing. That's what I wanna know. I mean I didn't even feel involved enough to think of taking it to the next level as far as taking her out on the date. She pretty much took charge of the situation and left me behind. I can't get with that. Nah."

"That's foul, Akil." I repeat with a sour taste in my mouth. Smacking my lips together I say, "Okay. So let me wrap this around my head so that I fully understand where you are coming from. From what I hear she didn't leave you behind, you left you behind because you didn't go with the flow. You want one of those types of chicks that go to the clubs only to hold the wall up all night waiting for a man to walk over to her and ask her to dance. I'm the type of chick that when I go out I actually go all out and have a blast. You don't see me holding no damn wall up waiting for a man to come and approach me to ask me for a dance. I didn't get all dolled up to be a statue for a damn wall. C'mon."

"Well, you're the exception."

"Not really. You want a woman to be incognito. She can't be herself if she dates you. You expect her to keep the inner woman tucked away so that you can feel like the man. You want her to be strong, confident, attractive, and sexy and a freak in bed. But you don't want her to make the first move if you ask her out on a date. But what I do not understand is if you never call her to set the date and she takes the initiative to do so, what's so wrong with that if she's confident enough not to wait on you?"

"It's just wrong!" Akil snaps.

"You asked, so how is that wrong? You showed an interest in her by asking her out on a date. She merely took charge because you probably were taking too long for her timetable. What was so wrong with her moving things along where you two could get more acquainted? Time waits for no one, Akil. And maybe, just maybe she has that mentality to get and go for hers. I don't see anything wrong with that. Unless you feel that since she slipped on her pants that she was taking your spot by not allowing you to call and set a day and time. C'mon. That's absurd. I'm sorry." I wave my hand at the air.

"Nah. Don't be sorry, be patient. Let me make the first move."

"But-but...who cares who makes the move."

"He does. I do. Men do."

I roll my eyes. "Akil, please, that's some bullshit. I don't think all men feel as you do. So you're basically saying that since she didn't wait that those are signs of her possibly being needy and/or a chaser or both."

"Look. It's simple. Let the man do the manly thing. Sit back and relax and wait for the damn phone to ring!"

I laugh out loud. "You are sooo stupid. I wouldn't be waiting for no phone to ring if you'd approach me. Freak that. I'll take myself out. Y'all men kill me for real. Some of y'all are cowards. You build us up just to let us down. And then, then when we have something to get off our chest you never pick up the phone or respond to our text or emails, you simply disregard us, why?"

"Whatever."

"See what I mean. You can never just answer the doggone question. Y'all always gotta talk over it. Or have a thousand and one excuses because you don't wanna deal with it. But know this for future reference, women are stronger than you think. We can take rejection. No, we may not like it, but who does. But we can take it."

"Av, I'm just saying let me be Chivalry, shit. Then when we get back to her crib she can be the freak I have no objections to that. See, Avery, I like a woman who can captivate my mind first, and then screw my brains out later." Akil laughs.

Tears pour out of my eyes from laughing so hard. I wrap my arms around my stomach trying to stop it from cramping. Akil is funny as hell!

"Stop, stop, you're killin' me!" I snort in between each laugh.

It takes me a minute to get myself together. I wipe my eyes with my forearm, while my body jerks from laughing. "Wait! Wait! Okay." Finally, I get a grip of myself. I revert back to the immediate conversation. "Akil, I agree one hundred percent. These young girls, really don't have a clue. I knew enough about myself to keep my body clean, but I still was one of those naïve girls when it came to the topic of sex. Poppa never talked to me about the birds and the bees, pimps, drugs, prostitution, nothing. Neither did Ma'am. I had to learn in school, reading books, and unfortunately witnessing stuff out in the streets."

I change the subject. "Did you ever find Mrs. Right?" I ask curiously.

"All depends on what you mean by Mrs. Right," he smiles, "You taking me somewhere I hadn't been in years. We people's so I feel I can go there with you," he grins, "Nah." he chuckles, "I can't."

"C'mon, Akil. It's me." I tilt my head to the side, bulge out my eyes, and stick out my tongue.

Akil laughs. "You are so goofy. A'ight, listen."

Akil's facial expression changes from upbeat to sadden.

"Are you okay?" I ask him. "Where did you go?"

"I was just thinking about this *other* woman I used to know," he murmurs.

"She must've been special telling by the look on your face."

"Yes. She *was*." He cracks a smile. "Her name was Geneva Franklin. She was from Paterson but she looked more like a New Yorker by the way she carried herself. She was different—unique in her own way. Sorta like you. The kind of woman I didn't mind spending quality time with. She'd make you laugh. Damn, she used to make me feel things I'd never felt before. She was a very special lady. And I loved her. Her flaws and all, yes, I loved. She was a natural black woman. There was nothing better to me. She was all that and then some. When I met Geneva, she was in between jobs. I didn't care because she kept it real with me. She had aspirations of becoming a writer. Sound familiar." He cuts his eye over at me.

I smile.

Akil's eyes get teary.

"Well, what happened to her? She sounds like a beautiful person, Akil."

"She *was*." A tear rolls down his narrow face. "Um," he sniffles, "Geneva couldn't handle the pressure, especially after finding out that she had to wait longer than she anticipated moving into an apartment she wanted. To have to live another hour, day, or week with her schizophrenic mom practically threw her over the edge. She leaped from the roof of a high-rise building in New York and plunged to her death." Akil shakes his head. "I-I-I didn't have enough time to even put that ring on her finger and ask her to marry me. She couldn't hold on as I had asked her to. Now," he shakes his index finger in the air, "she was the love of *my* life. That woman made me a very happy man." He lowers his head and breaks down. He literally breaks down in front of me. I am at a loss for words. I don't quite know how to react to his vulnerability. What do I do? What can I possibly say to make him feel better?

On my desk I reach for a Kleenex and hand it to him. He reaches for it and dabs his eyes and nose. A big part of me wants to reach my arms out to Akil and console him but I haven't touched another man since Xavier. I don't know if I should. "I'm so sorry, Akil, I-I didn't know." I say with much sincerity.

He sniffles. "How could you? We hadn't seen each other since grammar school." He lifts his head up.

I can feel my emotions getting the best of me just hearing Akil's story. It's so sad. God, it brings back memories of those I have loss. Every time I think about them I feel this lump the size of a fifty-cent piece form in my throat.

Akil wipes his eyes, while my mind drifts deep in thought of what other men and women go through behind closed doors.

What I would give to be a fly on the wall.

You Betta' Act Like You Know
MINERVA WEAVER

"PURNELL WEAVER! Mannnnn, you ain't *fuckin'* nuthin'! Stick the *dick* in the hole. You cock-eyed lookin' fool!" I narrow-eye him, tap my fingers against the cool white linen sheets. "Man, you betta' act like you know where the effin' *hooooolllleeeee* isssssss!!!!" My thick arms cross about my bosom feeling this urge to slap him senseless. "Purnell, do I have to map out where the hell the *hole* is?" I roll my eyes in disdain and suck the inner walls of my mouth. "You sorry son-of-a—!" I mumble under my breath.

I swear it feels like umpteen years since I had a penis in me. I mean all I want to do is get a goddamn nutt. You know, to take the edge off. But Purnell doesn't seem to have a damn clue. And I-I really don't have the patience to try to school 'im. My forehead crumples. Explain something to me. Why I should have to when these are the things *he* should already know. Lord knows he got my blood a boilin'. Pressure done rose so high I am 'bout ready to pop and punch his lights out. But I refrain from doing so. I manage to compose my anger. Baby, prison and Minerva Weaver are not a good fit. I can't do prison. No, no, no, I just can't. Not with all of this good stuff. Helllllllllllllll noooooooooooo!

Now I know every woman claims to have some good sweet pussy. But baby, I have a pussy that will make yo nappy-headed coochie bone-straight. I ain't lyin'. I ain't lyin'. I'd hate to break one of those bitches heart seeing how they ain't never had pussy as good as mine before. One taste of me, they'd be hooked. Wouldn't know what the hell to do with 'emselves. No. I wouldn't wanna hurt 'em with all of this good bitter honey. Those bitches wouldn't know how to act. They'd be fighting over me like wild cats in heat. I wouldn't have the strength to breakup no catfight. No, no, no...I might make a mistake and break a nail. And that would be cause for a *Nerva* ass whoopin'.

Dammit! I done got off track again. See this is what I mean when my coochie is starving for some affection. I can't even think straight. Got me

246

all discombobulated 'n shit 'cause I'm hungry for some dirty fuckin'.

Anyway, why am I bitchin' when I already know the situation between Purnell and me? I mean when we met at the Movie Theater I was nineteen and naive. Purnell was old and old-school to me. I mean *old* enough to be one of my uncles or daddy. With that being said, (wetting my heart-shaped lips) it was just something about that man that really made my nipples stiff and swollen. He had me right where he wanted me. But I tried not to let it be known.

See, women are good for this. We tend to think that we are being discreet, but truth be told a good man can see right through—a man who takes notice and sees beyond the surface. Chile, he can read you like a book. And you are none the wiser. Huh. I believe Purnell saw right through me but he never questioned me on it. He simply dismissed it. He gave me time to allow him to see me in my own time. That really made a huge impact on how I saw him as a person, as a man.

God was he one handsome man—dark and beautiful. Physically fit He had impeccable taste in clothes and shoes. He was just a well-groomed man with a lot of charisma. He was distinguished and debonair like James Earl Jones in *Claudine*. Actually, he resembled him. The only difference was he was a solid framed man but a few inches shorter than James. He was a man completely out of my league. Scratch that. I'll say he was someone new that I was unfamiliar with. I was so used to snakes, dogs, and rats that when I saw Purnell I really couldn't see me with him. And honestly, I couldn't see him wanting to be with me to begin with We just didn't seem to match. I know opposites attract and I guessed that was true when it came to us.

Purnell looked established. I mean based on his appearance. It said a lot. Me, on the other hand, I was still trying to find my purpose Dungarees, dingy white T-shirt and sneakers did not scream *bougie*. It screamed, *busted, broke, not a dime to her name.* I was young. He was older. It seemed like a misfit. But apparently it wasn't. I had to believe that this man was really interested in me. Minerva Swanson. And just not looking for a one-night stand 'cause if he were, baby, he was in for a huge disappointment, I didn't get down like that.

When Purnell opened his mouth and spoke all I heard were all the right things floating in my ears. That good-sugary-chivalry-shit that girls like me only dream to hear. I mean he was talkin' himself up as to what he wanted to do for me, to me, and how he would take his time while doing it all. I found myself sailing on his every word, but then I caught myself before I got too caught up. We had just met. I wasn't about to fall so quickly and find myself lying in his bed screwing his brains out with all of this fineness God blessed me with.

I found it funny that Purnell never initiated any conversation pertaining to the topic of sex. Nope. He was very respectful and well-mannered. The kind of man you didn't meet all the time. He had special qualities that really intrigued me.

Like for instance, he paid close attention to detail. He was very observant. He could spot things out that I hadn't even told him. I was always one to wear disappointment on my face. I could never hide it like some people could. He picked up on it right away, which I thought was rare. Most boys never paid much attention to me or my facial expressions. Half of 'em couldn't even tell me the color of my eyes. However, it truly amazed me how they always knew the label on the back of my thrift store bought jeans. I guessed to 'em my ass was my best asset.

Purnell gave me eye to eye contact as he asked a valid question that really caught me off guard. "Is there anything you want to get off of your chest? You seem very sad. I'm willing to listen if you want to talk. No pressure."

No man had *ever* looked me directly in my eyes when talking to me and asked me a question like that before. Did I *ever* want to talk? I mean I had so much heavy on my heart, but I didn't want to talk his ears off about my problems and possibly scare him away. So I kept my hurt to myself. And I tried to preoccupy my mind with him, but I couldn't. Not fully. I had too much baggage and nowhere to release it all. So I kept carrying it around with me like this homeless woman I usually saw in passing. I knew I lacked trust in people.

At that point in my life, I looked at boys, men, the same. But as I'd come to find out they weren't the same. Every boy, man, was different. I just had to learn how to weed out the bad apples.

Nineteen. I was nineteen when Purnell Weaver entered my life.

He had a *manly* scent that turned me on. And plus, no other *man* had *ever* approached me in such a way that he did that I was tempted to see what he really had to offer. Was he all talk and no action? Or was he a man who could backup his words? I'd come to find out that he was a man to back up his *every* word. After that my one hundred and twenty pound, five foot six inch, grayish-green-eyed self was stuck to him like honey. And my intentions were to *never* let him go.

In the beginning of our relationship, and no, let me stop you right there, I DID NOT give up the pussy on our *first* official date. I waited until the *second* date to give him a taste of my Honey Crisp apple.

Purnell was a romantic. I had never had a romantic man. I wasn't sure what to expect, but for some strange reason I felt like I was in the best of hands. Come to find out, Purnell Weaver was a dream come true.

That man gave me the world in that Radisson luxury suite in Secaucus, New Jersey. Anything that you could imagine having, I had. He did not penny pinch one thing. I had never been pampered, as I was that night.

Come morning, breakfast tasted sooooo doggone good I ain't want to go back home. At the time I was residing in Newark, New Jersey, and attending Rutgers University majoring in "Undeclared" while living in a studio no bigger than an outhouse shed.

I swear I didn't know what to do with my life or which direction to go down. At least if I had a sense of direction I would have had some idea of what I wanted to do. After a while college became expensive and my broke ass decided to withdraw while I could. Before I got heavily into financial debt and couldn't afford to support myself. That was probably the only decision I made that made sense to me. But where would I go from there with only a high school diploma, no money in a savings account, working in retail, a minimum wage paying job with no health benefits, what options did I really, really have? None. Not until Purnell. He became my lifesaver, security blanket. I wanted to stay with him as long as he wanted me to.

With open arms and warmth he invited me into his heart and home. And I so willingly accepted. Purnell made me very happy. He wasn't afraid to tell the world that I was his *lady* and that I was *more than a piece of ass*. He had given me a *title* that said more than just: friends, lovers, pastime pussy. We were unequivocally soul mates. That meant something special to me. That's when I felt he had captured my heart.

Back then I had no complaints. Not a one. As far as I was concerned, my husband was "the man." But as time went on, and his body began to shrink, so did his little peanut. It was like it vanished. Poof! The mind-blowing *fuck* was gone.

So, as you can imagine, sure I'm a bit livid. How am I 'sposed to get off when his dick is the size of my pinky and no thicker than my big toe?

***

"Sometimes you work my last damn nerve." I tell 'im. My face all twisted up and agitated. I shake my head. "You know it ain't easy being your wife, Purnell. I got needs. Needs that your lil'-limp-dick-self can't seem to meet. Have you ever thought of seeing a doctor? Maybe you can get a dick upgrade. My coochie needs to feel more than a brush of air. Baby, I am a woman in my prime...forty and fabulous, but I need to be spanked, fondled, and fucked sooooo hard I'd feel it into next week." I grit my teeth and strain out my words. "Can you make me feel that? Sweetie, make me feel something other than annoyed, please."

I know I am wasting my breath 'cause Purnell is a lousy screw. I love him, don't get me wrong, but I need to do something drastic to get him to see the doggone light. I am a good woman, a good wife, and a Christian woman, who is highly favored by God, but also a deprived woman who is *not* sexually satisfied by *her* man. And if my man can't do it, well, then, I need to find someone who can. It's just that damn simple!!!

"Minerva, baby, you mean to tell me you can't feel, all of this, good, *jumbo* sausage inside you?" Purnell asks, huffin' and puffin' and wheezin' and humping nothin' but thick layers of honey-toned skin.

I sigh heavily, before knocking him in the head with the steel bat that is in arm's reach.

CLUNK!

"Ouch!" He winces like a little girl. "What you gon' do that for?! I know how to please my woman."

If only he knew. He couldn't please a soggy dog in heat.

"Purnell!" I yell with steam flowing out my ears. "If you don't get your sad ass offa me!" I pause, chest rise, and then fall. I suck my upper teeth. "You gonna regret ever marrying me when I put your ass through this marble floor!"

Threats are easy to think of when it comes to my husband. But I am tired of thinking. I just want to unwind, and fuck.

BUT he refuses to obey. Look. Normally he would adhere to my sex cycle. BUT no, no, no, no...this Negro can't seem to keep the hell up!!!

Explain something to me as to what a woman is 'sposed to do when her *pussy* is in dire need of *dick?*

Well, I tell you what *I* ain't gonna do. First, I ain't gonna cheat on my man. I'm gonna work with what I got, and pray that he understands that his woman needs to be fed three squares a day of his sorry ass lovin'. I'm gonna smile and laugh and strut my ass and shake want my momma gave me until my man gets that feelin' back. And most important, I'm gonna be happy knowing that my man loves me unconditionally.

Okay. Minerva knows that sometimes you get fed-up with your man, but just think before you leap out of line and find yourself in a situation you can't easily get out of. Lust is a tricky bitch. Purnell is my man, and I love him to death. I do. Of course I get a little frustrated when my hormones get all out of whack. I'm only human. *And yes, he does annoy me when he farts up a storm. Nearly blows me outta bed. And yes, he gets on my last nerve when he wants to kiss me with stink ass breath. And yes, it irritates the hell outta me when he sits in front of the television with a beer in one hand and scratches his balls like he got fleas with the other. And yes, I get pissed off when he shits without flushing the toilet or forgets to lift up the toilet seat and pisses all over the seat and floor. And yes, he irks me something terrible when he doesn't wipe his ass and leaves skid marks of shit in his drawers. And yes, I get mad as hell when he gets into bed with smelly feet. Smell like somebody done died up in here. And yes, I can't stand when he digs up his nose at the dinner table and then says grace. Or when he makes that hacking cough sound that sounds nasty as aw hell, that shit makes me wanna gag. And yes, I can't stand when he mistakenly uses my toothbrush. I don't know where his mouth has been. Shit. He could've been eatin' some stank fishy coochie for all I know. And yes, I know he expects me to get all sexy for him when I climb into bed, but what about me? I want my man to come to bed sexy too. Why the hell do I have to be subjected to droopy drawers, white crewneck tee, and stinky feet? And yes, that's some BULLSHIT, if you asked me. And yes, I get embarrassed when he walks out of the house looking like a goddamn sugar daddy. And yes, I feel like I want to black the hell out when he scratches me with his sharp dragon toenails. And yes, some days I do feel like I could've done so much betta'. And yes, sometimes I want to pack my shit 'n' leave. And yes, I do realize that this marriage is what I signed up for.*

I find myself completely exhausted listing all of this shit in my head. Purnell is who he is but sometimes I wish I could blink and make his old ass disappear. Come back as a younger version of himself with more stamina. It just doesn't seem fair! I didn't sign up for old age. I signed up for marriage, happily-ever-after and all I seem to have is flashbacks of what-used-to-be. What happened to us? Where had *happy* gone? Did it suddenly pack its shit and creep out in the middle of the night and forget to take me? Obviously, because I'm still here, still living in this big ass house, staring at these same damn walls, ceiling, and floor wishing I could run the fuck away and into the arms of an Adonis who don't know shit about me and blow his friggin' mind!

251

Oh, why don't I stop dreaming? I always got my head in the clouds. When am I ever going to grow the hell up and accept the fact that I'm getting older?

Never! I know. Get over myself.

I revert back to my previous conversation with myself.

And yes, yes, yes, yes, if I really think about it...I am blessed to have a man who loves me inside out. Who treats me like a queen in spite of his deficiencies, and mine? I have a man that caters to my every need and pampers me like crazy. Why in the world would I give up all of this for a one-night stand?

Like I said my hormones were talkin', not my heart. Don't do it! Don't shortchange yourself for an easy lay. It ain't worth the trouble or the heartache.

When Purnell and I first met we used to have fun. We had great chemistry. There was a spark, but it seemed to have fizzled as he'd aged. With him being twenty years older than me, we had some minor issues. Like for instance, this '70s singing group he always played on the stereo, um, Jimmy Briscoe & The Little Beavers. I had no idea of who the heck *they* were. That was, until Purnell told me. They sung this one song "Forever" that Purnell played to death. Oh, that man loved that song. He played it on our wedding day. No, we didn't have an elaborate wedding. It was small and quaint with about twenty people who could fit in his favorite uncle's backyard but it was beautiful surrounded by nothing but nature.

On our wedding night Purnell played "Forever" to consummate our love. And from that day going forward, anytime he had something on his heart instead of telling me himself, he'd play "Forever."

After a while it became redundant and boring. I wanted him to do something spontaneous like makeup his own song and sing it to me. But Purnell had his ways. If it made him feel good, why bother to throw salt on it. So I'd make myself get hyped when he played "Forever" just to keep a smile on his face and rekindle some old flames. But it was never like before, not even close. I really couldn't get into his kind of music and he couldn't get into mine. He'd always say what I played wasn't music but a bunch of hyenas trying to sing about lust, not love. And we'd laugh, but behind closed doors I realized how different we really were. What did we have in common? Nothing. So here we were a married couple with no compatibility. All we had was love, and at some point it didn't seem like enough for me. Somewhere hidden in the dark space of myself, I realized I yearned for passion—something Purnell stopped giving me some time ago.

Back in the day I must admit I was a bit reluctant, but again, Purnell had a different smell to him. I didn't sniff in bullshit like with the other fellahs I had met and/or dated. Like for instance, my best friend, *now* ex-friend Swindle Hickmann. Thinking about him, Lord only knows where I should begin.

Swindle and I had been friends for like forever. I say about five or six years. I met Swindle at the food court at the mall. I think I was about thirteen. I was standing in line about to order me some Wendy's when he mistakenly bumped into me. He wasn't watching what he was doing or where he was walking. He was too busy clowning around with what looked like some friends of his. They were all huddled in a circle trying to catch these girls attention that were sitting at a table behind me. It was about six girls, all white, all blonde.

"Pardon self," he said, looking and sounding like he could've been Wesley Snipes younger brother.

"You're excused," I replied.

Had he not bumped into me I would have never noticed him. Maybe it was the sweet baby voice that caught his attention to focus in on me. I really couldn't tell yah.

"What's your name?" he asked with a strange look on his face.

"Why you want to know?" I asked.

"'Cause. I mean it is not every day I bump into a chick like you."

"A *chick* like me. What is that 'sposed to mean?"

"Nah. You're taking it the wrong way."

"Well, how am I 'sposed to take it?"

He massaged his full thick lips. "Do-over."

"What did you just say?" I asked.

"Do-over. Why?"

I broke out in a smile.

"Ohhhhhhhh. You like, do-over, too, huh?"

I didn't tell him on that particular day, but I had a habit of saying 'do-over' too.

"Maybe."

"Well, my name is Swindle Hickmann."

"Minerva Swanson."

He asked for my phone number. I saw no harm in giving it to him. He made me laugh, and I think at that time in my young life I needed laughter in my inner circle.

I knew then that Swindle was a complete clown because he was steady cracking on people. And when we developed our friendship that surely didn't change, he always made me laugh. That's what I liked about him, always the life of the party. I never knew when he was serious or not.

Swindle was also a *ladies'* man. Girls were his weakness—all kinds of girls, especially girls you had money. He didn't have a preference like some boys, but he did have standards. He wanted his pockets to be fat as well as his bills paid. And if it didn't have to come out of his pockets, the better for him. Swindle would cater to them all, but just like any boy if he'd get bored or considered them to be a nag, he'd bounce in a heartbeat. He'd disregard their calls. Then disregard 'em unless they happened to catch him off his guard. Then he'd play the role as if he missed 'em sooooooooooo much.

One thing about him though, he was selective in who he dealt with, and he didn't, according to him, stick his dick in anything. I'd beg to differ. 'Cause if the pussy had a hundred dollar bill stuck between the lips, you best believe he'd be down there eating it out, while slipping that hundred in his back pants pocket.

None of his girls approved of our friendship though. They just assumed that I had to be giving it up for him to want to chill with me. They were sooooooo wrong. I never looked at myself as Swindle's type. And I never thought he looked at me in that way either. We considered each other...*boys*. You know, best guy friends even though I was a girl. Swindle didn't see me as a girl. And if he did he never let it be known.

For some reason his little girlfriends looked at me as a threat of some sort. I guessed 'cause they saw me as a girl. Why get salty with me? I could only assume 'cause of how close Swindle and I were. I knew him inside out and he knew me just the same. We were *boys* like I said.

We didn't have secrets, at least I didn't. I couldn't speak for him. We talked straight up and open about a lot of things. We were there for each other in times of need. You know, an open ear, shoulder to lean on, pat on the back. Those chicks were wasting their energy being insecure about me. I was no threat. They were. But I never expressed that to 'em. Never showed it in front of 'em either. I kept my cool as if I had no concerns. And honestly, I really didn't because I knew the truth. If only they'd befriended me they would've been able to see the light, but no, no, they figured I was in their way, taking up all of their space that should've been spent with him. Are you serious? They caught Swindle's eye, not mine. I was like a backdrop, no lie, no one really noticed me even if I was sitting right in front of their face. They only noticed me when I was with him. I was invisible. Yet still a threat. I could never understand why they were giving me drama or rolling their eyes at me. It didn't make much sense to me 'cause we all had a pussy. Just in different shades and sizes and smells. It's just that I wasn't giving mine up.

As Swindle and I got older our friendship began to change. We changed. Suddenly those teenagers were growing up. And my outlook on life had a different view of what I wanted in a young man. I was single, had been since my childhood sweetheart had died...on all days, Valentine's Day. I took it real hard. A young girl's first loss is so devastating. I wanted to drop dead. Just die along with him. Climb in that silver casket and lie on top of him and just die! God I was so crushed. That type of love hurt so much, so deep, so long that I never wanted to fall in *love* with anyone *ever* again.

Then, one day in March, of the following year, Swindle looked me in my eyes and said, "I love you, Minerva. I love you."

I didn't know what to say, how to react to his feelings. Love to me was a strong, powerful word that tugged at my heartstrings.

"How do you feel about me," he asked.

I-I-I didn't know if I should share. I didn't take Swindle seriously. He'd been a prankster most of the time. He was never serious enough for me to think of him as someone I would love as in a relationship. I loved him as a friend, a best friend.

Then it dawned on me that the best relationships stemmed from friendship. Swindle and I knew each other. So much stuff we'd have to take to our graves.

Love was not a word I freely expressed to anyone. Not after Sheldon died.

Did I love Swindle? Was I in love with Swindle? It was hard to say — difficult to release those words without having acid reflux. I felt comfortable in his presence. But did I feel that he would be worthy of my love? My love was delicate, longing, hard. And I desired the same from my mate. I just didn't know if Swindle had it in him, to give so willingly, openly, and generously without completely demolishing me in the end.

Girls were drawn to him like flies on shit. He was dark chocolate, soft curly jet-black hair, thick long black lashes, big beautiful brown eyes and soft juicy swollen lips. He was gorgeously handsome, not to mention melodramatic. Oh, and he was a bullshit artist. He was always scheming and plotting. Knowing this, girls fell for his shit each and every time. He had those bitches wide open. It was just too much competition. I didn't feel the need to compete. So I never pursued it any further. However, I did answer his question.

While Swindle was lying on top of me, I looked him piercingly in his eyes and said in a soft-spoken tone. "Yes, Swindle, I love you." The look on his face spoke in volume. We had great chemistry, but I knew that it wouldn't last. Call it girl's intuition.

When Swindle told me that he loved me I felt it in my heart. I really did. But I also felt that Swindle had more growing to do, and so did I.

I felt his 'love' was a casual love, one that *didn't* require seeing me all the time or talking to me over the phone every day, one that *didn't* do sweet romantic gestures. One that *didn't* respect the word: *relationship*, one that *didn't* see himself with one girl.

He divulging his love for me was used so trivially. He used 'I love you' at a moment of vulnerability—at a moment that took years to develop into one night of casual sex.

My mind wasn't thinking. My heart was numb. Here I was in a state of grieving over my mom who had passed so unexpectedly. Swindle had come to console me. After the wake and funeral after the repast I found myself crying on his shoulder. Somehow one thing led to another. I had been a friend with him for so long that I didn't shun him away. If anything, I was able to see a softer side of him. One that I never knew existed. It just brought me closer to him.

In all the years that I'd known Swindle he always hid his feelings. Blocked them behind this thick wall inside of himself. I never questioned why. I figured he had good reason. Losing my mom was unfathomable. Surreal. But at a time that was crucial my best friend comforted me.

Often, quite often I wonder, was it just something to say or was it genuinely real on his part? Till this day I can't truly say. The feeling wasn't the same. He spoke words that I think his mouth or heart wanted me to hear, but Swindle never backed his words up, which made me realize he hadn't a clue as to what true or unconditional love really meant. And plus, the *very* next day my phone stopped ringing. I was now placed in the category with the others: *just another piece of gullible ass*.

Swindle's past relationships he was able to run buck wild. His last relationship, the girl gave him too much rope to come and go as he damned well pleased. I didn't have it in me to be that generous with my heart.

Girls were like vultures when it came to Swindle with no respect for me as a friend. What made me think that they'd respect me as his *girlfriend*? My heart was too fragile to withstand any more hard blows so

I distanced myself from him. I guessed I wanted to see if my absence from his life would matter. You know make his heart grow fonder. Can't say it did. Nah, I surely can't say. Swindle was Swindle—looking out for Swindle.

I don't know why but I felt if I had tried to build a monogamous relationship with Swindle I'd have to kill him later. A strong part of me felt that he would cheat on me as he had done with the others.

What set me apart from the rest?

The only thing I could think of was that I wasn't willing to share. I was too headstrong. I was not that desperate girl to allow myself to settle for half a boy when I knew one day a whole man would enter my view. One that was willing to give me all of him. So I chose to wait it out. Explore my options. Live out my teen years and enjoy my life.

His silhouette sits upright. Nude buttocks imprint the soft sea-foam green sofa. My eyes pierce the whites of his eyes. Heat engulfs in me. Bare feet move slowly, hips sway in a sensual motion. Firm breasts expose, nipples protrude, and then harden, as I get closer to him. Tongue swipes across my bottom lip, starved for my husband's affection

His strong dark-skinned legs open as I slither in between them. I then kneel down on my knees. Breathing hisses, anticipating the taste of his chocolate that stands erect before my famished eyes.

Body heat rises, mouth waters, eyes connect as I blow warmth upon his throne. His head tilts back resting upon the backbone of the sofa. Eyelids close. Miles Davis "Lonely Fire" ignites from the Bose system as my moist lips peck between his muscular legs and hot thighs.

My upper lip brushes against his coiled pubic hair. With my front teeth I pull one strand and wet it with slimy saliva. His head moves to the left as my mouth opens wide and swallows his manhood whole. He moans softly. I lick gently. Twirling my sodden tongue, deeply I devour his deliciousness so in-tune to the music that makes my body burn with intense heat.

My eyelids close as I make puckering sounds with my lips and tongue. His head moves to the right as juices ooze from my naturalness.

Mmmmmmmmmmmmmmm, I moan. Then rise to my feet, adjust myself as I sit upon his throne, slither up and down his hardness. My eyelids flutter, heart races, heat is sweltering inside me, him.

Our tongues twist, as he tastes himself off of my tongue. His massive hands smack my ass. I motion up and down his penis like death is lurking in the dimness.

Uhhhhhhhhhhhhhhhhhhhhhhh, I groan. Sweat beads his face, chest; I run my fingers through his natural jet-black hair. It is damp, feels like silky semen between my fingers.

I stick out my tongue and lick the side of his handsome face. Pinch his left nipple with my index finger and thumb, suckle it hard, then do the right.

He groans, roars with delight.

Harder, I ride him as sweetness gushes down from my candy apple, trickling onto his thighs, sofa.

His eyes roll underneath the lids. My sweaty face presses against his head, pelvic squeezes.

"Give it to meeeeee," he sings in my ear. He cups my waist, pushes me downward to go harder, faster. I do as I am told. Thrusts go harder, sensual, rotate my hips, and seduce him into me, a wet reality, and not a dream.

He flips me onto my back, digs himself deep, deep, deep into me. Tongue in my throat, dick in my stomach. Legs mid-air, twist around his neck, ankles cross, feet rest upon his sweaty back.

He sings, "Oh, damn, oh, damnnnnnn... that feels sooo good, good, good...so, so, so hot, hot, hot...ooohhhh, baby!"

Wrap my arms around his neck, motioning up and down; body shudders as I pee onto him.

It makes me go faster, harder, sensual, slipping up and down, peeing, peeing, peeing, heart beating, pouncing like fists are in my chest punching my inner walls.

He grips my ass, kisses me wildly, erotically, holds me tightly, his body shudders rhythmically with mine.

Our eyes lock as we settle down. I rest my head upon his left shoulder, and smile feeling so damn sexy and satisfied.

***

I was giddy like a-a schoolgirl with Driven Smalls. That was my lover's name. Driven Smalls. Just the thought of him, my face beamed a smile that I thought had vanished forever. I was flattered by his kind gestures. And it reeled me in to *want* to get to know him more personally. I was so gullible. Where I went wrong was when I offered my cell number at the department store. No. He did not initiate any exchange of his.

If I was thinking, I should've realized that that was a red flag. To not even go there, but I did. I reacted on impulse.

The truth of the matter is Purnell and I seem stuck in a marriage that isn't going but so far. Yes, we have a history. But it's *now* a tainted history. The trust is gone as well as the lust. It's been gone for so long now. Oh, maybe three years, to be exact.

I got fed-up with my man at home and I stepped out of our marriage and into the arms of another man—a man who showered me with gifts and sweet chocolate kisses. This man, who mind you was twenty years older than me, made me feel again. He thawed my heart and brought me back to life. I had been missing this lively feeling in my marriage. Purnell and I seemed detached. We became roommates, instead of husband and wife.

I *never* stopped to think maybe it was the chase that thrilled Driven? Or maybe he just wanted to see if he still had *it*—that charisma to pull a classy lady in and foolishly play with her head. Or maybe he was just being nice? Or maybe he was just in heat and in need of a warm soft sultry body to bed? I couldn't really say. All I knew was that at the end of the day I found myself withering in the dark of my indiscretions, alone. I felt this want to stretch my arms out to my husband, but I didn't have the courage to do so. So I kept reeling back to a man who didn't give a damn about me.

"I'm restless. Tossing and turning. My body is afire." I said softly into the receiver as I sat on the couch in my living room on my residential phone.

"Afire?" said Driven.

I proceeded to explain, "In great excitement. My energy is above its normal temperature. My body is moist from head to toe...blazing." I breathed deeply into the receiver hoping he was turned on. "Nipples are solid as stone. Vagina is silky. Your image roused me out of my sleep. Trickles of warm sweat stream down and in between my cleavage. You are sexin' me mentally. This is new for me."

"It's a full moon," Driven murmured.

"Is it? You are a distance away, yet your energy makes me ooze. I want to burst. I need to burst. It feels almost like foreplay. My skin is dewy. I am soooooo turned on."

"Go ahead and release," he said.

"I don't want to. I'd rather suffer and wait for you. I yearn for your touch. I want to burst inside you. It's torture, but I'll wait for you to want me unless you no longer desire me...then I'll release." I told him. "If you no longer desire me, honey, please say so."

"Are you gonna suffer through the night?" Driven asked.

"Sugar, I'm already suffering. Answer the question. 'Do you no longer desire me?' Be honest."

No response. All I heard was his breathing on the other end of the phone.

I pressed my lips together annoyed. "You're stalling to answer the question. Be honest."

Again, I got no response.

"Am I 'sposed to read between the silence. Tell me the truth even if it hurts me, then it hurts me, but I deserve the truth. Was I just a past-time, just something to do when the mood felt right?" I raised my voice into the receiver forgetting where I was...home. "Don't leave me hanging here. Express yourself." I sighed. "Yes, I care deeply for you. More than I thought I would, but if you don't feel anything for me, why even do it? I am open with you, maybe more than I should be, but that's me when I'm feeling someone. I'm not out here with every joker that steps to me. I save me for you. That's what I choose to do. You mean something special to me. I cherish that. I'm not looking for more from you. However, my energy is when we are close, that's who I am. It does not say that I want a relationship. Just says that I'm content sexually with you. That I prefer it just be us and not a third party. You agreed with that...unless you are digging someone else or have dug into someone else. Respect me enough to be honest. I'm not sharing myself with anyone, not even my husband."

"Content sexually? Care deeply? Honesty? Just us? No third party? That's saying more to me." he pointed out.

My face scowled. "Yes, I said content, not happy. There is a difference. Why are you so afraid of someone caring for you or expressing how they feel about you? A woman must've crushed your heart at one point and time in your life for you to be like this. Oh, and what the heck were you saying when you slipped that hundred in my suit jacket pocket, huh? Were you trying to imply that you paid for sex? That I'm some kind of whore? What was that all about?"

He remained silent.

I continued to scowl as I said, "Look. I don't see you all the time. We don't have sex all the time. We kiss to show affection. I express when I want to be close to you, what's wrong with that? When I said I would back off you said just give you some time because you were going through some things? I could see that you were stressing but I didn't pry. Figured if you wanted me to know you'd share. You didn't say we should stop seeing each other. I opened the door but you remained here. You didn't walkout to say that you no longer desired me, but it feels like your saying that right now. If so, then honey, say it. Make it clear. I'll understand." I scrunched up my nose. "What you think I'm gonna sex you and others? No, I told you that the other day, and you made it seem like you agreed, but apparently you want third, fourth, fifth probably six parties, then baby, do you. I love me too much."

He disregarded what I'd said. He made me feel insignificant. But I didn't share how I was truly feeling. I swallowed the hurt back down my throat. Then I toughened up.

"Door... to what? Seem like I agree?" he retorted.

I sucked my teeth. "What? All of a sudden you got amnesia? I told you the other night that I only deal with one person at a time. That I don't bed you and someone else because I don't want anything I can't get rid of. YOU agreed with that. NOW you're actin' like I'm losing my mind in hearing you say that." I huffed. "Obviously that's what you choose for you. Then do you. I can be intimate with you and not have a relationship with you. It's called an Understanding between two, mature Adults, but I can't continue on like this with you sexing every kitty that purrs. You pretty much answered my question. I hear you loud and clear. Sorry to have wasted moments of.." I paused, no need to go there getting all sentimental 'n shit.

"Wow. You're not losing your mind. Those are your personal choices," he said.

"So why agree just to turn around and disagree? This is the reasons why I express myself, ask questions when my spirit tells me to, it save me from a lot of headaches."

He raised his baritone voice. "Intimate with me? You said it was just SEX!"

I murmured. "If I knew then what I know now I would've never had oral sex with you. It is just...SEX. I chose the word 'intimate' so what. You are reading too much into everything I say. I haven't done one thing to imply anything other than what it is. We have SEX when we feel the mood. I'm not like these women...what I say is how it is. Go by my actions. I don't crowd you. I express when I want you through text, when we talk. That's all!"

"Imply? Revisit what you said tonight," Driven said.

"I don't consume myself with you. I meet people but just because I meet them don't mean I want to fuck 'em. I'm very selective in whom I pleasure." I said.

"We don't need to have a conversation about whom you meet or whom you fuck and pleasure." he reiterated.

I squinted my eyes. "Let me make myself clear. Yes, I care 'deeply' for you, which does not say that I am in love with you. It just says that I care for you. Your well-being. Yes, I'm content when we are 'intimate' which does not imply anything other than I am fulfilled until we meet up again. No, I do not choose to share myself if I'm with you in a sexual manner...that's my choice. Had you said that you do, well, I don't know if I would've considered you as my lover, but at least I would have known ahead of time. You didn't give me that option and that's what frustrates me. Yes, I feel you're playing with words instead of just saying 'I no longer desire you.' I made it very simple for you all you had to say was no."

"Playin' with words? Why would I do that? No... to what?" he asked baffled.

I placed my hand on my hip. "That's exactly what you are doing! You're dissecting anything that sounds remotely close to implying the 'R' word. I make it very simple and *you always complicate it for whatever reason. You can't just go along and enjoy the moments. Shit!" I heaved. "All I wanted was someone to get off with from time to time. Someone I trust where I can be sexually free, no strings, no complications, just honesty and pleasure. So what, I express myself. That's what women do! Last I checked, I am a woman, so stop reading into shit that isn't there. We had this discussion before when you asked what role you played. And I said no role. You are a man; I am a woman who yearns to be pleasured. Just make me feel good. That's your only role! Let your guard down, and stop thinking that every woman wants the happily-ever-after with the white picket fence. If you must know I already have that with my husband. And for your information, baby, there are actually some women who don't require all of that. Some women can handle a little hanky-panky and carry on with their daily lives. It is not uncommon for a woman to have an affair and not get caught up with the lover she is fucking. Think about it, some women have traits of a man."*

"Won't you just stop reading into things all the time? Let my guard down? Complicate things?" he snapped.

"You heard what the hell I said! I just wanted a handsome man to 'rock my world' from time to time. But you know, mista, you don't free yourself when we're together. I do. You let me do all the work. The first time we had sex you suckled my nipples, squeezed my ass. The last time we had sex you only smacked my ass. You have yet to free yourself sexually with me. And you think I would not feel that. Well, I do. I did, but I accepted it. Yes, it is only about pleasuring you, what you want, what you feel is right for you, then why even go there with me? Even when I went down on you, you said my energy said more than just sex. SO friggin' what! I was feeling extremely good pleasuring you. Seeing you enjoy me pleasuring you. Seeing you watch me pleasuring you. That shit turned me on! What the fuck! Last I heard that is not a crime when a woman wants to pleasure her man." I shook my head from side to side, with a grimace on my face.

He yelled into the receiver. "Blame! Blame! Blame! Have a good night!" CLICK!

I stared at my phone. "OH NO, HE DIDN'T!" I quickly pressed his ten digits. He picked up on the second ring. As soon as I heard him breathing I said, "The truth. You can't handle the truth. I take the blows from you, but you can't handle the truth. Wow. No blame here. I haven't blamed shit on you. I'm just stating a FACT!" I pursed my lips. "Let me tell you something, mista. When a man doesn't take off his clothes while engaging in sex with a woman he claims he is digging, he has not freed himself and he will not be free with that woman because of his own hang-ups. If a man, your so-called mate does not touch you because of his own issues that woman instinctively knows to pick up where he won't and show that man regardless of his lack of performance that she is still aroused by him. Twice I've felt more from your kisses than I did from your dick. Yet, you still excited me because I was/am into you. I have a lot of patience, darling. But how do you think I felt when you didn't respond to me. I stood right in front of you naked as a jaybird and you simply looked at me, then shutdown. You didn't ravage me to the point where I knew you wanted to fuck me. You didn't throw me down on the bed and lick my pussy! Break into a profuse sweat from pouncing on this big ass! No, no, no, you didn't do any of that! I desired you. You didn't show that you desired me. My body pulsated for you and your dick and you had no reaction. I found that to be odd, considering. When we first got together, baby, you used to make me holler, catch a charley horse. Sometimes you fucked me so good I thought I was going to collapse from coming so hard but now..." I stopped to catch my breath. "BLAME?! There is no blame. I'm just DISAPPOINTED in myself. I felt the distance between us, yet I accepted it. I will not bother you ever again. I just needed to express myself so that I can NOW get you OUTTA MY SYSTEM. Good-bye!"

I slammed the phone back in its cradle with discontentment flooding in my eyes. I stormed back to my bedroom and cuddled with my man.

So, you see, I don't have to wonder why my husband doesn't want to "rock my world." The fact that I had sex with another man made him lose his desire for me. I played with what we had and caused us both a world of pain. It was me who selfishly invited a stranger into our home and allowed him to play between my legs.

Cheating on my husband was one thing I could live with. But living with *knowing* that I had contracted a disease outside of my marriage was something I didn't think I could live with, especially after knowing that I had shared my body with the man who loved me more than his own life. I thought I was doing the right thing by not depriving him as he'd done me. I made a vow. And at one point and time I did and didn't take my vows seriously. But when that itch between my legs got the better of me, I lost my cool and collectiveness. I scouted for someone, anyone, who was willing to oblige my needs. I was willing to binge on anyone who was willing to bend over backwards to indulge in me.

I became weakened by the illusion of lust climbing inside my hole, filling the void of emptiness...a sexless pothole that had been dug over time. Nothing seemed to fulfill me like a penis. I needed the real thing not some imitation. I wanted that penis to penetrate every inch of me, feed me, and then feed me some more until I felt as if my pussy would drown in its own sex juice. I wanted to feel my insides throb with each step I took. I wanted to feel the sensation of his motion as a reminder that he had journeyed through my habitat, coursed through my safari like an untamed wild lion.

Let me tell you something. A woman can have anything her heart desires as long as she has a functional pussy. From the smallest to the biggest, women have the power to control a man's mind if she *fucks him good, feeds him well,* and *gives him his free time.* If that woman is laying it on a man he will lavish her with exquisite shit as long as she keeps her *body fit,* her *legs open,* and her *mouth shut.*

See, this is the reason why I gave up the pussy on the second date. Why wait to find out if this joker could hang? Hell no! I'd rather know right away. I'm not going to invest time, energy into getting to know him and then once we hit the sheets I find out this muthafucker can't fuck! No, no, baby, I ain't feeling that shit!

Look-a-here...a woman has to be fulfilled just like a man. I don't care how you slice it. It is a known fact!

Purnell knew exactly what I had to offer. And he was pleased with his choice. Had I not fucked up our marriage, we would still be living in marital bliss.

Look. I know I'll be eating *guilt* for the rest of my life. But I can live with it as long as—

Purnell really took me by surprise when I told him the truth. The unemotional expression on his face really tore me to pieces. The silence. God. It was torturing. But what really threw me for a loop was when he said that I didn't have to tell him because he'd already found out on his own. How? Is what I wanted to know? Who snitched on me?

Come to find out, no one did. Well, actually, *someone* did. Someone I never thought would snitch on me.

"Sit down, Minerva." Purnell said in a strong, baritone voice.

I sat down on the sofa in one of my many faded nightgowns with rollers in my hair and Queen Jubliee green facemask on my face.

Purnell remained standing in his rust plaid pajamas, navy-blue bathrobe, and taupe-colored slippers.

He said, "One evening while you were out, I knelt down on my knees and had a deep conversation with God. This was while you were out on your rendezvous with your lover. I spoke candidly to God and I told him how our marriage used to be opposed to how it is now. It wasn't like He didn't know, but I needed to verbalize what I was feeling before I drove myself crazy. God listened as he always does. Then He spoke to me and said, 'Purnell, close your eyes.' So I did. God said, 'which do you want: to be told or shown?' I was puzzled. I didn't know which would hurt more.

So I took a minute to really think about it. Then I opened my eyes and looked God in His eyes, and said, 'Shown.' And God said, 'Are you sure, Son?' And I replied, 'Yes, Father.' So God said, 'Look deep into my eyes.' So I did. "Minerva, God showed me everything that you had done with that man. The places y'all had sex, including in our bed, bathroom, kitchen, living room, dining room, basement and attic and garage and backseat of your car. How he maneuvered your sexy body, had your legs up in the air, wrapped around his neck, how you licked his hairy chest, while he fucked you with pea green dress socks on. C'mon, Nerva, *dress socks*? And you, you sucked his penis like you were punishing it, beating it for being bad or something. What was that about, huh? Then you switched it up by pretending you were making love to it. I was so jealous. Mad at the fact that he was squeezing your beautiful breasts and sexy ass with his grimy hands. He kissed your lips and tongued you down. I really got angry. How he lusted for your body, not your mind or your spirit. I was floored. Floored! Then the grand finale stomped on my heart as I watched you turn on your stomach, face buried in the pillows as he stroked you with inward outward motions from behind. I heard you moan full of delight with a smile so wide on your face." Purnell paused, and took a deep breath. "I called home, and you answered the phone like nothing was taking place when all along you were being fucked in our home, in our bed by another man. He had his *dick* in you anal while you were on the phone with me." My eyes remained low, staring at the carpet wishing I could disappear. He shook his head, and then continued, "He groaned. Then ejaculated all over your ass and massaged it into your skin." He paused again, lowered his head, and then lifted it back up. He took deep breath, then continued, "But then, then something transformed inside you. Nerva, you turned the tables on him. There was this look in your eyes, a look I had never seen before. It was a sultry, seductive look that said that you were about to fuck him up. Minerva, you ass fucked that man! I could not get a grip of myself after seeing that and how much you enjoyed pleasing him. You never did that to me. Just seeing you two interlocked in our bed, on top of our sheets really messed my head up. I wanted to slap you silly and hard. Throw your ass off a 16-story building or push you in front of a freight train. It hurt seeing you two as *one* like we used to be. You might as well have kicked me in the balls when you had that *man* in *our* bed. You might as well have. I saw the sexy and provocative negligees you bought from Victoria's Secret, too, that you modeled for *him*. You were just a switching your beautiful ass around showing off all of your assets for *his* eyes. But what about mine, what about how I'd feel, huh? Did you ever think about that when you were undressing and standing before him in the nude? He didn't seem that interested, if you asked me. I guessed he saw it so much that he was no longer impressed. That's just the look he had on his face. And what about the stilettos you bought from Bloomingdale's with *our* money. You had the nerve to wear 'em for *him*. I was so disgusted! I didn't know what the hell to do. Just, just seeing you two engage in: missionary, 69, doggy-style really made me want to throw up. I felt like I wanted to kill you and him." He scratched his throat, and stared blankly at me. My head remained bowed. "This is the kicker. You ready? Minerva, God even showed me you going to the doctor and getting your test results back, where the fuck was *he* then, huh? That scary look on your face, in your eyes when the doctor told you that you tested positive for HIV was something that dug a hole in my heart. That *man* did you dirty and you did me dirty, so, I guess we both were at fault." My eyes searched for a crack so that I could climb in. Purnell continued, "I say that because marriage is a package deal. When you fuck up I fuck up. When I fuck up you fuck up. And he, he gets off scottfree and into bed with another woman and do the same shit all over again. So, you see, baby, I knew all along. The *very* day you found out and walked through our front door with that fake smile on your face. I knew deep down you wanted to breakdown and cry, but you held your ground. And I-I held mine."

Purnell glanced up at the ceiling, and then continued, "Do you realize the strong bond God and I have?" He paused again. Finally, I lifted up my head and looked him deep inside of his soul. This bright light illuminated from the smile on his face. He proceeded to explain. "It's like that song Kurt Curr sings, 'I Almost Let Go.' Minerva, without Him at that point and time in my life I'd probably done something stupid knowing that some other man was sticking his dick in my *hole*. But I kept my composure as He told me to. Baby, He knows my heart. He knows that I take my faith very, very seriously—just as I had my marriage to you. No matter how bad things were getting between us, not a day went by that I felt the need to be with another woman. I chose you. But I realized that I was the only one in this marriage who saw it this way. All you had to do was talk to me, tell me what you needed. It had to be more than just the lack of sex or my sexual performance for you to step out of our marriage. I say this because it was never about the dick. It was about the whole package. I don't think you quite looked at me the same. I turned you off, and on to him." Purnell nods his head up and down. "Okay. Yes, we stopped doing the things we used to do, as we got older, I'll admit. Sometimes men get set in their ways and we have a tendency to lose sight of what's important. Sometimes we have to be reminded of certain things. And no, I can't stand here and say that you didn't remind me time and time again how much you needed 'Baller' (penis), how much you wanted it, but you have to understand that when a woman, not just *any* woman, but the woman he loves with: mind, body, and soul shits on her man's manhood he begins to diminish down to nothing. There is nothing left of that man. He shrinks inside himself. He is not thinking about *her* or her *pussy*. He has nothing to uphold him as the man in that marriage, so he becomes shattered and withdrawn from his woman and others around him. You see, some men go out and have flings to boost themselves back up. Some go out to the streets and buy pussy. But that's not me. The only one I had to hold me up was God, baby. God. Not my wife. No, *she* was too busy holding another man up, while she got down on her knees and sucked his cock. So what do you expect from me, huh? Tell me. Talk to me? Tell me what more could I have possibly done that I hadn't already done to try to please the woman I chose to be my wife?"

Purnell stood still waiting for a response, but I had none. I was left speechless. I really didn't know what to say or how to express myself to him face-to-face. It was easier just to brush things off, but he wasn't trying to hear that. He wanted answers that I could not give him.

Purnell was asking all the right questions but I didn't have anything that I felt was justifiable for my actions. I had hurt him enough and I didn't want to speak out of term as I had already done. So it was best to keep my mouth shut.

Purnell looked at me with those piercing brown eyes and said, "So, you're just going to give me silence. That's all I'm worth to you?"

Vigorously, I shook my head. I couldn't find the strength to open my mouth and respond. I had said too much. It was best to remain silent. So I did.

In between the silence Purnell told me that he had gone to the doctor too. I'm more than certain he was waiting for me to confess and divulge my infidelity. I knew he wanted that strong, black woman he'd fallen in love with so many years ago to reappear. I was still she to some degree. I mean, I didn't tell him right away. No. I waited until a year later.

Honestly, it wasn't until I was walking past this bookstore, OPEN

BOOK when I noticed this book, *Sleepin' Wit' the Virus* in the storefront window. I don't know why but I seemed drawn to that book. So I went inside to purchase the paperback. The female store clerk with the prettiest hair and eyes ever informed me that there was a saga series: *Anonymous*, being the first novel and then *Kreepin' Wit' the Virus* being the third, so I purchased the series to follow the story. I can't remember the last time I read a book, other than the Holy Bible, of course.

That evening I engrossed myself in those books, one after the other and I felt lousy after I turned to the last page of each one. I felt lousy because Avery's story hit home for me. I needed to share with my husband what I had done and suffer the consequences of my actions.

I know I waited too long but I was in denial. I didn't want to believe that I had an incurable disease. I didn't want to talk of it or think of it or anything, so I pretended that it didn't exist. That it didn't reside within me. And while doing so, I didn't do what was necessary to keep myself in good standings as far as my health was concerned. Yes, I took a huge risk by not getting the proper medical treatment. I could've put myself at risk of having full-blown AIDS. How stupid could I have been? I asked myself that question a million times. And even my stupidity had no response. All I could think to say was that I was scared, that I suddenly felt undesirable to my husband that I missed the magic that we once shared, that I was yearning for passion, but I didn't say it directly to Purnell. I didn't know how to articulate it in a way that made him feel something good about himself. I didn't want to make matters worse than what I had already done. I know. I know that I abandoned my marriage as well as myself. It would take a lot for me to stand before my husband, confess, and then admit that I had a disease that I didn't get from *him*, then build up my nerve to ask *him* to stand by my side while I dealt with everything that I was going through on a mental and emotional and physical basis. I just couldn't find a smidgen of courage to do it. So I didn't do anything, nothing at all to help myself. Like I said, I took a huge risk. I compromised my health because of fear.

It was then that Purnell said something that really astonished me. He walked up to me, knelt down on one knee, extended out his hand, as I reached out for it, and he said with tear-filled eyes. "I promised to love and cherish you through sickness and health and that *is* what I am doing. I have a friend of mine, who happens to be a doctor. The same doctor you went to see. And I asked him to go against all that was moral. I asked that he give me the prescriptions to try to keep you healthy in your time of denial. And he did. He didn't hesitate to help me out. So I had your prescriptions filled and I slipped your medication in your food, milkshakes, and juices to make sure I kept you here with me. I'm talkin' a lot of pills, honey. That doctor could've lost his license but he did it on the strength of my character. I am a man! You hear me, woman? I am a man! Doc knew that I would never divulge what he had done for me, but I'm telling you because you are my wife, as well as his patient. But you must promise to never speak a word of this to anyone. Promise me, Nerva."

He stood to his feet.

My pain-stricken eyes scrolled up to Purnell's tall frame and looked into his jaded eyes, then parted my quivering lips and said in a crackling voice. "I promise."

The hardest part of facing my husband was looking him in his eyes and admitting to him that he wasn't enough man for me. As I swallow, the words hurt going down my throat. It hurts me to my heart *now* as I remember saying those harsh words to him. I wasn't thinking. I was caught up in my own love triangle. Honestly, I didn't care one iota about him.

It wasn't until Purnell shared his truth with me about being "HIV-*negative*" that I felt a knife in my back. The fact that his test results were *negative* left me numb. No. I couldn't and can't say that I was happy for him. No. I can't. I know it sounds selfish but all I could think about was: *what about me?*

What about me meant: *who would want me, hold me, kiss me, like me, love me, accept me, befriend me, embrace me, make love to me again*...should Purnell decide not to.

Purnell was free to leave whenever he chose. He wasn't exposed to the virus; so therefore, he could've easily asked for a divorce and left me without as much as a second thought. I thought, perhaps he would, and especially after saying that he wasn't enough man for me. Now the tables were turned. I was his wife infected with HIV. He was my husband who tested "negative." Was I *now* enough, woman, for him?

Seeing Purnell stand tall and take those bullets that I lashed out at him really opened my eyes. It made me realize that Purnell was more man than I'd ever respected and known. How did I miss it?

I missed it because I was too busy worrying about meaningless shit that I lost focus of what was important. Had I looked at how he treated me, how he respected and adored me I would've seen what I had was someone who was deeply in love with me. But I took what we had, him, and our marriage for granted. I cherished the material things, and not the man. Even if I spoke it, my actions blatantly stated that I didn't mean it. My actions said I didn't give a damn.

God knows I wanted to bawl my eyes out that day, but I managed to hold back the tears. And Purnell, huh, he didn't pack his bags and leave me. No. What he did do that took me by surprise was that he sat down next to me on the sofa, took me in his arms ever so gently, tenderly pulled me close to his heart, lightly kissed me on my forehead, and softly cradled me in his arms as he hummed "Forever."

Somebody Catch Me Before I Fall
MAXINE STILES

SPENT EYES STARE AT a picture of a little black girl ogling a reflection of her babyface in a storefront window. I used to know that girl quite well. I used to like her too. I used to fit inside her skin like a hand inside a glove. We used to be one when life smelled like heaven. We used to smile where all you saw were teeth and pink gums. We used to dance with two left feet off of Curtis Mayfield "Little Child Running Wild" and we used to be boogying like we were on *American Bandstand* twisting, swirling, dipping, and two-stepping to the groove of his sound. I was trying to flee from my own woven blues. Vanish. I felt as if I was floating on a fluffy cloud. God. I used to weep for me as if death was upon my shoulders. And any and every time it grew in abundance I used to soak my dozy eyes in King James, recite scriptures, and pray. Pray. God. I used pray for a better me, better days, better ways to live my life. Sometimes I used to sigh deeply as I caught a spell of Donny Hathaway song "Giving Up" streaming through the porch screen as if I was at the Astrodome listening to him sing it live. Then I'd weep inside 'cause I felt so bad, so disgustingly ugly. I used to cry...just bawl for all that I had lost—mostly my soul. And I used to say underneath my breath, "Dear God, please forgive me for my sinister ways." I used to silence myself 'cause I knew I was asking for too much. I'd close my eyes and erase the misery away and pretend that it never happened. Never happened to lil' ole me.

"He Has His Hands On You" unobtrusively streams throughout the desolate and kempt rooming house on Summer Baldwin Street. Attentively I listen to Marvin Sapp's grief as it climbs up and into my suffering heart—ripping it more and more. His sorrow pains me, drains me. His loss smothers me. My heart literally feels like a heavy bag, weighed down with brick hard misery. I can't wrap this pain around arms of a grieving mother. Uh-huh. It squeezes too much life up out of me.

Rolling over on my side, red-rimmed glassy eyes I mourn in silence. The mayhem and misfortune strangles me so tight. Amazingly surprised. I am still among the living even though deep down inside I have died a dreadful death.

Hattie Daniels, another tenant, sings along as she briskly mops the foyer with Mr. Clean. Hattie is up at the crack of dawn, always cleaning to keep her mind off her troubles. Life hasn't been so kind to her, as she'd say. Not after losing her entire family in a house fire. Thirteen people Said she ain't knows what to do with herself. Said she'd probably windup losing her scruples and end up in one of those funny farms somewhere in boonies.

Hattie, a big, burly woman with peach fuzz on her chin was the first tenant I met when I came to the rooming house. She stood before me in slate black skin dressed in a racer back tank and a pair of faded gray sweatpants with flip-flops on exposing her pretty feet. That woman sure has some pretty toes. She wore her hair braided back in neat cornrows. Her eyes were big, clear, deep chocolate brown. And when she spoke it sounded like she'd been straining her voice and as a result it had grown hoarse.

Mrs. Odessa, the owner of the rooming house said Hattie is trustworthy so she asked her to show me in while she went to fetch for the keys. Mrs. Odessa put me in mind of a housemother. She also kind of resembles Octavia Spencer. They sure could pass for sisters.

Mrs. Odessa was tall in stature, wide childbearing hips, and fragile motherly look in her eyes told me that she was a righteous woman doing what God called upon her to do. Help women in need.

Hattie told me after Mrs. Odessa's husband passed the house seemed too big for just her so she put a sign in the window seeking only women tenants to share her living space. Hattie came up from Florence, South Carolina, but she couldn't find an apartment she could afford right away, so she inquired about the room here. Said Mrs. Odessa was so sweet and kindhearted. She told her to come right on over. Hattie said they sat in the kitchen while Mrs. Odessa served her hot tea and tuna sandwiches. They ate, while Mrs. Odessa told her about her belated husband, Oscar and the house. I assumed Mrs. Odessa was trying to get a feel for her. See what type of person Hattie was and find out about her background and if she could trust her in her home.

When I showed up on her doorstep, Mrs. Odessa took one look at me. It wasn't one of those looks as if to kill, no, but more of a look of consoling. She smiled, gently, and then invited me into her lovely home as we sat in the living room chatting over a cup of fresh brewed hazelnut coffee. I assumed she knew, could feel my bad energy. It wasn't like I could hide the misery I felt inside. Grief was not easy to hide, at least not for me.

Mr. Clean cascades inside my untidy room as a whiff bypasses my nose and fills it with an inviting fragrance of lemongrass. Bedraggled clothes lie sprawled on the floor that I had yet to pick up. It rained the other day. I swear it poured like God was furious with the world or maybe just with me.

I become teary-eyed as it brings back memories of how I used to keep house. I see myself with an apron on and headscarf wrapped around my head steady yelling at the boys to not run on the wet floor and track it up with skid marks from their sneakers. I see my husband, Ernest Charles sitting back at the kitchen table with his long legs stretched across a kitchen chair engrossed in the sports section of the Sunday newspaper. I can smell the aroma of baked rosemary chicken in the oven, baked macaroni and cheese, fresh collard greens atop the stove, and homemade cornbread in the cast-iron skillet set aside on the granite countertop with a freshly baked three-tier carrot cake with cream cheese frosting as a centerpiece on the dining room table.

I retain it all as I listlessly lay in this single bed atop disheveled green sheets and a beautiful grass-green afghan my grandmother made thinking about all that has left me.

Mom passed the afghan down to me when I was a teen. And since then I have cherished it as if it were a wedding ring. The color is filled with richness and the fabric soft as cotton against french coffee skin.

From what Mom told me, my grandmother was dirt poor. But through every penny she earned working on the crop fields she had a deep affection to leave her family something of her behind. This afghan is more than just an afghan to me. The time she put into crocheting it says a lot about her strength of character. Grandma was a phenomenal woman. My only regret is not living in her time to have met her.

When I feel the world is too weighty of a burden to bear I curl up in this afghan feeling all of my grandmother's spiritual energy permeating this feeble temple of mine.

As I slightly lift my head off of the pillow I look around at the furnished room, which puts me in mind of a suite I stayed in once when my *fifth* boyfriend and I first began courting. Oh, Derek Best was a helluva guy. I never met anyone as sweet as him. I guessed you could say he was a little too sweet. Of course that relationship did not last long, but I kept him as a good friend. Eventually he found his soul mate. I respected that. Gradually our friendship dissolved. But I still have fond memories of him.

This room is small, but quaint with a lot of colorful character, hardwood floors and lots of natural light shine through the wide windows. Often I wonder if God is shining His light on me. It's dark inside of me. Yet, God is able to seep through.

I tune back into Marvin's lyrics, "...*when you cry He says He'll see you through*..." as if he, himself is here mirroring me with *his* eyes—witnessing me fall so far down that I can hardly see myself rise above the anguish.

I sniffle in the loose mucus as my fingers clench the afghan wishing it were arms to hold me, console me. I pain with much animosity that only He can comprehend why, why this affliction burns to the flesh.

I was never a malicious woman, wife, or mother. But when something so delicate, so pure, so precious is taken from you, you change at a rapid pace. I changed into this woman I never perceived myself to be. A woman named Maxey.

Four months ago, I couldn't see, couldn't feel a thing. Blood that ran through my veins was bitter cold. Everything before me turned pitch black. I was swollen like someone had filled my emptiness with embalming fluid. My face down to my narrow feet was swollen. Swollen with revulsion and angered due to the fact that I never got a chance to say: "I love you. Mommy loves you all."

Then, one bleak evening, while I was lying in bed, afghan up to my neck, body trembling with hot tears in my eyes my soul began to reopen and the abscess of my pain quickly resurfaced.

I found myself in search of, looking for answers, reasons. Yet all I heard was silence in the background. And the silence literally cracked...me...open. My emotions unraveled. The anger erupted. The anguish exploded inside of me like a hollow-point bullet. The memories, they took a hold of my mind and I felt flashbacks of my past repetitiously haunting me. My feeble heart began to feel as if it was ripping in two. God. I felt as if I was crumbling bit by bit until there was no more left of me. I, Maxine Stiles, had vanished from eyesight and climbed into this dwelling that had a crack in the flooring of my temple. It hadn't any windows or doors. So I wondered, how the hell did I invade this place to climb into the crack? I don't recollect. I had no escape other than to climb out of the crack that was slowly closing in on me. I felt claustrophobic as if the world was squeezing every little ounce of energy I had left. I was locked down in this cold and dreary misery. Lying in a pool of blood that was not my own. It was then that things began to resonate.

"Mommy, Mommy! Shepherd, won't help me tie my shoes." Ernest Jr., yelled at the top of his little lungs.

I hollered from my master bedroom. "Shepherd, help your little brother. I'm trying to find my car keys."

"Yes ma'am."

I made my way downstairs to the first floor to the family room to search underneath the sofa and loveseat pillows to see if they might've fallen in between the cushions.

"Douglass. Joseph. What did I tell you two about running in this house? This is not a playground. Now I done told y'all if you break it, you bought it. And neither one of you are old enough to get a job, so cut it out before you make my blood pressure rise!"

"Sorry, Mom," They both yelled back in unison.

I retrieved my keys from behind the loveseat throw pillows. "Boys get your coats and backpacks. Your lunch is in those brown paper bags; go get them off the kitchen table. Shepherd, Ernest, y'all come on now before y'all are late for school and I am late for work."

"Coming Ma," Shepherd said as he trotted down the stairs with Ernest Jr., on his heels.

I press my lips together trying with all of my might to stifle a scream from bellowing out. I try to push the memories far back in my head. Fight back the sound of their voices echoing through. God. I watched them grow, crawl, walk, talk. Saw their big bright eyes and small faces light up Christmas morning as they ripped open their presents. Saw them dressed in their Halloween costumes. Joseph as Spiderman; Ernest Jr., as Michael Jackson in the video *Thriller*; Shepherd as Frankenstein; Douglass as Buckwheat from *The Little Rascals*. They were so amusing that day as I snapped photos of each one with silly poses and happy faces.

And on Easter, how they looked so handsome in their suits and polished black shoes. They had such fun at the Easter Egg Hunt.

A tear escapes from my eye and rolls down my cheek as I wipe it away with quivering fingertips. With my inner palms I massage my face as my mouth fills with saliva. Saliva that tastes sour. My emotions are scattered like debris on sidewalks and in sewers.

If I close my eyes I can still get an imagery of each room in that house—a house that used to be our home. I visualize reaching out and touching each one of their happy faces. Plant my soft lips on their mahogany, caramel, sienna-brown and honey-toned skin. Kiss them on their forehead and tickle them under their armpits into cute giggles that made me giggle. Listen to them crackup with adorable laughter. And Ernest Jr., smile that showed off his buckteeth.

With the back of my hand I smear tears about my eyes. Sniffle. It is a *hard* hurt to intake. The hardest I'd ever encountered in my entire life.

If I have to revert back in time I'd choose not to. But since this is the only road to recovery I have to believe in something. Something that will help me find the serenity I used to feel back when my life was so fulfilling. I was rich with love and full of hope and happiness. But a lot has changed since then. More than I ever anticipated happening to my family and me. Suffering crept at my front door...waiting...waiting for the right moment, right time, and right opportunity to ambush

Why didn't I get off earlier? When that feeling hit me, why didn't I just up and leave? Run. Run out the door, jump in my car and speed home.

I bow my head, and then shake it from side to side.

I remember it like it was yesterday. Only it was four months ago. Four months when my happiness dissipated from my heart

It was Tuesday, April 1st, the worst day of Maxine Stiles' life.

Wounded eyes affix the 28-inch TV screen. I am deeply moved by the sermon Bishop T.D. Jakes is preaching. I don't recall turning the TV on, or changing the channel. I don't recall moving at all. All I am doing is lying still...numb.

I hear his voice. See sweat profusely dripping down his face. I see his movements: bouncing, arms swinging, feet shuffling, head bobbing in front of his congregation. I wish I were there, at this particular moment. Lord knows I need a healing. Maxine Stiles needs a healing.

The 1st had significance. It had a great impact on my life. It was a painful, heart-tugging day of gut-wrenching reality. It was the day my *four* sons were murdered.

We lived in a modern one-family home. My husband; Ernest Charles

Stiles and I had bought many, many years ago. It was a suburban neighborhood on a quiet street in Pearlbrook, New Jersey. We were newlyweds building a foundation to one day start our family. That was our American dream.

I always wanted a big family. Stemming from about twelve I knew that I wanted to get married and have babies. I wanted lots and lots of babies. I was blessed to have four healthy sons—such beautiful little people. My children brought forth enormous joy to my life, our lives. I couldn't have been happier.

Losing my boys nearly knocked the wind out of me. But somehow, through prayer, I began to slowly regain consciousness. I began to see images of whom I had been and who I was becoming. Yes, I was Maxine Stiles, but I also knew that *Maxey* had to rediscover herself all over again. And although we were one in the same...we both had our own burdens to bear. Our lives had changed so drastically. And quite frankly, *I* wasn't prepared. I did not foresee this happening to me, to us. My children were to bury me, not the other way around. Maxey was hot tempered, disheartened, and severely beaten down.

If I had to tell you about Maxine Stiles, well, Maxine Stiles was a woman who went out of her way to help anyone in dire need. She was a volunteer for Big Girls Do Cry. You know, mentoring young girls about how to care for their newborns. She was a "Big Sistah" for juvenile delinquent girls too. Huh, Maxine Stiles always found herself involved with educating young people. She felt it was her calling in life. She was heavily involved in her church too. Her family was loyal members of Pearlbrook Baptist Church. She was an usher for six years too. Ernest sang with the Men's choir. Their boys sang with the Children's choir and also attended Sunday school. She was a woman who had spent countless hours working as a House Manager for Crown Jewels Overnight Shelter for Young Mothers in Crown Jewels, New Jersey, for nearly fifteen years. But that *Maxine Stiles* had seemingly disappeared. And no, no, I didn't know if she'd ever be found.

I remember when I first interviewed for that job at Crown Jewels.

It was an informal interview. No need for a suit and pumps. More less Capri's or sundress was sufficient. 2:00 p.m., was the scheduled time for me to meet with Ms Lordell. I understood that she had to be very particular in whom she allowed in her, if you will....home. I was a stranger so I had to really sell myself to convince her that I was the best candidate for the position, which meant I had to bring up some painful experiences in my past. I had to do what I had to do to be able to articulate how I'd be a great asset to Crown Jewels. It sure wasn't a pleasant feelin' but it was necessary to be fully understood. And yes, Ms Lordell disclosed that she was a recovering addict, but during her drug days she'd done some unflattering things that gave her some jail time. But what really got to me was when she said that the thing that really woke her up was when she found out that she was pregnant. It was the worst news in the world, she told me because she had no idea of who the baby father was. Like I said she'd done some things out in those streets with men she barely knew or didn't know at all. She said she hated herself for many, many years up until it was time to give birth. Sadly she gave the baby up for adoption and she never looked back. I guess during her dreary days she became closer to God. It happens, so I'd been told. I let it be known that I wasn't there to judge. I just wanted to be presented with an opportunity that could possibly change my life.

Upon my arrival at the facility which looked like a spacious house, I rung the doorbell, a petite female with long, straight black weave and caramel complexion greeted me at the door. She wasn't smilin' or anything. And she wasn't mean to me. She just didn't appear to be very friendly. She was about five feet tall, rather fragile looking little thang. I thought if the wind blew she'd fly away. That's how doggone skinny she was. Toothpick. And she had the squeakiest voice I'd ever heard on a grown woman. Sounded like a little chipmunk. Well, technically looking at her she looked like a child in knee-high hooker boots. But she was woman—full-fledged woman.

I was told by "skinny thang" to go right on up to Ms Lordell's office on the second floor. I trotted myself up those stairs. Near the top step, I needed to catch my breath. Nearly took my breath away climbin' those doggone steps, but I made it up.

I used these here hard knuckles to knock on Ms Lordell door. She was so bright. On the account she had on a bright fuchsia floral blouse like she just came back from a cruise and them loud yellow Capris. Honey, all that was layered upon her thickness was deep dark chocolate skin.

I walked into her office and she smiled with her eyes, and then white teeth. She was listening to gospel music too. Sangin' kinda off-key, but I gather she was catchin' the Holy Ghost sittin' down. Yes, siree. That woman was justa sangin' her heart out and praisin' Him for all His good deeds He had given to her and her children. I could tell she had younglings without her sharing it with me. Uh-huh. Oh, yeah, and I could tells she'd been through some heavy duty stuff in her life too. She was lettin' it be known that she made it through the storm! Hallelujah! She was justa swaying her head and tappin' her feet. I wanted her to get a fill up of the Lawd so that she'd praise me and give me that job. 'Cause Lawd knows I was in need of a change of scenery. I was so tired of wastin' away on frivolous things. My soul was sleepin' on borrowed time. I had things to do before I traveled that long ways to the Other Side.

I'd worked in many fields, yet I never truly felt fulfilled. I found something gratifying around young people. I'd always come alive when I was talking to 'em. Unbeknownst to them they kept me sane in some ways and some ways they didn't. Most of my happiness I realized had to come from me—from within myself. Took me sometime to realize that, but eventually I did, especially after getting married and giving birth to my firstborn.

I kind of thought Ms Lordell was a country gal. I don't know why. Didn't ask her. Just felt it. She was tall in height like Tyra Banks. Voluptuous in curves. She wore her jet-black hair in a pageboy. I noticed she had a glow. I'd never forget that glow justa shining on her oval face. Justa beam of light. Could've been that bright ass Capri's making it so bright in that small office too, now that I think about it. She had such an amicable presence. I felt right at ease as I sat in her chair across from her listening to her continue to sing off-key. Chile thought she was another Yolanda Adams or possibly Shirley Caesar. Hell, I didn't care if she thought she was Tamela Mann. I needed some faith and favors. So she could be any doggone sanger she wanted to be. Didn't make no never mind to me. I was on the outside lookin' in and I wanted to be on the inside lookin' out. So therefore I needed Ms Lordell to look a sistah out and see my potential. Use that spiritual eye and look deep inside me. Heck, I ain't has dilly swat to hide.

In the privacy of my own bathroom I had a tendency to ask momma (God rest her soul) to help me out in the Afterlife. I figured, hell, you done paid your dues in full while you were here on earth and Lawd knows you had some heavy duty dues to pay so I assumed that God would give her a pat on the back and maybe some of that patting could somehow sprinkle down on my shoulders so that I could get this job and sprinkle a little sugar in (good faith) here and there for these young pregnant and troubled girls.

Like I said the interview was very informal. Ms Lordell went over some things. Asked me some questions. I answered her questions. Asked her some questions. And within fifteen minutes the interview was over.

Damn. That was simple enough—90-days for a fifteen minute interview. Lawd, things sure had changed when it came to interviews, I thought. Ms Lordell handed me a shitload of papers in a manila folder that I had to fill out. Also, I had to get my fingerprints taken at a facility of their choice. Not to mention a physical examine from my primary doctor. A primary doctor I didn't have. Heck, I didn't even have health insurance at the time. So I had to apply for Charity Care in order to get the physical done in order to get this amazing job.

With no medical insurance I was up shits creek. And with the expectancy of my last check from the retail store that I had been previously working I could at the very least afford the forty dollar fee to pay for my fingerprints. And lastly, after I met all of the requirements then I'd have to meet the head honcho, Mr. Russell.

I'd heard rumors about Mr. Russell that did not put him in the best limelight, but at the time I could care less. Everything was right at my fingertips. The job was literally in the palm of my hands.

All I had to do was fulfill all of my obligations in a timely manner. Mr. Russell was the one holding me up because he just didn't seem to know how to return a phone call. And without he and I meeting that would have delayed my start date. But I kept my cool.

Ms Lordell was kind enough to help me out by giving me Mr. Russell's personal cell phone number. I called and called and called and the brother would not pick up the phone. It was so frustrating trying to connect with this man. I took in full consideration that Directors had a lot on their plates, especially when you oversea several departments within a facility the size of Crown Jewel, but come on. All I needed was a callback and an interview to get my foot in the door. I used my diligent skills, a lot of woosaing, and faith to get me through until this nick wit decided to pick up his phone.

It was a dizzily day in June, when Mr. Russell finally picked up his phone. "Hello, Mr. Russell speaking," he said in a deep, strong baritone voice. I heard what sounded like a lot of commotion in the background so I knew that he was at the facility. I had to raise my voice a few octaves so that he could hear what I was saying. He probably thought I was a teenager by the sound of my child-like voice. Little did he know I was a forty-something year old African American woman in need of a job that would give me a sense of fulfillment. I was *not* purposely trying to misrepresent myself as having all the answers because I had no prior experience working with young people. I always loved children so I figured why not try something different. See if I like it. Possibly grow to love it. I was a *novice*. And this new position was going to be my "lesson plan." And that it was.

I drift back to reality.

While lying in bed Maxey heard a voice that vaguely sounded familiar to her. The house was dim. The voice echoed from the living room. She was startled. She called out for Ernest. Then realizing Ernest was not there. She was all alone, scared and lonely, hurting and hungry for the love that had vanished from her life. She wanted her family back. But God didn't deliver that blessing back to her, to me. I was so angry with Him. So Maxey rebelled. She stopped going to church, stopped going outside other than to work. She just stopped everything that mattered to me.

I do recall it being the 1st. Of which month, I don't quite remember. I remember feeling this tingling in my fingers that shot all the way down to my feet. My palms were itching like crazy. My scalp prickled. I was all tingly inside. I guessed one could say I was feeling *alive* again. I damned near danced outta my wig. But honestly, Maxey didn't want to feel *alive*. She wanted to mope and wallow in her grief. She wanted to shrivel up and disintegrate. She wanted to perish. With all the anguish that was weighing heavy on her heart, to her it was senseless to keep on living.

Mostly every Sunday prior, Maxey would sit unglued. Eyes puffy and bloodshot red ogling at the four little faces that were hung in silver and gold frames mounted neatly on the wall of this room. Laden by an ache so great it nearly ripped her insides to shreds. A loss so severe it cut through to her spirit and buried her soul. A loss so traumatizing she was disoriented, immobile with deep-seated despair.

I'd kneel on my achy knees every night and ask God to kiss my babies for me. Read 'em their favorite bedtime stories. Make sure they brushed their teeth and said their prayers. And most important, tell 'em that Mommy and Daddy love 'em.

Most of Maxey's days were spent rewinding time. Her nights bypassed as she tried to get through to the next agonizing day. Often she felt a haste to run or hide or climb out of herself and just take matters into her own hands. Just be done with living this sullen life. But something so profound grabbed a hold of what was left of Maxine Stiles and pulled her back to deal with life on life's terms—to mourn the loss of her children and her husband of thirty-five glorious years. And find the strength within to carry on. Maxey was defiant. She could care less about living.

Today, the 1st, I find a smidgen of hope and a heart full of courage to sit and receive this message—a message that seems most relevant to my life, my loss.

Body sprawled across the hunter-green leather couch in her cotton pj's was something Maxine Stiles did often. She'd hibernate for long weeks at a time. After her sons murder she took a leave of absence from her job. There was no way for her to function at work dealing with young mothers every day. She needed to get away. Honestly, she didn't care about mortgage payments, food, nothing. None of that mattered. Maxey was too fragmented to care.

Maxine Stiles' whole world crumbled around her, inside of her, too. Then reality sunk in. She was now a childless mother and a wife on the verge of becoming a single woman. She lost everything that meant anything to her in four months' time.

Days were the worst. It reminded Maxine Stiles of her children— waking them up for school, preparing their breakfast, packing their lunch, and riding them to school. Normally, Ernest or she took turns dropping them off, especially if she received an unexpected call. And off she'd go to rescue one of the girls at the shelter. Ernest would hold down the fork like any other loving husband, father, would.

With all of them now gone, Maxey couldn't stand morning or any other part of the day. She couldn't function with normalcy. Living was a hindrance to her empty life. I'll admit, breathing was also impossible to tolerate for me. The thought of committing a heinous act traveled slowly through her head, on numerous occasions. But memories of my boys distracted me, as I'd look around at my surroundings—an empty place with a hollow soul. I'd glance at my once picture-perfect family and I knew that I was not bold or daring enough to take my own life. At least, not sober.

My crimson eyes are glued to the TV as I listen to Bishop T.D. Jakes's sermon. This is surely a sign that faith has found its refuge back in my heart. But it took time, four months later...time.

Each 1st day was a hefty burden. It took enormous patience. Maxey had no patience. She'd fallen numerous times and found she was unable to get back up on her feet. Each 1st was misery. For me, it took asking for God's guidance to come this far. And even with Him, Maxey struggled. Every day, every night, ate her up inside. She blamed God. And she wasn't about to bring herself to terms of forgiveness. The last time she'd ask for help the man she loved with heart and soul left her in a state of bereavement, hopelessness and helplessness. He'd abandoned her as well as himself. And since that time, she vowed to never submit herself to ask for help ever again. The memories of her beautiful children began to stifle her. The loneliness impaired every aspect of her life. Maxey became nonexistent. In her manic-depressive state of mind, Maxey died by multiple gunshot wounds too.

It seemed everything around her was falling apart. The images of her children: Shepherd, Douglass, Joseph and Ernest Jr. death blocked light from her sight. *Twelve, nine, seven,* and *five*...the ages of her sons especially burdened her. They were so young, so full of life. And now, now they were dead and gone.

Her marriage to Ernest Charles suffered the day of the funeral. Four sky-blue caskets with sketched pictures of each child's face atop of them, aligned next to the other, it devastated them both. Ernest Charles took it to the depths and collapsed atop of Ernest Jr.'s casket. He went into shock. Six of the twenty-four pallbearers: Nick Everstein, John Peterson, Randall Murray, Connor Tillman, Buddy Fork and Tim Moley tried to pry his pained body off. But his strength was overpowering. I tried to keep my melancholic composure and not fly off the deep end, but I, too, felt a twinge of rebellion. I wept, screamed from the top of my lungs for my babies, and then strapped my angst-ridden body atop of Shepherd's casket, bawling for mercy on my soul.

Some of my close neighbors and friends ran to my aid, but Maxey was too long lost to bring back to civilization. She had lost so much that day, including herself.

Paramedics arrived and rushed Ernest Charles, six foot five, late forty-year-old self to PUMC (Pearlbrook University Medical Center) for careful observation. His dark brown eyes filled with pang of guilt as they locked with mine. How could we have been strong at a time like that? How could we pretend? Move out of our own way and continue on with life as if we were living in bliss? I shake my head no. No, no, no bliss...we were now residing in hell!

Ever since that despairing day of April 1st, Ernest Charles Stiles couldn't bear the sight of me—his wife's attractive, yet youthful-looking face that seemingly transformed with anguish. Her almond-shaped chestnut-brown eyes once filled with euphoria were now stressed with desolation and self-blame. He couldn't bear the feel of her once supple skin, which now felt like abrasive sandpaper. Or her full-bodied shoulder-length ash-brown hair that was now stripped to thinness with patches of bald spots. He couldn't bear looking at her 5'7" curvaceous frame that had shifted from a size four to a size twenty-four. He couldn't bear the sound of her soft-spoken voice that now cracked full of dismay.

Or the echo of her wails in the dead of night. He couldn't bear starting anew without his precious children. But more important, he couldn't bear the fact that he was on duty fighting crime when the call came through of a home invasion at 619 Rescue Me Ave that took his sons lives. He couldn't bear to look at his wife every waking day knowing that he could not save his own family. Nor could he shake the blame that he bestowed upon his own shoulders for allowing his *twelve* year old son to mine the house until his mom got home from work.

The anguish eroded the family structure and wore him down to become a severely disturbed and mean-spirited man. So he left me. He walked away from his career of twenty-six years as a Pearlbrook Police Officer. Packed his bags and left his ruined wife to bear the weight of *their* loss alone. Ernest Charles Stiles was now a recluse from Maxine Stiles' life.

The death of her sons crippled her. So much she had repressed over the months. So much she had to relive in heart and mind. So much she was unwilling to accept. Maxey, she was at her wit's end not knowing how to move onward. So she found herself stuck in time and strapped in a straitjacket behind steel doors and padded walls. Maxey went stone crazy.

The 1st being the day of her release from the mental institution Maxey found herself homeless and broke.

What was she to do?

While I was contemplating of what to do, Maxey took matters into her own hands and hitched a ride to anywhere anyone would take her. Her final destination was Paterson. Feeling as though she had hit rock bottom Maxey used every attribute and got what she knew she needed.

First, she needed money to provide a roof over her head, food in the fridge. Secondly, she needed to melt the heartache and anguish away. Third, she needed to forget the past tragedy, her husband and all the other stuff she'd endured. So Maxey brainstormed and reinvented herself. She turned Maxine Stiles inside out and let her anger pave a way to survive.

Maxey worked the hell outta her body to get back on her feet. Then one day, out of the friggin' blue she heard this soft-spoken female voice say, "Maxine Stiles. M-a-x-e-y, what are *you* doing?"

Maxey snapped. "What the fuck does it look like I'm doing?! I'm selling my cooooooochieeeeee! These men out here don't care what I lock like. How old I am. Coochie don't have a face."

"Turn to your left," the Voice said. "Think back. Now, say it again."

"Say what?" Maxey replied.

"What you said about... coochie."

Maxey placed her ashy hands on her bony hips. She smacked her bone-dry lips. "What I saaaaaiiiiiidddd was coochie don't have a face!" Then she slowly turned to her left as if she dreaded to look.

Who *I* saw was, me, as a young twelve-year-old girl standing on the corner turning tricks. I squinted my eyes to get a better look. Oh yes, I had seen this girl many times in my traveling between Newark, Jersey City, and Paterson. Although, I never stopped to ask her *why, how, when*. I didn't even think to ask... *whom*.

Why? Momma didn't have any food in the fridge to eat. We were hungry. There was no one to call on, besides God. All the pantries were empty. The churches were empty. And Momma refused to go to Hurston's House, where they fed the homeless. She didn't want anyone to know that she had fallen on hard times and couldn't afford to feed her family. We had nowhere to turn.

I did what any other daughter with a loving mother would do. I tried to fix the destitute in our home. And I did. But no one, not even Momma could fill the hole in my soul. I had been living with this hole inside of me for forty-something years.

My chest heaved. Fists balled tighter and tighter. Eyes were angry and teary. Jesus. She was so young, so beautiful, so, so full of potential and options and opportunity and hope and promise and sorrow and bitterness and agony and blemishes and scars and...

The Voice continued, "Now that you see that coochie *does* have a face—a face that you've seen many times in passing. What are *you* going to do about it?"

What could I do? I didn't know. I didn't know what to do.

It had been so long since Maxine Stiles walked in those *caring* shoes.

Did I still have *her* in me? I had my own baggage—painful baggage.

As I was pondering, a burgundy sedan pulled up. The girl opened the passenger's-side door and hopped in.

I sighed, helplessly.

As the car passed me, the girl looked me dead in my face as I read her lips that said "Help me?"

I was in no position to help her. I'd let myself go. I couldn't do anything but watch her drive away with the window rolled down and the radio playing. It was then that I heard "My Testimony" flow into my ears and slither down to my young girl's heart. Tears streamed from eyes as I felt the message through a young girl's plea. It was then that everything gelled, including Maxey.

I knew. I just knew that I couldn't say goodbye and lose her. You understand me. Lawd knows I needed *her* just as much as she needed *me*.

Oh Damn, I Had a One-night Stand With My HUSBAND!
BURN BENTLEY

"HELLO, SUZETTE, did I catch you at a bad time? I really need to talk, girl." I anxiously say.

"What's going on, Burn?"

"Girl, you ain't gonna believe how bad I messed up."

"Whatchu do?"

"Girl. Girl. Girl, I *slept* with my *husband*."

"You did what! With *who*?!"

"Yeah, Su, it's true." I shake my head from side to side feeling as if I want to drop to my knees and repent to my Maker.

Suzette cackles. "Well, how was it, girl? I mean, can he *still* hang?"

"Mmmm-hmmmmmm," I reply.

"So then what's the problem?" Suzette asks.

"The problem is, I slept with my husband! Su, I'm so mad I can kick myself. I can't eat, sleep, and it's beginning to affect me at work."

Suzette remains silent.

"Girl, are you there?" I ask.

"Yeah, I'm listening. Burn tells me something."

"Yeah."

"Exactly how did all of this happen? Maybe it wasn't as bad as you're making it seem."

I get quiet all of a sudden. "Well, listen to this and then tell me if it wasn't as bad as I'm making it seem."

Suzette smacks her lips into the receiver. "Okay, girl, lemme hear it."

I scratch my throat, then glance down at my journal and repeat what I've written.

"*I feel the fire as he enters my domain*
He is slinging his whip
Penetrating my shit
Like he starving
We switch positions and I ride him strong and steady
Feeling all of his inches
But then I wonder why he is here?
Confident brother who claims he's like no other muthasucka
Why he giving all of his skins to me?
Of course this is after the fact
Of him breaking my skin in
I sprout rain onto his stomach
Making him aware that I am coming hot and heavy
I was riding him strong
Thinking along the lines of: is he really digging me or is this a fantasy where I am sticking my finger in my own hole?
It was clear that it was real
How he made me feel
I got a lil' emotional
Thinking this and that
Shit that I wanted back
But then realized it was irreplaceable
I had to let it go
Deal with the here and now
I was skeptical
Did I mess-up
By giving in
To someone on a whim
I mean, I find him attractive and shit
And I like the way he maneuvers his whip
But isn't there more to it?
This is where I'm somewhat stuck
Wondering if he really gives a fuck about me
Certain things have been proven
But I often wonder if we are grooving to the same beat

I mean, it is not about just the meat
It's about the conversation
The interaction
That gets my coochie all roused
The stimulation between minds that makes me climax
Sometimes I wonder does he really feel me
Not sexually, but mentally
Right now, I can't say
All I know is that at the end of the day I'm pulling the throw over one
Did I shortchange myself?
Sometimes I wonder
But then he proves himself again and again
It leaves me baffled
If you get what I'm sayin'
I mean, I don't think he's playing with my mind or anything like that
I think it is all about the timing
Dang, here I go feelin' that itch
Where is he now?
Good question."

I pause. I feel myself getting choked up.

Suzette doesn't bite her tongue. "Well, girl, he's probably with that bitch. That skank he shacked up with."

"Yeah, probably, but now where does this leave me, huh?" I ask.

Suzette doesn't hesitate to respond. "I guess where you've always been, girl, without his chocolate stick." She cackles, loudly.

I roll my eyes and pout. "I'll talk to you later, Su."

"Later."

We hang up.

"I don't find anything amusing," I say to myself. And the fact that Suzette does says a lot of how she feels about me. Doesn't she realize that this is difficult for me to accept? Couldn't she hear the distress and disappointment in my voice—the discontentment, the dismay that leaves me at a standstill as to what to do, how to react, how to view what has taken place. I once loved this man with all of my heart and soul. And somehow I allowed my feelings to project outwardly by being a willing participant and having *unprotected* sex with my husband.

The way Kenyatta made me feel my body had been yearning for that feeling for eons. And now that it has finally happened, yes, a door has reopened, what I am supposed to do with all of this *stuff* festering inside? I lower my eyes, shake my head. What am I to do?

I sit contemplating. And as I do, I hear these words, "*Yeah, she's out of my life, but I can't get her out of my mind*" by Glenn Jones, and it makes me wonder if he ever thinks of me in this way. Of us, where he knows he has a family here, wanting and needing him under the same roof. I never realized how much I miss him. Seeing him come in and out of that door never really sparked any feelings, but when we made love all that was hidden inside came pouring out onto him. I still love him. Never thought I'd admit that openly, but it's just God and me here behind closed doors having a profound conversation about what's missing in my life.

I see that I put myself in a compromising position because Kenyatta has moved on. I'm the one stuck in time, holding on to a marriage that has severed its ties a long time ago. I'm the one who won't get out of my own way and find my own inner peace and happiness. Why am I holding on to a man who no longer wants me as if wife? Why am I still hoping that he comes to his senses and realizes that what we had can become something good and wholesome, something that was missing from the very beginning? *Where is all of this coming from, Lord?* Yes, I slept with my husband, and it felt like I had been introduced to someone new and warm loving. I never felt him in that way before, when we were as one. I never felt his heart in the way that I did that night. It felt so free-spirited and willing to appease my every need. It did something to me. Something deep and meaningful and beautiful and scary is wrapped around my heart. I've fallen in love for the second time with a man who doesn't seem to love me back. So I say to myself, "where does this leave you, Burn?" and I answer myself in the same breath, "where you've always been: Alone, lonely, and afraid to give your heart to another man."

Tears flood in my eyes and slowly roll down my cheeks. The truth does severely hurt. And the fact that he has found someone to love him hurts too. I'm not trying to break up a happy home. I shake my head. No. That's not my intentions at all. I feel a self-lift coming on. And as I do, I reassure myself that I can and will be the bigger woman. And under no uncertain terms will I allow myself to stoop to low levels of underhandedness for a man. Not even Kenyatta. I mean I love him. I do, but I-I have to let go of what was, and allow God to guide me in finding what is...best... for...me.

But first I need to cut the ties with Kenyatta and file for a divorce. No need to wait on him. 'Cause the longer I wait the more time is just passing me by. I mean, truthfully, what's the point of holding on to a man who is already spoken for?

The Gutter of My Soul
WYNDOW PAIN

EVERY DAY YOUNG GIRLS live vicariously through other young girls. We idolize those who have more. We pretend. Pretend to be down with whatever they're down with. We want to bite their style, their talk, their walk. We want to fit in. You know, be accepted by our peers, which are the cool girls. And in the process of wanting to be accepted by them, somewhere along the way we tend to lose ourselves. Someone we never really knew or met because we were too busy pretending. As we get older we gradually mature, at least some of us do. Even as preteens we are still pretending, fantasizing about our lives. We see ourselves as grown women, married to the greatest man in the universe. A family oriented man. We pretend to have these wonderful lives, wonderful, adorable, great children, the perfect husband, wonderful career, *blah blah blah*, but behind closed doors our $500,000.00 house in a walkable suburb of Edgewater, New Jersey, is about to go into foreclosure. Our *adorable, great* children are a menace to society. And our *perfect* husband is having an affair with our best friend, Melanie. The last but not least...our job, well, little do we know we're on the verge of getting fired come Monday at 4 p.m. Yep. That *wonderful* career as a Buyer/Manager Merch Planner for Barney's New York in the Big Apple is gone too.

But grown women know how to make it *seem* like *everything* is ok. Yep. Even as adults *they* are still pretending.

As a teen I awake out of that dream, that fantasy, that reverie and return to my daily life. I know better than to sleep walk into a fairytale that won't come true.

I see the wear and tear on these women makeover faces. I hear their conversations. Not that I'm eavesdropping or anything. But I hear. I mean they wear it like a garment of clothing. Like a pair of worn shoes. Or a ripped pair of hosiery. They don't grasp exactly *how* or *why* or *when* this happened to them. They're such liars! Such bad liars!

Their bodies suffer. It's not like they can hide it, although, they try to,

289

but I still see. Don't they know that I have 20/20 vision? I see the weight gain, especially the midriff section. I see the weight loss. I see their roots turning gray. I see them aging seemingly overnight. I see the crow's feet. Quite often they let themselves go, and then they come here to try to spruce themselves up. To pretend that everything is ok. You know dress to impress. They are such terrible liars. They don't know that I see it all, as they come and go, pretending, week after miserable week.

But who am I? Just the wardrobe room girl, who gives them what they ask for, accommodating, complimenting, smiling, even when I don't feel like it I size them up. Constantly hearing them in their annoying proper speaking voices: "Oh, Wyndow, can you be a sweetheart and take this blouse back to get another one in a different size or color or style." That's me... Wyndow Pain...I am always at their beck and call. My eyes sparkle like diamonds as I watch them flash their fancy credit cards: American Express, Visa, MasterCard...unfortunately, we don't accept Discover at PRISSY MISSY. It's too expensive according to my boss, Miss High-Mighty.

At PRISSY MISSY, we sell upscale business apparel, fragrances, shoes, accessories, unmentionables, jewelry as well as hosiery. We're located in the heart of Wayne, New Jersey.

You really have to have a great personality to work in retail. Me, huh, I am more of the behind the scenes girl, because I mainly work in the wardrobe room. According to Miss High-Mighty, that's the proper way to say...fitting room. You have to be able to stomach people from all walks of life. Cater to their wants and needs like whiny toddlers. Sometimes it is just too much to devour with one chew. But a girl has to eat. It's all in a job. Yes, job. This is not a career goal of mine. No. I have bigger dreams.

I've been here almost a year now and Miss High-Mighty still hasn't mentioned one word about a promotion or hourly increase. I haven't even received my sixth month review yet. No review. No raise. So therefore, she leaves me with no alternative but to look for other opportunities elsewhere. But every time someone calls her for a reference on my behalf she always finds a way to sabotage it, indirectly.

So every day I have to pull myself out of bed to come in with a happy-go-lucky attitude. Go home. And do the same crap all over again. I feel like pulling my hair out, but it took too long for me to glue my tracks in. I can't even afford to get a proper hairweave! Yet, I am expected to dress accordingly: neat, crisp and clean. To look well-groomed: nails, hair, and makeup—to speak proper English—to sound like I am not from the ghetto. To camouflage the fact that I was born and raised in the projects—a single parent household, just mom and me. I am 'sposed to transform from who I am into who Miss High-Mighty wants me to be. But I'm a bit baffled because Miss High-Mighty is from the same 'hood as me. Paterson, New Jersey. She lived in the same building as me: Building 2- Cookey Fourth Ward Projects. Well, eventually she got out and moved. Where? I don't know. The point *is*...she got out because her boss (the Regional Manager Mrs. Brinkley) saw her potential to lead others, yet I'm stuck. I feel like I'm being held hostage, although, I don't quite understand why.

I *thought* if I worked hard, applied myself, pushed myself with every fiber in me...I'd eventually see some progress too. I'd see some growth. I know my potential. But I wonder if Miss High-Mighty knows. All I want is the same opportunity as her. Often the thought slips in and out of my mind. *Is it the age difference?* I mean I know Miss High-Mighty is in her mid-to-upper forties. But then I think: *what does age have to do with it?*

Mrs. Brinkley hired me because I tested high on the assessment— higher than anyone else, including Miss High-Mighty. But she doesn't know I know. Mrs. Brinkley mentioned that once she went on maternity leave that she was considering me for sales lead (asst. supervisor). I was 'sposed to be in training before she left, but things didn't quite work out that way. Miss High-Mighty received a promotion from sales lead to store manager. I thought it was a great accomplishment. So I don't understand why she is not willing to expand my horizons. No. I'm not looking for a handout. None of that preferential treatment crap, a free ride, a boost up without blood, sweat, and tears. If she would take off those blindfolds she'll be able to see how hard I work. I mean PRISSY MISSY is like my second home. I don't have a life outside of this place. I can't afford to.

My mother always taught me by example—to work hard and allow my hard work to speak for itself. That my hard work would be noticed and that I would be compensated accordingly. Obviously Mom has *never* worked for Miss High-Mighty.

In spite of how Miss High-Mighty makes me feel, I do my job to the best of my ability. I give all of my *stylist techniques* and I make these women look like dime pieces. I sweep those mousy-haired mutts into prime of their lives polished divas. I tuck their folds of blubber with fine girdles. I boost their confidence by lifting those droopy breasts with a push-up bra. I make their flat butts look scrumptious with the latest booty pads. Slip them in a pair of sexy hosiery to cover-up those varicose veins. Slip their feet in a pair of stilettos to accentuate their sticks called legs. And by the time I am done I create monsters in them all. And yet, I still get paid the same friggin' $8.05 an hour.

I get no commission for the hard work that I do. I meet my sales quotas. Yes, sales quota. Wardrobe room girl is more than hanging garments, fetching clothing, being a personal shopper. I'm the *only* wardrobe room girl that Miss High-Mighty has given a sales quota to. Every day it changes from: $1500, $2500, $3700, $4250...and every time I meet my goal Miss High-Mighty raises the bar. I get no satisfaction or extra compensation for my efforts. I get nothing, but the same ole paycheck, week after miserable week.

PURE, JENNIFER, TAYLOR, WHITNEY, and Beth can never seem to make up their minds every time they come to PRISSY MISSY. Oh, they're my clients. I mail them out monthly coupons as an incentive to come back. And they do. They walk in decked out in their designer wear, expensive shoes, designer handbags, diamonds, French manicures and pedicures. And they smell like money—so sweet and divine. They love to be pampered. It makes them feel important. But each time they come they never know what the *heck* they want. They are so indecisive. It is quite frustrating, to say the least.

I figured by now they would have some sense of style, but no. I guess they get enjoyment out of seeing me run around like a chicken with my head chopped off to accommodate their needs. I am not their wealthy husbands, maids or butlers. I am just the wardrobe room girl trying to make ends meet. Sometimes I feel this devious streak in me beckoning to come out and grab a wire hanger and snag one of their outfits on purpose! But I don't because I actually love the clothes that they wear. I love the clothes we sell, too. It's just; I can't afford to buy any of them, even with my employee discount of 20 percent, because Miss High-Mighty refuses to give me a friggin' raise!

It must make them feel good, but WHAT about me? Who's worrying about what I need? How I feel? I need a car. An associate's degree, so that I can move out of the dump I live in—move up and out into the world. I want a boyfriend for God's sake! I need to get laid! Maybe it will take the edge off. I grimace. But no...Wyndow Pain, she can never have what she needs. I have to go through hoops and bounds to get whatever I need. I need a raise! Or, or, fire me! Miss High-Mighty won't give me the satisfaction, because I'm one of her best wardrobe room girls. Of course, she won't admit it to me. I have excellent customer service skills. I have to; considering I am the next to the last person they see. I have to convince them to buy excessively before heading toward our cashier station with: Veronica, Porsche, Maria, Eileen and Heidi.

Our wardrobe room is an open space. No doors to hide behind. I see it all. Smell it all too. But I actually love working with people...women. I like to make them feel beautiful, inside and out. It's the only gratification I get from this job. I know I have what it takes to make sales associate or even sales lead, but I have one person standing in my way. Yep. Miss High-Mighty!

So what is wrong with me? Why can't I seem to sell myself to Miss High-Mighty for a friggin' raise or promotion? I don't know. Or maybe I do. Maybe I do, and just can't bring myself to say it. Maybe I can't say because I don't want to believe that Miss High-Mighty is... See what I mean. The truth refuses to come out.

No, no, no this has nothing to do with race, at least not on my part. Currently there are only two African-Americans working here: Miss High-Mighty and me. One Yugoslavian. One Brazilian. Two Puerto Ricans. One Dominican. One Jamaican. One Haitian. One Polish. One Trinidadian. One Italian. One Russian. Four Caucasians. There were two other African-Americans working here, but one girl got caught stealing. The other girl was let go because she wasn't coming to work or calling to say that she wouldn't be in. She just didn't show up. I guess they considered that "job abandonment."

Since I've been working here I have yet to miss a day of work. Actually, I can't afford to miss a day, because I need every bit of money for rent and a little bit of groceries. Thank goodness, I don't have to pay for my own utilities or I wouldn't be able to eat.

Miss High-Mighty makes it difficult for me to find a part-time job, too. I mean with this rotating shift I can't work another job, or take night classes at the community college. And yes, I have asked if she could work with me so that I could bring in some extra money. Of course she did not accommodate me. I assume that she is waiting for me to resign. But I won't. I put in too much time and too much hard work to erase this company from my résumé. And plus, it took me too many interviews to luck up and find this job. And you think I'm just going to throw it all away to satisfy her. I don't think so! I have a plan. Get some time in under my belt, maybe I can get Pure, Jennifer, Taylor, Whitney and Beth to write references on my behalf. Then I can move on with my dignity still intact. Or, hopefully Miss High-Mighty will be moved up or shipped out and then my opportunity *may* come.

Miss High-Mighty fails to realize that if Mrs. Brinkley didn't take an interest in her résumé and her years of experience in retail she probably would have bypassed her résumé. I mean a résumé is the first impression, right? During her interview I'm more than sure she passed with flying colors. Miss High-Mighty is very articulate. You would never know she was born and raised in an urban environment. Obviously something caught Mrs. Brinkley's eye. She probably had a gut feeling. And too, if Miss High-Mighty didn't do well on the assessment, then she probably wouldn't be working here anyways. Everything works hand in hand.

So, you see, it has *everything* to do with opportunity for me. I just want the *same* opportunity to advance in life as Miss High-Mighty was given. Why is *she* holding me back?

I drift back to what I need.

Pure doesn't care that *I really need her* to stop leaving her Odor Eaters in the wardrobe room because others have to use it. Jennifer doesn't care that *I really need her* to stop pulling the tags off of the garments. Taylor doesn't care that *I really need her* to stop whiting up the dresses with her deodorant. Whitney doesn't care that *I really need her* to stop trying on trousers with no panties on. And Beth, she doesn't care that *I really need her* to stop ripping the clothes because they don't fit her. All of these women want the attention that they are not getting at home. I am not, for the life of me, a shrink! I am a nineteen year old African-American wardrobe room girl. Oh, who am I kidding! Wardrobe room girl is just a nicer way of saying...*fitting room girl*.

Pure Sonnet, Jennifer Lewis, Taylor Gonzalez, Whitney Sweeny and Beth Cunningham are all compulsive liars, sluts, who drink Cosmopolitans and Apple Martinis for brunch. They love to go to the spa, gym, and meet up during happy hour at One-to-One Ratio to girl gossip.

One-to-One Ratio is 'sposed to be where the potentials hangout to unwind from a day of sitting on their asses doing nothing but chitchatting about how hard of a day they had shopping. Answering insignificant calls, going to insignificant functions, meeting insignificant people...*is* hard work, while I'm on my feet for at least four to six hours a day, with the exception of my one day off, selling women's apparel to these fake bleached blondes, brunettes and red heads. You gotta be kidding me!

How'd I come to meet these women is really nothing to brag about. Like I said they're all my loyal clients. According to Miss High-Mighty we have to call them...clients. But in all fairness they are nothing more than...snooty customers always coming in to look at the latest fashions. Try on whatever their eyes seem to think suits them. Don't get me wrong, they're committed customers, but their cunning customers, too. They're users—using their: looks, body, and status to mingle with the best of the best, while I go home to nobody. Watch DVDs because I can't afford cable until my brown eyes grow tired. Pet my cat, Buttermilk. And give myself a pedicure, because I can't afford to treat myself to one at the nail salon. I'm only making $8.05 an hour for a 25-30 work week. And it is just enough to cover my rent, nothing more, nothing less. *This sucks!*

I sit home on a Friday night, because no one has called to ask me out on a date. So I'm left cooped up in the house. I don't mind. Really, I don't. And if you're wondering, no, Miss High-Mighty has not given me my review or a raise. No sight of one coming in the near future either. So, as you can see I am one of those girls who live vicariously through: Pure, Jennifer, Taylor, Whitney and Beth.

I know. It's pathetic. But can't a fitting room girl dream?

***

BRIIIIIIIIIIIIIIIIIIIGGGGGGGGGGGG! Briiiiiiiiiiiiiiiiiiiiigggggggg!

I reach for my cell phone that is on the Ikea nightstand.

"Hello."

"Hey girl, whatchu doin'?" KiKi asks in a raspy tone. Her voice sounds strange. I guess from all the drug usage. One day I guess she'll get tired of abusing her young body. When that day will be? Huh, only God and KiKi know.

I check my phone clock. It's 8:20 p.m.

"KiKi, I'll call you back after 9:00 when my minutes are free."

KiKi laughs. "A'ight, girl."

I "end" the call.

My gut instinct says *not* to call KiKi back. I mean every time she calls I find an excuse not to talk to her. By now, you'd think she'd catch on, but KiKi has always been slow motioned. It's the drugs making her stupid. Yeah, it's sad, but there is no one to blame but KiKi. She's doing it to herself. And I hate to say it, but I will. I don't feel sorry for someone who is conscious of the hurt they cause to themselves.

It irritated me that KiKi laughed. I don't see what is so funny. She doesn't get it and she probably never will, but I have to be mindful of everything, especially money. I am on a tight budget. I don't have money to burn on constantly buying minutes. KiKi has no worries. Her mom's boyfriend spoils her rotten. Not to mention, her boyfriend Q.C. Heartthrob.

Q.C. is a big time thug in Cookey Fourth Ward Projects. All the young girls used to be trying to kick it with him. But he always had his eyes on KiKi. He's the reason why KiKi always looking so fly. The girl has never worked a day in her life. And from what I can tell she doesn't want to either. I don't know how she does it. I mean sleep all day, party all night. If I'm not mistaken, she dropped out of school to spend more time with Q.C., which of course was the stupidest thing she could've ever done to herself. But let KiKi tell it, it was her teacher's fault. Since I've known KiKi she has never been one to take to authority figures too well. She becomes very rebellious. I mean someone telling her what to do is basically asking for an ass kicking. I blame her mom, Karin. She treats KiKi more like a sister than a daughter. And her dad, well, he skipped out on them when she was five years old. I never knew my father. He was killed when I was a couple of weeks old. How? Mom has yet to tell me. She says it's too painful to talk about, so I don't pressure her. I never want to make my mom cry. I would feel like the worst daughter in the world, if I did that.

As I got older, like fifteen I really took a hard look at myself and the direction I was leaning toward, especially when my mom had a minor heart attack. That woke me up. Just the thought of being a motherless child was all the teachings I needed. Mommy is all I have, and the last thing I wanted to do was make her worry to the point that I stressed her out. No. I knew I had to stay focused. And change the people I hung out with. So I gradually detached myself—gradually stopped calling. Gradually stopped hanging out. I got more involved in school activities to give myself an excuse for not being able to chill with my girlfriends. I'm more than sure they felt a certain kind of way, but they knew that I was always the oddball of the crew. They accepted me anyway. I guess 'cause I didn't make them feel weird like I looked down on them. I never looked down on them. I just looked beyond their view, and saw myself somewhere else, around different people who inspired me to look at life with a set of different eyes.

Working in retail gave me the opportunity to meet: teachers, lawyers, doctors, nurses, firefighters, psychologists, social workers, and stay-at-home moms. Meeting those women of various ages really broadened my outlook on my life. I guess that's when I really decided to remove myself from the friends I used to chill with. Not to say that I am better than them, but I saw myself in a different setting. I didn't want to be chasing a dream. I wanted to be living the dream. Huh, my mom always inspired me to think big, apply myself, work hard, and I would see the fruits of my labor. So, I took the higher road and left that past behind. I grew up, sprouted out, saved up my money and moved out of Cookey Fourth Ward Projects to fulfill my destiny, whatever that may be.

I still chill with my girls: Tiff Simons, Steph Waters, and KiKi Washington when I go see my mom, but that is as far as it goes. I have priorities that come first. And plus, all Tiff, Steph and KiKi want to do whenever I do come around is smoke weed, jump bitches in the hallways and rob them for their jewelry and money, run up on guys in their Range Rovers, BMWs, and Lexus's or Hummers. They sit around in the parking lot and drink Henny, Remy or Ciroc, which are way too expensive for my pockets. I can't do it. I have other responsibilities that they know nothing about having. Either their boyfriends take care of them, or their parents, who mind you, are on public assistance. There is nothing wrong with being on assistance, especially if you hit a bump in life. But eventually those bumps become flat surfaces and if you have landed on your feet after five or ten or fifteen years, then you never will. You become a part of the problem, and not the solution, so your children follow your lead to nowhere. And nowhere leads to nowhere. And no way out.

Either way you slice it, they aren't trying to change. It's the same ole thing week after week. I can't be around it every day. I can't stand to see them leading down several detours: pregnant, high school dropout, addict, alcoholic, inmate and I hate to say it, but hoe or welfare recipient with four incarcerated baby daddies. I am not trying to go out like that.

KiKi is only sixteen, but she looks a lot older because she is fully developed in all the right places. As of today, KiKi is dating a married man.

Tiff is only eighteen and has two baby daddies and three babies—two from the same father who is currently locked up—the other baby from a seventeen year old boy. Currently she is sleeping with the first baby daddy's cousin.

Steph is nineteen, but she acts immature for her age. She's so naïve and easily influenced. That's 'cause her mom ran out on her when she was a newborn. Her mom was a two-dollar-crackhead-whore. Steph's

297

been moved around a lot through foster care. She's loose. She's been that way since she moved to the projects with Miss Mable. Unfortunately, Miss Mable couldn't bear any children of her own, so she opened her door to children who were less fortunate. Steph was placed in good hands, but by the time Miss Mable got a hold of her, she'd been broken in so deep, even Satan had no use for her. She done had about three abortions from three different *men*, not boys. She's also had a couple of STDs too. Sometimes I wonder what she is thinking by some of the dumb stuff she does.

It is 9:15 p.m., when I pick up my cellular and call my mom.

Ring. Ring. Ringgggggggg.

Mom answers on the third ring in a sleepy voice.

"Did I wake you?" I ask.

"It's okay, honey. How was your day at work?"

Mom is always asking me about work. I don't like to exhaust her energy with my problems, so I usually say, "It's just work, Mom."

I figure she'll read between the lines.

I am a little hesitant when asking her the next question, but I ask anyways.

"How are you feeling?"

It's not like it's a bad question to ask, but sometimes I worry about her response.

"Oh, baby, I have good days, and I have bad days," she replies in a faint tone.

My eyes wander about my bedroom wanting to ask the next question, but not wanting to hear the response. Sometimes when I call Mom she sounds so drained. I try to see her on the weekends. The weekends that I don't work I spend the night. It gives us time to catch-up on things. And plus, I get to see for myself how she's really doing.

"What's today like?"

"Well, today is my okay day. Hearing your lovely voice helps, you know. What time is it?" Momma asks.

I check my phone clock. "9:20 p.m."

"Lord, has mercy! I'm just gonna sleep my life away!"

I lower my tone. "Mom, sometimes you need to rest. The doctor said..."

Momma hates when I say: "the doctor said..."

"Did you take your medications, today?"

"Chile," Momma snaps. "I know what the doctor said. It wasn't like I wasn't there. I am the parent. You the child, remember? I don't need you to be my ventriloquist to remind me. I-I-I-I'm sorry, baby," she says, and then sighs deeply. "Wyn, I didn't mean to bite your head off. It's just, just so frustrating adjusting to the 'new' me. With all these medications I can't do my chores like I used to on account I get shortness of breath. Can't eat what I want. And you know I love my fried chicken. I gotta lose weight so fat won't grow around my heart. It's hard, baby girl, real hard, with all these things teasing me when I go to the grocery store I feel helpless, you know." Momma pauses, and then says, "Oh, by the way, I saw KiKi the other day. She was prancing around half-naked looking like a jezebel. I'm so glad you stopped hanging out with that fast girl. Sometimes I see Steph and the other one, um, Tiff hanging out in the parking lot drinking and using foul language. Whatever happened to the rest of those girls you used to hang out with?"

My mind drifts.

Sanaa, Desiree, Juicy, Pumpkin, Beautiful, Princess and Preemie...got caught up in other things.

I knew Preemie, Beautiful and Juicy got caught shoplifting at Rainbow so, now they were doing community service down at the Daycare Center.

Pumpkin and Desiree were both locked up for possession of a stolen weapon and aggravated assault on this girl named Live Chambers. Live used to go to our school, but last I heard Pumpkin and Desiree beat her down so badly they had to put her on life support. Out of all of us I think Sanaa got the rawest deal. Her parents were killed in a car accident. We were still in grammar school when that happened. Just imagine losing both parents at the same time. She ended up moving in with her grandmother, but that was only to collect on the insurance money that Sanaa had got when she turned twenty-one. Sanaa wasn't smart about it. It wasn't her fault. Her parents died young. She didn't have anyone to guide her, especially when it came to having a lot of money. So, Sanaa splurged on unnecessary things. She bought two PlayStations and a slew of expensive games, Lakers jersey, sneakers, clothes, and she always kept her hair looking tight. But Sanaa never saved a dime of that money. The money was slowly dwindling from home to home. So when the money ran out, so did the welcoming family that had embraced her so willingly. She ended up being homeless. Jumping from friend to friend until that was no longer an invite. From there she started sleeping in abandon buildings. The stairwell of Cooley Fourth Ward Projects until the security guard, Felix caught her couple of times and warned her never to come back or he'd call the police and have her arrested for trespassing. The once pretty Sanaa looked rough, hard. I guess to support herself she let her pride go and got caught up in stripping in this dirty strip club called Nazty. From her stripping that only led her to tricking. From there she went downhill and she never recovered back to the Sanaa Browne I knew. Most of the time when I do see her, she's walking around the streets mumbling to herself. I could always see her lips moving like she was talking to someone. But of course, there was no one there, but her, and the ghosts in her head. So that leaves KiKi, Tiff, Steph and me left from the crew.

"Wyn, Wyn, Wyn...are you listening to me, girl?"

I come to.

"Yes, Momma."

"I said...I'm so proud of you for getting yourself out of here. You give me hope, baby. It's the only thing that keeps my heart ticking these days."

Immediately, my eyes well up.

I don't like when she talks like that. It sounds so final. Like I'm the only person keeping her alive. I don't want to believe that. Momma used to have spunk. I could always see it in her eyes when she'd wake me up for school. She was always energetic and fun. She always maintained a job. Sometimes during the holidays like Christmas she'd work at the local bodega to make extra money for presents. She provided a good life for me. Sometimes I feel bad because I left. Other times I feel like should move back in with her to help her out. I give her money every time I visit. But sometimes I feel like it is not enough. Maybe she needs me to take care of her like she did for me most of my life. I feel a lot of pressure on my shoulders and heart. I only have one mom and the thought of her not being around to hug and kiss and call really makes me sad and scared.

"Wyn, remember to always make your doctor's appointments. Don't think 'cause you feel all right that you are all right. As you get older your body plays tricks on you. Don't take life for granted because so quickly it can be gone with a blink of an eye."

My voice breaks. "I won't. I promise. You get some rest, Momma, okay."

"Okay, baby. I'll talk with you tomorrow."

"Okay. Good night. I love you."

"Love you, too, honey. Good night. And Wyn, you have a wonderful day at work tomorrow. Just rub whatever 'Miss-you-know-who' does right off of your shoulders."

"Yes, Momma."

"Don't forget to call me tomorrow."

"I won't."

I "end" the call.

I think to myself, *having a wonderful day at work is asking for a miracle. Maybe Miss High-Mighty will call out sick, or better yet get fired. Then I'll have a great day!*

Unfortunately, great it was not. While I was at work, Momma died. The next day, Miss High-Mighty used that opportunity to fire me because I called out to make funeral arrangements for my mother. The whole time of me working for PRISSY MISSY I had not taken one day off. Never called out sick. Never abused my privileges, whatsoever, I played by the book. Why? Why didn't I undermine them? Well, because my mom taught me better than that. But to have them in the end give me the boot because I took a day to bury my mom is foul. Grimy. Plain dirty.

Miss High-Mighty fought me tooth and nail to make sure I didn't get my unemployment benefits. But I kept appealing my claim. Look. She had already gotten what she wanted which was to get rid of me. There was no way I was going to let her just win without a fight. No way! I got penalized six weeks. Six! I had nothing. No income. Nothing!

I lost my mom, my best friend, and then my mind. I got evicted for non-payment of rent. I had no home. No address. I was homeless. What could I do with mom not having any life insurance? What could I do? I had to scrape up money from everywhere I could, and then some. Lord.

During those six weeks I had to step outside of myself in order to keep my head held high. I used every bit of my resources, my assets, if you get my drift. That money came out of my pocket. No matter who pockets it was pulled out of; it was placed in my hands, which came from my backbreaking work.

I lost everything! Mom, included. I-I couldn't fathom that this had all happened to me. I had to keep repeating it in my head to believe it. "I am jobless, homeless for burying my mom." Constantly I said it to myself. The woman I cherished. The mother I loved with every fiber in me. I'd given her my heart if it would've saved her. But that wasn't possible. It was completely out of my hands. God called her home. I tried. Tried to be the best daughter any mother could ask for. I lived up to every high expectation she had of me. I made her proud, but what about now? Look at me. I am an utter disgrace.

I am homeless. Motherless. My life has spiraled completely out of control. I have nothing to grip; grab a hold of other than my cat Buttermilk. And even she left me in my time of destitute. From there I began a pattern, which led to me walking the streets, which led to me working the streets, which led to me experimenting with drugs to block out the dirt that had accumulated in me, which led to me getting hooked on all the things I tried to get away from in my black community. Everything happened so quickly, I never saw it coming. And then it did. And when it did I had no other alternatives and no one to go to, talk to, or lean on. *Friends*, what does that word really mean?

After my mom's death, KiKi turned her back on me. She expressed her truest thoughts of me. Said that I thought I was better than her. There were no stretched arms to catch me when I fell. Tiff and Steph, they both took sides with KiKi, jumped me in the hallway of my mom's building, and then they vanished from my life. But in the end of it all I let me down by not fighting for what I had in the palms of my hands: my job, my independence, peace of mind, my ability to dream.

I am a nineteen year old young woman, who has sacrificed to have a greater opportunity in life, and I-I let death get the stronger hold of me, and I gave in to something I kept straying away from. I got weak! Where had my strength gone? Yeah. It's buried with momma. Momma always used to say, "You can't knock'a girl for tryin'."

Yep. If only she knew.

She knew. Momma knew it all. She knew how difficult it had gotten for me. Through all the loss and heartache I lost my grip on life. Can't say I knew this right away. Can't say. 'Cause when you get hit with a heavy burden your thought process get it scrambled up. So quickly you lose focus. Bit by bit you lose yourself. Get shuffled in the pain that you internally feel.

Yeah. I was getting up every day. Had this routine lifestyle, you know. Job. Home. Momma. Me. God. But there was a lot missing in between. A lot of gaps that had not been filled I wasn't happy but I was surviving. I figured that meant something.

This lost person I had become was not the daughter or young woman my mom had raised. It began to bother me, especially as I bypassed life as if it was waiting on me to get it together. I was fooling myself. Playing with my own emotions—senselessly beating myself up.

My window of reflection began to show me that I had some serious issues. I needed to take back what was rightfully mine. Me. I had to pull myself back and reflect on all that I had done to remove myself from all that madness that was surrounding me. And I did. At least I thought I did. But thinking comes from not knowing. And I didn't know how deep my pain ran. Nearly tore me to pieces having to bury my mom. She was everything to me. And when she died, everything withered along with her. I had no feeling left inside me. Felt empty like an empty box of nothing. It was the worst feeling in the world. The greatest loss I'd ever come to greet. But I had to survive. Survive off of no hope, no faith, and no purpose. Just suck it all up and say the hell with it all in the same damn breath.

It became a disgraceful way to live. And that certainly wasn't me. No. My momma had instilled beauty in me. And I let that slutty *bitch* in me fall to her knees and do her dirt. I saw no other opportunities coming forth and I felt like I was running out of time. Out of patience, you know. I had nothing left. Felt like pocket change. Like a penny or nickel, shit, I had not grown enough to become a dime or quarter. My self-worth had no digit. Wow.

Wow. That's right.

I was at a low point—my lowest point. I was getting sick and tired of just getting by. It wasn't me. The girl I had become was an imposter. I could not identify with her. We were opposites. But this was who I had become. It was time to rid of the bad sistah in me. Kick that bitch to the curb, quick. And focus on salvaging what I had left in me. That good stuff. That good 'n' plenty. God. I wanted it so badly, so very, very badly.

Most of the time I felt like I had ulcers bleeding inside me, painful ulcers, and the pain became too much. It was just too much to take. I was ready, ready for change.

"Good morning, Help Me, Help Myself Shelter for Women, Ms. Ernestine speaking, how may I *help* you today?" The amicable female voice sang.

Those words: '*how may I help you*' were like music to my ears. It turned my frown upside down. I literally found myself getting emotional while on the phone with her. It was like she cracked me wide open and all I could do was feel the pain like rage had ripped me open. Just slit me to no end.

"Hello? Hel-lo? A-are you there?" she asked hastily. As if she was trying to catch me before I clicked her off. I swear she sounded just like momma with her gentle disposition. Probably looked like momma too. I just had that feelin' in my gut. It was the warmth in her tone that resonated something in me. Feeling this kind of compassion allowed me to open my mouth.

"Yes, ma'am. Um," scratching my throat, twice, "I have nowhere to go. Do you happen to have any beds?"

"Ma'am," she said, "Have you been to this shelter before?"

"No, ma'am."

"Where are you located? Do you live in New York? We're located in Brooklyn." she said.

"No, ma'am. I live in the *gutter of my soul*."

"Pardon?"

"The *gutter of my soul*, ma'am. That's where I live. It's not a city, town, state, just the gutter. A place where no young girl or woman should *ever* live, but it's my residence for now. Um, I've been trying to move but the devil, that's the landlord. He just, just refuses to *evict* me. Said I'm one of his very best tenants. And if I *come* (cum) on hard times he'd let me stay in his apartment rent-free. But I'm tired of opening my legs and lettin' all these niggas run up in me like I'm some loose floozy. Like my *brain* stuck in my butt, and my *heart* tucked inside its crack, and my *eyes* shoved in the bottom of my feet where I walk hard over this solid concrete just stompin' all over my *faith*. I have been sleeping in abandoned buildings, going to public libraries when the days get too hazy and the rain pours like diarrhea. All this waste come flushing out of me. Sometimes I go to the bookstore and just sit and close out my life 'cause it just be too dark for my own imagination. Never knew I was a storyteller till I looked inside myself and began to write the chapters of my life with my used-to-be pen of integrity. I had high hopes, whimsical dreams, and the thought of so much happiness in the world I couldn't stand it. So instead I laid back spread my legs and let him stick his dirty dick in my hopes, dreams, everything and anything that meant some good to me. I let 'em fuck it out of me. Just fuck fuck fuck till they popped my cherry all out of whack. My patience is nearly crumbling to dust. And care, well, that's dangling on a frayed string. And prayer, well, ain't much of that left either. Ma'am, I'm on the verge of OD'ing."

The woman remained silent. All I could hear was her soft breathing in the phone.

I continued, "I got enough bus fare case you have an empty bed. With winter just approaching I'm running out of places to hide where people don't wonder if I'm homeless. But I am, ma'am, I'ma homeless soul seeking refuge."

The woman continued to remain silent.

"I don't have family. My mom just recently passed away. I've been trying to get back on my feet. Just need a fresh start. New surroundings, you know. All I'm asking for is some borrowed time. I'ma hard worker. Got strong work ethic in me. Got that from my mom." I chuckle. "And,

and I know within a few months' time I can be back on my own. All I need is a bed, some where I can breathe a sigh of relief, clamp my legs shut, and regain some self-respect and dignity."

"I understand." The woman said empathically.

"I have *ten* dollars to my name. Money I put aside for a rainy day. I can get there if you tell me the address. I can get there today if you have one empty bed. Lord knows I'm so tired. I can't keep this up much longer. I'm only nineteen, ma'am, but I feel so old inside like I'm deteriorating right before my eyes. I just need a little help in finding that *lost* young woman in me, you know what I'm sayin'."

"Yes."

I crack a smile. "Momma used to say: 'I chose to name you Wyndow 'cause of all of the things I yearned to do in life but wasn't fortunate enough to do. Honey, I saw it all in your eyes. When I'd look in your eyes I'd see myself doing 'em through you. Baby, my sweet, sweet bundle of joy, you're the reason why I dream. I look in those eyes of yours and I see so plainly all that God has in store for you. You gonna be something. You don't know it right now, but you gonna make a huge impact on life. Girls from all over the world gonna envy you. Some gonna hate you. Some gonna respect you. Some gonna admire you. I don't know what the Lord got in store for you, but it gonna be something big.' She had a lot of faith in me. She pushed me in the right direction and circumstances set me off track. I need to get back on the track so that I can continue to make my momma proud. Feel like shit right now. But I know, I know deep in my heart my momma ain't raise no *shit!*"

It's Just'a DICK Thang
SOOTHE-THE-WEARY-SOUL

I NEVER CONSIDERED tying the knot. You know...*marriage*. Okay, okay, I just told a white lie. When I was twelve all of my dreams started off with: Soothe Soul, do you take this man Spike Williams as your lawfully wedded husband. "I do! I do! I do!"

Of course, that never happened. Spike Williams was nowhere to be found. Who was I kidding? He was fine as white wine in my mind. Well off, too. I was black and raised in a household with my pimp daddy. Mom died a ways back. Her being one of many of dad's tricks, not his bottom woman, but trick, she got caught in crossfire at a lock door and died at the scene. Dad didn't even have a wake/funeral/repast for her. Said she wasn't worth the money. Instead, he buried her in the backyard with the bones of my dog named Dookey. And he dared anyone to snitch him out. I hated my dad. Deeply. But the more I watched him the more I learned. Intentionally he taught me a lot about men and their fucked up ways. I guessed you could say I picked up some of his bad habits.

As I got older I realized dad's habits weren't bad at all. He was. I couldn't wait to get grown and on my own. Just to get away from him. He exploited women, beat them, sexed them, and jerked them around because he knew he could. He was not a gentle man. He didn't know how to be that kind of man. Sometimes I wondered would I grow up to be just like him. Or, would I be fortunate enough to be the opposite. Honestly, it was hard to say.

Since I had trick DNA my worst fear was that I'd end up like my mother.

Trixx. Everyone used to call me...Trixx. I was in my late-twenties. Twenty-eight. Four children. My youngest was two years old. Two. Yeah. Two. DYFS came and took my children. They came unexpectedly. Uninvited. Just came and looked around at my dirty apartment, my dirty and hungry kids, and took 'em. My men's left me too. Men's, that's right. Men's. All I had left was a frown. My whole world had been turned upside down. My children, DYFS took 'em. Oh, yeah. I told you that. I was ruined. Needed to snort some coke. Thought it might make me feel a little betta'. Drink a little too 'cause my throat was kinda dry. Alcohol always did the trick. Been boo-wooing ever since even though it's been so long ago. Snorting. Drinking. Boo-wooing. Drinking made the pain go away. Faces of my children fade too. Damn, I was broke! Welfare cut me off 'cause DYFS took my children. I ain't have no TANF (food stamps, Medicaid, check), no children, no men's...shit! Soon after I got evicted. So then I started shackin' up with this guy named Red-Hot. He was mean and nasty. I didn't like 'im one bit. But we fucked. Had to fuck to keep that roof over my head. I needed money. And I needed it yesterday. Red-Hot and Bubbles (Red-Hot's bitch) wasn't gonna keep letting me mooch coke offa them. Had to get my own. Bubbles whispered in my ear. "You need money, right? Won't you try the Ho-Stroll." Not only did she tell me, she showed me where it was at. Bubbles took me there and left me there too. I had to fend for myself. Teach myself. One time, I said. I'm only doin' it one time. After that I'm sure I'll get the hang of it. But that's it. One time. How hard can it be? Car pulls up. I hop in. I tell him what's on the menu. He makes his order. I service. He pays. Done deal. Everybody's happy. Not quite. I didn't really think it went that smoothly, but I hoped so. I really did. I remember the first time so vividly.

Here comes a black Expedition SUV now. What street is this? I don't know. Ain't from here, remember. Church behind me though. Let me straighten up. Fix my wig 'cause it's showing my peas around the edges of my hair. He gonna notice me real quick 'cause I got this sapphire blue lipstick on. It's a pretty shade. Stands out like a sore thumb. He's gonna stop, watch. Okay. He's pulling up closer, closer, closer. He stops right in front of me and rolls down the passenger's-side window. "Hi." I say. White guy says, "Hop in." I don't hesitate. I betta' hurry up for that other chick makes her way up the street and steals him from me.

I jump in his ride. We stroll the block. He keeps staring at my thighs. I'm rockin' a mini skirt. No panties. Pussy itchin'. Body too. I wonder what he's gonna want off the menu. He doesn't talk much. Just keep rubbing between his legs. I bet his balls and dick is sticky and hot.

Okay. I'm ready to get this over with. C'mon, man, what the fuck! Finally, he pulls in a secluded area. Doesn't look familiar to me I'm not from here. All I see is factories, warehouses, train tracks. Like an industrial area. He parks. Leans back in his seat, unzips his cargo pants. Takes out his erect penis and massages it steady staring at my thighs.

"Hike up that there mini skirt. Lemme see what you got hidden under there, miss lady." he says in a southern drawl.

So I do.

The seat is warm on my butt.

"You like this here?" he asks jerking himself.

I nod. Pretend to be lovin' it.

"You wanna watch it do a trick," he says.

I nod. Pretend to be interested.

I'm waitin'.

Pussy gettin' moist, wet.

I'm waitin'.

Nipples gettin' hard.

I'm waitin'.

He slips his fingers between my legs, sticks his finger inside me. Kinda rough.

"Now won't you drive this stick for me, huh?"

"How much is it worth?" I ask.

"How much you worth?" he asks.

"Eighty dollars." I say.

"Well, I guess you gonna give me eighty dollars worth of blow, then, huh?"

I lean over. Neck stretches as far as it can go. My mouth touches his skin. I sniff. He smells fresh and clean. Shoulders bounce up and down as if to say, not bad.

I give him what he wants.

He gives me what I need.

Done deal.

One time.

I lied.

One time turned into an on and off again cycle of trickin'. Now I'm a pro. 'Ey, was betta' than nothin'.

Fast-forward...

I'm forty-eight. I'm not men bashing. But I ask you, ladies, what's the point of getting all emotionally involved when all he's gonna do is take what you are giving and give the best of him to someone else? I learned my lesson the hard way. I gave that man the sweetest parts of me. Personality. Pussy. Kept promises. Purpose. And in return, he, he so kindly and generously gave me his ass to kiss. I willingly pecked each cheek. And then that scared woman, that weak woman in me lured him into the shower and I lathered him from his neck down to his feet. I rinsed him off. Got down on my knees, water drenching him like rain and I sucked that man's dick like love depended on it. I loved that man soooo much and I wanted him to know and feel and taste my love for him. And he did. He moaned out my name. Closed his eyes and took all of my lovin'. He took it all. And after, after I-I found myself sitting in the empty bathtub, naked, while he was in the bedroom getting dressed to go somewhere. Somewhere I wasn't invited to go. So I sat there and I waited to hear the front door close. I waited to hear the car start and him drive out of the driveway. And once I knew he was gone, I screamed at the top of my lungs because I felt like a fool! Foolishly in love. That was me. Foolishly I allowed that man to play me for a fool by thinking that his love for me was everlasting. That nothing, no one said or did would ever come between what we had built, shared. But I was duped. And it hurt so deep to feel that type of pain.

I had been giving this man of mine *head* every other night. I pleased the hell out of him. Tried my best to. And he did his best to fuck my pussy *very* well. Then in the end he leaves me where if I wanted to forget him, I couldn't. How could I? I wouldn't. I'd done him wrong. Never suspected that my past would ruin the best relationship I'd ever had. But it did, and so quickly.

It was like the wind blew and suddenly all the bad that I had done uprooted from its burial grounds. I never told him about my four children. I didn't feel the need to since I was starting a new life. They had moved on and so did I. I thought it was best. Keep the past in the past, you know. They never wanted to see me after I'd abandoned 'em. I couldn't well blame 'em.

It seems someone from my past saw Kareem and me together. They didn't know that I was his wife, not right away, but Kareem was so proud of our marriage, and how we connected that he told everyone in sight. I never looked at it as a bad thing. I mean this man loved me unconditionally. And I-I was so proud to be his wife—so proud. I pushed the past behind me and carried on with my life as this married woman. God, I was so happy and very much in love.

In the beginning of our marriage, Kareem, that man. He made me feel like a black beauty queen. I didn't want for nothing! He showered me with love and affection. He gave me all the penis a woman could stand to have. I was in wayyyy deep with this man. Attractive. Tall. Dark. Magnificent in bed. He was my black prince. And I treated him as such. I poured my heart and soul out to that man. Felt like I couldn't live without. I gave too much. And in the end of him leaving me I lost the best of me. My heart turned cold. That softness I had was hard. I was like stone. Cold. Ugly. Who would want a woman made of stone? Exactly.

See, that's why the woman I am now tries to give insight to other women. As painful as it might be to share something as intimate as this I feel it is my duty to share. I don't want another woman to feel my distress.

So, ladies, here you are cleaning house and bawling your eyes out because it hurts that much. Everything you touch reminds you of him. You feel like you can't breathe. It's too much. But you gotta dry those eyes, pick up those broken pieces of you and either throws all his shit out or do like I did.

Everything that reminded me of him I kept as a reminder of where I went wrong. Yeah. I needed something to stare me in my face on a daily basis in order for me to evolve. Throwing his shit out is the easy way out. I didn't want to go that route. His 48-inch flat-screen TV I'd watch every episode of *Mary Jane* on it. His sweat hood I'd slip one of those babies on like it was nothing. And sleep in it too. His thick sweat socks, girl, after I finished taking a hot shower, honey, I'd Vaseline my feet and slip those socks right on without a second thought. His toothbrush I'd let it set erect in the toothbrush holder. His toiletries are still under the bathroom sink. His bathrobe is still hanging on the hook. And his slippers are still right beside the bed. And his body scent is still on the left side of the king-sized bed along with his three pillows. I haven't washed his scent off as of yet. Don't plan on it either. His aura is cascading throughout this house. If I open the windows it's still here. If I open the door it's still here. He ain't goin' nowhere. His picture is still on the living room wall. I look at his handsome face every day. It doesn't faze me anymore. I don' sniffed him in so much that I actually like his body scent. Yeah. Call me crazy. Call me whatever. I don't care. His energy can stay here as long as it likes. Don't bother me one bit. I ain't selling my house. I ain't movin'. I'm stayin' right here.

See, when you get to this point of not caring you know that you've regained, restored your power. This is the best I've felt since he's been gone. The best! Hell, I look years younger. I feel younger. I'm content with self. Content with being by my damn self! Girl, Girl, Girl, you don't know what you missin'. You gotta find out how it feels to be free. You can't be free worryin' about that man that ain't worryin' about you. That ain't freedom. That's incarceration. I refuse to do any time for any man. I refuse! I am not anyone's inmate. I won't even consider it. Life is too short, girl, too damn short to be confined in the house because your man, a man who couldn't stand by his vows, a man who left months ago instead of hearing your side of the story. No, he'd rather believe some dog that knew nothing about me, yet knew everything about that cokehead. If he were really listening he would've picked up on the fact that that informant wanted what he had, but he didn't. He merely left and never came back. Never called. Had he asked me, had he taken the time to talk to me I would've divulged it all to him. My face could've been streaking of tears, snot, but he would've known the truth. He never hinted or left any clue that he was disturbed by something. He hid it well.

A month later a strange man came knocking at my door.

"May I help you?" I asked.

"I take it that Kareem is not here." The unknown man said.

"No. He's not. May I ask who are you?"

"An old buddy from his past, my name is Jefferson...Jefferson Wrong, ma'am."

"He never mentioned you before."

"Well, I'm not too surprised about that."

"Why not?"

"Back in high school we were very competitive. As we got older that hadn't changed much."

"Really? Well, Mr. Wrong, I'm kinda busy right now, scoooo..."

"I guess you're wondering why I'm here. Actually I came to see you."

"Me?!"

"Yes, ma'am. You. The way Kareem talked you up I needed to see for myself. Can't say he was wrong. You sure are one attractive woman. He described you to a T."

"Why would he be talking to you about me?"

"Well, that's what some men do when they have something good at home. Men like to brag. Some talk too much, which is what Kareem did. He gave me too much information. I must say it left me curious. I wanted to find out for myself."

"Find...out...what?"

"Find out if you are as good as he said you were."

"Good... as far as what?"

"Kareem put it out there that you can suck the hell outta of a dick."

"He did... what?!" I snapped.

"Some fellahs and I were at the bar the other night and Kareem came walking in with this big ass grin on his face. Any time y'all had sex we all knew 'cause of the grin. All one of us had to do was ask and he'd spill the beans. He told us about you giving it to him in the shower. And he went into explicit detail too. Yep. He described you to a T. I was just hoping that I could actually find out. I'm willing to pay any price. Don't matter as long as it's as good if not better than what he described you could do."

If y'all could be flies on the wall you'd see my whole body stiffens up. I literally had to pinch my forearm to make sure I heard him correctly. The look on his brown-skinned clean-shaven face confirmed that I had. I could not believe my husband had done this to me. But it was evident that he had. Or this man would not be standing before me, lusting after me like a dog in heat.

Tears filled in my eyes. I couldn't hold them back even if I tried. I felt that dagger just cut me open. At that point I didn't care about this man seeing me vulnerable. I guess in a way I needed to be seen. He just happened to be there.

Strangely enough the man was teary-eyed too. It was the craziest thing I'd ever witnessed in my life.

He tried his best to reach out to me, but I felt so belittled inside. Jefferson slipped his hands inside his pants pockets. "Don't cry. Please. You gonna make this six-foot-four-inch of man breakdown right in front you. Please. Don't cry. I don't know what I was thinking. I wasn't thinking. It's just a dick thang, you know what I'm sayin'. A man thang. Stupid. It was realllll stupid of me to come to your doorstep and request such a thing from a beautiful woman like yourself. Please. Please accept my apology. I didn't realize what I realize now."

With tears streaming down my face I said, "Realize... *now*?"

He nodded. "Yes. I don't think Kareem realized it either. But as I am standing here God is speaking to me. First, He's telling me to look into your eyes down to pit of your soul. Now He's asking me do I see *her*. I tell Him no. No, I don't see her. So, He says keep looking, a little deeper this time. So, I keep looking. Just as I'm about to give up I see something. As I focus in more I see her. Her, which is *you*...twenty-eight year old you. He says, do you see her for her worthiness? Do you still look at her the same? Beyond the flesh? Do you see her? And I say, yes. She's a very beautiful woman. So, God says, ask to take her hand. Let her feel your spirit. 'May I take your hand, please?' God says; look in her eyes, deep in her eyes as she's touching your hand. Can she see you? Ask her? 'Can you see me?' 'Yes.' God says; embrace this moment and each other."

And that's exactly what Jefferson and I did.

From the day that God spoke to Jefferson we have been moving forward as a couple. And whatever we do in the privacy of our home stays in its sacred place: our hearts.

Life is funny. I never thought Mr. Wrong would end up being Mr. Right. But I'm soooo glad he is.

"Magnetic Couple"
PURNELL WEAVER

WHY?

It is the question that lingers in most people's mind. After all she's done to you, why, why in the world would you stay with a woman who disrespected you in such a way? Why would you engage in conversation with a woman who played with your life? Why would you even care to entertain her? Why accept her back, not as the woman you married, but as your wife with HIV? Why waste precious time with someone who has doomed her future and yours?

My response to that question would be that you don't know the woman I married. Minerva Swanson. When I proposed and slipped that diamond ring on her finger there was no doubt in my mind that she wanted me as her husband. No doubt. The sparkle in her eyes, teary and full of joy made me feel so wholesome inside. She loved me through and through. No doubt in my mind.

Let me backtrack for a minute, if you don't mind. I want to give you some insight on me, some history. Then maybe you'll be enlightened as to why Nerva is the woman for me and why I feel she is a value to me. She is my black diamond. She is a rarity—sweet and loving rarity.

Growing up my Dad was a dirty hustler, a womanizer too. I learned early on of who I did not want to become. I never wanted to become him. He treated my mother as if she was a piece of ass, never once did I ever see him kiss her or show her any type of loving affection He basically ignored her, talked trash to her, and my mother took it like a champ. By watching her accept the abuse only made me look at her with anger and empathy in my eyes.

As I got older I began to understand that Mom did it to keep him around, and in my life. But had she known then what I know now, she could've let him go a long time ago. She was only protecting me, and trying to keep the family structure intact. Sorry to say, it only made matters worse for me because all that I had seen and heard and didn't see and hear but witnessed with actions only intensified the rage, the beast growing inside of me.

Witnessing this, I ended up despising the man I called Dad. But never did I share openly how I truly felt for him. Never did I divulge what I felt for Mom either. I kept everything bottled up inside. I was determined not to become him, or her, for that matter. So I worked on myself day and night, night and day until I felt I had me under control. In control enough to meet a wholesome woman who would understand me as a man, and appreciate the little I had to offer in wisdom and respect, something my own Dad didn't possess.

Then is when I saw *her*. This beautiful, young woman who took my notice, she had me as soon as I spotted her. I knew it in my spirit, in my soul; I knew that she was going to be my lady, my wife. I just knew it. And I acted upon what I knew, what I felt.

You have to understand me being a man of God, I allowed Him to guide me in directions that I was unsure of. I listened to His word before my own conscience. I patiently waited for signs to show me the way. Signs that stated I was in the right place at the right time.

When I saw Minerva there was this afterglow that surrounded her as if she was protected by angels. I took that as a sign, so I approached her with no hesitation. And when I did I noticed something in her face, a sadness I understood. A sadness I once encountered when I was young watching my mother pretend to be in love with a man who no longer loved her back, but remained in our home, under our roof, and provided for the family as if he was the man of the house. Yes, he did provide, but the hell that we had to endure in the process was something that sticks with a young boy and can either turn him into a replica of his dad or a man of his own. It messes with a young boy's mind and could either turn him into a cold son-of-a-gun or a gentle man.

During that time of my dad's absence other men chose to fill his shoes. Those men mentored me and gave me good insight on life and choices and repercussions— men who took me willingly under their wing and nurtured me with wise wisdom that had and has carried me through to identify myself as a man. I was blessed to have learned from them. Through them I especially learned a lot about women.

I saw what hurt and burdens could do to a woman as I watched my mother damned near lose herself right before my eyes. The disparity, she wore like a bathrobe. The misery, she carried in her eyes like a purse. The disappointment, she wore like shoes on her feet as they dragged through life, slow and grievingly as if she wished the Lord would just take her quick and painlessly. All of this I carried within myself, never had I buried it because it became a compact mirror for me, something my mother often reached in her purse scrambling to find, pullout, open it and look into the eyes of herself, seeing all the damage my dad had done to her, and what she allowed him to do.

Every time I looked at a woman I saw some piece of my mother. Their eyes, facial features, curves, the way they spoke, their mannerism, their softness, the texture of their hair, their scent of joy and pain and insecurity and confidence. All those fragrances of woman reminded me of my mother. And when I looked at Minerva, God, she reminded me of what my mother deserved...a man, not a deadbeat, a whole man willing to give his whole self to another, to love and cherish until death do them part. I was willing to give Minerva all of me, and I did.

So, in regards to her indiscretions, yes, it took me back a bit. I almost let go of her, but then I remembered something so important, my dad. How he dismissed my mother even in her presence. I never wanted to become anything remotely close to him. It was bad enough that I resembled him in facial features but I did not become him in mannerism. There was no-way no-how I could leave Minerva, no matter how bad it burned. First, second or third degree, I loved that woman to death. To death, I said. I would never leave her.

That may not have helped you understand a doggone thing. You're scolding hot over what she'd done to herself and our marriage. And I'm not going say you shouldn't be. It hurt. Hurt like the devil himself was shadowing boxing with me and knocked me the hell out! When hasn't a person hurt from love? I mean true, genuine love.

I learned that *love* is the epitome of Mother. It is said that Mom is the backbone to the family structure. Mom is the sergeant in command. She embodies church, hospitals, places where sick people seek a healing. Mom is earth. The soil. The root. She is the love that most children would die for. Most men will cry for. Most daughters would either confide or emulate at some point in their lives. Mom is a teacher, a preacher; mom is a woman—soft and supple—radiant—a glow of imperfection. Yes, even Mom is not perfect. Mom has a love that is so nurturing that it literally hurts when you defy her. When you go against all that she has instilled in you and you become other than what she had hoped you'd be, man, it is a hurt that splits one open. Mom hurts from your hurt because the love is that damn strong. The distance of that love is so powerful that she can still feel your hurt 3000 miles away. And being that Mom is the first woman you'd ever love; you are being molded into pieces of her. No matter how hard you try not to, her love cannot be dismissed. You cannot destroy what is already embedded in you since birth. It is a seed that has been planted from your beginning and will remain till your dying day. And too, those who have lost their moms early on, the rule still applies. Even if she never had the opportunity of holding you in her arms, her love for you while you were in the womb will guide you through life because she was love.

When she took you in her arms, cradled you, you felt that nurturing spirit cover you in her love like a blanket. A secured blanket filled with nothing but unconditional love. She vowed not with words but with heart that she'd love you for life. Even when she departs this earth, her love so spiritually grown that you can still feel her love inside of you, around you, beside you walking hand in hand.

As you grow you may go against the grain and try to find that significant one or you may just sit back and wait for the signs of *love* to come streaming through. And you will know if she is real or a fake. You will know because mom's love will come reflecting through. You'll feel her energy. You'll know by what your spirit tells you. And then, as Mom would do, she'll leave it in God's hands and allow you to do as you please.

Love is a word that should not be used loosely, and those who defy its meaning, oh, you know they will catch the mighty hell.

One thing about love, she don't play on emotions, and if you so try to, best believe it will come back to haunt you.

Love is a weapon—a deadly weapon that should not be used to inflict pain. But placed in manipulative hands, love becomes a deceitful bitch in a skimpy red dress. Much harm can come to one dueling with that type of love.

So, as you listen love comes in all different ways, but the most powerful of love, is truth. That kind of love will feel as if it is yanking your heart out of your chest. When you feel that, then you know you were truly in love.

Minerva, that woman is a gem to me. She is what keeps me alive on days when I feel I want to die. One look at her, in her present state, I-I literally cry. Oh, I'm *not* ashamed to cry in my woman's arms. No. Our love has deepened from the circumstance. It depends on us. You understand where I'm coming from?

God spoke to me in my dying days. That's what it felt like when I felt my woman was cheating on me. I felt it! I just couldn't prove it. But God, He spoke to me. He showed me all that I felt in my spirit!

God as my witness I never felt so loved in my life. Momma had come and wrapped her arms around me so tight, that I felt her presence on me. Felt her breath on my skin. Felt her hand wiping my tears away. She came to me in my time of grief. Her love had never died for me, and mine will never die for her, even after I'm dead. My spirit will live on.

Here *I* am. Here *we* are. No doubt a change has shifted in our lives. But now our love is stronger, than strong. Even disease couldn't tear us apart. There is no doubt in my mind that we were meant to be as one.

You see, love is to never say you're sorry. Love is to embrace the bad with the good, good with the bad, terrible ugly with the undeniable truth. Truth is, Minerva, (tears flow down my face) this woman gives me all I need. She completes me full. Not a day goes by that I stop loving her. Everyone makes mistakes. And yes, Minerva's is a huge, huge one, but *I* vowed to love her. And I do. I-I truly, truly do. I couldn't be happier simply because the love of my life is still with me. Yes, we are a "magnetic couple" her HIV-positive, me HIV-negative. And for as long as she has breath I will cherish every single day, *forever.*

Oh Damn, I Had a One-night Stand With My WIFE!
KENYATTA J. BENTLEY

IT'S OFFICIAL.

Burn and I had *sex!* As much as I feel the need to regurgitate after saying that, it's the damn truth. Damn. DamnDamnDamn! I can't get it out of my head. You don't understand the depth of this situation. But, but I'm here to plead my case, if you're willing to listen.

First, let me grab a Heineken 'cause this is going to take a lot out of me to explain. Better yet, let me grab the case. Put it on ice 'cause I need someone to listen before I plead my case to my girlfriend, Kindred.

I can't sleep, can't eat... can't think rationally neither.

This shit is fucking me up. My conscious is eating at me 'cause I know I got a good lady at home, and, and, she deserves to have a genuine man. I can't even make love to her right now. And that's fucking with me too. My dick won't get hard. That's fucking with me too. I mean, all of that beautiful, sexy mahogany at home, and I can't make a move to please my lady all because of this shit.

Guilty as Charged!

I, Kenyatta D. Bentley, had a one-night stand with my wife, Burn.

Fellahs, if you're listening.. FUCK. ME. UP!

Damn! Damn! Damn! I think.

My face leans into the palms of my hands. My head shakes from side to side. Then I whisper to myself, "I fucked up. How the hell—" I pause. Look to my right seeing Burn lying beside me, naked as a jaybird, snoring up a storm.

I lift up the fluffy floral comforter and see "Swing" limp on my right leg like he's drunk. And I know. It happened.

I hear my alter-ego Slo-Bro' badgering me. *Brotha' Kenyatta, what have you done? She's not even your flavor anymore. You're drawn to the afro centric sistah. The spiritual sistah. Now, back in the day, titties, ass, thickness used to make you bark, but now that you've matured and developed into the spiritual brotha' you are now, that don't even faze you. You don't even see those types of women anymore. You and Burn, man, what y'all had is history. I can't believe you fucked your wife! This is not good bro'.*

I know. I know, Slo-Bro'. You don't have to tell me twice. I mean, damn. Of all people, why her? Why now?

All... maaaaaaaannnnn! It is too late. She's already gotten the *dick.* What is a brotha' to do when he just had a one-night stand with his...*wife?*

I have to gather my thoughts. Reenact in my head *exactly* what happened for this shit here to have happened. All I remember is us having a discussion about our kids, Kriss and Troy. I said something about being hungry because I had just stepped in from work as a security guard. *Oh,* I was bunking on her couch yesterday so I came to get my stuff today to take home with me. Yesterday was...Sunday. I had spent the weekend with my kids, which usually led to me bunking on the couch. Ah, where are the kids though? I don't hear any ruckus throughout the house. That's a good question. Oh, that's right. They are still at one of Burn's girlfriend's house. I nod. *Juliette? Margaret? Peaches? Simone? I know it was one of them chicks. Why are the kids there again?* Think bro'. *I know she said something about a meeting at the school.* Burn is a third-grade schoolteacher. Ok. Vaguely it is all coming back. But not enough to explain why *we* are in *bed* together...*naked.* Think bro' think.

It's Monday. My forefinger taps against my full thick lips. Recapping...I said I was hungry. Did I mistakenly ask her to join me? I don't remember. Why didn't I just leave after I got my stuff? Good question. I don't have an answer though. Shit.

This is not a good thing. Trust me when I say: it is not a good thing. We aren't even connected enough to be having sex. Burn is the mother of my children. But we don't have an understanding as husband and wife. Look. I've been married to this woman for ten years and I realized in those ten years we have no spiritual bonding. We are friends. Not lovers. This, this was all a misunderstanding. A mishap. "Swing" whipped it on her. Look at her. This is not a time to be gloating. This is not a good thing because this could cause me more havoc. Fuck!

My index and thumb pinch the inner corners of my dark brown eyes. I sigh. Damn! Damn! Damn!

I fucked up big time. What am I going to tell Kindred? Oh, Kindred, um, I didn't come straight home from work today 'cause I was preoccupied with screwing my wife's brains out. Yeah, right. She would never understand that, even though, Kindred is very confident in her spot. She's not the jealous type of chick I'm used to dealing with. That's what attracted me to her. Not only is she sexy as hell, beautiful, with short natural mane, she is smart, funny, spontaneous and a freak in bed. Kindred keeps her pussy bald. Just the way I like it—hairless and odorless. Just clean chocolate pussy. That woman makes a brotha' go crazy with her *fiine* self. And plus, she has no qualms about me spending the night at my wife's house on the weekends because I need to bond with my kids. See, *Burn* is the one that has a problem with the kids being around Kindred. It's all about control with Burn. Kindred didn't put me in a compromising position of choice. Nah. She knows my kids mean the world to me. That's what I love about her too. She gets me. She stands by her man. And she accepts me as her man even though she makes more money than I do.

In our home, Kindred acknowledges me as the man of the house—the head of *our* household. I know it's a bunch of baloney, but 'ey. She knows how to make her man feel special. I am completely in love with that woman. No doubt. And if I so choose to tell her I wouldn't blame her one bit for being upset. Upset enough to leave me. I was in the wrong. Me. Totally in the wrong.

Kindred's a good woman, very understanding woman. We have a strong connection: mentally, spiritually, and sexually. There is no way in the world she would *ever* understand something like this. Nah. The way I see it, I'll have to take this one to my grave.

My eyes scan the bedroom floor: boxers, pants, socks, shirt, belt and shoes. Condom? No condom wrapper. I don't see a condom wrapper. My eyes widen with regret. NO! CONDOM! WRAPPER! Oh, hell no! I fucked her RAWWWWWWW!

Oh, Allah, what have I done?

My eyes scan the nightstand, dresser, and armoire looking for a bottle, a wine glass...something to put blame on—anything at this point. No alcohol in sight. Damn. That means I fucked her *sober*.

Slo-Bro' yells in my head. "You idiot! How could you!"

I ball up my fist and try to punch myself in the face. I can't believe I fucked her *raw*. Damn. What was I thinking? Obviously I wasn't thinking. I was too busy...*fucking* to think. I wasn't thinking with the right head. The one attached to my shoulders.

Ok. Get a grip. It's not as bad as it seems. You know Burn. That's true. She's not the type that gets around. She's a Christian woman.

"Take it easy. Breathe, bro'." I say to myself.

I mean what are the chances of Kindred *ever* finding out, huh? Burn is not that type of chick to air out her dirty laundry. Nah. That much I can say about her.

Slo-Bro' interjects. "Need I remind you that your wife is a woman who has been deprived? She is a woman who hadn't had dick in nearly ten years, bro'."

Good point. I think. *You're right, Slo-Bro'.*

Burn *doesn't* have a man. I can't remember the last time she'd told me that she'd gotten any either, so therefore, ah, ah, ah, this could cause some complications, if you know what I mean.

I mean, c'mon. She'd just gotten a taste of "Swing!" and I know she ain't felt like that in awhile. Damn!

This situation called for a meeting with the fellahs. So I gather the troops together.

Bob, Tim, Duke, Charlie and Ralph, we all sit huddled in a circle in my man cave. The garage.

I stand to my feet. Look all of them in their faces. They look at me. I pace back and forth, forth and back. Words. I need *words*, something to explain my predicament and why I called them here today.

Tim reaches his dark-skinned hand in his shirt pocket and pulls out his box of Newport 100s.

Duke leans back in his chair with one eyebrow raised.

Charlie sits quietly.

Ralph keeps giving me the eye like he knows something. Those cat eyes of his are making me feel very uncomfortable.

It's disturbing looking at Ralph.

I open my mouth. No words, no words come forth.

Ralph breaks the silence by scratching his throat. He sits upright in his seat dressed in wrinkled, faded heather-blue khakis and tangerine LaCoste polo shirt with his flip-flops on his ashy feet. "Why are we here, Kenyatta? Exactly, what did you do? I know you did something because we wouldn't be here if you didn't. What you do? What you want us to cover up for you? Spill it, dude."

Ralph is the skeptical one. Always prying and speculating. Sometimes he makes me sick. He is tall and fat. How you tall and fat, is beyond me.

I shrug my shoulders. No words. No words.

Charlie interjects as he pulls out a cigar from his dress shirt pocket. "Give him a break, fellahs. Can't you see this man is having a mid-life crisis? Can't you see the pain in his eyes? I'm here for you, dude. Take as much time as you need."

Charlie is always the optimistic one. The peacemaker. The one we all can count on to make us feel better in times of crisis. I love Charlie.

I nod my head.

"Nah. I ain't buying it. He did something. I can see it in his eyes. Those dark brown eyes don't lie," says Bob with conviction in his husky tone. He stands to his six feet dressed in a business suit and tie. It is the weekend but every day is business to Bob. He does not know how to dress casual. Bob reaches his hand in the garbage can filled with ice and Heinekens and pulls one out. He pops the cap and takes a long swig. Then he returns to his seat and leans back in his chair, sipping and waiting.

"Hand me one of those Heinekens, Ken, will yah," says Charlie.

I walk over to the garbage can and reach my hand in the cold water and pullout five cans of Heinekens. I hand them each one. Then I take a deep breath. Grab my balls from between my legs, and begin to say what I had them come to hear.

"If you were to ask me if I love my wife, Burn, I would answer, yes for various reasons of course. But if you were to ask me if I *am* in love with my wife, Burn? I would have to answer, no. Now, if you were to ask me if I *ever* was in love with my wife, I would have to answer, no. Now that may or may not put me in the category of: *asshole* and to some extent there maybe some truth to that. I'm sayin', why waste valuable time trying to shade the truth to save face? It's not worth getting a headache over. Burn and I had come to a realization that we might've made a mistake. Ok. I've come to the realization. I can't speak for her. However, the ultimate question is: *Why did I get married?* Y'all saw that movie by Tyler Perry. Brotha' should've gotten discovered way before now. He would've saved me some goddamn money and my freedom. Anyway, my response to that would be: my mother, Georgia Bee Bentley. Now, I am not taking the easy way out by putting blame on mom. I'm not that crass. But I will say that mom had a lot to do with influencing me in marrying Burn."

Swig. Swig. Swig.

I continue, "Yes, I'll agree. I had the final say. BUT...in all fairness Mom kept reiterating certain things in my head. Certain things coming from your *mom* can trigger a *young* man to react in a certain way. That's all I'm sayin'. Based on mom's influences I might've reacted impulsively. Ok. I did. But the truth is, Mom had some valid points that gotta brotha' to thinking in a different frame of mind. Her words really sunk in deep. Which made me think, bro', you gotta step up your game and be the man mom raised you to be. And plus, I didn't want another joker to be dictating to my child what she or he could and should not do as if he were their daddy. No. That was my job. I planted that seed; so therefore, it was my duty as a *man* to raise she or he in the presence of me, Kenyatta aka Daddy. As you figured out, yes, Burn was pregnant. And, yes, mom saw fit to speak her piece. We were young and having fun. And a result of that *fun* turned into a baby, which in turn (with Mom's advice) ended in a marriage proposal, which Burn did not hesitate to accept, might I add. Ok, fellahs, I'm getting a little frazzled here."

Swig. Swig. Swig.

I guzzle one can of beer down. Then reach in the garbage can for another. I pop the cap and take a long swig. "So, here we are two young people with child getting married. Now, fast-forward. It is twenty-something years later, two kids, me out of the house, and both of us raising our children. Isn't that the way it should be when two people grow apart? But what about us: Burn. Me. Well, fellahs, the truth of the matter is, I had a one-night stand with my wife."

Beer spews out of Charlie's mouth. "YOU DID WHAT?! WITH WHOM?! I KNOW YOU DIDN'T SAY YOUR WIFE! NO! NO! NO!" He turns to face the fellahs. "DID HE SAY HIS WIFE?"

Ralph, Bob, Duke and Tim nod their heads in confirmation.

"OH, HELL NO!" Charlie yelps. "Man, you done lost your goddamn mind. That beautiful, succulent, piece of ass you got at home and *you* gonna go and stick your dick in BURN! Have you no shame, my brother? I need a joint. Anybody got any crack?" He throws his arms up in the air. Shaking his head he says, "This is fuckin' unreal."

Tim's body cringes to the thought. He then asks with a crumpled forehead, "Dude, what the fuck?!"

I try to reason with them. "Look. Fellahs, this is the reason I called this meeting. I need your input. I need to plea this case to Kindred. Y'all already know how passionate she is about her career."

"Yeah," Charlie says, "She's the best damn attorney in all of Harlem, New York, if y'all forgotten."

I exhale.

Bob pipes in. "Look. You have to look at it from our point of view. Have you looked at *our* wives lately? I mean really looked at 'em. No offense but Charlie's wife, Sarah looks like a homely bag lady. I gotta ask. What the hell did you see in her, Charlie?"

Charlie shrugs his shoulders with this dumbfound look on his face.

Bob continues, "Ralph's wife, Jennie looks like she hasn't missed any meals. The woman is a beach whale. I don't even know how you're able to find her pussy with those big ass thighs of hers."

Ralph scrunches up his nose.

Bob continues, "Tim's wife, Shirley. Oh, dear God, don't get me started with her grizzly bear lookin' ass. She is a sight to be seen. She looks like a fuckin' linebacker. Have you ever really looked at her? The hair, face, body...train wreck. Disaster! One look at her, she'll spoil a good nutt. She makes my dick never wanna come out of hiding. There is no way in hell I'd fuck her. Even with a paper bag over her head. You couldn't pay me a dollar to fuck her."

"Damn, ease up, man that is my wife you're talking about." Tim says with a grimace on his face.

Bob continues, "And Duke with his wife, Melissa. We all know that the only reason he married that wide load was because she come from money. But even with money I still wouldn't want her. All that flab shaking and thighs rubbing together is enough to make me turn gay. I dunno how you do it, man." He shakes his head. "Now, as for me, my wife, Charlene, that toothpick looking crackhead makes me want to slap myself. What the fuck was I thinking to marry her tired ass? I should've known better than to marry a stripper. But I got caught up in her looks. Y'all know back then Charlene was the bomb! She had ass for days. Titties the size of watermelons, and her pussy, man, her pussy used make a brother go berserk. Damn, back then she had some good ass pussy. But then, I dunno what the fuck happened. Bitch got comfortable. Once we tied the knot she decided she didn't want to strip anymore. Not even in the privacy of our home. I was okay with that, but when the bitch stopped sucking my dick, oh, hell no! It was time to slap some sense back into her skinny ass. It was bad enough she couldn't cook but I didn't mind because she gave a brotha' that sweetlicious. Being home with nothing to do, she got lazy. And I got tired of looking at her lazy ass. I find myself doing the house chores, going to work, coming home to cook dinner, do the laundry, I mean, what the fuck I need her for? All I am tryna say, Ken, is you got the muthafuckin' life. Our wives look like busted bitches, but Kindred, man, she looks like a fuckin' movie star. Kindred have body, looks, career, and money, what I'd wish to have a woman like that in my life. Fuck, in my bed!" Bob walks over to the garbage can grabs himself two beers and leans against the garage.

Duke stands to his six feet four inches of solid man and just looks me dead in my eyes and says in a baritone voice. "Dude, you need the ladies' on this one. We are men. We don't know how they'll react to something as significant as this. You fucked up. Big time! But where there is a will, there is a way to fix it, hopefully. You are not dealing with the average woman. Kindred, she's articulate, smart, witty, and crafty. She's a lawyer and a woman who is completely out of your league—all of our leagues. And you, you snagged her. How? I don't know, but whatever you did you managed to have that attractive woman fall head over heels for you. If you want to keep her, man, you gotta reach out to women. Different women. Do it as an assessment. Talk to them. Feel them out. Listen. That's important. You must listen to what they say and watch their body language too. That says a lot. And you must get into their heads. That's the only way to save yourself from the embarrassment and ass-whooping that Kindred is going to put on you if she ever finds out. And you better *hope* that they don't squeal or your ship will sink."

I massage my chin. "Hmm. That's a good point." I say. "I never even thought to involve women. Now, what women are you referring to? Your wives?"

"Oh, heavens no," says Tim. "Not unless you want your business on the twelve o'clock news."

"So, you're saying reach out to women in general, right?" I ask for confirmation.

All the fellahs nod their heads.

I smile. "Fellahs, I think we have a plan."

"Look, man, I don't wanna rain on your parade but I think you should consider getting tested for HIV." Charlie says.

"Why?" I ask with a baffling look upon my face.

"Let me ask," Charlie says, "did you have your raincoat on while you were handling your business?"

I chew on my bottom lip.

"Exactly," Charlie sways his head from side to side, "Man, listen, not saying that Burn is out there likes that, but you don't know her every move. I mean, she could be seeing someone on the sneak tip. Just think about every woman you've ever fucked. You have history running through your body. It may not feel like it but it's there lying dormant. Then suddenly it wakes up, and you find yourself in a fucked up situation. Now since you fucked her raw think about it like this. Let's say one evening Kindred wants you to put it on her. You know how you get down. What you gonna do? Tell her no. I don't think so. Just think smart. You love Kindred. Burn is the mother of your children. But you can never really know a person. You feel me? You can never really know."

"He has a good point, man," says Tim, "I know this is gonna sound crazy but one time I thought my wife was cheating on me. See, the thing is, we may not see our wives as hot babes but best believe there is someone out there who will look beyond the exterior and really want to get to know her personality. Once they do that and realize that she is actually a very nice woman their status goes up. So, yeah, I thought she was cheating on a brotha' when she had joined the gym, Planet Fitness, and she'd come home all smiling and shit. I knew those smiles weren't because of me. At the time I wasn't thinking, I was too busy speculating because of what I wasn't doing for her. So, one day, I stopped at one of them Medical Mobile Unit (Paterson Division of Health) and got tested. It felt good to know that I was uninfected. That same day I went home and she'd come in with that smiley face again so I asked, 'why are you so happy lately, honey?' And to my surprise, she said, 'because I lost ten pounds. I feel like I'm accomplishing something. Look, I know that you've lost that passion for me. I see it in your eyes. At first, it hurt, but then it made me look at myself. How big I had gotten over the years. I felt like I needed to do something about it, not for our marriage, but for me. I figured if you liked what you saw you'd let me know, in your way of letting me know.' I can't tell you guys how stupid I felt. But I'm glad I was stupid because it pushed me to go and get tested. Something I probably wouldn't have done if everything seemed normal. But it was the best thing I've ever done, besides, marrying my wife."

"Damn, I never really looked at it like that. You think you know a person, you know. But in actuality, you really don't. I would never want to bring something home to Kindred. Never. Man, this shit is crazy." I tell them.

"Well," Ralph says, "At least you are open to suggestions. Some men think they know it all and then find themselves in a predicament they can't get out of. You have to take accountability when you screw up."

"Yeah, man. Do the right thing," Bob says, "You have a beautiful woman at home. I'd hate to see you fuck that up by being stupid. You and Burn haven't been together in years. Sometimes we as men assume we know our ladies' but often we are wrong. They are no different from us. They're looking for someone to bed too. Shit. They get horny just like we do and if the right motherfucker is talking with his pockets, shit. *they're* liable to bed him that same night. You can never be too sure of a motherfucker." He pauses, realizing what he said and tries to clean it up. "Not-not-not to call Burn a motherfucker, but-but you know what I'm tryna say, don't you?"

I nod my head up and down. "Yeah, man, I gotcha."

The Coldest
Muthafucker Ever
MR. FUCK-YOU-NOW-DISS-YOU-LATER

I LIE BACK on my king-sized bed. Arms cross behind my head, hands as my pillow, as I reminisce about a time I wish I could forget.

I come to.

Wipe the tears that scroll and curve down my maddened face.

"Shake it off," I tell myself. "Shake it off."

I jump up and back into my Mr. Fuck-You-Now suit.

Marvel myself in the dresser mirror, "Yeah, this feels much better," I tell myself.

Some women know a good thing when they see it. Instinctively they know if they want to bed me or cut me up with their mouthpiece, especially black chicks. Look, I'm my own billboard. I self promote. I'm articulate. But on the flip side I can deliver that gift of gab too. It all depends on my surroundings. I'm a well-rounded guy. Every woman cannot, I repeat cannot win me over, especially those overconfident women who think she can wow me with their pussy. Nah, nah, nah...wrong muthafucker!

Not to sound conceited but if I weren't me I'd want to get to know me. Sounds shallow, right? Yeah. That's what this black chick named Dream told me. Other women think of it as sexy. Yeah. Those high maintenance chicks, they *love* me. That's an understatement. Those ladies loooovvvvveeeee themselves some...me! With the exception of this fly chick I had met a few months ago. Yeah. I'm talkin' about Dream.

Dream was a lil' different. She had a different flow. She had something—something more than the norm.

Till this day I don't know exactly where I stand with her. I mean, I do. But I don't. That chick knew how to get to me. She reminded me of a nasty hair bump. Not that she was nasty but you know how it goes after you get one of those damn things! If you keep fuckin' with it, eventually it bleeds and leaves a dark spot.

And that was her—a fuckin' dark piece of *mmmmmmmmmm* pussy that left an imprint on my inches!

Don't get the wrong impression! Nah. She didn't give me any STD or STI or anything like that. She was a slim honie. Yeah. And I was sticking the big, dark dick in her a few months ago. And yeah, her real name was Dream... Dream Passion.

Now, Dream, huh, that chick was bold and sexy as hell! She was the type of chick that stole the fuckin' show. When she walked into a room—all heads turned in her direction. She owned that muthfuckin' room. Took control like it was her nigga. The bitches hated her! But I loved that shit because she didn't give a FUCK!

Slender. Sexy. Sassy. Liberated. Independent...that was Dream. All the ingredients of a baaddd muthafucker.

Don't get me wrong, she had lady-like tendencies. I mean she wasn't confused about her sexuality or anything like that. It's just she preferred to chill with the fellahs. She saw herself as one of the 'boys', which in the men's eyes was some bullshit because Dream was too fine to be considered as such. Even *I* knew that.

She had striking features that put you in mind of a custom-made piece of black art. Gorgeous! And yes, she was a little rough around the edges and definitely straightforward, but she was real, raw cut.

It was a turn on and off depending on how you looked at it. I was physically attracted to her because she knew how to maneuver herself. She controlled the room like I said. She dressed stylish, different from the ladies I was seeing out and about, even the bougie bitches. She knew how to put shit together. And she wasn't one to go to those expensive department stores to do either. But you would never know unless she told you. She was a thrift store junkie!

She was never seen hanging on any man's arms. She always did her thing solo. That was mad attractive to me. And the men, man, shit they loved her swagger! I gotta admit she had mad, mad swagger. You know, um, one of those confident chicks that could get something dead...jumping. She had *it*, that shit men weren't used to seeing or having in their possession. Dream fit in wherever she wanted to. And she was extremely good at it. Men? Women? It didn't matter. And the haters, oh, she gave them a performance of a lifetime. Just being herself was enough to piss women huddled in a corner or holding up the wall off. She knew how to role play with the best of them. And have a good muthafuckin' time doing it! Get in. Get out. That's how she got down. That was until me ...Mr. Fuck."

My reflection shakes *her* head. "Really?"

"Word. I was that *safe* joker. Or so *she* thought. You know, the kind of joker that didn't pressure her, didn't crowd her, didn't feed her ego, didn't overstep my boundaries, didn't extend too much of myself, didn't try to buy her love or like. I pretty much stayed in my lane, and drove my car, while she did her thing on foot. She could stop traffic with her walk; it was sexy like that. Shit. Huh, that chick didn't have to live a life of struggles. Dream chose to. And that shit was what connected us because she wasn't out to get mine; she was out to seek and get her own.

In other words, she had her freedom and I had mine because Dream didn't blend in my shit either.

Out in public she did her thing regardless if I was around or not. Her world did not revolve around me. I was impressed! I mean she was into her, but she was down-to-earth with hers. People gravitated to her because of her realness. Not to mention how beautiful she was.

Okay. Keeping it real, Dream was someone I would fuck, but bringing her home to meet my parents was something I could not see myself doing. I knew I couldn't love her, because honestly, she didn't possess the qualities that I felt were adequate for me, my lifestyle, or the entourage that I connected with. She was something to do, and do again if the opportunity presented itself. No strings, no commitment, just straight...*fucking*. But then-then something happened. Yeah. I think I got too ahead of myself. I lost focus. Got too into me to the point where I disregarded how I made her feel. Of course Dream brought that shit to front street like no other chick I know would do. She let a joker feel his fuck up. Not only did I feel it, I saw it. And no, it was not a pretty sight. If I had to backtrack that evening it went down something like this.

Before I begin to explain let me just say, I found myself bending because that shit hit me in the balls and brought me down to my knees in understanding. This was *one* of the reasons why I *don't* subscribe to real, raw talk.

I nod my head in acknowledgement.

I continue, "See, man, it was a rainy Thursday, as I recollect. It was pouring, thundering and lightening. The deejay at Glass Ceiling was having speaker issues. The sound was distorted and he was having a fit.

Rulle was a perfectionist. Everything had to be right when it came to his work. He was very particular about his sound, especially knowing that it paved a way to his success. He was pissed. I mean he had every right to be. This shit had happened two hours before the party was to start.

We were trying to rectify the problem. Of course this was a major issue because with no music that would ruin the evening and we didn't want that. Especially with the night crowd that usually flowed in.

Anyway, in walked Dream beading from head to toe in rain water. That shit looked sexy as hell. I mean just picture beads of water streaming down supple brown sugary skin.

I just happened to be at Glass Ceiling because I was promoting the party. Normally I'd checkout the scenery before everyone else arrived. I had to make sure everything was in its place. It was all about order for me. I wanted to make sure everyone would enjoy themselves, you know. The theme had to set the mood. I made sure the lighting was just right. The bathrooms had all the necessary supplies. The wine, light and dark liquor and beer were all well stocked. I did everything to make a smooth and enjoyable night.

So when it came to the speakers not working properly that might've put a snag in our whole night. Most of the time during the party I did my usual networking, handed out my business cards to let potential customers know that I did practically any event known to man.

Rulle was very popular. Almost every event he'd deejay, at the customer's request, of course. Indeed I felt honored to be in his company because when Rulle was around that meant money was going to be made. He was one of the reasons why I got into promoting parties. Brother didn't have to chase the paper, the paper chased him. And I was right on his heels, on my grind, getting digits as well as my due share.

Rulle cut his eye over my right shoulder, which alerted me to turn around. Man, Dream was looking good and wet. She sported an earth-tone tie-dyed halter dress that brought out her flawless complexion, a pair of custom-made wooden spear earrings and a beaded African necklace that accentuated her ensemble. And of course her signature cut that brought out her strong features. She was definitely model material. I kid you not! I wanted to stick my tongue down her throat right then and there. But I couldn't. I wouldn't simply because I had an image to uphold.

That night, Cinnamon was the barmaid. She was a veteran. And up in age. I'm talkin'...70-something. The manager Pooh just couldn't find the words to tell her to simply hang it up. You know, just retire from the lounge scene and stay her rusty ass home and learn how to knit shit.

Cinnamon brought in the older crowd. Mostly widows that formed their own support group called the Wrinkled Bitches Club. They'd drink and talk and then take their old selves home.

Cinnamon was a sweet old lady, but honestly speaking, it was time for her to call it quits. Stay home and care for her grandbabies, play Bingo, do something other than barmaid. Anyway, Dream and I were chitchatting. I mean one minute she was telling me about all of her life's failures. Next thing I knew I found myself being pulled in by her energy. Scared the shit outta me." I shake my head. "It was an interesting evening. I mean I expressed my views on how I saw Dream."

"Why were you scared? Exactly what did you say, F? Probably something slick, knowing you." The reflection of me says, and then rolls *her* eyes.

"Well," I hesitate a bit, "All I remember was us sitting at the bar. Dream was sipping on absolut, cranberry, and pineapple. I asked Cinnamon to make me a Ketel One with grapefruit juice. Cinnamon came back to tell me that she ran out of grapefruit juice, so I said orange juice as an alternative. Dream and I were engaged in general conversation. How we got on the subject of us is unbeknownst to me. I know that Rulle had already left. Dream mentioned something about us being friends. Well, I was feeling myself up and I told her that we weren't friends. Just the look on her face caught me by surprise. I mean her eyes immediately got watery. I think it was the tone in which I said it. I mean I spoke with truth, conviction, harshness. There was no way to deny what I meant. It was obvious of how I truly felt. I guess it stunned Dream. She said, 'You don't consider me, *me* a friend?' I said, 'NO! I don't.' She looked me dead in my face and spoke in a crackling tone. 'That hurts.' And I replied, 'Really?' I expressed it as if I had no feelings in me. As if I had no cares. That's when the tears welled up even more in her almond-shaped eyes. She excused herself and ran into the ladies room. I sat there at the bar as if I were this big shot with huge balls. I was popping my collar, you know. Showboating. One cocky muthafucker, for real.

"When Dream returned to the bar and sat down I noticed her eyes were swollen and puffy and red. Still, I felt nothing. If anything I dug into her a lil' deeper to get my point across. I said, 'Friends are people who invite me to meet their families. Friends are people who invite me to their sons or daughters events. Meet their parents. Invite me over for barbecues and housewarming parties. Those are friends to me.' Dream just gazed at me as if she didn't know me, didn't understand me. Here I had *fucked* this woman numerous times, and I never considered her to be my *friend*. Dream said, 'Then what do you consider me, if not your *friend*' We share intimate moments, yes, but after the fact I still look at you as my friend. Why go as far as fucking me if you can't look pass the fucking and see me as a woman, as a friend. I care for you even when you don't care for me. No, I might not get all mushy wit' it 'n shit but I know you feel it. Wow! I guess I have misconstrued fiction with reality. My poet ass! Always living in a fantasy world of my imagination. I guess that's the writer in me, huh?' she paused. 'You know, I'm sitting here looking at you, Fuck, and, and suddenly it dawned on me that I've read this book before, but this is a revised edition because the book I read didn't read this way. The protagonist had what I've yearned to have. True friendship. Men, you *muthafuckers* kill me!' Her gaze was piercing as she looked deep inside of me. I mean through me. She said, 'Your way of thinking of 'friendship' is foreign to me because I look at friendship as you and that individual. Should that individual *not* have family shouldn't change how I perceive him as a friend. Us being friends as I saw it was two people getting to know one another. Spending time together. Talking. Fucking. I don't care if I *never* meet your family or friends because it is not about them. It wasn't like we jumped into this! It took what???? Three to four or five months before we even hit the sheets! I wasn't an easy lay. And as I recall, when I met you *they* (family/friends) weren't there. When I was fucking you *they* weren't there. It was about *you* and *I*.' Dream paused again, then swallowed hard and tried her best to hold back the tears that had welled up in her eyes. Again, she had an insightful point. But it *didn't* bring me back down to earth. I could see the hurt that I had caused her, but I didn't react on it. Nah. I was too busy trying to play this role, you know. I tell you no lie, I felt like shit that evening but *not* bad enough to call Dream and apologize. I pushed her out of mind, out of sight, out of my life, far, far, far away. And she never stepped foot back in Glass Ceiling *ever* again."

"Wow. You never tried to find her and reconcile the situation?" My reflection of woman asks curiously.

I sigh. "Nah. It was too late even if I wanted to."

"Why?"

"Me and my big mouth," I say, then massage my face with my hands. I get quiet all of a sudden, too. Seem distant.

"What's wrong? Tell me, Fuck? Talk."

I scratch my throat. "Well, come to find out Dream was sick. Real sick. She had Lupus. But she never divulged it to me. The fucked up part was that I think she would've had I not acted like the coldest muthafucker born. She looked at me as a friend. And I totally dissed her. Yeah. I dissed her by looking down on her. Sad to say, she died before I ever got a chance to say, 'Sorry.' Dream changed me. And I never quite looked or treated women the same again.

"Now, don't get it twisted it took time. I say about...Fawn Hearthstone time. Damn, as I recollect that woman was a breath of fresh air.

"Fawn looked me dead in my face and said, 'First of all, *every* woman is not for all that gift of gab bullshit. Babe, babe, babe, just stop! Stop! Please. Look. I see past all of that. Of what you are tryna say. Been there. Done. Done it again. I ain't tryna go there. So I'd suggest you come with a different approach. Now, I ain't kicking you outta my home, but you best get outta my face with that nonsense. Look at me. Really look at me. I am a woman. Not some little girl looking for a little boy. I am a grown ass woman. I got grown titties. Grown ass. Grown hips and thighs. Grown pussy, too. So when you come to your senses you hit me up, but for now I ain't got nothing left to say, because I'd done said it all.'" Fawn shook her head and exited the guest room.

"I sat quietly in her guest room. My eyes scrolled around her eclectic apartment and I realized something that I hadn't before. Fawn was her own person, woman. She had her own shit. She never asked me for a dime—wouldn't take money from me even if I had offered. One time I had to literally slip some money in her pants pocket and asked that she not look until she was out of my presence. She never questioned me. She was straight-up. There was no way for me to manipulate her or come between whom she had groomed herself to be. She knew who she was. She knew what she wanted. And she was not afraid to fail whether it was: personally or professionally. She had been hurt I'm assuming numerous times. And, and, she wasn't about to go there again with me. It was either I shaped up or shipped out of her life. She was hard. Harder than any woman I had ever known. So hard that sometimes I had to check to make sure I still had my dick attached to my body. It was obvious that she had been through her share of heartache. And she wasn't about to go through anymore. She'd rather be single, than hurt again.

"Men. They trashed her. Talked down about her. Some claimed that they had had her. You know, *hit* it. Others wished they had. Everyone had a past and Fawn made it clear that she was no saint, but she wasn't a gold-digger or a skank either. She was woman who at times had needs that needed to be met with someone she selected. She made many, many mistakes when it came to men, but she was always upfront and real with it. And I truly, truly respected her for that.

"Fawn saw right through me. She knew the game way before I became a player. The language was pretty much the same. Genre was a little different. But she knew a boy's mind. She'd been with one or two to the point that she had grown tired. And she voiced it many times.

"I didn't know. I simply didn't know that I was acting as a boy. I thought I had grown into my manhood. But it took more than height and length and width between my legs to define me as a man. Intellectually, I was not there. Morally, I was not there. Spiritually, I was not there.

"I didn't know how to like or love a woman. I just knew how to *fuck* a woman. And actually I didn't even call them women. I called them bitches. I didn't know how to be gentle. I didn't know what intimacy was. I didn't know how to connect with a real woman. I was never taught. And truthfully, all the women that I had encountered weren't taught either. It was like the blind leading the blind. That's kinda how we got down.

"I'll even go as far as saying I didn't know how to communicate with a woman. Speak a language of love and romance. Show with my actions and words how I truly felt. I assumed the more I came through, the more I slept in her bed, the more I ate her cooking, the more I fucked her, she should have known that I was digging her based off of all of that. If I passed off a couple of hundreds that pretty said something. But in all honesty, it ain't say shit. And if it did I *never* knew.

"I got some serious On-the-Job training from Fawn. Yeah. That woman really showed me some things, insightful and empowering things that truly blew my mind.

"Damn, am *I* that bad?" I asked.

"Fawn didn't hesitate to answer. 'Yes.' She said, 'You are *that* bad. And I don't know if I want to continue to deal with it. I mean, what do I need you for? Oh, yeah, that's right. You don't consider this a relationship. You're just my pastime *lover*. What are you contributing to this, this, whatever *this* is?'"

Silence.

"Fawn continued, "Well, see, that's where we differ. Understand where I'm coming from. I'm an investment. I'm time. I'm energy. You have to punch the clock because this, me, I'm your job. Now, if you don't show up for work, that's on you. You take the risk of getting either laid-off or terminated. I know you have great potential to even become 'Employee of the Month' but I don't think you realize it. You abuse company policy. You've taken advantage of: sick and personal days. Not to mention that week's vacation. And those bereavement days when you claimed your grandmother died. You never brought me a copy of the obituary. You call out every other day claiming you're sick. Never come in with a doctor's note. You really can't hold a job but for so long. Yet you call yourself a *man*. I think you've been misinformed. I really do. Because this 'thing' that we have I pretty much control it, not that I want to, but because I have to. B-because if I have to rely on you, I'll be homeless and heartless. And you-you'll let me, because you don't know any better. All you think about is yourself. You've never had a strong woman. You mostly chose women who you could *control*."

"After Fawn spoke her mind I sat quietly the rest of the night. There was nothing left to say because she had pretty much said it all. I wasn't speechless. I was clueless. And she, she busted me wiiiiddddeeee open.

"Fawn continued, 'Any man that comes to you and tells you that they had me, ask 'em, ask 'em, 'what she did for you?' and I guarantee you they will be baffled by that question. And I'll tell you why they will be baffled. I might've slipped and fucked one, but even that one can't say that he truly had me. That woman I used to be was going through some serious life shit. I wasn't myself. I had to grow into me again. So I know for a fact that he didn't have me. He had that vulnerable woman. Not me. But you, you have had the pleasure of indulging in the authentic me. That man was never in my space—my personal space.' She paused, briefly. 'Remember when we had that heated argument and you left and I called your cell phone and left you a voice mail message?'"

I nodded my head up and down. "Boy, do I remember that." I said to myself.

Voice mail message:

He shut his eyes
Like shutters or blinds
Didn't or possibly couldn't see her reality
He closed her out
Shooed her away like flies get shun
Scrunched up his nose by her fragrance
Utterly repulsed
He turned his back
Something an old wino taught him to do
Took a long swig of her
Like she was whiskey
Then spit her out
Like she was piss
It was there all along
Staring at him like an owl in the night
Yet, he refused to let light in
It was too bright, too blinding
A depiction of her
Yet, he refused
Chose to shut his eyes
Squinted a little harder
Shooed her away like flies get shun
What is it?
Who gives a shit!
He didn't
Even though once a upon a time
He claimed
Usedta speak her name with a southern twang
Claimed so many things
None ever held true
Words toppled upon words
No significant meaning
Dark, the complexion of him
Tall, the height of him
Large in his mind
Small to others larger than him
Not prouder, puffier, slightly irregular

335

Similar to her
To him, not
Nowhere close
Not even a smidgen close
She was fragile
Small behind him
Yet, her voice as child-like as it was sung so loudly, so proudly
Deafening to his ears
Refused to listen
To her reasons, her pleas
Even if she had fallen to her knees
He'd merely about face
Couldn't stand to look in her face
Wonder why?
He shoved his reasons down in the pit of his soul
Let it wither
Let it die
Let it just grow old
Like him for the love of her.

"And that it did. Even a blind man who had never laid eyes on Fawn would know that she was a genuine woman. Loving. Sexy. Beautiful inside out. Generous. Unselfish. Intelligent. Different. She was a loner-type by choice. She was a homebody. Just a good person. I-I needed to put a lot of thought into what she had said. I had other women. Hell, I had a girlfriend. We didn't live together but I had one. But, but there was something about Fawn that set her apart from the rest. Something that made me feels comfortable. At ease. Special. Her warmth. Her energy. She knew how to treat a man like a million-dollar muthafucker. I didn't know how to be a man because I was still acting as a boy. Wanting my cake and eat it too. Not every woman was going to fall for that shit. But Fawn, she kept it real with me and told me she had another nigga on the side. And she had no intention of writing him off. Even with the new man in her life, huh, she never treated me any differently. Nah.

"Why would she not want someone to treat her like the queen that she was? I mean, this joker was giving her the world, mostly his time. He made love to her mind. I was living here in her neck of the woods and she barely heard from me. I wouldn't call her every day. I seldom called, seldom texted her. I never asked her out on a date. I waited for her to invite me over. I never cooked for her or ran her bathwater. I just kept her company. And I gave her some dick from time to time. We had limited conversations. Even with the distance, the excuses, the disregard, she never squabbled about it. She just accepted it. Took the little I would offer. Took the little time I would give. She took the dick as I had given it and went on with her life. Nothing stopped on her part. Life continued.

"So you see, I get when she said: *'What do I need you for?'* What did she need me for? I mean she pretty much had her shit together. She was focused and on her grind to really find her happiness. I mean she cut a lot of men loose just to have a sense of peace.

"It was then that *I* realized that maybe it wasn't *her* who needed me. Maybe it was *me* who needed her as a *friend*, but wasn't man enough to say it."

My reflection of a woman nods her head. "Hmm. I see."

19

Lounge
Out
Poets Café
Montclair, New Jersey

THE TIPS OF MY fingers feel numb. Heart is in my throat. I feel weak in the knees. Mouth is watery as if I am about to vomit. Tongue tastes pasty. Armpits are dewy. Hands are clammy. Toes are tingly in my boots. Do I have butterflies? I 'spose. It feels more like a first boy crush. My eyes are getting misty. Why did I come here? Just seeing this place takes me back to November 4, '08, and Anonymous.

My voice cracks as I begin to speak. I pause to take a sip of spring water. I glance over at Tyde and I swear that I see Johnnie standing right beside him. I am startled at first, but then warmth comes over me with another push to get me going. My eyes are closed but then I open them, take a deep breath, exhale, and stare at everyone in the audience. I can feel little beads of perspiration rolling down my armpits. I see blind spots in front of my eyes from the vibrant lighting. I literally feel like I am about to faint. Holding my ground, I begin to speak again, but this time with confidence. Looking over the audience for the second time I begin to recite my history.

"Look at me and tell me what U see?
Yes, I am African-American,
Stand about five-feet-eleven inches tall,
My hair is natural,
My lips are full,
Nose is wide,
Eyes are brown,
But other than the obvious of me being a woman,
Look at me and tell me what U see?

338

"I am not the woman I used to be
I was fierce,
Men fiend for me,
Like I was displayed on a silver platter,
And every desire within my body was fulfilled,
No questions asked,
No time to have regrets,
I was in my prime,
Climbing the ladder to my success,
But with a blink of an eye,
My world crumbled,
I became a hermit in my own nest.

"Why?
A stranger premeditated my death,
Wanting to pave a path of his remembrance,
Inflicting me with taint-taste of torment,
So, I ask that you look at me?
Use your eyes to magnify.
"Why?
'Cause even with me sharing the truth with you,
You still can't see what resides within me.
I am absolutely,
Unequivocally,
HIV-positive.
Wake Up!"

It's quiet. My voice cracks and I swallow and speak with my head held high. That's when I noticed Travar, Aja, Danell Blu, Zaelyn, Mr. Clyde, Ms. Sweet, Mr. Clausen, and Mrs. Jenkins-Rollin and Mr. Xavier Combs III standing in the crowd. I keep my head high and speak from the heart.

"The piece that I just recited is about how I became HIV-positive. I was raped and 'til this very day my rapist may still be on the loose. I almost allowed him to destroy my life, but fortunately I had a best friend who pulled me out of my hell. He later died from AIDS, but during the time that he was here, he influenced me enough to believe that I could accomplish almost anything. He encouraged me to be honest about being raped. I never told him that I was HIV-positive, never was bold enough. He was my role model and now I hope to be for others living the same lifestyle. It's not easy and I *still have a long ways to go, but I am ahead of the game because I have both feet inside instead of one in and one out the door. Tyde, you have also inspired me tonight. You've opened up my eyes to see true artistry. You my brotha' are an amazing character of strength. And I feel blessed to be in your presence. Everyone in this room has given me hope to nurture my baby, Anonymous. Thank You."*

The audience applauds loudly, whistles, and nods their heads in relevance.

I have overcome my deepest fear and all the bricks that were overlapping me have fallen to the floor. I have love from my extended family and my life has changed forever. It is difficult to sum it up as to how my life has changed in words, but I am no longer the reflection of what I used to be. I am reborn into a shell living with HIV, but I am living my life to the fullest. Filling my circle with positive folks with caring hearts that has helped mold me into the woman I am today. I have been fed plenty from total strangers. Gratitude and appreciation is just a small fraction of what I feel. To sum it up, I am truly blessed!

I come to.

Indeed. I did feel truly blessed.

I remember how excited I felt each time I'd get on Anonymous stage and perform spoken word or introduce upcoming artists. Goodness, I used to feel so energized—so full of life.

I look at the silhouette of my reflection in the tinted glass double doors and I wonder, what happened to me? And as I do, I feel this strong energy from behind these doors pulling me in. Just as I feel my energy pulling me back. What the heck am I afraid of?

"Go, Avery, go inside," Avona encourages by motioning her hands for me to take a step forward.

My body turns to go back, but the energy sort of spins me around. My face is toward the door, yet I still won't open it to walk inside. My left foot moves forward, then right. My right hand grabs the door handle; my left tries to stop me from pulling it open. But the energy is most powerful. I cannot stop this force that is deliberately battling with my spirit. At this point all I can do is submit.

If I turn away and run it will catch me. If I comply it will embrace me. I can't lose. The worse that can happen is that I have to face reliving the experience of loving something so much, and then, let it go. Honestly, I don't think I'm strong enough. I really don't.

I bow my head feeling ashamed, but the force lifts up my chin and continues to pull me in. Why am I feeling so down on myself? Everybody has a choice to make in life—some good some bad. I can't say if my choice was for the best or worst. But what I can say is that I did it for love. And love retaliated by swiftly kicking me to the curb. Why? I can only assume for compromising my love for it. Why did I choose? Why did I feel I had to choose? Why couldn't I have had both and still love? I wanted to give Hellman all of me: mind, body, and soul. Maybe I thought Anonymous would take up too much of my time. Intervene in my marriage. I didn't want Hellman getting jealous of a *thing*. I mean I was in a committed relationship with Anonymous, so it wasn't just a thing to me, but would I have been as committed to Hellman in the same way? Those are the questions I should've been asking myself back then. But I guess love got in the way. Or what I *thought* was love.

I should've stayed home and buried my eyes back in Mary Monroe, *Red Light Wives* novel I was so engrossed in before leaving out of the house, or, stuffed my face with that quart of Friendly's Cookie 'n Cream ice cream I got on sale from Pathmark that was calling me, but I didn't feel like being bloated tonight, or alone. And plus, it will only agitate my lactose intolerance. I can do without the scratchy throat.

Lately, I'm always alone. I thought to call Xavier to ask if he'd like to come, but then I thought against it. He hasn't been feeling well lately. And every time I ask to come by he always has some lame excuse as to why I shouldn't. Or he'd say, "Go and do something fun. Don't worry about me." That seems to be his favorite line these days. That really pisses me off. But I don't want to start an unnecessary argument so I keep quiet. He's probably home. More than likely he is snuggled in his bathrobe watching a western or golf or CSI.

Finally, I enter the doors of Poets Café. As soon as I walk into the dim lit room the energy within these walls instantaneously inspires me. I stand mid-center of the spacious floor and let my eyes wander about. I swear it's like a replica of Anonymous. Again, my eyes get misty. Surrounded by all these strangers I refrain from breaking down.

This is a good-looking crowd, I think to myself. Some people are dressed casual, but chic. Some are dressed in business suits, both women and men. They look like they came straight from the office. My eyes scroll down to my attire. *Not too shabby*, I think. I didn't go all out to be dressed up. I threw on a pair of twenty-dollar jeans, H&M chocolate brown turtleneck and a pair of rust ALDO boots (that I had since two years ago). I didn't come here to impress anyone. Need I remind myself? I gotta man. He just happens to be home.

This place is colorful with bright orange, green, fiery red and purple.

341

There is a winding stairwell leading up to the second floor. As you go up the stairs there are pictures of African-American writers such as: Omar Tyree, Eric Jerome Dickey, Michael Baisden, James Baldwin, Langston Hughes, K'wan Foye, Mary Monroe, Bernice L. McFadden, Sistah Souljah, Terry McMillan, Carl Weber and the late E. Lynn Harris and Bebe Moore Campbell hanging proudly on the walls.

As I look down at my feet I see that the hardwood floors are cherry wood. Nice. It adds richness to the decorum. *I wonder who owns this place.* I maneuver my curvaceous body through the handsome crowd. I can see a walkway leading toward a backroom where there are two sliding glass doors. There are chairs and tables decorated with burning candles in candleholders, fancy tablecloths, and shiny silverware. The glass ceiling is perfect for when spring and summer comes—just you and your man having a romantic dinner while gazing up at the moon and stars.

My thoughts are distracted when I hear the emcee of the evening, Hall's sexy voice. "We have a special guest in the house! I'd recognize *her* anywhere!"

I turn my head to look around to see who the "special guest" is.

Why is the spotlight on me? Where is the "special guest?" I don't see anyone walking toward the stage. Why is everyone staring at me?

"Let's give it up for our next poet...the lovely... Ms. Avery Love!"

Oh snap!

I-I-I didn't come here to perform.

I don't believe he is putting me on the spot!

I'm not prepared!

I didn't rehearse!

I don't have anything in mind to share!

Why is he doing this to me?

Blah, blah, blah...

"Avery, what are you going to do?" Avona asks with her eyes popping out of her head.

"I dunno," I reply.

"Well, you better think quickly. Everyone is staring at you, girl." Karma pipes in.

"I know. I know. Don't remind me."

I grimace. Through clench teeth I whisper, *Asshole!*

Hall has a way of getting the crowd revved up. He is one handsome man. Look at all of that scrumptious dressed in a pair of denim Levi's and V-neck black T-shirt with camel-colored Timberland boots on. Look at all that butterscotch skin, gray eyes, and muscular body. Too bad he's spoken for. Uh-huh. Sun is a very lucky woman. If he wasn't spoken for, and I wasn't in my current situation, oh, sistah could really get some mileage out of him.

I take a step, step, step, then plant my feet onstage. I let my inner pain become my outer deliverance. I feel a little shaky, but confident. *Voice; don't fail me now*, I think to myself, while gazing out at a full house of multicultural folks.

I feel their eyes burning in my flesh. It's been a while since I've been onstage reciting poetry. But I always feel alive when I do.

I pucker my glossy lips, close my eyes, and say a little prayer, then release what I've envisioned; the words just flow like minutes in a day.

Oh, no!

Suddenly, I feel Karma's up to no good.

"*What are you up to?*" I scowl. Then remind myself that I am in front of a crowded audience.

"*You have no choice but to play along, Avery. I got this!*" *Karma says with a big ass devious grin on her face.*

"*You wait till I get home.*"

"*Then whatchu gonna do?*" *Karma places her hands on her hips.*

"*You'll see!*" *I say with fury in my eyes.*

Karma steals the moment. And I have no alternative but to comply. God only knows what she has up her sleeve. Lord, help me? Suddenly, my mouth opens and Karma's words have a life of their own. *Oh, no!*

"This poem is entitled: I AM MY OWN BITCH."

I blink, three times. I know my face is every bit of beet-red.

"*I am not looking to fall in love like some of these whiny, needy bitches who can't see themselves without a man. I'm the kind of woman who is a self-gratifying chick; I know how to work my shit. See, all I want is what you desperate and depraved bitches don't. I want an UGLY man. You bitches don't have a clue, you don't understand, and definitely don't know what y'all missin'.*

"*'Cause when that zero gets in the kitchen he burns those pots. He caters to my every want, every need. He wipes the shit from my crack of my ass with a smile on his face, tilts my wine glass that I sip from, and he towel dries his queen and lubricates me down to a shimmering sheen. He makes my bed, washes my sheets and makes me feel like Cinderella 7 days out of the fuckin' week. He knows how good he's got it, and he ain't try'na fuck it up messin' wit' you sometimey bitches who ain't got no mo' than he got. So, you see, I want me a broke-ass-low-down-dirty-dog-of-a-man. A worthless*

343

son-of-a-bitch! I want a man who can scratch my coochie when it itches and fulfill all of my fairytale wishes—a man who knows how to do me right.

"See, I want a man with no ambition, no driver's license, or future goals. A man who knows if he ever got a chance to sink his dick in this hole, he had betta' takes full control and fucks this dime-piece into a drug induced sleep.

"I want a man who I have to tell to go wash his stank dirty ass. Nah, nah, don't take a shower, soaks that funk in a hot bubble bath. I want a man I have to show how to scrub his balls. Clip his toenails. Shave. And tell him when to go get a fuckin' haircut that I pay for. I want a man who can't hold his own. I want a man looking for a strong Ho to hold it down fo'a Negro. I want a man who is not a freak in bed, one that does mind eating pussy, ass, and suckin' on my tits. I want a man who can't work his dick and loses his breath when he tries to stroke my shit for long hours at a time. I want a man who can't see the head of his pecker 'cause his beer belly is in the fuckin' way. That's right! A fat muthafucker. I want a man who is the epitome of idiot. I want a man who has felonies—a grammar school dropout type of joker. I want a man with no college degree, nor a high school diploma, let alone a GED. I want a man who can't spell his own name. What is it? Hank. How do you spell it? Hnk. See, what I mean. I want a man who is on his last fuckin' leg and doesn't have a pot to piss in or a bucket to shit in. Yeah, I want all those things. Why? So that I can turn that muthafucker out and have every bitch envious of me. Y'all might think I'm kiddin', but I ain't.

"Yeah, I gotta story to tell. One that might make me seems like I got low self-esteem, but I assure you, I don't. I'm an over-confident bitch who can turn a mutt into a bluenose pit. Every dick I trick is a fuck investment. My drive to transform garbage to greatness is what keeps me ho' strollin' these streets. In spite of what others think, I make a difference in this fucked up world. I contribute back to society. I do my part. And I do it well. And in doing so, my pussy gains the respect it deserves. My ratings go up higher. And my body catches fire every time a john places that cha-ching in my hands.

"Trust me when I say, no other trick wants my position. They'd rather tend to their dogs at home, because they know their grade of shit.

"See, most hos want either: material things, marriage, money, multiple orgasms, moments, memories, but a trick goes for what she can, when she can. All I want is your man's money to groom my man at home. I don't need a man to stick his 'meager' dick inside of me, because I have a dick of my own. And when I need to pull that motherfucker out, best believe I do. I AM MY OWN BITCH—a bitch that has the capability of stimulating her own clit. I don't need a man to give me no lip. I call the shots...'Cause I'm the shit...I AM MY OWN BITCH—black owned entrepreneur of the

Afro centric pussy."

I nearly choked on Karma's words. I lower my eyes and bow my head. God, I am so humiliated. Palms meet and clap, loudly. I slowly raise my head. That's when I spot a familiar face staring back at me from out in the crowd. I can't believe that it's...tall, dark, muscular, and ever so deliciously bald...Blu McDowell.

I walk offstage. Dash out the door, and head back home to bury my head under my goose down pillows kicking and screaming...*Karma, you bitchhhhhhhhhhh!*

20

LOUNGE OUT POETS CAFÉ is home away from home. A place I can come to and let go. Just-just shed all of this worriation off of me. God, I feel so lucky.

My concentration is broken when I see Hall wave his massive hand at me. It's time for me to get onstage for my performance.

I stand before the mike; my eyes penetrate this one gorgeous guy in the audience. "Isn't he dreamy," I say to myself with a sly smirk on my face. His facial features are strong. His eyes, dark like tar. I wonder if he can see. See all of my pain and suffering. I ache every day. Every night I break deeper and deeper inside of myself. I wonder if he can feel the rage. Hear it scream out in anger. See the beauty inside of me too. Why is he looking at me? I guess 'cause I am looking at him. I see something mysterious in his eyes. Lies. Truth, I can't say. I want to take him in my arms and rock him with my world. Shake him up a bit to see my reality...HIV. What does he see in mine...my world, my eyes, I mean? FEED me, LOVE me, CLAIM me, MOLD me into a woman with less scars, less heartache, less pain, LUST me, HOLD me, KISS me, HUG me, TRUST me. These are the things my eyes say to him. Profoundly, shedding light on who I am—what I crave. Can he hear me beyond these walls—above the volume of music and voices? Can he feel my heart beating rapidly? My spirit is speaking to him, and only to him. "Listen," I mouth to him, "Listen, please. Listen to what I am about to say simply because, I may not live long enough to say it again.

I wrote this piece at 1:32 a.m., while Mrs. Silva was up talking up a storm to no one but herself. I want to seduce him into my poetic gaze. Give him something to think about.

I speak softly into the mike. "This piece is entitled: SEXUAL ENCOUNTER." I plant my eyes on him. Scroll him from shoes to face, face to shoes. I then open my mouth and speak as sensually as I possibly can.

"First gaze, my tongue rotates 'round and 'round my shimmer of 'Star' lips.
Mmmmmmmmmmmm he piques my curiosity. No. I won't let on that my boy shorts

are moist. Just look at him. My, my, my...

"His facial hair above his upper lip is a mixture of salt-n-pepper. So glad he doesn't use Just For Men. I like him natural. His root beer brown eyes are sexy as hell. Nose is proportioned to his oval face—lips, full and delicious. His physique: strong and fit—muscular chest and upper arms makes my insides creamy. Ooh, look at that. Nice waistline. Tight ass.

"His baritone voice makes me leap on the balls of my feet like a ballerina. I clamp my legs together to stop the flow of moisture that builds like silky saliva between fleshy folds of woman. His height is tall. I come to his chest; can bury my head in his armpits. Sniff his aphrodisiac of 'hardworking black man.' His wide smile and thunderous laughter takes me missionary, doggy-style, and 69. I feel like I've traveled around the world on his dick, even though I haven't been as far as down South. He makes me feel: tingles, butterflies, and quivers. I breakout in a sweat behind closed glass doors and I try with all of my pelvic squeezing might to repress my composure on the outside. I want to keep him a secret. Shhhhhhhhhhh. Nobody needs to know how he makes me beam within.

"I know that this is the beginning phase of sexual encounter. Small talk. Sexin' our minds with our eyes. There is a stack of hidden thoughts of what we wish to do to one another. Will we be friends before lovers? That's what our minds ask. There is most definitely chemistry, a blazing sexual attraction. Our bodies speak in French dialogue. Oh, how he makes my body dance. Not as in praise, but more as in striptease. I want to take it all off and let coochie lap up his milk.

"My voice sounds a bit nasally—child-like, too. I'm sure it's irritating to his ears. Yet he doesn't bruise my self-esteem. My body is not that of supermodel—breasts that barely fill the cup of a 34C. I might have to resume back to my 34B. I'm sure he won't be disappointed. It's still more than a mouthful—waistline of between 28 or 29 accentuated by cinnamon skin. The roundness of my ass tantalizes him. I see his eyebrows rise on more than one occasion. Shit. I adore his high self-esteem. He gives me a lusty gaze of sinful thoughts. I wish I could read minds. I'm sure his will be naughty.

"He makes me feel incredibly desirable. It's unspoken. Yet I can see it in his eyes. It makes my mouth water. Slips in and out of my sodden mouth and spirals around my tongue like Blow Pops. The sweet taste makes my dark nipples tighten into knots of painless pleasure. My stomach flutters in anticipation. I wonder what his saliva tastes like: warm, wet, and exotic like foreplay. He gets my mental motors running 100 mph. I never want to get a speeding ticket for constantly having him run through my mind. He keeps me guessing, gazing at his intersection. How big? How long? How thick-skinned? So many questions go unanswered.

"*What could possibly become of us: friend, foe, or lover—a love like no other—fulfilled unadulterated fuckin'. Slow down. I'm getting ahead of my consciousness. Slow down. Pace myself. Brace myself. Before I stumble and fall head-over upon his flesh of stiff erection. I love to get straight and to the point. No need to beat around the bush with him. Oh, shit! I need to shave my naturalness. Make it sheer like my long legs. I'm sure he'd appreciate the feel of soft sensual milk chocolate. The center filled with sweet tasting cherry jubilee. Just thinking about it makes my body glisten. A strong sexual desire has come over me. One touch I may engulf in flames. I know he can put my fire out. He's confident. I see it in his stance of vertical. That really turns me horizontal. Off and on like a switch. He says he adores my subtle strut of Lady. My knock-knees don't turn him off. Thank God! They're sturdy for when I feel the impulse to wet his whistle—trance him with my spoken word. I want him to feel my poetry in motion. Let it bring him to a head as I pop it like a cork and drizzle like ice cream. I want him to explode like a piñata that spells out my protagonist initials...A.L. Send chills up and down his spine as my tongue lusciously licks his baldhead. Damn, I can see it so vividly. Our naked bodies entwine into sweat, erotic moans and groans. His massive hand, massages my tits, squeezes my ass, and tease and pleases my clitoris. Paint the pages of my cinnamon skin with his shade of mahogany. Tilt my head back and lick my smooth, hairless crown—neck, earlobes, and face with the brush of his fleshy organ. Slowly and meticulously journey down to my earth and make my height and inches quiver. Relinquish all that burdens me, murders me, and toys with my emotions. I want him to sex me into a mindset of mind-blowing. Serenade me with his love ballad as we write the pages to this new release: Climax.*"

"Oh shit, that's what I'm talkin' about!" A young gentleman with jet-black twisties that look like he has a thousand worms on top of his head says standing mid-section of the room. Palms clap, heads nod with huge smiles on their faces. I hear the same guy say, "That's what's up! Man, that's what I'm talkin' 'bout!" He nods his head up and down with a smile on his face.

I tilt my head back and laugh even though deep down I feel like crying. My eyes surveillance the crowd. That's when I notice Blu dark piercing eyes gaping at my chest area. I guess he might be wondering, why? Why wear his name like it's some kind of mate that I am madly in love with? Why brand him on my skin so vainly? Why tell the world in this fashion? All I can think to say is: He isn't going anywhere, anytime soon, so why not accept it, embrace it, and let it be known without fear. HIV is a part of me. And in essence he is my life partner. Maybe it does feel like I am flaunting him around, then so be it. At least I'm not hiding him from the world, or from myself. I'm not pretending that he doesn't exist. It takes a strong person to do something like this. I guess you can say that I am finally coming into my own—dealing with my issues woman-to-HIV.

I've done my deed for the evening. Now I can go home, take a cold shower to cool Hella (vajayjay) down. Then I'll call my honey, Xavier to see how he's feeling.

I sigh full of relief as I walk offstage dressed in a black blouse that shows off my cleavage, black mini skirt with black "wish-you-could-fuck-me-now-boots."

Blu has his arms wrapped around some redbone's waist. Her bony ass! She is dressed in a cherry apple red skimpy mini-dress with matching hair and shoes. That whore! I eye him down dressed in all black with a black fedora tilted on his head looking like a pimp-daddy. He eyes me down, and then wets his lips. I walk pass him as if I never saw him before. And as I do, I sniff a whiff of his cologne of "Want Me, Don't You" in each nostril as I amble by. God, he smells so damn yummy.

I sashay pass 'em as if my shit don't stink. My mini-skirt sways from side to side. I am poised. "Straight, look straight ahead," I say to myself. I cut my eye over my right shoulder and see that they both are eyeing me. Is she bisexual? Oh, yeah. She is. But I am not bothered by her. Him? Well, he is definitely a distraction. Nonetheless, I am feeling myself. And she, too, is feeling me. I don't have what she wants, but Karma does...sweet nectar. And she has what my body craves...a masculine man with all the fixings to rock my world.

I have to block them both out of my mind. But I am minutes too late. Blu has already excused himself from his chick and is making his way over to me. I grab a plate and help myself to some spicy buffalo wings and celery sticks with chunky blue cheese.

"So, look-a-here, look-a-here," Blu licks his fingertips with a damn sly grin on his gorgeous face. "Ms. Love."

I try to act coy. Don't want to lead on that I am feeling his swagger. I know. After all he put me through, especially after he threatened to *piss* on me. Ooh, that was sooooo lowdown. And oh, the *hand sanitizer gel* thing...that ripped me open.

"What dragged you here?" I ask with a hint of sass in my tone.

Blu laughs. "Listen to you. Boy, haven't we changed from the damsel to the diva." He glances at his Gucci wristwatch.

I smirk.

"What you think you're the *only* one who *likes* poetry?" he says.

I lift up my index finger and wag it in his face. "Correction: I happen to *love* poetry. If you knew anything about me you'd know that."

He takes a step back. His walnut black eyes scroll up my tall frame as he steps forward and whispers in my ear. "I know *enough* about you, Ms. Avery Love."

I smirk, and then whisper back in his ear. "You're not the only one who knows *that*, Mr. Blu McDowell. My story has been out for a while now."

Blu raises both of his hands as if to call a truce. "Okay...my bad. So, I didn't know you had it in you. Back then you seem so, so, so...."

"Had *what* in me? Seemed so, so, so, what? Maybe I was timid. It's not easy to divulge something as personal as *that* to someone you *may* have *had* feelings for. I did what I did because I cared unlike you." I cross my arms about my chest.

"And you think I didn't. I reacted like any other individual caught completely off guard." He sighs. "That's in the past..."

Past? No. I think to myself.

Instantly my thoughts revert back to that ugly scene.

I take a deep, deep breath and say, "I'm HIV-positive."

My eyes widen. Blu snatches his hand away, and moves quickly away from me. His eyes bulge out. He opens his glove compartment and grabs his sanitizer hand gel, massaging it between his fingers, inner palms, and the outer surface of his hands. I swallow hard as the tears continue to slow motion down my face. He is making me feel worthless. He turns to look at me with sharpness, and then turns away. A roar of scathing bullets release from his mouth as if I am being shot in the face, eyes, and one last bullet finishes me off in the left temple.

"Avery, when the hell were you going to tell me?" He turns away. "Were you going to wait until after I started having feelings for you and then drop this time bomb on me? Oh, no, maybe you were going to wait until after we—"

He plays with his upper lip by pulling it, and then he turns to look at me again and I swear his eyes seem to have changed colors. He starts rubbing his crotch area. It's like his whole persona has changed.

"I ought to whip my dick out and piss on yo infected ass," he says smugly while gripping himself like he's opting to masturbate.

My ears can't believe what he has just said to me. The distraught look upon my face stresses it. What happened to the "gentleman" that was wooing me? The nice guy? The respectful guy? My head is spinning.

"BIIIIIITCH, GET THE HELL OUTTA MY CAR!!"

I literally flinched.

I come to.

"Let's just leave it there." Blu says, and then he changes the subject seemingly with a blink of an eye. "Look at you," his dark eyes scroll me from feet to face. "Damn, that sweet cinnamon brown sugar! But how could I have known when this is the first time I've actually seen you perform. Correction: second time. That shit up there that you just did was..."

Oh, boy, here comes the bs, I think as I tap my foot waiting for this melodramatic man to start some bullshit.

"That was so damn...sexy! Shiiiittttt you got a brother blood flowin'." He grabs his crotch with a firm palm grip.

I tremble, and then squeeze my thighs together. Roll my eyes. Then laugh softly trying to distract those erotic thoughts that are dancing around in my head for this *succulent* man. He is killin' me standing so close to me—inhaling his warm peppermint breath. This only intensifies the sexual arousal. Man, he smells so good and looks so tasty, and I bet with everything in me he is every bit of a nasty freak in bed. Fight it, girl. Fight that testosterone off of you!

I cut my eyes over to Redbone to see what she is doing. She has a 'tude with her face and lips all twisted up.

I cock my head to the side. "Hmm. Insecure isn't she. Don't you think you better get back to your redbone chick?" I say.

"Why are you so, so, antagonistic?" Blu asks. "I sense some pent-up frustration in you. I can feel it. Won't you let me help you out, you know, give you a massage or something. Let my magic fingers penetrate those deep tissues. Help you release those impurities that are obviously dying to come out." He winks. "Think 'bout it."

"There is nothing to think about," I say to myself. Not since Zaleyn do I ever want to display that kind of submissiveness for a man again. I let my guard down with Zaelyn. I let him in. We made love—passionate *love*. God, I adored that man and he completely ruined me. I told myself never again would I allow a man to get so close to my heart. But I lied. Xavier is the closest any man has ever gotten to my heart. I lied on several things because I said I'd remain celibate. Fuck *dick* and every man who had one! I was through! Done! Or so *I* thought.

Blu walks off back to Redbone and I finish nibbling.

Hall jumps back onstage. "Ladies, we have a special guest in the

351

building. He really needs no introduction, but since he is my brother from a different mother, and a good brother at that I'll welcome him into our home properly. Let's give a round of applause for 'LNS' otherwise known as 'LATE NIGHT SEDUCTION!'"

When this gorgeous man walks up onstage I nearly drop my chicken bone on the floor. *It's him again.* Man, he puts me in mind of Dwyane Wade. The Shooting guard/Point guard for the Miami Heat—Six feet four, two-hundred and twenty pounds of dark sexiness. *Mmmmmmmmmm.* Any woman who thinks No. 3 is not, huh; send her crazy ass to me. I'm not one who is into sports, but if they all look like Dwyane Wade, shoot, I am liable to change my mind.

I place my plate on the table, and I engross myself in him dressed like a friggin' angel. All that dark suited up in a white Valentino suit. Shoot, I know I have died and gone back to heaven!

"Ladies," LNS says in a deep, strong voice. "I'm not going to embellish you with candy kisses." This high yellow woman with a quick weave and southern drawl in her tone says, "Why not?" He smiles. And when he does, oh, my God, my legs get wobbly. My mouth is dry. I need some water. H2O!

"Because, my Queen, all I want you to do is...
Escape with me
I want to bask in the sun and melt inside of you
I want to run through your bloodstream to the warmth of your heart
And sigh relieved as I course your haven
I want to breathe with you, not apart
I want to feel your iridescence
Take me on a brown sugar Ferris wheel ride
Then let me lie in you
Reside in you as my final destination
Use my skin as your handkerchief for when your eyes get misty from missing me
Let me die inside of you
So that you never have to be lonely again
Let my spirit linger while I count your blessings as God grants you each wish
Let's go now, and return as one entity."

That same lady fans herself then drops to the floor like a pair of shoes. Plop! Another lady standing in the middle row with a hoochie dress on and fake blonde hair and fake blue eyes with a big gap between her two front teeth yells out, "C'mon, baby, let's go now!" Oh, yes, "LATE NIGHT

SEDUCTION" sho' has a way with the ladies and his words aren't so bad either.

LNS remains standing onstage looking out as if he found something or lost something. *"This here is no stretch of my imagination. It is okay to want what you think you may not be able to have,"* he says. And I swear his hot eyes are staring directly at me. I feel the heat burning down in my soul. He has definitely got my attention I am all ears.

He continues, *"I love U"* with this longing look in his "come-and-get-this-woman" eyes.

"U makes my toes numb
My mouth dry
U makes my eyes tear... just because
When U appear in my mind
U makes my body shake like an earthquake gazing into your beautiful deep-set
brown eyes
U makes my spirit dance and come alive
U makes me a very wealthy man
Richly in love
U make God smile from up above
Because He knows that U love me true
I feel whole, never half of a man with U
U gives me profound inspiration
A reason to hope
U gives me daylight, brightness
U gives me strength
U gives me U
I give U me
We give each other golden
U gives me SOUL
I give u MATE.
Let's not pretend
This here is FATE
Don't walk away
Don't let it slip another day
Embrace the NOW
Let the PAST subside
God is here

353

In your eyes, in my eyes
Open up, and allow me entry into your celibacy
Not your bed
Allow me to love your heart
Not mess with your head
Allow Him to mold us into something great
Something real
Allow your heart to feel
Just feel the purity that escapes from my mouth
Into your ears
I love U."

"Girl. Girlllll, if you don't close your mouth!" I hear Karma say, "Girl, come back to earth, damn. It is just a poem, not a marriage proposal. Girl, you are sooooo pitiful."

I am at a loss for words. Oh, this man has opened up a door. *Girl, stop buggin'!* Like Karma said, it is *just* a poem. But how do I wish...Oh, never mind.

When I arrive home I kick off my boots then head straight upstairs to my bedroom and plop down on my bed. I don't even bother to get undress or take a shower or bath. I close my eyes, and then quickly doze off to sleep with "LNS" slow dancing around in my head.

The feel of smooth skin gently grazes across the side of my face. It jolts me out of a sound sleep. Body shudders uncontrollably.

With my quivering hands I peel back the scarlet duvet from my body. Cautiously, I sit upright. Blouse clings to dank skin. My stomach feels unsettled.

Slowly, very gently my eyes shift to the right of me, then, the left, as my mind wanders, wary as to where *he* might be. *Today is the day*, I think. *I very well might die.*

And if this day should be my last breath to take, I feel it necessary to share my thoughts to my beloved Xavier.

I reach for my iPhone on charge. Scroll across until I reach the Utilities. I click on Voice Memos. Press the red button to the left as the record plays. Already I am emotional. But that lets me know that what I am about to share has truth and meaning. It speaks from my depth of my heart, my spirit. I speak into the microphone.

"Xavier,

"I once told a man that I had nothing to offer him. I had nothing, but my body, my mind. I had nothing, but words that had no monetary value, but were priceless pieces of me (my spirit). A starving artist destined to make a mark with something unique sparked from a dream. A woman entered my view named Avery Love. And from there this bond emerged.

"I once told a man that I was lonely, and alone. I was depressed because my life was in shambles, because I had taken more steps back than I had planned to. Some things are beyond our control. Some things happen because it was already written to. Some things just occur, out of the blue. Some things are inevitable.

"I once told a man that it is possible for me to fall deeply in love. He grew silent. He just gazed at me. The look in his eyes spoke in volume. And when he opened his mouth and released his wisdom in an abridged verse, I broke down and cried inside. I cried because I felt "love" for the very first time.

"No, I had yet to rise from falling so far down in burdens. I had yet to see the fruits of my labor. I had yet to see the doors to my agony spring open and shed light on my troubled soul. I had yet to embrace that wonderful feeling of successful. The kind that made you smile so wide, eyes spread so big, heart flutters with butterflies. Confused and amused, simultaneously. I had yet to experience so many things that I dreamed of, visualized myself doing. I had yet to accomplish my life's goals.

"But I have now. And now has me. And I have moments of clarity of what I want: peace of mind, honesty, loyalty, fire and desire, trust and commitment. I don't know what He has in-store for me. But what I do know is that life is of breathing, wishing, fulfilling those long awaited dreams. I have passion flowing through my veins. I have laughter that is bursting to come roaring out, instead of screams. I have tears that cry not only in misery, they cry of joy. I have gifted hands along with an imaginative mind that keeps me alive at times when I feel like I'm...I'm dying inside. I have me.

"So, I once told a man...no, I have not risen to my destiny as of yet. But I plan to keep trying. To never stop dreaming or soaring with imagery. But first, I need to relinquish someone so near and dear to my heart. It hurts, yet makes me smile, cry, and wonder all at the same time. I have to relinquish a time, a person, and a love that today, does not exist. I have to relinquish moments we'd shared. Remember him for who he was, how he was, find closure, and then gracefully move on.

"I once told a man that there is beauty from all the pain.

"And He told me when there is rain; there is sunshine and sunshine when there is rain."

With my forefinger I press the red button to the left, then press 1:45

AM to highlight, then SPEAKER as I listen to myself recite what I feel from within. After listening, I press SHARE at the bottom of the screen, then EMAIL. In the SUBJECT line I type: "From My Heart to Your Ears" then I press SEND.

I rise from the bed and head downstairs. I begin to hum, and then sing an old folk song Poppa used to sang during his spells of midnight. Often he had dark nights but he always knew how to cope. Sangin' was his way. Poetry is mine.

Before entering the bathroom, my home phone rings. I about face like a neglected animal released from a grungy cage. Clumsily, I trip over my pumps lying in the middle of the walkway. I hear my toes crack as I scurry to get to the phone. Anxiously, I pick up on the third ring remembering I never did call Xavier last night.

"Xavier?" I answer breathless, voice shaky; eyes gaze up at the high ceiling.

"Collect call for Avery Love from Edna Mahan Correctional Facility for Women (EMCFW) in Clinton, New Jersey. Will you accept the charges?" the nasally female voice asks.

"Yes." I murmur with a perplex look upon my face. I bite down on my bottom lip.

"Hello." The unfamiliar female voice says.

"Hello?" I murmur. "I'm sorry. I didn't catch your name."

"Oh, this is Mrs. Xavier Combs III speaking." The female voice retorts.

The contortion on my face stresses...pissed off! My eyes droop and blacken. "Excuse me?"

"Listen, bitch, you heard me right!" the female voice snaps.

"*Who* is this?!" I ask with soreness in my throat, body tensing up.

"This is JaVonna...Xavier's *wife*. That's who the fuck it is!"

Breathless, "I don't believe you," I tell her barely able to contain myself.

"Believe it. You see I *had* a good man who didn't want his baby to be born a bastard. He proposed to me. And of course, I accepted. We got *married* last week! Oh, it's so exciting! I'm so happy!"

I close my eyes to take in what she has just said. "WWW-What?!" My heart nearly drops to my feet. All I feel is *boom boom boom* in my chest.

JaVonna cackles. "And *you* thought he didn't believe that *I* was carrying *his* baby. Now who's having the last laugh, huh?"

I shake my head, baffled. Disbelief entwine with belligerence. "Xavier wouldn't do that. He loves *me!*" I snap.

She giggles, knowing that she is ripping me apart. "Well, obviously you didn't know him as much as you *thought* you did. Xavier was a noble man. That was my *husband* for yah."

I grit my teeth. "Why are you calling me? How did you get my number?"

JaVonna snickers devilishly. "Xavier gave it to me. He told me to notify you in case anything happened to him."

I inhale, and try to hold back the tears. "I don't believe you. Xavier wouldn't do anything like that."

"Believe it." JaVonna says in a smug tone.

Nervously I say, "I'm going to call him myself."

"You can call all you want, but he won't anssssssssswwwwwer," she sings with amusement.

I roll my eyes. "What do you mean...*he won't answer?* Exactly, what are you trying to say, JaVonna?"

"Xavier *died* last night," she says unsympathetically.

"She's lying. Why would *she* lie?" I say to myself.

"Are you serious? You're actually going to believe this chick! She's doing it to get to you, Avery!" Karma voice bellows in my head.

"Girl, call your man. Don't listen to that bitch!" Avona murmurs. "Click that bitch! Hang up and call, Xavier!"

I slam the phone down in its cradle. My hands shake as I press Xavier's 10-digits. The phone rings, repeatedly.

Blink. PLEASE answer! Blink. PLEASE answer! Blink. PLEASE answer, Xavier, I mumble under my quavering, warm breath.

I hang up.

Then think to call the hospital to see if anyone there can tell me anything.

The phone constantly rings and then this annoying voice picks up.

I hang up.

Then think to call one of his doctors. *What is his name? What is his number?* Xavier has been so distant from me. Everything kind of slipped my mind.

Dr.? Dr. Drew? Yeah, that's it.

I have his card because Xavier gave me one of them. *Where did I put it?*

I grow frantic.

Think! Think! Think!

It's in my hobo bag!

I fast pace it over to the closet and grab the bag and dump all of the contents out and onto the saffron coffee table. My hands meddle through some loose papers, makeup case, pens, notepad, and paperback. I unfold my green Anne Klein wallet. Flustered I quickly rummage through and find the card and call.

The phone rings three times, and then someone picks up.

"Dr. Drew, speaking." the baritone voice says.

I sigh relieved.

Take a deep, deep breath. "Hello, Dr. Drew. My name is Avery Love. I'm Xavier Combs fiancée. I know that this is going to sound strange..." I sigh inwardly. "Xavier has been distant for a couple of weeks. I've been trying to give him his space to deal with everything." I'm rambling. "Anyway," my voice cracks, "I just received a disturbing call telling me that Xavier *died*." I close my eyes and swallow hard, "Can you confirm this, please?" I'm sure he can hear the desperation in my tone.

He speaks with great control and compassion. "You said your name is Avery, right?"

Tears pour from my eyes. Quickly they scroll down my anguished face. "Yes, sir," I move my face away from the receiver and sniffle.

"He talked of you. I'm sorry, Avery, but I can only give information to immediate family or his wife, which you said that you're his... *fiancée*."

"I understand," I murmur.

"Do you know any of his family?" He asks.

"His mother and father and sister are deceased. I don't know of anyone else, besides me," I say, a face full of streaky tears.

He sighs, heavily into the receiver. "Okay. Okay. Listen, I know that this must be a terrible, terrible time for you. I'm so sorry."

I sniffle. "Thank you. Thank you for your time." I say with body-jerking tears. The phone slips out of my hand and drops to the floor, as do I. I just want to crumble to dust.

iPhone rings. After four rings the voicemail picks up.

"You have reached the voicemail of Ms. Love, please leave a brief message and I'll kindly call you back at my earliest convenience."

Beeeeeeeeeeeeeep.

"Hello, Ms. Love, this is attorney Norman Fest, give me a call so that I can go over the details of the annulment with you. Things are looking good for you. You'll have your freedom back very soon."

iPhone rings. After four rings the voicemail picks up.

"You have reached the voicemail of Ms. Love, please leave a brief message and I'll

kindly call you back at my earliest convenience."

Beeeeeeeeeeeeeeep.

"Avery, this is Dr. Cristal. Is everything all right? You've missed two sessions. Call me."

"This is not happening," I repeatedly tell myself, while scratching my scalp. Then swipe my long fingers across the rawness of my nose smearing snot above my upper lip. Salty tears stream hard down my grief-stricken face.

He isn't... gone, I think.

"Baby, he's gone," Avona says in a melancholy tone.

I shake my head in utter disbelief. My eyes skyward the ceiling looking for answers, something to give me comfort. I am diligently waiting for Him to respond. But He doesn't. So I talk to Him.

"Lord, one minute he was here, the next he's gone. God...why?" I sniffle. "Why does my life constantly wreak havoc? Why am I constantly going through these emotions? Why can't I get *love* right, just once?"

I was so close to getting *love* right.

Out of the three: Blu, Travar and Zaelyn, Travar was the *only* man who came back into my life. Those were some hard days. I crack a smile. But he didn't seem to mind. It makes me think of how wonderfully he treated me that day he invited me over for dinner. Goodness. I felt so beautiful that day. So like my old self.

"Ms. Love, your dinner is served." He holds out his left arm with his right arm holding the folded towel that dangles as if he's a waiter. I smile.

He escorts me to the table, pulls out my chair and sits on the opposite end. The table is delightful with lasagna, chicken Parmesan, salad, dinner rolls, and a strawberry cheesecake for dessert. I get up from my chair, walk over to him and kiss him on the cheek to show my appreciation.

He stares in my eyes and says, "Avery, you look very beautiful."

I am already melted but the butter is bubbling on a high flame of lust.

"Thank you, Travar."

In between my legs is burning hot cream that is coating my lips. I am foaming at the mouth.

"You look edible, if I may say so myself, Travar." I lure him in by wetting my lips.

I swallow hard trying not to become teary-eyed. I truly believe that he feels I am beautiful just by the look in his eyes.

After dinner, we sip a cup of gourmet coffee and sit on the loveseat talking and cuddling. He unbuckles my shoes and massages my feet. Oh...my...God! The man massages feet. I've died and gone to heaven, for sho'. He starts kissing me on my neck, while his other hand strokes my thigh. My body grows fiery hot. I want to just spread 'em and invite him in. I tease his earlobe and find it's his sensitive spot. Travar moans and I start kissing his neck. I feel the bulge in his pants knowing that things are heating up. My conscience is speaking, damn near screaming at me. Avery! Avery! Stop! But I ignore that inner voice because I want him so bad. I want to feel him inside of me. We continue on until he has my right breast in his hand, sucking on my nipple. I moan.

"Travar, please stop." He knows that I don't mean it. I know that I don't mean it. I don't want him to stop. If anything, I want him to keep on going until he pops my precious gem allowing me to release my built-up juices onto him. The look in his eyes alerts me that he is into it and trying to stop him now is going to be difficult. But I have no choice in the matter. Damn.

"Travar, please stop?"

"Avery, what's wrong?"

I get a little choked up because he is staring me in my face. I clear my throat several times before speaking. Taking deep breaths, I pause, deep breaths, pause and then begin to speak. I dangle my head low and then lift it back up. I am a strong woman. I can do this. My eyes wander the room for my purse, shoes, and keys before actually saying what needs to said.

"Avery, what is it?"

"Um. Travar there is something you need to know about me. First, you made me feel like a queen this evening. Dinner, the candles and dessert; everything was beautiful. I want everything to remain beautiful this evening, so what I am about to say can either change that or the evening can continue on." My eyes are watery and a tear falls. He looks concerned and takes my hand. I lose it at that point and just start crying an ugly cry.

Travar stands, wraps his arms around me so gently and says, "Avery, whatever, it is we can get through it."

How I've longed to hear those words.

I hold my head high, look him in his hazel eyes, and say, "Travar, I'm HIV-positive."

His eyes became watery and he put his hands up to his head. He sits down slowly. I can tell he is in shock. More like a silent shock. And I see the tears drip down his face. There is silence between us and only the music is playing. He doesn't curse, yell, or scream. He has no reaction. He sits there staring at the floor with tears flowing, dripping one-by-one. I remain standing, and then pick up my shoes, purse, and keys and walk towards the door.

But before I walk out I say to him, "Thank you for treating me like a lady."
I walk out of Travar's apartment never anticipating seeing him again.
I come to.

Body curls in a fetal position on the living room floor as I cry my eyes out for *my* man...*Xavier.*

21

January 2011

> *Ring. Ring. Ring.*
> "Hello."
> "Hi, Avery," *Xavier says in his baritone voice, and then sighs.*
> "Hi." *My right hand rises to my chest, waiting.*
> "I just left the doctor. Are you home?"
> "No." *I blink, twice.* "I'm at the bookstore."
> "Okay, Avery, ask," *I say to myself.*
> "What did the doctor say?"
> "You don't want to know."
> "Yes, I do." *I say calmly.*
> "Well," *Xavier sighs deeper this time.* "Doc says he found some spots. I have to have a biopsy done."
> *Okay. Okay. Spots. Get it together, girl, I think.*
> "O-kay. We'll be okay." *I tell him, while browsing from aisle to aisle, eyes scanning the bookshelves of Barnes & Noble. My mind is hungry for a good read—a read that will take me away from my troubles. Put me in a happy mood. In spite of everything that I am currently going through sometimes I just want to fade away. Take me away from all this sickness stuff.*
> *Xavier remains silent, and then says.* "Well, babe, I'll call you later."
> "Okay."
> *I "end" the call.*

January 29th

My cellular lights up, and so do I once I see the name staring back at me...Xavier. I feel butterflies in my stomach like always. I am deeply in love with this man. And I never want anything to happen to him. I don't know what I'd do if it did. I really, really don't.

It is weird because just recently we've both gotten sick within the same week. Actually, that's not true. Xavier hasn't been feeling well way before I had gone to the doctor on January 25th, which was the day after the snowstorm. I have bronchitis. I am not sure what he has as of yet. He still has to go to the doctor.

From Friday, 26th to 29th I haven't heard from him. He's been kind of distant. I left him two voice mail messages on the 26th letting him know that I was getting a little better, but that I wasn't one hundred percent me. I told him that I loved him. Still, he never returned my call. I found that to be quite peculiar, but I figured he'd call when he felt a little better. At least I'd hoped he would.

My thoughts drift back to a couple of weeks ago; I remember Xavier complaining of possibly having another kidney stone. His stomach had been bothering him and he wasn't having regular bowel movements either. That was alarming to me.

"Baby, I had two kidney stones that passed before. It's probably just another one," he said. He'd know better than anyone especially since he'd already had two before. That's what I told myself but in all honesty I felt he should've gone to the doctor way before now. Men will be men. They hate to go to the doctor.

The last time I spoke to him, he was lying on the floor because he said standing, sitting, or even trying to lie in bed, hurt. I could hear the pain in his voice and I felt completely helpless. Here we were living in two different places, still, trying to salvage our relationship. I asked if he wanted me to come over. He said no. I didn't press the issue, but I can't say that it didn't hurt. I wanted to be there for him—to show that I was in his corner one hundred percent. But I felt as if he was pushing me away. If this was anything minor I probably wouldn't have let it get to me so, but this was serious. Again, I felt like people shunned me when I felt they needed me the most. What was I trying to prove? I guess I wanted him to know that I would be there in sickness and in health. With JaVonna being arrested, the baby situation, and me trying to get my marriage annulled from crazy ass Stacy, yes, I needed him to know that I was in this for the long haul.

My eyes begin to well up. All I can do at this point is pray that I take better care of myself and not develop pneumonia. I hope Xavier does the same. "It's just a kidney stone," I tell myself. At least that's what Xavier seems to think. Hopefully it's nothing. Nothing major. Nothing serious. Nothing.

I pray, because I have this eerie feeling come over me. I am having strange thoughts too—thoughts that I do not want to be having about us. Like someone is going somewhere. I am having bad thoughts of me being shot and raped again. Xavier even stated that he had a dream about being shot too. He said his dream book gave him numbers that symbolized...death. It was creepy. The only place I hoped we were going was to be picking up the keys to our new home.

I push the thoughts out of my head, but they still linger. I know exactly what I am thinking; I'm about to lose again. In some way, shape or form I feel like he is going to be leaving me. Whether leaving me as in breaking up with me or otherwise. He says he'd never leave me. That the only way he'd leave me is if God calls him home. That's the only way. I believe him. But it doesn't lessen these thoughts I am having. Something just doesn't feel right. My spirit is at a tug-of-war. This isn't a good thing.

I need to be at peace. And at peace I am not. Something is coming. I can feel it in my bones—something difficult to understand, to face, to accept. I try to be strong in front of him but I'm hurting inside. I cry most of the time. Pray. Cry. This is my regimen, besides, writing to express my inner woes. It helps me get through the nights after I get off the phone with him. There are so many lonely nights, lately. Unpredictable days, and quite frankly I am tired of going through the motions of life.

Just a few weeks ago I told Xavier everyone I love I lose. And it is the truth. Poppa. Ma'am. Johnnie. Antwone. Jewell. And let me not forget Anonymous. Well, I relinquished Anonymous at my own freewill and it was the worst decision I'd ever made. It is a lot to take in. So I am reluctant to get close to anyone. God forbid something happens to Xavier. God forbid. Love doesn't seem to be in the stars for me. Men don't stick around. Relationships don't seem to last. In Xavier's case, this is not his fault. This is out of his hands. Mine too. We both have to leave it in God's hands and pray. Pray like we've never prayed before.

January 31st

11:20 P.M.

I call Xavier. The phone rings three times. He picks up on the third ring in a low tone of voice.

"Hi."

"Hey, baby."

"What's going on today? Did you find anything out about the biopsy?" I ask.

"The doctor didn't call yet. What's that called when they put that gel on your stomach?"

We both say simultaneously. "Ultrasound."

"What about it?" I ask.

"They called and told me they found what looks like a cyst or tumor on my kidney."

I sigh deeply. "If it ain't one thing it's another."

364

"Yeahhhh, you're right," he sings.

I take in inventory: a cyst or tumor on his kidney. Oh, boy.

"You're not getting any sleep over there and I was up pacing last night. I made a trail in the carpet. I'm in a little pain."

I close my eyes and say a little prayer. Then change the subject.

"I called the storage today. I'm going to take care of it, okay."

"That's not due until the 6th or 7th," he says. "If the doctors don't call by Thursday I'm going back to work. What's today...Monday? Tomorrow's...ah, Tuesday. I'll go back to work on Thursday."

We both pause.

Xavier continues, "I don't have any money. I won't until Friday. And I know you don't have any money, either. I'll have some on Friday," he says.

"I'm not concerned about money. I know how to make due, haven't I told you that. I'll go there and pay the storage myself. I have it all figured out: Phone bill. Storage."

"No." Xavier adamantly says. "Listen. I'll pay it. I'll use my credit card and pay it up for two months. You just pay the phone bill."

"I'm trying to help." I say in a soft tone.

"I know. Just pay the phone bill. The only way it won't get paid is if I'm in the hospital before Friday. I can't take another day in this house. I gotta do something so I might as well go back to work before I go crazy."

My forehead crumples. I'm not mad, but frustrated and somewhat aggravated. I am frustrated because it is taking too damn long to do the biopsy. The longer it takes the worse things can get. And plus, once they do the biopsy he'll still have to wait at least another week or two before getting the results back. It is beginning to piss me off!

"How are you going to do that in pain, huh? I mean it's not like you have...please...think about it. Don't make matters worse for yourself. I'm not trying to tell you what to do, but think first, okay. Why is this taking so long?"

"Uh-huh. I'm looking into another hospital. I told you about the one in New York...Sloan or something. The doctors there want me to do the biopsy here and then have me bring all of my information to them there."

"Well, I wish somebody would do something, and fast." I brush my left hand across my scalp and blow out hot air. "Time is of the essence," I say, flustered.

My heart is beating fast. Nerves are frazzled. It takes me back to Poppa all over again. Time. Time is very crucial. Early detection is my biggest concern. My mind drifts. I knew once I got that general assistance ($140.00) check to put fifty aside just in case. I smile, knowing that he wants to continue to keep things as they are. Who am I to stand in this man's way? I am his lady—the love of his life. That's who.

365

"I'm worried." I say with the tips of my fingers pressed against my chest.

"I'm worried, too," he admits.

I sigh again. Feeling relieved that he is not living in denial. Good, good, he's dealing with reality, I think.

"Well, I'm not going to keep you on the phone. I know you're tired. You keep your head up. We'll get through this. I love you."

"I love you, too," he says.

"Talk to you later."

"Okay."

I toss and turn all night. The heat isn't making it any better. It is stifling me. I have night sweats thinking unpleasant thoughts. I am definitely scared for the both of us.

February 3rd

6:23 P.M.

I smile.

"Hello."

"Hey, Beautiful."

I love when Xavier calls me Beautiful.

"Hi. Baby, are you okay?" I ask, pacing the kitchen floor.

"I've been in the hospital all yesterday," he says.

Xavier sounds like he is in his SUV.

"What's wrong?" I ask, shaking like a leaf.

Xavier continues, "Ah, they found two spots on my pancreas and a spot on my liver. The doctor tells me not to worry myself because it could be just a spot. He's trying to figure out how they're going to do the biopsy."

Honestly, I don't hear anything else except "pancreas." My legs feel weak. My heart feel like it is about to explode. Tears flow down my cheeks. I feel soreness in my throat. My voice lowers to a faint tone. It cracks when I speak. "Let's not think the worse, we've got to stay positive." I tell him.

Deep down I am thinking: God, please, please, don't take this man away from me? Already I am a body of nerves.

"I have to go back on Monday," he says.

My mind drifts back to Antwone. All I hear or thought I heard was something about Monday.

"Okay." I say softly, while sniffling.

"Look, I started not to tell you." He murmurs.

"Why?"

"You've been through this with your nephew...Antwone. Avery, you worry entirely too much."

This man knows me to the tee. I manage to crack a smile.

Xavier pays close attention to me. I like that. He has stood by my side through thick and thin. Come hell or high water, Xavier was right there—toe to toe. Don't get me wrong, we'd get annoyed with one another. Cuss and fuss like the best of 'em, but when push came to shove this man had my back. He refused to let me fall. That was, of course, before JaVonna. Back then I always said that he was my guardian angel. I don't know how many times I've told him that. It was the God's-Honest-truth. And now...now things are slightly different but I still feel the need to be there for him.

"Listen, don't worry about me. What did I tell you? Look out for you. Put you first, Avery." He speaks in an authoritative tone. A tone I respect to the utmost. But even though I respect it doesn't mean that I am going to comply with it.

My forehead crumples. "I don't want to hear that. I'm not going to do that, you hear me." I say, firm and strong. I try to keep my voice soft, but he knows that I mean every word I have just said. I can be tough when I need to be.

"Well, let me get out of this cold," he says.

I want to say: "Make sure you put your seatbelt on before you pull off." I can hear the, ding ding ding in the background so I know that he doesn't have it on. But I don't bother. I just close my eyes and say a silent prayer in my head.

"I'll call you later," he says.

"Okay," I reply, still tearing up and sniffling.

"Stop worrying," he says again.

I nod my head up and down.

"I'll talk to you later." I say, while I "end" the call.

After I hang up with Xavier, something changes in me. Whether his tumor comes back benign or malignant our relationship is going to change. Either we are going to make it or this "pancreatic bastard" will break us apart. I don't want to think the worse, but I refuse to live in denial and be crushed later because there will be no one to help lift me backup, no one. I don't want to lie to my heart because it is so fragile for him. And I don't want this love to end. I dread the thought of losing this beautiful man.

I look around at my surroundings, which is a one-bedroom apartment. No jobs has called as of yet. The phlebotomy class is becoming a bore. I am getting depressed not just from a job not calling but also from being in a place that makes me feel so burdened.

I quickly storm into the bathroom and look at myself in the mirror with tears rushing down my face. After my little meltdown I find myself getting pissed. I have someone who means the world to me (tears rush harder down my face) and whether we have a year, five, or ten, which I pray faithfully we do. I do not want this wonderful man to "possibly" leave me and my life still is in shambles. Oh, hell no! I feel and mean everything I am saying with mind, body, and spirit. I am not going to spend whatever time we have left in this situation. I've had it! Why Xavier? Why cancer? Why are you doing this to me, to us, to him, huh? Finally, I find a man who loves me. Me. Lord. Me! And here this shit comes creeping in. Look, I don't care that I am being selfish. It is 'bout time, don't you think. I feel free with Xavier. I can be me with Xavier. And here this comes! I don't mean to be disrespectful, Lord, but I mean come on. Haven't I experienced enough heartache and loss in my life? I need, want, and desire this man. Xavier needs me. We need each other. We are in love, Lord, love.

"I need to start thinking about me, myself, and I." I mumble under my breath. Xavier has preached this to me so many times. And I hate to say it, but it is finally registering, because it is now matters of the heart. My heart! I can lose him, permanently. And it hurts like hell thinking about it.

God forbid, (swallowing hard) if something does happen against our will, me being in a state of peace of mind will be better than where I currently am. If anything happens to Xavier, I will no longer have the love I need. And that will destroy me because I can't let go. I need love so.

February 4th

3:00 P.M.

I browse through Barnes & Noble in Hackensack, New Jersey, trying to unwind and relax my nerves. I have the biggest headache. I feel lonely, and alone, waiting for my cell phone to ring. Xavier had a doctor's appointment at 10:30 a.m., at Jaysen University Medical Center in Hackensack. He had to go there to see how and when they are going to proceed with the biopsy.

Finally, my cellular rings.

I answer it on the second ring.

"Hello."

"Hey. I'm at Red Alert—came to check on things."

"How are you feeling, honey?" I ask.

"Oh, I'm in a little pain. Nothing that I can't handle, so don't worry, baby."

I know he is still in his SUV because I can hear the ding-ding-ding, which means he doesn't have his seatbelt on.

I cut to the chase. "So, what did they say?"

"You don't want to know," he says.

"Yes, I do."

"Well, they say I do have pancreatic cancer. The doctor said that they are not going to do surgery because two spots are on my pancreas. A cyst or tumor on my kidney. Now it's on both kidneys. And spots on my liver, too. It's spreading so rapidly that they are just going to treat it with radiation and chemotherapy. But first, they are going to do the biopsy to see what type of pancreatic cancer it is: non-aggressive or aggressive. The doctor said he's normally seen the aggressive. He said that he's not going to say that I'm going to die or anything like that because he doesn't know. It's not like he's God, so therefore, I won't know until after they do the biopsy."

I exhale, and then look upward toward the ceiling with feebleness in my eyes.

Calmly, I ease out. "Okay, okay," while pacing the navy-blue carpet of the bookstore. That is all I can say at the moment. I have to allow it time to absorb in my brain. I am not shocked because I have already dreamt it. I saw a lot that I didn't want to see the other night. So I prayed, and cried, and asked God not to take my man away from me. I buried my head in my pillow and cried so caringly for this man I love.

"I knew I shouldn't have told you." He says.

My forehead crumples, and I snap. "Why wouldn't you tell me? I'd find out anyway."

"Your voice has changed already. Listen, don't worry about me."

I raise my voice. "Stop?! Stop saying that to me! I'm going to worry, you already know this!"

"Where are you? I know how you like to hop on the bus and go to the city."

"No, I'm in the area, kind of. I'm at the bookstore in Hackensack."

"I was going to pick you up for a few minutes."

"I had a shitty day today. I needed to get away. But if you want I can meet you somewhere. I would like to see you too."

"If I come back out, I'll call you. I'll see you tomorrow morning. I'll be out early."

I don't want to press the issue, so I say, "Okay."

"I'll talk to you later, babe."

"Bye, honey."

I roam around the bookstore some more. Then I ask this young white man who looks to be in his early twenties (who looks to be employed here) if he can assist me in finding a book The Last Lecture by Randy Pausch. I knew from watching Oprah of this *professor who had given a lecture about his life of terminal cancer. I remembered it being pancreatic, too.*

The tall, nerdy-looking, thin man, with brown hair escorts me to where the book is located. He hands me the book. I say, "Thank you." He replies, "You're welcome, ma'am," and then walks off back to what he was previously doing.

I open the rust hardcover book and begin to read, pacing about the bookstore absorbing the author's words and thinking about Xavier, simultaneously.

The part that really grabs my attention is when the author shared that he had ten tumors on his liver. Ten! Wow. My hope at the moment is that Xavier beats this monster. I feel myself getting teary-eyed so I walk over to the cashier station and ask the young brown-haired woman if she can hold the book for me until tomorrow. Hopefully I'll have enough money to come back and purchase it.

I walk out of the bookstore with Xavier heavy on my heart.

While sitting on the jitney, my thoughts drift back to a book I read To Be Young, Gifted and Black; Lorraine Hansberry in Her Own Words. But when I think of her a gray cloud hovers above my consciousness. She, too, died from pancreatic cancer at the age of thirty-five back in '65. How proud she must've felt to write her play "A Raisin in the Sun." I read about how she raised the money herself to stage her play at the Ethel Barrymore Theatre. How proud I feel to know that her play was the first drama by an African-American woman produced on Broadway. I smile, and then lean my head back against the synthetic fabric and dream of one day making a success before my demise. I know I failed with Anonymous, but I am undefeated because trial and error allows one to try, try again.

When I arrive home I decide to schedule to take the Registered Phlebotomy Technician test since I have been approved from the American Medical Technologist (AMT). I've scheduled and rescheduled it like twice already. Life was getting in my way and I kept allowing things to distract me. But now I'm ready. I'm moving forward no matter what the outcome.

I call Pearson VUE Call Center in Lyndhurst, New Jersey, and speak with a female representative to schedule my test. Yes, Avery, it is time to make some changes for the betterment of you, I think to myself. I love Xavier with every fiber in my being, but as he has said numerous times: "Avery, you come first." Finally, I'm able to see it too. Life is not guaranteed. Nothing for that matter is guaranteed. Not even time.

February 11th

"I lost thirty-two pounds." Xavier says in a voice of panic.

I cringe to the thought.

February 12th

"What do you want to do about us? Do you still want me?" I ask, dangling my head low, my fingers gripping the door on the passenger's-side of his SUV.

"The question is: 'Why would you want me?'" Xavier says in a low voice.

Tears burst from my eyes.

Does he think that I am that sha'low to only want him when he was healthier than he is now?

I shake my head. "Look, I'm not like these chicks out here. I'm different. I don't love you and leave you." I press my lips together, and then sigh. "That's not me."

Xavier gently wipes the tears that are running down my left eye. His eyes are teary, but he holds back his tears. It is an emotional moment. And honestly, I feel useless. But there is no way I am leaving him. He'll have to leave me first.

"Remember when you told me that the only way you'd leave me is if God calls." I say.

He nods, slightly cracks a smile.

"Well, knowing you as I do, the only way I'll find out if 'God' did call is if I read about it in the obituary section of the local newspaper." I tell him.

He remains quiet. And so, do I.

This is our reality, and I know I have to prepare myself because things don't look good. Either he'll survive or I'll lose him. Or he'll die, and I'll lose him. Either way, I'll lose again.

February 14th

12:02 A.M.

"I don't think I can do this." Xavier murmurs.

"Why?"

"I just don't think I can."

"Listen, you might not like what I'm about to say. So don't snap at me, but you don't have a choice. You have to keep on fighting. It's in you."

"All I think about is... how long..."

"Stop that. Think positive."

"How can I not think about it!" he snaps.

"Look, if you are able to, get out of that house. If your strength is up and you feel up to it go to the golf course. Hang out with your buddies. Just do the things you used to do. If you do these things you wouldn't be thinking about... how long. Being cooped up in the house is not helping you. How long...is all you're going to think about. I don't know what else to tell you because I'm not in your shoes. I'm going through some things, too, where I wish I could run as far away as possible, but I have to tough it out, too. We have to tough it out together. And that is exactly what we are going to do. Do you hear me?! You have two weeks to start chemo, right?"

"It might be sooner because they have to put the catheter in sometime this week."

"Good. Once you start chemo, get back to somewhat of a normal life; you'll be able to enjoy the things you like to do. Xavier, I get what you're saying. I do. I really do. Honey, try to relax your mind."

"I'm lying on the floor."

"Oh, I didn't know that you were on the floor. You don't have an air mattress you can lie on?"

"I'm laying on two-inches of carpet," he says.

"Oh."

We don't even bother to say, "Happy Valentine's Day" to one another. I guess it slipped our minds. And as it do, I feel Xavier is slipping further and further away from me.

22

THROUGH BLURRY VISION and bloodshot red eyes I view the colorful photograph of my beloved Xavier Combs III in the Obituary section of the HeraldNews. I feel such agony, such rage.

I lower my eyes clasp them shut. More tears stream from underneath the lids. God, it's like an unfathomable nightmare come true.

Index finger traces his distinguished-looking face. My eyes pierce his eyes. I raise the newspaper and press my lips against his lips. I touch his soft velvety hair remembering how it used to slip through my fingers—remembering his body scent of Dial body wash.

Eyes scroll down to the obituary, then widen, as I read the words in parentheses. *That bitch* is all I can think to say. *Why is she doing this to me? What? What have I done to her?*

SWOLL FUNERAL HOME, INC
Visitation: Monday, December 23, 2011
(11:00-12:00 p.m.)
Service: Monday, December 23, 2011
(12:00-1:00 p.m.)
Cemetery: Arlington Cemetery
Kearney, NJ
(PRIVATE SERVICE FOR FAMILY ONLY)

I blink, and then open my mouth wide. Screams bellow out, Whhhhhhyyyyyyyyyyyyyyyyyyyyy???!!! I stomp my feet down on the floor wishing it were her face. Grit and grind my teeth. *That bitch!*

Forehead crumples. Thoughts project louder and louder in my head. *No, no, no, no, no...JaVonna you're doing me a favor. I don't need to see Xavier as he is. I have fond memories of how he was. So, I say, "THANK YOU, JaVonna for sparing me the heartache of seeing him lying in that casket. Thank you for making this easier for me. I have Xavier in my heart. And bitch, you, you can never take that away from me! Never! Ever."*

I place my hands up to my face and sob so irrepressibly. I try to compose myself, calm myself down, but it is not easy to do. How vindictive! My head sways from side to side. *That conniving little skank bitch!*

After my breakdown I finally get a hold of myself. This has been the greatest loss my heart has ever endured. The pain is unspeakable. I feel a big part of me has died. My eyes open and gape at the ceiling, "Xavier, I am so deeply in love with you." I bow my head. God, I miss him soooo much. I can't even begin to fathom that he is truly dead. It all seems surreal. Even with seeing his picture. Not receiving a phone call. Not hearing his voice. Not seeing him smile. Lord knows he had such a winning smile.

I sniffle up the clear drool driveling from my nostrils before making its way to my parted lips.

Come out. Come out wherever you are. I wish I was courageous enough to say those very words, but the words won't release themselves freely from my mouth. My stomach bundles in knots—twists tighter and tighter like rope.

God, what are you trying to tell me? Talk to me, please.

Silence. I hear nothing but inaudible silence.

I bow my head, grief-stricken.

In that exact moment, my heart pleads. Professing, begging, dolefully I ask Him to listen to my soul eloquently speak.

I want to dive
Swim under crystal blue-green water
Come up for air with the taste of love on my tongue

I want to remember its essence
Preserve its existence
Crave it until my belly aches
I want to dream its scents
Inhale
Escape with its residue on my lips
Swipe my tongue across its heart and taste it
Again and again
Until the taste dissipates from my taste buds
Then and only then
Will I allow my tears to stream?
In the tranquil ocean of His soul
Then and only then
Will He see me in my purest form?

23

Lounge
Out
Poet's Café

WITH ALL THE STRENGTH left in me, I walk up onstage. If I don't say what is truly on my heart I never will. I can't keep bottling up my inner feelings because I'm worrying about what folks may say about me. At this point and time in my life it really shouldn't matter anymore. Karma kind of showed me that with her ghetto ways of doing things. I ain't mad at her 'cause that chick does what is necessary to get her point across. In other words, Karma lets it be known: Don't *fuck* wit' me if you can't handle the repercussions. Finally, it is all sinking in. I know she doesn't mean me any harm but sometimes she does get a little carried away. *Relax, shake the anxiety off, say what needs to be said, and leave.*

My state of being is to purge. To just let go of everything that hinders me. Tonight I feel the need to relinquish this grip that has been strangling me over the past few years. The thought of self-freedom seems so stimulating to the mind, but I wonder how it will make my body feel, my spirit feel? I don't know. I just don't know.

My eyes give an once-over to the audience as I see, an old school chum, Akil standing strong and proud. This gives me the support I need. I want to voice out what hurts. No, it's not my usual, but it feels more profound than anything I've ever recited.

I am the canvas and my words are a portrait of me. I hope they can appreciate and comprehend the validity of this verse.

I stare out at the crowd, and then say in a crackling voice into the mike, "This piece is called ..."REFLECTION.""

"I am more than ass, pussy and tits

375

"I am ears, eyes and lips
"I am pretty face and cinnamon skin
"Gates, locks, and knocks of pain
"Door of legs that open
"Reality spreading likes Hellmann's mayonnaise

"I am a hip curved to bone
"Tunnel, deep and long
"Lightening of uninvited storms
"Expose me
"Quiver that resides within me
"Blood streams crimson
"Mixed with bad cocktail
"That holds ounces of insecurities

"I am spit on tongue
"Colored 365
"Hidden 24/7
"Volatile
"Mood, temper, or desire
"Unfixable

"I am gift
"Unwanted
"Voice of neo-soul

"I am frigid, bitter cold
"4 seasons of 'Positive' woman
"Winter. Spring. Summer. Fall.

"I am Woman as the Face of Broken Silence."

I walk offstage with this piercing in my heart. It feels like someone has stuck a straight pin in it and I am bleeding out. Everyone is staring at me, but I don't appear to be disturbed by it. I exit out of the doors of my familiar, and step back out into a world of unpredictability.

24

I HAVE NO INTENTION of staying up to midnight to watch some friggin' ball drop. And I *especially* don't want to hear a crowd of folks yelling and screaming and hooting and hollering, "Happy New Year's!" What is there to be sooooo doggone happy about? *Hurray!* It's a new year, big damn deal.

Look. I'm hurting right now. The man I love is *dead*. DEAD! My parents are *dead*. My best friend in the whole wide world is *dead*. My estranged sister is *dead*. My nephew is *dead*. My ex companion is *dead*. Friends that I have grown to know and love are *dead*. Even my enemy is *dead*.

There is nothing left to get happy about for me. I have tried numerous times to look at life from a different perspective, but currently I can't see beyond demise. I'm blind. I can no longer see my purpose.

If God were to take me now I would gladly surrender. Because truthfully, this sistah is sooooo tired. I'm tired of trying to knock down that thick wall. I'm tired of being in the predicament that I'm in. I'm tired of reaching out and no one reaching back. I'm tired of loving those who do not love me. I scream in my head: I'M TIRED OF FUCKIN' LIVIN'! Do you hear what I am sayin'? God, can you hear me? Just cremate me and throw my ashes in the Passaic River with Teka Miller. Please. Just do it. I'm tired of livin'!

I lean back in my chair and breathe out hard. With my forefinger and thumb I pinch the inner corner of my crimson eyes to stop the tears from falling.

Stretched out on the chaise longue is Akil. I can't believe I completely blocked him out. I didn't realize that I had, but when I come to, there he is with his head leaned back and his eyes closed. I don't bother to wake him. I let 'im sleep.

I reach for the manuscript, *Ev'ry Ho Gotta Daddy* and soak my eyes in it. I need to escape from my own worries. Maybe Daisy's story is the medicine that my spirit so desperately needs.

I get up and walk over to my book shelf and reach for *Anonymous*. Flipping through the pages I come to the page when I first met Daisy's acquaintance. It takes me back to Red Alert.

"*Thank you for calling Red Alert Hotline Service, my name is Ariel. How may I help you?*"

"*You said your name is Ariel? What the hell kinda name is that, Ariel? Who's your mama so that I can slap her silly?*" *The vulgar woman says.*

"*Excuse me, ma'am?*"

"*Ma'am, damn you make me sound old as shit. Dammit, this is Daisy. Ya' hear me? I am thirty-five-years old. I got three children that I can't find. Do you know where they are?*" *she asks defiantly.*

"*Daisy, unfortunately I don't, but I bet they are good children.*"

"*Well, Ariel, if you should see 'em tell 'em they momma say she love 'em.*"

"*I will Daisy.*"

Daisy yells out to someone named Jessie.

"*Jessie! Jessie, where are you going with my beer? You think you slick trying to sneak behind my back and drink all my fuckin' beer. I bought this beer with my damn money. Hand me a cigarette!*"

"*Ariel, are you there?*" *Daisy asks.*

"*Yes, I'm here, Daisy.*"

"*Yeah, I'm gonna sleep good tonight. Ariel, you know my children?*"

"*Daisy, I'm sorry I haven't had the pleasure of meeting them.*"

"*Yeah, someone came and took 'em because I was high. I left 'em in the house by 'emselves for a week. I was flying high smoking crack. I was chillin'. Damn babies were home hungry many times while I's out tricking. Gotten beaten pretty bad from some of my clients. And my pimp, huh, he almost killed me leaving me sprawled out on the ground in the back of the Rainbow Motel. Not once, but several times 'cause I didn't make 'nough money for his muthafucken pockets. Ain't that some shit? It was my pussy! Ariel, he whooped my ass 'cause I didn't have 'nough clients or 'cause he was in a bad mood and wanted to fuck with somebody. Sometimes I would only make $10.00, $15.00, or $20.00 dollars per dick. The lowest was $5.00 and I had to be pretty desperate to spread my legs for $5.00 bucks. But I did. Wha' the fuck. Ariel, hold on for a minute?*"

"*Jessie! Where the hell is the rest of my beer! Ariel, you know what I am so damn tired. Body wore the fuck out by being turned out by these worthless muthafuckers poking my shit all out of shape. I used to be pretty white bitch. I used to catch a man at a drop of a dime. I had legs to die for like Tina Turner. I had a good job and got mixed up with the wrong crowd. I started skipping work, staying out late on the weekdays when my children needed me the most, and got hooked on damn crack. I was messed up* pretty bad, but after four or five years of suffering I got into a Narcotics Anonymous NA program, but after a few weeks I messed that up 'cause didn't let the program get me. I was too busy tryna get it. I got got. I relapsed. Uh-huh. I craved crack like it was dick. I was obsessed with it. Damn near sprinting to 12th Ave, Alabama Projects, Governor Street, and 10th Ave. Fuck my children! Fuck me! That's what I said to myself as I was staggerin' from block to block. I said it so much that I believed it. Just sellin' my soul to the devil like it was nothin'. Shit. If I wanted to get high I got high. Next thing you know, I lost my job, been evicted a couple times, and I was living single after my funds ran low. Then I started working the corners of Broadway. My children used to look up to me. Now they probably won't even look at me, let alone recognize me. I'm not the same person I used to be and I am ashamed to even look at my own reflection. I'm paying the price living with AIDS. Ariel, I'm drying up like a damn prune, but Jessie doesn't seem to mind. He says that I am sexy in his eyes."

Rae and I look at each other because Daisy is no joke. She knows that she has messed up badly, but never in the conversation did she say that she was trying to get her life together to possibly get her children back. I don't feel empathy for Daisy, but I do admire the fact that she's honest about her lifestyle. She doesn't blame it on anyone else. I wonder how her children are doing, coping with the fact of having an addict for a mom. Let alone a mom who is infected with AIDS. It is heart wrenching, I'm sure.

"Ariel, are you there?" Daisy asks.

"Yes, Daisy."

"Yeah, you saw my children?"

"Unfortunately, Daisy I haven't."

"Well, if you should let 'em know that I'm sorry."

"Daisy, I will."

Daisy sounds so sincere and it makes me swallow and feel a slight lump in my throat. Rae's eyes become watery and she puts Daisy on mute. She grabs one of her tissues out of her box, dabs her eyes, and returns back to the phone. It is difficult for me listening to this one call. Daisy seems both ill mentally and physically, but through all that she has endured she still has not forgotten about her children. She is an unfit mom, but she's still a mom who cares immensely for her children.

Rae completes the call with a perplexing look on her face. It's possible that after every call she analyzes the circumstance and it troubles her deeply. Women losing their children for a three minute high. Torturing their bodies allowing anyone to enter them And when their job is finished, they clean themselves up, and go back out there to repeat the same thing for possibly twenty dollars or less. Damn, is it worth it? I wanted so badly to ask Daisy that one question, but I knew I couldn't. There are creases

379

forming on my forehead because it's so disturbing. Obviously she feels regret, but she's a junky and that sickness won't allow her to stop. For some reason, I see Daisy as a motivational speaker. She's telling it like it is and she doesn't give a damn if you get it or not. She speaks her piece.

I come to.

Sit back down and reenter back into Daisy's world. *What a life to have lived,* I think. I sit still for a few minutes to take it all in. Daisy's story...it has so many layers that so many folks can and cannot relate to.

Lord knows I know how it feels to want to be wanted and be rejected. I know how it feels to love and be rejected. I know how it feels to hurt and be surrounded by no one, but my shadow. Lately, huh, I find myself holding myself up, hugging myself, and wiping away my own tears. Yeah. It's tough. It really makes you thankful for the life that you have. My life isn't all chocolate and strawberries and I love you's, but it's still a life.

I wish there was more that I could do to express my gratitude to Daisy.

I take a minute to think.

Then this light bulb goes off in my head.

Akil rouses out of his catnap. He yawns loudly, stretches his body to get the kinks out and wipes the drool from the crease of his mouth. "I see you've come back to earth, Av," he says in a sleepy voice.

"I'm sorry. I-I just got caught up."

"Girl, stop trippin'. You know you're taking a huge risk with this book. Think about it. This is the beginning of your writing career. Honestly, do you want your career to end before you get it fully off the ground?"

"I know." I shake my head. "No, I don't want it to end, but I feel like this is what I have to do."

Whoever sent me this manuscript, apparently wanted it to be done this way. I can't just go against someone's wishes to benefit myself. I just can't do it. This is how she wrote it. Who am I to just take liberties that are not mine to take? This is her voice, her life, and her pain, not mine. I'm just a messenger.

I cut my eyes over at Akil and lean back in the chair. "Akil, it really doesn't matter." I pause. "Tell me something. Um, have you ever felt like you were put on this earth for a purpose?"

Akil sits upright on the chaise longue and crosses his right leg over his left. "Every day. Look at *me.* I'm a teacher. Who would've thought?

Me. A teacher. You gotta point." He uncrosses his legs. "I gotta give it to you; you're sticking to your guns. Most people would just give in to make it to the *New York Times* best-sellers list."

I lower my eyes and sift through the printed sheets of paper. I shrug my shoulders, eyes still glued to the sheets. "Yeah, I know. I guess I'm just different, huh?"

"That you are. It's refreshing to see. You wouldn't be you if you tried to change just to satisfy others. Ms. Avery Love; continue to be true to yourself. I find it very attractive."

My head rises and my eyes meet Akil's as I look him directly in his handsome face. "Really?"

"Sure. Not only do you have brains, beauty, but you also possess a good spirit. I don't know about any other man, but that's certainly attractive to me."

"You know what, Akil that means a lot coming from you."

We both smile.

Akil changes the subject. "Are you performing at Lounge Out, tonight?"

I twist up my lips. "I dunno. I haven't written any new material lately."

My cell phone rings.

"Hold that thought." I tell Akil.

I reach over near the printer and pickup my iPhone that Xavier bought me.

"Hello?"

"What's up stranger?"

I don't recognize the male voice.

"Who's calling?" I say.

"What you've made it to the big time and forgotten about the little people? It's Jordan, Avery."

"Oh... my...God!" I smile with my eyes. "How...how have you been?"

"Good. Can't complain. I saw you performing at Lounge Out last week. You look good, girl. I started to say something to you, but I thought against it since I wasn't alone. I didn't want to ruin your night. I figured I'd call first. I wasn't sure if your number was the same. I figured I'd give it a try."

"Smart move," I say, as my teeth bite down on the inner wall of my mouth.

He laughs, loudly. God, I miss hearing his laugh.

I cut my eyes over to Akil.

He's staring at me.

Let me get off this phone.

"Listen, Jordan, I'm actually in the middle of something. Can I call you back? Maybe we can do lunch or something."

"Sure, Av."

"Talk to you soon, okay."

"Bye."

I "end" the call. And then place my iPhone back by the printer.

Akil makes this annoying scratchy sound like there is something caught in his throat to get my attention. I just look at him. I guess he's waiting for me to volunteer some information about who Jordan is. That's not going to happen. I'm keeping Jordan Seymour all to myself.

"Now what were you saying, Akil?"

"I was saying that I'm sure you can think of something—all of this madness out in the streets. C'mon, you got something percolating in that head of yours to perform."

I smirk.

Akil is right. I do have something percolating but I don't want to talk about it or think about it. If anything, I want to forget it ever happened.

"I'll see what I can come up with. I take it you'll be going tonight." I say.

"Yep. So get to writing. I want to see my favorite poet onstage doing what she loves. You know you're going to make it, don't you."

I lay the manuscript down on my lap and look in outer space. "I feel like I am."

"You will." Akil assures, "Don't ever stop dreaming. And never stop pursuing what your heart tells you to. It's destined to happen for you. I feel it. It's coming. This year, it's coming."

My eyes meet Akil's. "You know you are really good for my ego."

He smiles. "What are friends for? Look, the way I see it, you make it. I make it."

I lean my head back and chuckle. "How so?"

"We have something in common, Avery. Something you know nothing about."

"Entertain me, why don't you?" I say.

"When the time is right, sweetie, I will. I most definitely will." He pauses. "You know we should checkout this spot called CHURCH."

"CHURCH?" I scrunch up my nose. "What kind of place is that?" I ask him.

He laughs.

"Is it a restaurant, bar...?" I ask.

"No. It's a strip club, but I think you'll like it because it's something different." He says.

I frown. "Different...how?"

"There is no drama. Most of the women are dancers so they don't have time for the b.s. I go maybe twice a week. You should come with me tomorrow. What'd you say?"

I hesitate in answering. I have never been to a strip club before.

"I don't know, Akil. That might not be my thing, you know."

"Well, you won't know if it is or not until you actually go to one."

He has a point.

"Girl, why you so doggone stiff? Loosen up. Go and see how the other half live. It can't hurt," Karma says in a voice of optimism.

"Okay, I'm game."

Akil's eyes light up. "Yeah!"

"Yeah!" I smile.

Akil stands to his feet. "Listen, I have some errands to run. I'll get up with you later, okay."

"Okay." I walk him to the door.

After I shut the door, I head into the bathroom. Peel off my layers of funk. Turn the nozzle to the shower on until the water gets lukewarm. I reach for the Colgate mint toothpaste and my electric blue toothbrush and brush my teeth. Then rinse my mouth out with Listerine. Kneel down underneath the sink and reach for the block of almond milk and honey soap, stand, then step inside the bathtub.

8:45 P.M.

RING. RING. RING.

My fingers fumble to pick it up my celluar lying beside me.

"Hello." I say in a sleepy voice.

"I thought you were coming, Av." Akil says.

"Coming...where?"

"Lounge Out, remember?"

"Oh, I guess I fell asleep. I'll have to do it next Thursday, sorry. I've been reading the manuscript all night."

"Okay, well, go back to sleep."

"Bye."

I "end" the call, roll over on my back, and gaze at the ceiling thinking about my life, and Xavier.

I feel achy all over my body. Cough. Sneeze. And when I talk I sound nasally. Dang. I'm sick again. I'd just gone to see Dr. Fulmore maybe a week and a half ago. He prescribed me some antibiotics (the kind you take for 5 days) and cough syrup. Dang. I was back to myself again. And now I'm sick.

Ah-coo!!!! AH-coo! AH-COOOOOO!!

I reach over on the nightstand and snatch a Kleenex out of its box and blow my nose. It sounds like a bugle. I pull apart the thin tissue and stare at it. Yellow mucus clings to it. *Yuck.* This nasty tasting saliva fills my mouth. Soreness swells in my throat as I swallow. My forehead feels clammy; eyes glossy, watery, yellowish and itchy. I feel like crap.

I sniff feeling as though I am inhaling dry air. The edges around my nose are already forming raw skin, which means in the morning it will be hard and scaly-looking. That's just great. I frown.

I don't even have the energy to go get my 'do done. I need a fresh cut, but walking around with a baldy right about now ain't a good look. I can't get that off being sick like this. I'll wait to call Sha.

My eyes shift over toward the nightstand as I stare at the near empty bottle of Tylenol Cold & Flu Severe Honey Lemon. There is less than half of a teaspoon of orange liquid floating at the bottom of its plastic container. And I still have the six-flow ounce of maximum strength Mucinex is set by the night lamp, unopened.

I went crazy at CVS trying to find the right medication to help me get better, sooner. I have a lot of work to do, but unfortunately I am detained by this friggin' cold.

If neither of these works, I guess I'll be back in Dr. Fulmore's office for another prescription. Or he could just call Clyde's Pharmacy for a refill of the antibiotics. Hopefully, I won't have to go there.

Dr. Fulmore can be a bit nerve racking at times. And so can Mr. Clyde. I mean both cares immensely for me, and I am glad, but sometimes they get a little too paranoid. And when that paranoia kicks in is when Dr. Fulmore wants to run all these different tests on me or send me for MRI's and whatnot. He'll have Violet calling me every hour. And Mr. Clyde would want to damn near take me home and care for me himself. Before I go through that I will try to self medicate myself.

Shaking my head no, no, I am not overreacting.

Look. The last time I stepped foot in Dr. Fulmore's office I had to reassure him that it was nothing but a bug I had caught. I understood his concern, though. But my CD4 count was normal (above 500) which meant my immune system was strong. But if the number of CD4 cells in those pea size drops of blood ever drops below 200 CD4 cells, I'll be classified as having AIDS. My immune system will no longer be strong enough to prevent illness and infection. I don't even want to think about that. That is the reason why I stay on top of the little things before they turn into bigger things.

I feel really blessed to have Dr. Fulmore. I know that he was just looking out for me. Making sure my health remained in good standings. I gotta love him for that.

Along the edge of the nightstand sits my violet-blue mug that was once full to the brim of Celestial honey lemon zinger tea. The teabag and sliced lemon are dried out and stuck to the bottom of the cup. I guess I'll get to wash it later, once I get control of this coughing.

My neighbor, Mr. Vincent heard me coughing and sniffling on the elevator the other day and suggested that I drink a hot cup of salt. I nodded to his suggestion. Poppa used to do that. He'd put about three good pinches of Iodine salt into his mug and pour searing hot water over it, and sip until the mug was empty. Three pinches was a decent amount considering Poppa had some big hands. Come to think of it, I do have some sea salt; maybe I'll use that.

A rumbling in the jungle is sounding off. I don't have an appetite ever since I got this cold. I've been nibbling on these Club buttery garlic crackers. I don't have any energy to cook. And plus, with these taste buds everything tastes yucky.

I have two cans of Campbell's Chicken Noodle soup in the cupboards. Poppa used to say: "You can't go wrong with chicken noodle soup."

I feel a sneeze coming, but instead I cough again. I lift both dry hands and rub my closed eyelids in a circular motion. I feel miserable. My body feels hot, then cold, then warm, then sweaty. I sniffle in more dry air. Then cough. All I hear is a rattling in my chest. Phlegm buildup. Dang.

I reach for the bottle of Mucinex and untwist the white cap. I know I have to drink plenty of water. I also should try to eat something. It's bad to take medication on an empty stomach. I know. I know.

I need to get up and use the bathroom. This is the *fourth* time. How many times am I going to do number two, today? I mean I haven't eaten much. Oh, yeah, that's right. It could be backed up from days ago. I learned that in my phlebotomy class.

My cellular rings.

"Hello." I say all nasally.

"Tell me you... do... not.... have... a cold?" Akil sounds a bit disappointed. "Boy, don't we sound lovely. I guess this cancels CHURCH, huh?"

"Not in the mood, Akil."

"Grumpy aren't we." He laughs.

"Not in the mood, Akil."

"S-o-r-r-y."

"I'm sick."

"Again?"

"Yep."

"Is it that love sickness again?"

"Nope. I have a cold."

"You sound like you can barely breathe, honey. You need me to bring you anything...possibly a handsome hot-blooded man. I don't mind slipping one under the door for you." He laughs.

"Funny. Ha! Ha! Maybe some Progresso chicken noodle soup, if it's not too much trouble."

"Well, I'm not driving my ride. I'm hanging out with my boy Jerome. Listen, I'll see if he won't mind dropping it off, okay."

Jerome. Oh, God. That broke and confused drama queen.

"Call before you come." I tell him.

"Why? You have company or someone special coming over that you don't want me to see?"

"No, Akil. I was just going to meet you in the lobby so that you wouldn't have to come upstairs."

"Oh."

"Bye." I say, then "end" the call.

After I get off the phone with Akil I have this impulse to call this tall, good-looking fellah I met at Lounge Out Poets Café named Frederick...something. For some reason I can't remember his last name. It'll come to me later. Well, I think against it. I don't think I'm ready to start talking to someone new even on a platonic level. Something as innocent as a phone call can easily get misconstrued for something else. These days you have to be careful whom you call, invite in your space, in your house, in your heart, in your bed.

A few minutes later, I hear that nut Akil yelling for me from out in the hallway. He can be so doggone ghetto sometimes. I laugh it off, because he is looking out for me by bringing me medicine. I go and answer the door. "What nut?" Akil laughs, then hands me the brown paper bag, I say thank you, and then shut the door. Hopefully come morning, I'll feel like my old self again.

Morning is upon. I get out of bed feeling a little better, but not one hundred percent me. I make my way downstairs and sit on the sofa staring at Sis pondering over what to do about this book situation. I need money in order to get this book out. So that means I need a jay-o-bee.

I warm-up Sis, then I type in: Google and click on the link for employement opportunities at a few retail stores. I just need an easy hustle, nothing too complex or strenuous. I need most of my mental energy for writing this book.

After surfing the web for close to an hour I come across a women's apparel store, ECLECTIC in Paramus, New Jersey, that is hiring. So I fill out the online application and upload my résumé.

A week later I receive a call from a Spanish-speaking woman named Lizzy.

"Hello?"

"Hola, may I speak to Avey Love, please?"

"Speaking..."

"This is Lizzy from ECLECTIC. You filled out an application and I was wodering if you are still intereted in a position here?"

"Yes."

"I jus' need to ax you some questions."

"Okay."

"What is you availability?"

"I'm flexible."

"Do you have a probem workin' after store hours? The store closes at ten, Monday through Friday, but on Saturday we close at eleven, which means we won't leave until after the store is cleaned up. Will that be a problem for you?"

"No."

"Have you ever worked in retail before?"

"Doesn't she have my application and résumé in front of her," I say to myself.

"I used to own my own business so I have an idea of what you're looking for." I tell her.

"Oh yes, I do see that on your application. Anonymous, right?" she asks.

"Correct."

"Well, we are scheduling group interviews for ah, the tenth. Are you available to come in?"

"Sure."

"Okay, Avey, I'll see you on the tenth. Bring two forms of ID with you. Take the escalator upstairs to the Customer Service station and tell the girl that you are here for the group interview, okay."

"Sure."

"Goodbye, Avey."

"Goodbye."

25

GOOD LAWD, IT FEELS LIKE eighteen degrees outside. Thin sheets of ice layer the asphalt as I exit out of ECLECTIC. I carefully look down at my boots as I make my way through the parking lot toward the bus stop near the overpath hoping not to fall on my behind and completely embarrass myself.

Fine rain comes trickling down. It's that cold rain too. The kind that makes your bones shivers in your skin. I tuck in my plaid angora scarf around my neck and bundle up in my full-length camel wool coat with matching knit hat and chocolate brown leather gloves as I wait for the jitney to pull up. I am freezing.

Ten minutes pass when the jitney finally pulls up. *I hope it has heat.* I think to myself as I fall in line with the others.

The cold air blows in my face making me sniffle as I enter the jitney and hand the Hispanic man my two-dollar bus fare. I sit next to the last row near the window and gaze out deep in thought.

I exit off the bus at 6:02 p m., and walk the six blocks home as the howling wind bellows in my ears. My eyes run. I sniffle again.

I enter my studio 6:45 p.m., immediately kick off my boots, unravel my angora scarf, unbutton my coat, snatch off my hat, and peel off my gloves and hang 'em on the coat hook.

I press the "On" button to the heater to take the chill off. Before I head into the bathroom to take a hot shower I turn on the kitchenette light to see if the pack of lamb chops I took out this mornin' thawed. They are.

I enter the bathroom and check to make sure my nightshirt is hangin' on the hook on the back of the door.

I get undressed. Then reach in for the nozzle and turn the shower on. The hot water steams up like a misty fog. I step in the shower and reach atop the shower rack for my washcloth and begin to lather myself with the bar of almond milk and honey soap.

The hard, lukewarm water feels so good against my skin. As I am rinsing off, I think I hear my cell phone ringing. I jump out of the shower, don't bother to wrap a towel around my nudeness and run to answer it.

The caller hangs up as I am saying hello. I "end" the call and return back to the bathroom.

I towel dry myself, and then pull over the nightshirt. Don't bother to put any panties on. My coochie needs to breathe.

I check my cellular to see if there is a voicemail. There is. Danell called. Yes, you heard me right. Danell Owens. Yep. The same Danell who kissed me. Uh-huh. I saw her at the fish market downtown. We got to talking and decided to squash all of that silliness. JaVonna was out of the picture, so we really had no one interfering in our friendship. That was, if we really wanted to be friends. I had no issues with Danell, other than the kiss, but I have since put that behind me. She's a beautiful person, and beautiful people are pretty damn hard to come by these days. So here we are friends again. I do wonder what she wants this time of day. Normally she'd still be at the hospital wiping butts or catering to the needs of the ill. That chile sho' hates her job as nurse's aide; I can't very well blame her 'cause just the smell of sickness makes me want to puke. I don't have the stomach to work in that type of environment, but Danell was in a predicament with her business. And plus, with the economy as it is, she had no choice but to take on a second job.

"I'll call Danell in a few." I say to myself.

I prep my lamb chops and season 'em good and place 'em in cast-iron skillet with a thick sliver of butter. Cut up one Idaho potato in cubes, add a little butter, salt and pepper for taste and dump 'em in a small pot, add some water, and let 'em slow cook.

I reach for my cell phone and call Danell back.

Ring. Ring.

"Hi, girl," I say in a tiresome tone of voice.

"You must've just gotten home from work, Av," says Danell.

"Yeah, chile, it's been a day. Why are you home so early?"

"I called out today. Didn't feel like seeing that place. I needed a break. Did you get my message?"

"No. I didn't bother to listen to it. I just picked up the phone and called you back. What's up?"

Danell briefly pauses.

"Danell, girl, you still there, is everything okay?"

"Yeah, girl, I'm here. Everything is good. Lemme ask you something, how are you *really* doing? Don't get me wrong, you've been holding up pretty damn well since Xavier has been gone. I know it's been difficult, but you've come a long way. You seem a little blue lately. I don't mean to pry but I hate to see you so sad and selling yourself short. With Xavier your face just lit up the way you used to talk about that man. God, I wished I had had the opportunity to meet him. Avery, you were so happy, so very much in love. I could see it on your face every time you talked about him. You just didn't seem the same with Zaelyn. That's all I'm tryna say. Maybe you two weren't meant to be, you know. Maybe you need to *now* just do Avery, at least until someone worthy comes along."

"I'm alright. I could be better though. But I'm making it, you know, trying to get back on course. I have a lot of catching up to do. What s really up, Nell? What are you *not* saying to me?"

Danell pauses again. I can hear her breathing heavily into the phone.

"You're scaring me. Is everything okay, Nell? Talk to me."

"Have you ever read one of BLAB magazines?"

I scrape my top teeth against my bottom lip.

"What are you talking about?" I ask with a befuddled look upon my face.

Danell stammers. "I-I-I..."

"Talk, Nell, tell me what's going on?"

"You really don't know, do you?"

"Know what?"

"Well, girl, I hope you still have your kickboxing shoes. I suggest you get to reading. That uncle of mine is a trip. He's blaming you for his business failing as well as his marriage. He needed money so he contacted Narlena Scott to badmouth you."

I press my lips together. "How bad?" I ask.

Danell's voice softens. "Call me back. I'm here for you, okay."

I cock my head to the side, and then twist my lips. "Yeah."

I "end" the call, take a few deep breaths, and then head back into the kitchenette. I reach for the stainless steel tongs and turn the lamp chops over so that the other side can get golden brown.

The curiosity is killing me. Why did Danell say she still hopes I have my kickboxing shoes? Exactly what did Zaelyn say? I wonder.

My forefinger shakes as I reach in to touch the screen on my iPhone and download the attachment.

As I press OPEN, I feel my pulse rising. My eyes scroll down the screen and my mouth makes an O formation as I read the headline.

BLAB

MAGAZINE
"Where we SCOOP your GOSSIP JUICE"

"Jus' a Hoochie
with a
Wanderin' Coochie"

by
Narlena Scott
Editor-in-Chief

BLAB: "Let's talk a little bit about your affair with Avery Love. I mean you were married at the time, correct?"

ZAELYN: "Okay. And yes, ma'am, um, my wife and I were separated at the time that I met Avery."

BLAB: "How long did you two date?"

ZAELYN: "Not long at all. I had recently relocated and wasn't really looking to get into a relationship. I felt somewhat pressured into it. Ah, Avery was very persuasive. She knew how to treat a man like a king. A man could get quite comfortable with a woman with such manipulating powers."

BLAB: "Hmm. Manipulating powers? Is it possible that her energy was just that inviting? Um, perhaps she had/has a nurturing spirit. One that was/is sincere in treating men well. You know women can go through life being dogged by men and still retain that inner woman who won't allow herself to treat others as she had been treated. Possibly Avery was one of those women. You might've had someone very, very special and didn't even know it. Where did you two meet? Was this love at first sight?"

ZAELYN: "Yes. Manipulating powers. I dunno 'bout her having a nurturing spirit. All I know is she knew how to cater to my needs. She'd cook. She'd clean. She'd fuck the shit outta me. Um, she'd do any and everything possible to keep me satisfied, and she did it very, very well. But she had to really work on herself. You know, clean herself up and stop the drugs. I couldn't and wouldn't deal with her under any other circumstances. But she did the work. She really got herself together. She got into an NA program. Ah, she got herself a sponsor. She was doing really well. After seeing that she really wanted us to work I found myself being drawn to her. And eventually I wanted the relationship too. Where did we meet? Well, that's kind of an interesting story. Avery and I met at a supermarket. She was panhandling to get money for I can only assume…drugs. A brotha' has a kind heart so I offered her some change. I just hate to see my 'sistahs' selling themselves short like that when all it takes is a little polishing, primping, and know-how of utilizing those hustling skills and applying 'em to finding a job. As far as if it was love at first sight. Naw, it wasn't for me. I can't speak for her. I was full of ambition. Avery was more of a slow pace type of chick. Everything with her required a plan. Everything had to map out. I was a chaser. She, she was still trying to figure hers out. We clashed in that aspect of the relationship. Not to mention she was a slacker. She'd never complete a task. I saw that as a negative. I saw myself progressing while she was still at the starting line trying to catch-up. It was stressful. I got tired of trying to boost her confidence. And providing for the household was a strain too. I could only do so much. She wasn't pulling her weight. It put a wedge between us. Near the end I wanted more than I wanted or needed her. She became a doormat that no longer said: Welcome."

BLAB: "So it sounds like she was a burden of some sort. Is that how you saw it?"

ZAELYN: "Exactly. I was on a different path and I wanted and needed a woman who was in sync with me. I had a thriving business, whereas Avery wasn't even working one job but was steady complaining about what she didn't have. I think she was envious of me—of the fact that I was driven. I intimidated her. I mean look at me, listen to the way I speak, the way I carry myself. Avery could use some polishing to keep up with a well-rounded man like myself."

BLAB: "Wow! That's serious. Then what was the attraction?"

ZAELYN: "To the naked eye Avery is a gorgeous forty-something year old woman. But behind closed doors, with her clothes off it is a whole different saga. It is no longer a mystery, more like a horror flick."

BLAB: "Ouch!"

ZAELYN: "Tell me 'bout it. That's all I used to hear while having sex with her. She'd claim that I was too well endowed—that she couldn't handle what I had to offer her in bed. During sex she'd wince, or cry, or squint, that shit is not sexy while you're at the peak of climaxing. Not sexy at all."

BLAB: "How often did you two have sex? Were you ever in love with her?"

ZAELYN: "Well, if you're talkin' good sex. I had to get her high and drunk to have good sex with her. And that was probably three times a week (with protection)."

BLAB: "Wait a minute! I thought you said she was in an NA program. She had a sponsor. She was getting herself together. Then you say that in order for you to have good sex with her that you'd get her high and drunk. So you had her relapse to satisfy your sexual needs, is that correct in saying?"

ZAELYN: "Yeah, that's correct. If not, she'd just lie there. I tried. I'd eat her out, suck her nipples and tits, finger-fuck her, whatever it took, but she didn't reciprocate. Yeah. I did have her relapse because I didn't wanna have to go out and buy the pussy. Why do that when I had some pussy at home. I knew what I had at home. And I knew how she used to get down. I just had to bring it out of her with booze and weed. I mean without the booze and weed she'd give me no foreplay. She wouldn't suck my dick. She did nothing to arouse me. I mean it got to the point where I didn't even want it anymore. I was completely turned off by the sight of her naked. As far as being in love with her and having love for her, it was two different things. I had love for her because she was a nice person, but as far as being in love with her, naw, I was never in love with her."

BLAB: "Did you ever cheat on her?"

ZAELYN: "Naw. I just took a lot of cold showers and watched me some porn and beat my dick."

BLAB: "Oooookkkkaaaayyyy. Do you think she cheated on you?"

ZAELYN: "Oh, I know she did. She was jus' a hoochie with a wanderin' coochie. I caught her in the act with my boy giving him a blowjob."

BLAB: "Really? But she wouldn't suck your dick. Hmm. How did that make you feel?"

ZAELYN: "I wasn't mad. At least I found out early in the game."

BLAB: "Soooooooo, you'd never consider reconciling?"

ZAELYN: "Naw. That's a book I don't care to read a second go-around. The first time I read it I thought it was going to be a best-seller, but then I realized that it would have never made it to the best-sellers list because it was poorly written with no character development or plot. It had no substance. And plus, she got issues. She's a liar. And, and, and...."

BLAB: "Don't stammer now, Zaelyn. Spill the beans."

ZAELYN: "Well, I'm not one to put people's personal business out there, but Avery got that shit."

BLAB: "What, shit?"

ZAELYN: "The Package."

BLAB: "And how would you know this? Inquiring minds are dying to know."

ZAELYN: "I did some digging. Come to find out she been trickin' wit' the virus for a while now. I feel sorry for the next man that gets a piece of that ass. Of course all of this new information came 'bout after the fact of us having sex. I couldn't believe how foul a scorned woman could be. Why didn't she care enough to inform me? You know, give me an option. Naw. Not her. She's angry at the world and took her anger out on me. I dodged that bullet by wearing a condom. Boy, I tell you. God is good."

BLAB: "So are you saying that Avery is out spreading the virus? Is she having unprotected sex?"

ZAELYN: "Yeah. All I got to say to the jokers who come in contact with her: Run, nigga! The bitch is trickin' wit' the virus."

BLAB: "Oooooh, that's a bit much to chew and swallow. I hate to be [Avery] right about now. On a more serious note, would it upset you if Avery told her side of the story? I mean with you just putting her out there in BLAB this becomes a serious topic for America. I'm sure the public would want to know her side, from her own perspective."

ZAELYN: "Naw, not at all. Everything I've said I can back up."

BLAB: "Are you currently dating anyone special? Have you used that experience with Avery as a choice to get tested annually?"

ZAELYN: "Oh, I have someone on my radar, but I haven't made any moves. I'm kind of leaned back observing her from afar. And yes, I have used that as a reason to get tested. Undetected is serious business."

BLAB: "Well, well. When you are ready to let the cat out of the bag as to who she is, remember to call **BLAB** and give us the scoop first."

ZAELYN: "Will do."

After reading this shit, I blink, three times 'cause I can't believe this jerk is telling all these lies on me like this!

Hot steam is bursting from my ears. Eyes fill of fury. That bastard! How could he! How could he purposely put my personal business out in the streets like this?! Why would he do this to me? Does he hate me that much? Obviously.

Tears well up in my eyes, I am stunned by his accusations. So *he* says he was *never* in love with me, huh? *Ain't this a blip!* So he says that I was a panhandler, huh? So he says that I was a *horror flick,* huh? *A hoochie with a wanderin' coochie...*out here *spreading the virus.* So, basically he's calling me a *hoe, junky and an alcoholic.* Hmm. *Ain't this some shit!*

I bite down hard on my bottom lip, while pacing the floor.

I think to myself, taking the easy way out would be to sue him and BLAB magazine. But I'm not going to take the easy approach. I know. Folks may think I'm stupid—that I should seek retribution. Reparation. But no. Since the cat is out of the bag, I'm going to use this as an opportunity to reach those who are hibernating behind closed doors afraid to live their lives. I'm going to use this opportunity to reach out to the young girls who are promiscuous—to the men and women who are incarcerated, temporarily residing in halfway houses and shelters—to those who are sleeping on the streets and in abandoned buildings. I am going to build a platform and tell my story in hopes to save others. I am going to hug these streets in hopes of hugging these women who don't know who love is or how to even love themselves enough to stop and look at what they are doing to themselves. If I have to portray the role of: mother, sister, aunt, then that's what I'll do. I'll do whatever it takes to prevent unnecessary anguish. I'll do whatever it takes to get the right information out there. And I won't stop just here, no, I'll step out of my comfort zone and spread the message as far as my feet will take me. I'll do it. And after I do it I'll make it my business to thank Zaelyn personally. I'll let him know that he didn't break me, if anything he encouraged me to break out of my shell.

I walk into the kitchenette and open the fridge and reach for a bottle of seltzer water. I twist off the cap, tilt my head back and quench my thirst with a long swig.

The thought of all of this happening is really disturbing. I never thought it'll come to this between Zaelyn and I. Things ended so amicably between us. After I wrote him that letter I never heard from him again. And I was cool with that. Often I thought of him but I never attempted to reach him. I just let everything end on a good note. But now this, this tells me that he was already angry with me. I gave him options and he chose the one that he thought was best. I didn't force myself on him. He gladly came to me. And I didn't refuse him because I wanted him. I wanted him so badly, but not this badly. Not to be going through this. It makes me wonder how deep his pain runs. Is it so deep that he feels the need to destroy my life? Doesn't he know that I've already been down this road? Yes, he knows, because I was the one who told him. He asked and I told him the truth, as painful as it was to talk about I shared it all with him. So why, why hurt me in this manner? Why tell the world in this way?

26

WEDNESDAY, it comes too quickly.

I rise from my bed and head straight downstairs in my nightgown to the bathroom to take a quick shower. Daisy's service is from ten to twelve today. I figure I'd go early and say my farewells. I don't have to be to work 'til five o'clock.

After my shower I head upstairs to my bedroom. I walk to my closet and slide the door open. I pull out my black sleeveless dress and olive-green J. Crew blazer. I glance over to my dresser and think to wear my pearl necktie necklace and bone-colored earrings that look like ribbons dangling from my ears. My eyes scan my shoes so I reach down and pick up my Steven by Steve Madden gold mules. I walk over to my dresser and open the drawer for a pair of panties and a lace brassier. I get dress. Then I take a few minutes to add on my makeup. Open my three dollar bottle of Midnight Fantasy oil and dab about my neck and behind my ears. I reach for my cellular and call a Yellow cab to take me to the funeral parlor on Rosa Parks.

As I enter JESUS LOVES ME FUNERAL HOME there are already a slew of folks sitting down. I nod my head to greet a man standing in the entranceway way talking to a Muslim woman. They both acknowledge me as I make my way to sign the book to the far right of the room.

A few heads turn, probably wondering who the heck I am. I try to keep a pleasant look upon my face. But deep down I feel a bit uneasy and queasy. Funerals and me not a good combination, but I'm here now. I might as well stay.

My breathing is silently erratic. God I pray I don't have a panic attack. That will be so embarrassing, especially since I don't know a soul in here.

The room has a soft breeze like a light whisper in ones ear. The carpet underneath my mules is of plush thick faded bluish-gray.

Thirteen tan leather chairs align crossways in a row. There are four chairs in a light mauve color to the right of the room with two end tables and two lamps with two boxes of Kleenex on them.

The lights are dim lit so it gives a spine-chilling feel.

As I turn there is a picture of Rosa Parks by Paul Collins hanging on the wall framed in an elegant gold frame. The sign-in book is a couple of feet away with scribbled names and addresses in blue and black ink of those who'd come to pay their respects. Muffling voices chatter as the music, "I Know I've Been Changed" bellows from the speakers. I can't recall who the songstress is, but her voice is strong and determined to get her point across of how she's been changed.

In walks a man I used to see in the streets from time to time. His lanky stature is clean to the bone. He has a sharp haircut and gray suit with striped tie and glasses on his clean-shaven narrow face. He looks like a completely different person compared to the window cleaning/sticking up his middle finger/grouch I'd see panhandling in the streets of downtown. Kicking jitneys and cussing out Transit bus drivers.

The family sits in the front row, four women, two teen girls, and the clean-shaven guy. He might be a son or uncle. Who knows? He might even be Jessie, Daisy's boyfriend.

The fourth row sits one gentleman dressed in a blue suit. There is an empty seat between him and a loving couple who sits gaping at the heather blue casket that holds the deceased, Daisy.

The fifth row is empty.

The sixth row seats three gentlemen, one in a black suit, tan suit with mahogany framed glasses on, the third guy is dressed in a pinstriped black or navy suit. He is wearing glasses too.

The seventh row is empty.

Seated behind it is three empty seats, but sitting alongside them is four men: one Asian, three African-American, all of light complexion and elderly. They could pass for white.

The eighth row is where I sit to the right of the room, in the first seat. The remaining chairs in this row are empty. I don't bother to go up and view the body, like I said funerals and I, not a good combination. I take death too personally. It is not a good look, especially around a bunch of strangers who will probably think I'm crazy if I happened to fall on the floor bawling like my momma took my candy away from me. It is that painful so I'd rather not even go there and display a temper tantrum.

I cross my glossy legs as my mule dangles off of my right foot.

Folks are flowing in little by little. Children are chewing bubble gum and laughing. More muffling voices chime in.

I see a couple of familiar faces. Folks I've seen in passing in the streets of downtown Paterson and folks from the library.

In the front of the room hangs a beautiful throw in a black and white photo of Daisy. It's a photo that one could have framed and hangs it over a mantel in their living room for eyes to admire. Daisy looks so poised and sophisticated—a real dime.

A brown-skinned guy dressed in a black vest with trousers to match and a white collar dress shirt pats one of the women in the front row on the back to console her. It might be a sister or aunt or daughter. It leaves me in curiosity if it is one of her daughters.

Gospel music spills through from the above speakers along with coolness that hovers over my head.

Everyone is quieting down as the pianist has arrived. She is dressed in a stripe red and white blouse with thick black belt and black flare skirt with strapless silver shoes on her feet. She has on sheer black panty hose that have a run at the heel. I hope she has some clear nail polish before the run gets worse. Her jet-black hair is styled in a short cut, which accentuates her dark brown skin tone. She wears a choker of pearls around her thick neck and pearl earrings to match.

She sits. Slips off her shoes and begins to play the piano. Her voice is rough and crackling as she bellows out, "Amazing Grace."

As she sings I find myself getting emotional. I drift in thought of Johnnie. Suddenly I feel this heavy weight on my shoulders. It is too much to bear, so I rise from my seat and walk straight toward the door to exit out.

As I do, in walks a familiar face. It is none other than Javis Cline.

Our eyes meet.

"Avery?"

I can't compose my emotions any longer and find myself falling as he moves in and catches me before I make a spectacle of myself.

"Are you all right?" he asks while gently bringing my limp body toward his broad chest and slowly walks me to a chair. The smell of his minty breath and the look of concern in his golden brown eyes say so much. More than I expect.

My nostrils inhale his Polo Black cologne. It reminds me of our departed friend, Johnnie. Tears leak from my eyes as Javis gently wipes them away with his silk handkerchief.

"Do you want to talk?" he asks.

I can't even find the strength to open my mouth, so I nod my head up and down.

"Sit here. Let me pay my respects, then we can go." he says.

I nod my head again.

Javis makes his way into the room dressed in an expensive designer suit. Navy-blue really complements his eyes. He signs the book and then heads up the aisle to view Daisy. He then turns and greets the family, then makes his way back to me.

He helps me to my feet, and we walk toward the door and exit out.

He opens his passenger's-side door to his black BMW, and helps me inside.

I sigh, and then buckle my seat belt as Javis gets into his car and gets comfy in the driver's seat.

"How did she look?" I ask curious as my heart throbs in my chest. Body a bunch of nerves. He turns and looks toward me and says in his Italian accent, "At peace. She looks like an angel dressed in a white Anita Pasha dress I bought her from Pasha, Inc. Now, where would you like to go?"

"Anywhere you care to take me." I reply as I sit back and close my eyes.

Our destination leads us in Javis's hometown of Philly. Javis parks in the parking lot of the elegant Latham Hotel located in the heart of Philadelphia's Center City district. It is so quiet, so much greenery and beauty. I can see why Johnnie wanted to be here. It is so serene where you can hear nature. The smell of the air is clean and fresh.

"Avery, what happened back there?"

I look down at my fingernails. I shake my head. "I don't know. I-I..." I pause to unscramble my words.

"I understand. It kind of brought back memories for me too. Johnnie was a big part of our lives," he says.

I nod in agreement.

"How do you know Daisy?" I ask.

"Actually I don't. I know her son, Colby. Good kid. Lived a hard life, but if you ever talked to him you'd never know. He hides it well. I think he was ashamed of what his mom had become. But he never denied her as his mom. He just, just wanted to have a normal life like normal people. I heard him speak at this event I had gone to. Adolescents were talking about family members living with HIV/AIDS and how it impacts their lives. Colby said, 'My mom is an addict. She has AIDS.' It was the way he said it, I felt his words so intently. He spoke of how their family used to be before the drugs, the disease. How Daisy took care of them. How she loved them. It was a profound moment for me. I grew attached to him. Colby has a good heart, good head on his shoulders. He wants to go to college and become a social worker. He wants to help kids like him." he sighs. "So," he scratches his throat. "I, ah, took it upon myself to make sure he gets that opportunity. I've setup a college fund for when he is ready for college. His sisters, Jody and Molly, I'm sure they will follow in his footsteps. So I've made sure they have college funds too."

I remain quiet. I just listen. And as I listen I can't help but think that I feel the same exact way as Colby. *Why can't I have a normal life like normal people?*

Javis leans back in his seat to get comfortable. He unloosens his silk champagne-colored tie and unbuttons the first three buttons on his light gray dress shirt. His dark bushy chest hairs are very thick, yet sexy. He cracks the windows as we inhale the sweet lavender air.

"What are you thinking over there, Avery?" he asks.

I stare out of the passenger's-side window. "So much," I reply. "Just," I squirm in my seat. "Just wish things would just get easier. I feel like nothing is working in my favor. Like the whole world is against me. Things are so difficult. The simplest things are difficult for me. All I want is a little peace. To be able to clear my head and think without worrying about the next catastrophe that may enter in my life. There is always something going on to distract me from what I need and want to do. I need a break, Javis—a real vacation away from Paterson. It's changed so much that sometimes I dread going outside. Folks are so angry and bitter and shiesty. No one seems to care about the next person. Everyone seems to be looking out for self. And they don't care who toes they step on or who's body they step over either. The violence and killings are out of control. I don't know what to expect anymore. When I walk out my front door I don't know if I'll be walking back in. I think about that a lot. And then I think who will miss me or even know that I am gone."

"I know what you mean," he says. "I'll miss you, Avery." he says with a sincere look on his face.

I turn and look in his direction.

Javis continues, "Avery, everyone, including me, is going through a rough time. People barely have enough money to survive. Everything is so outrageously overpriced. People are barely able to eat. Businesses are going under. Crime has increased. I see more homeless people than I've ever seen living on the streets. It makes me count my blessings. Some of my tenants have some of their family members or friends move in to make rent. Yes, I know that they are not on the lease, but what am I supposed to do kick them out and force them to live on the streets. No. I refuse to do that. Because I understand how difficult it is to make ends meet. And if they have to depend on family and friends to support themselves and make rent then that is what they have to do. My mortgage is paid on time. So why should I make matters worse for them by evicting them when I know that they are only trying to do the best that they can do. At least they are trying. I can't ask for anything more." He runs his fingers through his hair, and then taps his two forefingers against the steering wheel. He continues, "You know, sometimes people look at me and think that I have the life. I have a nice car, properties, businesses, money, but it is not all it's cracked up to be. I have more stress than I need. I never really have a moment to myself because my phone is constantly ringing. Someone needs this, someone needs that. They think I'm a walking bank. And I'm not. I'm just a person who made some good investments that happened to work in my favor. I worked hard to get what I have, but some seem to think that I was born with a silver spoon in my mouth. I wish it were so."

"Wow. That's a lot." I say.

"I never shared this with anyone but I'm going to share it with you, Avery. I always wanted to have a wife and kids—three kids. Live in a quiet suburban neighborhood and live a normal life. You know, have wifey stay home and take care of the kids while I go out and be the breadwinner. But with everything going on I don't have time to even date. And the small amount of time I do have no woman is going to want to date me by my clock. So I find myself consumed in work to fill that void of wanting a family of my own."

"I thought I had it bad when it comes to dating." I say.

"*You!*" He says somewhat surprised. "I can't see it. You're beautiful. You're smart. You're caring. Who wouldn't want to date you?"

"You'll be surprised, Javis."

"Really?"

"Really," I tell him. "It's not as easy as you'd think. I-I, have some issues that kind of get in the way. It gets lonely sometimes but I'd rather deal with the loneliness than deal with the heartache."

"Wow." Javis says.

"Wow, what?" I ask.

"Hearing myself talk, I kinda sound like my dear friend, Reilly. Reilly is single, childless, and girlfriendless, um, he's a great guy, but he has no life. He's consumed in work. Even took on a second job because he overextended himself when he bought his home. He didn't pay close attention to the numbers as he was buying this and that to renovate. He never really considered how high his taxes would be either. Things began to really manifest when he realized that his money did not stretch as long as he would have liked for it to. So um, he loses out on so much because he won't stop to smell the friggin' roses. Indulge in life, while he still has air to breathe. Money, it's good to have but it can ruin you, if you let it. That's why I share my wealth with others. I give, and I receive so much more in return. I receive life lessons. And it, it inspires me to continue to work harder, think smarter, so that I can remain in a position where I can help people like Reilly. He needs a break, but he seems to think that life will wait on him. Not gonna happen, dude. So I took it upon myself to give Reilly the freedom that he deserves. He, um, always wanted to travel, write a book, so now he is able to do those things and more." He smiles. "It feels good to give. Real good."

I reach my hand over and pat Javis on the outer skin of his right hand. Javis turns and looks at me. We both gaze into each other's eyes.

Javis leans in and so do I.

As our lips nearly touch I pull back and shake my head.

Javis reclines in his seat. I turn and face the passenger window and blankly stare out.

We sit quietly for a few more minutes, then Javis starts the car and we drive off.

27

"MS. LOVE..."

I lift up my head and look her in her eyes.

"Or would you prefer that I call you Avery?" Narlena asks in her throaty professional voice.

"Ms. Love is fine," I say in a soft-spoken tone as I scoot back in the red leather chair. I do feel slightly uncomfortable with the bright lights shining in my face, sitting across from the incomparable Narlena Scott of BLAB magazine. Seeing her up close and person, I see that she can be a bit antagonizing.

Narlena shuffles her cue cards, and gets comfy in her seat. "Okay, Ms. Love, as you know I asked you here to discuss your former relationship with Zaelyn Homes. How's he doing?"

I flutter my lashes.

Narlena cracks a devious smile.

"Well, I *wouldn't* know. I don't follow his every move. I mean, I do have a life of my own," I say with a hint of sarcasm.

She nods her head, and then makes some kind of erotic moaning sound. I really don't know how to take that, so I simply dismiss it.

"Well, let's begin." Narlena says.

"Let's," I say, then crack a smile to ease the tension I am feeling.

Narlena scratches her throat, then reaches in for her glass of ice water set on the table alongside her leather chair. She takes a sip, and then places it back down onto the table, looks up at me, and smiles, wickedly.

It is something 'bout that smile that makes me feel *real* uneasy.

"Ms. Love, is it true that Zaelyn caught you in the act of giving fellatio to one of his friends?"

My eyes like to fall out of their sockets. Mouth dangles wide open, "Absolutely *not!*" I snarl.

"Um, Ms. Love, can *you* elaborate a bit more on the alcohol and weed during sex? According to Zaelyn he admits to getting you high and drunk to have 'good sex' with you."

The interview has just begun and already I cannot compose myself. I swear I feel like snatching off this mike, leaping out of this chair, and heading to my attorney's office. But no, I'm bigger than that. I'm better than that. I will not let Narlena get under my skin. And I especially won't let Zaelyn get the satisfaction of breaking me down.

Inhale. Exhale. Nostrils flare. "Mrs. Scott, I have never met his friend. As far as me being a recovering addict, yes, there is some truth to that but I was not with Zaelyn when that occurred in my life. Someone I dated exposed me to crack-cocaine and I became addicted. But I was never an alcoholic as he claims. And he never had to get me drunk or high to have sex with him. I was a willing participant." The contortion on my face stresses, watch it. *How dare her!*

Narlena seems unconcern about my facial expression and digs in a little deeper. She puckers her heart-shaped shimmering peach lip-gloss lips and says in a rather nonchalant tone of voice. "Well, based on Zaelyn, he stated that you go both ways. Is there, any *truth* to this?" she cut her eyes over at me in a devious way.

A cold chill runs up my spine. I do a double take by her question. "I'm not following you. What do you mean by... *go both ways*?" I ask.

With her left eye she winks in a flirtatious, yet uncomfortable teasing manner.

At this precise moment I feel another frigid chill run up my spine. *I just know this trifling heffa doesn't think that I'm bisexual*, I think.

Narlena continues, "If I may, according to Zaelyn he states that you are *unequivocally* ...bisexual. He said, and I quote: 'She likes it both ways.' He said something about you get bored very quickly and need a variety to keep you sexually stimulated. He said you have that, that *sickness* like in the movie: *Black Snake Moan*. He also mentioned that you had a threesome with, ah, a gentleman by the name of...Keith Watts," she glances down at her cue card. Her eyes light up as if stunned. "Wait a minute!" she opens her mouth wide. I can literally see the cavities in her back teeth. Her eyes are spread so wide they like to pop out of her head. "OMG! Is this the same CEO Keith Watts of *Well-Endowed*...the multi-billion dollar mogul? You go, girl!" she snaps her fingers, twice.

I roll my eyes in the back of my head.

Narlena cannot contain herself. "According to Zaelyn, Keith, his wife, Naya, and you have this 'swingers' thing going on where they compensate you for sex. Is this true? So, ah, how much did you receive? Twenty thousand? Thirty? Forty? Fifty? Chile, inquiring minds are dying to know."

406

I squint my eyes and scrunch up my nose. "Excuse you. Don't you think you're stepping out of bounds? You should really think before you speak, Mrs. Scott." I tell her with fire burning in my eyes.

She breaks out in a devilish smile that makes my skin crawl. I take that as she thinks I have something to hide, but I don't. Truth be told, if I had gotten paid money like that there would be no need for me to be sitting here talking to her. I would be heading Interstate I-95 right about now.

I cannot believe she just asked me that question. I cannot believe it.

I shut my eyes, squeeze them tightly, while I silently ask the Lord to give me the strength I need before I climb out of myself and rip off this mike and leap on this heffa sitting across from me gloating like she thinks she has something on me.

My head is throbbing. Heat is building inside of my curvaceous body. I feel like I want to blow a fuse. Black the hell out and knock this shrewd chick out. But I keep my composure by woosaing in my head. *I can do this*, I think to myself. *It's all good.* But in all honesty, hell, no, it ain't all good 'cause this nosey bitch needs to stay in her lane.

I have no other alternative at this moment but to handle it. With me being under the spotlight I have to keep in mind that whatever I say or do can and will be perceived differently. No matter what I have to at least come off as a woman in control. I cannot go ballistic and whoop this bitch ass. Because if I do, the tabloids will eat me up—my life will be ruined. Zaelyn is, is not worth the humiliation.

Question after question I respond in a delicate tone of voice to Narlena.

"That's simply *untrue*." I say with conviction.

Inside, I pant.

"Oh, no, *he* didn't *say* that!"

I roll my eyes, and purse my glossy lips.

"WHAT?! Oh, *he* went there, huh?" I sigh, heavily.

By the time Narlena gets to the twentieth question I am nearly on the verge of tears. I do everything in my power not to breakdown in front of her. I am beyond furious about the whole situation. I want to *kill* him for putting me through this humiliation. KILL!!!!

Why is he trying to tear me down, slit my wrists and throat, stab me in the back with a butcher's knife? I wonder.

All I've ever done for that *man* was give him moral support and this is the thanks I get. I worked my ass off to please him, and, and, and, ooh, I am *heated*!

I sigh again. I try with everything in me to wrap my head around all of these lies. Why would he want to hurt me like this? Why? What had I done to him other than have sex with him and love him?

I sit here with a pensive look upon my face, while Narlena crosses her bare-skinned legs and dangles her Manolo Blahnik black stiletto off of her right foot, steady scrolling her eyes up and down my conservative attire: black pencil skirt, purple silk blouse, and strapless black pumps. My natural salt and pepper hair is cut low to the scalp. Makeup is minimal. I like more of a natural look. If I didn't know any betta' I would think that she was Zaelyn's other piece of sweet potato pie with that crafty look she has on her face. Why is *she* so interested in my heartache? Why does this gorgeous, fair-skinned sexy woman want to dish my dirt? Does she really look at me as some cheap thrill trying to freeload off of this scumbag? *If only she knew the truth*, I think. I can tell that she is studying me through her wire-rimmed glasses. Those big brown eyes are analyzing me with all sorts of corrupt thoughts.

While I am inspecting her, she pushes her brunette hair behind her left ear, and then leans back in her seat. I am trying to regain myself, and keep a hold of my dignity. I know she is eager to get the *exclusive* on the breakup between my former ex Zaelyn Homes and me. How eager is she? Is what I wonder. How far will she go to get what she wants? I guess far enough to invite me here to get the other half of the story.

Why is he trying to ruin my name and reputation? I have to pull myself up somehow, and grabbing *my* twelve inches between my legs oppose to Zaelyn's eight is the only way to rise above this madness.

But before I can, Narlena bludgeons me with her next question. "Apparently, Zaelyn is very upset about you not divulging your status to him. He feels that he was duped, unwarned about..." she pauses trying to find the right words to say.

At this moment, my "female penis" comes swinging out and I give Narlena a dirty look. Her brows rise, which tells me that she knows I have something brewing in this head of mine, I narrow-eye her. She leans forward with her long index finger ready to push 'Record' on her Sony tape-recorder, while drooling at the mouth, anxiously waiting for me to talk. This is one thirsty bitch.

I satisfy her curiosity by saying, "I am an African-American, forty-something year old woman. I am in my sexual prime. I have urges like any other woman. I have had men before and men after I was diagnosed of having HIV. I am appalled by Mr. Homes' accusations of me spreading the virus. I am appalled at him fabricating that I never disclosed my status to him. I told him the truth of how I contracted the disease. I was raped. As so many women in America and outside of the United States of America are every day. I gave him options. He chose to fulfill his sexual desires with me. And I'm not going to sit here and say that I wasn't elated, because I was. Living with HIV puts a woman in a cardboard box with no one by her shadow. I managed to come out of seclusion. Every day is a challenge. But I serve a greater purpose by allowing others to see me out and about. I am no longer hibernating behind closed doors. I'm out in the publics' eye, open, seen and heard. So yes, to answer your question, Narlena, yes, Zaelyn and I did have protective sexual intercourse. And it felt exhilarating! But what Zaelyn *failed* to share with you was that the condom did come off in the midst of him still being inside of me. He reached in and pulled the condom out. And I rushed into my bathroom and douched. There is where I made a huge mistake, but I didn't know this at the time. I panicked. But after reading an issue of *HIV Plus* I'd come to learn that if the condom should break after ejaculation, you should pull it out slowly and carefully, and then go take a nice soapy shower or bath. Do not, women of the world, do not douche or use an enema because both set the stage for infection. And if you are both HIV-positive you really should both see your doctors and explain the situation and talk to them about possible reinfection.

"After the condom came off Zaleyn and I really didn't talk much that evening. I think I scared him off. He left my place having a difficult time even looking me in my face. Can't say it didn't hurt because it did. I mean this man had wooed me up till that evening and then BAM! Everything suddenly changed. I cared deeply for Zaelyn, but he was the one who had lied. I never knew he had a family, a wife and children. He never informed me of this need-to-know information. Had I not gone over to his house I wouldn't have known a thing. He never told me. I saw the pictures on his mantel. There was nothing to question, so I never stirred up any conversation for him to explain. Upon me finding out, upon me feeling duped and heartbroken I immediately ended our relationship. Me. Not him. Me. I found a greater purpose, more inviting than a man in my bed, and I sought out to fulfill that purpose. I'm no different than any other woman who wants to be loved, who wants to fall in love. There is more to me than meets the eye, but I realize that only a true man, in mind, in soul, in spirit, can appreciate a woman like me. I have a lot to give, but just like other women sometimes my judgment is off.

Sometimes I leap. Sometimes I fall. Sometimes I overanalyze. Even fantasize. And when things go left, I give myself five days to mourn my dilemma. And by the sixth day I should be refreshed enough to carry on with life because life has its ups and downs. Sometimes in my predicament I get discouraged because folks are so misinformed. But instead of educating themselves they'd rather live in ignorance. I have so much to do with my life to be bogged down with trivialness." I smile. "I hope you got what you needed, Mrs. Narlena Scott. As an intelligent black woman to another intelligent black woman I wish you nothing but success in your endeavors. I appreciate you giving me the opportunity of meeting you and telling the public my side of the story. Hopefully I've inspired someone. If we don't stick together as black women and pull our sisters up, who will?"

I feel I have accomplished my goal. I kindly pull off the mike, stand to my feet; walk off set with lightness in my step.

28

I PULL OPEN THE MAGIC CHEF fridge and pull out the garden herbs of: rosemary, sage, oregano, fresh garlic, red onion, and Hotel Bar butter, while simultaneously opening the freezer and pull out the Ziploc bag of two and half chickens I bought from the butcher the other day. I kneel down in the fridge and reach on the second shelf and grab the one sweet potato I have left. Then shut the doors.

I open the cupboard and pull out the family size bag of Uncle Ben's long grain and wild rice that is on the lower shelf, along with the carousel rack of herbal seasonings.

I reopen the fridge to pull out the last bit of fresh string beans to cook before they go bad.

I slightly turn to the left and turn on the faucet to the sink and let the cold water flow out. Grab the small bottle of vinegar that is to my right and an aluminum pan and fill it with cold water. Then I unzip the Ziploc bag that holds the chicken and place them in the water to clean. Then wash my hands.

I reopen the cupboard and pull out my small rice pot and plastic measuring cup. Fill the pot halfway with cold water and place it on the stove, then turn on the knob for the first right side burner to heat up. I unclip the bag of rice and pour three-fourth measuring cup in. Then cut a thin slice of butter and add it to the water as the heat makes it dissolve

I untwist the plastic bag that holds the string beans and cut them up, then rinse them off. Grab another pot and fill it halfway with cold water and add some seasonings in it to give the string beans some flavor.

I turn the knob to turn on the oven allowing it to preheat for the chicken and sweet potato, when I feel my cell phone vibrating in my back pants pocket.

I slip my iPhone out and say, "Hello?"

As soon the caller hears my voice she automatically starts crying hysterically and talking simultaneously I can barely understand what she is saying. "I lost everything. Everything!" she bellows in my ear.

"Who's calling?" I ask with a perplex look upon my face.

"Av, its YaYa...Yancey Lopez from the job."

"Who? What job?"

"Y-a-n-c-e-y. We both work at ECLECTIC."

I have to take a moment to think. *Yancey?* Doesn't register.

"Hello. Hello." she says in a voice of hysterics.

"Yes, I'm still here. I'm just trying to picture who the heck you are," I say.

In between her now bawling uncontrollably she tries to catch her breath. "I-I-I-I'm the chick with the big mouth—big titties, big brown eyes, kinky bleached blonde hair and long acrylic nails. The chick that is always farting in the clothes racks, and cracking on people in the break room—the one who be running around the store like a chicken with its head chopped off."

I raise a brow. "Oh, *now* I know who you are."

Yancey continues, "I-I-I-I just needed someone to talk to. I was looking in my phone and I realized I had your number. I just need to talk to somebody. You're probably thinking: *how dare this trifling bitch call me this time of morning.*"

I am not thinking anything of the sort, but I am curious as to what brought this call on because Yancey and I aren't close like that. I mean we aren't friends. We barely interact at work; unless we are making a run together (putting clothes back on the racks) and here she is calling me at 2:06 a.m. Some people gotta lot of nerve.

"I'm sorry to have awakened you," she says trying to compose herself.

Yancey and I work as sales associates. We only exchanged numbers when she asked me to switch a day with her so that she could take her daughter to the doctor. I took her hours because the first of the month was just around the corner and I needed the extra cash to get me through the rest of the week.

Why am I up this time of the morning? I can't sleep so I thought to cook before the food in the fridge goes bad. With my hectic schedule it is the best time for me to get it done. Or grab takeout for a few more days, which really does a number on my pocket change. I get tired of eating out and just wanted a home cooked meal.

I've only been working for ECLECTIC for a short time. I had since informed Social Services of my employment. My caseworker advised me to write a simple letter stating that I no longer was in need of the $140.00, but that I could still use the food stamps until I landed firmly on my feet. At the time I was getting $200.00, but then that was reduced down to $194.00 once I started working. Then that was reduced down to $176.00 and then the final reduction was $140.00 after the government took back about thirty-six-something dollars from me. Shit. At the rate that things were going I'd be close to bone and no skin fooling w_th them.

Before I was due to get another paycheck I sat down and calculated all of my living expenses, which of course, included food. I figured I'd come off better depending on myself, so I peeled a piece of loose leaf paper from one of my college notebooks and sat down at the kitchen counter and wrote a simple letter.

Dear Ms. Roberta (caseworker)

Case Number: 11111
Food stamps: $140 (on the 3rd of each month)

Due to my flu-like symptoms I'd figured it best to write instead of coming to your office and spreading my germs all over the place. I got sick at work.

Anyway, living on my own I feel that I can budget and fully become self-sufficient again. I truly appreciate your help in my time of need, but my need is clearly in its right state of mind right now and "we" both feel that "we" can lean on one another. So therefore I won't be in need of your services at this time. Should it come that I will be I will surely look for other employment opportunities first and if that should not work in my favor then I'll come to you as my last resort.

Thank you,

Ms. Avery Love

I mailed that letter off and was quite content with my decision. I've been working for ECLECTIC for probably four months now. At the time that I got hired by ECLECTIC I had recently got back in contact with this Jewish woman named Adina Ashire I used to work for back in the day to see if she had any vacancies as a barmaid. She was excited to take me back on at FIELDS OF CREAM for four nights a week and nearly every Friday and Saturday evening but I told her with my rotating schedule I was hoping she'd work with me. She didn't hesitate. And I was so relieved and pleased.

While working FIELDS OF CREAM the evenings that I did my

413

eating habits were atrocious with all the greasy foods I was eating there. I had to come from one job and hurry to the next without any time to go home and cook me a home cooked meal. With the money I was making from barmaid and ECLECTIC it still wasn't nearly enough for me to make ends meet so I sought out to find other employment opportunities but had yet to find anything to meet my needs.

Yancey breaks my train of thought and voluntarily tells me of what had occurred for her to be calling me in the wee hours of the mornin'.

"Av, he kicked me and my kids out of the house. My house!" Her voice sounds hoarse. I can hear pain in her voice too. "I have nothin', Av, nothin'."

Calling me Av is already starting off on the wrong foot. My parents did not name me Av. My name is Avery and if that is too difficult, Ms. Love will suffice.

I shake my head, annoyed. "First of all, honey, my name is Avery. And what do you mean...you have *nothin'*, YaYa? You have your kids. *Who* kicked you out?"

"You don't get it. When I come to the States mami 'pecifically told me to get a man. It took me *five* baby daddies before I got Enrique. I'm nada bout to lose another man because of my *seven* kids. I was at work, girl, when my son called me. He was like: 'Mami, Enrique kicked us out of the house.' I was like: 'Boy, stop lying, Johan. Don't you fuckin' play wit' me!' He said, 'No, Mami, really he did.' Girl, I started screaming 'n' shit. I know they thought I was goin' crazy at that fuckin' job. I can't believe this shit." Her voice gets low and somber like. "Now my kids don't have no daddy. I have to start all over from scratch. I can't believe this shit."

My brows knit. "Did you call the police?"

YaYa remains silent.

"I know you heard what I said. Did you call the police?"

"No," she says.

I shake my head. "Why didn't you call the police?"

"I love Enrique. My kids love him too. Enrique's just goin' through something right now. It's hard for him to find a job, so he drinks."

"I don't wanna hear any excuses from you. You sit and let that man kick you out of your house, where *you* pay rent. Did you say that he is *still* looking for a job? And drinks?"

YaYa remains quiet.

"I'll take that as a yes. So your kids are standing outside in the cold with no coats and no shoes on their feet, and you talkin' 'bout you...*love*...him. YaYa you betta' be glad I'm not one of your kids 'cause I would've...Oooh, girl!" I purse my lips. I am hot under the collar. I lean the small of my back against the sink and try to calm myself down. I open my mouth and express, "Woosa! Woosa!"

Yancey is bawling now. But I don't have a caring bone in my body.

I continue, "Look, you have to get your priorities in check. Now I don't know how thangs are handled in your country but here, girl, you have to put your children first. A man is just that, a man. And any man who puts his hands on you or your children or goes as far as kicking them out of their home is not a man. Now it's cute that you love Enrique but you cannot allow yourself to be blind by false love. If that man really, truly, loved you, girl, your ass would not be in some dirty ass motel room with seven kids calling me."

Yancey bawls, even louder.

I remain silent and just let her cry. I mean what else I can possibly say. Oh, I can think of some mo', but I think I've gotten my point across. The ball is in her court.

"YaYa, winter is here and it is just beginning to get colder outside. This January chill can be a cold son-of-a-gun. You can't afford for your kids to be getting sick. And you sure as hell cannot afford to miss work. Not with Gilda as our manager. Now I don't really know her that well but she seems like a stickler for perfect attendance. I haven't been on the job that long but I already peeped that out. She seems like a perfectionist. Everything has to be in its proper place and order. With the economy as it is, girl, you need your job. What you gonna do, get fired? You know as well as I do that ECLECTIC is not going to allow you to collect your unemployment benefits, so your only option would be welfare. Girl, please, gets it together."

Yancey sniffles. "What am I gonna do?"

I swallow the lump that has swelled in my throat. "You are going to do what you've always done...take care of business! Grab those balls between your legs and call the police. Why you letting that asshole lay up in your house while you paying for some nasty motel room with all of y'all stuffed in there like friggin' sardines. Chile, take care of you and your kids, forget that man!"

"I might've lost him." Yancey cries in hysterics.

I tilt my head back and let out a loud; "effin' bitches!" then "end" the call.

I open the fridge and grab me a seven-flow ounce Budweiser to help take the edge off. I am frazzled. I cannot believe her. I feel like I am two steps away from being homeless my damn self, and this stupid bitch is gonna just let her so-called man put her and her children out in the street.

Within a nanosecond my cellular rings again.

"Hello?"

"Avery, I need to talk."

"No, chile, what you need is Jesus. Talk, Yancey, talk my doggone ear off, why don't you." I take another swig off of my beer and listen to her yap, yap, yap.

"Av, I ran up to where the cashiers are screaming at the top of my lungs. All the customers' heads turned. I screamed, 'my house caught fire! I gotta go! I gotta go!' That's when the customers intervened and told Gilda to let me go home. Gilda felt a certain type of way like she was being accused of being the bad guy. The customers were in an uproar about my house. I know I was wrong, but I needed to get home to my man."

"You sound realllllllll...*stupid*." I snap.

"Anyway, Gilda turned her slender self around and flung her shoulder-length jet-black hair and those charcoal black eyes of hers bulged. She started yelling back at the customers. Girl, I was hysterical. It had to take LP (Loss Prevention) to come and try to calm me down. I think I was having an anxiety attack or something."

"I cannot believe you." I tell her again with a crumpled forehead, and then click her off. I do not care to hear any mo'.

I guess YaYa gets the hint because she doesn't call me back. I resume back to doing what I was doing before that stupid bitch called.

I guzzle down my beer, then open the fridge and reach for another.

I am reluctant to go to work, today, but I know that I need to 'cause I finally have some real hours. And plus, I need money for the book. For the past couple of weeks my hours have been lowered to two to three days, ten to fourteen hours.

The store manager Mr. Mark Drayton, who stands about six feet five inches tall with pale ghostly skin and deep sea-blue eyes, tapered short dirty blonde hair with the most irritating screechy voice I'd ever heard from a man, announced the cutbacks two days after Black Friday. He said that hours should pick back up in March. I was highly upset after hearing that. It just put a major snag in my plan. Shit.

The Seasonal employees had already been advised that their assignments would probably end after Christmas or New Years. Some of the employees, who weren't hired as Seasonal assumed that they were permanent, ended up being released of their duties.

Before Christmas my schedule was looking pretty good. It gave me a chance to catch-up on my bills, and start a little savings account. I can't say I had a very good Christmas because a dear friend of mine had died. I couldn't even go to the funeral 'cause I didn't have the money to travel to North Carolina. I thank God that I don't have any kids because I am not financially secure to be bringing no babies into this world that I know good and well I can't support. And I especially am not going to get sucked into thinking that if I am in a loving relationship that my man is going to be there with me through thick and thin. No. I am not going to be the one to fall for that. I see how things can change once a baby arrives. Love runs its course. People grow apart. Arguments start. Next thing you know fights erupt. And who suffers in the end. The children. Those poor innocent babies who didn't ask to be here.

Don't get me wrong, someday I'd like to have children, but I prefer to be married when I do. Listening to some of the women at ECLECTIC it is the best thing for me *not* to do.

Most of the ladies working here are either single mothers or unwed mothers shacking up with their baby daddies or boyfriends. Some of the older women are married and have been for eons. And they have no qualms 'bout growing old with their husbands. I have too much on my plate to even think 'bout babies or husbands. My main objective is to make my money so that I can get the hell out of Jersey, and start a new life somewhere else.

29

I MEET THIS HAITIAN woman named Tish Boyd in ECLECTIC. She is a shopaholic. Her cart is full of the latest trends. Tish happens to notice me folding a new shipment of fashionable merino sweaters and comes over to give me a compliment on the bone structure and features of my face.

"Hi." she says, with this beaming smile. Her whole face lights up.

"Hello."

"I hope you don't mind me saying but you have beautiful features. Have you ever thought of modeling?"

That was the last thought to come to my mind. *Me? A model? Been there, done that. No, thank you.*

"No," I reply. Okay. I lied. Look, I didn't feel like revisiting the past because then I'd have to remember that I am still married to that asshole Stacy Blazman. And I am really not trying to go there.

She pulls out a business card from her purse and hands it to me. "Hi. I'm Tish Boyd. Independent Senior Sales Director for Burnt Sugar Cosmetics. We are having a WOW Event on the 27th two days after Christmas at the Chambro House in Teaneck, New Jersey. I would love for you to come and be my guest model. What does your schedule look like for next week?"

All I can think to say is, "Full."

"Well, should it change give me a call. Let me take your number too, just in case some other things come up."

"Sure. It's ...." As I am reading off my cell number I can't help but look at her face. Her skin and makeup is impeccable. She looks refreshed like she feels like a million bucks. I always wanted to know what that feeling felt like. And by looking at her, it makes me want to know even more as to what her secret is for looking youthfully rejuvenated.

Don't get me wrong I am flattered, but I don't think that it's for me. I might go and check it out. The week of the event I never make it because of my work schedule. I couldn't afford to miss work.

As fate would have it, the following week I end up running into Tish at the store.

Call it coincidence or not. but by the *third* time of us bumping into each other I wonder if this is fate. Is there a reason for me to hear what this mocha-complexioned lady with the dreamiest chestnut-brown eyes and long luscious golden brown hair has to say about becoming a Burnt Sugar sales rep?

At this moment I can't really say, but after the new. year rolls in I receive a text message from Tish about making extra income. So I immediately texted her back and tell her that once I get my finances in order I'll be giving her a call. It's either that or tries to make a way with what little I am making between both jobs, but it really isn't making a significant difference.

At the end of the month there is no extra for me to go crazy and splurge. I'm basically living from paycheck to paycheck. And truthfully, a girl needs a new pair of shoes!

30

BY THE TIME I arrive at ECLECTIC, the word is out 'bout Yancey, and the *"fire." I can't even be bothered with her foolishness*, I think.

I make my way to the escalator and head upstairs to the second floor, bypass the Customer Service station, enter the door that says: EMPLOYEES ONLY, and walk down the narrow corridor into the break room to locker #62.

"What's up, Avery?"

I turn around and see that it is Josie sitting in the chair texting someone on her cell phone. Josie is in her early twenties with thick black curly hair. She's a big thick boned girl with a pretty face and sweet disposition.

"Hi."

"You heard what happened to Yancey?"

I nod my head.

"That's messed up, right? I'm texting her now to see how she is doing. Girl, she was a mess on Saturday. That shit scared me halfta death. It was so embarrassing. That chick was out in the parking lot running in circles and screaming and throwing her arms up in the air saying, 'Jehovah, why? Why are you punishing me like this?' like a raving lunatic. I thought I was going to have to drive her crazy ass to the psych ward. Ooh, I wanted to slap some sense back into that crazy bitch."

"Yes. The unexpected always happens at the most impromptu times." I say.

As soon as I say that I get a text from you-know-who. I don't even have to look. I just know. Call it...woman's intuition.

January 26, 2:51 P.M.

"Oh, you wanna play dirty, huh? Well, you messin' wit' the wrong muthafucker. Bitch I will bury you with words!"

Okay. I guess the word got out that I had had the interview with Narlena Scott. Problem is I don't know exactly what Narlena printed in the article to make this man as furious as he is.

I see that Zaelyn still has the same cell phone number. There were so many times I wanted to reach out to him, see how he was doing, but something always stopped me. I am so glad I didn't. I would've made a complete fool of myself. Had I known this was all going to happen, no, I wouldn't have been as supportive as I was with him. But at the time Zaelyn *was* my man. And I was willing to support him as much as he needed it. Naively I never expected him to diss me or speak so ugly of me or viciously attack me like he is.

"See you downstairs," I say to Josie. I punch in at 3:00, and then enter the security code before entering the Customer Service room to see if there are any returns that need to be taken to the stockroom, before heading to my section on the floor.

With everything in me I try for the remainder of the day to keep my mind clear, to focus on work. But I can't seem to. Every time I feel my phone, *ping*, I know I just received a new text or email. From who? I don't know but I can only think of one person...my ex Zaelyn Homes.

It's 4:45. In fifteen minutes I go on break. I can't wait. I am dying to know whom texted or emailed me. The suspense is killing me so bad that I cannot concentrate on anything else.

I make my way toward the escalator and step on. I land on the second floor and head into the ladies bathroom, enter one of the stalls and pull out my cellular to see if Zaelyn had sent me another *nasty* text.

To my surprise, it wasn't a text from Zaelyn but rather an email from Narlena Scott. She sent me two attached files. I download the first attachment, which is a PDF file of an article entitled: *"Jus' a Hoochie with a Wanderin' Coochie"* ooh, my blood is still boiling. Just the headline alone still pisses me off. I cannot believe she did that. But then again, I can She's none other than Narlena Scott known for pickin' bones.

As perturbed as I am, and as much as I am dying to read the article, I think against it for now. I'd rather wait until I get home just in case I have a spasm attack.

I exit the bathroom and make my way to the break room. Pulling a dollar out of my front pants pocket I insert it in the vending machine for a Dr. Pepper.

I sit down, pop the cap, and engross in a little television for the remainder of my fifteen minutes.

I throw the empty can of Dr. Pepper in the trash, and then head back to the bathroom. Before heading back downstairs I make my way over to

Customer Service. I enter the security code and wait for the light to turn purple, I then enter.

I check the bins by pulling out clothing to see if there is anything for my department. Pulling out designers such as: Head Honcho, Voluptuous Diva, Pretty-'n-Petite, Condemn, Conservative Lady, P.O. Box, Casual & Relaxed, Hissy Fitness, Right or Wrong, Snazzy, JT Inc., Apples, Oranges, Berries and Cherries, NJ, and Y.O.U.

The designer clothing that is hanging up, I collect and make my way toward the escalator. Take the clothing to the stockroom for the ladies to sort out. Then head back upstairs.

The loose clothing I drape over my arm and take downstairs to the stockroom. Back up I go to get the last load of clothing. After I make my way back down to the stockroom.

As I enter the stockroom, my supervisor JaChelle is already in the midst of paging me.

"I'm here, JaChelle," I say, as she places the phone back in its cradle.

Her forty-five year old light-skinned complexion stands out over the navy ribbed turtleneck she is wearing. Her black trousers hug her size zero frame. She smiles when she sees me and her one gold tooth sparkles.

"Honey," JaChelle says in a thick Ghana accent. "I need you to be the floater because you're the only one on the floor."

"Isn't Biella here?" I ask.

"No, hon, she left a few minutes ago," says JaChelle.

"Oh."

I exit the stockroom to make my way out to the floor where I am stationed to be.

JaChelle yells from the stockroom doors. "Just circulate the store and straighten up the tables. Oh, make sure you pickup any clothes you see on the floor, okay."

"Sure."

JaChelle continues, "And focus on the Clearance racks in all the other sections too, 'kay."

"No problem."

As I am heading toward Pretty-'n-Petite to pick up a blouse off of the floor this blonde-haired middle-aged woman with wire-framed glasses stirs up brief conversation with me.

"I know you get tired of picking up after grown folks all day long." She says.

"Yes, it can be tiresome." I say, while straightening up the racks.

She shakes her head. "It baffles me why grown ass women can't pick up after themselves. I make it a point to put stuff back on the hangers and put the clothing back where I found it. Sometimes it makes you wonder how they live."

I nod my head, and then smile.

She continues, "You go to their house and you probably have to sip tea with a towel not to spill it on their Persian rug, you know."

I laugh inwardly because she makes a valid point.

In the middle of our conversation, this young slender redhead woman approaches me. "Is returns done upstairs?"

"Yes, ma'am," I say.

She heads toward the escalator.

I turn around to pick up another piece of clothing off of the floor, while the same blonde-haired woman browses.

"Excuse me, ma'am." I raise my body up and look in the brunette's direction. "Um, do you work here?" she asks dumbfoundedly.

I just look at her as if to say: *No, lady, I'm just here for my damn health. Pickin' up these clothes off the floor like I'm back home pickin' cotton.*

Some people ask the stupidest questions. Can't she see that I have on this laminated nametag with ECLECTIC advertised across it in big hot pink letters?

I nod.

"Can you tell me where your black dress pants are?" she asks.

"There's not a specific section, but I'd check Conservative Lady or P.O. Box. Check Clearance. you might luck up and find some there."

"Thank you."

"You're welcome."

I make my way around to circulate the store. I stop in Apples, Oranges, Berries and Cherries 'cause the Clearance section looks like a bomb hit it. Clothes are strewn all over the floor. Hangers are sticking out with garments dangling from them. Clothes are toppled atop of the racks.

I straighten 'em out, then make my way to the next section and repeat the process.

I go into the fitting rooms to see if they're full. They are.

The rack is overflowing with clothes. The rooms are congested with clothes.

On the floor, hangers are scattered everywhere. Open packaging of hosiery, leggings, and tights are all over the floor. I find a pile of jumbled panties and bras underneath the seat that looks like a customer might've tried 'em on.

Eew! I think.

I pick 'em up with the hook of a hanger and place 'em in the bin. I find two empty earring holders on top of the mirror. Somebody stole 'em. I take the empty holders to Jewelry Junkie section and give 'em to the sales associate Abigail.

"Agun," Abigail says in broken English.

I shrug my shoulders, and then head back to the fitting rooms.

Thank goodness, it is 9:17 p.m.

I fold the last of the cashmere sweaters, and then make my way to the escalator. My back, neck, and the heels of my feet are so sore.

As I am entering the bathroom to wash my hands I look in the mirror and see that my eyes are red and my face looks beat.

I exit out of the bathroom, enter the EMPLOYEES ONLY door, walk the narrow corridor and make my way into the break room to my locker.

I turn the combination lock, pull the locker open, grab my belongings, put on my coat, hat and gloves, and make my way to the escalator, out the store, and to the bus stop.

The chill in the air is brisk. I watch where I am walking because I know that there is some black ice that I can't see. I don't want to fall like my co-worker Consuela did the other day.

I can see that there are a few people waiting at the bus stop. I walk up the walkway and stand by the pole shivering in my full-length black goose down.

The jitney is coming so I get my fare ready, board the bus, and sit three seats from the back. *I'll make myself some soup for dinner*, I think, *and then take it down early tonight. I'm beat, and feeling a little under the weather. Hopefully I am not getting another cold.*

When I walk into my place, I undress, take a warm shower, and throw on an old faded T-shirt.

As I massage a quarter-size scoop of Noxzema on my face I stop, gape in the mirror at my reflection realizing I have on one of Xavier's shirts.

I lose it.

Just completely lose myself in grief and pain-stricken wail.

I fall to my knees, and ask the Lord to help me.

31

AT A SNAIL'S PACE I walk downtown Paterson. I cross the street in front of Bank of America and walk a little ways down and sit on the hunter-green bench occupied by two elderly women.

As I sit I stare into S & A, which is flooded with Hispanics and a handful of blacks.

"Good afternoon, miss." This dark-skinned woman with a southern drawl greets me with a smile on her oval face.

Sitting next to her, is a light-skinned slim woman with a floral print headscarf on her head. She nods.

"Good mornin', ma'ams." I say, as we watch three police cars siring, as they zoom down lower Main Street.

"You're not from here, are you?" the dark-skinned woman asks.

"Yes ma'am. Born and raised." I murmur.

"Doesn't she remind you of back home in South Carolina, Luella Jean?" the dark-skinned woman turns to the light-skinned woman and asks.

The light-skinned woman nods in agreement.

"I'm Offa Mae," she says, "And this is my best friend in the whole wide world, Luella Jean."

"Nice to meet you both," I say. "My name is Avery."

"Likkkke wiseeeee," Luella Jean says in a stuttering tone.

They both drift off in deep conversation as I drift back in my own world of gloom.

"I ain'ttttt never wannnt nobooody thatttt ain'ttttt nevvvver waaaant mmmmme." Luella Jean blurts out with a grimace on her narrow face.

"I sho' know that," Offa Mae chimes, and then chuckles as her hefty body shakes like Jell-O.

Luella Jean laughs.

"Luella Jean, you just as crazy as ever. Ever since the first day I met you in Charlie's Sweet Shop back home."

"I-I-I-I ain'tttttt nevvvver gooonnnnaaa chhhhange."

"I'd imagine not. We's old. Too old for change." Offa Mae says.

"Weee'ssss ain'tttttt nevvvver tooooo ollllldddd forrr chhhange, chilllleee. Doooonnnn'tttt leetttt theee deeeviiiilll maaakkkeee yoooouu aaaaa lllllllliiiiiiiaaaarrrrr," Luella Jean says.

"I receive. Yes, Lawd, I receive," Offa Mae says, and then nudges me with her meaty elbow, "Whatchu so deep in thought about, chile?"

"Snap out of it, Avery, don't you hear that old lady talkin' to you," Avona says.

I come to.

"Ma'am. I'm sorry. What did you say?"

"Talk, Avery, tells us what's troublin' you. I can see the blues in your eyes. Ain't no good to hold so much hurt inside. It will eat you up. You can trust us two old ladies. We ain't gonna harm your heart."

Did I tell her my name? I can't remember if I did or not.

"Did I tell you my name?" I ask her.

"Sure you did. How else would I have known, chile?" Offa Mae replies. "Are you feelin' okay? You feelin' ill 'cause I got some Castro oil in my medicine box at home."

"No, ma'am, I'm not sick. I'm just..." I pause.

"Well, spill it, sweetie. You too young and pretty to be troubled, sugar. Life is so full of brightness. God blessed us all with air to breathe, honey. Take a deep breath and exhale those sorrows. Let that demon know that you ain't gonna inhale no mo' pain. No mo' from this here day forward, you hear me? Tell 'im!" She shakes her head from side to side. "Tell 'im to leave you be!"

I lower my head feeling as if Poppa is towering his massive body over me. "Yes ma'am."

"WWWWhaaatttt seeemmms tooo beee trouuuubliinnn' yoouuu?" Luella Jean asks.

I heave, not knowing where to begin. Before I get a word out Offa Mae pats me on my left knee and starts reminiscing. And I don't bother to interrupt her. I just listen to what she has to say.

"When I met my husband, Ethaniel E. Bolden, he was a tall, handsome fellah. He was dark as coal and as sweet, if not sweeter than sweet tea. Shultz, he could make lemons tastes sweet. He worked in the cotton fields back home. I was so smitten wit' that man. Still gives me goose bumps whenever I's mention his'a name."

"Ohhh, I'ss 'mmmmember wheeeen yooou firrrrst sawwww hhhhim, Offa Mae. Averrrrry, ssssshe ddddidn't knowwwww howwww tttttoooo accccct. Hurrrr hairrrr wassss mooooist frrrrom hurrrr swwwweatin' likkkkkkeeessss aaaa piggggg." Luella Jean says.

I smile, showing nothing but teeth. I kind of feel my spirits uplifting talking to these two women. I really do.

"You two remind me of these ladies that were at the doctor's office I was at one day, but this was years ago." I tell them.

"Who's your doctor?" Offa Mae asks curiously.

"Dr. Fulmore."

"Oh, Shultzzzz!" Luella Jean shrieks.

"What? What!" I say excitedly.

"Yep, that was us." Offa Mae says.

"Really?" My eyes light up in surprise.

"Yessss." Luella Jean confirms.

Offa Mae nods her head.

"You know how long ago that was?" I say to 'em both.

"Ain't been that long. We were there to get tested for HIV. Jus' 'cause we's old don't mean we don't still have our needs. We are still vibrant women, chile. How you think we's still livin', honey." Offa Mae says all bright-eyed.

I smile, as she amuses me.

"If you don't mind me as'ing is that what's troublin' you?" Offa Mae asks.

Instantly, my smile turns upside down.

"Did I says sumptin' wrong, baby?" Offa Mae asks, as she looks at me with such sweetness in her big bronze eyes. She surely reminds me of an older woman I once knew as child. What was that woman's name? Oh yeah. Her name was Miss Sissie. She was a very troubled woman, who kept to herself. I rarely saw her with anyone. It was like she lived in her own little world. I was sore when she passed away. It was so painful to accept. Still I hold her deep in my heart. I don't mention her much, actually this is the very first time.

My eyes begin to well up. My thoughts drift back to Dr. Fulmore giving me the unexpected news: "*Avery, I regretfully have to advise you that you are HIV-positive.*" I blink, and then snap out of it. "No, no, I-I, just have a lot on my mind, that's all." I fake a counterfeit smile.

"Well, sugar, let us take some of that load offa your heart."

"I don't want to impose on you. You two were enjoying the weather and..."

"Lemme ask you sumptin'?" Offa Mae says in a strong, grandmotherly tone.

I give her my undivided attention because she kind of reminds me of Poppa when he had something near and dear to his heart to share.

"Yes ma'am." I say.

"Do you believe in God?"

"Yes. But I'm not a religious person. I think I'm more of a spiritual believer."

"Faith is faith, baby. Who's to say that God or a spirit didn't put me and Luella Jean here waitin' specifically for you?"

I remain quiet. I just listen.

"Do you believe that?" Offa Mae asks me.

I take a brief second to think about it. "I dunno, ma'am."

Offa Mae looks at Luella Jean as if they both can read each other's thoughts. They both speak simultaneously as if they were joined at the hip.

"We's Weeee's gonna gonnnnnaaaa help hellllppppp you yooooouuuu buuuiiilllllddd up uuuuuppppp your yyyyoooouuurrr faith faiiiiittthh, chile chhhhilee. Jus' Jussss' like liiiiikkkkkeee building buiiiiilllding aaaa house hoouuussseee from frrrommmm the tttthhheee ground grrrroooouuuddd up uuuppp."

I smile, and then say, "Okay."

Offa Mae leans forward, and turns her body around, and looks me dead-on. She puts her wrinkled hands on top of mine. "Sweetie, God uses anyone He feels is worthy of delivering His messages. He uses humans and animals, believe it or not. Think 'bout it. God don't want His chil'ren to hurt. And He, and only He will do everything in His power to make sho' if you do hurt you don't hurt for too long. See, God has to teach us all a lesson 'bout life and the choices we make. He is not going to babysat us, but He will be there when we call upon Him. He wants us to experience life, bad or good and come out a believer. You are highly favored, Avery. Jus' think, baby. You can be walking down the street with a frown on your face and someone; a total stranger will cross paths with you and say: 'Smile.' Or you can be so down on your luck burdened by your own aches and pains and someone will see it in your eyes and say: 'God loves you.' You can be down and out wit' no money in your pocket to feed you'self and someone will come along and invite you to have lunch or dinner wit' 'em. Might even hand you a coupla dollars not knowing your situation. Honey, that ain't no coincidence. That's God. Almighty, God. I know. I usedta hurt like you. Oh, when my son Malcolm died. Chile, the world felt like it had been snuffed from under my feet. I had nuthin' to grip my hands onto. I ain't have no one to call at that time. I didn't want to bother Luella Jean on account she's always been there for me. I didn't want to wear her out wit' my problems. God knows I felt so alone. But then I realized I wasn't as alone as I had thought I was. God is always listenin'. No matter where you are God is there, waiting for you to talk. So I talked and talked and talked myself till my voice grew hoarse. I reminisced about the good times with Malcolm. I talked 'bout the bad times too. It's good to spit out your feelings. Don't keep that sickness buried inside 'cause it will bury you to your grave." Offa Mae smiles so endearingly, and winks at me.

"Yeessss, LLLorrddd." Luella Jean praises, and then claps her frail palms together likes she's sitting in the pew of Temple Cross Baptist Church.

It does kind of feel like church sitting next to them. Sho' does bring back memories of Poppa and Ma'am. Sho' does.

Offa Mae continues, "There is one thing you should always 'member, baby. Someone out in this world got it just as tough, if not tougher than you—than us. God is testing you. He wants you to put your faith in Him. Believe, honey. Trust. He won't put no mo' on you than He knows you can handle." She smiles. "Avery, never forget that in this life: 'everybody's dyin', ain't nobody cryin' but love-love, my chile, love.'"

After that profound statement I take a deep breath. I let Offa Mae's words permeate through. "She has a point," I say to myself. Everybody's dying. People are suffering.

I stand, and then turn in the ladies direction and say, "Well, I guess I'll be heading back home. Thanks for the talk."

"Anytime," Offa Mae says, with pleasantness in her tone.

"Byyeee...Averyyy." Luella Jean says.

"Bye." I say, as my mind drifts to the only person who presently means the world to me.

As I cross the street, my head dangles low.

32

THE FIRE ENGINE SIREN awakens me out of a sound sleep. I stretch out my arms and yawn, loudly inhaling stink breath. Working has really worn me out. With all the bending and stooping and kneeling, my body is sore.

Is it is Sunday or Saturday? I roll over on my side and reach for my cell phone. It's Sunday. Thank you, Jesus! ECLECTIC is closed on Sundays. They have that Blue Law for their county. Thank, thank, thank, you, Jesus! Sometimes I wonder what I've gotten myself into by working in retail. It is not my cup of tea, that's for sho'.

My spirit is famished for the Word, so I reach for the remote and flick on the thirty-two inch Philips flat screen. I flip from channel to channel until I stumble upon Joel Osteen as he says, "you must make a decision that you are going to move on. It won't happen automatically. You will have to rise up and say, 'I don't care how hard this is, I don't care how disappointed I am, I'm not going to let this get the best of me. I'm moving on with my life.'" I listen for a few more minutes, and then flick to the next, which is Creflo Dollar as he says, "*Satan* is not a fictional character or a figment of the imagination. He is a real spiritual being who has a specific agenda; to destroy people's lives and lead them to Hell. *Every* human being will have to go before Jesus and give an account of the life they lived. What will your story be? Honor God with your body by abstaining from things that defile it." Then I flick to the next, which is Bishop T.D. Jakes as he says, "You got a devil to fight. If you got to walk around with your eyes closed-go ahead and do it-'cause you got a devil to fight. If you got to be lonely and stay by yourself- go ahead and do it- you got..."

Each one gives me something to think about, but not enough to refill my spirit. I guess I got the Sunday blues.

Sunday is usually a peaceful day. Not a lot of commotion, arguing from the neighbors to my left or right. Mrs. Silva doesn't make a fuss on the Lord's Day, which is kind of bizarre. I take what I can get from *her* because when she gets riled up, she gets rilllleeeed up cussing the walls and ceiling out. And don't let there be a pigeon on the windowsill, oh, that really triggers her to go off.

I spend my morning cooking a healthy breakfast, egg whites, turkey bacon, toasted plain bagel with spinach cream cheese, and a cup of herbal tea. I sit down and eat in my wife beater tee and plaid boy shorts.

I think to myself, *hmm, it has been a while since I stepped foot in Temple Cross Baptist Church and heard the new Pastor preach. It sho' wasn't the same as Reverend Giltroy. I tell you that.*

I think that last time I was there the ceiling was leaking, paint was peeling, stairways were crumbling, the air conditioner wasn't working and the heaters were as cold as the snow on the ground. And as I recall the new Pastor was driving around in a spanking new Bentley.

For some strange reason my spirit is nudging me to get out of this bed and go to Temple Cross and see what this new Pastor's sermon is about today.

I contemplate, what should I do? The ill feelings I get after walking through Temple's front door is one of mixed emotions. Sometimes I find myself more confused when I leave than when I arrived. And that really, really irritates me. Not to mention the throbbing headache that comes along with it. It's like the floor, walls, and ceiling simultaneously goes boom, boom, boom in my head. If I don't carry Bayer aspirin with me I d be in a world of trouble. Sometimes I wonder is it me, or, just the fact that the new Pastor and I don't have a spiritual connection. But isn't my connection supposed to be with God? Isn't it about receiving the Word?

I get up on my feet and put my plate in the sink.

It's pretty sunny and bright in my place. Wonder how the weather is though.

My mind drifts as I head upstairs.

Ma'am's little pocket Bible comes to mind. I reach for my Jimmy Choo shoebox in the top of my closet and find the Bible.

Ma'am wore that Bible out so badly she had to tape it with yellow tape to hold it together.

I crack a smile.

On the navy-blue cover it has the faded words that read: NEW TESTAMENT.

I open it up. Feel the worn pages. Touch the pages that she touched and I allow myself to drift back in time—back to a scene in my bedroom when Ma'am came in to talk to me.

"ST. MATTHEWS, 6," Ma'am said.

"12 *And forgive us our debts, as we forgive our debtors.*

"13 *And lead us not into temptation, but deliver us from evil: For thine is the kingdom, and the power, and the glory, forever. Amen.*

"14 *For if ye forgive men their trespasses, your heavenly Father will also forgive you:*

"15 *But if ye forgive not men their trespasses, neither will your Father forgive your trespasses.*"

Yeah. I remember so vividly. Ma'am then walked out of my bedroom, and back into her own little world. Two days later Poppa threw me to the wolves.

Closing the Bible feels as if I am closing those chapters of my life. Feeling this way makes me decide to pay God a visit.

I head downstairs to take a quick shower.

"It is not this difficult," I say to myself while stepping in the bathtub.

While drying off I decide to wear my tangerine dress, the brighter the better.

Exiting the bathroom and heading back upstairs I get dressed, apply on some makeup, rub a dime-size amount of shea butter on my scalp, grab my keys and purse, and then call a taxi.

I head out the door, down on the elevator to the lobby, and exit out of the building, feeling nervous tension.

It only takes the taxi five minutes to get to my building. I open the back door and climb in, pay the cabdriver six dollars, and lean back in the seat feeling nauseous.

It's just church, I tell myself. Why am I buggin'?

I exit out of the taxi in front of Temple Cross Baptist Church, sighing deeply.

Heading up the set of six steps, I open the door. Breathe in deep. Take a step, then another, then another until I reach the door to enter the church where I hear what sounds like Rev. Paul Jones singing, "I Won't Complain."

I open the door and step inside. And as I do, I slowly look up and I see that it is he. Immediately I tear up. Each step I take feels likes a boobytrap. *The devil is a liar*, I think. Sooner or later I'm going to trip and explode into thin air. *The devil is a liar.* God has been awaiting my arrival and I have been distancing myself from Him. In His home, not mine. I carry Him in my heart, but I guess sometimes He wants me to come visit Him in his house. I understand. It's just sometimes His home is not as inviting as it used to be for me.

432

I can't change overnight. I can only be who I am. Right now I seem flustered and a little apprehensive 'bout God, spirits, me...about everything. I want a relationship with Him, but it seems so overwhelming, so judgmental, and so over-the-top that I can't handle the pressure. So many booby-traps surround me. *The devil is a liar.*

Listen. Listen. Listen. Listen to the message that Rev. Jones is preaching to you in song.

I sit down. And I allow his words entry into my head, my heart.

I rise to my feet, sway my head from side to side and clap along.

I feel the message taking over my mind, my spirit. I raise my arms mid-air and praise Him.

"Thank you, Lord!"

I've been talked about.

"Thank you, Lord!"

I've had some hills to climb.

"Thank you, Lord!"

I've had some weary days.

Some sleepless nights.

I've been misunderstood.

And when I look around and I think things over, all of my good days outweigh my bad days. I won't complain.

"Thank you, Lord!"

Lord, why so much pain. But He knows what's best for me. I won't complain.

"Thank you, Lord!"

I leave out of church pouring with sweat. My head is soaking wet. I caught the Holy Ghost and literally danced outta my shoes. Hallelujah!

But—

Before I can exit out of the lobby I run into Reverend Kriss-Kross. This burly looking man with cashew-colored skin and dark menacing eyes dressed in a tan suit with matching shoes and a dark brown attaché case in tow. He used to be Reverend Giltroy's deacon.

Immediately his mid-fifty year old self notices me heading toward the door. He ceases his conversation with one of the ushers and focuses in on me, hastily walking toward the exit.

In his croaky voice he calls out, "Hello Sunshine!"

The edges of my mouth curl up and I nod to greet him. My feet keep moving. Two more steps and I am home free, but he manages to stop me in my tracks before I can push the door open.

"Hello, Reverend Kriss-Kross," I say with this eerie feeling swarming around in my belly. I done heard some things about Reverend Kriss-Kross that ain't too kosher. I know. I know you shouldn't believe everything you hear, but sometimes Reverend Kriss-Kross makes me wonder. He really, really does.

A smug look outlines his chubby clean-shaven face. "Yes...it is I. The Reeeeeeeeeeeverend!"

"I know," I reply dryly as I stare at his salt and pepper wavy hair.

"So...why haven't you been texting me like the rest of the congregation?" he asks.

"Excuse me," I say with a baffling look upon my face. *"Now why in the world would I be texting him,"* I say to myself. *Lord forgives me for I am about to sin. Reverend Kriss-Kross is asking for it and I'm the one to give it to him!*

"Look, Reverend Kriss-Kross, I got a lot of *shit* going on. But I'm still standing by the grace of God." I smile so proudly. I don't know what happened but suddenly I hear Lyfe's "Made Up My Mind" in my head, and suddenly I concur with Lyfe about church folks. Reverend Kriss-Kross is a perfect example of a man playing devil's advocate. Steady lusting and cussing and fucking up these women's heads 'cause of his status. I grimace. Lusting after me like a depraved dog. He should be ashamed of himself.

Reverend Kriss-Kross forehead crumples as if he is bothered. He gives me a penetrating glare, and then says, "Wait. You got *shit* going on? What kind of *shit*? Shit, shit? You on the toilet kind of *shit*? Or you stepped in *shit* and it stinks? Or you wanna take a *shit*? What kind of *shit*?" Those threatening eyes of his are burning a hole through my skin.

"Life *shit*!!!!!" I snap.

"Wait a minute. Life *shit*? Ooooh. Ok. That kind of *shit*. Oh, alright. Ok. I guess I better haul ass then."

I give him the evil eye. "You best."

Before I take another step toward the door, he blocks me like a security guard. "Damn. That sounds bad. Ok. Hope you feel better. Text when you do...love you...ok."

For some reason Reverend Kriss-Kross gets under my skin. I mean deep under and I let it rip. "Oh, oh, I get it! You can only text when *shit* is good, huh?"

"Avery, honey, why are you so angry?"

"ANGRY! ANGRY! Do I sound...ANGRY? I'm not angry! That's your imagination."

"Yeah like the Temptations...*just my imagination running away with me. It was just my imagination running away with me..."*

"You oughta keep that in check, Reverend Kriss-Kross," I say with a scrunch up nose. "You don't want rumors to spread in an unholy fashion, now, do you?"

He cuts his eye over his left shoulder then takes two steps closer to me as his hot breath grazes my ear. He speaks in an undertone as his right hand slithers down his trousers to his crotch area and he begins to massage himself in a vigorous motion. "I can't when it comes to *you*. Sometimes I wonder what it would be like to make love to you. You are so drop dead gorgeous."

My mouth opens wide as my feet quickly make their way out of the church.

I stand in front of the church, a body of cast-iron as my discouraging eyes skyward the cloudy sky and I speak in an irate tone of voice. "And You wonder why I don't come to visit as often as You'd like."

I shake my head and walk up the street pouting mad because Reverend Kriss-Kross messed up my Holy Ghost high.

33

WHEN I ARRIVE HOME, I enter the kitchenette to boil me some hot water, and then make my way into the living room. Before I sit down I hear my cellular buzz so glance at it and notice that I received a text from an unfamiliar number... (973) 123-4567.

"Hello again; r u busy?"

"Who r u?" I text.

No response.

34

IT IS A WINDY TUESDAY. I walk downtown to OPEN YO' EYES to discuss the possibility of working on consignment for my upcoming book. I am quite excited and a little sad about it too. Well, I don't want to dwell on Daisy's passing. I have my own burdens to bear. I know it might be a hard sell because of the subject matter, but I don't care. One thing people fail to realize is that living with HIV is just that—living with HIV. People infected with the virus are still human. Still have everyday lives to live and dreams to fulfill. It's definitely not a death sentence, as most seem to think. People are still ignorant to a disease that has so much to say. I guess that's why I write poetry to vent out my frustrations before I blackout on an innocent bystander.

For some reason the novel, *Anonymous* is on my mind. I decide to go to the Paterson Free Public Library.

I walk into the Paterson Free Public Library and I see the African-American fiction section in the far corner of the library. I make my way over to see if I see *Anonymous*, *Sleepin' Wit' the Virus* or *Kreepin' Wit' the Virus*, which I don't see on the book shelves. I happen to see a dark-skinned woman standing at the desk assistanting an adolescent girl. I patiently

"Yes, may I help you?" she asks in a deep husky voice.

"Um, I was wanting to read one of the author Karla Denise Baker's books, but I don't see any on the shelves. Have they all been checked out?" I ask.

She places her fingers on the keyboard in front of her and starts clicking away.

"Yep. They all are, ma'am. But if you'd like I can put a hold on them when they are returned."

"That would be fine. Thanks. Wow."

"You seem surprised." The library assistant says.

I nod. "I guess I am."

"Well, I can understand that. People are fickle. You never know what they'll like."

"Hmm."

"This is a great thing, if you asked me. With the way these horny teenagers are today, huh, she is putting it out there. Listen. This shit is real. HIV/AIDS does exist. At least she has them reading about it. She has to pull them in any way she can. And let me tell you, that she does. Slowly, but surely she's getting the message out there. Patrons come in here looking for her books and there all checked out. Or if they're stealing her books or not returning them back, then obviously they must like what she's writing. I, myself, haven't heard of anyone else writing several books on the same subject matter, at least not locally. However, she sees fit to bring awareness about, so be it. I ain't mad at her. At least she's trying. And she doesn't care about the stigma that comes along with it either. I mean, you ain't heard this from me but when she first released that novel *Anonymous*, everybody and their momma thought it was a true life story. 'There ain't no Avery Love,' they'd said. 'She's hiding behind her character. This book is *her*—all *her*.' Yep. That's what they said and thought. And that just drew me in even more to want to read the book. I mean I had every intention of reading it, but every time I'd go to check it out, the book would be gone. I guess I'll have to download the e-book. That seems like the only way I'm going to read her books." She nods her head. "It takes guts to put yourself out there like that. A whole lotta guts."

I nod.

"Have you ever met her?" I ask.

"Oh, yes. She's a nice, down-to-earth lady. Not like some authors who ain't got the time of day for you, but expect you to buy their books. Pulllleeeassseee. No, Karla, she'll take the time to talk. Listen. Laugh. She's real, you know. I can tell she's a people person. She has a great personality. Something tells me she likes to stray from drama though. You know how *women* can be. Always got to turn their nose up when they see someone doing something different to better themselves. Why women can't get along and be happy for one another is beyond me. Especially black women. Personally, I don't deal with the bullshit. I ain't got the patience or the bail money," she chuckles as her whole body jiggles.

I nod, and then smile in agreement.

"You did say that she comes here frequently?" I ask.

"Oh, yes. Being around people gives her ideas for *her* books. We talk here and there."

God, I hope they embrace mine. I know Daisy will be so proud.

"Well, thanks for all your help."

"Don't mention it. Come through anytime."

"By the way, um, I'm Avery Love," I extend out my right hand.

Her brown eyes widen. "Not..." She pauses, and then waves her hand. "Nevermind," she says, and then reaches out to shake my hand. "Nice to meet you, Avery, I'm Hazel Croxford."

"I'm sure I'll see you again, Hazel." I tell her.

She shakes her index finger at the air. "You know, I was just thinking the same thing."

"Bye."

"Good-bye."

As I am exiting out of the library I receive another unexpected text. This time I disregard it.

Every day, since the day, Dr. Fulmore gave me the news of me being infected with the virus I feel empathy for those I have yet to meet. Contrary to what folks may think, the worst feeling in the world is to be told that you have an incurable disease. That sticks in your head, your heart, and every waking day of the rest of your life. Every day I rise from my bed I take a moment to think about those who I've come in close contact with. Mostly, I think about my best friend Johnnie Rivera. Johnnie was *sweet* (no pun intended). He was a very endearing man. Fragile. Spiritual. He was my very best friend.

One thing that I can say about Johnnie was that every day since the day he told me he had AIDS, he lived life to its fullest. Man, I miss his laugh, his smile—I just miss him. I'm more than sure he had good days and bad days, which is typical, but somehow he used every negative thing that he'd ever endured and changed it into a positive. To me, it's phenomenal to be able to discipline yourself to think, to feel, to carry on with life as if life is good knowing in the back of your mind that any day could very well be your last. I admired him for being so courageous. I just-I just wished that I could've been there for him. Yes, I still have regrets of not being able to say "see-you-later" properly. He was my best friend. How else am I 'sposed to feel? I hold that regret close to my heart I don't know when I'll ever be able to let it go.

35

"YES, THIS IS Ms. Love."

"This is Mr. Witherspoon from OPEN YO' EYES." He says in a husky voice.

"Yes."

"Eugene gave me your number. He said that you wanted to speak with me about consignment. Are you an author, artist?"

"Author."

"Oh, really. I have a lot of writers, authors come in to my store. I love the ambiance. A place that is great for poetry, things of that sort."

"Yes, it does have that feel to it."

"Well, when is a good day for us to talk?" he asks me.

"You tell me."

"What about, um...ah, Sunday?"

"Sunday's good."

"Okay. Say around noon. I'll talk to you then."

"Okay. And thanks for returning my call."

"You're welcome."

I "end" the call.

This particular day I was walking down lower Main Street, when I happened to notice this storefront OPEN YO' EYES so I decided to stop in and browse. There was this short, slender brown-skinned older gentleman standing in front of the store who looked like he worked there. I stopped and asked if he was the owner. He smiled as if flattered. Then in a deep baritone voice said, "No, unfortunately, you just missed him. Was he expecting you?"

"No, no, I was just walking and I happened to notice the store and wanted to speak with him about... consignment." I told him.

"Well, if you'd like I can take your name and number and have him contact you." He said.

"Okay, that would be fine," I replied, then followed him into the store.

As we were walking up the walkway leading to the back counter, the older gentleman turned slightly around and said, "By the way my name is Mr. Eugene. I'm the store manager." I nodded in acknowledgement as I was drawn in by the decorum of the store.

As I looked around the store it had a quaint, cozy feel to it. The scent of African Musk incense lingered this insatiable fragrance in the air that uplifted your spirits as soon as you inhaled. Mmmmmmmmmmmm it smelled so divine.

The 60s theme of furniture and zebra and leopard printed pillows, earth-tones of mud cloth, dashikis, assortment of oils, artifacts, books, spiritual, urban, self-help, an a array of colorful jewelry, which happened to be my favorite things. There was music playing overhead. Soulful music. The kind of music that made you snaps your fingers, sway your head, and do the two-step while entering the store. It had that kind of feel to it. The kind of feel that tingled in your toes and electrified your whole body making you feels good when you left out of the store. The ambiance also set the scene for Spoken Word to me. It had a good vibe to it. A place I could see myself coming to again and again and again.

My cell phone rings. I hesitate to answer it. After the third ring I finally pick up.

"Hello."

"Oh, don't we sound better." Akil says. "What are you up to, Avery'"

"Nothing, really. I just got home from work maybe an hour ago." I say.

"Want to grab a bite to eat?"

I shrug my shoulders. "Why...not?" I say dryly.

Actually, I had already planned my evening. Take a hot bubble bath. Paint my toenails. Then think to get lost in that *New York Times* bestseller by Pink Khocolate, *The Darker Side of Pussy*. Seeing *her* interview on Nitelife really piqued my curiosity to read her erotic tale, but now I have plans with Akil. I frown. Bummer.

"I'll come and pick you up in a half hour."

I glance at my wristwatch. It's already 8:15 p.m.

"Okay." I "end" the call. Then rise from the sofa into the bathroom to take a quick shower and get dressed.

By the time I slip my feet in my boots and zip them up, my cellular rings.

"Hello."

"I'm outside." Akil says with music blasting in the background. I'm sure everyone can hear "Share My Love" by R. Kelly on the block.

"On my way down," I say loudly into the receiver.

I grab my silver-beaded (bootleg) Jimmy Choo clutch, give myself an once-over in the bathroom mirror, grab my off-white three quarter length leather jacket, and head out the door.

My heels are clicking so loudly in the desolate hallway to the elevator. I press the down button. *Ding!*

Within a couple of seconds the elevator door opens and I step on.

On the lobby floor I quickly check my mailbox and then exit out of the door as I adjust the off-white fitting sweater dress, not to put a snag in my french coffee pantyhose as I admire my Michael Kors off-white leather boots in the glass doors. And of course, I am rockin' a pair of fierce earrings to complete my ensemble.

The sun is dim. The air is slightly nippy. Akil unlocks the door when he sees me sashaying toward his Benz. He looks distinguished in his navy suit with white-collar shirt. His dreads are pulled back in a chic twisted ponytail.

As I sit in the passenger seat, Akil turns the music down. His car is immaculate. And it smells like clean linen.

"Where are we going?" I ask.

"Remember that place I told you about?" he says looking directly ahead. Akil is a cautious driver. I like that.

"What place? I'm sorry; I have so much on my mind lately. Refresh my memory."

"CHURCH."

My nose scrunches up. "Oh. That *place*. Why do they call it CHURCH?"

"Because 'church' is a place where you worship God, whereas this 'church' is a place where you worship Strippers. You still game?"

The light turns red. He turns and looks at me.

I shrug my shoulders. "Why... not?"

"Loosen up, Av."

He sounds just like Karma, I think to myself. *Am I that much of a bore? I must be with both of them telling me.*

"Have you ever just let your hair down and let go?" He asks.

I cut my eye at him. "Ha, ha, Akil, you know I don't have any hair." I burst out laughing.

His warm hand touches my left knee. "See, that's what I'm talkin' about. Have fun, girl!"

I smile.

Akil pulls up in this spacious parking lot. The place seems full to capacity. Akil parks. I step out; run my hands down my dress to smooth it out.

"Come on, Akil. I have to pee." Akil scurries behind me.

I step inside CHURCH and the place is dim lit. The bar is full with Caucasian men. Some are dressed in dress shirts with unloosened ties dangling from their necks. Some dressed in tees and khakis. Others dressed in causal shirts and jeans. I see potbellies, flat board stomachs, tall, skinny, and medium built men. Where are the *brothers*? Akil must've read my mind because he says, "It ain't that type of party here, Av. The only dark meat in here is me." He grins.

I frown.

By the front door there is a booth where the deejay is housed. There are a handful of dancers onstage. What the heck are they doing? All you see is beanpoles with blonde, brunette, and red hair. Do they eat? Oh, my. This is anorexic-ville.

I point to one blonde-haired chick. "Cute shoes," I say to myself.

Oh, they actually have a black chick in here. Oh, my God! Girlfriend makes all black women across the nation look bad with this getup she has on. What the hell?! Girly is dressed in an American Flag getup looking right stank. Did she cut the spandex pants up herself? All you see is black ghetto-ness!

To my surprise, there is another black chick that looks well groomed sitting all hugged up with this tall, older white gentleman with cropped mousy blonde hair. He has on a white dress shirt. His grayish tie is unloosened and dangling from around his neck. You can tell he just left the office and came here to unwind. He looks like a stockbroker or insurance sales rep. Maybe he's a lawyer, but I highly doubt it. I hope his breath is fresh 'cause he is breathing all up in her face. He is into her. Territorial, if you ask me. Go get 'em, girl. I ain't mad at her one bit. Get that cheddar, boo.

The chick with the American Flag getup has changed into some skimpy-looking outfit with her breasts and ass cheeks hanging out. Do I see a sore on the backside of her right thigh? I lean in and look closer. Outbreak. Yep. Herpes. Girly got herpes. I make a cross sign with my two index fingers. Ooh, chile, stay the hell away from me.

With the lights so dim I have to squint to see if I can see where the friggin' bathroom is. Akil finds a seat at the bar.

I walk toward the left where I see the symbol for RESTROOM, but it's the Men's room. This tall, white guy with wildly blonde hair points me in the direction of the Ladies room, which is down yonder. All the way on the other side of the bar, I quickly head in that direction before I pee on myself.

I enter the ladies room thinking that it is going to be this elaborate spacious bathroom that lingers a flowerbed fragrance. Only to be highly disappointed when I am smacked in the face with burning white girl hair from the flat iron this dirty blonde-haired babe is frying. She stands about 5'5" with a mountain of hair toppled on top of highlighted streaked hair. Her skin is pale like a friggin' ghost. She looks kind of spacey, too.

There is another young white chick that looks to be in her early twenties sitting down close enough to rub my skin. She is thin, brunette-haired with a rockers tee on. She's dressed in jeans and Converses. She looks zombie in the eyes.

The small space is claustrophobic to me. I just want to pee and head out.

"Is there anyone in there?" I ask.

Either one can respond.

The dirty blonde-haired chick replies, "No," in a raspy, sluggish sort of tone. Dang. What is she speech impaired? This chick is high. Maybe she's high off of hairspray. I don't know if she's one of the dancers or not, but if she is good luck.

I enter the cramped bathroom. There isn't even a mirror in here. *Sad*, I think. I pull down my leopard thong, and squat above the toilet bowl. All I hear is a ravine of hot liquid flowing out of me. Dang. It feels so good to have gotten that out. I have a hard time trying to yank the tissue because it's stuck in this damn tissue holder. I'm getting frustrated so I just rip the tissue and wind enough around my hand to wipe myself with. I dump the tissue in the toilet bowl. Pull up my thong. I use my foot to flush the toilet. Then turn to wash my hands. No soap! Are you friggin' kidding me! I want to scream...these cheap bastards! Can't even afford to buy soap! Or a friggin' mirror!

I rinse my hands with hot water and wipe them dry with toilet paper. I exit, and head to find Akil. *I need a drink.*

It seems darker as I stroll through trying to find the only dark meat in this dump. I retrace my steps. I can't find Akil anywhere. I see this dark arm standing erect and swaying from side to side. There he is. I walk over and sit down on the uncomfortable bar stool.

Akil sits taking in the view of pale faces, loud talking, balls smacking from the pool table, flat-screen plasma TV blasting, and retro music bellowing in our ears as he sips his wine.

This young woman greets us. She's cute, but can do without the makeup. A little goes a long way, honey. It's on the tip of my tongue but I don't dare say it. Don't want to hurt her feelings, especially with her making my drink. Oh, hell no! She ain't spitting in my glass.

"Hi. I'm Frankie. Can I get you something to drink?" she says all bubbly. Another blonde, God, can someone come in here with pink or blue or purple hair, please!!!!!

"Hi." I mock her sounding all bubbly, too. "May I see your wine menu?"

"We don't have one," she says rather nonchalant.

I purse my lips.

Akil turns in the other direction because he knows I am going to cut my eyes at him for bringing me to this sleaze dump.

He takes another sip of his red wine.

"Ok, well, Frankie, read off the names of what you serve."

She looks at me dumbfounded like I just asked her to recite the alphabet backwards.

Girl, don't play with me! I need a friggin' drink!

Breathe. Avery, breathe.

"Ok-ay. Ah, tell you what, Frankie, I'll have a 'Goody Two Shoes'." I just throw a name out there. I don't know if it's actually a drink or not.

Frankie nods, and goes at it.

Cool, I think.

Within seconds I have my drink sitting in front of me. Okay, she's efficient and knowledgeable. I like that.

Frankie and I engage in small talk. I want to see where her head is. See if she's one of those dumb blondes people always talk about. She doesn't appear to be to me.

"Who's the owner?" I ask her.

"You see that guy with the black shirt on," she says pointing her index finger toward the right side of the room.

I turn and see this older white dude in a black dress shirt with his shirt unbuttoned showing off his gray hairs. Who does he think he is John Travolta in *Saturday Night Fever*? His hair is wavy blonde and cropped to his wrinkled face. He appears to be a gigolo with the ladies. And since there aren't many women in here I know without a shadow of a doubt that he is dipping and dabbing with the help. He definitely doesn't appeal to my taste buds. He looks like he might have worms. Eew!

I put on my professional voice. "So, how long have you been a barmaid?" I ask Frankie.

"I've been working here for seven years," she replies.

"Really."

She thinks I'm interested, but honestly, I'm not. I'm just a new face in a sea of white people. Of course I feel a bit out of place. So I use what I have to blend in: my personality.

"I'm Polish," says Frankie. "When my mom found out that I was working here she hit the roof. My family is very religious. Mom thought I was a stripper. I said no mom. I'm just a barmaid. It took me two weeks to tell her. But then after I started contributing to paying bills, she lightened up. She likes the money."

I smile, seeming engaged in her storytelling. "I'm sure."

I take a sip of my drink.

"How is it?" Frankie asks.

I give her two thumbs up. I never had a "Goody Two Shoes" before so I wouldn't know if it tastes like one or not.

After polishing off my drink the retro music is beginning to appeal to me. I jump up off the bar stool and twirl my arms in the air. Akil smiles at me. I feel buzzed. Oh, I'm loosening up now.

"Avery, what are you doing? You actually like this music?" Akil asks.

"It kinda grows on you." I say grinning like a Cheshire cat. 'Ey, he said, "loosen up" so I'm loosening up.

Frankie comes back to check on us.

"You guys want another?"

"Sure, but I'll have a 'Gimme More,'" I say with a stupid grin on my face.

Frankie's eyes widen.

"Av, you shouldn't mix your drinks." Akil advises.

I wave my hand at him to nix him off. *I'm grown*, I think to myself. My words slur when I speak. "Youuuu saiiiiiiid thaaaat I-I-I-shouuuuuuuuld 'looseeeeeeen uuuuuuup'. Soooooo, Akillllll, I'mmmmm looseeeeeening uuuuup."

"Yeah, but..." he huffs feeling defeated.

Frankie shrugs her shoulders, and then smiles.

"Frankie. I'll have another wine, please." Akil says with a look of frustration on his face.

Frankie walks off and does her thing.

Within seconds Frankie comes back and places his drink in front of him.

Akil and I chitchat for a bit. Well, Akil talks and I grin. That's when the strippers start making their rounds around the bar, shaking their boobs, clapping their butt cheeks and puckering their lips, batting their

446

fake eyelashes. They use whatever it takes to entice these doggish men.

As soon as this brunette-babe comes Akil's way he pretends that he has just gotten an important phone call. After a few times I say, "Knock it off. Stop being so cheap and give her a dollar." He looks at me dumbfounded like I don't know what he is doing. *Cheapskate.*

The next girl that comes to us is sporting a cute little yellow baby-doll. Akil generously gives her two dollars. She leans forward showing off her boobs and he slips one in between her tight cleavage. The other dollar he slips in her G-string. She smiles and heads on to the next victim. It doesn't bother me one bit. I'm out to have fun. And plus, Akil is not my type. Don't get me wrong he's fine. Nice. All the things a woman would want to have lying beside her, but he is not the man for me. I mean after being surrounded by these hunks makes my taste buds salivate for something vanilla. I've always been partial to white meat.

I place the tip of my index finger in my mouth and bite down, not breaking my nail. Hmm. *Look at him: tall, dark, and mysterious with those gray eyes of his*, I think to myself. *Look at that flat ass, thin lips, and gold plated money-clip.* I rub my belly in a circular motion as if famished for the likes of him. He looks eatable. I raise a brow. But can he hang? I wonder. I need a man with some stamina, good credit, career oriented, loves to travel, and no kids, not married, doesn't want to get married, no baggage, well, some baggage, and most importantly, he needs to be head-over-heels for some A. L.

I know. Can't a sista dream? I'm sure it will be difficult to find someone like that. Not that I'm looking.

I turn my focus on Akil. "What do they have here to eat?" I ask him.

He seems entranced with the blonde bombshell and her well-endowed beige-colored tits. She turns to do a seductive dance in her bikini thong. Goodness, at least pull the string from out of the crack of her flat ass.

I smile because she is working it by grabbing her tits, squeezing them, jiggling them, and then pulling on her firm taupe-colored nipples.

Akil hasn't blinked once. She has him spellbound.

"Earth to, Akil," I snap my fingers.

"Huh?"

"Akil, hand me a menu, please." I ask.

He pulls the menu toward him without taking his eyes off of her and slides it to the right.

I scan it while Akil makes eye contact with big tit chick.

"'Ey, Frankie, how's the food here?" I ask, and then take two sips of my drink.

"It's good," she replies. Of course she would say that. Let me be the judge. The pricing is reasonable. I decide to take a chance and order the fried shrimp and French fries, which cost $6.00. Frankie takes my order, and then I drift to la-la land again.

I remember when I used to hunger for white men. I'd practically leap bounds for them. But that was merely an escape. I was hurting so deeply inside all because of Poppa. I've been hurt by the first man that had ever held me in his arms. Never did I want to feel that kind of anguish again. Never did I want to be punished by the arms of blackness. I'd rather go jungle fever before I submit back to my culture. That's how I used to feel. Since then I've overcome some of the heartache. I still have a long ways to go.

I come to.

"Damn, she got a nice tight ass," I hear Akil say.

I follow Akil's eyes. And yes, I have to agree that this other brunette babe does have a cute bottom. Her hair is shoulder-length. Her skin tone is eggshell. Her waistline looks to be between 24 or 26 inches. She's very shapely with flawless skin, and very attractive in the face. I can see how men would drool over her. She's a nice piece of ass. Uh-huh. I've been hanging under the fellahs too long. I know. I'm beginning to sound like 'em.

Finally, after twenty minutes my food arrives piping hot. Akil and I share. Drink. And enjoy the evening.

By now my attention focuses on the guy sitting next to me. He's dressed in a navy-blue suit with an expensive paisley silk necktie on. He's far from frugal. His skin is tanned to perfection. Brows well groomed. Fresh manicure. Brunette hair trimmed. And he has a sexy smile. Oh, that's a deal breaker for the coochie. Yummy. I can't keep my eyes off of him. But this whale of a man with sweaty dark hair distracts my concentration. His obese potbelly sits a few bar stools away from Sexy Million Dollar Smile. He stands and makes his way over to Sexy Million Dollar Smile and completely steals his spotlight with his overactive mouth.

One thing I can't stand is a self-absorbed arrogant man. I'm turned completely off. Instantly I come back to the Motherland of my black brothers.

I sip on my drink, somewhat bored. The retro music is beginning to nauseate me. This blonde chick with Tina Turner wig comes sashaying her flat ass over to us. She smiles all up in my face. Akil's too. She's trying to make her way through to us. Akil gives her a dollar and slips it in her bikini top to shoo her off. But she doesn't budge. She's a talkative one. She is just talking Akil's ears off. Better him than me.

I take another sip of my drink.

"Aren't you a sexy number," she says looking in my direction.

"Don't embarrass yourself," I say to myself, "be nice to the blonde bitch." I give her eye contact and say, "Thank you."

"Ooh, that voice of yours in turning me on. It's all sultry and shit," she says in this Rosie Perez voice. You remember that movie Rosie played in with Woody Harrelson (as Billy Hoyle) and Wesley Snipes (as Sidney Deane) in *White Men Can't Jump* God, it's irritating to my ears.

I turn to look at Akil. "What's up with this chick?" He shrugs his shoulders, and then rubs his hands together. "This is about to get good!" He says, and then leans over and whispers in my ears, "That bitch must've dabbled in some ecstasy or something. She's a wild one." He nudges me in the side with his elbow, as if to imply...what?

I turn away from her. Don't want to give her the wrong impression that I'm interested. This is a strip club so I know that anything goes.

One other blonde chick completely dismisses us.

My mouth opens wide. She walked passed us as if we weren't even sitting here.

"Don't let it get to you, Av. Some of these strippers are prejudice," Akil tells me.

Bitch, I mumble under my breath.

This brunette-haired barmaid keeps eyeing me. Akil nudges me in the side with his elbow letting me know that he sees her too. She's sexy, sensual-looking with those Angelina Jolie lips of hers. Her eyes are green and dreamy. They resemble cat eyes. There is some naughtiness and innocence behind them. She's highly attracted to me, yet she doesn't say it. It is all in her look.

"You have beautiful eyes," I tell her.

She smiles, her whole face lights up. She's beautiful. But still, I don't roll that way. I can't see myself licking nobodies' carpet.

Akil must've read my mind. "There is nothing wrong with a little bump-'n-grind. What goes on in *Church* stays in *Church*."

I shake my head. "Not gonna happen, Akil. Dream on."

I guess to these strippers I'm a mystery too. They can't figure me out. I mean the haircut speaks in volume. The body, the face, and the eyes...they're reading too much into me. I'm a woman—a full-fledged woman who is not interested in women. I like men. And I love me some penis, not pussy. So therefore, nothing can sway my decision. Not even Akil.

Miss Ecstasy returns. *Oh, damn.*

This time she comes to where we are seated. There is an empty seat alongside Akil, but she asks him to scoot over one so that she can sit between us.

I frown.

She starts yapping as soon as she sits down. She rubs on Akil's shoulder blade. That's right honey indulge in that dark meat. You know you tired of eating the same ole thing for dinner. Then she takes her focus off of Akil and turns to me. I sip my drink. Hopefully she'll return back onstage and leave me the hell alone.

"Which one of you will buy me a drink?" she asks flinging her hair. I look at it hard and see that it is not a wig. It's actually her hair. I hope this chick don't have lice and shit. Flinging that shit all in my drink. I move my glass over. Then take another sip.

I look at Akil. Akil looks at me. I know good and well cheapskate isn't going to buy her a drink.

I cave. "What would you like?"

She starts talking a bunch of nonsense. "Oh, I'll have a glass of juice. No milk."

I just look at her wondering did she lose her brain on the Parkway somewhere.

"No, I'll have ah, ah...Ass-Smacker." She says as she cuts her eye over at the owner.

"What is his name?" I ask her.

"Him? Oh, that's Rip. He has liver spots on his dick."

"How would you know that?" I ask curiously.

Miss Ecstasy turns and looks at me as if to say, "girl, been there, sucked that."

She raises her hand waiting for me to slap it. We greet palms.

Akil burst out in laughter.

I don't find anything funny.

"'Ey, Frankie, give her a...Ass-Smacker." I say. Just saying the words makes me crackup too.

Why did I buy her a drink? This is only going to make matters worse for me. Akil will enjoy it, but I think I might soon regret it.

Frankie places Miss Ecstasy's drink in front of her. She takes one sip. Next thing I know she is rubbing on her breasts. Then she looks at me peculiarly.

Sensual-Looking comes towards me to grab a napkin for one of her patrons. "I like your earrings," she says, and then eyes Miss Ecstasy down.

Ooh, that stare would've cut you. What the hell is going on? I just know these two aren't...erase it from your mind, girl. You ain't all that, I remind myself. *Ain't that the truth!*

Next thing I know Miss Ecstasy is getting all touchy feely with me. She takes liberties that no one takes by rubbing my baldhead. I'm about to black the fuck out. "Keep calm," I tell myself.

I take another sip of my drink.

"Ooh, I love your head," she says, her voice gnawing my eardrums, her thin hands motioning to other places on my body. She swipes her hand down my left breast and tries to inch its way to my crotch. I smack her hand away. I cut my eyes over at her with "kill" in them. She's all giggly and shit. Little does she know she's beginning to irk my nerves?

Finally, the retro music eases in and I stand and start motioning to the beat, completely ignoring her. I sway my hips, twirling my arms, poppin' my coochie, shaking my moneymaker. I rub my baldhead. I am feeling myself up. I grab my tits and squeeze them like they're the best tits in the world.

Miss Ecstasy finally gets up and leaves to go back onstage. *Thank God!*
I sit back down on the barstool.

There is this brunette-haired woman talking to this tall, dark-haired man across the bar, while she's eyeing me down. I get up off the bar stool and start dancing, feeling the retro music vibrate inside of me.

The woman across the bar raises her hands and bellows out funny sounds. Then she points to me and winks. I take a double take and point to myself asking her if that "wink" was directed toward me. She nods her head.

Oh, shit!

I get up and head back to the ladies room to pee for the second time. All eyes are on me. *These chicks are in need of something delicious to eat, but it won't be me.* I think.

Within seconds the woman across the bar enters the ladies room, too. The same sluggish speaking chick is still in the mirror frying her hair. I take a seat because the bathroom is being occupied. The music is blasting through the door.

The woman across the bar starts dancing. She turns in my direction and shakes her round ass in front of my face. *How rude!* She then moves back and grinds my knee giving me a sultry lap dance.

I can't believe this is happening. There are two other chicks in the room as well. They are smiling from ear to ear.

Who's ever in the bathroom, please hurry up, I think.

After a few minutes the door swings open. I push her away, get up, and lock myself in the bathroom.

I pee, wash my hands, and exit.

As I am about to open the second door, the woman across the bar flicks the light off. There are three young women in here with me.

The woman across the bar says, "We are going to *fuck* you."

I try to feel for the doorknob so that I can get the hell out of here. These bitches are crazy if they think they are going to gang rape me. Fuck that!

I rush back to my seat, sit down, and gulp my drink. Akil looks at me strangely. I can't think of anything else except what that woman has said to me: "We are going to *fuck* you." I turn to Akil and say, "You are not going to believe this!"

As I am telling him the story, Akil grins from ear to ear. He bursts out laughing. *This is not funny*. I think.

Miss Ecstasy is back onstage in a revealing getup. She is seductively motioning her curvaceous body, squatting to entice the eyes of these horny men. She comes back over to us and I say, "Buy me a drink?"

"You want me to buy *you* a drink," she repeats as if in shock.

"Yes."

Akil has this 'oh, shit' look on his face as if to say, "Damn, Av, you got this stripper buying you a drink. Oh, you are a bad bitch fo' real."

"Okay." Miss Ecstasy replies, "I've never bought anyone a drink since I've been working here," she tells me, "You're the first."

Boy, do I feel special.

"'Ey, Frankie, I'll have that 'Gimme More', now. It's on Miss Ecstasy."

Miss Ecstasy nods her head.

Frankie prepares my drink and sits it in front of me. I sip, and then engage back into the music.

Next thing I know, Miss Ecstasy takes it too far when she lifts up *my* glass and sips from it.

I blink, blink, blink. "No this bitch didn't." I say to myself. .

I quickly turn to Akil and say, "No, this bitch didn't just sip from my drink."

Akil nods.

My brows knit. "Oh, hell no, this bitch done crossed the line! I don't know where the hell her lips have been. This bitch done lost her mind!"

Akil remains silent because he knows that I am about to pop!

"'Ey, Frankie, come here for a sec." I yell with a grimace.

She scurries over judging by the look on my face.

I soften my tone. "Can you replace this drink? Girly, sipped from my glass. I don't play that shit."

"Sure," Frankie replies, and cuts her eyes over her shoulder and scowls at Miss Ecstasy.

This brunette-haired guy sitting next to me dressed in a baseball cap, blue T-shirt and dungarees turns in my direction. He's deliciously handsome. Obviously he overheard everything I've just said. Does he find it appalling? Disgusting? I know I do.

"Frankie, give *her* a drink on me." The baseball cap guy says.

I turn and say, "Thank you." I try to put a warm smile on my face, but I'm not in the smiling mood. I'm livid!

He nods.

He points his index finger toward our direction. "And give her *friend* a drink too." He tells Frankie.

She nods her head.

"As soon as you finish this drink I'll replace the other for you," Frankie tells me with 'I'm so sorry' embedded in her eyes.

Miss Ecstasy must've overheard me talking to Frankie about the drink, so she sashays herself back over to Akil and me.

She's not as perky as before. Oh, she's changed faces very quickly. This bipolar bitch!

Miss Ecstasy gets up in my face. My right hand rises to let her know I ain't one to fuck with especially under the influence.

"Who does that...sip from a strangers drink," I say to her.

She turns her nose up as if she smells...*shit*.

I do my rendition of "Joan Clayton" on the sitcom *Girlfriends* right about now. My eyes expand the size of saucers.

That squeaky, screechy Rosie Perez voice is deafening when she says, "Oh, girly, this is a strip club. You don't have to get uppity with me, bitch. I bought you that drink!"

I narrow-eye her down like the white trash that she is. My forehead crumples. "So what are you trying to say? That because *you* bought me a drink that you can sip from my glass! Get out of my face," I demand with "I-will-fuck-you-up" burning in my pupils.

She twists up her lips and walks off mumbling to herself.

The Baseball Cap Guy turns in my direction and says, "Miss, she just called you the "N WORD."

Akil looks me dead in my eyes. He nods his head and says, "Yeah, Av, that's what she said. She whispered it. I'm surprised you didn't hear her as keen as your hearing is."

I flip! Completely lose my ladylike fashion.

"WHERE IS THE MUTHAFUCKIN' OWNER! GET HIM OVER HERE...NOW!" I command. I am yelling at the top of my lungs to anyone who cares. It's on and poppin' now!

I pace back and forth pissed the fuck off, while impatiently waiting for this old ass gigolo to bring his slow ass on.

That bitch!

That white bitch!

Finally!

This old slow walking cowboy boot wearing muthafucker comes with a grimace on his face.

I scowl.

What the fuck is his problem! Already I can tell this is not going to go well. Call it women's intuition.

"Are you the owner?"

He nods. "My name is Rip."

"Well, Rippppp, I have a complaint. One of your strippers bought me a drink and then sipped from my glass. I don't appreciate that. Now, I was kind enough to buy her a drink first. Because that's how I do, but..."

He interrupts me with, "I'm sorry that that happened to you."

I raise my forefinger and sway it from side to side. "Oh, I'm not done yet. Oh, girly, then had the audacity to call me a...Nigger."

"I apologize for her," he goes on to say.

I interrupt him. My voice gets loud and raspy. "Oh no, I don't want *you* to apologize. I want *her* to apologize. And you're going to make her do it...now!"

"You don't tell me what I am going to do," he retorts.

"Oh, no!" My breath is hot! Smoke is coming out of my ears. "That bitch is going to apologize directly to my face."

"I will handle it," he says with a glare in his blue eyes.

"No! Either you're going to do it, or I'll take matters into my own hands," I tell him.

He grimaces.

I move in closer. We are nose to nose. The music stops. Eyes stare.

The dancers continue to dance slipping and sliding up and down the strip poles.

I take one step back; look over my left shoulder to surveillance the place. Akil remains sipping his drink. The Baseball Cap Guy remains sipping his drink too.

Where is she?

That bitch!

Herpes chick rat's her out by pointing her finger. Miss Ecstasy is creeping toward the door.

I scowl.

"I dare you to touch me," I tell Rip.

He doesn't move.

Miss Ecstasy tries to run out the door, but I get there before she has the chance. I grab her by her Tina Turner hair and fling her ass down to the floor.

I snarl. "You called me a ...Nigger!"

Miss Ecstasy begins to whimper like a whiny toddler.

And that just pisses me off more. "Bitch, you ain't seen a Nigger yet, but I'm about to show you how a Nigger like me gets down." I ball my right fist as tight as I can make it, and punch the shit outta her. *Whack!* Across her face. I then drag her into the ladies room, squat over the toilet bowl, piss, and then dunk her head in it, repeatedly. "Swallow, bitch, swallow my 'Nigger piss'." Next time she'll think twice before she opens her fuckin' mouth.

"Next time, you choose your battles wisely, bitch." I scowl. Then leave her in the bathroom gagging and spitting and crying her eyes out I slam the bathroom door. I sashay back to my seat. All you hear is the click clacking of my boots.

As I walk pass Rip, I can't help but say, "You watch your back you weak ass muthafucker! The next time I hear you fucking your help I'm going to come back here and fuck you up! You liver-spotted dick bastard!"

Rip eyes grow big, but he remains silent.

I sip my drink, pounce the bar with two balled fists making my, Akil, and Baseball Cap Guy's drinks splash in the air.

Baseball Cap Guy shoulders bounce to the loud bang.

"Let's get the fuck outta here!" I snap at Akil.

Akil doesn't budge. He doesn't even blink.

My voice roars. "I SAID; LET'S GET THE FUCK OUTTA HERE! NOW!"

I never saw Akil jump up so fast before. Looks like Akil won't be inviting me to "CHURCH" with him ever again.

I push the door open with full force. My adrenaline is pumping fast as I walk briskly out to the parking lot, heading toward Akil's car.

"Avery! Avery, slow down. Listen, I have something to tell you." Akil pleads.

I ignore him. I'm too mad to listen. I just want to go home and drown myself in a Rachelle Ferrell CD.

Akil catches up with me. "Avery, please, listen...listen to me. There is something I need to tell you."

I keep walking with a disconcerted look upon my face.

Akil jumps in front of me to slow me down. Finally, I stop, breathing heavily. My heart is throbbing in my chest.

"Things got out of hand," Akil says.

"What do you mean...*things got out of hand*?" I ask in a salty tone.

"This...all of this, it wasn't supposed to happen this way."

I narrow-eye him, "What are you talking about, Akil?"

"You were setup."

"What do you mean...*setup*?"

I purse my lips. Akil sighs. Then he throws his arms up mid-air and slowly brings them back down to his sides. "Hear me out?" he murmurs.

I tap my foot. "I'm listening."

"The Baseball Cap Guy is my boss. And the woman who you just beat-up, well, that is his wife. Well, soon-to-be ex-wife. They are in the process of a nasty divorce. His name is Emerson. He asked me to help him out by finding someone he knew his wife would be attracted to. With short notice the only person I could think of was you. Emerson paid me fifteen hundred dollars to seek revenge on his wife. He's a really good guy, but he snapped when she pulled his kids away from him. He's torn up inside. He's a good dad and the thought of him losing his kids really bothered me. I could see if he was a deadbeat but he's not. She's got a restraining order on him. Avery, he has a reputation to uphold being the principal of the school. This is destroying him. I had to do something to help him out, especially when she lied on him and said that he put his hands on her. He never did, but who's going to believe him. He can't go see his kids until this ugly divorce is finalized, but by then who knows how his kids will respond to him. We have been friends since I've been teaching. I could not sit back and do nothing and watch Emerson drown."

I can't believe my ears. I squint my eyes and cock my head to the side, and just look at him with an impassive look on my face. "So, let me get this straight. You'd rather compromise our *friendship* to help your boss? Are you *fucking* him?" I say in a belligerent tone.

"No! I don't fuck men. I fuck women. It wasn't like that, Av. I needed the money. I mean these car payments are kicking a brotha's ass." He smirks.

I don't see anything funny.

With a tight face I say, "Where's the money?"

"Huh?"

"Where's the money?"

"I have it in my wallet. Why?"

"Give me the money."

"What?"

"I SAID...GIVE. ME. THE. MONEY. You want me to do all the work while you two sit on your asses and watch me make a complete fool out of myself. Give me the money!"

"C'mon, Av, we peoples."

I shake my head. My eyes grow dark with fiery-red flames burning in the pupils. "I can't believe you. Did you *not* tell me that he said his wife called me the 'N WORD'? No, no, we're not...peoples. Now, I'm going to ask you *one last time*. GIVE. ME. THE. MONEY!!!"

"You're serious? Oh, it's just about the money now, huh?"

"Don't try to patronize me, Akil, just fork over the money." I have this cold look in my eyes. And Akil knows that I ain't playing. "Let me explain something to you. Hear me real good and clear. I want to thank you for proving me right about you. I'm not mad one bit. Nah. See, I've learned that real men hold their heads up high, real men swallow their pride when they cannot follow through. Real men speak up even when they can't fulfill their words. Real men are true to their heart. But Dogs, Dogs show their true colors even when they think they're not." I smirk. "God is so good in revealing a true man. It is obvious that you have no concept of what MAN really means. You may have a penis but even that does not make you a man. I'm happy today because I've learned a lot about you. But it's funny because you always speak of knowing men who only want sex, men who cheat, men who dog women out, but have you ever looked in the mirror and asked yourself: 'Man, what kind of man am I?' Real men know who they are. But Dogs, Dogs are still trying to figure it out."

Akil reaches in his front pants pocket and pulls out his wallet. He opens it and pulls out the fifteen hundred dollars, and places it in my hands.

"The next time you want to make a fool of someone, don't bother to call on me. Do it yourself. Don't call me! Don't think of me! We are through!" I snap.

Akil walks off with his head dangling low. He gets in his car and drives off.

I place the money in my bag and strut off like I'm the shit. With everything in me I try not to breakdown, but I know once I walk through my front door, it's a wrap. I'll be bawling like a big ass baby.

When I arrive home and open the door. God it feels so heavy. The burden has taken over me. I flick the light on.

Sluggishly I make my way over to my CD player. I search through my CDs and find Rachelle's. I open the case and slip her CD in the CD player. Then I reach for the remote and plop on the sofa.

Bursting from the speakers is "I Can Explain." I lean my head back against the fabric and close my teary eyes and float away in mind, in spirit with Xavier.

Poof. I seem to have vanished from this life.

36

GILDA PULLS ME FROM Snazzy and has me work with this Hispanic woman named Ola, who looks to be in her mid-forties.

Ola is petite in size with short red-dyed hair and round chestnut-brown eyes. Her English is broken but not as bad as Abigail's.

I button up my knit sweater and button three buttons on my denim jacket because it is cold back here.

I greet Ola, "Gilda sent me back here to help you out."

"O'ka. I'm repacking these," she shows me a bunch of cardboard boxes with opened hosiery packages, underwear, socks, tank tops, and T-shirts.

This is tedious work. I feel caged in this cold room. The heat ventilation above my head is blowing, but with the doors in the far back open cold air is coming in due to the trucks delivering shipments of cargo.

The tip of my nose is cold as if I am in frigid Alaska.

I can't wait for 5:15 p.m., to get here. I'm ready to go home. Instead I go on my fifteen-minute break.

"OOOOOOHHHHHHHH, Gurrrrrrrrrrrrrrrrrllllllll, say it ain't...!"

I hear this screechy echo coming from behind me. I can't make out if it's a female or male by the high-pitched tone of voice.

"Yeah, I'm talkin' to you." the screechy voice says again. "Yeah, *you* in them skinny jeans, whatchu gonna do? You gonna jus' let *him* get away with that! Just accept it and let him run over you like a doormat. Gurl, gurl, gurl, it couldn't have been me. Lies!"

I turn around before getting on the escalator and see this dark-skinned dude with a peasy Mohawk walking up behind me. All I hear is the click-clacking of his hard bottom shoes as he catches up with me.

My eyes scroll him up and down. *Fashion don't*, I think to myself.

Boyfriend is lookin' tired. His stripe button down shirt is wrinkled along with his snag pinstripe navy-blue trousers that do not end at the heel of his dress shoes. Dress shoes, might I add, that he is wearin' with white sweat socks. I said, sweat socks! This is a fashion tradgey. How you gonna work in fashion and don't look the part?

I scrunch up my nose and shake my head.

Boyfriend rotates his thick neck. "Uh-huh. Don't even try to clown me, beeeetttt-cha!"

"You talkin' to me," I ask with a bit of 'tude in my tone. I am *not* in the mood.

"Look, I know the scoop on *you*. You can run but you can't hide. Not with BLAB hot on the press. I read the article and I was like...*wwwwwwwwwwhatttttttttt*?! Oh, no, *he* didn't say that about *her*. Oooh...oooh, no, no, *he* didn't! That's right! I was too through. Hmm." He presses his lips together and crumples his forehead with this mean glare in his eyes.

I keep quiet. Don't want to stirrup any drama at work especially with this nappy-headed drama queen.

Boyfriend throws his arms up mid-air and places 'em on his wide hips. "Well? Whatchu gonna do?" He fans his fingers to stress a point. "Okay." He purses his lips, then smacks them loud. "Gurl, listen, it was all nicey, nicey with the interview you had with Narlene Scott. But seriously, tell me that *you* aren't going to allow him to just diss you like that, are you? I mean I get the 'black sisterhood thing' you workin' it and all, but c'mon. The man disrespected you to the world. He blurted all of your personal business out like you were some low-class ho to him. He practically ruined your reputation. And oh, let's not forget him blurting your HIV status to a magazine. Wow. You cannot be that stupid as to let him get away with it. Tell me you're not that stupid. And that you're not gonna let him get away with it. Listen, girlfriend, we *women* have to stick together. If you let that bastard throw you under the bus what do you think the other 'sisters in the 'hood' are gonna do? Your name means something whether you want it to or not. Women look up to you. They respect you and admire you for speaking up. So it's no longer your fight. It's all women's fight. I don't think you realize what you've done. You started a frenzy so I suggest you finish it. Do you even know who you are?" He rotates his neck. "Honey, wake up, and smell the *Anonymous*! That's right, I said it! It's time for you to start smellin' yourself. You really have to see your work, worth, and appreciate what you've accomplished thus far. Run with it. Don't just let that that man do you dirty because he thinks he can. Giiiiirrrrrrrllllllll, you got the power in your possession and if you don't use it to your advantage, then you might as well as stop now. Don't say another word and don't do another thing. Just disappear."

I suck my teeth. "What business of it is yours?" I say with my hands on my hips. This dude is beginning to get on my first and last nerve.

He gasps, and then presses his right hand to his chest so dramatically. "What business!" he says in a high-pitched tone. "What business?!" his voice gets louder and louder trying to attract an audience.

I turn to see if anyone is looking, listening. No one appears to be entertained.

He doesn't seem to care even if they were. This melodramatic civa definitely missed his calling 'cause he doggone sho' should've been an actor.

He makes a hand gesture like he is about to claw something. "Girl, I oughta snatch— if you had hair I'd snatch it bald."

I burst out laughing 'cause this character is something special. And I don't mean special as is unique. I mean special as in ...coo-coo.

He clicks his heels together. *Oh, now he thinks he's Dorothy in the Wizard of Oz*, I think. Yeah, he is truly special.

He changes his tune real quick. Now he's all bubbly and whatnot. "Hi. My name is Divine...aka Go-Diva. I'm here as a shoulder to lean on. You gotta be hurtin' after that bastard put you out there like that. He put you on blast, girlfriend. In print at that! With Narlena Scott...the 'Blabbermouth Guru'...of all people! That beeeetttttt-cha can't hold water. And her fans love it! In my opinion she's on a low scale but fans respect her like *Oprah*. She has a great following, bigger than Wendy Williams." He adds, then purses his thick lips and rolls his big dark brown eyes and plants 'em on me.

There is no way I can deny that it is even me. And with this queer I won't even bother. He is too much for me to handle and I don't even know him. We have never even said hello to one another but he finds it necessary to give me advice. I wonder how many others know. I bet by the time I come from break and head back downstairs the whole store will.

My eyes scroll him from feet to face already I can't stand him. It never even dawned on me that someone from my job would be a fan of Narlena Scott. Dang, dang, dang!!!!

I cluck my tongue as I often do when I feel someone is so full of themselves and barely got their shit together.

"I ain't through with you," he says, while shaking his jug head as he makes his way toward the Men's room and enters.

This is all I need for this drama queen to be all up in my business. Isn't it punishment enough for me to be embarrassed by Zaelyn? Now I have to worry about this out-of-the-closet queen spreading gossip about me on the job.

I enter the break room feeling like all of Zaelyn's lies are growing out of my back. And just like Pinocchio's nose they just keep on growing and growing and growing until I can no longer stand the weight of 'em and I just simply collapse.

I must admit Divine asks a very good question: "What am I going to do?" A part of me feels like blowing Zaelyn's spot up and suing him for defamation of character, but then the other part of me says no. Everything that he is doing to me will surely come back to haunt him. I am not going to exert my energy on him. I know the truth. God knows the truth. What would I gain by lying...nothing, but heartache, grief? And that is something I can do without. My time will come. With me working my tail off like I am, things are bound to work in my favor. I'm stacking my chips away to pursue something that was never mine. If it weren't for Daisy I wouldn't have come this far. I would still be home moping around grieving over Xavier, and just letting life pass me by. I know I'll never be able to tell Daisy how much she has given me, but I can show her by keeping my word. *Ev'ry Ho Gotta Daddy* will be in print. As long as I have air in this body, there is no stoppin' me now. I am on a mission!

Eight o'clock rolls around rather quickly. I grab my stuff and dash out the door into the cold night's air to avoid any more distractions from Divine or anyone else.

37

RING. RING. RING.

I rise to my feet and answer my cell phone.

"Hello?"

"How was your evening?" the male voice asks.

"Fine." I cut my eyes to the side. "May I ask whose calling?"

"Still don't recognize my voice, huh. After all these years, Ms. Love I am appalled."

I shake my head. "Jordan?"

"Yes. Ms. Love, I have been waiting by the phone forever. Someone was supposed to be calling me so that we can do lunch. What do you say? Are you free?"

Free ain't the word.

"How long do I have to get dazzling?"

"Baby, you are already dazzling. Can you be ready in let's say...half hour?"

I nod. Then smile. "Yes. I have to give you my new address."

"I'm listening."

"124 Struggling Artist Ave."

"Got it. See you in a half."

"Okay."

My eyes skyward the ceiling, "You are always on time." I giggle. Then rush downstairs into the bathroom to take a quick shower.

I dash upstairs butt naked to my bedroom and slide open the closet doors. *What am I going to wear today?* Hmm. *Maybe this, no, maybe that. No. My eyes light up. This one!*

I remove the tie-dyed fuchsia, orange and purple halter dress from the wooden hanger. Head straight toward the full-length mirror and place the dress in front of me, then pose, still giddy.

I walk back to the closet and grab my fuchsia four-inch stilettos. teardrop purple earrings that hang to my shoulders, and get dressed.

I head downstairs and into the bathroom to add some cocomango hair butter to my scalp. Apply minimal makeup. And await Jordan's call.

Ring. Ring. Ring.

"Hello."

"I'm in front."

"Okay."

As I step outside, it feels about 80 degrees. The sun is blazing. The heat feels so good on my bare-skinned back. As I walk up to the car I can see that Jordan has bought a corvette—shiny midnight blue. The man has impeccable taste. I still for the life of me can't figure out what he sees in Dolce. I never thought her to be his type. Or maybe I am just being bias because in my eyes and heart Jordan Seymour was meant for me. Dang, he looks so good. I wonder if he just left from the gym. I know how much he likes to get his workout on. *Why doesn't he do his workout on me...just once? Doesn't he know how happy that would make me? Just once, Jordan, do something outrageous. Do something I would least expect like pull me close to you, whisper sweet nothings in my ear, tell me how much you want and desire me, and then throw me down onto the bed and toy with my body. Make me beg for more.*

"Girl, stop dreaming. Wake up and smell the roses for goodness sake. HE. DON'T. WANT. YOU. AND. YOU. KNOW. WHY.

"Shut up, Karma! You're always trying to ruin a good thing!"

"Bitch, you don't need any help in that department. Chile, you fuck your own shit up without any help from me. It's you, Avery. You!"

I nix Karma off. Then enter on the passenger's side and sit down. God, he smells so fresh. Like morning rain with a splash of "I Am King" body oil. My body feels exhilarated. I'm actually going on a date with...Jordan Seymour! I smile inwardly.

"What's up stranger?" Jordan says with a huge smile on his face.

I turn to him and smile. He looks so casually dressed in his black tee and a plain pair of dungarees. I see he recently got a haircut. It looks so smooth that I have the urge to reach out and touch, his clean-shaven head, but I don't.

"Nothing much," I say. "Well, actually, I'm writing a book," I say, and then smile.

He turns and looks at me. "What's it called?" he asks surprised.

I blush. *"Ev'ry Ho Gotta Daddy."*

Jordan bursts out in laughter. "Wow! Never knew you had a book in you, girl. You are full of surprises."

I nod. Then smile again. "Yes, I am. Well, you never know what you can do until you do it. And plus, it's a collaboration with another woman." I tell him, while gazing out of the passenger's-side window.

"That's awesome, Avery!" He says, turns the music up a little and turns and looks at me with this gleam in his eyes.

What's up with that? I wonder.

Surprisingly, there is minimal traffic. We ride for maybe close to an hour and a half. Jordan takes me to this fancy restaurant called BEEHIVE on the outskirts of Philly. I surely wasn't expecting this! Jordan parks the car, exits out, and comes around and opens the passenger's-side door for me. *Okay, what gives?*

I step out nearly bumping heads with him. He still makes me hot and dizzy. I don't care what anyone else thinks...Jordan Seymour is panty dripping fine!

As I walk into BEEHIVE I am stunned. The place is exquisite. Sea-foam green marble floors, stained glass rainbow ceiling with beautiful aqua crystal chandleries. There are high walls in gold, bronze, violet, crimson and lavender. The crown molding of black stone adds a little oomph along with the shiny gold sequins on chocolate brown silk drapery really accentuates the place.

Red, lime-green, orange, pewter, magenta, turquoise, and amber yellow throw pillows about the floor. The aquarium of exotic fish and waterfalls in the center of the spacious room adds a nice touch too.

The dining area is of satin and linen with rich cherry wood tables and chairs, fine china and crystal glasses. The restaurant is full of color and eclectic beauty. It is simply gorgeous.

As we stand by the entranceway a slender woman who looks to be in her early thirties greets us with an illuminating smile.

"Welcome to BEEHIVE," she says in what sounds like a British accent. "My name is Golden. Please follow me."

I nod.

I can't seem to take my eyes off of her. She is beyond gorgeous. She has flawless eggplant-colored skin and soft coal-colored eyes, full thick lips, and a round face with exotic features. Her hair is cut low in a kinky afro. It looks healthy with a glistening sheen. It brings out the brownish-red tones that shimmer in the light. I can't pinpoint where she may originate, but she is 100% imported *Egyptian fineness* to me.

Over dinner Jordan and I talk, laugh a lot, and eat a delicious Mediterranean meal and reminisce about back in the day. I really enjoy his company, mainly because there are no distractions from Dolce.

"There's something I need to tell you, Av." Jordan says with assertiveness in his tone and seriousness on his face.

Oh boy, here it goes. I think.

I place my fork down to the side of my plate. "Is everything all right?" Jordan just stares into my eyes.

What is it? Just tell me and stop gawking at me like I have a booger on my nose.

"This is not easy to say, especially to you," he says. "But...I'm... married."

My head is spinning. *Did he just say.... the "M" word. No, I must be dreaming.*

"But your eyes are open... stupid ass!"

"Karma, back off! I am really not in the mood for you."

I am at a loss for words.

"Smile bitch. Act like you don't care. Do something, other than look like a dork in front of this gorgeous, sexy man."

I stammer. "Oh, oh, oh, um, I mean...that's wonderful." I bat my lashes, stunned. Deep down I want to reach over this table and punch his lights out. *How dare you get married on me! And then have the nerve to bring me here to gloat in my face that you have someone at home. A wife—a life partner—someone to grow old with—someone to get fat and gray-haired with—someone to eat with every single day. A warm body to lie beside you every freakin' night! I can feel MBW (Mad Black Woman) wanting to rise up out of me and give him a piece of her mind.* I try with all of my might not to. But it is difficult. *Why, Jordan? Why would you of all people hurt me like this? Can't you see the connection we share? Why are you so damn blind? Blah, blah, blah...*

Quickly I get a grip. Calm, my sista, calm the fuck down.

I bat my lashes. "So, so, when did this all take place? Did you have an elaborate wedding?"

"No. Jack and I decided something small would be better."

Jack! Who the fuck is...Jack?! What happened to Dolce? Is he gay? Oh, Jordan tells me that you are not getting bent over.

I blink. "Jack?"

His brown eyes spread wide. "No, no, I don't roll that way, Av. Jacky. That's her name. I know you're probably wondering what happened to Dolce. Well, to simply put it she was not the woman for me. We clashed on so many levels. So we decided to call it quits before we ended up killing one another. It was pretty, pretty bad. Dolce can be somewhat of a she-devil." He cocks his head back and laughs. It echoes throughout the restaurant. A couple of heads turn in our direction. I look to the side trying to figure out what the hell is going on with him. *Why do this to me? Here in this beautiful restaurant around strangers. Why humiliate me again? Wasn't once enough humiliation? You had to wait four months to share this news with me.*

You could've told me this over the phone, sent me a postcard, or wrote me a letter, or not tell me at all.

I am breathless. The news is too much for me to handle. I rise to my feet and storm out of the restaurant.

Jordan leaps to his feet. "Avery! Avery, what's wrong?" He yells.

I don't bother to stop. My feet are moving pretty damn fast in these stilettos while tears roll hard down my face. All I see through blurry vision is Karma standing before me with a picket sign that reads: YOU MIGHT AS WELL BECOME A FULLBLOWN LESBIAN, GIRL. THESE MEN DON'T WANT YOUR HIV ASS.

Up goes my middle finger. Bitch!

I hop on a train to head back home.

I sit with weariness on my face and sadness in my eyes as I think about Xavier. Slightly I crack a smile. I think about how much he spoiled me, and how much I miss romance, dining out, trips away from the here and now, spending nights in exclusive hotels, room service, waking to breakfast in bed, rose petals at my feet, and shopping at the finest boutiques in the city. And then, I think, *Avery, you don't need a man for all those things, because eventually you can give yourself that and more.*

I lean my head back against the smooth pleather seat and think it would be the ideall life for me. And even though I cannot give myself it at this particular moment, I know that I am working towards it as long as I continue to work as hard as I am doing. I am in my early forties and I've only been in love once in my life. Xavier *was* the man of my dreams. He *was* the only man for me.

I know I shouldn't have accepted Jordan's invitation. And I know that the only reason why I did was because I wanted to be in the presence of a man. I trusted Jordan. He was my safety net.

I feel vulnerable at this time in my life. I guess I just wanted to be wanted. Even for a couple of hours would've sufficed. But Jordan ruined that without as much as a second thought. How could *he* be so insensitive to my heart? He knows I how feel about him. Why would he hurt me so badly?

I swear, in that exact moment, I hear a female's voice say, "What had I done to deserve a life like this?" It is as if she took the words right outta my mouth.

467

38

I WIND MY NECK and then crack it to get the kinks out. Stretch out my arms and legs to get the blood circulating before I stand to go to the bathroom. I still can't seem to get Daisy out of my head. It just-just amazes me of how much she went through. It seems hard to fathom one person going through so much. But then again, it doesn't because look at all the stuff I've gone through. Why would she lie? I see no reason for her to conjure up a make-believe story as this. I can't see her as that type of person even though I don't know her personally. I felt something as I was engrossed in her words. It felt so real, so brutal, and so unfair. I just can't see her lying about something like that; especially knowing that she is trying to reach out to young girls. Daisy doesn't come across as a woman who plays simple-minded games. Not at all.

I lay the manuscript on the saffron coffee table, then stand in my white men's nightshirt from the saffron futon and walk over to my computer and insert my poetry demo: *Lady of Leisure* before heading to the bathroom. With the apartment being so quiet I attentively listen to myself recite this poem I am thinking about performing at Lounge Out Poets Café this coming Thursday.

I get up off the futon and make my way into the bathroom. As I pull down my boy shorts and sit my behind on the cold toilet seat so many thoughts race through my mind. *Man, the rush I feel flowing through my veins when I stand before a crowd is something...beyond beautiful.*

After using the toilet, I flush it and wash my hands and towels dry them on the deep plum-colored hand towel. I then, walk barefoot over to my full-length mirror and study myself. There is something bursting to come pouring out of me.

I tilt my head to side, and stare. Then I pretend I am standing before a crowd of folks. Green, gray, brown, blue, hazel eyes stare back at me. They feel me—sex me down with their eyes. Looking at myself, I feel sexually free. Having the freedom to expose myself through speech, and having it without being put on pause, silenced, or shushed. It is the most unbound I've felt in a long, long time.

I wake up out of a daze with a devious smirk on my face. The whites of my eyes glow in the pitch darkness, and vivid memories flash across the bedroom wall. I ease my tense body up and lean my back against the headboard. I feel my pulse rise, temples throb, heart pounding, eyes narrowing, and adrenaline pumping.

I lean forward with my mouth dangling open. Eyes widen, forehead crumples as I hear the keen sound of *click, click, click...*

Visibly, I can see myself walking downtown Paterson. Quickly my fingers grip the tangerine sheets. I ball my fingers into a knot, then tightly clench the linen fabric and squeeze and twist it as if to wring a wet towel.

I feel a stranger's arm wrap around my neck—him dragging me in the alleyway—in the back of the Electronics store.

God, why?

"Why are You making me relive this again?" I ask Him in a whisper. I hear nothing but the sound of the radiator, fridge, and toilet running. Then the sounds all vanish.

My ears tune in to the soulful sound of Ann Nesby singing "I'm Still Wearing Your Name" permeating through the paper-thin walls of my crazy ass neighbor, Mrs. Silva's apartment.

Every day I think, I feel, I relive that moment knowing that I am wearing *his* name inside of me—flushing through my veins having a good ole laugh at my ass. Although it is not *his* real name, it is *his* acronym just the same: HIV-Human Immunodeficiency Virus.

My mind drifts.

I sit back and recollect when I was sitting in the Assembly Room of the Paterson Free Public Library and speakers from Hyacinth AIDS Foundation came out to share their stories of how they became infected with HIV. It was truly an eye-opener for me.

There were so many young and older men and women of different ethnicities divulging their darkest secrets, aloud. There were various ages standing before me just peeling away at their pain. While listening to them, I felt so disconnected. I felt set apart from them even though I knew that I was in the same inner-circle with them. Why? Why didn't I get up and share what happened to me? Why did I sit there engrossed in their stories and said nothing as if my mouth were cemented shut? Why couldn't I stand before a crowd of strangers and admit how scarred I was/am? How come I couldn't say that being raped twice was nothing compared to living with HIV? No, it didn't matter that I didn't self-inflict this on myself. No, it didn't matter that I wasn't a junky or promiscuously whoring around the streets of Paterson. No, no, it didn't matter that I didn't shoot up. Honestly, none of that mattered! But what did matter was that I was in the right setting at the right time and I did nothing to include myself. I was undetected. And I wanted to keep it that way.

I sat quiet; yet attentive, feeling disgust swarm around in my belly. I said nothing. And I have regretted it every waking day. But then, I eased up on myself and thought *it wasn't my place to share*. I wasn't associated with Hyacinth. I was just there. Listening to them educate others before it happened to them. But it had already happened to me. I was punishing myself. Blaming myself. Beating myself up, for no apparent reason, it happened. And I have to live with it.

It is then that I realize that I don't have to share what is inside of my body. This is my business. My life!

I *choose* to be upfront and honest with those I may be attracted to in a sexual way. But other than that, if I feel as though whatever I share with someone may be used against me I have a right to keep my personal life to myself. I have a right as long as I am not doing harm to anyone. I have a right and a moral obligation to me, first and foremost. Me. Every waking day, and every lonely night, there is no one in my bed, mind fucking me, but HIV.

Dizzily, I rise to my feet hearing myself humming the lyrics as if I can relate to Ann's tale. I drag my feet across the hardwood floor, nearly tripping over the long pants leg of my tatty jeans, simultaneously feeling emptiness pitting away at my heart, still in tune to Ann singing from the depths of her soul.

I struggle to amble over to the fridge and stretch my limp arm out to reach atop for my meds, Omega-3 fish oil caplets and Strovite One multivitamins. I pull open the fridge and pullout a bottle of spring water. Untwist the white plastic cap, tilt my head slightly back, and pop the pills in my mouth, one by one. Then take a long swig of the cool refreshing water to wash them down with.

I cut my eyes over to the wall-mounted clock. It reads 1:15 p.m. I sigh, as if my body feels completely lethargic. What have I done to be feeling so drained?

"Stress," Avona says, "Girl, you've been under a lot of stress lately. You need to get out of the house and get some fresh air. Inhale the world and let God do the worrying for you."

I nod, and then take a few steps toward the closet, slide the doors open, and slowly extend out my arm to reach for my black goose-down from its hanger. Sluggishly, I put it on. Tiny beads of moisture crowd my forehead as my hand slowly reaches in the coat pockets and pulls out my black leather Anne Klein gloves. I slip them on.

Lazily, I reach my hand atop the closet shelf for my chocolate brown knit hat and snuggle it on my head. Take a step or two toward the left and snatch my keys off of the key hook. I then head straight toward the front door. I stop; look down at my feet noticing no socks or shoes.

Feeling exhausted by now, I stand in place trying to catch my breath. I turn back around and climb the steps back up to my bedroom. By the time I reach the top step I am pooped. Where has my energy gone?

With my right hand I pull out the second drawer to reach in for a pair of wool socks. I sit on the edge of the bed, barely able to raise my left foot and slip it on, then the right. Already I am out of breath. Sweat is trickling down the sides of my face. I sit for what feels like eternity but I know that it is only a few seconds. I rise to my feet and walk toward the small closet and pull out my black leather Coach boots. I pull out a chair sitting in the corner next to the small bookshelf, sit, and struggle to put them on. Finally, I do. I have no energy left, so it seems, yet I manage to go downstairs, walk out of the door, down to the elevator, land on the lobby floor, and exit out of the building walking toward downtown Paterson with that song still embedded in my head.

Honestly, I want to stop hurting. Just lock away this pain and stuff it in my closet somewhere. I feel so hung over. *"Get out of your head. Move out of your own way,"* I hear what sounds like Johnnie's voice. My body shudders.

Things are tough. The current situation is mind-boggling. And being truthful, I really don't know what to do or how to face it. It is right here in front of my face. I wish I could run from it, but I can't. I won't. No matter what I promised myself I wouldn't.

My right hand slides down my cleavage, down, and then rests upon my lap. The silver bucket rests on the saffron coffee table with a bottle of Sweet Bitch "Shiraz" chilling. My wine glass is half full as I lean my clean-shaven head back against the fine leather of the black swivel chair.

The crystal edge of the wine glass touches my lips. I sip the smooth and fruity. It pleasures my tongue.

I savor it for a minute and then swallow it down. Take another sip, and put my earphones to my phone in my ears as I plug it into my HP

Desktop and let out a soft *ahhhhhhhhhhhhhh*. My body feels so relaxed.

I prop my feet up on the saffron ottoman and listen to some of my favorite blue-eyed soul artists. "Sisters Are Doin' It for Themselves" by Anne Lenox (of the Eurythmics) with Aretha Franklin. Jon B. "They Don't Know" eases in. Then Christina Aguilera "You Lost Me" sets the scene clear as day for me. Joss Stone "Free Me", Duffy "Distant Dreamer", Adele "Set Fire to the Rain" and Amy Winehouse "In My Bed."

Robin Thicke smoothly glides his fine self in with "Lost Without U" and "Sex Therapy." I know Paula Patton is knocking that down every night. Or perhaps not.

I fade. Completely lose myself in the lyrics. My thoughts glide effortlessly to another place. Another time. Another me. I feel as if I am floating on cloud nine. No worries. No cares. I'm doing...A.L.

I sway my head from side to side enjoying myself. I take another sip of wine, then lip-sync along with Robin Thicke: *"I'm lost without you/can't help myself/how does it feel/to know that I love you baby."*

After listening to the music, I rise to my feet in my terrycloth sky-blue bathrobe and enter the bathroom. I sit on the edge of the bathtub, turn the nozzle, and let the warm water flow freely in the bathtub until it reaches mid-level. I pour some lavender chamomile bubble bath in the water. Unloosen the belt to my bathrobe, hang it on the bath hook, then slip down my panties, and step in the silky water.

I reach over in the soap dish and lather the Dove pampering shea butter with warm vanilla scent in my Cain and Able bath sponge, exfoliate my body, then rest my head on my fluffy bath pillow. And as I do, my mind drifts replaying all the memorable moments I shared with Xavier. I smile, feeling a sense of inner peace. God, I miss my man.

My cell phone rings, but I don't dear budge to run and answer it.

Let 'em leave a message, I think to myself.

Ahhhhhhhhhhhhhhhhhh. It feels so good to have complete serenity. I bathe for half hour, use my big toe to flick the handle to drain the tub, and step out in my birthday suit. Exit the bathroom and climb the steps to my bedroom. Sliding open the door to my closet and remove my satin kimono robe from its hanger and cover my damp skin.

My cell phones rings, again.

Jesus!

I rush back downstairs to the living room to answer the phone.

"Hello?"

"Hey, Av."

I roll my eyes. "Akil?"

"Yeah, the one and only," he says, in a low tone of voice.

"I thought I told you we are no longer friends. Don't call me anymore!"

Before I click him off, Akil intercepts by saying. "Hear me out before you hang up on me, Av?"

I cut my eye to the clock mounted on the living room wall.

"Why are you calling so late? It's 1:00 a.m."

"I miss you. I know I shouldn't have called. But I needed to talk to you about something. Look, I didn't realize how cold this world was until you left. You were my blanket."

"Well, welcome to my world." I sigh. "Can't this wait till morning?"

"No. Not really. Since you've been gone I haven't slept, ate, and stopped drinking. I feel so alone. No moments to share with anyone that I want to be with. I'm fucked without you! I don't like your world, very dark and lonely."

"Yes. It is. Lord knows I know that to be true. What's going on?" I cock my head to the side to hold the phone with my ear as I tighten the belt to my robe.

"Well, remember when I said that we have something in common?"

"Yes."

"Um, there is something I need to ask you."

"Okay. Ask away."

"Do you know a man named Zaelyn Homes?"

I remain silent. Blood rushes to my head. Suddenly, I feel light-headed. Dizzy.

"Av, you there?"

I blink, "Yes. I'm here. What about Zaelyn?"

"How well do you know him?"

Should I tell him that we dated? Should I play like I don't know him? What do I say? I can't tell him that we had sex. I can't tell him that the condom came off and Zaelyn freaked the hell out and went home and tried to drink himself to death. What do I say? How do I explain what we shared?

I pull on that tough skin. "It's really none of your business, Akil, but to satisfy your curiosity, yes, we dated for a little while."

"Did you know that he was *married* at the time that you two were dating?"

"No. He never told me directly. I kind of found out on my own."

By now I am getting annoyed with the twenty questions.

Akil pauses.

"Why are you asking me about Zaelyn, Akil?"

"Well, actually I need to tell you about us first," he says.

"What do you mean...us?"

"How well do you know your mother's side of the family?"

"Not well enough, I guess. Why?"

"Avery, we are third cousins."

"Get the hell outta here!" I snap.

"No. It's true. My mom was doing some housecleaning and came across your mother's obituary. I don't know why she was holding on to it. Well, there's more..."

"What? What are you trying to tell me, Akil?"

"Zaelyn," he says.

"What about him?"

God, please tell me that we are not cousins, too. I wouldn't be able to live with myself.

"Well, not Zaelyn per say."

"What are you trying to tell me, Akil? Please... just say it."

"I found out that Zaelyn's *wife* is *our* cousin."

"What!"

"Calm down, Av. Her name is Vett. I didn't know how to break the news to you. But it's been killing me to tell you. I couldn't hold it in any longer. I hope you are not mad at me."

I remain silent, then hang up the phone completely baffled.

Massaginge my forehead in a circular motion, I think, *oh, God, I had sex with my cousin's husband. I'd fallen head-over-heels for my cousin's husband. What kind of woman does that make me?*

"Avery, you didn't know," Avona stresses in my defense. "Don't beat yourself up. It was an honest mistake."

I wonder if Zaelyn knew that we were related. I think. This cannot be true. Lord, tell me that it is not true.

I walk over to the silver ice bucket and pullout Sweet Bitch and take it to the head.

I sit in my living room indulging in Sweet Bitch until the bottle is empty. I can't believe this is happening. Xavier. Now Zaelyn and his wife, I swear I sure know how to pick 'em, don't I. Of all the people I pick one that is married to my cousin. What are the odds of this happening? I really don't know. All I know is that I am not buying into it just yet until I get some proof. Akil has to come one better than an obituary or word of mouth. What other concrete evidence does he have?

As far as I am concern, what's done is done. Nothing can be changed. It happened. I had sex with my cousin's husband.

I walk into the kitchenette and grab the bag of Wise potato chips. I open the bag and pullout two at a time, and slip them in my mouth.

Crunch. Crunch.

I walk over to Sis and sit down and surf the web. As I am doing so, I feel this urge to get out of town, so I see what the new happening spots are in New York.

I come across a place in Harlem on 310 Lenox Avenue between 125th and 126th called Red Rooster Harlem. I checkout the menu and read up on the place and the history of the owner Chef Marcus Samuelsson.

"*Make a reservation tomorrow,*" Karma suggests. "*It's time to do something spontaneous for a change.*"

Zaelyn creeps in my head again. Our night of passion is wearing me thin. Life is too short to be waiting to enjoy my life. I can't change the past. All I can do is live for now. And that's exactly what I'm going to do. Live, laugh, and enjoy the comfort of becoming a successful woman in transition!

"*How you figure that?*" *Karma scolds me like I'm some teenager.* "*You got to do the work in order for you to be successful. What you gonna do this time, Avery? First, you were working at Red Alert. Xavier got in your way. Then you tried with Anonymous. And you let 'love' with Hellman Middleton get in your way. Then you decided that you wanted to learn a trade so you tried phlebotomy. Passed your final exam, but you still haven't taken the national test. Then you decided that you wanted to be a writer. Ain't nobody gonna buy that whack ass book of yours, Ev'ry Ho Gotta Daddy. You ain't no real author. Girl, stop dreaming. You got all of these brilliant ideas, but when are you going to execute one, and stick with it? When? Okay. You're sticking it out at ECLECTIC to support the book, but for how long? Just stop while you're ahead. Just stop. You know you had success with Anonymous. It was your dumb ass that let it go. Know what, Av, you really make me sick!*" *Karma rolls her eyes and sucks her teeth.*

"Hold on, Avery, just hold on," *Avona says.* "*Don't let her discourage you. She's just jealous.*"

"Hah!" *Karma cackles,* "*Jealous of what? A failure. A has been.*"

Avona interjects. "*Don't listen to her. She'll see. You'll bounce back and show 'em all what you're workin' with.*"

"Yeah. I will," I say to myself.

I smile from ear to ear.

Zaelyn slips in my head again. We had great chemistry. He made me feel so good, so beautiful, and so alive. But that is in the past. It is time to let it go.

Focusing on the here and now I contemplate how I can accomplish two things at once. The book is in its final stage. I've already contacted a few printing companies for quotes. I'm leaning towards one in Nebraska. I downloaded software to do the PDF (portable document format) myself. I also attached everything I needed to the printing companies site. Based on their email it will take approximately two weeks for me to receive a proof before the book goes to print.

For my first signing I want it to be more than just a book signing—more than just a speaking engagement of socialites. Actually, I prefer that there aren't any socialites. Not to say that they can't relate, but I'd rather focus on those who are actually living the life. Prostitutes.

39

CUN EL TRI BETREAT
TRI

"No Daddy

to

Sing Me

No Mo' Blues"

LE TRE LI BER BOO TONING
IN EC

Avery Love
June 28, 2013
Teaneck Rhonda Center
250 Celestial Ct.
Teaneck, NJ 07666
10:00 PM—12:00 AM

G

Ev'ry Ho Gotta Daddy for $14.95
* Clean pajamas, bathrobe and slippers.

I SLIP Anthony Hamilton's CD in the CD player, "Best Of Me" speaks to my spirit as I lip sync along. *"Giving you the best of me, amazing, outrageous..."* Sing it, baby!" I shout as I scrunch up my nose feeling the message, while heading up Rt. 4 toward Teaneck, New Jersey.

I park the (rental) black Beetle and sit in the car, lean my head against the headrest and just listen to my future make-believe husband sing specifically to me.

After I listen, I flick the switch to pop the trunk open. Exit out of the car, and open the trunk for my promotional packages and books that are stacked neatly in my traveler's bag.

I pull out the bag and set it upright on the ground. I shut the trunk. Then wrap my fingers around the handle and pull it as the wheels make this annoying sound against the asphalt.

As I get closer to the building I can see some women standing in front smoking cigarettes.

"Hello," I say as I bypass them. Some heads nod, others don't. The women go back talking amongst themselves.

"Is that her," I hear one woman say with spiked hot pink hair. *Pink!*

"I think so," another woman replies with bone straight brunette hair.

"Damn, she's classy and pretty," I hear another woman say, but I don't turn to see what she looks like.

I pull open the glass door to the redbrick-faced Teaneck Rhonda Center and enter.

The lobby is decorated in lavender and eggplant with dark wood boarders. There is a large vase sitting on a smoky gray oval glass table to the left side of the room with magazines atop. There is a security station for the guard who must've stepped out. I see a sign in book so I sign my name to alert of my arrival time. Then I head down the marble floored corridor mobbed with women.

My body grows warm from all of the unknown women staring at me. I wonder if they can tell that I am nervous.

I shake it off, and then enter the Ballroom.

As I step foot inside the spacious room, heads turn. Mouths gape open as if surprised by my presence. I smile. Make eye contact with several women who look in my direction.

Between the women in the lobby and the women in this room it looks to be about one hundred and fifty wounded, battered, bruised, brokenhearted *tricks* that look to have paid dearly to come out of hiding and hibernation to attend my slumber book signing. Jesus, it is so packed and humid. Goodness, already I feel stifled.

I tilt my head back, eyes heavenward the majestic ceiling admiring the crystal chandeliers dangling like ice sickles. Unfortunately, the air-cooling system must be on the brink 'cause it's hotter than a hoochie-momma in this place. These hot-bloodied heffas need to cool down a bit before it gets ugly all up in here. I mean the tension is so thick a knife couldn't even cut through it.

Listen, I do not...I repeat...I do not have time to be refereeing no catfight should things get *ghetto*. They betta' act like they know 'cause I don't want to have to act other than myself and step to these hussies' toe-to-toe.

I wave my left hand in front of my face to catch a mild breeze. It does me no justice. I swear it has to be about ninety degrees in here. With my fingers I knead at the nape of my neck, while glancing downward at my Simply Vera Wang loungewear. I smirk. I am delighted with my ensemble. My long waffle white bathrobe feels soft against my smooth skin. The white silk pajamas I have on feel like a second layer of skin. And my toes feel quite comfy in these fluffy white Isotoner slippers too.

Sometimes I surprise myself. What I mean by that is even in my distressful state of mind I cannot be seen looking all busted and disgusted. Contrary to what folks may think, Ms. Avery Love has a reputation to uphold.

As I look out into the crowd of women my brows raise high, then low, disconcerted by what I view. Thoughts race through my head as to what type of torment they might have endured. I make eye contact with: brown, hazel, green, gray and blue eyes, and I see a vacancy of aloneness and uncertainty. Some wonder where to go, how to repair themselves, how to rebuild or mend a broken spirit and heart God, it is written all over their faces. Flashing red, pleading for someone, anyone, to stop the agony, the merry-go-round of mayhem, and just let them fall and shatter to dust. I have answers, but I question if it will help, heal, or even encourage them to look ahead—to see brighter days to come—to see the woman they all used to be before they got manipulated into becoming "Ladies of the Evening."

My eyes continue to surveillance the spacious hall. What I see woven on some of their dejected faces is blatant misery, deep-seated unhappiness, disappointment and bewilderment. They have so many questions, so many doubts, so much regret and grief. All I hear in their voices is cracked emotion and scalding belligerence. I look at their presentation of how they feel about themselves. It's dismal. They all are shadowing, shading their outer beauty possibly for fear of anyone seeing them for who they really are. Camouflaging every inch of their angst-ridden selves in shabby-looking pajamas, raggedy, holey bathrobes, and dingy dirty slippers with pink and black sponge rollers in their hair, and fishnet hairnets on their heads says that they don't want to be seen. Travesty is an understatement. This is an embarrassment. Lord knows I really should give Dr. Cristal a call. These 'dilapidating bitches' need an emergency pick me up. No, no, no...this is more than Dr. Cristal can handle. This calls for Iyanla Vanzant. Sister-girl knows a thing or two about *PEACE from Broken Pieces.*

"How you gonna play these hoes like that, huh?" Karma says with a grimace on her face.

I cut my eyes to the side. "How am I playing them?" I shift my eyes to the right of me. "What you got to say?" I ask Avona. "I know your lips are burning to jump right on in." To my surprise Avona stays quiet.

"First, you invite them out, and then you have the nerve to talk about them in front of their faces." Karma retorts. "You can be so shiesty at times."

"Mind your business because you don't know what you're talkin' about. I am helping them, or at least I will be."

I shake my head. Then purse my lips a tad bit annoyed. "You always got something slick to say. Sometimes it is good to say nothing! Won't you crawl back in your hole and shrivel up. Do that!"

"Oh, you gonna wish you ain't go there." Karma snaps back.
I nix her off.

As I was saying before I was rudely interrupted. Oh! The promotional card specifically read in fine print:

*Clean pajamas, bathrobe and slippers.

Not one of 'em listened. It's like they woke up, got out of bed, and walked straight out of the door. I swear all I smell is rump-dump-dump all up and through. Can you believe *they* didn't even bother to wash their funky asses. Ain't this a blip! I know how *they* feel. Been there, done that. But...come on. When I'm down and blue I clean up, listen to some music, read a book, watch a movie, drink a hot cup of herbal tea, take a bubble bath...I do something other than walk around the house smelling like *death.* Ok. Three times I let myself fall, but it was after the rape, finding out that I was HIV-positive, and after I got word that my best friend Johnnie had died.

But now, on my really off days I may shed a tear or two, but I'd be damned if I let another man drive me to the point of no return. I'd be damned!

Look at 'em. I shake my head, and then cluck my tongue. *One chick looks like she hadn't been to sleep in months. She's fidgety. She is constantly looking over her shoulders. Face swollen, eyes puffy, and where the hell did she get that fat lip? Huh. Yeah. Uh-huh.*

And this one...she looks like she done had a collision with somebody's fist and they broke her nose. Oh, don't try to hide, missy. I see you, too. Now how the hell did you exactly fall on your arm and break it? I'm listening. Yeah, yeah, yeah, yeah...okay. That's the best excuse you can give. Girl, please. Save that one for your momma.

And you, yeah you, you with the auburn hair, you got that shiner, how exactly? Oh, you just happened to walk into the cabinet that's how many feet high?

I bite down on my bottom lip and gnaw at it. *I can't take no mo' of this lying. And you's have the nerve to defend them like they're men to be worshipped. Woo! The nerve!*

Lord. Jesus. Did they even stop to take a moment to look at themselves in the mirror? I mean *they* could have at least washed the crumbs out of their eyes. Those babies are swollen and red as if they have been crying for days at a time. Looking in their faces, they all look starved. Dang. Fucking done broke these hungry heffas down.

My objective is to give them insight—to assist them in finding a way out and closure. Look. I am not standing up on this stage with these bright hot lights beaming on me sweating bullets for my health. These women are going to feel my rage. And hopefully they will be inspired to get back on the bandwagon, hopefully in the process clean themselves up enough for some wonderful man to want to date them. But first he has to notice them. And the way they're looking right about now, huh, a dog wouldn't even want to hump them. Well, maybe a dog would. Yes, they are pitiful. But I fully understand because this is a sensitive thing to be going through. Their "Daddies" are the closest to a father figure/man they ever thought they'd get to have. I'll be gentle and guide them with great care and caution. Truthfully speaking, they all look too broken to even conceive of the thought of dating a fellah. First and foremost they need to work on repairing themselves.

If you see what I see, huh, you'd be saying the same exact thing too. I shake my head again.

As I look in the array of pained faces, I plainly see their emotions festering on the outside of each and every one of them. Resentment and desperation seem to pour out through their tears. This room is filled with heartache; so therefore, I have to be sensitive, yet firm in my approach to get my points across. I don't want them to hurt, but I also don't want them to become the individuals who hurt them either. Hurt does hurt. And regardless of how one sees it, no one wants to experience a hurt that nearly destroys...them.

I stand before these hoes in honesty, openness, and brokenheartedness. I'm not exempt. I, too, am tired of being a fool to a foolish game called "Fuck-A-Bitch-Heart-Up."

Maybe? Just maybe my downfalls will awaken them to see that "love" is not to be compromised. It is not to be gambled, or, accessorized in G-strings and hooker boots to lust one. Love is eclectic. It has a soul of pureness. Love is heaven twinkling in the stars. It is an emotion that can heal as well as harm, if placed in manipulative hands.

I put on my headset and adjust it along my left ear as I remind myself that these women have come because they look to me for guidance and understanding. And as I do, all I see are reflections of my many selves: me, myself, and I. But currently, all I feel is gloom in this hot ass room.

I bring the small microphone closer to my lips. I sigh, and then feel a smidgen of pity for these ladies. The room is filled with mixed nationalities and of various ages. Too bad my arms are not long enough to hug each and every one of them, simultaneously, but hopefully my message will empower them enough to mend themselves back together. Because the sight I'm seeing is a serious case of "raggedy bitches."

The muffle voices die down as my forefinger taps the miniature mike.

"Testing one two, testing one two." I say. All heads turn. All eyes are now on me. I feel a little uncomfortable, but a nudge of confidence sets me straight. "Remember. This is not PCCC (Passaic County Community College)," I remind myself. "These are not grammar students. They are grown young, middle-aged, and over-the-age of fifty women. Don't get ahead of yourself. Don't fumble and fall. Think positive. Different time. Different circumstance. You are going to be fine, Avery, just fine." I tell myself.

I brush my hands down my silk pajamas. I stand on the balls of my feet and look out into the audience of women.

The crease of my mouth curls up and a glow of white straight teeth shine as I open my mouth to speak. "Welcome. I am so glad you came out to hear me speak. I took the liberty of placing your sleeping bags out. I hope you don't mind your neighbor. We have a buffet of varieties of food and desserts to the back of the room. Please, help yourself. The ladies' room is outside through the double doors to the left. The EXIT signs are to the left and right should an emergency occur."

With a grimace on my face, I blurt out my thoughts without

thinking.

"Do any of you know the domestic violence hotline for NJ: 800-621-HOPE (4673)? This is a 24 hour, 7 days a week service.

"Answer these questions for me, ladies:

"Are You in an Abusive Relationship? Do you even know if you are or not? Well, here are some questions that will help you decide:

"Are you ever afraid of your man or woman?

"Does your mate threaten to hurt you?

"Does your mate control all the money?

"Has your mate ever pushed you or shoved you, thrown things at you, or forced you to have sex?

"Does your mate *stalk* you or show up uninvited at your job or when you're out with friends?

"If you said *yes* to one or more of these questions, you may be a victim of domestic violence.

"I'm not trying to scare you, because some of you are already shaken up."

I stop talking and just stare at them. The concerned look in my eyes speaks in volume of how ticked off I am. No. It's not my life, but dang. Can't they see that "love" shouldn't leave marks? These are not love taps. They are getting their asses whooped by animals who have no say in their lives. Animals who picked them up from stray kittens and molded and manipulated them into selling themselves out on the streets and in their own homes to keep his pockets fat. Here standing before me are basements tricks, housewife tricks, streetwalker tricks, that have been beaten like puppets on a string. When is enough, enough? When????

Oh, I guess when Heaven Gatte Funeral Home comes to pick up their broken, bloodied lifeless bodies? Is that 'sposed to be the end result for them to get out and move forward in their lives? Death? I scratch my scalp. I must be missing something here.

My hands massage my head. Yes, I am flustered. Why? Denial.

"Ok, now that I've gone over that. I wanted everyone to be relaxed for this speaking engagement, so I thought what better way than to have something like a slumber party. I think I'd gone to one as a child. The only difference is, we won't be sleeping over, but we will have discussions as well as a book signing for my first novel, *Ev'ry Ho Gotta Daddy*. Oh, the books are stacked on the table in the back near the sculpture of the African woman. That wonderful masterpiece is called Blak Butta. It is one of my special pieces by an upcoming artist named Kybuu. There are also some lovely Burnt Sugar Cosmetic products to purchase for those who are into body butters, lipsticks, blushes, eye shadows, liners, lipgloss and foundation and concealer. I also took the liberty of baking (from scratch) you all some of what I call: Love's Cakes for those of you ladies' who have a bit of a sweet tooth. I'm only asking for two dollars per slice, which the proceeds will go toward my independent publishing house: *PINK PINSTRIPES PUBLISHING*. Ladies, I want you all to unwind. Let your hair down. Let your burdens go. How does that sound?!" I say with enthusiasm in my tone.

I see no smiling faces. The negative energy up in here is killin' a sista. Oh...my...God! These *hos* got it bad.

"Girl, you have your work cut out for you with these homely bitches," Karma *exclaims with her arms crossed about her chest. She shakes head. "Tsk, tsk, tsk. Look, girlfriend, I ain't tryna be funny, but just look at 'em. They hungry, Avery... HUNGRY. Feed these sloppy bitches some dick, please."*

I shoo her away.

What can I do to put them at ease? Put myself out there first. Women will embrace another woman putting the spotlight on herself. Well, it is certainly worth a try to bring these ladies back to earth.

I feel the tension in my body loosening up. "Let me ask you all something. And please, take a moment to think about everything that I am about to say. Have you ever felt like people who don't even know you from Thelma and Louise find themselves constantly gossiping about you? I go through this almost every day, if not, every other day.

"According to people, Avery Love is dating this guy and that guy and this guy and your guy your momma's guy, maybe even your daddy's guy. According to people, Avery was dating a guy who gave her HIV. According to people, Avery is just getting her groove on—another Stella in the 'hood. But see what these 'particular people' don't know is that even with what I have running through my bloodstream their men and women still try to kick it to a sista. I don't initate, they do.

"Hear me out clearly; I am not interested in any rebound-broke-down-Negro-with-a-drunken-dick-and/or any chick with an eighteen wheeler-twat. I can do badly all by myself."

Heads nod up and down.

"Okay, I'm making a little progress. I have to keep the momentum going," I tell myself.

I continue, "There are reasons as to why a person does reckless things in their life. Some things can be explained, but the person who is doing it may not know how to articulate it with words. They may find themselves acting it out in behaviors that may seem inappropriate to those on the outside looking in. But in most cases there is a reason for the mayhem.

I look out at the many women and I say, "One has to dig deep inside to pull out that anguish that is linked to the behavior. And if one is not cautious, they can and will self-destruct.

"It amazes me how people, professional people who have studied people with major issues seem to psychoanalyze us. They babble of how many years they have been in the profession, but it makes me wonder: have you ever endured what I have? Have you even come close? Most, I find have never experienced any of the issues they try to resolve. They have the credentials, years of college background, clinical, but do they have personal experience? Text book smarts, yes. Personal experience, some.

"Those who have endured much pain are the physical text books. We are able to speak our pain, tell you where and how it hurts, we can point to where the scars exist. They have to flip from page to page to reiterate word for word something someone else has written. We just speak in our natural tone of voice. A voice that may crack between each word, yet, still a voice that can depict what had/has occurred in our lives.

"I am not bashing the *professionals*, but what I am saying is that these who do not have an address, medical insurance, money, an open ear find themselves stagnant, lost. And when this occurs they have no one to help them out of bondage. They have no refuge. They have no home to place themselves in. They have no start over. I was once one of those people. And I thought I had no start over, but through each phase I found the strength to conquer all. However, there was still a lot missing. And it took years of reflecting on who I used to be to who I am now. I had to find those missing pieces within myself. The most profound for me was that I discovered that, I couldn't love her. Once I discovered that...everything else began to mend.

"Look, I'm not as broken as people make me out to be. I'm a classy sista. And any man, that is, a man would prefer to have a lady on his arm than a tramp. I keep myself up. Keep my cut tight. I eat a little better now. Sho', I go up and down in my weight. No different from any other woman. People make more out of nothing, simply because they have nothing else better to do. I guess I should feel privileged that people feel the need to talk about me behind my back. But I don't. I prefer that they tell me directly to my face. People who gossip like that aren't anything but cowards. And I've come to realize that the *new and improved* 'Avery

Love' don't give a damn about what people say or think or feel, anymore. 'Cause when it is time for me to leave this earth, those same sorry ass-good-for-nothing muthafuckers will still be talking about me after I am long dead and gone."

One jet-black haired obese woman dressed in what looks like maple syrup stained all over the front of her red flannel bathrobe breaks her silence. "Yup. Yup. Dhat is soooo troo. Till it susta," she says in a thick southern drawl.

I smirk, and then continue, "As it may sound, yes, I need to vent out my frustrations. I have a lot heavy on my heart. And if I don't talk about it I am liable to do something stupid. 'Ey, I'm only human. I have feelings like everyone else. Yeah. I know I can easily call my therapist, Dr. Cristal. But to be perfectly honest, I don't want to talk to her about this. I rely on her for more personal issues. You know soul-searching shit."

One blue-eyed redhead woman with black mascara running down her eyes onto her apple cheeks nods her head in relevance.

I walk back and forth across the stage so that everyone can hear and see me.

"Question: Do you ever wonder why Men take women for granted? Men underestimate us intellectually. Have you ever asked yourself why? Think about it. Have men conceived this notion that women are so naïve that we can't see that we are being used? Are we that oblivious? Or are we so Internet desperate that we allow ourselves to be used for the sake of male companionship? I mean once we have indulged in Internet dating we have just submitted in our application to be 'played.'

"In other words: he knows that he's in there, especially after we've handed over the car keys without even checking to see if he has a suspended driver's license. Especially after we've handed over the credit card, bank card (with pin #) without even checking to see what he has purchased or how much of our money he has withdrawn from our checking and savings accounts. And especially after each and every time we've wanted to have sex, all of a sudden, he has a goddamn headache, stomachache, or the ultimate...he farts to stress a point. A point that eloquently says he is not in the mood for our stingy pussy. You know how our dumb asses can get. Too busy listening to that lonely bitch in our left ear. You know...your girlfriend." I cut my eyes at them all. "Oh, let me rephrase that: your lonely manless girlfriend who hasn't been screwed in years. Keep on listening to her, and see how far you get in getting or keeping the man you have. And another thing: women have a tendency to use sex as a weapon. Bad move. All that does is encourage our men to go and find someone else. Now understand. If you don't have any tricks to your trade. You better learn some, because these bitches out here are tricking up a storm. They are feeding our men. How romantic is that? Yeah. So when your man resorts to farting to spoil the mood that, my dear, is a dead giveaway that he has someone new on the side. C'mon, ladies, wake up!

"Think. When has he invited you over to his house or apartment? Um, you have been dating almost a year and a half now. Have you even been inside of his car? Ah, something just ain't right. But even knowing this, feeling this, seeing it for yourself, what you do? Stay like some desperate broad.

"Are women 'sposed to have telepathy? No. We are 'sposed to use our intellect, which we dispose of once we are 'in the moment' with a man (who mind you is not who he says he is). But do we care? No. Once our 'woman's intuition' tells us that he is 'no good' something happens inside of us. We become stupid! Brain dead. We lose all of our smarts. Our dignity diminishes. It's quite pathetic! We are some lost kittens. Our identity has transformed to the person he wants, not the woman we were. Dang! Penis takes full control—access of our mind and body. And Vagina, well, she obliges his every need. And you wonder why Men treat us sooooo good." I snarl and purse my lips.

"Women create these monsters by giving in too easily. And as our gullible asses do, Men will continue to use us up, spit us out, and screw us over again and again and again as long as will allow them to.

"So, can we blame it on the alcohol? I think not! Not if the stupid ass is a recovering alcoholic."

Everyone, including me, bursts out laughing.

I compose myself. "We have to blame it on our gullible selves. Don't get me wrong...Men do contribute 60% of the madness, simply because *they* are visuals. The Eyes, as I like to call them. The remaining 40% is women, simply because *we* are the Ears. We hear what we want to hear. And turn a deaf ear to what we don't. Majority of the time we ignore that little voice inside of us and release our frustrations out to the enemy." I smirk deviously, "Other women."

They all gasp as if *they* don't know.

I frown. Then shake my head, disappointingly.

"Listen, ladies, the art for destroying a relationship is divulging our deepest, darkest, demoralizing secrets to another woman. This is ground for termination of that relationship. Once you allow another *woman* get inside of your head, your bed, ladies, you may as well give that trifling heffa the key that locks him inside your heart. Just hang it up because *you* just hung yourself."

All the women clap and whistle. They are beginning to get riled up. "Finally," I say to myself. For a minute there I thought I was talking to myself.

I sigh, as my eyes shift from right to left, left to right. "I am going to give you something to think about." Now I have their undivided attention. This makes me feel powerful. I move closer to the front of the stage. Sweat is drenched upon my face. Pj's are clinging to my skin. It's gotten hotter in here.

"Okay. Follow me on this." I reach under the podium and pullout a copy of *Ev'ry Ho Gotta Daddy*. I part the paperback book open to the *Foreword*, look out at the women's faces and begin to read.

***

Having lost track of time, I pause, as I glance at the clock. It's after two in the morning. Dang, I'm surprised security didn't come to escort us out.

With red eyes I look out at all the women faces. They look back at me. And in unison they all harmonize an, *awwwwwwwwwwww* when they hear me say, "The End."

This one mid-forty-something year old lady with the letters: M A X E Y in black lettering on a white nightshirt nods her head. She then ties the belt on her Betty Boop bathrobe and looks down at her fluffy slippers as if she is ashamed of something. Just the look on her face tells me she's been through something traumatic.

Unexpectedly, a burst of energy erupts from this dark-skinned obese woman with big eyes and wide hips—she steals my thunder. She opens her mouth and out comes strong vocals. Everyone gives her her moment to relinquish her frustrations.

Soft and angelically she sings, "*It's gonna be a long long journey, It's gonna be an uphill climb...*" with her head dangling low. All the women circle around her as the light from the chandeliers shine above her head.

As she *feels* the lyrics, she unloosens the belt to her tattered yellow-stained bathrobe. "*It's gonna be a tough fight...*" she sings as she lifts up making eye contact with her fellow homely sisters in the room. Slowly, she opens her robe and exposes her chocolate ice cream stained pajamas with whip cream and two maraschino cherries stuck to it with a sense of pride beaming on her face. And with what once was somberness in her eyes, now is elation. She's come back glued to the woman she once knew—the songstress.

This bleached blonde-haired scrawny woman with sea green eyes and black and blue bruises on her face, strapped in her shabby soft pastel pink terrycloth bathrobe joins in. *"It's gonna be some lonely nights..."*

This brunette-haired medium build woman with sapphire blue eyes with puffy dark circles underneath them and monstrous breasts with two missing front teeth, dressed in her frayed floral pink fleece bathrobe finishes her sentence. *"But I'm ready to carry on ..."*

Next thing I know, everyone follows suit as we all join in, *"I'm so glad the worst is over, I can start living now, ooh..."*

The women get so caught up in their inspirational anthem "The Living Proof" by Mary J. Blige that they yank off their hairnets and fling them in the air singing with heartfelt revelation. This honey-toned woman who looked to be in her mid-forties with big loose curls catches my attention. With her red robe open she has on a red nightshirt that reads in black lettering: "Minerva Weaver ain't trippin' no mo'." Then she parts her full lips and bellows in a strong gospel voice, *"You can't deny the truth, 'Cause I'm the living proof!"*

I smile so big with tears welling up in my eyes. I am so happy. So very, very happy! Nothing can bring me down off of this natural high. Nothing!

40

WHEN I ARRIVE HOME I check my mailbox before heading upstairs. Junk mail. Junk mail. Junk mail. Bill. Bill. Bill. What's this? A forward letter addressed to: Xavier.

Immediately, I head upstairs by elevator.

Once I get inside my apartment, I walk straight over to my computer and sit at my desk. *Ping!* I hear e-mail come through on my iPhone, but I don't open it. I pull open the desk drawer and place the envelope inside next to a photo of Johnnie.

I smile; hark back to us sitting on the plaid blanket in Central Park, gazing at the sky, absorbed in one another. It was a memorable day—one that will never fade from my heart and mind.

Sadness breaks my smidgen of pleasantness as I think about how folks come and go in my life. They use me. Abuse me. Reuse me. Abuse me. And then as soon as I come to my senses and remove myself from the pain...here they come wanting *me* back. And *I* always find a way to weasel them back in fully knowing that they are going to just use and abuse me again. What is it about me? *Do I have a forehead banner that reads:* "Just do me any ole kind of way?" *What do they see that I don't? Am I that damaged? Does it show how vulnerable I am? Do I seem desperate? Weak? What is it?*

These are the questions no one will honestly answer. Maybe because they don't want to hurt my feelings, yet they seem to find great pleasure in hurting my heart. I don't get it. I shrug my shoulders. Maybe I'm not supposed to. Xavier slips in my head. And this achy feeling comes over me. I never had anyone out of all the men I have encountered as a full-fledged woman, not young girl treat me like I was worthy of love. Not until, Xavier. He had a way about him that just made you feel safe and secure. The way he held me in his arms was with such care and gentleness. The way he brushed his lips against my skin and kissed me so passionately, and whispered how much he loved me in my ears. God, I loved him soooooooooo much.

I bow my head. Then sigh heavily, remembering the *man* who explored every inch of my mind, my soul, and embedded his love in my heart. A man who contributed to making me sees that I am a phenomenal woman. That I have in my possession qualities that should not be taken for granted—qualities that should not settle or reduce standards just to have a man in my life or in my bed. Xavier taught me a lot about what it takes to be a real man to a good woman...more than my own dad.

As I look around at my place I see that I have everything I could've hoped for. My health is in good status. I feel incredible. Look the same. I have a foundation again. I am building a future for myself in hopes to help others. Something I yearned to do. Something I have done with Anonymous. I guess falling helped me find my way back to me.

I'm soon to greet forty-seven, come November 4th. God willing. How lucky I am. I feel joy, pain. My stomach churns. I guess I'm a little on edge because this is a time to be celebrating with my very best friend. A friend, who now, and who has been for some time...dead. So many years have gone by. But I've been productively working hard—harder than I've ever worked before. It gives me less time to grieve—less time to carry the dead weight of all the misery.

January 2013: I launched my fourth book signing at "Read Between the Lines" in Harlem.

February: Black History Month. I held a release party at Hustler 'n the Poet. I also did a reading and book signing at "Necessary" and "Blue Moon," here in Paterson and also one at "Saturate" in Newark, New Jersey.

March: I met up with Zye Anderson at WOBS 99.3 FM, and did a radio show presenting the listeners to my book. I also ordered more books for my next event.

April: I had a book discussion at several libraries: Paterson, Newark, Hackensack, Elizabeth, Camden, Somerset, Fort-Lee, New Brunswick, Trenton and New York.

May: I did a lot of promoting. I even thought about writing a second book. I launched my e-book and also worked on uploading my website: *PINK PINSTRIPES PUBLISHING*.

June: I had already done the Tricks Retreat, which was a huge, huge success! I did some networking with other authors. Met some folks at a book function I attended. I hung out at some book events and listened to some seasoned writers tell their stories of how they got started, their disappointments and whatnot. I handed out some of my business cards I ordered off of Vistaprint.com.

July: I take a breather. Replenish my mind and spirit. I find myself grieving over Xavier. Johnnie. Still, I yearn for both to come back home to be with me.

From *January 9, 2000 to July 28, 2013*, I've been mourning—damned near suffocating from my own misery. I felt myself calming when I began to feel the written word—along with the feelings I have buried. I find them freely relinquishing. Now, I am beginning to feel alive, free, and at home again.

I smile. And now, now I am back to that beginning of losing someone so dear to me. *July 29th*. God, this day is a day of complete and utter agony. The *day* Johnnie died. Somehow, I try and make it through.

I keep capturing that moment when we were laying on the blanket in Central Park. The way Johnnie looked into my eyes—the slow dance to "Ready for Love," with India Arie serenading in the background. I think about the shopping spree—Nuyorican Poets Café. The poem: *Farewell, my Love*—the money—the love—the friendship. I nod. I remember. I used that money to birth *Anonymous*. The drive I had. Ambition. Persistence. Johnnie. He was my rock, my water, my hope, and solid ground. He held the torch to my heart. Never had I ever had such a beautiful friend. Often I feel as if I didn't deserve him. I was selfish. Shallow. Reckless. Yes, I'd agree, back then I was a piece of effin' work. But I've changed. Life changed me. Pain changed me. Anguished changed me. Rape changed me. HIV changed me. Destitute changed me. Prejudice changed me. I'm a different me. I still haven't fully grown into myself. I'm still catching up, still trying to find my fit in this five foot eleven inches of woman...my "fit" to deal with realities that aren't easy to deal with. I've been through a lot. And I perceive myself going through much more. It's all a test of faith.

Thus far, I wonder how God thinks I am doing.

41

AMBLING INTO Nordstrom Rack in Bergen Town Center, dressed comfortably in a pair of black leggings, white button down tunic shirt, black ballerina shoes and my black with silver stud hobo hoisted from my left shoulder. And as I do, I feel so vibrant, so not like my old self. I feel I am evolving. Turning into the woman I always saw myself to be: successful. I feel it. I feel success coming into fruition.

But am I ready? I mean really, really ready for all that comes with it?

I sigh, and then mull things over in my head.

Suddenly, I'm not sho'.

Pushing these thoughts to the wayside I browse the store hoping to find something eye-catching. The sway of my hips says I'm feeling sexy. But reality says I need to work on this small muffin top before it gets out of control. Some sit-ups should do the trick. I hear my stomach growling. I cut my eyes over my left shoulder to make sure no one is walking behind me. Oh dear, what did I eat this morning for breakfast? All I had was an Activia Mixed Berries yogurt and two boiled eggs and a bottle of spring water. No wonder I am famished.

As I am heading toward the dress aisle, this blonde-haired sea blue-eyed slender woman cuts her eyes at me. *I know she is not checking me out*, I think.

I walk over to the designer dresses looking for my size when the same blonde-haired lady finally approaches me dressed in a Rachel Roy black business suit with four-inch Charles David faux patent leather pumps on what looks like size six feet. Her hair is shoulder-length and cut evenly at the ends. She wears minimal makeup with a thin layer of peachy-colored lipstick on her heart-shaped lips.

"Excuse me," she says all bright-eyed. "Ah, I don't mean to stare, but I am a bit star struck."

Turn around looking for the 'star'. Then turn back around and look at her.

She's smiling from ear to ear. "Aren't you the author of *Ev'ry Ho Gotta Daddy*?"

She kind of takes me by surprise. Haltingly I say, "Yes."

The lady gets even more excited. "I thought so! You look just like the woman on the back cover. I kept saying to myself, 'that's her! I know it is!'"

Lady, take a breath. I think.

I bulge my eyes. "Yes, it's me!"

"God, I can't believe that I am actually talking to an 'author' in the flesh. That book..." she presses her freshly manicured hands to her chest, "it really took me to a place within myself...somewhere dark and disturbing. Oh, the protagonist suffered. Her story had me on this emotional roller coaster ride. My mood kept going up and down throughout the book. She was one brave cookie, if you ask me. More than *I* could've ever been. I mean."

I nod.

I can tell she's a talker.

"Is there something you want to share? I mean, we can go and have a cup coffee or tea, if you'd like to talk." I say with sincerity in my tone.

Her blue eyes stretch wide. "Really?"

"Sure."

"You really are different from what I'd expected," she says.

I really don't know how to take that comment.

"What do you mean?" I ask with a perplex look upon my face.

"You're different. Oh, dear, no, not in a bad way. You know how some people can be. They accomplish something phenomenal and then they change." she says.

"I don't see a need to put on airs. I'm just trying to get ahead; you know what I'm saying?" I say.

"Oh, wait until I tell my book club that I actually met you! They are going to die!"

I raise a brow. "Book club?"

"Yes, we call ourselves...Pynk-Ghetto."

"Interesting name," I tell her.

"Well, Paige is the President. She's the one who started the book club about three years ago. We have about twelve members, thus far."

I nod.

"Oh, where are my manners. I'm Faye...Faye Roxenberg-McDowell."

All I hear is...McDowell. And of course Blu pops in my head.

"Avery. Nice to meet you," I say.

"Did you come here to shop? I don't want to intrude," Faye says.

"No intrusion. I can always come back and browse. No big deal."

"You sure?"

"I'm positive."

"Ok, well, we can go to Whole Foods, unless you prefer, somewhere else in the mall?"

"Whole Foods is fine."

"Shall we?"

"We shall."

We step into Whole Foods and Faye orders herself a cup of decaffeinated coffee, no sugar, while I get a cup of lemon ginger herbal tea with fresh lemon and honey, and a raspberry scone.

We sit nearest the entranceway.

"Where did you purchase my book?" I ask.

"Chelsea, she's one of our members. She bought the book off of Hear It Voiced (HIV) website."

"Please don't take this the wrong way, but how many of the members in your book club are African American?" I curiously ask.

"None." Faye says.

"Latino?"

"None."

"So, what other nationality, besides, Caucasian is in *your* group."

"That's it. I mean, Paige tried to recruit others, but no one wanted to join our book club. Some said that we were too lame because all we read were Harlequin novels."

"So what would make, ah, Chelsea wants to read an urban fiction book? I'm sorry. I'm just a little baffled."

Faye laughs. "Chelsea has a mind of her own. She does what she wants to do, not want others expect her to do. I guess that is what set her apart from the rest of us. Paige was the one who wanted to keep everything the same. She'd drift in a Danielle Steel novel like: *The Kiss* with no problem, while we all suffered. I *despise* Danielle Steel novels because of *her*. Gag me with a spoon, would you please? So, when Chelsea joined the group she came in with an open mind. She was eager to read something different, things that Paige was set against doing. We realized that if we didn't stand together and support Chelsea we all would be drowning by now in romance. So we spoke up and told Paige how we really felt. Eventually she caved."

"So, what would make Chelsea pick my book?" I ask again.

Faye chuckles. "We asked Chelsea that same question. but she never really told us. Normally we'd engross in Nora Roberts, Nicholas Sparks, or Jennifer Weiner. But Chelsea was always the one who thought outside of the box. She'd surf Hear It Voiced (HIV) for the upcoming releases. If anything piqued her interest she'd purchase the book, read it, and then come and tell us about it. She'd only give up minimal details. But she was good at hyping a book up. If she saw that she was able to draw us in, everyone would put their money together and purchase individual copies of it. We'd give ourselves deadlines to finish reading the book. If it were a short read, we'd have discussions that following week. If not, we'd give ourselves two weeks, no more than that though. Then we talk among ourselves if it was or wasn't a good read."

"Do you have a website?" I ask.

"Yes. Pynk-GhettoBookClub.com. We review books and write our opinions about it on our site along with Hear It Voiced (HIV). We rate the book between 1 and 5. (1) Being the lowest. (5) Being the highest. Oh, yeah, and one of our members, Lillian has some connections with this radio host named Zye Anderson. He interviews new authors on his show every second week of the month. Would you like to contact him so that he can interview you about your book? Zye is great at promoting!"

I don't hesitate to respond. "Sure. But do you think he'll think it's too in your face?"

"No. It's right up Zye's alley."

"I'm going to level with you, Faye. This is all new to me, you know." I take another sip of tea. "I mean the book has only been out for a year. I'm about to run a second print soon." I take a bite into my raspberry scone.

"That's the beauty of it. Can't you see it?!" Faye says with lit up eyes and enthusiasm in her voice. "You see what happened to Pink Khocolate, right?"

"Who? Oh, the woman who wrote that erotic tale, *The Darker Side of Pussy*. Everybody's talking about it." I say dryly.

"Yes. That's our next book club pick! I can't wait to sink my teeth into that baby!"

I frown. "Great."

Faye lifts up her cup. "Yes, it is! Women are eating it up!" She takes a sip of coffee and then places her cup back down on the table.

I wonder why, I think to myself. *Read one provocative novel, read 'em all, right?*

"What makes her book so different from the rest?" I ask Faye just to see what she thinks.

She cocks her head to the side with a bewildered look upon her oval face. "I don't know. Maybe the sexual acts they perform? Could be because *she* is a control freak? Who knows? All I know is that I must

496

read that book! Maybe I can learn a thing or two from her," she giggles.

"Hmm? I never looked at it like that, maybe because I don't have anyone presently in my life."

Faye raises a brow. "You will, trust me."

I force myself to crack a smile.

Faye chuckles. "This is the most fun I've had sitting here talking to you," she says, "The women in Pynk-Ghetto all have children. One or two have teenagers soon off for college. The book club is pretty much the most fun we have. Our kids take up most of our time. My husband is a respected corporate attorney. He works lower Manhattan at Brumar & Prescott Law Firm. Besides, the kids the book club is how I spend my free time. My husband works really, really hard, so I try to keep our household in order. It's what my wifely duties require to keep my man and children happy."

My eyes light up and mouth slightly dangles open. "Bruman & Prescott is one of the most prestigious law firms in New York." I say with a little too much enthusiasm.

Faye gives me a peculiar look. "Oh, you're familiar with?"

"Years ago, I used to work there as a paralegal."

"Really? Why'd you leave?" she lifts up her cup and takes a sip of her coffee.

I sigh inwardly. I find myself staring in outer space. "I was raped." I don't know what comes over me to just blurt it out like that.

Coffee spews out of Faye's mouth and onto her suit jacket. Her eyes spread wide and her face turns beet red. "Oh...my...God! I am such a ditz," she plants both hands to the sides of her face and shakes her head. "I'm sorry. I shouldn't have asked. Please. Please, forgive me."

I grab some napkins and clean the table off. Hand her one to wipe her suit jacket off.

"It's okay. I've come to terms with it." I say convincingly.

Faye changes the subject. "It must've been nice going to work every day. Doing something you liked and interacting with other people."

I hear a bit of envy in her voice.

"I'm a stay-at-home mom. That's how Tucker wanted it. We've been married for about ten years now. It hasn't been easy. We had a lot of setbacks with *my* parents butting in our business, especially my Dad."

"Why didn't they like him? Did he mistreat you?"

"Dear, no. Tucker is a gentleman. Very respectful toward me ever since the very day I met him. He's a hardworking *black* man."

I raise a brow.

Faye catches on quickly. "Exactly. Tucker had to grow on them. My dad was very old fashioned. It took time for him to accept my husband. It split the family up for a while. I mean I had to stand by my man, you know. There was no way in hell I was letting Dad ruin what Tucker and I had built. We were in love. And love is not easy to find. I knew the first day I saw him that he was going to be my prince. And he is. I tried to explain to Dad that not all black men are out here selling drugs, getting high or street hustling to make a dollar. Tucker had high expectations. He worked his ass off to become someone to admire. Tucker works with disadvantage kids at the juvenile delinquent shelter too. I mean coming from a household of abuse. Seeing his mom gets smacked around and having a dad who didn't know how to be a father. His dad was a womanizer. I never had the chance to meet him. A woman murdered him in his sleep for sleeping with her mistress. My dad was very impressed when Tucker passed the Bar and showed that he could provide for the family. With me being a stay-at-home mom, huh, Dad saw that I was well provided for. Tucker gained his respect." Faye cuts her eyes to the side then downward.

I can tell that she has a lot on her mind. "Faye, there is nothing wrong with taking care of your children. At least you get to watch them grow up and know that you had a huge part in molding those little people into independent, responsible, positive people."

She cracks a smile.

"I understand, trust me." I tell her as I notice she has this shattered look in her eyes. "Are you okay?" I ask.

"Ms. Love..."

I raise my right hand and fan it in front of her. "Call me Avery."

"Daisy's story got to me: in my mind, in my heart. I know it got to Chelsea too. She can't stop talking about it."

"What is it about the book that seems to be stuck in *her* head?"

"She won't tell any of us. I know for me her mom, Daddee. God, that woman was a wicked witch. The disgusting things she had Magnolia (Daisy) doing to support her drug habit. The way she talked down to her." Faye shakes her head from side to side. "It's a shame to have to be subjected to that type of mistreatment. She was a child—a fragile girl."

I remain quiet. I need all the feedback I can get on my first book. So I listen attentively to what Faye has to say.

Faye sips her coffee and then changes the subject again. "Avery, you know that June 27th is National HIV Testing Day."

I cock my head to the side wondering why she is telling *me* this. "No.

Actually, I didn't know that. Where did you hear that?" I ask her.

"I receive emails from Black AIDS Institute. I also get free Greater Than AIDS community materials to pass out to make awareness known. I distribute them out at Young User Body Abuser Center I volunteer for."

"Young User Body Abuser...?" I ask.

She lifts her cup and then places it back down on the table to explain. "Oh, one of Tucker's nieces entered the program. She was a user. Her daughter was maybe three or four years old at the time. Tucker was able to get her into the program once he felt she was tired of getting high. I mean she was a young mother for God's sake. Amirra is doing really well now. Her daughter is getting so big," she smiles, "Once Amirra completes the program she'll be able to live drug-free, get housing, and care for her daughter. She'll be eligible for public assistance for about a year or two until she gets on her feet. They also provide training for her to give her options to take some college classes. She says that she wants to be a social worker. With the proper training she'll be able to get a job. It's a really good program for young mothers."

"Really?" I say.

"Yes."

I lift my cup and take a sip of my tea. "You mentioned Greater Than AIDS?"

"It's like a movement—a cause to inspire others to get tested—to use condoms—to love themselves enough to protect their bodies. Nourish their minds with knowledge so that they won't be subjected to living with the disease—to be mindful of their partners too. I am Greater Than AIDS says that you are spreading positive knowledge of a disease that has a stigma attached to it. I can give you their site: www.greaterthan.org."

I search in my bag for a pen so that I can write the website down.

"Faye, can you say the website again?"

"Sure, www.greaterthan.org."

I jot the website down on the back of a receipt, and then slip it in the side pocket of my bag.

I snap my fingers.

Faye flinches. "You liked to scare the dickens out of me!"

I look at her strangely. Why is she so jumpy?

Faye composes herself, and then asks. "Is everything okay?"

I should be asking you that question. But I don't want to pry, I think.

"Oh, everything is fine. I just forgot to call this place. No big deal. I can call later." I glance at my wristwatch. "It's only 2:30 p.m."

Faye cell phone rings.

"Excuse me, Avery, it's my Dad calling."

I notice her hands shaking as she takes the call.

"Hi," she says, "No, no, that won't be possible. I can't make it today. I have to go pick up the kids. We have to do it some other time, okay. Bye."

Faye seems frazzled. What gives?

"Avery, I have to get going. It was nice meeting you. We have to keep in touch. Let me give you my number. Maybe one day when you're not busy you can come to one of the book club meetings. Meet some of the women." She reaches her left hand in her Louis Vuitton and pulls out a Pynk-Ghetto business card and hands it to me. Then she reaches for her cup and takes one last sip of coffee, then hightail it out of Whole Foods.

I sit back; raise my left brow in wonder of what she is hiding.

I take a hefty bite off the scone.

42

FOR SOME REASON, I'm having a difficult time discussing my issues with Dr. Cristal. I'm on the defense simply because she opened a can of worms.

"Safe? Cautious? Speculative? Curious? Adrenaline rush? Butterflies? Tingles? Attraction? Mannerism? Freedom—a depiction of what drew me in—an invite into the world of a broken wounded woman who Band-Aid herself back. Safe. No slaps, kicks, punch, no forceful sex. no attempts to rid of me with killer hands. Safe." I explain.

"Hmm," she replies.

"Had I felt or seen differently the brick wall inside of me would've formed. And I would not have sight, sound, or feel for him. My body would've become lifeless—dead ...in a metaphoric sense."

"Your feelings and sight are valid," Dr. Cristal says. "Go on."

I sit upright. "So, if you absorb that then for future any person you meet who has been harmed: domestic violence, rape, incest...whatever, and one finds themselves attracted to her my thinking is she probably won't divulge her pain to him right away. It all depends on the person. Most or some women may play it SAFE by not sharing for FEAR of pushing a man away. I was never afraid to push a man away. I was afraid..." I pause. "I was afraid of letting a man in."

Dr. Cristal nods. "I understand the fear. But it doesn't only apply to women...children and men have the same choices to make. Not in the physical sense or relationship kind of way. You may not be able to tell, Avery, but my senses and instincts are sharp. Well," Dr. Cristal smiles. "This is the profession I've been in for over twenty years."

"I'm aware of that, Dr. Cristal. That *you* understand. But I'm just speaking of me right now. Every case that walks through your door is different because every person is different. Even those who have been in a profession for umpteen years can still learn something new. Being in the profession and actually living the life is totally different. You may have over twenty years, but I have you beat by over 40 years of *experience* stemming from the age of five. There is a difference whether you like it or not. Because, you see, I don't need a text book. *I am the text book.* And yes, there is more for me to learn too. I have to learn how to: cope, understand, and heal. This is where I currently am in my life."

Dr. Cristal scratches her throat. "That is a great place to be. It speaks to your resilience."

After my session with Dr. Cristal I stroll down Jitter Street enjoying the weather and to clear my head. Dr. Cristal bombarded me with questions, questions I answered without hesitation. It was a very emotional session. I felt layers falling from my skin. So much pain I harbored over the weeks. Xavier, the baby...pretty much everything that hindered me I released in that session.

As I am walking I bypass a same gender couple holding hands. Two white men not afraid to express their devotion. They are bold to declare their love in front of the world, in front of God.

There are four black boys throwing rocks at a tree. A Hispanic man sits on the steps of his residence and gazes out at the cars passing. Soon I approach the end of the street, stop to let a car go by, and then proceed to cross.

I approach the redbrick building of Father Michael's Pantry, I see a man, sable skin tone, tall, massive in weight with a low cut and waves standing inside the gate. My heart begins to flutter in my chest. I keep my eyes looking straight. Don't bother to look his way as I come up close to him, near passing him, I breathe heavy.

Did *he* recognize me? I ask myself. How could he not? He still looks the same in the face, maybe a little chubbier around the cheeks and chin, and neck, and well, he gained a lot of weight around the midsection too probably from drinking too much red wine. We used to be inseparable at one point in my life. I used to be his best friend, his shero, his blanket, his shield. I used to be his road dawg, his partner, his boy, and his woman. Things were so complex between us back then mainly because he couldn't distinguish the two: boy, woman, and other women. Yeah. *That was Deron Bridgeport for yah.*

At any given time he'd switch boy, woman, to satisfy his needs, and as for me, well, I was left in the cold. I refused to be as his other woman. Her pain weighed her down to gain all this extra weight. She was deprived of him. Soon she began to hibernate within, slowly drift into another state of mind. She was lonely, very alone, and unhappy while he gallivanted from mate to mate. I refused to become her. I could no longer accept him as my friend, lover, man, so I vowed to let him go. And I asked that he let me go, but he wouldn't, he couldn't. So I was left with the ball in my court.

The friendship was already strained with all the lies he'd told. His need to feel pampered and wined and dined and catered to as if the woman. Sometimes I wondered if he were gay. I tried to reason with the fact that he was a great listener. Women craved his attention for whatever their needs were, but in the midst of it all he forgot about me, and the love he professed to me while making love to me.

Many times I tried to explain how I felt, how he made me feel. It didn't seem to register.

"Deron, we have been boys for two years. And now you are finally confessing how you truly feel for me."

"I do *love* you," he said.

I shook my head. "You take me for a joke, don't you? You don't know what LOVE is but let me explain it to you. Love is when you think of that someone more than you think of yourself. Love is when you do things for that person (that doesn't always require spending money) because you want to. Love is when you go the distance without thought or reason. When she is constantly on your mind and no one, I mean no one can get in the way of how you feel for her. Love is when you feel a disconnection from that person and, and you try so many ways to mend that love back to you, because without her you feel vacant. Even in the presence of others you feel this great loss. You don't love me. You love to *toy* with my emotions, which will only make me *despise* you in the long run. No, no, you don't love me. Because I shouldn't feel like this...hurt. You say you love me, that you want us to make this relationship work, but then I go to my favorite restaurant and there you are being wined and dined by another one of your ladies."

"I spoke to you," he said.

"I'm supposed to be thrilled that my *man* spoke to me while he is being fork fed from his bitch."

"She's just a friend. Why are you overreacting?"

I shook my head. "You still don't get it." I sighed; head was spinning round and round. "Look at it like this," I said, "Here I am on the phone with you professing how much I love you while in the midst of having another man's dick digging in and out my pussy. I moan because it feels so good to me, but you don't hear it because you aren't actually listening to anything that I am saying. Your mind is preoccupied with dollar signs and other women. So I am saying things that I think you want to hear. I'm layering it on thick because he is hitting all the right spots. God, I feel so fuckin' good, yet while I am talking to you I feel so fuckin' badly.

What's wrong with this picture if you're supposed to be my man? But here someone else is pleasuring me because you can't seem to meet my needs on any level. It is more than just sex, baby, much more. You don't know how to commit to one woman and I don't have any more energy left to waste on you. Let them do it."

"Damn," he said, "That's a deep analogy. I never looked at it like that. I'm sorry if I hurt you."

"You're sorry. Funny thing is when you get off of this phone and another chick calls you, you'll get up and leave with no regard for me. See I can answer all of my questions because I know you that well. Two years well."

He interjected. "After Brenda left I began to feel free, I'll admit."

"You were free before Brenda left. She gave you too much leeway. And you ran buck wild with it. You never really appreciated her. I know how that feels. You're selfish. It is always about Deron. Deron and so-and-so. You're always plotting, scheming to get into someone else's pocketbook just so you'll have more for yourself. You have no conscience at all. She loved you and she put up with it because she was in a situation. She gave you too much and in the end she had nothing left for herself to remove herself from the situation. I understand completely of how she felt. I feel the same way, only thing is I haven't given anything monetary but I allowed you in my heart space. I knew that you wanted freedom because of how you looked at me, single and free. But I didn't use it to my advantage. I could've. But I'm looking for more than just deep pockets and a nice ride and a long stroke between these thighs. I'm seeking a man, a decent man who wants to be a part of my life. I don't want to go to bed angry with my man. I want to go to bed happy. I told you that we trying to build a relationship would not work because you love women, all types, all sizes as long as you get the perks in the midst of dealing with them. You have to be getting something out of it or you won't waste your time. I know you."

"But I'm not fucking them...all. I enjoy their company. They share things with me that they don't even share with their boyfriends or husbands. And if they want to treat me in the process why not let them. I don't see the big deal."

"Just the fact that you need to fuck any says a lot to me. It hurts. Basically says I am not enough, woman for you, that you would do me dirty as long as I allow you to. I won't allow myself to become Brenda. I won't."

504

Body shivered
Heart slivered
As I internalized
Eyes discovered the scratches upon his back
Initials still intact
Slightly faded around the "O" and "K"
Stem of the "J" curled up
As if a hook to grip him away from me
"E" sticking it through me, to me

From a lie like that...

I was wounded
Assumed so much
As he took me for granted
I lost trust
I wanted to walk, just walk into the arms of TRUTH
I wanted to undress him
Seduce him
Admire him before I sat down to eat
Salivate like table food
Inhale his scent in my nostrils and hold it there
Never did I want to let him go
Oh, no
Oh, God, I wanted to disappear
Seep deep inside him
I wanted to ride on his strength
As he stroked my misery over and over again

From a lie like that...

I was thrown
Bitter to the coldness of my bones
Oh, he had me dark, darker than black
I couldn't see, feel, or believe that this shit
Was happening to me

505

From a lie like that...

I became frozen
I chose to remain numb
I no longer felt like I could come With
On, forget about Inside
I was done
The love I had for him instantly was gone

From a lie like that...

All I saw was her legs mid-air
His head tilted back
Digging more and more into the wound
While she took all of his inches in
Grinning, sweating, pretending that I didn't exist
Oh, how did I wish?
Wish that that erotic kiss that stained his lips had faded
He walked in the door, pressed his lips against my skin as he'd done before
But this time he left an imprint on my cheek
And I literally felt her kissing me
Then he looked me dead in my eyes
Brick layered lie atop of lie
I stood still as a rock
Contemplating if I even gave a fuck
Yes, it had come to this
But what really brought everything to a head
Was when I found her panties in our bed?
Tucked under the sheets: silk trimmed in lace, size 3
It infuriated me!

From a lie like that...

I could no longer turn a deaf ear, blind eye
Act as if I didn't care
Because I did
I did in the worse way

I cared for that man
More than I could say
But my eye was twitching
While I was wishing for this misery to dispel
Inside I was scalding,
Burning from the ferocious flames of infidelity
I stood stagnant,
Melted and badly scarred beyond recognition
As he stood there with a smirk on his face
Not concerned with my condition
I shook my head from side to side
Pierced his bone dry eyes with my teary eyes
And I said, "You must think I was born yesterday!
You come be-bopping your ass up in here without as much as a care for me.
You climbed atop of another and you think I can't smell her pussy on the covers.
No, you ain't slick!
I've been keeping track of all your dirty shit!"

From a lie like that...

I hope you fucked her good
I hope you gave her all the inches that you could
I hope you made her holler
Just know while you were hitting the skins
I was getting my second wind
I was smacking my lips
Gyrating my hips
Yum! His thick skin tasted like
White c-h-o-c-o-l-a-t-e
He was giving it to me over and over and over again
My head was bobbing, my pussy was popping
Singing that Luther song
You know the one
"A House is not a Home"
We were doing it
Getting it in
Coming, sweating, coming

507

Again and again
It was incredible!

From a lie like that...

Changed every thought I had of you
The way I felt
The way I looked at you
I just took it all in
Then simply walked away
And no, no, I didn't run into his arms
Baby, I leaped
His strong arms held me so doggone tight
I could barely breathe
Pressed himself against me as if we were one being
I couldn't help but grin, and then smile
All the while thinking that all of this happened

From a lie like that...

I guess the J.O.K.E is on you
'Cause this woman here,
is most definitely through.

With my thumb and middle finger I pinch in the inner corners of my eyes. I don't want to shed another tear for that man. Two years! Two doggone years of bullshit! Not another tear do I want to shed but another falls, then another, and another, until I break down and cry. Sob in my palms as if it is all reoccurring again. It was two years of wasted time! Two years of witnessing and dismissing his actions. Two years of stroking parts of him that weren't mine to stroke. Two years of bickering and then making love. I gave him two years of me and he gave me two years of grief!

Here he appears out of nowhere. I don't think he recognized me.

I step one foot off the sidewalk when I hear, "Avery...Ms. Love. Hold up. It's me Deron...Deron Bridgeport." His voice is so close I can literally feel his breath on the nape of my neck. It is not music to my ears. If anything, it is misery coming alive from the dead.

I proceed to walk across the street hoping he doesn't follow me.

Here I thought I was slightly out of the woods, but no, no, that would be too easy. There is always something lurking around the corner, waiting. I stop questioning why and just accept what is. What is the point of masking pain when all it does is continue to unmask itself? What does this all mean? I have the foggiest idea. All I know is "D" stands for DISAPPOINTMENT something I don't need any more of.

43

SITTING IN MY LIVING ROOM staring in outer space I hear music coming from Mrs. Silva apartment. Joss Stone's "Spoiled" seeps through as if a mist of truth potion. I've given up on understanding of how Mrs. Silva knows what I'm feeling and going through. It's like she's a fly on the friggin' wall.

Trying to tune the music out, but can't I find myself extending my index and middle fingers and touching my lips. And as they do, I can literally still feel Xavier's coolness against my warmth. It is torment. Torture—to see, to say, to believe that he is truly, truly gone. It is still unfathomable to my heart.

My eyes wander about the room, scroll up the tall walls, roll across the high ceiling, then back down eyeballing the floor. And as they do, so does my head. I sit pondering over all that he has left me. The most sentimental is the *coat*. The black goose down "coat" (he bought from Macy's) is all I have left that I can physically feel. And on those cold wintry days he still metaphorically keeps me warm. But it is not the same. And I've resented him for that—for loving me, and then leaving me. I am still angry, still deeply, deeply angry.

I refuse to relinquish the coat. It is all I have left of him, other than the memories. And it becomes more than enough for me. Lonely days, empty nights I can always snuggle in my coat and think of him holding me, kissing me, and loving me enough to shield me from the bitter bite of pain.

I shake: body, hands and fingers, shake as I open the drawer to my desk and reach in and pullout the letter addressed to Xavier along with my silver letter opener. I slice the letter open, slip out the folded acid-free papers, unfold them, and begin to read:

July 19, 2013

Dear Xavier,

Yo' man, Devil tapping on my window—the mirror to my dark soul. Why can't a nigga breathe? Gimme some sunshine on this bleak day of my existence—lemme see the muthafuckin' light before he snatches it away. I know I don't deserve it. But can't he find it in him to let bygones be bygones?

Whoa! You ain't have to go there.

I know I fucked up. I don't need you to tell me shit. Who the fuck is you? Oh, so you tryna tell me that you perfect. That you ain't never fuck a bitch, leave a bitch, knock a bitch out, and then fuck her some more?

Nah. Nah.

(Laughing) Ain't this some shit.

I THOUGHT you'd understand where I was coming from. I THOUGHT we had a connection. But I see, I see I was wrong again.

This fuckin' medication got me trippin' 'n shit. Piss is red. Red, nigga! Red. I'm pissing blood.

Yo', why you actin' up?

Yeah, man. It's yo' boy, long time no hear from me. I know.

Well, see, um, I need your help. Nah. Not money this time. Um, I need to tell some people something. Well, bitches. Chicks. Women. Ladies. I'm rambling. Me rambling, what the fuck! Nigga changing fo' real.

I'm sorry. Nah, man. I know that this is gonna sound crazy coming from me, but I got depth. I ain't that fucked up.

You and I both know that I made a lot of mistakes in my life. Since college. But this, man, this one takes the cake out of everything I've ever did. I'm tryna humble myself. Before....

Look, man, I know you might not believe me. You probably think I'm bullshittin' again. But I'm not. I have to make amends. Make peace. You know what I'm sayin'. I fucked up! I can't take it anymore. The guilt. It's killin' me. Literally killing me.

I need you to locate these women for me, man. I hope you can. I wrote a list of names down. The list goes on and on, as you can see. Ah, their addresses are written below along with an informal letter. You have to make copies of the letter and mail each one one. Hopefully they all still live at the same places.

Xavier, I'm only sharing this wit' you. I know you'll do the right thing. You've always been loyal to your friends. Who knew? We both had goals, dreams, aspirations, but I guess only some of us got to actually do what we said we'd always wanted to do, be who we said we wanted to be when we grew up. I was on the right track. And then something snapped in me. I found myself going down a dark path—shooting dice with the Devil himself.

Do me one solid, man. I mean this is the cause you fight for: HIV/AIDS, right? I can't trust anyone else, but you, man.

Well, hopefully we'll meet again in the afterlife. Maybe God will give a nigga like me a free pass.

Your dude,

A. T.

Gasp. Swallow. Breathe. Gasp.

I cannot believe my eyes as I continue to scroll down reading name after name off of this list. Almost one hundred or more women's names appear before my watery bloodshot red eyes. Oh, the pain I feel in my heart for them. I sway my head from side to side, fingers touching quivering bottom lip. Why, why would someone do this to *them*? Having my own speculation—dreading the reality of my thoughts.

Hot tears stream fast from my eyes, as I continue to scroll down to the last name. Heart palpitates.

Avery Love

The sound *truth* makes me wanna *holler*!

About the Author

It was February '95, when the *twenty-six* year old *single mother* of two little black boys endured the greatest pain any loving parent fears, when her six year old son, Anthony was diagnosed with a malignant cancer (brain tumor) called Glioblastoma.

Due to his illness, Anthony influenced his mother to find *her* happiness. But all the she could do at the time was pray for inner strength to keep her child comfortable and happy.

By November 2, '95, Anthony lost his battle with cancer. He was seven years young. And the author lost her way. But having to care for her oldest brought her back to life.

Still grieving over the loss of her youngest son, and having moved out of Paterson, New Jersey, she began to tap back into her love for poetry. She found comfort in exposing her most intimate thoughts on paper, but after a while it didn't seem gratifying enough. Something was missing.

By '05, Karla felt she needed more, but she didn't know exactly what *more* was. Unfulfilled in her pursuit to find happiness, the poet was challenged by a dream.

With no face, the novice writer was frustrated by this unknown woman who seemed to come in her sleep. With no name, she tried to tune her out, but the spirit seemed persistent in her quest to be heard. Finally giving in to the voice, Karla began to listen. And what she heard astounded her.

From there she seemed drawn in and a bond between her and the protagonist Avery Love emerged.

By '06, Karla persistently sent her manuscript out to literally 30 literary agents, and received back 30 rejection letters stating: Not interested.

Her first initial thought was to let the manuscript collect dust. But the voice persuaded her of how crucial her story was specifically for minority women from all walks of life.

Feeling obligated to finish what she had started, Karla decided to educate herself on how to self publish.

By '08, Karla relocated back to her hometown of Paterson, New Jersey. Life became more of a struggle for the aspiring writer, but her pursuit to get her novel out and into the hands of readers pushed her to continue to pursue her dream as well as be a mother to her oldest son, C.

April, '08, she established her imprint: the Write Message.

April 8, '08, her first groundbreaking self-published novel, *Anonymous* was available to the public.

With the uniqueness of the novel, it became a unisex hit! Readers were so engrossed in her tale that they requested more from the novice writer. Wanting to give all she had, Karla penned a sequel, *Sleepin' Wit' the Virus* (November 2, '08).

Within the following year she pushed herself to write what she calls her: Avery Love Saga Series.

June 26, '11, her third novel, *Kreepin' Wit' the Virus* was released.

In 2014, her fourth novel, *Trickin' Wit' the Virus* was released.

Knowing that writing is her passion, within her free time she utilizes her knowledge by providing a service as a consultant for other aspiring writers. *Daddy's Little Bitch, He Died Inside of Me, How She Became a Hoe, The Andre Williams Story, It's All in My Head- A Schiophrenics Life, The Paterson Pimp* are just some of the projects she has worked on.

She resides in Paterson, New Jersey.

Currently she is working on her next novel: *Pink Pinstripes (the final saga)* due to release in 2015.

Coming Soon!!!!!

The Final Saga:

Pink Pinstripes